Nightrealm V

Diabolus Lapis

Alexander Z. Kautz

I0564011

Ahead of the Press Publishing
St. Louis, Missouri

Library of Congress Cataloguing-in-Publication Data

Nightrealm V: Diabolus Lapis/ Alexander Z. Kautz

ISBN   KINDLE   978-1-950392-43-8   (ebook)
ISBN   PAPERBACK   978-1-950392-42-1

Ahead of The Press Publishing
St. Louis, Missouri

TABLE OF CONTENTS

ACKNOWLEDGEMENTS

I believe that the greatest experience of an adventure is not its final destination, but those met along the way, and sharing the journey. In saying this, I thank you dearly for having shared this one with me.

Special thanks are extended to my dear friend and editor Ole' Papra. For endless nights spent cursing over my manuscripts, patience, dedication, and for always being there!

I would also like to give honorable mention to Kagome Lynn Dirksmeyer, Carrie, Scott and Patrick Dayment, Ray and Deb Merrill Carlson, Jen Valdez, Richard Brent MacDonald, James Stewart, Pamela Dawn Montgomery, Harold C. Black, Wayne Marshall, Neil Dobson, Mark Kokopelli Watkins, Lawrence (Duck) Handley, Jay Leonard, Marie Dawn Fischer, Robert and Ruth Sampson, Dr. Edward Wong, Jesse Whyte, Jerry Langdon, Ted Cowan, Danny Scott, Dennis Monroe, and dearest, Merlin.

I would also like to respectfully acknowledge, Martin Ruland, Lexicon alchemiae sive dictionarium alchemistarum. (1612). Martin Ruland Lexicon, Alchemiae (1661). Archidoxis magica. Paracelsus. Johannes Huser of Basel (1591). The Vampire: his kith and kin. Montague Summers. Kegan Paul, Trench-Trubner & Company. London. (1928). The Hound of the Baskervilles: Another adventure of Sherlock Holmes. Sir Arthur Conan Doyle, George Newnes, London (1902). Beowulf, David Henry Wright. London, Panther. (1970). Warren Comics Magazine, Warren Publishing, (1963), Dick and Dee Dee, The Mountain's High, The Wilder Brothers (1961).

I would also like to express my gratitude and sincerest affection for dear friends and publisher, S.L. Kotar, J.E. Gessler, and Amy Zimmerman. For decades of support, endless patience and tireless efforts, I am forever grateful.

"Where there is love there is always hope."

Alexander Z. Kautz

PROLOGUE

A strange and solemn stillness now hangs upon the old estate. It's an unsettling veil of doubt that haunts every waking moment, and torments me through the seemingly endless nights. Caitlin and Eva have abandoned our home for the safety of an ancestral keep in Ireland, as securely confined upon the hallowed ground, love endures.

Tim now resides in the guest-house, as spellbound within its walls all are protected in the presence of an ancient and unseen guardian. It was more than a matter of security that had convinced both Rich and Raymond to take residence in the estate. It was a bond of friendship that extended well beyond the simple meaning of the word. In all truth, I would have certainly lost all hope and possibly even my mind without them. Existing beyond the sight of an unwary world, Sanctum Arcanum has become a prison of fear, and our living tomb...

The time seems to slip past all too quickly as I drift through a terrifying and endless dream. Although Marlowe remains, the demon is my only companion through the deepest hours before the dawn. The research continues, but answers are few and far between. I can only hope and pray that we find salvation before the evil returns for us all...

CHAPTER ONE

Friday, January 24, 1975.

It was just shortly after eight when I had attended the breakfast table with Rich, Raymond and Tim. We had shared as a family would, as taking turns while working in pairs, prepared and managed the meals. It was something foreign to four bachelors, but a system that presented some semblance of sanity to our chaotic existence.

"So, you've finally managed to get a weekend off?" Winking, Rich grinned as Raymond served ham, toast, and scrambled eggs.

"That's right--," Raymond joined us at the table, "Three blissful days of lying around on my butt and wishing that I could get some sleep."

"At least you have a job to go to--," Tim followed closely from behind with the tea and coffee, "Now that the repairs are done to the parlor and the property is for sale, I don't even know what to do with myself. The loss of sleep doesn't really bother me much. In all honesty, I haven't had a good night's rest since I was a kid."

"Living in a funeral home might have that affect on a person--," Rich scoffed while poking a finger under his glasses and rubbing at the dark circles beneath his eyes, "I wish that I could get just one good night or even day of sleep. I'm so tired most of the time now that I'm starting to see things."

"Well that's a relief--," Raymond huffed while looking around at all of us and chuckling, "I was beginning to wonder if I was the only one."

"I notice them too." Shuddering with the thought, Tim's eyes flashed in obvious fear, "Those creeping shadows, and dark things that move in the corner of your eye. But when you turn to look—there isn't anything there…"

"In most cases it might just be Merlin poking around—," Attempting to take the edge from off their nerves, I presented another possibility, saying, "You all know about his midnight snack runs and endless naps in all corners of this old house."

"Of course we do--," Replying in a somewhat sarcastic tone, Rich had suspiciously peered back at me, "But somehow I doubt that he can wander across the ceiling or vanish into walls…"

"I see them out there in the snow-drifts--," Appearing greatly unsettled, Raymond dropped his teaspoon while saying, "Early in the morning, when I'm clearing the driveway with the bobcat—and just before dark…"

Unable to offer much in the sense of comfort or relief, I had looked around and into my friends' dismal faces, and simply said, "As frightening or disturbing as these apparitions might be—according to Marlowe, they're perfectly harmless, and, in the presence of the vault guardian, no evil energy may trespass on these grounds. It's most likely that they're just the spirits of the old owners of many of the things we've gathered here."

"I wish that I could say that your explanations made me feel better--," Sipping at his coffee, Raymond shook his head, saying, "But the thought of anyone or anything sneaking around while I'm showering or sleeping just gives me the creeps."

"It's not just that." Tim poured coffee and tea, thinking for a moment, and said, "It's a sense of being trapped here and suffocated with the fear of what's waiting out there for us. Not to mention that I've been feeling completely useless just waiting around. Although it really wasn't much, the funeral parlour kept me busy and gave me a sense of purpose."

"Well, for whatever it's worth? I don't consider any of you to be useless, you've been a blessing around here," I thanked them all, "And I don't know what I would've done without you over these past months. With everything that's happened, and my wife leaving, I'd likely have lost my mind or something even worse."

"Nonsense--," Grinning mischievously, Rich said with a wink, "You can't lose what you've never had. Not to mention you would've likely starved alone in this place. You can't go through life eating nothing but toast and drinking tea."

"Especially that stuff--," Raymond sneered at my unbuttered whole-wheat toast, "Without butter or anything, I really don't know how you manage to get that stuff down?"

"Believe me--," Looking down at my plate and sighing, I said, "It really isn't easy."

"I spoke with Maya last night on the telephone--," Rich had directed the comment toward me with a nervous glance, "Apparently she had something of a skirmish with Caitlin. It seems that she got it in her head to come home, regardless of the danger."

It bothered me to even hear news of them. Though I dearly loved her, Caitlin had forced me into becoming a reluctant stranger.

"Oh—and what did they make of it?" Sipping at my tea and attempting to appear reserved, the emotions seethed within me.

"Caitlin had taken the phone at that point--," He sadly exclaimed, "And I had to promise that we'd come there for them just as soon as we resolved this thing. She's really regretting their decision to leave now, and starting to fall apart..."

There were no words in any vocabulary that could have properly described the emotional devastation that she had left within our parting. While caught in an emotional hurricane of frustration, confusion, and utter despair, tears had been my only companion on most nights. On several occasion I had even considered taking my own life and ending the nightmare for all involved, but the demon had always intervened. There had even been occasions wherein Caitlin had pleaded with him that we join them. All in vain though, as we were all still helpless before an unseen, silent, and deadly force...

"We have to be careful not to give them away--," Nervously tapping at my tea cup with a finger, I looked about the table, "We still don't know what we're dealing with here—or what it might be capable of doing..."

"Their location has been kept so discrete that even we don't know where they're staying." Raymond reminded me, "So, even if this evil could see into our thoughts, what would it find?"

"After what happened with Harry, let's just hope that it can't sense and locate things through telephone signals." Tim added in, "Or we might all be in for some ugly surprises..."

"But, we don't even know if it used Harry's body to contact us by phone." Rich paused thoughtfully over his breakfast, "Or whether it can somehow pass into the energy flow traveling through telephone signals and power lines."

"Well, it can't do that anymore" Raymond shrugged, "In order to get into our phones, it would have to come through lines passing over our property, and from what Michael was saying about the guardian—it won't permit that."

"We really don't know anything for certain--," Looking between my distraught friends, I shook my head, saying, "All that we can do in our current situation is hope that they remain safely hidden on hallowed ground."

"Well, I still need to have my property blessed--," Rich picked at his ham, and said, "It's not like anyone would even suspect anything. It's fairly common for most Catholics to have their minister bless their new homes or residence."

"I thought that you didn't believe in religious hocus-pocus?" Surprised at Rich, Raymond had looked to him curiously, and said, "You're always going on about how much you hate the church."

"I have faith in the word—I just don't care for the politics of the system," Pouring more coffee and shrugging, Rich said, "And besides, it seems to be working for our wives. So it was the least that I could do to try to protect Tanya and the boys."

"Fair enough--," Raymond played with a fork in his eggs, "I have to admit that my opinion of faith and religion has changed a lot lately. Let's face it—something is better than nothing."

"I'll find some answers soon." Unhappy while nibbling at my unbuttered whole-wheat toast, I tapped it against the plate, and watching it crumble, said, "I've been reading through that old Grimoire of Marlowe's. Hopefully, I'll find some reference to this thing—or possibly something we can use against it."

"Maybe we should've asked the priest? I'm sure that the Vatican archives are filled with ancient spell books and forbidden knowledge. They've got their fingers in everybody's proverbial pies, and know everything that happens." Contemplating for a moment, Rich frowned, "In fact, I'm surprised that they aren't investigating us yet?"

"Bite your tongue—we don't need any additional attention," Raymond smirked, stirring cream and sugar into his coffee, as he said with a snicker, "Not that sneaking up on you guys is really all that hard."

Appearing somewhat offended by the comment, Rich scowled, remarking, "Well, normal people wouldn't suspect others of going around and sneaking up on them, now would they?"

"Raymond has a point." Agreeing with our friend while dipping the dry toast into my tea, I grumbled, "Not that there's really anything normal about us or our lives anymore..."

"Normal is just a word used for anyone who isn't in jail or locked in some looney-bin." Rich spread strawberry jam onto toast, and looking around the room, said, "And this is both, really, so what should we expect?"

"It seems that somewhere along the way, we've all stopped living and just started surviving." Salivating while gazing upon the jam jar, I looked away, "It's hard to believe that beyond this estate, our lives could end in something as simple as a dark basement, corridor, or deep shadow."

Cautiously sipping at his steaming coffee, Raymond pondered, "I wonder how long most people could live with that knowledge before losing their minds?"

"What makes you so sure that we haven't?" Wagging his eyebrows at Raymond, Rich winked, "I don't know about you guys, but I really wouldn't mind a 'hug-me' jacket and a nice, safe padded room."

I would have laughed, but the ridiculous remark bore some strange semblance of sanity. Looking around the table and into the wearied and worn faces of my companions, dismay caused me to sink even lower in the chair. We looked nothing like the post-apocalyptic heroes and survivors of adventure films. In fact, we had become little more than mere shadows of our former selves, terrified and exhausted, as we feared the coming night. At one point I had even wondered if they had all become prematurely old during the experience. But then again, I was always so utterly fatigued that I couldn't even trust my own eyes or judgement anymore.

"I often wonder--," Gazing blankly into the wearied faces of all that were gathered around the table, Tim queried, "How much longer we can all continue going on like this?"

It wasn't so much what he had said, but the way that he'd said it, that now left us all sitting and quietly thinking.

"Because there's no other choice at the moment--," Picking at a tooth with a fingernail, Raymond muttered, "And the alternative is worse..."

A moment of dark reflection descended upon the breakfast table, and then, clearing his throat, Rich had waved toast at Raymond, saying, "I know that this is a sensitive subject, but speaking of surviving in this sad state, you should really consider retiring from the department. No offence, but you've been cutting it really close on making it home before dark on some days."

"I know—believe me, it's always on my mind." A shadow passed over his face as, looking to Rich, Raymond groaned, "So far, I've managed to get out of the office early, and always found some excuse, but it's coming down to the edge now, and I'm not sure what I'm going to do..."

"There really isn't any reason for you to keep doing this to yourself." Speaking with the greatest of compassion, Tim slowly shook his head, "I realize how important that job is to you—but it's just not worth losing your life over..."

"He's right about that." Wiping at my mouth with a napkin and looking over at my dismayed friend, I said, "In all seriousness, we could employ you at the office and warehouse as security. And most of it would be a tax write-off at the end of the year."

"Please don't think I don't appreciate what you're all trying to do--," He declined in the kindest way possible, saying, "But for the moment, I still need that job. Aside from inside information, it also provides certain liberties, and permits me to carry these." He patted the revolvers beneath his suit jacket.

"You wore your guns to breakfast?" With bulging eyes Rich sat over his meal in utter disbelief.

"I'd rather have them and not need them--," Raymond gazed blankly from over his coffee cup, "Than need them and not have them."

My hand slowly slipped down while resting upon the cane that stood against my knee from beneath the table, and I could hardly blame him. There was sullen comfort in these objects which was a narrow bridge between the sanity of security, and border of blind terror. So in fact, just the canes presence would have been enough to have made me a hypocrite for having said anything disagreeable in the matter...

"We're your friends and we're scared for you—can't you see that?" There was a depth of sincerity in Rich's expression and eyes that caused us all to become utterly silent, as he quietly said, "So, if you should happen to change your mind about the offer, it stands open."

"Thank you..." Swallowing hard, Raymond had just nodded and looked away. It was apparent from his expression that, although willing to concede, some kind of self-induced sense of false pride had forbidden it. Having immediately recognized this, Tim had reached out to our friend, and quietly said, "There's no shame in changing careers—and no dishonor in working for a friend. I did it for years and would willingly do it again."

There was a moment of silence as Raymond contemplated and seemed to weigh the content of each word. Then, peering up and looking into the faces of all who were gathered there, he said in a solemn tone, "It took me years to make Detective and get the seniority that I have at the department." The words came hard and slow, but Raymond seemed to have finally accepted the inevitable, saying, "And please, don't get me wrong, I'd be honored to work for any one of you. But, for the moment, I'm just not willing to give this up..."

Gently patting his friend on the back and speaking in an understanding way, Rich nodded, saying, "When that time finally does come—just let me know, brother, the door is always open..."

"I realize that none of this has been easy for anyone--," Looking between my friends and feeling disheartened, I dropped the dry toast on my plate, saying, "And that we've all been forced to make sacrifices. But they've all been necessary for safety's sake."

"The idea of being safe anywhere seems so unrealistic now." Gulping at his coffee, Rich frowned, "It never meant much to me before—but the truth being said, it means everything now."

"Do we even know that Caitlin and the others are really safe out there?" Adjusting his glasses, Tim looked anxiously around the table, "I mean—wouldn't they be safer right here, and with us?" He turned to me, "You said it yourself—we've done everything possible to secure the estate."

"I'm not really sure about anything--," Confused and emotionally tormented with the thought, I remembered the words of Marlowe and the demon, and looking sadly to my friends, said, "According to Marlowe and his companion, there are reasons for this distance between us. And, it's a matter of safety for all of us—one way or the other..."

"But we all know that once this things gets into the dead—," Swallowing hard, Tim almost whispered the words, "That it can wander anywhere, and even onto sanctified ground..."

"Please--," Gesturing for him to halt with a trembling hand, I shuddered with the realization, looked pleadingly, and quietly said, "You might be right about all of these things—but we have to just be patient and wait. And believe me, I'm being held together by mere threads of faith in Marlowe's words."

"I'm sorry--," Realizing the effects of his words upon me in Caitlin's absence, he apologized, "I guess that I'm just on edge like everyone else, and I really didn't mean to make things any worse than they already are."

"Don't feel too bad…None of us are sleeping properly or thinking right--," Rich rubbed wearily at his eyes, saying, "I've been trying to work on some new projects just to try to stay focussed. But I keep forgetting things due to sleep deprivation and short term memory loss."

"Tell me about it--," Stabbing a spook into his coffee cup, Raymond groaned, "I've been trying to memorize passages from a book that Michael lent me called *Beowulf*," he admitted, saying, "It keeps my thoughts occupied—but keeps me completely frustrated as it's almost impossible to remember anything."

"I pilfered a book from his library too-," Appearing somewhat guilty, Tim smiled mischievously while looking over at Raymond, saying, "It's Sir Arthur Conan Doyle, *The Hound of the Baskervilles*, another adventure of Sherlock Holmes. But like you said, I could read the whole thing over again, and it would seem like I'd never even seen it before. It's like daydreaming instead of actually retaining anything of substance."

"Is that the red book with the black hound on the cover, dated from 1902?" Looking to him with certain concern, I had raised an eyebrow.

"Yes it is--," He thought briefly, asking, "Why do you ask?"

"Well, just please be careful with it--," Feeling a little unsettled, I added, "It's a first edition and one of my favorites among his works."

"Weren't you thumbing through some big old leather-bound volume the last time that I knocked on your office door?" It had been a subject of Rich's curiosity from the beginning, and was a book that I felt necessary to conceal from my dear friend. Being rather reckless, his endless fascination in enchanted weapons and their forging made this particular volume very dangerous to him…

"Oh, that 14th century Grimoire that I'd taken out of the vault--," Attempting to imply that it was of little use to anyone, I looked carelessly to where the glow of the sun peeked in between the dining room draperies, and said, "It's not much different than most alchemical dictionaries, with a flash of mysticism and drama on the author's part to keep the reader from putting it down."

"In any event, just be careful--," Obviously disappointed, he tapped a spoon upon the table and quietly said, "We don't need to accidentally invoke anything else."

"Oh, there's no need for concern with this volume--," I had assured them all while feeling a little guilty for misleading my friend, "But I'm afraid that a recipe for carrot cake might be more dangerous than this book."

The disappointment became obvious dismay as Rich's attention now fell surprisingly to his breakfast, and using a knife to better spread the butter and syrup over his pancakes.

"It's been much too quiet lately." It was obvious in the way that Raymond had looked around the table that he didn't trust the sound of his own words, "I get the feeling that thing is up to something. It's like the stillness before the storm."

"Oh it's out there alright--," Rich shoveled a forkful of pancake into his mouth, and wiping at the dripping syrup that ran onto his shirt, said, "We're out of its sight for the moment, but not beyond reach. It knows that we have to leave this place sooner or later—and has all the time in the world to wait…"

"We can't sit around here forever--," Raymond nervously tapped a finger on his coffee mug, "We're over-tired, not thinking clearly and already starting to lose our minds."

"It's well aware of those facts--," Using coffee and a napkin, Rich wiped at his syrup-stained shirt, "It also knows that we'll get desperate and make a mistake sooner or later—so it's just a matter of time."

"Something will happen soon." Promising even while feeling utterly destitute, I looked hopefully toward my friends, "According to Marlowe, there is a tool or weapon of some kind that we can use against this thing. It might even influence or help to open another portal into another dimension."

Wiping at his goatee with a napkin, Rich appeared suddenly enthusiastic, "Do you mean like the beryl or the sword?"

Feeling utterly exhausted, I stuttered in thought, "I'm not exactly sure of what it is—but we'll know it when we see it. But, it might be something that occurred in all three locations where the previous portals were opened?"

"That's rather vague--," Tim chewed at a fingernail, "It could be a charm, an article of clothing—or even some common mineral that existed in any of those places?"

"It could've been almost anything." The confusion darkened Rich's features, "Or anyone?"

"It had to have been something that was present during all of those incidents." Repeating the statement and attempting to rationalize, I looked to Tim, and gasping said, "Of course, Sherlock Holmes!"

They had all just looked to me as though I had finally lost my mind.

"No—not the man himself--," Explaining while motioning toward Tim, I said, "He was reading Sir Arthur Conan Doyle, so naturally--."

"Of course, the process of elimination--," Snapping his fingers and nodding, Tim said, "We may not know what or who it was—but we can certainly define as to who and what it wasn't."

"Then we can start with Caitlin, Tim, Harry and Raymond--," Rich pointed out, saying, "Because none of them were with us at the warehouse."

"But then again, Michael was alone with Eva and Caitlin at the Duff Glenn--," Tim reminded everyone, "So that completely eliminates all of us."

"Maybe it was something that was already there?" Tim pondered, "Possibly something from the Duff Glenn, or that you might've been carrying?"

"We've basically brought everything from the Duff Glenn here--," Rich appeared haunted with some sinister thought and strangely guilty, "I've even recreated the pentagram with the marble angels from the mausoleum, but none of those things had anything to do with the warehouse or the hospital..."

Slowly turning to look at me, Rich suddenly gazed wide-eyed and pointed, "The amulet—that pendant that you took off the mausoleum gates!"

"No—," Slowly shaking my head and peering back at him in certain disappointment, I said, "I returned it and even wrapped it around the gates where I'd first found the damned thing."

"Well, that wipes out the possibility of this having been anything taken from the Duff Glenn." Rich appeared defeated, "And, it wasn't your Silver Celtic cross--," Pulling the talisman from beneath his shirt, Rich held it up for all to see, "Because you gave it to me long before the incident at the warehouse or hospital."

"You know, even if we do manage to open a portal of some kind--," Raymond peered up from his coffee, "How do we get that thing into it? I seriously doubt that it'll go willingly."

"These portals seem to draw anything ethereal or unnatural to this dimension." Pausing, I thought briefly before saying, "But then again, it also almost took me and Caitlin at the Duff Glenn…"

"We could all get killed just trying—," Looking increasingly unsettled by the conversation, Tim swallowed hard and said, "And I can't even imagine what would happen—or where we would end up if we got swallowed into some portal into another dimension?"

"You already know my opinion on that." Dipping his soggy toast into his coffee as we all cringed, he chewed at it, saying, "We're screwed either way—but at least with this we have a chance of sending that bastard back to hell, where it belongs."

"Well, we won't exactly be sending it to hell--," Sipping at the tea that became cold in my cup while talking, I winced while saying, "Just into a different dimension, and where it'll likely continue its reign of terror in another civilization, just like it did here and with me—sooner or later we'll possibly be confronted with this same nightmare, all over again…"

Raymond coughed on his coffee, "Isn't there some way to just destroy this damn thing?"

"Energy can never be destroyed, just transmitted or transferred." Rich finished his breakfast and, looking to Raymond, shrugged, "Even if it means playing tag with this thing through eternity, it's better than being killed now…"

"According to what Marlowe said--," Feeling unbearable guilty, I muttered, "I've done this before while existing in a different time and dimension, and that within doing so, I am entirely responsible for its being here now…"

There were some very dark and suspicious glances in reflection, and then appearing utterly distraught, all around the table became painfully quiet. Although the guilty party had been revealed, none had passed judgement…

"It never comes down to the actions of a single person." Tim said thoughtfully, "It's always cause and effect, and generally due to group efforts and interaction."

"I'm sure that we all earned our part in this one." Raymond agreed, "And let's face it, we're all here right now—so what says that we weren't somewhere else in time, and in this mess before, together?"

"It shouldn't really be that surprising--," Eyeing me skeptically, Rich groaned, "It wouldn't be the first time that you stuck your nose where it didn't belong, and pissed off something really nasty."

"He does have a point--," Tim looked to me and quietly agreed, "It's a natural talent that you've always had—and honestly, if you did it before, that explains while you're still doing the same thing in this world."

"He was likely killed in the last life and didn't learn from his mistakes--," Rich contemplated, "So now, fate brought him here, and he's stuck dealing with the same mess that he caused before."

"You seem to have forgotten something?" Slumping back into the chair and curiously examining at Rich, I offered a thought, "If it's true that polarities attract, then just the fact that you're even sitting here substantiates that it wasn't just my stupidity that got us into this mess in the first place."

"Assumption and theory--," Looking between Raymond and where I sat, Rich suddenly grinned mischievously, and pointing a fork, said, "But from where we all stand, you're still the protagonist."

It was obvious by his expression and tones that he had just attempted to brighten what was swiftly becoming a very dismal breakfast conversation. There had been some raised eyebrows and a few grins exchanged, and the matter was immediately dismissed.

"Is it possible--," Having remained exempt of the conversation, Tim interjected, "That along with this nightmare, something else has followed you into this world? Maybe what we're looking for isn't something that existed here before, but something that's just arrived?"

"Assuming might take us in a million directions--," Rich shrugged, "And likely all of them wrong. It's even possible that whatever we're looking for is not related to any of the previous events, and might just be something that we need to find?"

"The list of possibilities is endless--," Rubbing at my eyes, I looked over at him, "All I know for sure is that we need to find it, if we hope to ever fight off this evil."

"Just a second here--," Rich reached some epiphany, "If this thing's been waiting for us all this time—how long have we actually been up against this nightmare?"

"From what I gathered during the conversation with Marlowe--," Pondering the thought for several moments, I quietly looked back and said, "Through distant dimensions, endless worlds, and for possibly aeons."

The toast suddenly dropped from Raymond's fingers, "Are you saying that we've been juggling this bastard through time and space, forever?"

"Assuming that we were even aware of its presence in time--," The thought terrified me, "And that it didn't just kill us all first—it's a distinct possibility..."

"But—if this thing knows that we can't destroy it, and that we're hardly even a threat--," Tim slipped down into his seat, "Then why is it trying so desperately to stop us?"

"Oh—but we are a threat..." Grinning devilishly, Rich said, "We may not be able to ultimately destroy this thing—but we might be capable of stopping it."

There was a moment of dead silence.

"I don't see how?" Raymond gestured with a nod at me, "From what this Marlowe character told him, we're just tossing it back and forth through time, and leaving it for others to deal with until we run into it again, somewhere."

"Not if we could somehow open a passage into a black hole--," Rich spoke as though having uttered some dark and terrifying spell, "And send that thing on a direct pathway to oblivion."

"Is that even possible?" Stirring far too much cream and sugar into his coffee, Raymond raised an eyebrow, "Has it ever been done before?"

"Yes--," Gasping, I turned suddenly while realizing that he may have stumbled upon an answer, "I saw something written about doing exactly that—trapping souls and demons in oblivion. I just have to remember where?" Exhausted, my mind refused to reveal the source, as frustrated, I slipped slowly back against the chair.

"But if something went wrong--," Tim played devil's advocate, "Wouldn't that also mean that anyone lost during the process would be trapped forever with that thing?"

"And how would we even be sure of the gateway that we were opening--," Rich pondered over his coffee, "Or where we would be sending that thing from here? None of has any real clue of what we're doing here. It would likely be hit and miss..."

"He has a point there, wouldn't that be kind of like trying to tune into a station on a radio with millions of channels?" Tim sipped at his tea, his eyes darting about the table, "You could be sending the damn thing right back here without even realizing it."

"Marlowe might make the difference--," I had reminded them, "Maybe he has some way of influencing portals and dimensional voids. I know that he uses them in some ways…"

"If he can open a portal into multi-dimensions--," Rich slowly nodded, "Then anything might be possible."

"I'll speak with him this evening." I felt a cold lump form in the pit of my stomach. We had either stumbled upon a possible conclusion to this nightmarish dilemma, or were about to make an even worse mistake.

"At least it's a chance--," Nursing a glass of orange juice, Rich nervously tapped at the lip of the glass, "And besides, I really don't feel like waiting around until it runs out of patience…"

"I don't think that we'll have to wait long--," Raymond's eyes glistened in dark anticipation, "Once that thing figures out what we're up to—it'll come at us with everything that it's got…"

"Hopefully we'll have the gates up before then--," Rich's confidence seemed to leak away as looking around and muttering, he said, "All that we can do now is hope that the guardian will keep us all safe…"

"When Marlowe summoned it, he said that it would watch over the grounds and anyone here." I remembered the mystic's warning, and said, "Which means that it's familiar with all of you and that you're safe out on the grounds--," I reminded them, "But, for no reason should anyone ever enter the guest house without Tim."

"Why, if the guardian knows us we should be fine--," Confused, Raymond looked upon our friends with a shrug, I mean—what's the difference between being out on the property and in that building?"

"Because the vaults are the guardian's domain—and only Tim holds the key to that world--," Rich answered, "So anyone entering the building without Tim and that key—might as well be committing suicide."

"It seems that the nature of some elementals is very similar to the animals in this world." Looking around apologetically, I sighed, "I'm afraid that this one is rather territorial, to say the least."

"So, what would happen if a stranger entered the property?" Raymond's curiosity got the better of him in a string of questions, "Or another animal, birds, squirrels, and maybe even bees?"

"Being an elemental and a nature spirit—most would be perfectly safe." Looking between my companions while recollecting all that Marlowe had explained, I said, "The guardian is like a psychic watch-dog, and will only react to a direct threat, or anything with a generally malevolent nature."

"At least this one's on our side--," Appearing somewhat skeptical, Raymond glanced back at me, "We're sure about that, right?"

"It seems to be on the side of whoever holds the key--," Gesturing to Tim with a motion of my hand, I looked back to Raymond, and said, "And anyone directly involved with them."

"Have you ever seen it?" Dreadfully serious, Rich revealed an obvious concern, asking, "Has it ever done anything—or given you any reason for doubt?"

Somewhat apprehensive, Tim had wiped at his mouth with a napkin, and quietly said, "Well, to be honest—it did startle me a few nights ago."

"Oh—did it?" Raymond was immediately suspicious. None of us had been comfortable with the prospect of having an elemental on the premise, and this only served to heighten the paranoia.

"What happened?"

"I was restless, and since I couldn't sleep anyway, decided to take a little walk. As you all know, the halls in that place seem to go on forever." Pouring more tea before continuing, he cleared his throat, saying, "As you all know, it's nothing like what it seems on the outside. It's more like a three level museum filled with display cases, dimly lit corridors, dark stairways, and a windowless basement. In the daytime it's pleasant enough, but it's very different in the night. It's more like a network of dark halls with the faintest of blue glows from strips of track-lighting on either side of the halls."

"Those were just added as a courtesy--," Rich explained with little interest, "Initially we never planned or expected to have anyone staying there."

"Anyway--," Tim continued with the story, "I was coming down the stairs from the second floor, and encountered something in the East wing of the corridor." A faint sweat glistened upon his brow as he spoke, and sipping at his tea, he said, "I think that we surprised each another, odd as that may sound."

"What did it do and what did it look like?" Fascination brightened Rich's eyes and features with a child-like enthusiasm, "And did it make any sound?"

Shuddering with the thought, Tim looked to Rich, saying, "I first noticed it in the darkness at the far end of that hall. It was like a deep green shadow that moved through a trailing and translucent, emerald mist. If it had been in the forest, you would likely never have even noticed it between the fog and leaves."

"How did you feel at the time?" Raymond inquired, "And was there anything like that chill that we get whenever the darkness or something other-worldly comes around?"

Tim thought briefly, and then licking at dry lips, spoke through a memory, saying, "Yes, there was a definite feeling. It was like walking through a dense forest and encountering a grizzly hidden in the brush. I could sense an ominous presence—but could only see a faint and drifting, greenish fog."

"What did it do?" Raymond appeared enthralled within the strange experience, "Did it approach you, or threaten you in any way?"

Rubbing at his arms, Tim shook his head while gazing blankly, "No, it just lifted into the air and, slowly drifting—passed through me as though I weren't even there. I was terrified at first—but then became aware of a strange, foreign intelligence, a benign presence." His fingers searched out the golden, key-shaped whistle that hung from its chain about his neck, and he whispered, "It just drifted back down the corridor, and then fading, vanished down and into the floor."

"That would've scared the living day-lights out of me--," Looking around at everyone with wide eyes, Raymond gasped, "But at least we know that this key deal works. I'd hate to have to find out the hard way, and in the middle of the night, that it didn't."

"Not really much of a monster if you ask me?" Appearing strangely disappointed, Rich frowned, "And I don't know how that's supposed to protect us?"

"Just trust me on this--," Obviously unsettled with the thought, Tim's eyes narrowed, "I don't think that any of us want to find out what this thing really looks like—or what it can do…"

"Let's all just stick to the rules on this one." Unnerved for some reason, I turned to Rich, and said, "If Marlowe has reason for concern, I would not take it lightly for even a second."

We were both well aware that appearances hold little significance in the nether-worlds, but it seemed that he had been hoping for something more substantial, and evidence of a true monster.

"I still have to run over to my shop and finish making those new symbols for the gates." Already focused upon other matters, Rich gulped down his coffee, "I'm replacing the others with something that looks noble, and a little more sophisticated."

"You have a real natural talent with working in iron." Paying Rich a true compliment, Tim lightened the moment with a smile and change of topic, saying, "I wonder if you could make swords like the Katana of the Japanese."

"It's funny that you would ask--," Tapping his butter knife against his tea cup, Rich grinned, "I've always had an interest in sword craft and even looked into it when I was younger. The Japanese created the first "uchigatana" and "tsubagatana" in the Kamakura Period and have been refining it ever since. Did you know that they even have their own specially smelted sword material? It's a steel called 'tamahagane' and Japan is the only place in the world where it can be acquired."

"I'm guessing that he might have some idea of how to make a sword." Chuckling, Raymond smiled at Rich, "You never cease to amaze me."

"I still wish that we hadn't lost that mystical sword at the warehouse that night--," Speaking as while lost in some other thought, he said, "I wonder if you could invoke power into steel while it's being forged, or whether spells were cast after it was already made?"

"Easy there friend--," Raymond waved a hand in warning, and snickering, said, "You're treading into some pretty dark territory, aren't you?"

Utterly captivated in both the moment and thought, Rich had turned curiously toward me, and asked, "Marlowe's book—did you notice any mention in reference to the forging of magic weapons?"

"See what you've started now?" Shaking my head at Tim who mischievously grinned, I looked back to Rich, and said quite adamantly, "I really don't think that we should start dabbling in black magic, especially not in matters concerning death and killing…"

"I would imagine that invoking a demon into a sword might make it unbreakable--," Tim considered the possibilities aloud, "Maybe even undefeatable?"

There was a dark desire burning in Rich's wide eyes. It was a wanton and sinister light that shone from the darkest depths of his soul. We all suffered the temptation of demons unique to our own design, and I now saw his as a dark and mighty blacksmith, forging hell on earth.

"And at what cost, I wonder—to the craftsman or its wielder?" My words had been a proverbial 'cold shower' that swiftly flooded and drowned the conversation. I knew that Rich had always been fascinated with mystical and sacred weapons and desired to own or possibly create one. The subject had come up between us more than once, and so had mention of Marlowe's book in reference. It was due to this dread of his infernal curiously that I had hidden the book where no mortal would easily find it…

Ashamed as while realizing that he'd unintentionally drawn Rich into a personal darkness, Tim altered the topic slightly, asking, "Are you working outdoors—or is your shop big enough to house all the steel that you're using for the gates?"

The spell having been broken, Rich had spoken as though awakened from a particularly dark dream, saying, "I have too many projects happening at once and far too many tools to do things. So, I managed to make space—but it's a tight fit and very cluttered."

"Oh—I was also going to ask?" The thought had just come to mind, "Do you have any idea when those new guide rails for the main gates might be done?"

"We have them all measured and cut out." Raymond announced, as still somewhat concerned about Rich, who appeared strangely stunned, he looked to his friend and said, "We just need to finish the mounting brackets and get everything painted. Or was there anything else that you were concerned about, Rich?"

"No—no concerns--," He thought briefly, and then appearing to have recovered, proudly said, "But, I did manage to make a remote with buttons that will operate the gates and both sets of garage doors." Tapping his knife upon the table and peering over at me, he said, "I've also hired two crews to handle all the installation, so that'll save us a lot of time and stress."

Pouring more tea, I shuddered with the thought of struggling with those gates far too often, and near dark, saying, "The gates are heavy and we're not getting any younger—that automated system is an absolute blessing, regardless of anything else."

"Well, not to worry we have it covered--," Offering a thumbs-up, Raymond turned to Rich and asked, "We still have to get everything ready and done for your place…"

"No problem, I have that all figured out as well--," Tapping his fingers at his coffee mug with a confident smile, he looked to me, saying, "I'm using all the same style iron fencing and mechanized systems over at my place. But my gates aren't quite as fancy as yours."

"I'll feel a lot better once that's done." The thought had escaped before I had even realized to have said anything, "I've been really concerned about Tanya and the boys…"

"I know, but it really couldn't be helped." Dismayed but speaking frankly, he shrugged, "The damn snow and frozen ground have made everything ten times worse, and it's an endless battle to get anything done. We're working as fast as possible—but there's only so much that we can do. That's why I've hired extra crews to get this project done."

"He isn't kidding--," Frowning, Ray huffed at the thought, "If the work wasn't already tough enough, try being out there and freezing your backside off while you're attempting to get something done..."

"Other than for the sake of Tanya and the boys--," Picking at his breakfast, Tim swallowed hard, "Finishing the work at Rich's place is more important than we might assume." There was something very unsettling in his tone, as looking over at me, he said with certain deliberation, "If for some reason things should go badly here—it will be the only place left to run..."

"And as true as that may be—when I'm done with this place, it'll be tighter than Fort Knox" Rich promised while appearing absolutely confident and pointed to Tim while saying, "And nothing will get in here unless we want it to."

"Well, don't get me wrong here--," Tim looked around the table, "I have absolute confidence in all of you. But even though we have all this mystical protection against spirits and evil forces--," He made the motion of making quotations from his head with his fingers, and said, "Without those gates, we're almost helpless against those squishy, bloated and freaking disgusting, walking meat-bags..."

Looking down at the ham that remained on his plate, wincing, Raymond slid the remainder of his breakfast away.

Noticing this, Tim had promptly apologized, saying, "Sorry—I didn't mean to be quite so colorful in the description."

"Oh—it wasn't you--," Sighing and looking back at his plate, Raymond shrugged, "I just remembered a burn victim that was at a scene that I attended last week. The smell was still in my sinuses somewhere, and just made me feel a little sick..."

The fork had dropped from Rich's fingers and into what remained of his eggs, and where it remained as breakfast had ended for him as well.

"At the moment--," Feeling rather unsettled with the descriptions and recollections shared about the table, I swallowed hard, "We really don't have much defense against the dead. There just isn't any possible way to generate an intense enough heat to utterly destroy them before they can re-manifest."

"Well, that's not exactly accurate--," Pulling a page from the breast pocket of his flannel shirt, Rich began unfolding what was quite obviously a diagram, "I came up with an idea."

Picking up the page and closely examining the illustration, I was immediately fascinated. The image depicted what appeared to have been three small and adjoining glass cylinders contained within a spring-loaded arrow tip. They were about the size of a cigarette in length and diameter, and with a long shaft and feathered end, were obviously designed to travel fast and shatter easily.

"It's only the basic design—but here's how this works." Sipping at his coffee, he pointed while explaining, "We already know that we can destroy the dead by fire. Our problem was being able to produce an intense heat at a close range, regardless of conditions. So, I came up with an idea. Those three glass cylinders contain three separate elements. The first is filled with Potassium Permanganate crystals, the second is Glycerin, and the third contains water. "

"You're going to use water to start a fire." Tim appeared confused and fascinated at the same time, "Now this I have to hear."

"The crystal components in the tubes are harmless on their own." Rich explained, "But when combined and mixed with water, they produce an intense chemical fire. So, when the arrow strikes its target--," He pointed to the diagram, "A spring-loaded metal plunger shatters the tubes, and the protective plastic casing slide back in unison."

"That's brilliant!" Raymond appeared absolutely ecstatic, "Lawn dart, fire-bombs!"

"Well, they'll be fired from a hand-held and light-weight cross-bow, but I'm still ironing out the bugs." Rich swallowed hard, and rolling his eyes, said, "The problem right now—is that if anything should happens to leak, the arrow tip will explode."

Tim frowned, his eyes widening behind his glasses, "The probability of getting killed using this weapon seems a little high, don't you think?"

"I'm still working it all out--," Slowly nodding while thoughtfully examining his diagram, Rich frowned, "It might still be a little while, but its close."

"Um, just out of curiosity--," Raymond leaned down to closer observe the diagram, "How big of an explosion and fire are we talking about here?"

"It would be more like an ignition than an explosion." Appearing a little uncertain, he tapped nervously at the diagram, and said, "And a really intense, giant flare."

"Seriously, if something did happen to go wrong--," Swallowing hard, Tim appeared increasingly concerned, as he asked, "How bad would it be?"

"Well, that all depends on how many arrows the individual was carrying--," Rich replied, closely examining his illustration, and thoughtfully said, "Like I said, it only takes a few crystals in a spoon-full of water to cause a nasty chemical fire. I'll be using considerably more than that. So, if only two in our group were carrying four arrows each--," He thought briefly, "It might be enough to incinerate the four of us and anything within twenty feet in circumference."

There was an abrupt silence and stares from all around the table. Rich had simply shrugged in reply, "I know how it sounds—but if I can make this work it would greatly improve our odds."

"The dead are wet with decay anyway--," Tim shuddered, "I'm not so sure that we would need to include the water cylinder. After all, that is what makes it so dangerous to us in the first place—correct?"

"Some corpses are mummified—and dry as a bone," Rich reminded him, "Are you willing to take that risk?"

"I'll take my chances with those arrows--," Raymond poured more coffee, and said, "We have no idea of how fast this thing learns. If it figures things out—we're finished…"

"I'll do the best that I can." Sipping at his coffee, Rich appeared suddenly distraught, "But, nothing in life is ever truly guaranteed."

"I'd rather risk having those weapons--," Offering Rich some positive support, I handed the document back to him, saying, "Than chance going without them."

"Is that the time, already?" Raymond glanced over as the clock chimed nine, "We should get busy with those gates before it gets any later."

"See you guys at dinner time--," Moving from his seat and folding the diagram, Rich looked to me while slipping it into his pocket, "Do you need anything while we're out?"

"Yes--," I began assisting Tim with the breakfast plates and cutlery, "We'll need coffee, cream, and more sugar. Tim's planning a grocery shop—so we can pick up everything else later."

With a wave they had both hurried toward the door, but I had halted them, saying, "And please watch the time, it still gets dark very fast around this time of year."

It was an unsettling thought and received its rightful attention. Waving, they had quickly and quietly left. We were all aware of the horrors that awaited us in the shadows, but had become somewhat careless in its absence. It troubled me to have to keep their nerves on edge, but I feared that the paranoia was the only thing keeping us alive.

Tim had already begun clearing the breakfast plates as I busied myself with the mugs and condiments. The entire effort had taken less than thirty minutes between us. After washing the dishes, he had dried and put them away. We had shared only light discussion, and mainly matters concerning the groceries, cleaning supplies, and other daily requirements.

We had decided to share tea before continuing our day and soon enjoyed the warmth of a well-stocked hearth. The sun had shone in from between the parted draperies, but I had found no comfort on that morning. There was an unusual and suffocating shadow about the place. It caused the room to appear smaller, the atmosphere to seem stagnant, and the air subsequently harder to breathe. It wasn't the usual and presiding tension that had for so long hung about the place. It was more appropriately surmised to have suited that old adage, the one referring to the stillness that came before the storm.

We had sat quietly while watching the flames crackling and dancing in the hearth. It might have been somewhat pleasant, but I was immediately disturbed with his unusual silence. He had always been congenial, and quick with a joke to offer a smile. So, it was very unlikely if ever that he would have entertained such an absolute absence of general character. Whatever now bothered him had to have been prolific. It had become all too apparent through nervous little side-glances, and long quailed sighs of which he had uttered all too often. He had done this so much in fact, that I could no longer just sit there ignoring it, and felt obligated to inquire.

"I realize that in our current state this might sound like a stupid question--," I had peered into the crackling flames of the hearth, and sipping at my tea, quietly asked, "But, are you going to be alright?"

He had not answered right away and lethargically gazing into the hearth, thought for several moments. It wasn't insulting as this was his usual manner, and as while caught in some deep or disturbing thought. Allowing several moments to pass, he slowly looked up and adjusting his glasses, quietly replied, "Well Michael, and quite honestly, I'm feeling completely lost at the moment."

"Lost--," I had contemplated the statement, and considered every aspect of the word before looking back at my friend, "Do you mean in respect to giving up the funeral parlor, being here, or our current circumstances?"

"It's all of that and more." Leaning closer, he spoke as though fearing to be overheard, "It's also this place, the house, it's all slowly falling into darkness--," He struggled with the words as they slipped like a poison from between his lips, "This estate plays host to the horrors of the Duff Glenn, and to all of the evil things that you've gathered along the way. Michael--," He stared wide-eyed, "This has become a dwelling place of demons and is nothing more than a glorified prison."

Peering to where the dull morning light crept in through the partially open draperies, I nodded, "I'd be lying if I said that I didn't agree. But what would you have me do—just surrender to this evil thing that's come after us?"

"You're like the brother that I never had--," He swallowed hard, "And, you know that I would do anything to see you and Caitlin reunited and happy again. I would give almost anything just to see all of us able to return to some semblance of a normal life. But, I'm scared for you. You're spending more and more time locked away in that office, with Marlowe and that demon. I'm scared that we're already losing you."

"We need answers to things, and knowledge that can't be found in books, or by any other means." Watching the sunlight slowly creeping across the room, distraught, I looked back at my friend, and said adamantly, "There is just no other way…"

"Can't you see what's been happening to you? What's happening to all of us? The greater the threat becomes, the darker we become—and the further into Hell we wander…"

"Time, we just need more time to figure this whole thing out." I had pleaded, realizing that the borders of our sanity were slowly being compromised, "I feel it in my heart—in my soul. Things are going to come together—and everything is going to work out."

A sudden north wind howled at the window pane and we both glanced over, gazing fearfully beyond the draperies. It was as though something monstrous had overheard our discussion, and now reminded us of its presence.

"Michael, do you honestly feel that you should be writing all of this down?" His features became taught, his eyes suddenly large, "You said that the main reason that the general public was safe from most evil—was because they had no true awareness of its presence. Even though most will consider your books a work of fiction—what if even a few of them suddenly have their doubts? What if they start looking deeper into the details, obituaries, and newspaper articles? What if--," He pondered briefly, "Someone gets the idea to start poking around into those dark and old places?"

"They won't find them. I've changed the names of the people and places to protect the privacy of those involved, and anyone else that might stumble into anything." Scratching at my brow and brushing the curls from my eyes, I swallowed hard, "The chances of anyone finding anything would be extremely remote."

"It didn't take Raymond very long to put one and one together." He fell silent.

"I really don't think that my books are even that popular--," I had attempted to be optimistic, "Scholars wouldn't waste their time with them—and the general public wouldn't take any of this serious for a moment. What rational person would?"

"All that it takes is one to start a chain-reaction." His words fell like a hammer, "And, what if you're wrong? What if people do react—and those things that exist out there in the ether, realize that they're being exposed—and decide to fight back?" His eyes were huge and his tone weak, "Instead of just a few unexplained deaths and freak accidents—it would become a slaughter and genocide of the human race..."

A recent dream had suddenly come to mind, and images of utter chaos and the fall of humanity flashed before my eyes. Silently moving from the chair, I poured brandy for the both of us, and offering him a glass, returned to my couch.

He nervously sipped at the drink, and then draining a large portion, looked back at me. There was a desperate anticipation in his features. It was something that now creased and paled his brow with an unnatural and premature age. I knew that he had expected some kind of an answer, but I was at an utter and complete loss for words. I wondered if he had even realized how deep that insinuation had gone. It wasn't that I might've placed a few people in harm's way, but condemned humanity to hell...

"So, what would you suggest that I do?" Gently swirling the brandy in my glass, I sniffed at its soothing bouquet.

It came in the form of a stuttering explanation, which was entirely unlike him. The glass almost slipping from his trembling hands, he looked to me as though questioning his own sanity.

"I don't have any answers. All that I do know is that we need to protect others—and avoid making things any worse than they already are." He paused to finish his drink and I had quickly moved to pour him another, and placing it into his hands, returned to my seat.

He drank deeply before continuing, as speaking just above a whisper, said, "Maybe, you should inquire about this with Marlowe before continuing any further?"

"Agreed--," I gazed upon my friend, "If Marlowe shares your concerns—I'll destroy the manuscript without any question."

"I'm truly sorry." His features were long and drawn in the shadows as he apologized, "But I just can't sit idle when we might be jeopardizing so much more than ourselves."

"Not half as sorry as I would be—if what you're assuming holds any truth"

"We all know that you would never have done any of this if you had known the possible consequences."

"I'd rather have fallen into that pit at the Hedley mine as a child, than brought this down upon any of you."

"Don't say things like that."

"It's the truth—and I'm having a very hard time living with many things, especially after what happened to my mother, and poor old Harry."

"You know that wasn't your fault." His gaze softened and I was forced to look away, as he said softly, "Those things in Hedley might've killed all of us if you hadn't come when you did."

"I can't help but wonder if it hadn't all been done by some evil design." I swallowed down the remainder of my glass, "And if, whether by destiny or fate, and due to the things that I've done at one time or another, I've somehow condemned us all."

"That's utter and complete rubbish—and you know it!"

"Tim--," I stared down into the glass held tightly between my hands, "I really don't know anything, anymore."

"All that you really need to know right now is that we are your friends, and come hell or high water, we will stand together."

The words failed me as the sound drowned in my breast, "I wish with all of my heart that I'd never started any of this."

"Oh, my dear friend—you never started anything." The compassion shone in my friend's gaze, "It was the evil that brought us into this—and hope that still binds us altogether. All that anyone can do now—is make an ending worthy of whom and what we are."

"Its people like you, my dear friend, who make this life and world worth fighting for."

"Michael--," He feigned a smile, "Goodness and hope are always worth fighting for—even if it just means leaving a better world for those who follow."

I could only bow my head in silent reflection. I could hear the distant words of my mother resounding painfully within the echoing halls of my empty heart. "Do you really believe that he is so bad? Perhaps, if you keep an open mind and heart, you will discover that he is so much more than you might have ever imagined." She had been right about him and so many other things in life. I wished that I had listened more…

"I'll go to Marlowe and discuss this matter of the book with him."
Moving from my seat, I gathered our glasses, and pausing to look back at
him, said, "I'll likely lose track of the time, would you mind knocking?"

"Of course—when did you want me to call on you?"

"I'm doing my mother's Goulash recipe tonight. I put her cookbook on
the counter by the stove—while I remembered. I'd like to get dinner started
around four—it needs time to simmer."

Realizing the intensity of our conversation to have been overwhelming in
my current and exhausted state, he had attempted to lighten the mood by
changing the subject.

"Of course--," He nodded, though still looking very concerned, and added,
"Try to have a nap if you can. I'll get all the prep-work done according to
the recipe, and have it waiting for you."

"Thank you, I haven't prepared this meal in many years." I moved into
the kitchen and washing the two glasses, sighed as he followed, and I said,
"I sure hope that I get it right."

"Even if you get it half-right--," Smacking his lips with the memory, he
sighed, "It'll still be the best meal that we've eaten in ages."

Patting his shoulder, I nodded toward the hearth, "Maybe you should try
to have a nap before dinner--," Pointing to the dark circles beneath my
eyes, I said, "We're all starting to look like raccoons."

"Burglar rodents that sneak around in the night—it almost sounds
appropriate--," Making his way back toward the couch, he called back,
"I'll make the chocolate Mousse before I come up to get you. It'll save us
some time and counter space."

"Thanks again, Tim—for everything…"

"When this is all said and done--," He had looked back at me, "I was
thinking of asking Tanya out for dinner. How does that sound to you?"

"That sounds terrific. When this is finally over—maybe we should all go
on a long vacation—somewhere warm." It was the first truly pleasant
thought that we had shared in what seemed forever. He had smiled, and
making himself comfortable on the couch, turned his attention back to the
hearth.

Moving toward the stairs, I glanced back as he fluffed a cushion and
shoved it beneath his head. He had always had what my uncle referred to
as 'intestinal fortitude.' Although he might have seemed rather 'mild
mannered' to the general public, there was a Saint and warrior residing just
beneath the surface. He never failed to surprise me. In that moment, I had
regretted the many years that we had lost together over a terrible

misunderstanding. I could only hope and pray that we might have the time to make up for it.

CHAPTER TWO

10:35 a.m.

That strong north wind had found its way around the house, and was now howling from beyond my office window. It rattled the pane and incessantly moaned among the gnarled and snow-covered branches of the old willow. Standing before the parted draperies, I felt mesmerized by the fatigue now clouding my mind, and gazed silently into the pale oblivion. The worst of the snow had ceased several weeks prior. Danny and Dennis had cleared the drive and walks, but all else still lay deeply buried. I had been greatly relieved when Raymond and Rich had finally removed and put away all of the festive decorations. As within my mind's eye I could still vividly see the storm ripping and tearing at the Nativity scene. It was a ghastly vision of the manger being destroyed, and the baby Jesus being spirited away. Carried upon bitter and blackened winds, it was deeply buried beneath the dark and frozen drifts. Distraught at the sight of such a terrible scene, I would soon after discover that it had been an evil omen of things to come...

The tall pines creaked and groaned as they swayed in the gusts, casting icy veils down upon the stone pillars of the main gates. In a blurred moment, I had thought to have seen the crucified form of poor old Harry. As still hanging from the spiked gates and staring through dead eyes, his entrails poured down into the deep snow. Then, and to my absolute horror, he looked back at me, extending a beckoning arm! His eyes were suddenly cast upward into the heavens, as his coat billowed like the blood-stained wings of a fallen angel.

Unable to watch any longer, I stared upward as the wind wailed high in the tree-tops. The heavens had become gray and overcast and the shadows crept ever longer, in passage and from beneath the tall pines. Looking to where I had seen the gruesome apparition of Harry, I stared to where some part of him still remained. They had removed the corpse, but a dark stain could still be seen just below the gates. It spread ever outward, and could be seen from just beneath a light layer of fresh snow. A crimson shadow in memory, a bloodied stain that, marking the property, also seared my soul...

Slowly moving from the window, I went back to the desk, and slumping into the chair, placed a hand before my eyes. My head hurt and even my eyes felt as though they were throbbing from some internal pressure. It felt as though a dozen hammers now pounded from inside, fighting to escape from within my skull. I had never experienced headaches before, and squinted to avoid even the dullest of light.

Looking away from the mid-day gloom of the window, my attention traveled to where the raven now solemnly gazed back. It made no sound or movement, only watching with those brilliant and flashing red eyes. Without realizing what I was doing, I had reached out and gently caressed the blackened feathers of its crest. The demon reacted curiously, as even to the bitter cold of its unearthly touch. I continued with the sincerest of affection. Remaining absolutely silent, it just watched as though having understood the unrelenting torment of my broken heart.

"You who would bare the bitter wages of sweet sorrow--," It whispered, as leaning down, its eyes became twin spheres of ethereal fire, "Speak of this burden which now weighs so heavily upon your soul."

"They are matters concerning things that I had done, and continue even now." I remembered Rich and Tim's concerns lucidly, but all else seemed to be fading and lost in thought, "I need to know of portals into possible oblivion—and whether my works condemns us all…"

"Such a thing is possible—but power of this magnitude comes at great risk and terrible cost." Marlowe's voice boomed from the dark abyss of my mind.

"If this could be done—a passage opened into a black hole. I would willingly assume all responsibility, and accept whatever penalty that may come. And as long as the consequences fall only upon me—and the others remain safe…"

"You would wander into places few dare to tread…" Marlowe appeared as a shadow that lingered in the deepest corners of my office. As with the hood of his black cloak drawn closely about his face, pale eyes shone out of the darkness as he spoke, "There can be no promise as to the safety of your companions. Such things reside upon individual choices, and whatever fate and destiny rule, accordingly."

"Those are still reasonable terms--," Agreeing, I still pursued a hope, saying, "And I would still agree."

"The pathway brings many changes—the cost of which might very well be your undoing, and even damnation. Once you have chosen—we all share in this destiny. Do you still dare consider such a thing?"

"What do you mean by changes? Will they affect Caitlin and the others in our group?"

"All shall be affected and all shall suffer the consequences or redemption of our actions in the here and now. The pact seals your destiny—but not your fate…"

"Then I accept—and without any regret on my part."

"Before the stone can be cast into destiny's pool— there is another who must decide and agree upon this path…"

"Another?" Startled, I looked to where Marlowe now solemnly gazed upon the raven. It hadn't occurred to me previously, but even this mysterious and ominous entity had the right of choice within such matters. We would all share in this fate, be it freedom or damnation.

For several moments all that I could do was look down while tightly clasping my hands together upon the desk. Nervously fidgeting, I had looked to the large and grim bird as though seeking the answers in its burning, crimson gaze. But not a single sound was uttered or any motion made, as it just silently sat perched atop the hutch, and blankly stared. And so, we had remained in this moment for what seemed an eternity. It was almost as though the bird, having already decided within decline, considered in what matter to express the denial.

At this point, and overwhelmed by emotions, I had looked up pleadingly, and quietly said, "I've made so many poor decisions and terrible mistakes through time." I looked deeply, desperately into the demons burning gaze, "And, because of this—so many have suffered and already been lost…" A tear of fear and frustration dampened the heated flesh of my cheek, "If I could give life and love back to you, I would willingly do it, even at the cost of my own."

Obviously sensing my sincerity, the bird dropped from its perch, and stood staring from directly in front of me. Moving within inches of my face, the large sharp beak tilted ever so slightly as a single burning eye focused intently upon me.

"Why would you dare offer such a thing—knowing what I am?" The raven whispered. There was something between shock and amazement reflecting from the depths of its fiery gaze, as it asked, "And to what purpose does this serve you—and why do you seek this for me?"

"Because, you have suffered this fate long ago and while saving me--," Swallowing back the tears with the memory of the boy and fiend in the forest, I said, "And, you are the dearest of friends, sincerest of souls—and certainly did not deserve the evil that has befallen you. If by life or death I could somehow release you from this sinister servitude—I would do so willingly and without remorse."

It appeared as though some long lost and distant memory now returned to the creature, the flames flashed as it blinked, and leaning closer, it said, "I serve only the masters and Marlowe—of what do you speak within calling me friend, and savior?"

"The answer shall come to you soon enough--," Marlowe interrupted, as pointing a long and withered finger at the demon, he spoke in a commanding voice, "Not all things may appear as what they may seem, even unto you…"

The demon now appeared confused, as hopping back and forth across the desktop, it moved even closer, and looking directly and deep into my eyes, whispered "What is this matter of which you have knowledge—but is lost to me? I must know…"

Marlowe uttered silent warning and I said nothing, thinking briefly before saying, "If it's enough for me to trust you and risk everything—then isn't it worthy of discovering for yourself?"

"Beware—for now you taunt the demon of which possessing, has bound an innocent soul in darkness through time." Marlowe whispered in my thoughts, "The two now struggle within as the soul awakens and remembers…"

The raven now looked indecisively from side to side, and while revealing a strange duality that visibly questioned itself, it was as though two entities now occupied the same form, and fought for consciousness and dominion. I felt frightened in that moment, but held steady and struggled to conceal it. I knew that any sign of weakness in the face of the demon could provoke an attack, obsession or possession! It was now apparent that this creature, of which I had first assumed to have just been a demon, was in reality a possessed soul!

The raven walked from one side of my desk to the other, slinking rather than moving in the fashion of a living bird. There was something insidious, terrifying about the creature. It now revealed some kind of truly sinister and evil inner force. I had forgotten how the darkness had concealed itself within corpses, and never considered how a demon might use a soul in the same way. It now also horrified me with the realization that this creature had also evaded the guardians notice. What could have possibly spared us from the darkness if this was possible? Of course, it had initially been the power of the cane to dispel spirits… As in fact, and quite different from the evil that was banished from beyond the gates, I had willingly welcomed this demon into my house and home…

The raven returned to where it had stood only inches from my face, and staring blankly, asked, "And, would you truly choose damnation in my place?" The red eyes flashed like beacons in the long shadows of the dismal room.

"Beware—speak only to the soul and not the demon…" I swallowed hard with Marlowe's warning, thinking for a moment before speaking, and saying, "Given no other choice and at the end of all things, I would never abandon the soul or break my promise."

The bird fell silent, its eyes softening as something else now looked back at me. It was like someone that awakening from a terrible dream now saw the world again though new eyes, and for the first time. Reaching upward and gently stroking the feathers at the crown of its head, I whispered, "Do you now remember me?"

There was a moment of silence between us and an understanding that words could never have properly expressed. As suddenly sensing a strange change in the entire demeanor of the mystical creature, something shared from deep within us emerged in that moment. Then, something caused me to suddenly withdraw the hand. It wasn't fear, but astonishment, as the once bitter cold creature began permeating with steadily increasing warmth.

Slowly turning to look upon the demon, I glanced at my hand in amazement while saying, "Is it possible—are you truly resonating with the vitality of life?"

"An act of sincere self-sacrifice--," It spoke softly in that haunting and child-like voice, "A gift of love by no other name and a force beyond all others."

Something happened in that moment, as no longer fearing the demon, I felt something far more powerful and binding that grew between us.

"The choice has been made." Marlowe's voice boomed as he vanished back into the shadows of mind and space, "A pact sealed within an unholy trinity—and so begins the journey upon the pathways to oblivion..."

The enormous black bird began trembling violently, its eyes flashing wildly as leaping down from the desk, it dropped into the chair beside me, its form altering, growing, as it became the boy once more. Yet something had changed. He appeared strangely different. Touching at his arms, he had looked to me in utter astonishment. I knew at that moment that his heart and flesh had taken on some new semblance of life. It was warmth beyond the bitter cold of space and the stillness of the grave, and although I could not explain this event, was humbled in the moment.

There was a sudden hesitation in his features, as slowly moving from the chair, he stood and looked down at me. It had been the first true expression of emotion that I had ever seen from him, as without another thought, I suddenly understood. Leaning forward, I opened my arms in offer of gentle embrace.

There had been slight hesitation on his part, but then he had come forward and accepted the gift in friendship. There was sudden warmth surging like a shining force from between us, as clutching tightly, we silently held one another as dear friends would.

"I feel the light of your soul--," He had whispered, "And the truth within the steady beating of your heart."

"A greater gift I couldn't have possibly asked for." I held him near while gently stroking the long white hair at the back of his head, "Please forgive me for leaving you on that night in the forest. The night that you saved my life from the witch at the cost of your own immortal soul..."

His expression had suddenly gone blank as he leaned back and stared in utter disbelief, "The witch of the horde in the forest" The words came as though through some distant and almost inaccessible memory, as squinting, he repeated the words again, "The witch of the horde in the forest..."

Looking deeply into the blue fire of his wide gaze, I saw the memory realized as his confusion turned to recognition through sudden tears, and he whispered, "I know you..."

"I swear on my heart and soul--," Weeping, I had whispered in promise, "That I will never abandon you to the evil ever again..."

"You look upon me--," He seemed saddened, "And yet still you do not truly see me in the way that I know you..."

There was a moment of stillness while something slowly came over him, and I sensed the demon welling as it reclaimed dominion, and gazed back at me. After releasing the boy, he had just stepped away as though having never spoken, and coldly whispered, "Accordingly and in order with the pact, as I enter into your world—so also do you submit unto mine."

"I will abide by the natural laws—and whatever they may bring--," Swallowing hard, I prayed to have not accidentally submitted, or unwittingly fallen into unauthorized treatise with the beast.

"Be warned—Michael--," The demon whispered, as moving closer and gently touching my face with a pale hand, it said, "For as the years shall still pass—they shall not scar you as they do others. You shall sense many things of this realm and know much of those beyond. You are a child of the sun—but shall exist in moonlight, do you understand..."

"Yes—I understand."

"You have released the child that was taken—." The demon's eyes flashed with starlight, a sinister shadow crossing its features, as it said, "I am now to become one—both fair and most foul, deliverance and damnation..."

Utterly terrified but fascinated, I remained absolutely still and silent. Ever so slowly it caressed my face, as speaking softly appeared as though it might tear out my throat at any given moment.

"There must be an exchange, Michael--," It hissed in a terrifying tone that sounded like some sinister song composed by the devil, "For all things to come to pass—you must offer the price of life for the living in this world."

"And what is it that you need from me?"

"Just this--," It took a firm hold upon my right arm and then, with a sly glance, slashed out at my wrist with a claw! As the blood ran, it had done the same to its other arm, and swiftly pressed our two together! Falling to my knees before the beast, the world swam as I felt the life flowing out of me! Lights in brilliant and flowing colors filled my thoughts, as demonic shadows spun while dancing wildly from all around us! Sounds that I had never before heard suddenly echoed in my mind, as songs existing in unknown languages were sung by shining seraphim.

In a flash it had all ended and I slowly slipped down with my back against the desk. Still nauseous, I had looked to my arm in sudden surprise as the wound had completely healed.

"And so it begins…" Unsteadily, the demon had taken several steps away from me, and then appearing as though caught in some strong and bitter gust, swayed as though it might fall. A pale light now shone from all about the boy, as his features began twisting and elongating. With eyes burning brightly, he grew taller and fairer, his white hair growing, lengthening while flowing about his pale and shining form.

Kneeling, I could only stare in astonishment as the boy's eyes shimmered with the bluest of star-light. If ever anyone had truly experienced the vision of a soul, demon, or angel, it surely stood before me now.

"You have released that which was once lost—," Marlowe whispered from the shadows of my mind, "And, with this first revelation—you must now seek the second of three to this destiny that we all share. But tread softly and beware—for the evil follows closely upon our heels."

"Marlowe, I need to know, why this change to our companion?"

"It is not what you see but sense in things that grants them power. There exists a mystery between you—and once solved, it shall either restore your souls, or commit all to certain damnation …"

"But how will I know how to find the answers?"

"The truth exists as it always has—all that you have to do is realize and accept it…"

The figure was no longer that of the boy, nor even recognizable. It bore no gender, and yet was strikingly beautiful in the way that an unfinished marble masterpiece might seem. It was hardly imaginable that something so exquisite might harbor the soul of a demon...

"Are you still in the service of the old and dark Gods--," I had questioned while still kneeling at my desk, "Or finally free of their bonds?"

"We remain in servitude—but not beyond redemption." Its voice was no longer that of a child, but still soft and seemed to emanate from all about me. Oddly, I thought to have heard the numerous echoes of multiple voices as it spoke. They were like the finest of crystal wind-chimes dancing in a gentle summer breeze, as it promptly replied, "Hope remains—for us all."

"What is the second mystery along this path that we now follow?" I spoke the words to both Marlowe and the entity while asking, "And where might I find it?"

"It shall present itself before you--," Marlowe replied, "But you must discover its secret for yourself—and beware, for few things are ever truly what they seem."

"Are you still a demon?" Looking to the shimmering form that stood before me, I fought with the words, "Are you truly still the boy that I had once known?"

"I am neither and both—what was, what is, and what shall be," It knelt before me, and looking up and into my eyes, promised, "And, until our paths no longer cross, I am your friend and in your service, always."

Gently taking its hand, I felt the warmth flow like a river of light through my entire being. Slowly nodding, I looked down upon the entity while thinking briefly, and then saying, "I will no longer refer to you as the demon, nor boy. From this day onward I will just know you as friend. And in Latin, a friend is called, Amica."

"Amica--," It repeated in approval and moving back to its feet, slowly bowed, "Amicus, we are."

Looking upon the beautiful and terrifying creature, I was utterly captivated, "Are you still in my service through bonds attributed between Marlowe and your masters?"

"We three are bound together through time and space—I remain for you as I always have." It gazed upon me with those brilliant and star-lit eyes, "And, shall always do so, until--," It faltered and suddenly fell silent.

Looking around the room, I questioned its last statement, "Until what— what do you mean?"

"Answers arrive as decisions force the wheels of time--," Marlowe answered, "Continually opening passages—doorways to destinies unwritten, and unknown as of yet."

Looking to Amica, I saw a strange sadness, which appearing utterly foreign, was like a shadow that dimmed its shimmering features. I knew at that moment that Amica had seen some distant vision, and feared what was soon to come. Sensing this, I hadn't dared to ask anything further. Stepping away, Amica's form began fading and falling into shadow as it changed once more. Ever smaller and darker it became, as blackened feathers erupted, and with wings stretching outward, clawed feet now rested upon the floor. It leapt into the air as swiftly fluttering past, returned to the mantel and hutch above my desk.

I had looked to where it now perched, those brilliant blue eyes shining where the crimson had once been. I felt saddened while feeling as though I had forever lost the boy, but then realized that within soul we bare no gender, or singular form. It was believed that angels were all androgynes and bore semblance to both. In which case, demons having been nothing more than fallen angels would have most certainly been the same.

Utterly astonished, I slipped back into the chair while curiously gazing upon the bird.

"A great power for good exists within all--," Marlowe whispered, "It is the strength that binds mortal hearts, delivers the damned and overcomes the darkness. But, we must also be aware of the darkness that causes man to commit evil upon men. They are the mortals who would willingly serve, simply by means of weak constitution. They are the desperate, frightened, and easily manipulated. The darkness poisons the souls and minds of the lost, and seduces them into its service…"

"It's becoming harder each day to trust anything or anyone. How can we ever possibly recognize, much less defeat such overwhelming odds?"

"All that we are destined to do is overcome our own darkness. With our victory comes a sway in the balance of things, which will then provide hope and opportunity for others. Ours, my dear friend, is only a battle in an ongoing war."

"I can only pray for the strength to overcome this."

"Have a heart, for though the shadows run long, so does the love grow from all about you. You are not alone in this fight—we stand together. All that you must focus upon now is discovering the next secret, for it contains the influence to set a great power free in this world."

"But how and where do I begin?"

"You already have—simply follow your heart and always remain true. For the answers reside within us all—if we dare gaze deep enough."

"Amica--," Looking curiously toward the Raven, I said, "At the Lumberton house you were able to send that demon into the abyss. What would prevent you from doing the same now?"

"There remains a hierarchy among all things--;" It replied, "A lesser being presents little threat to us. But what we face now is well beyond my ability, alone."

"Hence the necessity for combined effort--," Marlowe reminded me, "And, the necessity of the second key of which you must now discover."

Taking hold of the cane and nervously fidgeting with the hound's head, I bit down upon my lower lip. We now possessed the strength to fight off lesser demons, ghouls, and the souls of the dead. As between the great hound, Amica, and what lay spellbound in the guest house, the estate was sanctified and secure.

The enemy was aware of our presence, but was blinded and unable to penetrate our minds upon hallowed ground. But in the same turn, what would happen once I ventured out of Sanctum Arcanum?

"You have already cast several lesser entities into the void." Marlowe whispered, "Yet, we three still require assistance—which exists within the second secret. The third shall follow upon its own accord, and when summoned, in combination to the second."

"You seem to have all of the answers, but speak in riddles, old friend." I swallowed hard, "Aren't there any other clues that you might provide to guide me to the source of the second key?"

"I have provided all that I am able--," He replied, "There are many forces at work here. Have faith, stand strong and they shall present themselves before you in due time."

"Time is such a precious thing--," I placed the cane between the desk and shelving, "We lose so much in its passing."

"Time is a contrivance of the physical realm and merely an illusion." Marlowe muttered, "Effects of which you shall no longer suffer as others do. Focus upon what must be done—and allow nothing to hinder or cause you to falter upon the path…"

"I'm just one man--," The thought pained me, "It's so hard at times—I see the faces of friends lost and fear what follows us….Some things never fade from the heart or soul."

"Focus on the morrow and release the past—," Marlowe whispered, his tone revealing a sorrow beyond measure, "We all suffer within bitter loss—but this only broods weakness in the face of evil. We must not allow the darkness to use this against us. Look ahead now, and seek out the truth and solve the mystery…"

Marlowe's voice faded into the shadows as all fell suddenly silent. The world seemed to have been lost into darkness as a single spark of light came to mind. Then, instinctively drawing the black satin cloth from the golden sphere, I gazed into the shimmering golden globe. My thoughts were immediately sent drifting through the swirling and crystalline light, and I watched through the semblance of a shining dream. Through the mists of time I saw a woman in a long and hooded green cloak. She was gathering flowers from a little garden, and then knelt before a weathered and ancient grave. Drawing back the hood of her cloak, she allowed the fiery curls of her long hair to spill down into the clover at her knees.

My heart wept at the sight of my beloved, as with flowing tears, she had bowed and silently prayed. Although I could not hear the spoken words, I knew that her sorrow was over a broken heart that we shared. I had wanted nothing more than to reach out and comfort her, but my trembling hand was restrained by Amica's soft voice.

"Weep not for her, but be strengthened within knowing that she remains safe." Amica had softly called to me from its perch, "For the time may yet come when you return to her…"

Recovering the sphere and wiping the tears from my eyes, I turned back to the bird, "You are my light when none other shines, dear Amica."

"Marlowe—there was a question that slipped my mind--," Staring upon the blank page in the typewriter, I asked, "What will become of anyone reading my work and discovering the truth?"

"Those who might suspect the truth are already aware and at risk." He responded without hesitation, "These efforts will provide them with wisdom, protection, and hope. Do not misunderstand the power of the written word or forsake it."

"I thought that it couldn't reach us here?"

"Doubt is a mortal aspect of the darkness and is always with us— always attempting to mislead and destroy us. You must complete what you have begun and reveal all that we have shared. The future of many depends upon it."

I had never attributed much significance to the collective works, and was amazed when Marlowe referred to them as kind of alchemical, white magic, modern Grimoire. In this respect, I could justify everything, and would complete the project to the best of my ability.

"Nothing happens without purpose--," Marlowe whispered, "Do not hold your friend responsible for his fears and concerns. He speaks only out of love for all involved, and is an honorable and trust-worthy soul."

I had forgotten that Marlowe had always been with me, and most certainly known of our previous discussion. There was comfort in his words and tone, and they had a soothing effect that immediately put my fears and heart to rest. I listened to the ticking of the clock, its metallic heartbeat rhythmically pounding to the steady sound of my own. A shudder suddenly coursing through me, as while reaching an epiphany, it chimed several times and I turned back toward the typewriter.

It all seemed to happen without having even attempted a single thought. I slipped a new page into the carriage, and had begun with the title: *Nightrealm V: Diabolus Lapis*, which quite literally translated from its original Latin meant, "Devil Stone."

I was uncertain as to why I had chosen that in specific, but had assumed to have heard the title suggested from somewhere deep within my psyche...

The words seemed to flow almost flawlessly, as entering the events of the day, I began the fifth volume of the adventure. A book that due to current circumstance, I had not even been certain would become a reality. In fact, though I had completed the previous manuscript, it still lay untouched. Thinking briefly, I drew the page from the typewriter, and installing a fresh one, looked over the final page of the last book. I fully realized that there was a distinct possibility that I might not survive the days to come, but quickly wrote out a "cliff-hanger" to top them all!

"Well, Amica, let's hope that I survive long enough to finish the new project." Sighing deeply and looking to the bird, I added in thought, "It would be a real shame to leave the readers hanging."

"Have hope--," Fluttering across the room and perching atop the iron figure of Pan and the Maiden, Amica quietly settled while looking back, "Our journey only just begins..."

Peering over at the bird, I realized to have forgotten about the statue in all of the general chaos. I had promised Eva to have it moved into the guest-house at the first opportunity. Drawing a pad and pen from a desk drawer, I scribbled the thought down and left it where I would notice it. Intending to continue writing, I had paused and sadly looked to the empty chair beside the desk. In the dull gloom of the late afternoon I had imagined the shadow of my beloved, as smiling sweetly, she had sat there as though nothing had ever happened. Although I tried to continue with my work, it was impossible to focus without continually noticing the empty seat.

A furtive movement in the long shadows of the office caused me to turn. The raven had swooped over from where it was perched, and dropping into the chair, suddenly became Amica again. Pulling its long and pale legs up from beneath it and sitting as Caitlin had once done, it rested its face upon its knees, and peered back at me. Its long and white hair fell in shining locks from about its soft features, as those star-lit eyes seemed to gaze into forever. All semblance of the boy having faded, there was an uncanny resemblance to someone from a distant memory, and I felt as though it had not just been mere fate that had brought us together.

The pose had been familiar to Caitlin, but there was something about this entity that was hauntingly familiar… It was a distinct impression, and a sense of having known this being far longer, and previous to having ever known the boy. As through the subtle features, form and gaze, I felt the call of some distant memory. It was the strong impression that we had been together in a preceding lifetime, but shared in another world quite differently. Had this been another sacrifice before the evil that still pursued us?

It was happening as Marlowe had predicted. I was beginning to sense things in the now and hereafter… In that moment, I knew that we had always been together and regardless of the demon or whatever happened, that it was somehow eternal. And yet, there was a mystery, a shroud of dark intrigue that remained between us. It was something that had both fascinated and terrified me.

"We have all been drawn together many times through an eternity—and existed in many ways." Marlowe whispered, "Do not forsake the truth for fear of mortal misconceptions."

"Please—continue…" Amica settled back into the chair and silently watched. It shone ever so slightly in the dim glow of the dull afternoon, but its eyes darkly sparkled like diamonds. There was something both sinister and hauntingly beautiful about this strange and noble creature. Thoughts of the boy now entirely faded as its defining features were deeply impressed upon my inquisitive mind. It was neither male nor female, but became something resembling a woman, yet without baring gender. Oddly, I was troubled as while struggling with the memory that now sought desperately to identify the true identity of the incredible creature.

What was this uncanny and insatiable fascination for something that would have otherwise repulsed and utterly terrified me? And still, what was the purpose of this change and what part might it play before the end of all things?

"Look to me when the sadness takes you--," It sweetly whispered as though sensing my heart, "Know only me when you dream of your beloved..."

Inexplicably, its words had caused an undeniable love to well from the very core of my being. Not just for Caitlin, but for Marlowe, this enchanting creature and all other living things. Something was happening to me, a type of awareness, an awakening which now occurred while within direct interaction with the magic and mystery that was Amica.

"Is she truly safe--," The words had formed as swiftly as the thought, "Is she hidden upon hallowed grounds in a secret place, and kept far from harm?"

Amica gently placed a hand upon my cheek and leaning close, gazed deeply into my eyes, "See only me—for I am the light that shields your heart from the darkness, and will blind the eyes that would do you harm."

Drifting deeply into the bright and shining heavens that were the eyes of Amica, I could see a universe of endless stars reflecting from eternity and back. All doubt dissipating as I slowly nodded, pondering, questioning, "Is this how you truly appear—and what you really are?"

"I have been and am many things--," Sorrow now creased its pale and angelic features and it sadly said, "And will become others still..."

I sensed from deep within that it had been speaking the truth. It was apparent that what occurred now was happening out of necessity, and that it could not have been safely or successfully approached in any other fashion....

"Take comfort in my presence—dear Michael--," Amica whispered, as settling back into the chair formed the semblance of a smile, saying, "Soon you will become aware of many things and then—with the coming changes you shall remember..."

Beyond words, I had simply nodded as it gently caressed my arm. A fallen angel seeking redemption, it was the ghost of love and friendship immemorial.

I had continued typing, the thoughts flowing faster with every effort. There was a purpose in all things though we may never discover them in a single lifetime. It was all coming together. Strange and even terrifying events that had to reach some conclusion before life as we had known it might ever return to normal. The first key in the order of events was the revelation and redemption of Amica. The bonds between us strengthen even further as the mystery between us begins to slowly fade. Although

Marlowe and the entity remain in the sovereignty of an unknown evil, I can sense that the balance already begins to sway…

CHAPTER THREE

The telephone suddenly rang, sending me backward and almost falling from the chair as I grabbed to answer it! The voice was immediately recognizable, and old Ted laughed as he apologized, "I'm sorry, did I get you at a bad time?"

"No—nothing like that--," Rubbing at my eyes, I slowly leaned back into the chair, and replied with a smile, "I was just doing some research and you caught me off guard, but lately, that's nothing unusual for me."

"It sounds like you're keeping too many late hours again. I'm surprised that you don't just pass out?" Sighing deeply, he sounded troubled, and hesitating before speaking, said, "The reason that I was calling is because I have some bad news."

"Let me guess--," Swallowing hard I assumed the worst, and nervously asked, "Book sales are down and you're calling to cancel the sequel?"

"Hell no--," He laughed out loud, "They're doing just fine and you can expect another royalties- check sometime next week, in the mail."

"Alright--," Taking a deep breath and exhaling slowly, I felt the tension slowly slipping away, "So, what was the bad news that you were talking about, I'm all ears now?"

"Well, it concerns that sweet Kagome girl that was going to edit your book--," He puffed at a cigar and coughing, said, "It seems that she had a loss in the family and had to go back to Toronto to stay with her mother. It's a huge deal in her family and might take a week or longer, so I don't have any idea of when she might be coming back?"

Looking to where the completed manuscript rested in its metal basket beside the desk, I sank back into the seat, "Well, it's not like anyone can really do anything about that, but if it's just a week or two, it's not such a big deal, really. What did you have in mind?"

"We do have someone else that could handle the job." He tapped a pen on his desk while thinking aloud, "He was a professor of Linguistics in Germany, reads Latin fluently, and has a history with esoteric literature. I hired him to replace Hans. His name is Ole Papra."

"You sound a little hesitant about this." The tone of his voice bothered me.

"It's like I said--," Ted sighed, "He was a professor and has a history in occult material. I'm not sure as to how he might relate to your specific type of fiction. I usually only use him for educational material and historical books. He's sharp as a whip and doesn't miss a turn."

Feeling rather intimidated about using a scholar to edit my work, I mumbled almost fearfully in a barely audible voice, "He sounds absolutely fantastic—but um, is there anyone else available?"

"Only dear old Ruth Sampson--," He chuckled, "She's outstanding when it comes to romance, historical fiction, or religious material, but I just wouldn't have the heart to drop this stuff into her lap. She'd have nightmares for years to come."

I remembered the dear woman. She was short, stocky, mid-fifties, and always had assorted chocolates and candy bars on her desk. Her hair was white and styled in a bob-cut, her features pleasant, and her big blue eyes revealed a depth of sincerity and wisdom. In that moment I had also remembered an incident with a spider and that she was terrified of anything that slithered or crawled...

"You're absolutely right, I wouldn't even consider handing this to her. I feel pretty confident about Ole and he does sound like the right man for the job. He certainly has the qualifications--," I thought briefly, and putting a finger to my lip, said with a mischievous smile, "I just hope that he doesn't get nauseated too easy."

"He just completed editing a historical account involving the implements of torture used during the Inquisition--," Ted scoffed, and puffing at his cigar, chuckled, "It was a human slaughterhouse, so I think that he'll manage."

Looking up as the clock chimed, I noticed the time, "Well, in that case I can have it on your desk first thing tomorrow morning."

"It would be even better if you could drop it off this afternoon."

"Alright then, I'll run it down now." I had barely finished the sentence when Ted had hurriedly thanked me, and the line went dead in my hand. I had looked down as Merlin had crept out from beneath my desk and began rubbing against my leg.

"Hello there, old man--," I leaned down and scratching behind his ears, chuckled, "Did you want to drive down and drop my manuscript off at the office?"

He had just looked up at me with those golden and heavy, half-lidded eyes. It was obvious from his expression that he was so involved with the attention that nothing could have broken him from that mesmerizing moment. The instant had passed quickly, as wandering off he had suddenly taken notice of the raven, and halted in mid-step to stare. It wasn't fear but fascination that now held him spellbound. As leaping into my lap and cautiously creeping onto the desktop, he moved toward and gazed up at the ominous bird. There had been a moment of close inspection, and then satisfied, he had turned and hopped back down to the floor. Then, as casual as always he had sauntered across the office, and vanished into the hallway beyond. I had suspected that he had likely heard Tim working in the kitchen, and was on his way down for a treat. Tim and the old beast had renewed their friendship, which untainted by their previous acquaintance, had become a true fondness over the passing weeks. The others had teased and told him that it wasn't about Merlin desiring his friendship, but just how much extra food could be gained. Tim had simply smiled, and winking, replied that they knew nothing of the loyalty of animals, and especially the nature of cats. Having adamantly supported my friend on the subject, I had secretly felt absolutely terrible. As dearly as I had loved him, sometimes old Merlin could be such a conniving, little creep…

Looking back at the clock, I was reminded of the time, and gasping, leapt from the chair, "Almost two already, I'd better hurry—I don't want to get caught out after dark…"

2:22 p.m.

The drive to the office had not taken very long. The roads had been cleared by plows and the old Chrysler 300's weight and snow tires made the journey safer than anticipated. I had rushed up to Ted's office and admitted by the secretary, was surprised to meet another man. He was middle-aged, dark haired and sported a neatly trimmed beard and mustache. He was average height and build, and wore blue jeans and black woolen turtle-neck sweater. When he turned to shake my hand he smiled devilishly, his dark eyes sparkling within introduction. He appeared rather reserved and was an intellectual, a wild and passionate scholar if ever I had seen one.

"Ole Papra--," Ted had smiled with a wave, "I would like you to meet Michael Schreiber."

"It's a pleasure to meet you." He had firmly shaken my hand with a bow, which had been customary in old Europe and among the decadent aristocracy, saying "I have heard many good things about you."

"Likewise—Ted speaks highly of you as well."

We had sojourned to the chairs before Ted's desk as, dropping the manuscript before him, I said, "I don't mean to cut this short—but I have a Hungarian goulash simmering, and really need to get back home."

"My wife Anna also cooks a wonderful Goulash--," Ole beamed with the thought, "We share similar tastes."

"As European's I would have suspected that we might--," I winked, "Food and music are the universal language of the soul."

"I believe that we will get along just fine." Ole laughed, and looking to Ted, motioned toward the manuscript, "With all due respect, we should allow Mr. Schreiber to attend to his supper."

"Do you have any concerns?" Ted looked to me as I rose from my seat, "Or is there anything about the manuscript that you feel might need any special consideration?"

Thinking for a moment, I snapped my finger with the recollection, and said, "I used the old King James version for the 23rd Psalm. If you feel the modern version would be more appropriate, by all means feel free to change that. Also, I've made use of 12th century Latin of which I'm certain to be accurate, regardless of what more modern text implies. All the sources were meticulously researched, and I've made careful mention of any additional material in the acknowledgements."

"This is beginning to sound more like historical research and biblical archaeology—I thought that you wrote fictional books?" He appeared strangely amused while opening the manuscript to glance upon the introduction.

"No, it's just whimsical nonsense done entirely for fun." Shrugging, I added in thought, "I just like to add some fact to the fiction, I feel that it keeps it more colorful, and maybe even more interesting to some."

"It sounds fascinating." Nodding to himself, he looked through several pages before curiously glancing back at me, "How long have you been working on this project?"

"All of my life." My eyes kept passing between my friends and the clock, and I had a distinct sense of urgency, adding, "I'm learning as we go, so please feel free to call me with any questions or concerns." Handing him a business card that I pulled from a breast pocket, I smiled, "I work well into the night and am always available, except between six and ten in the mornings."

"I also do my best work in the evening." He seemed pleased, and rising to shake my hand in parting, said, "I will begin this afternoon!"

"Oh, can I speak to you for a moment in private?" Ted had called me aside as Ole took the manuscript, nodding politely, and departed the office.

I detected an immediate change in Ted's demeanor as, standing quietly at the office door, he said, "I just wanted to let you know that I'll be taking on a business partner in the next few weeks."

"A business partner--," Shocked, I leaned closer to my friend, "Is everything alright?"

He hesitated, and then smiling as though it mattered very little, said, "Well, I went to see the doc last month and he sent me out for some testing." His expression caused the blood to run cold in my veins. Gently pulling me away and back into his office, he closed the door and looking back at me, said, "Apparently, I've got advanced lung cancer. They gave me six months to a year..."

His words were utterly devastating. I leaned against the wall for support, staring back at him in utter and complete shock. His response had been a shrug as butting his cigar, reached into a shirt pocket for another, "That's what I get for smoking these cheap Mexican cigars." He scoffed while lighting another cigar, and coughing, said, "So, I'm taking on a partner—I can't just leave everyone high and dry when it comes time to check out."

"I'm so sorry..." There were no words of comfort that could be offered.

"Aw, it's going to be okay, kid--," He slapped my shoulder as he always had and chuckled while feigning a smile, "You'll like this other guy a lot. He's an old friend of mine. He's a private kind of guy, so names aside, we all just call him the Captain. His wife Joan is a real gem and his sister Amy is already working here. You'll all be like one big, happy family."

The emotions were overwhelming. After having already suffered so much loss, the thought of losing him was unbearable. Placing a hand before my eyes in a futile attempt to hide the tears, I peered back at him in disbelief, "This can't be happening—there must be something that they can do?"

He pondered briefly and then, looking me straight in the eye, said, "We're all responsible for our own decisions and actions in this world. And the way that I figure it—we should go proudly into the next. I could sit around feeling sorry for myself—but that's not how I want people to remember me. I'm sixty nine years old and I've had a terrific life—let's make the best of the time that we have left together. What do you say?"

Even while aware that there was so much more, the human condition within me refused to allow his mortality to pass without reaction, or escape within such simple release.

"I'm sorry—I'm not helping anything by being this way—but this is such a shock..."

"Hey--," Ted hugged me as family would, patted my back and quietly said, "The show must go on—and I know that you'll make me proud."

He had stood back and looked at me as though for the last time. There was sadness in that expression, the kind that we all share in final parting. His head had tilted in thought, and his features were hazed in the cigar smoke as he said, "You know, for whatever it may be worth, I wouldn't change anything, not for the world."

There was an old and familiar feeling in that moment, an impression of something that left me standing there bitter, guilty. As remembering the many times that he had invited me out on special occasions and I had declined, leaving him alone over the holidays more times than I could count.

"If there's anything that I can do—anything at all, just name it…"

"There is one thing?" He peeked behind the blind and appearing very concerned, looked back at me, and said, "Please don't tell any of the ninnies in the office about what's happening, I couldn't bare to watch them moping and making a fuss around me until this thing's done."

His courage broke my heart and I had to hide the tears, as even through it all, he still tried to make me laugh.

Ted had just forced that same smile he always had, and winking, said, "Don't make this any harder or worse than it has to be. We still have a lot of work to do together."

"I'm already working on the conclusion to *Nightrealm*--," The sentence were stuttered, but I couldn't find any other words, "I'm hoping to have it completed in a few months."

"That would be terrific--," He smiled, "I've been following it so far—and can't wait to see what happens next. You really do have one hell of an imagination." He placed his hands on his hips, thinking, and said, "Hey, listen—I want you to promise me something, right here and now."

"Sure thing, Ted, You name it."

"Promise me that no matter what happens, that you'll keep writing." His eyes reflected a deep inner sadness, "Promise, that you'll do it for me."

"I promise that I'll keep writing—for as long as I'm able…"

"That's more than fair--," He took a long hit from his cigar, exhaling and briefly vanishing into the thick cloud of smoke; "I'll introduce you to the Captain next month." He slapped my shoulder, and throwing the office door open, winked, "Now get going before you burn dinner and the house with it."

"Um—Ted?" Halting in the doorway I had glanced back at him, "Who else knows—about this?"

"Just you, me and the doc--," His features hardened, "There's no need for anyone else to know—at the moment."

For reasons that I couldn't quite explain, I asked him something that caught him completely off guard, "Ted—do you ever get the impression that something is following—or watching you in the night?"

His features had paled considerably. In a sobering tone he replied, "It's funny that you should ask that—all joking aside." He puffed at the cigar, coughing and clearing his throat, "I'm not sure if it's just age, or living alone for so long, but I've been getting a little paranoid, you know? It's almost like the shadows in your stories, the darkness moves around in the corners of my eyes. Odd thing though—I just had an eye exam and they're clear as a bell."

Removing the talisman from about my neck, I moved forward, slipping it around his, and said, "Please accept this gift—and promise me that you will not remove it, under any circumstances."

"What's the deal with this?" He seemed strangely amused as he toyed with the charm in his fingers, "Is it some kind of Voodoo gimmick?"

"Please—just trust me--," I pleaded, "And promise that you'll never take it off."

"Alright then—if it makes you happy." He slipped it beneath his shirt and tie, "I promise to never take it off."

"Thank you, Ted." Gently patting his shoulder, I nodded in departure, saying, "I'll be in touch—let's have that lunch that we're forever talking about, soon…"

When leaving the building I had felt as though I had left some integral part of my life behind. It was hard to swallow and my eyes burned. I felt light-headed and dizzy, and paused to lean against the brick-work outside for support. It was hard to breath and as I looked into the cloud-filled heavens, my heart sank.

"Are you okay?' A soft and familiar voice called from behind me. Turning to look back into the open doorway, I was promptly greeted by Ruth Sampson. She was dressed in white as always, and in the gloom appeared almost angelic.

"Michael, are you alright?" She moved down from the step to closer examine me, "It isn't your heart is it—can I get you anything?"

"No, I'm just fine—but thank you, Ruth." Straightening out and gathering what little wit remained, I forced a smile, "I didn't sleep very much this past week. The long hours are kicking my butt—I had a manuscript to finish."

"You really need to take better care of yourself--," She pointed a finger, those big blue eyes filled with sincere concern, "You're not exactly a spring chicken anymore."

She had the appearance of every 'apple-pie grandmother' that I could remember, and all that she needed was the apron and oven mitts. Noticing the half-eaten candy bar in her other hand, I could only smile.

"Go easy on those candy bars, Ruth--," I patted my slightly protruding tummy while saying, "If you're not careful, they'll get you in the end."

"Oh, I'm being careful--," She grinned from ear to ear, "I'm only eating four a day. They're just snacks, you know—and I'm careful not to overdo it."

"I have dinner cooking as we speak--," Politely excusing myself with a white lie, I looked into the dark skies before looking back at Ruth, "It's one of my mother's recipes, Hungarian Goulash."

"That sounds wonderful--,' She thought for a moment and then suddenly stared, "You didn't leave that cooking unattended, did you?"

"No, Tim is watching things--," I sighed deeply, "But I should really be getting back."

"Oh, one last thing--," She frowned sadly and softly said, "I'm so terribly sorry about what happened between you and Caitlin." She placed a hand to her heart, "But please, don't worry too much—because you can never really lose a true love…"

I looked back to her as a cold wind tossed the white curls upon her brow, and for just a moment, thought to have seen my mother standing there. Ruth had always been so very special and a blessing to all who knew her. She was a kind soul with a giving heart, and a walking Hallmark moment after having edited romance novels for twenty-five years.

"Everything will work out--," She toyed with the silver cross that hung from upon her white woolen sweater, "Have faith—and the good Lord will work everything out."

"Bless your heart--," Nodding and swallowing down the emotions, I waved and, turning to depart, called back, "You better get back inside before you catch a chill."

Smiling and with a friendly wave, she nibbled at her candy bar, and promptly hurried back into the building.

Standing there for several moments, I bowed my head while unable to leave that dark and empty doorway. Although I knew in my heart that we never truly lost the ones that we loved, I suddenly wondered if it was possible for them to momentarily return. In times of sorrow and weakness, had they reached out to us through others? Was it possible that within a type of symbiotic relation, that they existed for but a brief moment and in times of true need? The wind had whistled mournfully across the deep drifts and into the shadows of the alley. A newspaper had blown out from before me, and the headlines read: Anything is possible, look inside for more details…

Hurriedly climbing into the car, I paused to stare out into the street. Amica had been right and my world was changing, or perhaps it was just me? Where I had once accepted the physical loss of this mortal plane, I now sensed something far deeper. I had the distinct impression that just beneath this physical illusion there existed an eternity where life continued. The walls of reality were slowly fading, and I felt as though I were upon the breach of something unimaginable.

"What's happening to me? Am I falling beneath some misdirected illusion of reality, or has the veil been drawn from previous, mortal misconceptions?"

"If you do not take the swiftest route back immediately--," Marlowe whispered from in the shadows of the back seat, "You will most certainly discover the answer to mortality in the coming darkness…" The key was in the ignition without a second thought and the car roared to life.

5:15 p.m.
It was dusk when Raymond had finally closed and locked the main gates. Although we had strictly avoided being out in the night, they had accidentally lost track of time. Completing the task of assembling the last few iron symbols, they had hurriedly mounted the new seals. They stood upon all ends of the fences, as facing inward and out, also adorned the main gates. Rich had done an amazing job in their creation. They were roughly the size of large dinner plates, were comprised of wrought iron, and appeared more like a family crest than a protective talisman.

"That was cutting it just a little close--," Hurrying our friends into the house and swiftly closing the door, Tim locked it tight with a loud sigh of relief, saying, "You did a wonderful job on those crests. They look like they've always been there."

"Thanks—but they're still not as nice as I would've liked them to be--," Rich drew the draperies in the entranceway and kicked off his boots, "I'll feel a lot better when we get the new automated gate system installed and activated."

"We can get busy with that first thing in the morning." Raymond followed the two men into the dining room, "Everything is ready to go, we just need to call that work crew and then haul it all over here."

"I sure hope that they work fast." Rich was impatient with good reason, we could all hear the weather forecast over the radio that was left playing in the kitchen.

"They're calling for flurries--," Tim grumbled while placing ladles and cutlery into the appropriate serving dishes, "And possibly even a storm—later in the evening."

"Let's hope that we can get the new gates installed before dark." Rich frowned, peering nervously from out of the kitchen windows, "I really wouldn't want to spend a night without them…"

"Keep in mind that we're not alone here, my friend." Attempting to reassure him, I grabbed oven mitts, and hurried past with the steaming food, "If the need should arise, we have other means of defense."

"All the same--," Rich washed his hands in the kitchen sink, saying, "I'd rather not push our luck. Because, with every time that thing tests the boundaries and fails, the closer it gets to us…"

"Let's just cross our fingers and hope for the best." Raymond sniffed at the serving dish as I passed him in the corridor, "What smells so good?"

"It's Michael's mom's recipe for Hungarian goulash." Tim hurried back into the kitchen to assist me, "Cubed beef, pork, onions, mushrooms and peppers, all fried, and then simmered in heavy brown gravy."

"Dinner is almost ready--," I hurriedly mixed butter, milk, a touch of salt and sprinkle of nutmeg into the mashed potatoes, "But this will never be nearly as good as the way that mom or Eva made them."

"Maybe not to you—," Tim breathed in deeply as though indulging paradise, "But it's heaven to the rest of us."

"If that tastes even half as good as it smells--," Raymond beamed, "I'm never leaving home again!"

"Now I know why your folks moved to Florida." Rich winked as we began indulging our meal.

"I'll have you know that I moved out when I joined the military--," Raymond advised us, "And that I was just a mere lad of eighteen."

"At eighteen I was already running the parlor for my grandfather--," Tim snickered, "And taking the coach out for pick-up and deliveries."

"And while you were safe at home with your family--," Raymond boasted proudly, "I was saving the world from hostiles and terrorists."

"Oh--." Raising an eyebrow and leaning closer to him, Rich curiously asked, "And where were you doing that?"

"Well--," Blushing and shrugging, Raymond winked, "It was while I was peeling potatoes and working in the kitchen. No food, no soldiers, and that's how wars are lost."

"So now we know--," Tim facetiously grinned, "You've been fighting the battle of the bulge all of these years, and I see that you've been losing." He motioned to where Raymond's belly hung slightly from over his pants.

"That always happens over the winter--," Grumbling, Raymond poured more gravy over his potatoes, "It goes away in the summertime, when I can get more exercise."

"It's from ingesting too much salt and sugar--," Tim warned him, "That'll cause edema and clog up your arteries."

"And people wonder why no one likes morticians." Raymond buttered another slice of bread.

"How are the gates coming along at your place?" Offering a change of subject, I had looked to Rich.

"We have three teams working--," He replied, "The snow's been a royal pain, but they should have it installed within a week. As you know, it's not as straight forward as what we're doing over here. We had to install the entire fencing first, and then I still have to provide them with the symbols as well. We made a few extras while we completed the ones for Sanctum Arcanum, but they still need to be painted and fastened."

"It seems to all be coming together as planned--," Raymond blissfully loaded his plate, "And, if we can't beat the storm—we'll have to wait it out before we finish the job here." He looked to Rich, "There really isn't any reason to take chances by rushing this thing."

"Your absolutely right--," Rich had sighed as though a great burden had been lifted from him, saying, "I suppose that we're all a little unsettled and anxious, all things considered?"

"How are Tanya and the boys doing over there?" I thought for a moment, "Is there any cause for concern—have they mentioned anything unusual happening?"

"Well, it's funny that you should ask about that." He dropped a portion of green beans onto his plate and passed the steaming bowl to Raymond, "It seems that the boys wandered into my trophy room. They saw the turtle's claw and Danny was absolutely infatuated with Marlowe's old boar head. To tell you the truth, that bothered me right away. I don't like the idea of that thing being anywhere near Tanya or the boys. They may have killed the monster—but I feel like something's still lurking inside that rotting old hulk. So, I've decided to bring the beast and everything else over here and lock it away just to play it safe."

"I was going to suggest that to you, this evening." I sipped at my tea, "We should keep everything and anything of a questionable nature under lock and key."

"I've already spoken to Scott about that." Rich nodded in agreement, "The boys are going to help him empty my trophy room, and the vault at the warehouse as well. They'll haul everything over here and then load it into the basement, under Tim's supervision, of course."

Tim's hand instinctively slipped to the golden key that hung about his neck, "As long as you manage the heavier items, I'll see to everything else."

"And while we're on that topic, would it be possible to get some help moving that figure of Pan and the maiden out of my office? It really doesn't bother me—but I promised Eva that I would move it out of the house."

"Of course—we can do that just as soon as the gates are installed and working --," Raymond nodded, as shoving a forkful of mashed potatoes and goulash into his mouth, smacked his lips, "Hot damn, this is absolutely delicious! Bless your mother's dear heart—and recipe book!"

"Thank you, ever so much." I knew that she would have been smiling with the compliment, and it warmed my heart, "We made lots—so fill your boots."

"I still have to talk to old Red about using the truck." Rich interrupted, "As you know, we'll need to move everything during the day. So I'll have to double-check with him about any deliveries first."

"With everyone helping, it shouldn't take any longer than a few hours --," Raymond agreed, "Weather permitting, of course."

"Oh, Red Cloud called earlier--," Tim snapped his fingers as he loaded his plate, "Sorry—it completely slipped my mind."

"Was it anything important?" Rich appeared concerned.

"Well--," Tim addressed me while ladling more goulash over his mashed potatoes, "He was asking if we were still considering doing any field-work. I told him that I really wasn't sure, all things considered."

Although the thought hadn't previously occurred, curiosity caused me to inquire, "Did he feel that it was something significant enough to follow up?"

"You really can't be serious?" Rich almost dropped the fork onto his plate, "You're not actually thinking about going out there?"

"I'm just wondering—and nothing more."

"He was very disturbed about the event—to be honest--," Tim explained while heaping green beans onto his plate, "He received a telephone call late in the afternoon from an elderly woman. She owns a house in the lower east end district of Burnaby. Apparently, she was claiming that there was something creeping around in her basement. She told him that it was making strange noises, whispering in the night. And--," He glanced over at me, "That she was afraid for her life."

There was a time when we might have all just chuckled at the mere thought. It was likely little more than the battered nerves of an elderly woman, and the noises of an old house settling in the night. But those days had long passed. Instead, we had all just curiously looked to one another.

"Did she provide any details, or any possible reason as to why this might be happening?" It had been my experience, though few could offer facts, that many could corroborate certain events and present possible cause. It was a shot in the dark, but always worth the attempt.

"Well, they didn't speak very long and she didn't reveal any dark mysteries," Tim had waved the fork like a weapon before his face, "The story gets a lot more intriguing, because, when old Red had tried to call her back, he found out from relatives that she'd passed away, two weeks prior…"

"This definitely sounds like something is knocking at our door again." Rich had eyed me suspiciously. It caused my thoughts to suddenly return to the evening that Harry had called from beyond the grave…

"Did she provide an address?" The Detective in Raymond now joined the conversation.

"I wrote it down--," Tim replied, and tapping a finger at his brow in obvious frustration, muttered, "But I can't find the note or remember the address for the life of me. It was close to where the eastside borders Burnaby in the old district."

"It might just be a coincidence." Raymond glanced over at me, "A friend of mine came into the office pretty messed up a few weeks back. He told me that he'd attended a homicide out that way. It was a brutal murder involving an elderly woman."

"Coincidence—I mean, what are the odds?" Rich seemed to suddenly lose all appetite as he slunk back into the chair.

"I'd imagine that you get quite a few calls from that side of town?" There was a bitter reflection in Tim's tone, as frowning, he said, "The old districts used to be the crowning glory of this city. But sadly, it's all been deteriorating for years due to poverty, drugs, and crime."

Spitting his food into a napkin with some sudden and ghastly recollection, Raymond cursed, saying, "That's all true, but how many of those calls do you think include a corpse that was totally dehydrated in less than 24 hours? And I do mean completely—she was so dry that the she crumbled when they tried moving the body. They had to literally sweep her off the floor with a damn dust-pan." His eyes were glassy and features grim as he slid his food away, and grumbling, said, "I saw the crime scene photos and it wasn't a pretty sight…"

Unbeknownst to Raymond, both Rich and I had previously encountered this exact scenario at the Duff Glenn. The reminiscence of which now caused us to both linger over our food as though it were utterly rancid…

"They spoke to the neighbor who had seen her puttering around in the yard the day before--," He explained while swallowing down a mouthful of coffee as though attempting to clear some bad taste in his mouth, "Well, it seems that the next afternoon that same neighbor had noticed her front door open. So, naturally being concerned and having been on good terms with the old girl, had wandered inside to have a look around. They found what was left of her in the basement and near the washing machine. Needless to say, due to the poor condition of the remains, the cause of death was undetermined and the case remains open."

"It goes without saying--," Unable to deny the obvious and especially before Rich, I conceded, while saying, "There is definitely something in that place and it's left an undeniably obvious calling card." Peering to Rich, I muttered the words, "And one that we have both witnessed before at the McCreary estate."

"Sure, and we've both seen this kind of thing before. But going there is a bad idea--," Rich was adamant, "This is more like a dare."

"But why would it make something so blatantly obvious?" Disagreeing with Rich, Raymond looked to me, and said, "Unless it had a good reason in not wanting us anywhere near the place?"

"And it's almost as though it was guarding or trying to hide something?" A dark suspicion flashing in Tim's eyes, he slowly turned toward me while pondering, "Maybe the darkness has made its first mistake and revealed something here?"

"It still reeks of being a trap, if you ask me--," Still impervious, Rich openly denied the possibility, saying, "This thing has either become ingenious, or we're losing what little common sense we had left."

Frustrated and dropping both hands on the table before me, I had given in to my friend, saying, "Alright, maybe you're right and this is just some clever ruse to draw us into a trap, but keep in mind that this woman was quite elderly and likely running out of time. And realizing this, and possibly in a desperate moment, it may have created this scenario to provide itself with a little more time."

"The investigation will keep the place tied up for a while." Raymond agreed. Tugging at his mustache and leaning back into his seat, he curiously asked, "What would it need the extra time for if that was the case?"

"Possibly time enough to either possesses or reanimate something--," Tim concluded, saying, "And just long enough so that it could physically remove something from the residence..."

"This is all conjecture--," Rich still argued, "You're all building a profile out of thin air. Guys, let's face it, this thing is likely intelligent enough to realize that we'd do this, and especially after leaving its proverbial calling card. And then, it will have us right where it wants us. In the shadows of some old basement—and not a single witness around..."

The argument had been strong enough to cause doubts in the minds of all who now sat silently watching and waiting for my reply. The issue now was that both sides had provided valid points, but neither bore any true relevancy, only doubt. Thinking for several moments, I could only frown, while saying, "There really isn't any way to be certain either way..."

"There might be?" Toying with a fork in his food, Rich leaned back into the seat and then curiously inquired, "Wouldn't Marlowe or his minion have some knowledge about these things? You did say that they could see and sense things well beyond our physical limitation, why not ask them?"

"Within certain boundaries--," The thought had already occurred to me as I looked back, and said, "We have to remember that he's also bound and regulated by dark forces."

"That doesn't mean that he can't drop a hint here and there." With eyes widening hopefully Raymond had glanced between us, and suggested, "It can't hurt to try asking about the old girl's death, and if there's anything of significance hidden in the house, or somewhere on the property."

"Just for my benefit, and so that I can properly understand--," Removing his glasses, Rich rubbed at his eyes, asking, "Please tell me how it's possible for Marlowe and his demon, being part of the evil to begin with, to even be involved with the opposition without being noticed? Seriously here, isn't the universe and all of its diverse counterparts sentient and all-seeing?"

"I am but a current traveling among the dark tides of an endless sea—," Marlowe spoke as the room suddenly fell into deep shadow and his voice boomed from the abyss, "As unnoticed and insignificant among a far greater hierarchy, I remain able, though limited to certain freedoms..."

Tim's water glass was knocked from the table, as spilling without breaking, it rolled harmlessly away.

"We simply desire knowledge--," Respectfully, I had humbly inquired of the dark sorcerer, asking, "As to the reasons that you can or cannot provide answers to certain things."

"There exist secrets that must remain mysteries until fate and destiny are prepared to unveil them--," Marlowe's voice became little more than a whisper, "They are primary elements upon the path of cause and effect—and must never be tampered with until choices are made, and destinies met. For this reason I am not permitted to reveal, but by simplest of means, provide guidance."

"Then please answer this if you are able--," The shadows swirled from all about us as my friends cringed fearfully, and I asked, "Is there a secret hidden or being guarded from us in the house in question?"

There was an unsettling stillness as the anxiety now left us breathless and just staring. Never before had Marlowe appeared before anyone but me. The effect upon my friends was devastating, as absolutely terrified, they gazed questioningly upon me.

"From providing an answer to this question I am strictly forbidden--," Marlowe grumbled and then in a thoughtful tone, replied saying, "Yet, the old woman, whose soul might be questioned, is not..."

"And how might we accomplish this?" Swallowing hard, I watched the brilliant rainbows of ethereal lights that now flashed while flowing through the darkness from all about us.

"The golden eye in the stone sees all—you have but only to look..." His voice drifted into the distance and I suddenly understood.

The shadows suddenly faded as the lights brightened and light was restored to the room.

"So that was our ghostly sorcerer--," Still gawking, Tim had looked to me with a shudder and muttering, said, "He really is quite an imposing individual, even for someone who is dead..."

"I believe that I might've pissed him off just a little?" Wide-eyed and still staring, Rich sunk lower into his chair, saying, "I'll be more careful of the things that I question or say next time..."

"At least we've got some way to figure this out now--," Anxiously pointing a finger, Raymond turned back to me in question, asking, "But what's this golden eye in the stone that he's talking about?"

"It's a golden beryl crystal ball. We got in an anonymous shipment from Ireland some time ago--," Rich answered his question, saying, "It's something of a mystery and was connected to an Irish family here that had dealings with the McCreary's in the shipping industry."

"It was that old Irish woman who died in that warehouse incident in North Vancouver, right?" Raymond had looked to me, asking, "How was she tied into all of this?"

"It was her grandfather's corruption and the family business that initially brought her into everything." Sipping at his coffee and then refilling the cup, he squinted while saying, "She had some old deliveries in her warehouse than were never sent to the McCreary's, and discovering Caitlin to have been here, just delivered them anonymously to our warehouse."

"And this stone has some kind of power?" Utterly captivated with the thought of the stone and old conspiracy, Raymond gazed blankly between us.

"I'm not really certain if it's the stone itself--," Pondering, I looked back at him and said, "Or just the way that particular mineral affects the minds of anyone looking into it?"

"Can you really contact the dead when you look into that thing?" There was something deeply saddening in his expression, and I suspected that he now considered the possibilities of reaching someone dear to him and previously deceased.

"Not really--," Speaking quite frankly, I looked back at him and said, "Or at least not in the way that the stone seems to affect me? My experience has been more like watching scenes that are occurring in the now or hereafter, and images of people and places that seem caught in time."

"So, you might be able to see what the old lady was doing before she was killed?"

"I'll certainly do my very best to try and find out."

"And what about this demon of Marlowe's--," Appearing somewhat dismayed and visibly concerned, Tim asked, "Is it going to become dangerous to you or any of us, and what's going to happen when this all ends?"

"Whatever threat it may pose isn't clear to me at the moment--," Peering sincerely around the table and into the eyes of my friends, I said, "But I can assure you that it's not something to be immediately concerned about. And, if the times comes that I have any doubts, believe me, I'll be the first to inform you."

There had been some obvious mixed emotions on the subject, but faced with other concerns the debate over the demon's credibility had been dropped.

"I say that we just go over to that old woman's house--," Raymond growled, "And face down whatever the hell might be waiting there."

"And let it turn us all in leather hand-bags like that poor old lady?" Scoffing at the thought, Tim looked over at me and said, "I'll do whatever you feel is right—but I'm not interested in suicide."

"Before we discuss this any further--," Sliding my chair away from the table and dinner and standing up, I looked to my friends and politely said, "Just give me a few moments and I'll have a look into the stone and see if anything happens."

Not a word had been uttered, as turning and hurrying to the stairs, I swiftly made my way into the office.

Ever so carefully, I had removed the golden sphere from its place upon the hutch and desk. Then, placing it down upon the counter and removing the black cotton cloth that was covering it, I sat down while gazing into its light.

Clearing my thoughts of all other things, I focused upon the sad ending of the poor old woman. Several moments had passed and as while nothing happened, I stared dreamily into the crystals shimmering and golden hues. In the stillness of the long shadows the glow seemed brighter with every moment that passed. Then, in a moment when I had assumed to have likely been dreaming, I heard a voice from out of nowhere.

"Oma, what is that?" A child asked as the hazy image of an old woman and a boy appeared from within the crystals smoldering face.

"It is nothing, mein lieber, just one moment, Carl--," She spoke in a German accent as while hiding something in the basement, and saying in warning, "But you must never touch it—or speak about it to anyone, do you promise?"

"I promise, Oma—are we having cake now?" He appeared more interested in food than what she had concealed.

"Of course—," The grandmother lovingly laughed, saying, "I've baked your favorite, apples and cinnamon."

"I love you so much, Oma!" Throwing himself upon her, he'd almost knocked the dear woman over while tightly embracing her.

"Easy now, Liebchen, you'll break your Oma. I'm not as young as I once was!" They laughed, as taking his hand, she led him away and they had climbed the stair and vanished from sight.

At that point I was already trembling while having become endeared in relating to both. The golden haze danced before me once more, as the shimmering waves slowly parted while clearing upon another scene. In it I saw the old woman with a laundry basket while carefully making her way down the same basement stairs.

Already knowing her fate, my heart had leapt into my throat while fearing and predicting her terrible end. In that moment she had stopped while approaching through the sphere, and suddenly looked straight out at me!

With a livid horror that twisted her kindly features, she pleaded tearfully while reaching out to me with both hands, "Please, you must find it before others do and the monster takes all of your lives!"

Leaping back and almost falling over, I realized to have fallen asleep there and likely dreamed the entire event. Climbing to my feet, I had just been turning back to the desk when I noticed a shadow standing there.

"You must find it—you must…" The shadow of the old woman's soul that had been standing in the corner now vanished from before my eyes…

"Your perception grows stronger as you reach ever further into the beyond." The raven whispered while barely moving from its perch upon the hutch and desk, "But be wary that you do not travel too far—and find yourself unable to return…"

"I'll be back soon…" I promised as, half-stumbling and still shocked, I hurried toward the door.

It had only taken a few moments to share my experience with the stone and old woman's ghost, and then we had all sat looking to one another in question.

"Well then, I'd say that it was unanimous--," Rich had insisted while completely changing his perspective on the event, "If we don't investigate into this, we'll be doing that old woman and ourselves a great injustice, there has to be something there…"

"He's right--," Raymond wiped at his mouth with a napkin, "And besides, I'd rather go down fighting than sitting around here like a bunch of scared rabbits."

"Scared rabbits--," Tim had obviously taken subtle insult at the suggestion, grumbling, "Scared rabbits, really?"

"Yes--," Raymond waved a hand about the table, and speaking politely, had only attempted to share an opinion rather than offer insult, saying, "Take a long and hard look at yourselves in the mirror: We're all hiding in here like a bunch of boy scouts too afraid to walk into the woods for a piss, because we're all scared of the dark."

If there had been any pleasant ambience about the evening meal it had been carried off in the bitter wind of reality. No one had wanted to say anything after Raymond's remark, as though apprehensive, all had silently agreed as it was the absolute truth.

"He's right—it's become too easy to just sit here while hiding within a hope." Shrugging, I was at a loss for words, "While those we love are distanced and the world is slipping by."

"I'm sorry." Raymond shook his head, "I shouldn't have just rattled off like that."

"It had to be said--," Rich spoke with courage of conviction, "As much as we all fear this darkness—we need to get out there and fight back."

"So, now that we've established the facts." Tim nervously tapped a finger on the table as he looked to me for an answer, "What are we going to do about it?"

There was a complete and utter stillness in the room. I doubt that anyone had even drawn a breath in that moment. It had been so quiet in fact that as an ember cracked in the hearth everyone had jolted in their seats.

Removing his glasses, Rich nervously cleaned the lenses with a napkin, "I come from a long line of proud MacDonald men. They were clansmen who fought great wars and died in the cause, but as I sit here now, I feel as though I've shamed them all." He looked to me sadly, and slipping his glasses back onto his face, said, "Because, as hard as I try and as much as I love Maya, God forgive me, I'm just so terrified of this damned thing…"

"There is no shame in honesty—and likewise no dishonor in fear --," Looking to my friend, I spoke in his defense, saying, "We're all only human and faced with a terrible enemy. Anyone who'd claim to not fear such a thing would either be insane or a liar."

"My grandmother married an Englishman by the name of Emerson--," Raymond looked to Rich, and patting his friends arm, said, "But, we were all originally clan MacDonald and from the Isle of Skye."

"My great grandmother was a Stewart!" Tim blurted. Finding some humor in the coincidence, he laughed, "It's like an old-time clan-gathering! Let's kick some ass, lads!"

"Did you know that the name Stewart is believed to be pre-seventh century Old English?" I brought a little light into the darkness that had taken the table, "It's derived from the Scottish Stigeweard, and its literal meaning in translation is: Hall guardian."

"I guess that isn't just a coincidence." Raymond pointed toward Tim and the golden chain that hung from about his neck, "I suppose that there's more to names than we know?"

"There are more things in creation than man's lifetime permits to know, much less understand." I had fallen silent in contemplation, considering Marlowe and Amica, and the keys to timeless mysteries they might hold.

"Eva is a Scott, too--," Rich turned to me, and appearing quite serious, pointed a finger, "And, Caitlin came from Scot and Irish heritage."

"So are Scott and Carrie." I pondered the thought, "It's almost as though the ancestors of those who died defending the castles and villages of old have returned to stand against the darkness, together..."

"So, for this world at least, it all comes down to the ancestors of the Duff Glenn?" Raymond thought aloud while putting events into place, "Come to think of it?" He pointed an accusing finger in thought, "What about that old Irish woman, the last owner of that North Vancouver warehouse? Didn't you say that she had some connection to the McCreary family?"

"Coincidence--," Rich put a finger to his lip, "I think not... We've all been brought here together again for this fight..."

"It all makes terrifying sense--," Tim's eyes were huge, as speaking quietly, he said, "We have no idea of how many worlds or places in time and space this nightmare has traveled, but it seems affixed here, and to all of us."

"All things must take a name, and have purpose to manifest in specific places." I thought aloud, "Nothing can exist without meaning, or remain without becoming part and parcel to something, or someone else."

"So, we're born into this world under certain astrological signs which designate our general character, and then we're confronted by old obstacles that we need to overcome--," Rich contemplated the code of dimensional existence, "Nothing can just arrive or appear here. And everything must abide by similar laws of physics, pertaining to a specific reality."

"Rules are bent when mankind tampers with the natural laws--," I reminded them, "As we have seen with the darkness, Marlowe and the demon."

"That confuses me a little--," Raymond squinted in thought, "How did the darkness get here again? And if what Rich is saying is true—how does it manage to stay here?"

"It was sent into a portal that carried it to our galaxy and dimension--," I tried to break it down into simplest terms, "And now it's managed to manifest in some way, and is grounded."

"But, I thought that it was just an energy form?" Tim looked between us.

"The darkness has to manifest to some degree and have a place of origin to remain anchored in our reality." Rich explained, "It may be an energy form, but still has to exist on a molecular level."

"So, that's why it consumes the life energy of others to sustain its existence." Rich leaned down and picked up Tim's fallen and forgotten water glass, "It's been eating its way through our ancestors for centuries."

"Our monster has likely haunted castles and mansions throughout Gaelic and Celtic history." I swallowed hard with the thought, "With knowledge of time and space, it simply waited until destiny and time brought me to the Duff Glenn."

"With the known history and legends of battles against unspeakable nightmares, I wonder how many times this evil has already beaten us—in past lives?" Rich appeared far paler than I could ever remember.

"Regardless, it will not take us so easily in this one." Unwilling to succumb to my own fear, I slammed a fist down upon the table, "We are learning, we have a plan, and all that we need to do is follow this through."

"If that thing is using the Duff Glenn—then we'll know how to find it when the time comes," Raymond agreed, "What we really need to do now—is find out how to open that portal into oblivion."

"Marlowe spoke of three secrets—mysteries that we have to discover--," I finished the last of my meal and placed down the fork, "The first was the ascent of the demon. The second was something that he said would release a great power into this world. The third will apparently come to pass when the second is activated. Unfortunately, I'm not completely clear as to how this is all supposed to come together."

"But even so, how can we return to the Duff Glenn? Wasn't the whole place leveled to build a golf course?" Tim began removing the dinner plates.

"No--," Raymond assisted him as they cleared the table and prepared the evening tea, "There were several deaths, a few workmen that mysteriously fell from scaffolding. The place is still under investigation. And they can't do anything until the courts sign a formal release."

"I only wrote that into my book to dissuade anyone else from going there."

"So, all other things considered—this will end where it really began for us." The grim expression upon Rich's face caused something to sink in the depths of my belly. I could only nod in reply as our friend's returned with tea and coffee.

"Then, let me ask you this, about Marlowe." He hesitated as unsettling glances were exchanged around the table, "Are we absolutely certain that he's working to our benefit? I mean, what if we are all somehow being rounded up, and lead into some kind of a trap? You did say that he and his consort were both under the influence of darker forces."

"Yes I did tell you that. But, as you already know, he could have easily destroyed all of us long ago." The thought was absurd in my mind, but understandable considering the growing tension and paranoia.

"Is he actually this Marlowe character?" Tim peered nervously between us, "Or that sixteenth century black magician from Wittenberg, that Faust that you were talking about?"

"It's likely that he may be neither or existed as both. In the end it means very little." I had looked to my friends while drawing upon their sense and sensibilities, and saying, "If it was not for our friend and his ethereal companion, we would likely all be dead, or suffering something far worse..."

"Understandably--," Rich sipped at his coffee, "But still, it's just really hard to accept the fact that we're being assisted by phantoms and demons."

"My dear friend--," I had looked too Rich in certain disappointment, "You seem to have forgotten that we are all phantoms in one state or another, and that demons are merely fallen angels. On the path of hope none are beyond redemption. And in any case, if they were truly evil, they could never have entered this estate."

"Point taken--," Rich agreed, "But still, you have to admit that this whole consorting with demons thing is unsettling."

"Wittenberg--," Raymond snapped his fingers, "You may not be of Scottish descent, but your heritage is German, right?"

"That explains the mortal connection to Marlowe." Rich nodded thoughtfully, "You must have some distant, though direct link to the past with him. It might even be some kind of inherent genetic coding, or frequency beyond our awareness."

"Like someone tuning into a radio signal." Tim's eyes widened, "The Buddhists believe in positive thought creating positive flow. What if specific energies all exist on different frequencies and all that we have to do is mentally tune into them?"

"If energy can be directed in such a way--," Rich stirred cream and sugar into his coffee, "Considering your background, interests and pursuits—it's not so hard to imagine that Marlowe would've found you quite easily. And, on the subject of pursuits--," Rich raised a finger in thought, "Did you have an opportunity to discuss the gateway to oblivion with Marlowe?"

"Oh yes, the black hole theory--," I directed my attention upon Rich, "Marlowe agreed that it was possible—but warned against it. So, a decision was made and motions were taken toward the inevitable..."

"What motions were those?" Rich gawked, obviously fearing the worst.

"I'm not exactly certain—but Amica, which is the name that I have given Marlowe's familiar," I thought briefly, "Has somehow changed, and seems to be evolving through the course of events."

"Has changed—in what way?" Raymond looked increasingly alarmed.

"Well, the demon is no longer the boy—and yet it is." Looking between my friends, I struggled for an answer, "It's something different..."

"Oh—so that was what you meant by the ascension of the demon--," Rich clicked his tongue, "With everything that was happening it completely slipped my mind."

"As long as it's on our side--," Tim shrugged, "Appearances really don't matter anyway."

"Speaking of things not appearing as what they may seem," Raymond sighed deeply, "I realize that this is a sensitive subject for you guys, but it's important that you all know."

I had my suspicions, but simply motioned in gesture for him to continue.

"It appears that Detective Simms has run into something of a dilemma concerning your friend, Harry." Raymond's gaze became strangely distant as his demeanor darkened, "Although it was positively confirmed that he committed the murders at the Hope diner, there are some discrepancies."

"What discrepancies might those be?" Looking to Rich, I was becoming increasingly nervous. I felt that familiar, icy lump forming in the pit of my bowels...

It was apparent in Raymond's expression and the way that he now wrung his hands out upon the table that he felt the same. He had hesitated briefly, and then swallowing hard, said, "According to the police report, Harry walked into the Hope diner around nine p.m. and killed both employees. He then proceeded to make his way here, and was then discovered at your gates approximately two hours later."

We had all silently listened and just nodded as Raymond, looking at the antique wall clock, had cursed under his breath, "Well, here's the problem, gentlemen. The coroner's report stated that he had died of a massive coronary event on the previous night, and therefore was incapable of having committed those crimes..."

Startled as Tim had dropped his teaspoon onto his plate, I could only stare.

"Well, if they're saying that Harry couldn't have done it. Who will they blame?" Rich gawked, obviously dreading the possible implications.

"According to the coinciding events and irrefutable evidence, they can't implicate anyone else." Raymond poured himself more coffee and winked, "In which case, poor old Simms now has evidence substantiating a multiple murder case, committed by a corpse."

"Poor old Harry--," Tim held back the emotions, "I wish that we could have saved him."

Rich had gently patted Tim on the back, "We all do, my friend..."

"And how exactly is that supposed to hold up in a court of law? Can they charge someone who was deceased at the time of the incident?" Placing down my tea cup, I looked to my friend, "I mean, let's face it. We all know that it's physically impossible for a corpse to move about freely, much less commit a multiple murder."

Judging by his expression it was apparent that Raymond had not found any amusement in the remark. Instead, and appearing rather perturbed, he clasped his hands together while leaning back into the seat, "Unfortunately, and with everything considered, Simms has asked me to arrange a discrete meeting here with you."

"I don't like the sounds of this at all." Rich almost spat coffee at the statement, "What possible use could something like that serve to any of us?"

"I have a feeling that he's becoming a little more open-minded." Raymond shrugged, and looking back to me, said, "The final decision is yours—but I would suggest that you consider this as an opportunity."

"An opportunity for what--," Rich scoffed at the thought, his eyes becoming huge behind his glasses, "The possibly of getting us all committed to some sanitarium for admitting to having any knowledge of these events?"

"You all know that I'd never allow something like that." Raymond appeared insulted with the insinuation, and focused upon me, "But, this might be a chance to get that additional help that we talked about."

"We already know what will happen if we involve others." Tim became the voice of reason, "Things have only calmed down because we're staying low. God only knows what might become of this if we involved the police."

"It would be a mindless and horrifying blood-bath--," The words formed in thought, as looking sadly to my friend, I said, "We can't afford to risk involving others."

"What you all seem to be missing here—is that these guys are already involved. You once said to me that people come together for a reason." Raymond spoke quietly and calmly as he watched me from across the table, "I realize the implications, but maybe this is meant to be."

"As much as I hate to agree with him on this--," Rich thought briefly, "He does have a point. We all know that we need to gain entrance to that old woman's house and the Duff Glenn. It might help to have someone else on the inside."

"We talked about Raymond possibly leaving the department earlier." Tim shrugged, "Maybe this is the ticket to keeping the gold key to the proverbial crapper, without putting Raymond at risk on night shifts?"

"Listen, these guys are already in hot water." Raymond insisted, "And, the only hope that they have against those things is us. The question here is not whether we should be worried about getting involved, it's whether we'll be able to just stand by, knowing that they'll likely be taken without a chance."

"I don't like it any more than anyone else, but Raymond is right." Tim slowly tapped his teaspoon against his cup, "He is coming to us for help—do we just ignore him and watch them die? Or do we make whatever difference that we can—join ranks and fight back."

"I agree with Raymond and Tim--," Rich pondered briefly, "We have nothing left to lose—and everything to gain."

With a unanimous vote I had simply conceded with a nod, "Alright then, arrange a time and we'll all sit down and see what comes of this." I had the distinct impression that I might live to regret the decision, but we were desperate men in desperate times...

CHAPTER FOUR

11:15 p.m.

It had been another sleepless and miserable night and the heavens were darker than I could ever remember. The wind had howled while tossing the dark pine branches and Tim had hesitated before the open door. Having immediately sensed his reluctance, I had quite vigorously and happily invited him to stay! After all, he was family and quite honestly after dark I had preferred to keep everyone safely under lock and key.

Gathered around the hearth and sharing a very old and fine brandy, we played a game of chess while discussing Red Cloud's telephone message.

"Do you think that call really came from the old girl's ghost—or was it just the darkness reaching out?" Tim slurred his words terribly. A little too much brandy and a warm hearth were slowly getting the best of us all.

"It might've been either one--," Rich faltered in a move upon the chess board, and swiftly changing his mind, said, "The darkness would've sensed that she would try to reach Michael—so it could've been calling—or the darkness trying to scare us off."

"It's hard dealing with an adversary that always seems a few steps ahead." Faltering with a move on the chess board, Rich swiftly moved his queen while countering with a stalemate. Frustrated and crossing my arms before me, he had just winked and indulged his brandy, smiling.

"It's not easy playing against the devil." Tim shuddered, almost spilling his drink while attempting to place it down, and said, "Not when he knows all the rules better than we do—and will break them every time..."

Wagging his eyebrows while making horns at the sides of his head with his fingers, Rich asked, "Would you care to play another game of chess, sir?"

"I think that you've either become remarkably better at this game--," I pondered while looking down at the board, "Or this brandy is getting the better of me?"

"It's neither--," He sighed while grinning and shrugging, and said, "When you weren't looking I cheated..."

"And as always--," Slowly shaking my head and chuckling, I pointed an accusing finger into his face, saying, "Because of your crooked honesty, I'll forgive you."

"Did I miss anything while I was gone?" Rubbing at his eyes and drawing his robe closer about him, Raymond dropped onto the couch beside Tim.

Surprised, I had just looked over at my friend, "I thought that you had gone off to bed?"

"I couldn't get comfortable and I thought that I heard something outside my window." He groaned while rubbing the sleep from his eyes, saying, "I went to have a look, but even in the moonlight it was too dark to see anything out there. My nerves must be totally shot? Now I'm even jumping at the slightest sound or shadow."

"Maybe we should check it out?" There was something in the way that Rich had suggested this, which now caused me to suspect there was reason for alarm. I knew that his senses were keener than most, and something now told me that we might have an unwanted guest… But how was it even possible? Nothing in spirit or of an evil nature could trespass upon sanctified ground, and even so, the guardian would have most certainly sensed this and investigated.

"I'm still dressed—," Moving from the couch, I took the cane from where I had rested it near the hearth, "I'll just slip into some boots and a coat and have a quick look around."

"Not without me you're not--," Raising a hand in gesture Rich hurried from the room, "Just give me a moment, I'll get ready and be right back!"

Moving unsteadily from his seat, Raymond looked back at me, and speaking in a low and authoritative tone, said, "I've got a bad feeling about this. Don't you move a muscle until I get back—we'll do this thing together…"

Tim had attempted to move from the couch, but being utterly intoxicated, slipped back down into the cushions like a sack of potatoes. There was a desperate and dismayed expression crossing his face when he looked over at me. Stumbling over his words, he said, "I think that I might've had just a little too much of that two hundred year old brandy—I don't think I can walk?"

"There's no need for all of us to go rushing out there. You just stay right here, and watch the house until we get back, this won't take long."

As mild-mannered as he may have seemed to some, his courage had always astounded me. I was forced to gently shove him back down as he had attempted to follow, regardless of the probable threat or his condition.

"It's going to be just fine." Attempting to comfort my troubled friend, I patted his shoulder, "Seriously, just stay put…"

Appearing utterly lost, he suddenly faded out of consciousness and then slowly slipped back down into the cushions. Covering him with a woolen blanket and removing the glass from his hand, I made certain that he was quite safe and comfortable before hurrying away.

Slipping into boots and a coat, I turned as the others quickly joined me at the door.

"If we take one lantern each, we should be fine--," Rich spoke quietly while noticing Tim out cold on the couch, "Flashlights are useless as you both know, something ethereal can drain the batteries dry in a second and leave us all in the dark."

"Do you guys realize that we haven't left the house after dark willingly for months now?" Zipping himself into his green, hooded parka, Raymond checked the chambers of both revolvers, before saying, "And even after my big speech tonight—I have to admit it, I'm scared shitless…"

"And with good reason--," Looking nervously between my slightly drunken and visibly distraught friends, I asked, "Are you ready?"

Raymond had slipped his revolvers into their holsters at his hips, nodding, and watched as I reached for the door handle. He hadn't been the only one dreading this particular late night excursion. It was not even so much just wandering out into the night, but where this journey would take us…

Raymond had occupied Norman's old room which, situated adjacent to Eva's, had been down the hall from the front door. It faced the northeast side of the property, shared a wall with the garage, and was surrounded in dense pines. It was the darkest point of the property and, unlike the surrounding grounds, was still very wild and overgrown.

Leaving the safety of the house for the front porch, we were immediately assaulted by a bitter cold and unearthly wind. It bit painfully into the exposed flesh of our hands and faces, as swiftly penetrating our clothing, chilled us to the bone.

There was a pale and golden glow emanating from the lanterns upon either side of the doorway. Unfortunately, and as while frosted with ice, they barely illuminated the surrounding porch or stairs. A strong wind cast long veils of streaming snow from the barren branches of the surrounding pines. Pale and shimmering, they flowed silently downward while glistening in crystalline reflection of the moonlight. Even in the frozen darkness there existed a type of majestic beauty within the icy touch of winter's deathly embrace.

Holding the lanterns high, we had begun the journey across the dark balcony and down the snow-covered steps. Although the walks and drive had previously been cleared, upon entering the gardens, we soon found ourselves struggling through knee-deep snow.

"I don't remember it ever feeling this cold before." Raymond cursed while leading the way, "I never did like the winter much—but I've really learned to hate it living here…"

"It's an unnatural cold—," Trembling while attempting to hold the lantern, I peered suspiciously into the night, "It's more appropriate for Siberia or somewhere deep in the arctic."

"I'll never understand what anyone could appreciate about the season of death." Shuddering uncontrollably, Rich scoffed at the thought while following from close behind Raymond, and saying, "Once this is all over—I'm going somewhere warm to thaw out."

"No offence, gentlemen--," I looked between my friends as we struggled through the deep snow and alongside the house, "But you might want to pay closer attention to what's in front of you. And not be quite so loud about it…"

"It's the brandy talking--," Rich mumbled, as raising his lantern higher, he whispered, "It's deafening, and drowns out the common sense while soaking into your brains…"

"It's the nature of spirits--," Shivering terribly, I muttered, "They dull the senses while possessing your soul…"

Passing beneath my office window and before the massive old willow, I stared nervously into the twisted and dark boughs high above. Squinting, I could barely make out the gnarled and snow-covered limbs. No longer appearing as the wonderful old tree, the crooked and blackened boughs twisted like the charred remains of some frozen and long dead fiend.

In a moment of doubt and between endlessly streaming veils of snow, I had wondered, feared, had there been something there? Was there some vile secret concealed within the deep shadow of death's pale and frozen shroud? The wind moaned, and whistling among the blackened boughs, cast veils of snow down from all about me. The moon had vanished as while being smothered by blackened clouds, and the lanterns' glow lay pale from all about us. It would have been quite impossible to detect in any way if anything was truly stalking us…

Stumbling along, we were cautious to avoid the immense icicles hanging from the gutters. If they should happen to break and fall for any reason, we might certainly have sustained terrible injury, or possibly something far worse...

I could barely see the faint light shining from Raymond's bedroom window when an unfamiliar sound caused us to suddenly halt. Visibly frightened and pausing merely yards away, we raised our lanterns in hopes of a better view. The deep mounds lay pale and undisturbed for far as our sight would reach within the lanterns' glow. There wasn't a single sound or the slightest motion beyond the veils of ice that flowed from the winds in the branches. Utter stillness, without sight of track or trail: It was quite apparent that nothing moved in that forest.

"I'm sorry for dragging you guys out here for nothing." Raymond looked to the light as Rich waved his lantern into the deep and undisturbed snow, and he said, "There isn't a single track or trail of any kind out there—and nothing could've come through here without leaving some kind of print."

"Don't be so sure of that." Rich suddenly stared as the beam of his light breached the darkness beneath Raymond's window. For just from beneath the window, and caught within deep shadow, were several large and indistinguishable tracks. It was as though something had appeared in that one place, and then vanished without ever leaving a single track in passage, or trace of evidence in departure. An uncanny familiarity suddenly took me, and a chill beyond the weather sent icy fingers tingling along the length of my spine.

"You have to be kidding me--," Raymond stared in disbelief, "How could something just skate across the snow without leaving any other tracks?"

"Because, it didn't skate--," Leaning down to closer observe the tracks, Rich had solemnly gazed back while mumbling, "It flew..."

"Oh--," The whisper slipped from out of my trembling lips, still in denial, as I had curiously asked, "Was it a late night bird of some kind—um, possibly a large owl, maybe?"

Rich had just stared back at me as we both suspected the same thing, but said nothing to avoid unnecessarily frightening our already distraught friend. Casting our lights into the branches of the bordering pines, we pressed our backs to the outer wall of the house.

"I've never seen a bird that big unless it was an Ostrich or an Emu--," Drawing his revolvers and appearing terrified, Raymond struggled to maintain his calm, while saying, "And they sure as hell don't exist in this neck of the woods."

Several awkward glances were exchanged, as realizing that we could no longer retain our suspicion, Rich understood that it was time to share.

"That's because it wasn't any bird--," Holding his lantern high, Rich swallowed hard, and whispering, said, "It was an insect—and a very, very big one..."

Raymond had stared over at me, as speaking barely above a whisper, he asked, "If he's talking about what I think he is—didn't that thing burn up in the Dayment house-fire?"

"That's what we were hoping, too." My throat was dry and the words came out in short and raspy tones, "But lately, nothing seems to be working in the way that we'd expected…"

"If it's out there—then why hasn't it attacked us yet?" Raymond's eyes glistened fearfully in the lanterns light while tightly gripping his revolvers.

Moving closer ever so slowly, Rich motioned with a finger into the blackness near the main gates, "I think that I just saw something move out there, just by the edge of the gates?"

Cascading veils of shimmering snow had showered us while the wind carried it down from the roof. But standing there with our backs pressed tightly against the outer wall, we had just quietly stood and watched. I was trembling uncontrollably, my jaw clattering as I pulled the collar of my coat closer for warmth.

We stood there shivering, not daring to move a muscle as we watched for even the slightest of movement from the gates. It seemed an eternity as peering terrified, gazing endlessly into that icy blackness, nothing had even moved. But then it happened… A movement caused us all to hold our breath as something crept ever so slowly into view. My heart faltered, every muscle tensing while staring at the hideously thin and dark thing!

It stealthily crept outward from behind the gates, now peered out from between the tall iron bars. Two small and pale eyes, which flashing while blinking now stared back as we stood aghast! It was just for a moment and then the lights vanished as the shadow returned to the dark.

"I don't know what the hell that was—but I don't want to find out while we're standing out here." Raymond's words fell in little more than a whisper, as raising his weapons, he peered over at me, "Let's get moving— I'll take the lead."

"It's Trudy--," Rich gasped while hurriedly following from close behind, "I had a feeling that she escaped the fire that night—and knew that she was still out there somewhere."

"How could she have come on the property without being noticed by that thing in the vault?" Raymond seemed frustrated and even angry as we hurried back through our previous tracks.

"She's not inherently evil--," Explaining between gasps as we hurried, Rich whispered, "And being an insect, she likely possesses no spirit or soul in the sense that might be recognized by the guardian."

"If it was her--," Peering fearfully behind us, I said, "She may not have survived—and might be something very different now."

"Impossible—or like Raymond said, she'd never have slipped past the guardian." Rich suddenly leapt aside as an iridescent shower of shimmering ice passed within his lanterns pale glow. He'd gasped desperately, as the reflection of stark terror within being startled had undoubtedly taken years from his life.

"Keep moving--," Raymond insisted while speaking quietly and taking the lead.

In the night the property had taken on a sinister semblance and the place was unfamiliar beneath all the snow. I heard every step and each breath, and kept glancing into the blackness that seemed to follow closer the faster that we went. Had it just been the wind, or was it something else? My heart skipped a beat as the front porch came into view, and the door seemed too far away! I thought to have sensed something watching, creeping and stalking while following closely from behind. Terrified, and looking back continually, I stumbled several times while hurriedly making my way around to the front of the house.

"Wait…" Raymond suddenly halted us with a raised arm, and turning to look into the darkness, aimed his revolver into the shadows behind. The wind had seemingly cried out, then moaning among the dense branches, bitterly tossed the curls upon my brow. It became painfully apparent that, although none could see anything, we all sensed that something was there…

"I'm not absolutely sure--," Raymond whispered while holding the weapon is his trembling hand, "But, I have a gut-feeling that we're not alone…"

"That's because we aren't…" Whispering, Rich nodded in gesture toward the main gates as his features became withered and pale.

At first it had been almost invisible, but then I saw the slight movements in the dark. It was not some large and monstrous, lumbering thing, but a thin, and barely noticeable shadow. It swiftly weaved and crept from behind the iron rails, as peeking out, cautiously stayed hidden from view, its tiny and pale eyes burning like twin sparks as it crawled about while looking in.

"I don't know what that is--," Rich whispered as he looked back at me, "But, it's not Trudy…"

"I don't know or care to find out in the dark." Motioning with certain urgency, I quietly said, "Let's get back behind locked doors—and near the hearth."

Hurriedly making our way to the front porch, Raymond had quickly looked back and quietly said, "I thought that Marlowe said we were hidden and safe in here?"

"And he was right--," Rich had pointed back as while whispering, and said, "It can't really see or hear us. Look—it's just randomly looking in and between the bars."

There had been a brief hesitation in our movements as we had all paused to stare back and into the blackness of the gates. The hideous and thin shadow still moved blindly about, but never once did its attention entirely focus upon any one of us. Oddly, I noticed that it had also been very cautious in each movement, and as while avoiding any contact with the iron bars.

"Let's go--," Rich trembled as tugging upon my sleeve, now dragged me as we stumbled through our previous tracks and toward the front of the house.

The lights of the porch had suddenly come into view and my heart leapt into my throat! Never before had I been more terrified than within those final moments between the stairs, porch and opening the front door!

We had fallen into the corridor as though returning from some arctic adventure with a polar bear in close pursuit. Raymond had swiftly slammed the door closed, and promptly locking it, slid the heavy bolt into place.

"So, what happened?" Startling us from where he sat waiting on the hallway floor, limp as a rag doll, Tim had curiously peered up, and still utterly intoxicated, said, "You guys look like you must've seen something, because you're all white as a ghost."

"We found some tracks under Raymond's window." Rich informed him while removing his boots and coat, "We also saw something nasty that was sneaking around from just outside of the gates...."

"It wasn't the same thing that was at Raymond's window--," I had reassured my friend, "But I have a feeling that it'll make its presence known soon."

"I'm never going to drink this much again..." Stumbling, Tim followed us into the living room and slumping back onto the couch, groaned, "I'll end up dying from alcohol poisoning before anything has a chance to kill me..."

"You just keep telling yourself that--," Raymond dropped onto the couch beside him, "But if there was in any truth to that idea, trust me, there wouldn't be a drop of liquor left in this house."

"So what was it?" Tim burped while politely attempting to cover his mouth, "The thing outside the window?"

"Rich seems fairly sure that it was Trudy." Taking my favorite chair nearest the hearth, I rubbed at sleep-filled eyes while saying, "But for all of our sakes, let's hope that he's wrong..."

The sudden realization had been sobering, as Tim gazed fearfully into the flames.

"But don't worry--," Feeling a sudden sympathy for my drunken and frightened friend, I offered the only comfort that I could, "The guardian protects the property, but we still have Marlowe, Amica, and the hound."

"Amica--," Rich pondered briefly, "Oh, that's right, I'd completely forgotten that you'd named Marlowe's demon."

"It's the Latin word for friend--," I had explained, "And considering our circumstances it seems more appropriate, and a little less diabolical, wouldn't you say?"

"It's a demon—and in case you've forgotten, they're supposed to be diabolical," He squinted, "Does it really respond to pet-names?"

"And this is coming from the man who named his bug-daughter Trudy?" Raymond shook his head while indulging another brandy near the hearth.

"It might not be good to use the demons true name, anyway." Tim shrugged, "Wouldn't that be like invoking it every time that you did?" His eyes slowly rolled back into his head, as slipping backward, he silently drifted into a drunken slumber. With a grin, Rich had kindly covered him in that same woolen blanket that I had used earlier.

"Back to what we were discussing--," Rich reminded me, "About the name and summoning- would it make a difference, if similar demons have different names in other cultures? And why would Marlowe's demon even consider responding to a name suggested by a mere mortal?"

"This entity is different somehow." Thinking for a moment, I felt a little insulted at the mere insinuation. In fact, I had almost revealed the secret of Amica and her demon, but refrained at the last moment, saying, "We all have two sides to our nature, I simply named the less despicable aspect of the creature."

With eyes fixed as though utterly bewildered, Rich shook his head while saying, "You, my friend—have been alone and in the company of demons for far too long... Seriously, it's bad enough that you're consorting with evil, but do you think that it's really advisable to attribute pet names to demons?"

"I don't believe you guys--," Raymond swallowed hard, "If anyone had tried telling me any of this before, I would've been the first signatures on someone's 'one way ticket' to the booby-hatch."

"It's amazing what happens when you realize that the devil is knocking at your door, for real…" Muttering from somewhere in the realm of a waking dream, Tim giggled while stuttering his words, "I wonder what Michael will name those things at the gates—and do we get to have one also?"

"We should be sleeping--," Raymond's stern gaze awakened us all from the foolishness, "Simms is going to want answers—and I need you guys to be absolutely straight with him."

"The thought of involving more people really scares me." Sipping at brandy, I sighed to the soothing burn of the spirits, saying, "We don't need to cost any more people their lives just by simply knowing too much…"

"He's already on the hit-list, no matter how you look at it." Rich poured himself another brandy, and looking back at me, said, "It's just a matter of time."

"I'd start with the possession thing--," Raymond poured a Whiskey from our serving cart and took a stiff drink, "He already knows that he's dealing with the living dead. I'd keep it as simple as possible—and the rest will happen on its own, like it did with me."

"He has a point--," Rich agreed, "Once old Simms stumbles any further into this nightmare—I'm sure that the rest will follow soon enough."

"Agreed--," The clock chimed midnight and I pointed as the 'witching hour' passed, saying, "We should try to get a little rest—the morning comes all too soon."

"Morning, for some reason it feels like it's always dark." Raymond grumbled, as looking toward the slightly parted draperies, sighed deeply and said, "I wish that spring would hurry up and get here. Sometime I even wonder if I'll live to see another summer."

"Don't even say things like that." The comment having obviously unsettled Rich, he angrily shook his head, "Things are already bad enough around here without you being pessimistic."

"I just wish that this whole nightmare would end." Parting the mesh on the hearth, Raymond jabbed at the coals with a poker, and tossing another log onto the fire, quietly said, "It's getting harder all the time to keep a positive outlook, and especially with what's happening at the gates."

Without another word Rich carried our mugs and empty glasses into the kitchen, and filling them with water, left them in the sink to soak. It hurt to see him appear so utterly lost and hopeless, and looking to Raymond, I said, "For all of his nonsense he's really a sensitive soul, and is just very worried about all of us."

"The ending will be coming sooner than any of us might think." Unaware of my previous statement, Rich had returned, and dropping onto the couch across from me, said, "I'd rather just believe that there's still hope for some of us..."

"What makes you say that?" Moving from the couch as while preparing to depart, Raymond looked back at him. There hadn't been any immediate response from Rich, who just seemed to sit there while considering his own words. It was apparent by his dismayed expression that he was bothered with some ghastly premonition, which now made him hesitant to share.

Awakening and stretching, Tim fluffed a cushion, and noticing our expressions, remarked, "Let's face it, gentlemen—no one escapes alive from the game of life. All that matters in the end—was how you played it." Rubbing the sleep from his eyes, it was apparent that he fought a losing battle against intoxication and complete exhaustion, of which he soon lost.

"I'm still interested in hearing your thoughts--," Refusing to release him from the obligation, I joined both men in the hallway, "What makes you so sure?"

"Maybe, it's because I can sense that from somewhere out there--," Rich frowned, "That thing is purposely pushing us, because it knowns that we'll break..."

Sympathetically patting him on the back, I could only agree, "All that we can really do at the moment is pray for hope, and an ending to that thing."

"Amen to that." Raymond looked to where Tim had passed out and was sleeping soundly on the couch, "Well, at least one of us is getting some sleep."

Whimpering as he suddenly twitched in dark and troubled dream, Tim lashed out at some invisible assailant before our astonished eyes! Then, moaning almost painfully, he rolled over, and burrowing deeply beneath the woolen quilt, was gone again.

"If you're willing to call that sleep--," Glancing between my friends, I groaned, "Then I hope that the powers that be will have mercy on us all..."

"I'll have a quick look around the house before bed--," Patting my shoulder and nervously looking around, Raymond quietly said, "After the thing at my window and what we saw out there tonight, I'll feel better knowing that everything's locked up tight."

"I'll go along for the walk." Rich offered with a shrug, "It's not like I'll be sleeping any time soon..."

"I'll be working late—and watching." Attempting to offer them a little comfort within knowing, I moved toward the stairs, and looking back, said, "Try to get some rest—we have a busy day tomorrow."

In truth, none of us were even certain if we would live to see another dawn. It was becoming increasingly harder to live on a prayer while existing on a distant hope.

"Maybe--," Rich hesitated in the hallway and curiously looked up at me, "You could ask Marlowe about Trudy and if she's really a threat to any of us?"

"And if she is--," Raymond added, "See if you can find out what the hell she's up to. I'd rather not wake up in the middle of the night with some big, nasty bug hanging over me…"

"Believe me--," Rich glared back at him, "If she really had the intention of doing us any harm—you wouldn't know, because you'd never wake up…"

"I'll do what I can." The promise had sounded empty even as I had spoken the words. It left me feeling discouraged rather than hopeful, and helpless as they made off into the shadows and went down the hall. In parting I had said a silent prayer, and could only hope that someone or something from somewhere had been listening.

In turning I had almost stumbled and tumbled down the stairs. Meowing, Merlin had paused before me while upon another late night excursion to his food bowl. Smiling and leaning down to scratch behind his ears, I watched as he contentedly waddled off and down the steps. It was hard to believe the difference between what happened inside the estate and what lurked in the blackness just beyond. It was quite literally two entirely different worlds. One of warmth, compassion and love, and the other existed as a night realm. A dark place occupied by endless danger and unspeakable horrors…

Making my way into the office and switching on the lamp, I slumped into the chair before the desk. As always, I had left the door partially ajar so that Merlin could return, but upon second thought, swiftly moved and quietly closed it. Then, for reasons beyond explanation, I had decided to turn out the lamp and in the darkness, returned to the desk

Carefully feeling my way back and finally settling into the chair, I closed my eyes while dreaming into the shadows. There was a dull glow creeping in from beneath the door, and the light was enough to make out basic forms and shapes. My heart was heavy and head felt hot, and it seemed as though it might simply explode. The ticking of the mantel clock thundered in my thoughts, as each strike of the gears felt like a hammer from either side of my head.

"There are devils at the gates on this night." Amica whispered.

Looking to the enormous black bird, I swallowed hard, unable to find words in response. Curious, the raven dropped down from its perch and into the chair beside me. There was a pale and shimmering blue light that shone throughout the room as the raven transformed. As within mere moments of having moved, Amica stood quietly beside me.

There was something mysterious in those star-filled eyes that now haunted my soul. It was some distant recollection that left me mystified whenever we exchanged glances.

"I know—we saw something out there tonight." Rubbing at my eyes, I fought the heated pressure of the fever gathering in my head, "Amica, I'm scared for the others and especially Caitlin. I'm afraid that I'll never see her again..."

"She exists far closer than you might ever imagine--," The entity slowly drew its legs up from beneath it, and resting its chin upon its knees, gazed up at me, "And the shadows that gather at the gates exist without sight or senses from beyond the barriers of the estate..."

"But for how long?" Looking to the creature, my heart ached with fear and loss, "For how much longer will we be incessantly hounded by these horrors, and will I ever see my love again?"

There were several long moments of stillness between us, and I felt a strange urgency in its gaze. But then, a shadow of had passed between us while causing it to suddenly look away. Noticing that Amica had ceased to shine quite so brightly, I leaned closer assuming that it might have just been my eyes. It had avoided my touch or glances in those moments and cowered with each attempt that I had made. In fading, I could only assume that some of the magic that attributed life to this amazing being had somehow slipped away.

"Amica--," Concern now caused me to extend a hand and gently bring the creatures gaze back into my own, "Please speak to me, are you alright?"

Once again there was no reply and just that same wide-eyed and endless stare. Suddenly, I became aware of subtle changes that were now altering the physical form of the creature. The hair had become longer and fuller and the form more tangible than ever before. Still appearing strangely alien in some respects, it was visibly manifesting while assuming distinct characterises of human form.

"What's happening to you—and was it something that I have said or done?" Removing my hand from upon the creature's face, it despondently looked up at me. Its trembling lips had moved as thought to speak, but not a single sound would come.

"Please—speak to me, Amica, and tell me what has happened."

"She cannot--," Marlowe whispered from the blackness of my thoughts, "The change forbids it—patience, all will come in good time."

"She--," Looking down at Amica with the sudden realization, I saw the obvious, and gasped, "Marlowe—what have you done?"

"I have done nothing--," Marlowe moved from out of the deep shadows, his pale eyes shining from beneath his hooded cloak, "Destiny now moves our path as events are altered according to design. All are coming about according to your own doing and a wish fulfilled…"

"But why Amica--," I could only gaze upon the fair creature in fear and fascination, "What possible purpose could this serve?"

"Choices have been made, destinies forged, and the wheels of time now turn against us." Marlowe's voice became mournful as he spoke in barely a whisper, "You are still blind to many things—but are now firmly fixed upon the verge of discovery."

"But, I don't understand any of this--," Feeling a hand upon my wrist and looking back at Amica, she gazed with wide-eyed desperation. Words were not necessary in that moment, as her expression revealed a plea to accept Marlowe's guidance without question.

"Marlowe--," Speaking humbly, I slowly turned toward the apparition, "Is there any chance of a favorable ending for any of us?"

"Favorable perhaps--," His voiced faded, echoing while sounding miles away, "But there are never truly any endings…" The ghostly figure vanished into the ether.

Shivering and noticing the previous pressure from behind my eyes to have passed, I slowly rubbed at the tingling flesh of my wrists and forearms. Through little glances I had noticed that there was something very different about Amica now. Aside from the apparent, she still appeared so very pale, but the preternatural glow had altogether vanished.

Taking notice of my fearful glances, she looked back at me. Her eyes widened as to my shock and horror, her shining gaze faded into a pale and blind pupil. White, soulless and empty they blinked, but nothing looked back.

Moving away from her, I could only watch in utter dismay, soon realizing that the changes we had affected through the pact were slowly making her into something unimaginable…!

"As Marlowe foretold--," She once more found her voice and began to quietly explain, "I shall become what I should have been and always was, before the demon…"

"If you lose your abilities, what will become of us? What will happen to you if one of those things catches you somewhere?"

"The universe now guides us by design—and the choice is no longer ours." Gently rubbing at her eyes and blinking several times, she looked back at me. Her form began altering again, as though molded by some master artist, she became more tangible and visibly female. Pale and white and blank as slate, she appeared like an angel carved from the finest marble. It was almost impossible to avert my gaze as her transformation became complete. Ashamed, I had looked away, realizing that she knew nothing of humanity and even less about humility.

"One moment, I'll be right back." Moving from the chair and out into the hall, I quickly went into the bedroom. A swift search through the linen closet with fumbling hands and I soon located one of Caitlin's bath robes, and hurriedly went back into the office.

"This should suit you for the moment--," Gently assisting her into the long and green robe, I carefully showed her how to tie the cloth belt, saying, "But if you're going to appear in this form—you'll need to dress appropriately."

It appeared that modesty and humility were well beneath her experience, and that she was quite comfortable in my presence, regardless of clothing. Unsettled and admittedly excited by this, I felt certain shame in my own feelings.

"Please, go into the bedroom and find something to wear for the morning." Clearing my throat, I had focused upon the typewriter to avoid looking upon her again, and said, "You're welcome to anything in Caitlin's closet—and appear to be about the same height and build."

She had just looked back with those empty and ghost-like eyes, and nodding, still stood as while silently staring down at me. I had been caught in the moment and as while utterly captivated, drifted unintentionally into some lost and distant memory. It had been a time when Caitlin had sat in that very same chair and in similar condition.

"You must not think of her--," Reaching out and gently touching my wrist, she broke the spell, saying, "It only draws the darkness that much closer…"

Startled and speechless as while realizing that she had sensed my thoughts, I looked back in utter and complete shame. Taking hold of my hand, she slowly seated herself upon my lap as while wrapping both arms about my neck. Then, while I was gazing deeply into the white emptiness of her eyes, she whispered, "You must see only me—trust and remain true to what you believe. In spirit I could only influence dreams and imagination. But in body, I shall shield your heart from the darkness and stand at your side, when all other hope fails."

"Why do I feel as though I have always known you?" Gently holding her, I felt our souls meet while touching in the darkness, and quietly asked, "What's this mystery that Marlowe speaks of—and the secret that still exists between us?"

"I am forbidden to share such things--," Sorrow filled her fair features, "But in time all shall be revealed and then, shall you truly know me…"

It was apparent that her servitude to the elder gods held her from revealing such things, and I did not pursue the matter. Instead, I turned back to a previous concern and questioned her in the topic, "Can you still see beyond these walls and sense all things?"

"I still sense distant realms—know the truth of your heart, and feel the darkness at the gates."

"There is a creature—something that we fear is stalking, and might even possibly be hunting us." I shuddered with the thought, "Are you aware of it—or its intentions?"

"I felt its presence earlier—and in the night." Her pale gaze traveled toward the window and out into the frozen night, "If it had desired death, many of you would have already fallen long ago."

"If it isn't hunting us--," I licked at dry lips, "Then why does it seek us out?"

"She is the last of her kind—unnatural by design, and unlike any other creature upon this world. She knows only you and your companion, and especially the one that you call Richard."

"The last of her kind--," The words held a sudden finality and a strange sorrow struck me in some terrible way, "So, then we were successful in destroying the nest that I discovered in that mine."

"Yes, only death and the silent decay of generations occupy those dark and empty caverns now."

"And, how would we go about finding this last creature?" All things considered I had felt certain guilt in the whispered words, "And putting an end to this monstrous, genetic mutation…"

"Do not make haste in judgements—allies are few and precious in these dark times."

Slowly nodding, I swallowed hard as my attention was drawn toward the window and heavy draperies. Although nothing had moved visibly, I thought to have sensed something that stirred in the frozen boughs of the old willow. Intending to move and being gently forced back down by Amica, she brushed the hair from my eyes and quietly said, "Be still, there is nothing to fear on this night. The darkness dwells beyond the gates and is deaf and blind to your presence. There is much to be done in the days to follow. Use this time to rest and record all that you have seen and learned."

She then moved from off of me, and motioning with a hand into the hallway, said, "I will see to that clothing that you mentioned, and attempt to appear appropriately."

Nodding, I watched as she swiftly slipped out of the room and moved quietly into the hallway. There was a strange static energy in the air and it caused my head to swim in a dizzying haze, and flesh to strangely tingle. Was it just another adrenaline surge caused by the seemingly endless fear, mental fatigue, and complete, physical exhaustion? Or was something also happening within me? For reasons beyond explanation I somehow felt lighter, and as though some aspect of youthful vigor and vitality had been restored to me. Looking to my hands, I noticed that they appeared softer, and that the wrinkles that had begun had faded. Was it possible? Marlowe had said something about time no longer having the same affect upon me. Assuming to have imagined the changes due to poor lighting and exhaustion, I shook the thoughts from my mind.

Moving without another thought on the matter, I turned in my chair, and facing the desk, switched on the little lamp. Slipping a fresh page into the typewriter, I began recording the events of the day. The words came steadily and with their familiar 'machine-gun' rhythm of the keys striking the carriage. It was like thunder in the stillness as, while half-awake, I attempted to place all things into their proper perspective. Over time and with all the stress of continual interruptions this had become a considerably more complicated process. What seemed fair while written in the early hours of the morning, made little sense by noon the following day. This presented the issue of having to constantly rewrite things, and pray that the editor would not abandon the project for all its little inconsistencies.

Amica had quietly returned, and leaving the door ajar for Merlin, crept back into the chair. She had chosen a long white night gown and matching robe, and nestled into a comforter that she had also brought while settling into the chair beside me. In some respects her new form now bothered me. Rather than simply being divinity or entity, she was now a female presence in the house. I had sighed deeply as she curled up, and covering her face slightly, watched me as she drifted into a place I could only assume was shared by dreams. There was something angelic, mysterious, and terrifying about her. There was a definite magnetism between us, but no physical desire as my love and loyalty for Caitlin was far stronger. And this I kept telling myself, over and over…

Noticing a shadow in the open doorway, I watched as Merlin cautiously entered the room. He had paused curiously, and then approaching ever so slowly, sniffed at the soundly sleeping Amica. The interest had passed quickly as, after investigating, he made his way beneath the desk and to where he comfortably settled in his favorite place before the heating vent. His complacent behavior had brought about certain relief as I had been worried about his reaction to Amica. It had occurred to me on several occasions that my senses and sensibilities concerning the demon might possibly have been terribly off course. In this sense, I suppose that my faith in the basic instincts and nature of animals had always been greater than my trust in human logic. Marlowe and Amica had become precious to me in so many ways, but I still feared their servitude to the darkness. I knew that Amica harbored an unimaginable evil, but could never abandon her now. I would never break the promise, regardless of what happened…even if it terrified me.

I was suddenly startled as a soft breeze now caused the draperies to drift slightly open and move ever so slightly. Ordinarily, this would have been a common occurrence, except for the fact that the window had been tightly sealed… I had always suspected that the house had been haunted, and that the love of those previously lost still remained. I knew that whatever moved in the shadows of Sanctum Arcanum now watched, and guarded over all who dwelled within her darkened walls.

CHAPTER FIVE

Sunday, January 26th, 1975.

8:35 a.m.

Morning had come all too soon. I had awakened with my head down on the desk, and groaned while rubbing at a stiff neck. I was amazed to discover that Amica was still asleep in the chair beside me. She made no sound, but was clearly quite comfortable while bundled in the large and white patch-work quilt. I was even more surprised to see that I had managed to complete the entire events of the previous day and evening, the pages of which now rested neatly in their appropriate, metal basket on the desk.

The alluring smell of breakfast now caught my attention as the sounds of my friends echoed through the hall. A movement caused me to turn, as yawning and stretching, Amica had stirred in the chair while allowing the blanket to fall. It had been nothing short of utter shock to discover that she had undergone several more striking changes in the night. If there had ever been any question as to her gender, there would certainly be no mistake of it now!

Swiftly retrieving the blanket from where it had fallen, I had hurriedly recovered her and quickly slipped back into my chair. Assumedly having become too warm, she had disrobed during the early morning hours and simply covered herself with the quilt. In a slow but steady movement she had incoherently swung an arm, and swiftly uncovered herself again.

Looking away, I had considered other possibilities of preserving her humility, and then considered simply covering her with the robe until she woke up. There hadn't even been time to discuss the matter as footsteps in the corridor announced the arrival of a guest! A moment later, I stood there like a fool with the blanket in my arms, as Rich opened and walked in through the office door! My eyes had dropped to where the night gown and robe lay on the floor before me, and then I'd ashamedly looked to my friend.

"Are you coming down for breakfast?" He glanced inquisitively at the gown and robe, then back at me, and asked with a grin, "Or—did I interrupt something?"

I had been caught speechless, but then looking between the empty chair, blanket in my arms and the raven perched quietly atop my desk, gawked foolishly, "Of course not—don't be ridiculous—I'll be right down."

He had stood there for a moment analyzing the picture, and then slowly shaken his head. Then, taking a bite from an apple, he winked in departure without another word.

Returning my attention to Amica, I whispered, "Disrobing in your human form is not advisable—unless you intend to bathe or change clothes. And you can still become the raven—thank goodness for that!"

"Agreed—and it would seem so?" The bird looked back at me with pale and ghostly, haunting eyes, "Though I am not certain as for how much longer this ability shall remain?"

"How are you feeling?" The memory of the struggle between the demon and possessed soul had come to mind, and I feared the possible consequences.

"Feeling--," Amica pondered the question, "I am well…"

"It might be best that they don't see you just yet. After breakfast we can see to more suitable arrangements--," I felt rather awkward having another female presence in the house, "Maybe you can stay in the bedroom while I remain in the office?"

"I will do nothing of the sort--," She argued, "I am to remain at your side at all times now, within reason of course."

"We will discuss the matter once we have eaten." I spoke firmly but politely, refusing to accept any further argument, as I departed the room. Hearing a movement on the stairs behind me, I had glanced back and stopped suddenly, gawking in disbelief! She had followed in nothing more than the blanket, and looked curiously at me when I had questioned her actions. She appeared as pale as blank slate, a figure that awaited color. Her eyes were white and without pupils, though her every feature and even her hair flowed as natural as anything else in life. She was both beautiful and terrifying to behold. It was also quite apparent that Amica was a determined creature, and that I truly had little say in the matter. In any case, it was quickly and mutually agreed that she would remain at my side, but anonymously for the moment.

Although it had seemed strange, I hadn't minded the presence of the raven at the breakfast table. Rich and the others had seemed rather surprised that it had taken the seat directly beside me, and politely waited while the food was served. They were then even further shocked as it indulged a rather large meal from a plate that I had prepared for the bird.

None had uttered a single word in reprisal, but their expressions spoke volumes.

"Oh my, but our little friend certainly does have an appetite." Tim had spoken politely and with a curious smile, "It never ceases to surprise me." He had always been fascinated with the intriguing creature, and I knew that his remarks had been sincere.

"I couldn't possibly agree more," I stirred a little honey into my tea and received a scolding eye from Rich as I spread some over my toast. No sooner had I placed down the jar, than did he snatch it up and place it well beyond my reach!

"I just had a little in my tea and a few drops on my toast." I held up the half slice that I had barely coated. At which point, the raven snapped it out of my hand and presumed to gobble it down!

"I'm beginning to like that bird more all of the time." Chuckling, Raymond glanced over at the Raven in some new found admiration, "They say that ravens are very intelligent."

"Well, it seems to be a lot smarter than him--," Rich glared at me, "You know that you're supposed to avoid sweets and grease because of your heart condition."

The bird had eyed me suspiciously as my friend had returned to his seat. I sensed that she had discovered something new, information that I had previously neglected to disclose. It was also apparent that she had not taken kindly to it. Oddly, she shared a similar disposition to Caitlin. It was becoming increasingly harder to consider her little more than an ethereal entity.

"We've decided to postpone installing the gates today." Rich announced, "I'm worried about the weather—and I'm not too thrilled with the idea of being exposed after seeing that thing at the gates last night. I'll get the crew over here first thing Monday morning. It's supposed to clear up over-night."

"That makes perfect sense." I had sipped at my tea, and added, "I'll admit that the thought of being without those gates leaves me feeling a little exposed as well."

"Don't worry--," Rich had winked, "You're secret is safe with me."

It was the robe and gown incident—I knew that he wouldn't have just let something like that go unnoticed or without comment. Returning a sarcastic smirk, I purposely ignored him, saying, "We can use the time to try to catch up on our rest."

"Catch up, nothing—I hardly slept a wink last night." Raymond dipped toast into his egg, "I kept looking out of my window and expecting an unwanted guest....oh, and speaking of creepy crawlies? Did our friend say anything to you about the bug?"

Amica had paused over her food to peer over at me. It had not taken much thought to see the intent in her gaze, and so I presented the matter in a somewhat more optimistic perspective.

"Yes, several things in fact." I had placed down my toast and leaned back in the seat, "Firstly, I was reassured that she is in fact the last of her kind."

Rich had nodded in acknowledgement, unwilling to pursue the matter any further as the investigation and search for the mine vandals was still high profile. If the fools had only known what we had done there, they might have awarded us medals rather than started a man-hunt. Clearing my voice, I looked to Raymond, "It would also appear that she isn't a threat to us— but is in fact, a type of neutral element."

"I don't understand what you mean by neutral element--," Tim sipped at his coffee, "Is that to say that for the moment, we are safe? Or that she is simply undecided as to what side she stands on, at this point?"

"I was given every indication that the creature is more lost in this world than anything else. And, that she is simply searching for something, or someone familiar."

"What—like some kind of a lost pet looking for its owners?" Raymond scoffed at the thought.

"More like a child that's ended up homeless in a foreign place." Rich corrected him, saying, "Just before we'd lost her, we'd established that her intelligence levels were close to the skills and understanding of an average six year old child."

Raymond just stared, his expression revealing utter disbelief, "We're talking about a bug here, right?"

"Not exactly--," Rich had seemed somewhat reluctant at first, but then said, "From what we gathered, she was part of some government experiment. We aren't exactly sure what they were doing, but her genetics were different than the others."

"She was a queen--," I coughed in explanation, and putting a napkin to my mouth, said,

"Rich also fed her exclusively on steroids, fruit and vegetables, so she never developed the carnivorous traits of her predecessors."

"You forgot to mention that she also shares Rich's genetic structure." Tim had volunteered the dark secret, "So although he is a bit of a wiener—the creature might have an exceptionally high IQ."

"Just let the wiener thing slide—he did mention your high IQ." I whispered while motioning with a hand for Rich to remain calm.

"Dare I ask how that was even possible?" Raymond had looked to our friend, whom looking rather ashamed and very guilty, quietly said, "We discovered from previous victims and through the developmental stages of the insects, that these creatures absorb DNA and assume the physical traits and characteristics of their hosts. I was hoping that by introducing a more stable factor into the early development of the larva that it might become something more manageable."

"You created a monster that outsmarted you all, escaped, and then tore an almost unstoppable, killer hybrid to ribbons--," Raymond appeared completely horrified, "So in fact, what you're telling me is that it also survived a burning building, it's venomous, armed to the teeth, and that it's most likely looking for you…"

"More or less--," Shrugging, Rich attempted to appear optimistic while saying, "But due to the fact that we do know that she's very intelligent, we also have to keep in mind that she saved our lives at Scott and Carrie's place. So, it's possible that she may relate to us in some regard, and possibly even as a familiar species when considering the DNA? In truth, I really don't know how far she has advanced, well, at least not until I've had a chance to examine her."

"Examine her--,"Scoffing at the thought, Tim snickered nervously, "What we really need is a seriously big can of Raid."

"So, what are we going to do about this? Do we set traps--," Raymond looked to me for answers, "Or maybe try one of those new chemical fire arrowheads that Rich designed?"

"We do nothing at the moment. I was assured that she's harmless to us— and might possibly play some significant role before this all ends."

Raymond slid back into his seat and looked between us, "Well, I'd feel a whole lot better if we could just eliminate the thing from our current list of life-threatening issues."

"If she isn't a threat—maybe we can work with this." Appearing fascinated with the prospect, Rich pointed to me, and said, "Let's face it— we could use an extra watch-dog around here. And we all know that she's lethal against anything that she considers a threat."

"Oh great--," Raymond rolled his eyes, "So what happens if she gets it in her head that I'm an issue? Do I just get written off as a statistic, because I somehow pissed this thing off?"

"She's very simple to deal with--," Rich now appeared desperate, even frightened, "All that we have to do is remain calm around her, never raise our voices, and avoid eating meat near her. That always seemed to scare and get her excited. She isn't very different from a horse in nature."

"Sure she is--," Raymond cursed under his breath, "But if you excite a horse, it won't kill or eat you…"

"So what would you suggest?" Tapping a finger against his coffee mug and grinning sarcastically, Tim asked, "That we put some food and water out for her—and make a bed in the attic?"

Spinning to look at me, Rich's eyes revealed that spark of Frankenstein madness was reignited. I knew that feverish and desperate look, and feared it more than the insect itself. I felt that familiar cold and greasy lump forming in my guts and swallowed hard.

"That might not be such a bad idea?" Directing his attention to Tim after finding no support from me, Rich spoke thoughtfully, "She'd be right at home up there—and safely out of our way."

"Did he just say safely? Are you kidding me here?" It was apparent that Raymond could not believe his own ears or eyes, "Are you seriously considering bringing a giant killer-insect into the house?"

"She's more humanoid than insect, actually." Rich had looked to me, "Well, as far as we know?"

"Listen—I get where the mad scientist is going with this," Tim intervened, "And just for arguments sake, I say that we try to attract her here. If she's truly harmless, then we'll know for certain. If not—then we'll have a much better chance of destroying her on our own terms."

"Fair enough--," Raymond nodded, "But the first sign of trouble--," He pointed an accusing finger at Rich, "And we put her down, agreed?"

"Putting her down is not as simple as you might think--," Looking between the two men grimacing, he warned, "I've seen what the more primitive specimens were capable of doing—and gentlemen: They are a living nightmare…"

"Will your chemical weapons work against this thing?" It was apparent that Raymond intended to take as few chances as possible, as he said, "I need to know for sure…"

"Most definitely--," The promise came without a moment's thought, "Nothing can survive that."

"Alright--," Swallowing hard, Raymond had looked between us and said, "The first time that any of us feel truly threatened—we nuke the thing."

"Scouts honor." Rich raised a hand. I had heard and seen all of this before—and it was just before everything had gone terribly, terribly wrong…

They had all peered over at me and I felt centered out while being left to make the final decision in the matter. Amica had watched me as she gulped down a heap of bacon that Tim had kindly placed onto her plate. I sensed that she had shared Rich's opinion on the matter, and felt obligated to side with the ruling majority.

"The attic is full of furniture, boxes, and an old bed." I thought for a moment, "There's a large oval window, it's hinged and swings out from the bottom. It's been years since I went up there, but I'm sure that with a little 'elbow grease' we can put something together."

"I can't believe that I'm agreeing to this... I must have bugs in my belfry too." Raymond shook his head, "Well, since we put the gates off until Monday--," He agreed, "Let's see what we can get accomplished after breakfast."

"We have kitchen duty today--," Rich grumbled, and then looking hopeful, peered over at me, "Unless someone else wants to volunteer?"

"I need to run out and pick up groceries." Tim announced, and leaning closer, asked me, "Did you have any plans?"

"Um, actually--," I turned as the enormous black bird silently gazed over at me, "I have some errands to run as well."

"Do you mind if I tag along?"

It was apparent that I could no longer conceal Amica's secret from my friends, and that the matter could not wait until after dinner. Sighing deeply, I put down my tea cup and tapping a finger at the table, said, "Of course not, Tim--," Turning to look at Amica, I said, "Would you please go up to the bedroom and find something appropriate to wear out?"

Bowing, she leapt from off the table, fluttering off, and disappeared up the stairs and from out of sight.

Raymond gawked, as slowly turning to me with raised eyebrows, he asked, "Did you just tell the bird to find something suitable to wear? Is there something going on here that you might've forgotten to tell the rest of us?"

"Yes—by all means--," Placing his toast down and crossing his arms over his breast, Rich glared suspiciously, "Do tell..."

"Well, as I'd previously mentioned--," I spoke in an uncertain and disconcerted manner, "Amica has undergone some striking and unexpected changes." I felt extremely awkward attempting to explain matters and would have preferred that the demon had remained a boy, or simply the raven. It would have been far less complicated. The moment had passed quickly and judging from the expressions, I knew that she had already made an appearance. Looking toward the stairwell, I politely waved in introduction, "Gentlemen—I would like to introduce you to: Amica."

She had chosen a red, woolen, turtle-neck sweater, blue jeans and black, knee-high boots. She appeared to be a perfect fit in Caitlin's clothing, and it was all becoming a little too uncanny. Not a single word had been uttered, as all now moved from their seats and stood about the table. Brushing the long platinum hair from her face, the pale and incandescent eyes fell curiously upon each and every member of the group. She had all the appearance of living and breathing, marble statue.

"I thought that the demon appeared in the form of a boy?" Whispering from behind a hand while attempting to remain discrete, Rich failed miserably as Amica had heard him. Politely taking the seat beside me, she had silently looked back at Rich. His reaction had been one of utter embarrassment, and he stuttered, "But hey—it really doesn't make any difference--," He shrugged, "You can appear in any shape or form that you like…"

"Due to recent developments—and necessity--," I had announced, "Amica will now be joining our efforts in physical form rather than just spirit. Rest assured I was just as surprised as all of you."

There had been an awkward silence as none had known how to properly respond. Their shock and hesitation was well warranted, as we had no idea as to how she might react in a social situation.

"It's a pleasure to finally meet you--," Bowing respectfully before a lady, Raymond nodded before returning to his seat, "I'm at your service, young lady."

"So, there are gentlemen among you." Amica had eyed Rich suspiciously, and then politely nodding to Raymond, said, "I am both honored and pleased to make your acquaintance, sir."

"Feel free to call me Raymond—everyone else does."

"Brown nosing already…" Rich scoffed while mumbling to himself, "Typical…"

"Raymond--," Amica had politely acknowledged his request, "And thank you kindly, for making me feel welcome."

"Amica—isn't that Latin for friend?" Grinning mischievously from across the table, he nodded, "Welcome to our little extended family—and please feel free to call me, Tim."

"Guardian of the hall--," She had taken immediate notice of the golden whistle that hung from about his neck, "Keeper of that which walks in silence… I am pleased to meet you as well, Tim."

"And last and usually least, I'm Rich--," The skepticism was revealed in his tone and sarcastic manner, "Welcome to our own personal little hell. I'm sure that you'll fit right in…"

It was more than obvious that Rich had been uncomfortable with the presence of this strange, yet fascinating creature. Not in her mere presence, but basic nature and the way that she seemed to gravitate toward me. For in fact, few if any had ever witnessed a demon in the flesh, much less lived to speak of it...

"I know and understand your concern for Michael." She had quietly turned and gazed upon him, "But, do not fear me—for I could have taken you all long ago, had I wished it so..."

"Was that some kind of threat?" Rich laughed and slapped the table with a hand, "Um—tell me something—if you wouldn't mind?"

She only nodded in reply, never once removing her gaze from his eyes. It was obvious that she was not amused with his rude behavior. And for that matter, neither were the rest of us.

"If you're really a demon—and in league with darker forces—then why are we all just blindly following you? This could be a trick to take us all down!" Rich had blurted the words out without even having had the time to consider what he was saying, "What if Marlowe and his pet demon are just playing us until the last moment—and then bang—they nail us!"

"Rich!" Tim had shouted, "What on earth is wrong with you?"

"What you have all seemed to have forgotten--," He cursed, leaping up from his seat and pointing an accusing finger at Amica, "Is that whether it looks like a little boy or pretty young woman—it's still a demon. She is a concubine of the devil, a demonic force that you're all treating like some god-forsaken house-guest! What the hell has happened to us here? Are we in league with the devil and consorting with demons now?"

"It is true—I am a soul long damned--," She quietly responded without so much as a blink of an eye, "A captive in servitude upon a desperate path of hope and redemption... I had not intended to insult, or by any means threaten you..."

They had just stared upon one another, neither of them uttering a single word for what had seemed forever. Something strange had occurred between them during that time. It was almost as though they had shared thoughts through expressions alone. It was a sorrowful and silent understanding which now caused Rich to slowly nod and turn away.

"I'm sorry--," He rubbed at his eyes, and peering nervously around the table, said, "I don't know where that came from—please, forgive me..." Glancing at Amica, he slid back down into his seat, and slowly shaking his head, mumbled as he spoke. "Amica—please forgive me for what I've said. I'm so terribly sorry..."

We had all sensed something building in him for quite some time. Due to his strong beliefs he had always revealed a certain discontent for Marlowe and the demon, but we had not expected this sudden outburst. I had just looked around the table as everyone sat speechless. Amica had curiously watched Rich, unmoving, and seeming a million miles away. There was something about her stillness that now caused uneasiness among us all. It was almost as though she had slipped into trance, and left her body lingering upon the brink of life and death. The moment had passed suddenly, seeming as though having just awakened from a dream now, she spoke in a whisper, and said, "Your own false guilt and remorse brings you to the gates of doubt, mistrust, and inner loathing. Your parents did not suffer, Richard. They knew only a sudden sound and brilliant flash before departing this dimension. And as for the one thought that has forever haunted you--," Tears formed in her eyes as she quietly said, "Your mother's final thoughts were those of love and concern for you…"

Rich had almost spilled his coffee cup across his breakfast as he gawked in horror and astonishment. His eyes were huge, his jaw hanging agape, as he placed trembling hands before his face.

"Your father has traveled onward—," Amica continued, "But she still dwells in the shadow of this world, forever mourning your pain and loss. It is not I that must forgive you, dear Richard—but that you must forgive yourself… You must submit and releases this sorrow, so that you might both be set free from this sickness of the soul…"

Trembling, Rich had looked down as the lenses of his glasses hazed, and the tears flowed. Placing a reassuring hand upon his friends shoulder, Raymond leaned closer while solemnly gazing into Rich's face. There was a moment when I had feared another outburst, but instead, Rich only stared aghast.

"How could you know this?" The words were almost stuttered as the emotions flashed in his tear-filled eyes, "How is it possible that you can see or know these things?"

"All that has ever been said, thought, or done exists between dimensions, an eternal record for those who would dare gaze into eternity. All that you have to do—is forgive and let go…"

"The very last thing that I'd ever said to her--," Looking like he was choking on the words, Rich shuddered while forcing them out, "Was that I wished that they would just leave and never come back."

"It was defective machinery that was responsible--," Reaching across the table, she gently took hold of his hand, "Not the wishes of an angry and disappointed child…"

There was a sudden compassion in her voice, an expression that now moved Rich from out of his seat and to where he knelt before her, "I was so wrong about you--," The tears ran from his eyes, fogging his lenses as he clasped her hand between both of his own, "Please, forgive me…"

"I know the suffering of your soul—we are all lost to some extent, my dear friend."

If there was any doubt as to Amica's' intentions from among any of us, it had passed in those moments as Rich had bowed before her. She had lifted him from his knees, and gently taking him into her arms, said, "Our strength resides within healing, hope and the love that binds us all. For without it—we will certainly be lost. You are weakened by doubt and this grief that you have so long carried. Release this suffering, the hostility, frustration of disappointment, forgive and set her and yourself free…"

For just a moment Rich appeared to have become little more than a child in her arms. I know that I had not been the only one who had witnessed this, as both Raymond and Tim blinked and rubbed at their eyes.

Brushing the hair from his face, she spoke softly, "You have power in this world—sensitivities accrued through lifetimes. All that stands in the way of your full potential—is doubt and fear, let them go, my dear Richard…"

The boy and the demon looked upon one another, and it seemed that a light had grown between them. A moment later, Rich stood strong and silent before Amica. There was something different about him, a demeanour of confidence, it was courage of conviction that I had not seen in quite some time.

"I'm terribly sorry—everyone--," He had returned to his seat and looking around the table, humbly said, "I'm not sure what came over me—I just lost it."

Raymond had gently patted him on the back, "We're all coming apart in one way or another. Don't go beating yourself up for it."

The moment having passed, we had all settled down, only to notice that Amica had now focused upon Tim. Although he appeared somewhat disturbed by this, he had just glanced back at her.

"The reason that you feel lost in this world is because all that you were, or have ever been, was honorable to a cause, and not yourself." She thought for a moment as he listened, "Loyalty to your father kept you at the parlour, and honor forced your marriage. You once dreamed of escaping Hedley—but would not abandon a true friend. And now, with the loss of all others—love and friendship binds you still. You might not be nearly so lost as you might imagine…"

Tim had not responded or replied beyond a nod, and swallowing hard, peered over at me. I knew that she had revealed his inner-most thoughts and psyche, but he still struggled to accept them.

Raymond's eyes had widened as she had turned her attention upon him, and thinking briefly, said, "Forever, you are the loving, loyal and watchful hound. You have gone into battle without thought unto your own undoing, and given everything without ever taking. Whatever may come, you are a benediction upon all in your company, and forever blessed."

It was the very first time that I had ever seen Raymond truly blush. Then, somewhat embarrassed, he had shrugged and humbly looked away. It was apparent that he was not accustomed to accepting compliments.

All had fallen silent as she had slowly turned to gaze upon me. In that moment, I felt suddenly vulnerable and unsettled as those pale and empty eyes now seemed to look straight through me.

"And you--," She spoke as though walking through a dream, "The wanderer, and the ancient child that would dare seek out nightmares... Alone we would most certainly fall before this most bitter of enemies. But united, we become hope where none existed before..."

It was obvious from their expressions that Amica's retrospective had reinforced the failing moral, and foundations of hope. She had cleared the proverbial air to some respect, and everyone had taken a deep breath and settled back into their seats.

"Was there anything else?" She gazed slowly about the group while being greeted with nothing but shaking heads and solemn refrain.

They had all quietly returned to the breakfast routine as though nothing had happened. Yet, through the course of events something had ultimately changed about Rich. He appeared stronger, youthful, and as though a great shadow had been drawn from his soul. In my heart I knew that he had finally been released from the ghosts of a past that had been haunting him a lifetime...

Intending to break the tension with light conversation, I looked around the table and said, "I suppose that now that I'm not going to be followed around by an extraordinarily large raven, we don't draw as much attention."

"I disagree--," Raymond winked, "I'm willing to bet that she'll be noticed wherever she goes."

Amica had offered only the faintest smile in reply and continued with her meal.

"We'd better get busy with the breakfast clean-up if we expect to get anything done today." Rich sighed deeply, "It's pushing ten already."

"Well, I've got my grocery list--," Tim pulled a notepad from a shirt breast pocket, ""I'm ready to go anytime that you are."

Amica was ravenous, though staying polite: She managed to devour the remaining bacon, sausage, and toast in the short time that she had been at the table.

"If you're finished --," Looking over as she drained an entire glass of orange juice in a single swallow, I said, "I'd be happy to escort you to the mall."

She hadn't responded immediately, but looked over the contents of the plates surrounding her. Although appearing quite lady-like, there was something primordial and almost terrifying hiding just beneath the surface. It reminded us all that we were dealing with forces beyond our world or understanding.

"Yes—I believe that I've had a delicate sufficiency." She neatly wiped at the sides of her mouth with a napkin. There had been the slightest hiccup, and then she had blinked as though stunned by something. We had all just stopped what we were doing, and then stood and watched. Not due to her odd behavior, but the fact that she had begun to change again. Not in any great degree physically, but the tint of her hair and skin. The once completely opaque and marble tone had taken on a slight shadow. Not enough to suggest any true color, but in the sense that she no longer stood out quite so terribly.

"You look so familiar--," Tapping at his chin in thought, Rich closely examined her, saying, "But I just can't put my finger on it?"

"It's the utter and complete absence of color--," Tim nodded in thought, saying, "I know from doing cosmetic work at the parlor that it makes all the difference in everything."

"She's definitely remarkable--," Moving from the table Raymond adjusted his revolvers, and looking to Rich, said, "You just about ready to roll?"

"There's something else--," Stuttering while looking between Amica and the others, I fought with the words in explanation, "When she accepted this change, there were some unexpected complications…" She appeared frightened within the revelation, but nodded and slowly looked away.

"Well—don't keep us waiting." Gesturing at the clock with a jab of his thumb, Rich said, "We need to get going if we hope to get anything done today."

"When she previously existed as the demon—she wasn't actually a single entity—but two different beings that were bound together."

"So, what are you telling us--," Glancing suspiciously between Amica and the others, Raymond thought aloud, saying, "That she's no longer possessed?"

"No--," Turning to look at him, I spoke without hesitation, saying, "I'm telling you that the more human she becomes, the sooner the demon inside of her will separate and enter into our physical reality."

"Oh no--," Putting a fist to his mouth and biting at his knuckles Rich stared in utter disbelief, "And how long do we have until that happens?"

"I'm not exactly sure, but trust me: When it happens, we'll all know..."

"Alright—so we'll see physical changes, right?" Rich gasped, his eyes wide with fear and concern, "It won't just be a pop, bang, and surprise you're all screwed—or will it?"

"No—it will be a slow progression--," Sadly looking to the others, she spoke quietly, saying, "Until it finally takes my place in this world."

"This wasn't part of the original deal as far as I knew--," There was shame and bitter remorse in my words, as looking to my friends, I whispered, "She has to die in our world to give life to the demon, and then her soul is finally free of it forever..."

"So—we bide our time and make the best of things, such as they are--." The words had been the only few that Tim could offer in that moment. Looking to me, he said, "Nothing is ever truly written in stone—and a lot can happen before then..."

"Angel or devil, I'll be there for you, sweet lady--," Raymond hugged her in passing, and said, "And nothing is going to change that."

Overcome with the sentiment, she had turned and looked away.

"That goes for me too--," Standing behind her and looking away, Rich quietly said, "We all have our demons, but I'll never turn my back on a friend in need..."

"Bless you all--," She whimpered, and looking back, could only shake her head, "I swear on everything I hold sacred that I will never allow harm to come to any of you over this..."

Quickly moving to where she stood and taking her into a gentle embrace, I spoke to the others while holding her, "We can take my Chrysler 300. According to the radio it's going to be a nice day—so we should be fine."

"Michael, don't be gone too long--," Rich warned, "Watch the time—and don't lose the light."

"I'll be watching the time." Reassuring him, Tim pulled up the left sleeve of his jacket, and tapping at two watches upon his wrist, said, "I wear two now just in case."

"That's a damn good idea--," Obviously amused, Raymond looked closer and said with a smile, "Funny thing, I was eyeing up an old pocket-watch at the jeweler's the other day." He glanced over at me, "And now I have a reason to pick it up."

"It might be a good idea to have something that isn't battery operated."
Rich agreed, "I'll do the same thing. We can pick them up today—and
right after we get the attic sorted out."

"Alright, I'll see you all back here before dark." My words sounded more
like a threat than promise…

12:15 p.m.
The heavens were crystal clear and the sun blinded me even behind the
dark sunglasses. When we had stepped off the porch that morning I could
have sworn that our lives had returned to normal. Affectionately taking
hold of my arm, Amica had almost pranced as she followed along beside
me.

We were amazed as to how easily the Chrysler 300 had started even after
the bitter cold weather. Then, hurrying ahead as I warmed the engine, Tim
had shoveled away any additional snow and promptly pulled open the
gates.

It felt like the perfect beginning to what might yet become a wonderful
day. In passing I had slowly turned while noticing the crimson stain in the
snow before the gates. It was a grisly reminder of what would happen to all
of us if we forgot the time…

Hugging and then kissing my cheek, Amica whispered "Don't look—it's
just the shadow of someone that is no longer there…"

Pulling through the gates, we had patiently waited as Tim struggled to
pull them closed. There had been a little ice build-up around the hinges,
and it took more effort than usual.

That's when I first noticed the strange prints in the deep snow and all
around the outside of the gates. They were small and scattered, and most
people would've assumed them to have been left by animals. In truth, it
was amazing what the sun could do within melting, a fox print could
appear as a bear… This was the story that I had heard all too many times in
reference to the unexplained, and it was always worth a good laugh…

"You noticed the tracks, too—huh?" Tim hopped into the car while
blowing hot air into his hands for warmth, "The black sludge makes it look
like they were made by something that crawled out of a grave…"

"More like a lot of somethings--," Peering back out and into the deep
snow, I frowned, "They almost look like the melting paw-prints from a
racoon or opossum…"

"And almost like giant rats--," He shuddered with the thought, "But the
wind and sun will make short work of the evidence, it's already melting."

"Maybe we should get Rich to rig something up?" Looking down at the prints and around the gates, I thought aloud, "Maybe even some really big traps?"

Leaning close and placing her head upon my shoulder, Amica sweetly asked, "Can we please just be rid of this place and its horrors—just for a little while?"

She was warm, affectionate and spoke so sweetly that the nightmares had swiftly faded out of my thoughts. It was the first time since Caitlin had left that I had felt even remotely human again... With a wink and a smile I had nudged her playfully, saying, "Hold onto your hat—we're gone!"

The engine roared as the radio played and we swiftly sped down the street.

CHAPTER SIX

12:45 a.m.

Our destination was the immense shopping center known as 'Guildford Mall' in Surrey. It was a short drive from off the freeway and onto 152nd Street, and to where reaching 104th Avenue, we had soon found parking in the enormous lot.

The buildings occupied both sides of a busy street, and were joined by a bridged walkway that crossed over in the middle. It was always a popular location while providing almost anything that one could possibly want, and likely never required.

The morning passed uneventfully, and I was surprised that Amica had not been bothered by anything that had occurred from around us. Aside from selecting a few items of clothing, simple things and everything in black, we were done quite quickly. She spoke very little, avoided eye contact with others, and moved like a shadow amidst the aisles.

Oddly, I had soon noticed that she detested mirrors and avoided anything that cast an image. Assumedly, this likely pertained to the theory that spirits and demons feared being captured behind the reflection. Although she may have had little personal concern, I suspected that something within her might...

The grocery shopping had gone quite quickly. This was due to the fact that Tim had shared the list with Amica, and making it a game, used separate carts to collect everything. It was the first enjoyable experience that we had shared in a long time. While focused upon the meats and dairy, Tim had left the dry goods, tinned items, and frozen supplies to us.

In all truth, I would never have expected to have seen a soul possessed by a demon having so much fun. We rushed through the aisles laughing like children while hurriedly loading the cart. People had stopped and stared, but most had just laughed and waved.

Meeting Tim at the counter and till, he just gawked as our cart spilled over with things that he'd never listed. She had accepted a free sample, and then taken an immediate liking to sugary cereals of every kind. At another counter a kind older woman had offered her chili and assorted cheeses. Needless to say the samples went on and our cart became over-filled.

"Will this even fit into the car?" Laughing out loud, Tim had swiftly covered his mouth with a hand, "I'm glad that you're paying for it—we might just have to call a cab!"

When the total arrived the girl at the till had called several young lads to help. They assisted us from out of the store, and then carefully loaded the back seat and filled the trunk.

After tipping them quite generously, they had stumbled over each other while trying to help. Amica had laughed while indulging an enormous bag of popcorn, and then we all climbed into the car.

"I wonder if this thing will even move with all the food that we packed into it--," Chewing at an apple, Tim grinned while peeking past Amica to look at me, "I hate to admit it—but that's the first time that I've ever had that much fun while shopping."

"I like this--," Smiling, she chewed at a ring of figs while looking between us, "We should do this often."

"Hey, Amica--," Grinning mischievously and winking, he asked, "How would you like to try hamburgers?"

"Hamburgers--," She pondered briefly while curiously looking between us, and then leaning back to me, said, "Hamburgers—I would like to try them."

"Do we have time?" Tim asked while raising an eyebrow in question, "We could just hit a fast food place—heck, I'll buy and even run in."

Between his offer and her expression there was simply no possible way of avoiding it. Not long after we had pulled into a fast food burger place, and she had enthusiastically followed after him.

Sitting hungry and in a car filed with groceries, I kept looking at the time. They had been gone for almost half an hour and there hadn't even been any line…

There was a moment when I started to fear that something terrible might have occurred. I was just reaching for the door handle when, glancing over, I suddenly saw them coming out…

Shrugging and laughing as they carried several large bags, Tim shouted while pointing at her, and saying, "Don't blame me—she wanted them!"

We had taken the opportunity to indulge a quick lunch while still parked in the lot. Tim and I had eaten a double burger, while she finished off six 'Super Kings', four orders of onions rings, four French fries, and a large chocolate shake…

Being aware of her issue with the demons' ravenous appetites, this had not been altogether shocking, but was still increasingly hard to watch. In my entire life I had never known a single person capable of such an extraordinary act. A single "Super King' burger weighed a pound excluding the bun and fixings, and she had managed to devour six! Just the thought of her eating the additional fries and onions rings had left a cold and greasy lump in my stomach...

She was still working her way through the last burger as we both watched in utter astonishment. There was a belch worthy of a football player, and then she'd grinned happily from between us.

"Hey, anyone care for a little desert?" Tim sank back into the seat as I glared back at him.

"We should really get this food home, some of it is perishable."

"Oh--," Putting a hand to his mouth and looking deeply concerned, Tim gently touched Amica's arm, "Are you going to be alright?"

Alarmed, I leaned forward to closer examine her and gasped at what I saw! Surrounding in empty wrappers and with burger sauce on her face, the poor dear stared blankly and appeared as though she might be sick.

"Amica--," Speaking softly while gently wiping her face with a napkin, I leaner closer and in a whisper, asked, "Do you need to be somewhere private—are you going to be okay?"

"She's looking a little flushed--," His eyes widened with sudden guilt as while frowning, he sadly looked back at me, "It's my fault, I shouldn't have taken her into that place, and should've known better..."

"Flushed..." The word caught me completely by surprise, as swiftly leaning to look directly into her face, I saw what he meant.

"We need to get her home right now..."

2:24 p.m.

When we had arrived at the estate she appeared to have been fast asleep. Carrying her into the house, I carefully laid her out upon my bed. She was unresponsive but breathing regularly, and I saw that hues of colors now appeared from wherever the skin was revealed. Something was happening again, but I suspected that it had not been induced by the lunch... This was most certainly an inevitable part of her previous transformation. Something that now drew so heavily upon her life's energy, that its final stages were utterly exhaustive.

Removing her coat and boots, I had gently covered her with a quilt, and closed the door in departure. I would have to trust in Marlowe and the fates, for this journey she required to do discretely and alone.

"I'm so sorry--," Tim had greeted me as while unloading the car at the front porch, "I really didn't think that anything would happen or I would never have done that."

Gently patting my dear friend on the shoulder, I spoke quietly and with obvious concern, "It wasn't your fault—there's something else happening and it was inevitable anyway."

"She really is special--," The emotions overwhelmed him as he concealed a single tear, "I don't understand how a creature like her could have an ounce of evil, anywhere..."

"Because she wasn't the evil to begin with—it caught her in a helpless moment, and she was taken because of me..."

"What--," He was speechless and could only gaze in utter bewilderment.

"It was in another time, a different dimension—and we were not who we are now..."

"What happened—and how do you even know about this?"

"The beryl stone showed me--," Slowly shaking my head in the cold wind, I felt the sting of its bite upon my face and hands, and said, "The darkness manifested as a monstrous thing in the forests of a distant world. It had almost taken me as a child, but she saved me, and the demon liberated her through damnation from the horde witch..."

"The horde witch--," He swallowed hard, "Is that what the darkness used to be in a past existence?"

"It was just one of its many manifestations. It was a monstrous shape that it used to continue its path of terror and destruction on that world. I remember--," A tear stung against the cold flesh of my cheek, "It was a combination of every nightmare that you could ever imagine, and fed exclusively on young women and children. That's why the villagers referred to it as the horde witch—because it was never one thing—but all combined."

"And you sent the horde witch into a portal--," He slowly nodded, "It was revenge in her loss..."

"And within doing so--," Staring aghast, I whispered, "I sent it here..."

"The more that I think about it--," Shivering in the cold wind, he spoke softly while dreaming into the distance, "The more that I wonder how many other people in our lives were taken by this thing, without us even knowing?"

"It took Leigh that winter night--," The pain in reflection began burning, "And as while she was trying to cross the street."

He had spun to look at me, but I had never stopped staring past the gates, and saying, "It even took my mother on the day that I wasn't there..."

There were no words cold or cruel enough to describe or properly express the absolute hatred that I felt for the darkness, but in that moment, I think that Tim had completely understood, as embracing me tightly, he said, "Someday we'll see that god-damned devil burn in hell for everything it's done..."

"Hell is too good for that nightmare--," The tears froze against my face in the bitter wind, "And, I don't think there's any punishment severe or cruel enough to atone for the things that it's done..."

The blackness of the spiked iron entrance stood out against the darkening horizon. In the shadows Harry's body still hung from the gates with the ends of his coat flying like the wings of a dark angel. It was hard to distinguish whether it had been his ghost, or just the illusion of a weary and grief-stricken mind...

The wind had blown harder as Tim shivered and quietly said, "Michael, we'd better get these groceries inside before Amica awakens. She'll be worried and wondering where we are..."

3:23 p.m.

Surprisingly, it hadn't taken very long to unload the car and put the groceries away. The fridge, cupboards, and cabinets were overflowing, and we even needed to use the new freezer in the basement. When all was said and done, we had sat down in the breakfast nook in the kitchen and just looked at one another.

"That's a lot of food--," He wiped the sweat from his brow with a paper towel, "But if you think about it—that saves us going shopping again for a long time."

"I know that you'd find a silver lining--," I could only smile while saying, "You always do."

"I was thinking of making my world famous spaghetti and meatballs--," Raising an eyebrow in question, he asked, "What do you think?"

"As long as you can do it without the garlic—that sounds wonderful."

"Oh, I'd almost forgotten your allergy to Penicillin," He snapped his fingers, "Most people don't even know that garlic is the only member of the onion family that contains Alicen."

"It's a low dosage--," I agreed, "And it won't kill me—but I'll spend the better part of the evening in the bathroom for doing it."

"We can supplement onion salt for the garlic." He raised a thumb, jabbing it toward the ceiling, and said, "Maybe you should check on our friend?"

"Will you be alright down here?"

"I'll be busy making the sauce and meatballs. Besides, I want to have a quick look in the attic and see what the guys have been up to."

"Raymond's car isn't here--," I looked out the kitchen window, "They must have gone for those pocket watches that they were talking about earlier."

"Alright then, you look in on the little lady--," He began removing items from the fridge, "I'll get things started. We can have a look once the sauce is simmering."

"Perfect—I'll be back shortly."

Quickly and quietly making my way up the stairs, I was startled to discover Amica awake and sitting in my office. She had collected the parcels from the bedroom where I had left them for her, and was busily unpacking and placing them in my office closet.

"I wasn't aware that you were awake." I watched as she sorted the clothing from the bags and neatly placed everything away.

"I am better now--," She paused, and appearing saddened by something, said, "I thought that I should put these things away rather than leaving them lying about."

"You can use the closet in the bedroom--," I had suggested, but she swiftly disagreed.

"No—these quarters suit my needs—such as they are."

"Amica--," Moving closer, I had embraced her as burying her face into my chest, I said, "Are you really okay—I know that something happened, and to be honest, I'm very worried about you at the moment."

"Please forgive me--," She gazed up, as her pale eyes flashed while reflecting the light, and whispered, "This change affects me far deeper than just matters of the flesh."

There was a distinct change coming over her. I could see it in the way that the shadows played upon her flesh and the altering colors and tones developed. Her form was like an opaque palette being tested by some master, the colors only advanced by the slightest of degrees.

"I have needs that I have not required for aeons…"

"I'll do what I can to help you adjust--," Brushing the white hair from the pink tint of her face, I quietly said, "Just let me know if you experience any discomfort or issues—and we'll make the best of things, okay?"

"In that case--," She pointed toward the hallway, squinting, and politely asked, "May I make use of your washing room?"

"Of course—this is your home now, too—please feel free."

She had motioned for me to lead the way and I had immediately obliged.

"This is where we keep the linens and supplies for the bathroom--," Showing her the closet in the hallway, I opened the door, "As a proper lady, you will require all of these." I provided her with a towel, hand towel, wash cloth, and promptly led her into the bathroom.

Spending several moments acquainting her with shampoo, conditioner, soap, and toothpaste, I drew her attention to the shower and bath.

"That is an interesting piece." Her attention crossed the room, "Why is it standing in here?"

Looking to the far end of the bathroom, I squinted while observing the old mirror that had remained hidden beneath the sheet. Strangely enough, I hadn't even been aware of its presence for quite some time.

"It was a piece of antiquity that Caitlin brought back from the Duff Glenn--," Gently touching the smooth surface of its ornate framework while looking back at Amica, I quietly said, "It used to stand in the second floor washroom of the McCreary house. I'd almost forgotten that it was even here."

She appeared deeply disturbed by its presence, and I had assumed for the same reasons as with the others she had previously seen in the mall. Like a cat being forcibly drawn to water, she had recoiled at the very sight, and cringed while suspiciously peering back at me.

"Does it bother you?" Asking quite innocently while fully aware that it did, I attempted to avoid complications.

She had glanced between the mirror and where I stood several times, and then backed away as she said, "Would it bother you to know that you have a Beryllus in your possession?"

"Paracelsus spoke in reference of a Beryllus--," I had remembered while saying, "It's supposedly a magic mirror or gemstone that clairvoyants use to see astral auras. I suppose that it's harmless, since Caitlin owned it and it's no different than the golden beryl in my office."

"That is where you are sadly mistaken." Caressing the sheet covered frame with a hand, she suspiciously looked back at me and quietly said, "Unlike the golden beryl—this one may hold some dark secret, a passageway, or hidden evil..."

"I'm surprised that you've never taken notice or an interest in this before?" Dismayed, I put a finger to my chin in thought and said, "Usually you don't miss a thing."

"It is not dangerous as long as it remains covered and unbroken." She frowned, "But, should one gaze into the mirror by night—they risk being drawn into whatever lays beyond."

Shuddering with the memory of the night that I'd experienced something similar, I swallowed hard, "I'll see to it that it gets taken to the vault and is placed somewhere out of harm's way."

"I sense a cold emptiness about it--," Cautiously moving back from the large mirror, she pondered briefly, and then said, "But until it's uncovered in darkness I could not be certain..."

"Is it safe to have a look right now?" As I was reaching for the sheet, she had swiftly caught and stayed my hand. Frightened, she said, "Even by the daylight we could not be certain as to what might gaze back..."

"Caitlin always loved this old thing." Confused, I had attempted to offer an explanation for its presence there, "She said that it was made by an artist of whom she had once been very fond."

"It would serve you well to take greater care in matters of the unknown." Amica carefully covered the mirror before glancing back at me, "No matter what you are told or by whom..."

Her words had troubled me deeply. Not just for the blatant insinuation, but the fact that I had always been frightened of the old thing. Remembering the night that I looked into its blackness, a sudden shudder tore through my entire being.

Touching my cheek with a pale hand, she slowly shook her head, "Some things are not meant for this world--," She motioned with a nod to the mirror and said, "And I suspect that may be one of them..."

"I'll have it removed--," Feeling unsettled by tampering with Caitlin's personal treasures, I was now haunted by the guilt, saying, "When they come for the figure of Pan and the maiden that's being moved from the office."

"Please--," She took a gentle hold of my wrist, and gazing deeply into my eyes, pleaded, saying, "Understand that whatever I do or might say is in your best interest."

"I do understand, truly I do. But, at times, I don't even trust my own judgement anymore."

"An instinct that will keep you safe--," She spoke in barely a whisper, her face mere inches from my own. Contemplating briefly, she said, "I had better bathe before the others return."

"Yes—of course--," Turning to leave and pausing in thought, I looked back, "Oh, please be sure to keep the door locked when using the bathroom. It's so easy to accidentally walk in on someone."

There had been an awkward moment, glances exchanged, and I had quickly closed the door in parting. There was the tell-tale clicking sound of a door being locked, and I quickly made my way into the office.

The ringing of the telephone had startled me, as grabbing it from off my desk, I answered, "Schreiber residence—Michael speaking, how can I help you?"

"Michael, it's Ole Papra--," He sounded apologetic, "Did I call at an inconvenient time?"

"No, of course not, you just caught me a little off-guard! I was just doing a little reading and everything was dead quiet when the phone rang, I'm sure that you understand."

"Do you have a few moments? I have some questions about the manuscript."

"Of course—what seems to be on your mind?"

"First and foremost--," He flipped through pages, "I noticed that you used the wrong name for the town that you mentioned in the Lumberton adventure. I retraced your route on a map according to what you had written, and…"

"Ole—I tend to mislead the readers a little for privacy reasons and their own protection."

"Their own protection—now that is an odd thing to say. Would you care to enlighten me as to why they would require protection?"

"Old buildings, moldering architecture--," I thought for a moment, "I would never forgive myself, if an adept reader followed my direction to some nasty, old place and was injured there—or worse."

"Alright, that would be an acceptable answer. We can over-look the details of the directions. This is a fictional work after all, right?"

"Well, what do you think?" I could only laugh at the remark.

He had fallen silent for a moment as if lost in some thought, as suddenly he said in a curious tone, "When you mention that the shadows grow far deeper in certain places, and the night becomes colder than it should… something causes me to wonder about that?"

"They're the claims of numerous writers of ghost stories in countless books—I'm only one among many."

"I have experienced something similar--," He admitted, "They're moments that I could never quite properly explain. And might I add, for someone who claims to write fiction, you certainly seem to speak from personal experience."

"My mother always said that I had an over-active imagination. What can I say—except that I'm very flattered with your kind sentiments?"

"On another note--," He dropped the subject, "I have also decided to leave your religious rituals in their original format." He explained, "It seems rather appropriate to use the archaic forms rather than modern texts."

"I thought that it set a certain mood—didn't you?"

"Yes, I can agree, and as far as the manuscript is concerned, except for a little grammar and punctuation, it's coming along nicely."

"Fabulous—was there anything else that you might have been wondering about?"

There was a silence on the line once more, and then he quietly asked, "If I was to retrace your steps to the fictional Lumberton property—would I find it to be gated and sealed to the public? And—would there be a nefarious history and related, mysterious deaths?"

"There is always a little truth to all fiction…"

"I wonder as to how much—in this particular case?"

"Well, I have written several other books. If you enjoy wondering, they might catch your fancy?"

Ole' had just laughed heartily, "It was a pleasure speaking to you, Mr. Schreiber. If I should have any other questions or concerns related to the manuscript, I will contact you."

"Feel free to call me Michael—all my friends do."

"Thank you, Michael—you may call me Ole. Have a pleasant afternoon—I will be in touch."

It was apparent that he was a very astute and clever young man, and it was beginning to frighten me a little. Tim had previously warned me of this… what if someone follows directions and discovers the truth? There were simply too many things happening at once, and it was beginning to become impossible to properly focus upon any single one.

Turning, I heard the shower still running behind me. Slowly peering out the door, I looked into the hallway. Having almost forgotten Ole in that moment, my thoughts returned to Amica's physical manifestation.

"How could she have just appeared from out of the ether? It takes three components to become part of this dimension. It requires the Corporeal, Astral and Ethereal. She only possessed the soul and subconscious—where did the physical element come from?"

"You're doing it again—get a grip, old man." I fought back the fear and paranoia, "She manifested through mutual energy and nothing more. I'm sure that she'll explain—given the opportunity."

A billowing stream of steam escaped as Amica now came out of the bathroom. She was wrapped in a black towel, and closing the office door behind her, quickly hurried to the closet in the office. Averting my gaze as she dropped the towel, I listened as she quickly slipped into a dress. It was a high-collared, long-sleeved and rather simple gown that draped about her ankles. In some respects it reminded me of the styles of the roaring twenties, but without the sequins or frills. I had insisted upon purchasing slippers for her, but she had politely declined while preferring to walk about without them. It was a habit that Caitlin had had since the first time we met...

Slipping into the chair and drawing her legs upward again, she smiled back at me. It was a complete and sudden shock to see my beloved Caitlin now looking back at me! The change had come while she had showered and finalized as she had dressed!

Her hair flowed in fiery locks that tumbled down into the small of her back. The pale pallor of her ivory skin now radiated while having become exotically freckled. Her lean form was taut and defined by the subtle tones and physique of a dancer.

They appeared so similar in every regard, but with exception to those wild, shining and wolf-like eyes. Shimmering and even greener than those of Caitlin, they seemed to reflect like a mirror into another reality: A dangerous place, where wild things roamed and once were lost, and few might ever return from.

"Absolutely remarkable—you are her doppelganger..." Gasping, I slowly nodded while unable to resist staring, whispering, "But, different in an aspect that completes the image of what I had always imagined her to have really been... You're not the Caitlin of this world, but the one that has always existed in my heart and dreams..."

"Maybe more than you truly know." She touched my hand in gentle caress and sadly looked away.

Utterly captivated with her appearance, I became lost in the moment. It was like sitting beside an almost perfect likeness of my beloved.

"Amica, there is something that I need to ask you--," Desperation filled my entire being as I looked to her, and said, "And I need to know the truth..."

"Of course—if I am able to."

"How is it possible—how could you have become a physical part of this dimension?"

Some kind of terrible truth now reflected painfully in her brilliant green eyes. In that moment, I sensed that something terrible must have happened.

"The transference was not taken--," The explanation troubled her deeply as the words came slowly and with much grief, "The exchange was mutual—and exists primarily within the love that we share."

"The love that we share--," I had suspected this to have been a possibility, but needed to know more and asked, "In what way and how?"

Raising her left arm before me, a great and ghastly wound appeared. It was a gash made by a demon's claw and of which I had previously forgotten!

The wound swiftly vanished as she had sadly looked down, "The living energy that exists within you is now the power of my becoming …"

"Then, you truly are my one and only…"

Gently brushing the hair from my eyes, she pleaded sweetly and sorrowfully, "Please do not ask for what cannot yet be shared…"

"If you are sustained by my life and love—then we are something far finer than anything that has ever existed on this world. You're a mystery to me—but my heart tells me that you are true. When the time comes, I trust that you will share whatever secret still remains between us, my dear Amica."

"Though I cannot--," She looked sadly to me, "Your heart has answers to any secret that you truly wish revealed…"

A knock at the office door had us both turning to look as Tim appeared, "Sorry to interrupt—were you still interested in having a look in the attic? The guys thought that it would be better if you checked out to see what they've done."

"Of course—we can do that right away."

"Caitlin…' Tim almost fell backward from realizing the transformation "It's her—I mean, Amica's become Caitlin." He could only stand there gawking.

"That was the change that affected her earlier--," I said, "I told you that it wasn't your fault or the hamburgers…"

Cautiously lowering the old steps that led into the attic, I waved in a cloud of dust. I had insisted upon doing it myself, as the mechanism was old and had a tendency to snap back up if not properly done. It was apparent by previous disturbances and prints in the dust that Rich and Raymond must have struggled with the old thing.

It creaked and groaned beneath our weight, as moving in single file, Tim and Amica had followed closely as we climbed into the shadows of the attic.

A cold gust had caressed my face and drawn my attention to where Rich had partially opened the immense, oval window. Swinging inward, it appeared almost alien in the way that it provided an open gateway to the night stars.

At first glance, I saw that the furniture that had once littered the area had been neatly placed off to either side of the large room. In the center, and located before the window, they had shoved the old bed-frame and mattress. Amica had immediately pointed to where a large bowl of mixed fruit and vegetables had been made as an offering. This had been placed in the middle of the bed and surrounded in old quilts and assorted woolen blankets.

"An offering of friendship--," She had approved with a nod, "Your creature will understand immediately—and accept with the utmost gratitude." Then, in a moment of dark reflection, she had looked between us and sorrowfully said, "It has recently existed on refuse and whatever vegetation that it could find..."

I knew from her reaction that she had envisioned this through premonition, and the sympathy that now reflected in her eyes had opened my heart.

"Well, now it has a home to come back to--," Slowly looking around the room, I thought for a moment before saying, "I hope that it will feel welcome..."

Peering into the long shadows, Tim had taken immediate notice of something, and raising a finger in pause, moved to the far corner to examine it. Watching quietly from near the hatch-way, I saw him pick up a large and weathered, old teddy bear, and carrying it to the bed, gently place it nearest the headboard.

"That should do it--," He wiped the dust from off his hands while walking back toward us and said, "Well, according to Rich, she's at the age where she might appreciate that sort of thing, if she can relate to it?"

Gently stroking the side of Tim's face with a hand, Amica's eyes softened, "There is such great kindness within you for all living things. You are a blessing, even unto this lost and lonely soul of which you call the creature..."

"Thank you, but all the same--," He nervously looked around and into the long shadows of the rafters and each dark corner, "I'd rather not be here when she shows up. I'm still unsettled about what happened to us all in Hedley..."

"I still have nightmares about that too--," Shuddering with the thought, I remembered old friends and those lost, whispering, "The old diner, the mine, and Sergeant Steve Harris..."

As we stood in the shadows of the attic, thoughts of a young man and the bullet that had ended his suffering seared my conscience and soul. Having sensed this terrible vision in some manner, Amica had peered up at me while gently taking my hand.

"There is no sin within mercy--," She whispered knowingly, "Nor should there be guilt or suffering within reminiscence of the act..."

It was an angel in the form of my beloved, offering redemption and releasing the evils hidden within the depths of my soul. A gasp in the form of a sigh had escaped my lungs while lightening my heart. It felt as though the years of guilt for his death had suddenly and quite mercifully been released. Taking comfort within the moment, I could only bow my head in sorrowful reflection of the young man.

"We did the very best that was humanly possible in that situation--," Noticing my stillness within dismal reflection, Tim gently patted my back and quietly said, "I still thank God every time that I think about it—and I'm grateful that you were there with us..."

"We better be careful not to burn the sauce." Sniffling while brushing a single tear away, I directed their attention back to the steps, "We better get moving before it gets any darker up here."

"Is that the only way into the attic?" Pointing to the stairway, Tim curiously looked around the room

"No—there's also a hatch-way--," I pointed to a ladder in the far corner of the room, and said, "It leads to the widow's peak—but hasn't been used since Leigh's father was a boy."

"Leigh." Amica whispered while slowly nodding in recognition of the name. She knew all that I had ever done, ever known or experienced in this life. Her solemn gaze now reflected the sorrow of having sensed my suffering in the loss of Leigh and the dear old man. For my own part, there were no secrets or mysteries between us, and my soul lay bare before her...

"I wouldn't mind having a quick look up there—," Testing the ladder, he squinted into the darkness above, and then looking back to where I stood with Amica, said, "It'll only take a minute—if you wouldn't mind?"

"I supposed--," I followed to where he enthusiastically climbed the ladder, and then calling up after him, warned, "Just be careful—I don't know how solid this thing is!"

"It's just fine—these old places were built to last." Confidently slapping a hand against the ladder he looked back down with a grin, "Not to worry— I've been climbing trees and rooftops since I was a kid."

Remembering the time that he fell from the roof of my mother's garage, I cringed, "Oh, I remember alright—and like I said, be careful..."

Reaching the top quite quickly, he grabbed the latch, and then shoved with all of his strength against the hatch door. Grunting and groaning beneath the immense effort, he had finally conceded while calling back down, "It must be stuck or frozen—and likely even covered in snow?"

"Just forget it for now--," Something bothered me at that moment, and I feared that what he tried might be something other than ice and snow, "We can look another time—the sauce--," I reminded him, "We should really get back downstairs and check on dinner."

Disappointed, he clambered back down, and with a shiver, made his way back toward the steps.

"You two go ahead of me please--," Insisting, I peered anxiously back toward the partially open window, and muttered, "These steps are old and unsteady, and I'd rather be the last one down..."

5:37 p.m.

Sitting at the kitchen table with her husband, son, and Pamela Montgomery, Carrie suddenly and suspiciously looked around. It had been a long day at the office, they were all tired, hungry, and had just been disturbed by something not so easily explained...

"Did you guys hear that?" Carrie spoke in a low tone while listening to the wind at the windows, quietly saying, "It almost sounded like someone was trying to get in here?"

The doors were locked, windows sealed tightly, and the old building was constructed of solid brick. It was highly unlikely that anyone might break into the bookstore, but her 'gut-feeling' said that something was definitely wrong.

"I heard it too—something like a thumping, or pounding noise--," Scott turned upward while gesturing with a nod at the ceiling, "But it seems to be coming from up there?"

"Does this place have an attic?" Curious, Pamela glanced questionably between them.

"It's more like a crawlspace--," Patrick explained, "I was up there with a flashlight when we first got the place. There's nothing really up there, just insulation and a whole lot of nails sticking out from the roof." He rubbed at a mark on his wrist which indicated that he spoke from experience.

"Are you all wearing those amulets that Michael gave us?" Carrie stood, and leaning over the table to closely examine everyone, insisted, "You should always keep them on."

"I never take it off." Scott promised, and pulling the talisman from beneath his grey knit sweater, held it out for all to see.

"Mine's right here—I never take it off—not even in the bath." Patrick followed his father by example and Pamela had done the same.

It had only been dark for a short time. The weather report had promised a clear evening, but the sights and sounds from beyond the large kitchen window proved otherwise...

Although visibly uncomfortable with the idea, Scott had courageously volunteered, "Did you want me to go and have a look, honey?"

"Are you out of your 'cotton-picking' mind?" She just stared, her steel gray eyes wide from behind her large glasses, "In this family we do not go looking into things that make strange noises in the night. I'll have you know that policy has kept us all alive and well for countless generations..."

"Someone should have told Uncle Michael about that." Patrick shrank into his seat as his parents just glared.

"So—what do we do?" Pamela looked to the window and then anxiously between them.

"We get some candles and lanterns out from under the kitchen cupboards—," Carrie advised, "Eat our dinner and wait this thing out."

"The sound stopped--," Patrick peered up at the ceiling, "I think that whatever it was—has gone away?"

"It could've been a raccoon poking around up there?" Scott had seen the dark reflection in Carrie's eyes, and moving from the table, sighed, "I'll get those lanterns and candles..."

6:15 p.m.

Working later than usual, Red Cloud stretched and yawned while burdened with an excess of paperwork. It had been an exceptionally long day and they had received a larger order than expected. Insisting that Danny and Dennis went home before dark, he had make more coffee and gone about his usual inventory. It was nothing unusual for him to work late. He had also found that as while growing older, he had also developed an increasing appreciation for the peace and quiet. It wasn't that he didn't love the boys, but sometimes a man just needed a little time alone to think and get things accomplished.

Red Cloud had always considered the position to have been the next best thing to retirement. In fact, he liked keeping busy and enjoyed digging through the old treasures, and listing the new items. He would often spend hours unpacking, writing descriptions, researching prices, and carefully shelving the more fragile items. In many respects, he hadn't even considered this work but a privilege and a pleasure. Not to mention, there was always endless coffee, pastry, and assorted doughnuts.

He spent countless hours while pushing a cart of sorted treasures along the endless aisles of shelving. Often, his only companion was his own voice while thinking aloud, as he wandered beneath the steady hum of the fluorescent overhead-lamps.

The warehouse was almost completely silent, as he made his way around the pallets and sorted through numerous boxes and crates. He had been tempted to turn on the jukebox that stood next to the counter, but in a moment's thought had decided against it. Instead, he turned to the song of the percolator announcing that the coffee was ready!

Deciding upon making one last pot for the evening, he would finish the pastry for dinner before calling it a night. In Maya's absence he had admittedly been missing regular meals. Of course, he had justified this within having rescued all the baked goods that would otherwise go into the trash.

Taking a little break, he moved from the boxes to pour coffee, grab a cherry pastry, and take a seat behind the counter. Indulging his snack, he catalogued the details of the inventory, smiling as he fondly remembered an old lamp in particular. It now stood directly across from the counter and where he could closely admire, and consider whether to keep it.

Rich had insisted that if he liked something, that he should strike it from off the inventory list, and was welcome to keep it. In most cases, he had disregarded many things due to limited space and a sincere dread of living in clutter.

Stirring cream and sugar into his coffee, he returned to the counter and before the box of pastry. It was just one of many little breaks that he allotted himself to avoid being on his feet for too many hours. Nibbling at a pastry, his attention drifted, as smiling, he gazed lovingly upon the lamp.

It was an exceptionally beautiful Art Deco piece. Standing over four feet high, a figural beauty held an orange globe high in the air and in both hands before her. With her blonde hair tied back in the fashion of the day, a sheer veil daringly revealed her supple and nude form from beneath. There were bushes of orange flowers gathered at her sides, and she stood barefoot upon a pedestal of mauve, shimmering stone.

Smiling while slowly leaning back and forth, he was fascinated as the colors changed in perspective and according to the dappled glass. The deep tangerine ascending into golden honey colors before glowing in subtle tones of the setting sun. In that moment he had decided to leave it shining and enjoy its beauty while he considered taking it home.

Sipping at his coffee, a sudden movement caught his attention and he looked to the dark windows of the bay doors. Reflecting the pale glow of the florescent lights, the glass revealed only the tall lamp posts that shone back from the darkness beyond.

A moment passed, as writing it off to bad nerves, he assumed it to have been nothing, or the security lights would have certainly been tripped. Glancing over at the lamp, he hesitated as it flickered, then faded, flashed and suddenly went out!

"Oh no, don't tell me that the wiring is bad…" Disappointed, he moved to leave the seat as the light suddenly flashed and shone.

"Its old—maybe it just needs to be used again for a while—connections do tend to get oxidized over time." Rationalizing with himself, he sat down, and taking a bite from the pastry, returned to the inventory list.

The howl of the wind beyond the window caught his attention again and his eyes pierced suspiciously into the night. He had looked up several times within a few moments and then settled back into his chair. It was times like these that he truly appreciated the wrought iron security bars that Rich had installed. It would take a freight train to break through those cement walls, and even more to breach the iron barriers in between.

"You're just getting edgy in your old age—it's nothing…" Sipping at his coffee, he returned his attention to the last page of orders for the night. They had received several crates from an estate sale that he had recently attended. It had mainly been smaller pieces, and this was why it had taken so much longer than usual.

A loud thump caused him to start. Almost spilling his coffee, he spun around and stared out and into the night. There wasn't a single movement to be seen, but his keen senses now caused him to slip off the chair and slowly step back. Instinctively, his fingers found the talisman that hung about his neck. The lights flickered throughout the warehouse, his heart raced, and he now knew that something was there… He realized now that it wasn't old and faulty wiring, but an energy force stronger than all others, and within close vicinity…

It happened in degrees rather than all at once. He could see the gathering darkness beyond the bay windows, as everything was slowly consumed into the blackness of space. Then, appearing as thin tendrils of smoke that crept from all about the doors and windows, something began testing cracks and crevices while attempting to get in… Ever so slowly it had slipped from beneath the doors, and streaming like a fine mist, entered the warehouse.

Silently standing behind the counter, he watched in horror as the smoke formed into a smoky and writhing mass before him. Horrified, he suddenly realized the mistake… In sanctifying the office and apartments, they had somehow neglected to take the same precautions with the bay doors…

Drawing the talisman from beneath his shirt, he stepped back from the counter while holding it out before him. Terrified, he attempted to retain his composure, while speaking loud and calling out to the fiend, "You have no business here—or with me! Leave this place and return to the shadow world from where you have come!"

The darkness slowly moved closer, the tendrils expanding as its shadow began smothering the light. Forms began appearing from within the mass, and he stared upon the writhing nightmares than clutched outward as they struggled to escape!

"You have no right here! Go back to the world of shadows!" Moving forward, he held out the talisman, demanding, "Return to the blackness where you belong!"

Rearing, the darkness withdrew suddenly and erupted in dark and ethereal flame! A fiery face appeared from high above, with a mane of fire blazing from either side! It burned darkly in crimson with eyes that shone with all the fury of hell. From out of its smoking and smoldering core extended the arms and heads of a thousand, clawing and biting horrors that now tore and snapped before the bay doors!

Fearing to even gaze upon the fiend, Red Cloud tightly closed his eyes while uttering the words of a Cree prayer. He spoke louder and shouted, as with a trembling hand, extended the talisman to the full extent of its chain.

"You have no power in this place or over me! Return—return to the shadow realms where you belong!"

There was a sudden and mind-numbing screeching, and the sound sent Red Cloud reeling as he fell to his knees. Crying out, he desperately covered his ears with both hands as the inferno howled into the depths of his mind, and shrieking soul.

Raising the talisman in a trembling hand, he called out, invoking the power of tribal elders and his peoples' God. The words were spoken and the flames suddenly burst from beyond the bay doors. It became a gale force wind, a blackened hurricane of shadow and ice that bellowed, crying out in fury before vanishing into the night.

Struggling to make his way back onto the chair he shook uncontrollably. A sharp pain suddenly caused him to double-over, as slipping a hand to the place just beneath his left breast, he was paralyzed with the pain. Breathing became an effort as he struggled to remain calm, and fearing the inevitable, rested his head upon the counter. Several moments passed before the pain subsided, and breathing slowly, he managed to regain his composure.

Sipping at his coffee, he coughed several times before dropping back into the chair. This had been a recent development, and something of which he had not shared with the others just yet. In his mind he was just an old man and there was little need in upsetting them. He saw no reason in making things any worse than they already were.

Wiping the cold sweat from his brow, he slowly moved before the bay windows and looked out into the empty storage yard. Tossing the page of an old newspaper, the wind whipped it against the glass before carrying it off and into the night. His movements were rigid. Making his way back to the counter, he paused to look back at the antique lamp. Like a gentle orange and golden moon, it was his only comfort in the pale twilight of the neon glow.

"Okay, old friend—tonight I will take you home." He made a decision in that moment and then reaching for the telephone, dialed Michael's home number...

7:22 p.m.

After receiving a distressing call from Carrie, I wasn't really that surprised when Red Cloud called soon after. It had taken a considerable effort to calm them both down, but I had immediately contacted the others right after to make sure that they all wore their talismans.

"What should we do if something happens here?" Tanya was livid and sounded desperate as she sniffled, and said, "We don't even have any way to defend ourselves."

"Just stay in the house—and make sure that everything is locked-up tight. Rich is having crews put gates up this week. So, all that you have to do right now is try to remain calm—and make sure that all of you are wearing those protective amulets."

She had inquired of both boys as to whether they had their charms, and I could hear their frightened comments in response. I had breathed just a little easier knowing that they had all done exactly as instructed...

"Should we come over there?" She sounded panicked, "We could call a cab, and we're only a few moments away."

"No—whatever you do—just stay in the house. Please—trust me on this."

There had been a brief apprehension and then sniffling through tears of sheer terror, as she said, "Maybe we should move back to our apartment in the morning—we'd be closer to Red and the others. Michael—this big old place really scares me to death now…"

"If that's what you would prefer--," I could only agree as being frightened and concerned for all of them, said, "I'll see to it that we get you all safely relocated first thing in the morning."

Having overhead the calls, Rich now stood beside me, gawking in disbelief. I knew that he was doing everything that he could to reinforce his estate, but we just couldn't take the chance of waiting any longer.

"Thank you—I'll be right here beside the phone for the rest of the night." She swallowed hard, "Is it alright to call you if something should happen?"

"Of course--," Glancing at Rich, I sighed deeply, "You can call any time—and I'll be up all night working, as you know."

"See you in the morning." She didn't sound too confident, "And, please tell Rich that I'm sorry."

"There's nothing to be sorry about—this is about your safety, and nothing is more important to us." Looking to my friend who stood beside me in grievance, I gently patted his arm, saying, "I'm sure that he understands and completely agrees."

"Thank you--," She sounded terrible and my heart went out to her as she said, "Good night and God bless…"

After I had hung up I could only look to Rich with a shrug, "Tanya and the boys don't feel safe there anymore. And as you heard, I promised that we would move them into the building with Red Cloud, first thing in the morning."

"I completely understand--," He nodded in agreement, and quietly remarked, "It's not worth risking their lives just to have tenants in the place. I'll just check on it once in a while."

Patting him on the back, we both made our way back into the main room, and joined the others by the hearth.

Tim's dinner arrangements had run into over-time. It was partially my fault, as between telephone calls and explanations the evening meal had lost priority. Needless to say, we were now all famished and eagerly waiting for the call to supper when the phone had rung once again. Eagerly awaiting a call from Maya, Rich had hurried over and answered with a smile. For some reason I had watched my friend with a growing concern, sensing that something was very wrong…

Bowing his head, he had almost dropped the telephone. He had spoken quietly for a few moments, and then slowly hanging up, joined us in the dining area. His expression alone foretold of forth-coming doom, but the tears fogging his lenses revealed a broken heart.

"I'm afraid that I have some terrible news--," He took a napkin from the table, and blowing his nose, removed his glasses to rub at his eyes, "I'm so sorry--," He spoke as though he hadn't even believed his own words, "We—um, we lost Eva this morning—she passed in her sleep. Caitlin told Maya that it was natural causes…"

Looking away, I could find no expression that might offer comfort to anyone who now sat silently around me. Placing a reassuring hand upon my leg from beneath the table, Amica now watched my every movement with the greatest of concern. Overwhelmed with her compassion in that saddest of moments, I had conceded and gently accepted her hand.

"I'm at a total loss--," Raymond just stared, "To be honest, and with everything else that's happening, this was the last thing that I'd expected to hear…"

"She was a blessing upon all that had the pleasure of knowing her--," Raising a glass of brandy in her honor, Tim bowed his head while quietly saying, "May she find peace in the good grace of our Lord."

"I'm not feeling okay…" Trembling terribly, Rich had looked over at me and I had hurriedly gone to him and offered the security of a friend's embrace. He shook uncontrollability as, tightly gripping and holding on to each other, his silent tears flowed like a heated rain. We had shared the burden of that sorrow, as knowing how he had dearly loved the old woman, he now buried the only mother that he had ever truly known…

There had been silence from around the entire table, as while granting him grievance, everyone now quietly bowed their heads. We had stayed like that for a considerable time and as the minutes ticked away, and the half hour was chimed by the clock. Presently, his demeanor grew stronger, as slowly allowing me freedom from the embrace, he had tearfully looked up, "Thank you—I'm sorry, but I just can't take much more of this constantly losing the people that we love…."

Although there might have been words of comfort to offer in the moment, I noticed that the others had refrained from uttering a single spoken word. It wasn't for lack of caring or even intending the best, but out of respect for his feelings in the moment. There were times where tears might hope to offer closure in better measure than anything spoken by a friend.

Hoping to sway the balance of emotions, I turned to the subject of our wives, asking, "How are Maya and Caitlin taking this?"

"Not so good—they're both absolute wrecks," He had stuttered, as blowing his nose again, looked tearfully back at me while saying, "We should really be with them. This is all just so wrong."

"I know—believe me, I know…"

My own heart being broken, all things seemed to have grown darker. Gently patting his back, I quietly returned to my seat.

Amica had just curiously observed their reactions. The loss of the dear woman had come as a hard blow to us all. The only redeeming factor was that she had not suffered, or fallen and been taken by the darkness.

I knew that Amica was well aware of emotions and the human condition, but having been so far removed for an age, found it hard to relate on a physical level.

"We all loved Eva, dearly--," I had cleared my throat while attempting to offer solace, and said, "And, I know that she's gone into the good graces of eternity."

"Amen to that." Rich had whispered as though having spoken to himself, "God bless and keep her, always."

"Let's have a moment of silence in her memory, please." Clasping my hands together, I had silently bowed my head and said a prayer in passing. The pain came as it always did in those moments while gathered in the loss of a loved one. But together we endured, as with the eighth chime of the clock we had all looked up, and gazed mournfully upon one another.

"The food is cold--," Amica had pointed out, "Is there anything that I might be able to do?"

"It doesn't matter—thanks anyway--," Tim indulged the cold Spaghetti and meatballs, "It'll still taste good…"

"Did you have an opportunity to talk to Detective Simms?" I had changed the subject while addressing Raymond.

"Sorry, it slipped my mind--," He remembered while loading his plate, quietly saying, "As a matter of fact I caught him at home this afternoon. We can expect him tomorrow around noon."

"Will you be able to be here—or are you and Rich going to be over-seeing the work crews?"

"There's no need--," Clearing his throat, Rich chewed at his food while saying, "It's supposed to be a clear day—and they already know the routine. So we're free and will definitely be here."

"Perfect--," Looking to Rich, I had politely reminded him, while asking, "Is there a chance that you and Raymond could move Tanya and the boys first thing in the morning?"

"Sure thing--," Still preoccupied with Eva's passing, very little seemed to bother him, and he said, "All that they brought to the house was some bags of clothing and a few personal things. Everything would fit in your 300—if you don't mind me borrowing it?"

"Of course not—I'll leave the keys on the shelf by the door."

Returning my attention to Raymond, I pointed in thought, saying, "Are you sure that you want to sit in on this one? I know that the two of you have bumped heads a few times now."

"I wouldn't have it any other way." Raymond sipped at his coffee, "And besides, when you try explaining this whole nightmare a few extra witnesses will make a world of a difference."

"Can I ask you something?" Rich looked over at Amica.

"Of course—what's on your mind?"

"Well, Michael and I had previously discussed the transference and materialization of energy into matter." He spoke slowly, calmly and with a dark determination, "And, please correct me if I'm wrong—but doesn't that require some kind of an exchange with a living being?"

She had looked to me before replying and then, clasping her hands upon the table, looked to him, and said, "Yes, it requires what philosophers and alchemists refer to as 'Prima Materia' in order to complete a transference."

"Prima Materia—can someone explain that to me?" Raymond gawked, and toying at his spaghetti, said, "It sounds like a Pasta brand?"

"It literally means 'first matter'--," I remembered reading about it in the works of Anaxagoras and then Aristotle, and said, "And in alchemical tradition it's the universal starting material to create the philosopher's stone."

"And where exactly did she come across this 'Prima Materia' to manifest—if I might ask?" Rich stared as though I had committed some cardinal sin. We had exchanged glances, the expressions succeeding where words could not. He knew me better than most and all things considered, apparently understood my purpose in having remained silent.

"How exactly does it work?" Raymond appeared fascinated and frightened, asking, "And what do you guys know about this stuff?"

"From what I've read—it was believed to have been a power found in nature, both male and female--," I swallowed hard in description, "A hermaphroditic monster, the heavens and earth, all colors and all metals, it produces itself, conceives, and gives birth to itself…"

"Oh, I remember now—it went by many names--," Rich met with some distant recollection, and raising a finger in thought, said, "In 1612, 'Martin Ruland the Younger' wrote about it in his alchemical dictionary. He said that it was comprised of what he referred to as, the Primal fire, Light, and Mercury. But no one knows for sure, its true name was kept secret by alchemists."

"That explains the traces of Mercury that you found in the samples from the McCreary estate." Ponting to Rich, Tim pondered briefly and then said "And that's evidence enough to substantiate the existence of an entity having manifested there."

"Pardon me for saying it--," Rich peered back at Amica, and said, "But you never did tell us where you acquired this, 'life force'."

"Michael's ethereal energy sustains my existence here--," She answered quite honestly and without hesitation, saying, "And our continuing bond strengthens my ties to this world with the passing of each day."

"She's draining your life..." Tim dropped his fork and stared, "You've got your own personal vampire..."

"Not exactly--," Scratching at my cheek, I looked among the gathering, and said, "She is strong due to the demon and merely shares what she needs to sustain herself here."

"Hey—wait a minute?" Raymond slurped spaghetti and the sauce splattered all over his shirt, "If she can do this just by exchanging a little life force with someone, then what's stopping that nightmare out there from doing the same thing?"

"It too has this ability—and has likely used it many times before. But, flesh would make it vulnerable--," Amica spoke softly as though fearing to be overheard, "So it would only use such a guise to influence or betray unwary mortals." When she had said this she had shot a wary glance in my direction, and it had bothered me for reasons that I could not quite explain or understand...

"Well, if you came over to our side--," Raymond's eyes glistened fearfully with the realization, "Then you're--..."

"Yes, Amica's body can also be destroyed—but not her spirit." I swallowed hard with the thought, "It was the choice that was made—and a fate that she has accepted."

"No offense--," Raymond asked, "But, wouldn't you have been safer and more useful as a spirit—or whatever you were?"

"I only submitted to the powers that be. All that happens now occurs by fate and destinies path, the results will dictate the means to an end."

"That didn't sound too reassuring to me." Rich swallowed down the remainder of his coffee, "But thank you for your honesty, where Eva was concerned."

"Amica, how much longer do you figure that you'll be able to stay human?" Raymond appeared utterly dismayed, his eyes darting between us, as he asked, "This isn't permanent—is it?"

"The time runs shorter with each day that I grow more human. I am not a creature of this world, and the life fades as the powers flows from out of me. When that times comes—I too shall fall and--." She had stopped before revealing too much and simply fallen silent.

"So, no more black bird--," Tim swallowed hard, "Or magic tricks?"

"I still have the sight—," She explained, "And I'm still able to defend myself."

"We also have Marlowe--," Reminding them while rubbing at a stiff neck, I said, "So we still have the benefit of a spirit guide."

"If you don't mind me asking--," Turning to Amica, Tim politely inquired, 'Exactly how would you defend yourself?"

Appearing somewhat dumbfounded, she looked around curiously as though looking for or having lost something. It was apparent that she was uncertain as to what powers still remained, or how much longer they might last.

"When the need arrives--," There was something hauntingly sinister in the way that she peered back at him, "I will release the power in our defense…"

Sensing the demon lurking in the depths of her troubled soul, I prayed that none would tempt it into action… It wasn't so much a physical reaction, but a sense of diabolical presence that now gradually grew within her.

"If you keep sharp and stay on your feet you should be just fine, little lady," Raymond promised, "As long as I've got these beauties--," Waving his revolvers and smiling, he said, "You don't need to worry about any self-defence nonsense."

"I still have the sight--," She whispered as though failing to have even heard Raymond, and her eyes burning with an ethereal flame, turned back to Tim, saying, "Our greatest defense is the master of my undoing…"

"It must be terrifying to share a single consciousness between two entirely different beings." Sensing something behind her eyes, Tim looked on in suspended disbelief, "I could never imagine what it would be like to be reborn as an adult in a strange world, and have the wisdom of eternity."

"I think that it'd be downright terrifying--," Raymond sighed deeply, and pouring more coffee for Rich and himself, said, "Can you boys even guess at what that might be like? Existing lifetimes, and knowing that you've died over and over again?"

"I hate to sound like a pessimist--," Rich scoffed, "But, just the fact that we're all alive here means that we definitely died somewhere else. In which case—reincarnation is no longer just a theoretical possibility, but fact."

"Existence is all just an endless roller-coaster ride--," Tim sounded as though he sang the words, "Welcome boys and girls to death's carousel—your ticket's punched, and we're all on our way to the carnival of horrors…"

"Morbid, yet darkly poetic--," Rich smirked, "You might want to write it down."

Drawing the little notepad and pen from the breast pocket of my vest, I did exactly that.

"Have you managed to work out the bugs on those weapons yet?" Raymond appeared pale and as though he were grabbing at proverbial straws.

"Well—yes and no--," Rich retrieved a small metal crossbow from a shelf of the bookcase behind him, and placing it down on the table in front of us all, said, "I finally figured out how to provide a semi-safe delivery method for the flammable crystals."

"What's this?" Raymond swallowed hard, and retrieving the weapon to closer observe it, said, "Is this made of aluminum?"

"The base and bow are stainless steel--," Rich explained, "But the grip and casing is aluminum. I thought that it would help to keep it light."

"Will that be powerful enough--," Appearing fascinated, Tim accepted the weapon from Raymond and curiously tested the bow, "It seems fairly easy to flex?"

"I tested it. It's accurate and deadly for up to forty feet." Rich nodded as something sinister now shone in his deep blue eyes, "They had to be quick and easy to reload—and besides, if anything gets much closer than that, you're already dead…"

"What about the arrows—did you figure out a safer design?" Swallowing hard, Tim offered the weapon back to Rich.

"I made some alterations to the initial carriage design." The reply came somewhat reluctantly, "Instead of three tubes carrying different elements, we'll only be using one now."

"How can you mix those chemicals with water—," Raymond almost choked on his coffee, "I thought you said they'd ignite on contact?"

"Only when they're introduced to fluid--," Rich thoughtfully tapped a finger to his brow, "I needed a conductor for the crystals to travel in to be properly dispersed. But, being as we can't use anything wet, I finally figured it out." He looked between us while drawing a small canister from his coat pocket, and placing it upon the table before us, said, "The one fluid that isn't wet."

"Of course--," Tim picked up the glass container and closely examining the silvery liquid, looked back at me, "Good old fashioned Mercury."

"But, what about what you said about those stiffs being as dry as a board?" Doubt now resonated from all about the table, but Rich had only smiled.

"We'll all be carrying bows and darts—and will work in pairs. When I fire a live round into something, my partner will fire a water dart as well. This way we can reduce the risk to ourselves while still working at maximum efficiency."

"Is there still a risk of leakage?" Tim looked nervously between Rich and the weapon, "I mean—we are using glass tubes, so something could happen."

"I've designed a special water-proof holster for the darts in case of rain or any other unexpected disaster." Scratching thoughtfully at his goatee, he added in thought, "The pouch will be hermetically sealed—so unless someone pulls it open while going for a swim, theoretically, we should be okay."

"Well, that's a far cry better than our previous odds." Raymond anxiously tapped his fingers upon the table, "When can you have more of these things ready?"

"Just as soon as you get back to my shop and help me finish them--," Rich exclaimed, and drawing a larger canister from his other coat pocket, said, "I also made six of these." He held it before him and waved it for all to see. It appeared as little more than a plastic casing the size of a soda can, and was weighted at one end with a tapering metal tip.

"What is it?" Raymond reached toward the object.

"These contain a single large glass tube with chemicals and are encased in a soft plastic, water-filled shell with a detonator cap at the end." Rich plucked the object out of Raymond's hands, and holding it close, muttered, "They're lethal…"

"You made lawn dart bombs." Tim nervously chewed at his fingernails, "If the arrows are nasty--," He pointed in question, "Then what kind of destructive force can we expect from these?"

"Well, each one contains enough chemicals to annihilate something as big as a Greyhound bus, or turn an average sized house into an inferno. As far as personal safety goes--," He pondered briefly, "I wouldn't suggest anyone using one of these unless the situation was absolutely desperate."

Tim looked around the table, swallowing hard, and asked, "Um, how safe are they to handle?"

"If one went off, we wouldn't even notice it." Rich shrugged, "There'd be a blinding flash, a moment of searing pain, and then they could load us all into an ashtray when it was over."

"If it gives us an advantage--," Nodding in thought, Raymond agreed, saying, "Then it's worth the risk. I don't know about you guys, but if it there's no other choice—I'd rather be a crispy critter than get taken by those things…"

"My point exactly--," Rich agreed, as dropping the makeshift bomb onto the table and frightening everyone, he smiled mischievously, "It's just a prototype and isn't loaded…"

"I'm just wondering—for the sake of argument--," Tim raised an eyebrow and looking to Amica, asked, "You mentioned that you still had some abilities—what might they be?"

Glancing over at me as though seeking permission, I nodded instinctively, and she turned back to Tim. There had been an almost immediate panic, as wide-eyed, he feared to have placed himself in a compromising situation. But it was already too late, as concentrating all of her efforts upon the man, something sinister flashed in her eyes.

Once more I sensed that same diabolical force, and feared that through their symbiotic existence and use of this power, the evil was brought ever closer! The fire burned like blue sparks within her pale eyes, as ever so slowly Tim was lifted from his seat and drifted above the table like a feather! But the experience had not been pleasurable: Terrified and helpless, he suddenly sailed across the room and crashed heavily onto the couch!

"Telekinesis—she has the ability to move things with her mind." Rich nodded in approval, "And I'm willing to bet that Tim won't be asking her anymore questions."

Slowly rising from her seat, she turned and looked back toward the flames in the hearth. Having seen this, Tim had ducked behind the couch and crept beneath the woolen blanket.

She focussed intently into the coals and the fire in her gaze grew brighter There had been a moment where we had all doubted that anything further might happen, but then it did… The room appeared to grow slightly darker by each degree that she concentrated. Her focus becoming absolutely intense, the fire suddenly hissed and literally became frozen solid before our eyes!

"Dear God—I never thought that I'd ever live long enough to see something like that." Amazed, Raymond had cursed under his breath, "Remind me to never piss her off."

With a wave in the direction of the hearth, the flame suddenly returned, and Amica slowly slipped back down into her seat. There was brilliance to the emerald of her eyes, something more mystical than physical. In that moment I realized that the demon within was alive and growing with each moment, and every time that she summoned its power…

"She might have retained a few others as well--," Tim reluctantly returned to the table, nervously taking his seat, and humbly said, "But those can wait until the need for them arises."

"Maybe so, but I wonder for how much longer." Suspicion darkened Rich's glances as he directed his attention back at me, "According to what you said, sooner or later she'll become as mortal as the rest of us. And then…"

"And then, we'll deal with things to the best of our ability--," I had interrupted the obvious,

"In the mean-time—we need to take a look into that old woman's house."

"Alright then--," Pointing to the clock, Raymond nodded, saying, "Once we finish the meeting with Simms this afternoon, we'll head over to investigate the place."

"That's already too late--," Tim had immediately disagreed, saying, "If we do this—it's best to get an early start."

"He's right--," Raymond looked to me, "Let's plan this for a morning— the last thing that we need is to get caught out there after dark."

"What do we really expect to find there?" Tim looked between us, "And, do we even have any idea of what we might be looking for?"

"All that I know for certain is that we'll know it when we see it. Marlowe described it as being an item or object of mystery—or great secret. Something that will release a great power on this earth."

"And when we finally find some ending to all of this--," Rich's frowned, "Will our angel be lost to the darkness?"

Retrieving the crossbow from before Rich, Raymond glared down the length of the barrel, "Not as long as there's life in my trigger finger."

"I think that we're all agreed on that." Moving from the table, Tim looked back, "I'll get the Italian plum cake—would anyone care to help clear the dinner dishes from off the table?"

"I'll do it--," Rich sighed deeply, as moving from the table, he paused to look back at me, "Maybe the two of you might want to go down to the wine cellar, and choose something appropriate for what should have been dinner?"

It was something that I had always done with Caitlin, and looking to Amica, had just nodded, "Would you care to join me?"

"Why, Michael—you didn't expect to escape me that easily—did you?" She grinned, and for that moment all that I saw was Caitlin. But then my attention drifted into those burning, wild, and wolf-like eyes, which I won't even attempt to describe, because what I saw there existed between both worlds, and somewhere I feared to even imagine...

CHAPTER SEVEN

The stairs down into the basement appeared far darker than usual, or maybe it had just been the way that I was feeling? Amica had followed me down as I switched on the lights, and we entered the corridor leading into the wine cellar. It housed much of what we had brought from the cellars of the Duff Glenn, gifted bottles, and a few of my own favorites.

"I'm not sure if you have ever been introduced to alcohol?" I glanced back at Amica who knowingly observed my every movement. I had felt the fool when reaching up and drawing a bottle from the collection, she smiled and said, "Might I suggest the Château Haut-Brion 1930?"

Absolutely amazed with her choice, I stood there feeling stunned. It was exceptional red Bordeaux hailing from Pessac-Leognon in Northern France. Not only was it appropriate for the occasion, but it was also among one of Caitlin's favorites.

"Lest you forget, I have had an eternity to wander, listen and learn." Her eyes sparkled in the shadows of the cellar.

"I might have known—it's hard to grasp at times, especially in your current form."

"Do not allow forms to betray you--," There was danger in her eyes, "For even the most foul may become a blessing in the end..."

"And, will appearances truly fool this darkness into believing that you are Caitlin?"

Amica had turned to look up at me, her eyes widening as though revealing the world in a single glance, "The darkness could never be betrayed by anything less than the truth of your heart."

"Then why the change—what possible purpose--," I stopped in mid-sentence as she silently watched, waited for the truth to finally settle within my mind. And so it had, like a poison that now seeped from out of my soul, "You have returned to me—and become all that I have ever truly known and loved. To make me---..."

Placing a finger before my lips, she slowly nodded, "Do not allow anything to come between us—and only this shall betray the darkness. I am the shield—but my strength resides within your heart, and the others who now follow."

I remembered the valiant expressions of my companions when Rich had recited Amica's possible fate. Appearances held dominion over the heart, love provided strength, and hence faith to the spirit. It all made sense…

"I think that I finally understand what Marlowe meant--," My thoughts streamed like an ocean of seething fire, "We had better get this wine upstairs before we miss the dessert…"

It had been my turn to assist with the chores that evening, but Amica had insisted that we all retire. I had felt guilty while indulging an evening brandy as she had attended to the supper dishes. Glancing over my shoulder and into the kitchen, I had caught glimpses of her, rushing about with dishes. Something had changed about her, and this had not become more apparent, than when she had startled us all while humming a familiar Scots' ballad as she worked!

"The Bonnie Banks O' Loch Lomond--," Rich had immediately recognized the tune, and sadly said, "It's almost like some part of Caitlin and Eva is still with us…"

"It's nice to have a lady about the house again." Tim had remarked, drifting somewhere in thought, as he tapped a finger upon his brandy glass, "I'd almost forgotten what it was like."

"Speaking of ladies--," Raymond had peered about like a fox in the henhouse, "I've invited that pretty little Pamela from Carrie's bookstore for a meal. It's just an early afternoon dinner—and nothing too serious."

Stopping and just staring, we were all shocked and amazed that the confirmed bachelor had finally broken down! Under the circumstances, none of us had even considered anything beyond the impending threat.

"You asked Pam out?" Rich almost spilled his brandy, "Where are you taking her—or will you be bringing her here?"

"I'm not exactly sure?" He promptly pulled a notepad from the breast pocket of his vest and flipped through the pages while saying, "I asked her what she would prefer, and she said--," He read from the notes, "If it's a dinner at home, country ham, squash, mashed potatoes, and fresh sliced 'home-grown' or Heirloom tomatoes. No alcohol, only Iced tea—no sugar."

"You wrote it down?" Rich stared.

"I'm a cop, dummy--," Raymond rolled his eyes, "I write everything down…"

"What else did she say?" Tim took notice of additional notes.

"Well--," Raymond looked back at his notepad, "If it's dinner out, she loves Italian, and seafood tops the list. For dessert, she prefers 'Crème' Brule' or coffee, caramel Gelato."

"Well, you certainly are a stickler for details--," Tim shrugged, "When is this dinner supposed to happen?"

"I wanted to pick her up on Thursday depending on what's happening here." He thought briefly, "But she won't even let me do that. She said a lady should have her independence, so she'll pick me up in that little red Jeep of hers."

"I'm surprised that Carrie wasn't all over that--," Rich snickered, "You all know how protective she is of the girls down at the office."

"Carrie was the one who talked me into this in the first place--," Raymond admitted, sipping at his brandy and shrugging bashfully, "I never would have done this on my own accord, especially under the circumstances." He thought briefly, his face becoming pale as he looked over at me in wide-eyed fear of some unspoken realization, and asked, "You don't think that this'll draw Pam into the firing lane—do you?"

Expression of concern and confusion now roused my companions as Raymond looked to me for an answer. Although I shared his concern and thought long and hard, I simply could not offer a viable conclusion.

"She will only become significant if you allow her to." Amica returned from the kitchen, "We meet and know many people—the darkness only hunts the few and the most precious."

"Maybe—you should postpone dinner for a little while?" Tim had delicately suggested, "Just to play it safe and until we can figure things out?"

Nodding, Raymond had tucked the notepad back into his vest, "You're right—I don't know what in the heck I was thinking? I'll deal with it tomorrow."

"We need to call Scott and Carrie back—and fill old Red in on everything." Rich re-filled his brandy glass, and slurring ever so slightly, said, "I need to pick up the truck and get the boys, so I'll catch Red at the office."

"Detective Simms will be here around noon--," Raymond reminded us, "It might be best if you introduced Caitlin as the maid." He motioned politely to her as she moved closer to me on the couch, and he said, "With all due respect—we really don't need to complicate things here anymore than they already are."

"That's not going to work." Rich peered over at us, "Simms already met Caitlin—remember? I doubt that he'd even know the difference between them? And, to be honest, although I know Caitlin really well, the more that I look at Amica, the tougher it gets."

Casually flipping her fiery curls, she had slipped an arm about me from behind, and curiously looked back. It was perfectly uncanny as to how comfortable she had become in such close vicinity and intimate detail. If I had not known better, I would have assumed that this might actually have been my wife, and that some terrible joke had been played.

Pulling her legs up from beneath her, she moved closer, looking about as though confused by the dubious reactions from our companions. She had shivered, and similar to Caitlin, drawn the woolen blanket down from the couch while covering her legs.

"If I didn't know better--," Tim had agreed, "I couldn't tell the difference between them now either."

"Then it's unanimous--," Sipping at his brandy and then slowly swirling the glass in his hand, Rich winked as he said, "We'll refer to Amica as Caitlin in front of everyone else, from now on. That way there won't be any questions asked. Besides, I'm sure that the detectives would be wondering where your wife has disappeared to, anyway."

"He's right—and it'll work with Simms." Raymond frowned, "But, somehow I don't think that anyone else will buy it for a second. She may look like Caitlin—but she doesn't share the same mind or experiences."

"I know of their past and have seen her interactions through time--," Raising an eyebrow she had smiled at me, "You must consider this nothing more than a game, a masquerade—I do love a party—please play along, won't you?"

It was almost as though I could hear her speaking while something dark had gazed back at me. It was those eyes, those brightly and burning, deep green eyes, how they haunted me…Fighting back the ominous and growing anxiety, I was beginning to wonder if Amica was unaware, and slowly slipping away? Perhaps this facade was a game being played by something more sinister? What would happen when the guardian of the vault became aware of her—and if so, would the darkness then also discover our secret?

"Sweetheart--," She appeared concerned as brushing the hair from my brow, asked, "Did you hear what I said?"

"Sorry, Caitlin--," Affectionately patting her hand with a sweet smile in apology, I said, "I heard you, my love, my mind was just elsewhere." And then, in a moment of embarrassment after having realized the mistake, I blushed while looking about at my friends, "It would seem that she's quite convincing. I'll admit that just for a moment she even caught me."

"Call it whatever you like--," Raymond said thoughtfully, "As long as it looks and sounds real to everyone else, for the moment nothing else matters."

"As much as I hate the thought of lying to everyone--," Rich sighed in agreement, "Things could be far worse...

"He's right--" The thought bothered me as well, but there was little choice, and I said, "I'm just concerned about Caitlin hearing about this. Who knows what would happen if she came back in the middle of everything?"

"Then we'd better inform her--," Tim shuddered with the thought, "For her own good—and ours..."

"There is no need for her to be made aware--," Amica seemed strangely distressed, "In fact, it might be best for all if she never finds out."

"She's off in Ireland with no connections to anyone here but Rich--," Tim nursed his drink, as thinking aloud, he added in thought, "We need everyone here to believe that she's truly Caitlin—or this whole thing could back-fire..."

"He's right--," Rich agreed, "So—how should we go about this?"

Amica's expression had spoken volumes, as somewhere between sorrow and dread, I knew there could be only one answer.

"As much as I would have been against this before—," Rich volunteered as the messenger, saying, "We need to move ahead with this. I'll inform everyone that Caitlin has returned—and that Maya stayed longer to manage Eva's funeral. It goes against my grain as well—but it's the only way to assure that this will work..."

"If they all think that she's back—the darkness will sense it too." Tim nodded, "I'm agreed and disagreed at the same time. But you're right—it's the only feasible answer..."

"Then it's agreed--," I looked to Amica, "You are now Caitlin—until whatever end."

Raymond glanced at the clock and groaning with the realization, said, "Well, morning comes much too early these days." He coughed and placing down his brandy glass, stretched his arms, and said, "I'd better drag my sorry butt to bed before I just fall over."

"Well, I need the facilities--," Grunting while climbing from off the couch, Tim waved in departure, "Pardon me—I'll be back in a few minutes."

"And on that note, I'm going to pack it in for the night too," Moving from the couch, Rich paused to look back in parting, "Pleasant dreams, Caitlin."

"You shall be reunited with your beloved Maya soon enough—," Amica had gently taken hold of Rich's arm in passing, and peering deeply into his troubled eyes, said, "Things are not all as they may seem or to appear—but of this one thing I am certain."

Rich had smiled sadly, and looking down at her, slowly nodded, "Thank you—and bless your heart for saying it." Although it was apparent that he hadn't taken her words to heart, it was obvious that he had respected her intentions.

Slowly turning, he had waved in departure before quietly sauntering down the hall.

She had watched as Rich and the others had departed the room, and then curiously looked back at me, "Your thoughts stray—tell me what troubles your heart."

At first, the words had been upon the tip of my tongue, but they had somehow eluded expression. Placing down the brandy glass, I gazed listlessly into the crackling hearth while feeling disenchanted and utterly lost.

She had reacted quite instinctively, as moving nearer, had embraced and pulled me close, "Soon all shall be as it was—and time will cause the shadows to fade from memory."

"And—what will become of you?" As I had turned, she had seen the concern in my eyes, sensing the sentiment, and swiftly looked away.

"Amica--," I moved closer, gently taking hold of her, and asked again, "What will become of you when this finally ends?"

"I shall pass from this world and into the realm of shadows." The pain that now filled her features was beyond words, "Until such a day as redemption comes and we shall meet once more upon golden shores and at the dawn of all things."

"Aren't you even afraid--," I choked on the words for fear of her reaction, "Of the demon within you…and what will happen when it finally escapes?"

"I do not fear the inevitable--," The reply was said in little more than a whisper, as she looked to me and muttered, "But I fear that your taunting the beast with such questions shall bring it about that much sooner."

"I'm sorry—but you can't blame me for caring… and for wanting something better for you…"

"We are not destined for this world." She turned away and looked back in second thought, saying, "But Michael—I do love you. I have always loved you and will continue to do so, forevermore." Tears now welled in her eyes, as slowly shaking her head, she whispered, "You must trust in me—our love shall never fade. It exists in all things such as it did long ago—and shall continue until fate and destiny bring us together once more."

"And I love you both—to the fullest that life or love could ever offer. But there must be some way—some way to save you, and free you from the demon?" My heart ached for this selfless creature that had given so much and suffered so long, "Tell me—and I will do anything..."

There was a moment when, as her eyes had quite suddenly and brilliantly flashed, I moved back. It had not been any reflection of the hearth, but rather something that now gazed out from deep within. It had taken me by surprise, but I had known that the demon had reacted to my compassion and pleas...

"Overcome this darkness..." Her words came without a thought as she stared unflinching into my eyes, "Cast it into the depths of oblivion where it shall exist as nothing in the great void. Vanquish this destroyer of lives—violator of souls and horror, that through time forever haunts us."

"I'm only one man—but if I am able," Swallowing hard, I promised, "And if it's the last thing that I do in this world, I'll send that nightmare into the abyss..."

She gently took hold of my hand and paused as a sudden motion behind us caused us both to look.

"Pardon me--," Politely taking his place on the couch across from us, Tim raised a finger in thought, "I just looked out from the bathroom window—and it's a bitter cold and very dark night. Would it be a real bother if I just stayed here—for one more night?"

The journey to the guest house would have carried him some fifty yards through deep snow and the pitch-dark. We had not installed the posts for lighting as previously planned, and after several brandies, I could hardly blame him.

"Of course not—you know that you're always welcome—it's our home--," I had warmly welcomed my friend, saying, "In any event, I can hardly blame you." Peering into the magenta folds of the tightly drawn draperies, my thoughts drifted into words, and I mumbled, "Death whispers to the wary upon winter's icy breath—a gift in warning and parting, within the season of the grave. Still, there are far too many ghouls haunting these woods and a darkness that even now lurks at the gates..."

He had just looked over at me, and swiftly draining his glass, moved to refill it, "I don't know if you even realize it? But you're starting to sound a lot like that poor, old Sir Reginald from the McCreary place."

"And perhaps--," Entertaining wild thoughts in the late hour, I looked up at my friend as he returned, saying, "You were his dear friend and the good Doctor whose life was lost to the demon in the tombs…" Pulling a notepad and pen from a pocket, I snickered while quickly scribbling down the thoughts to later add to my book.

"You should not make light of such things--," Amica appeared disturbed and even frightened, as she said, "Who truly knows how many lives we have shared, suffered, and our bones made to rest within unknown graves."

Her words sent a shudder through my entire being as pausing only briefly, I hurriedly wrote down what she had said.

"Does it not seem strange to the both of you--," She now spoke as though in warning rather than a shared discussion, "That we have all come together and gathered in this place, much like the unfortunate souls of the Duff Glenn? Do you really believe that your discovery of the McCreary manor and the diaries was all simply coincidence?"

"Are you suggesting that we have all existed there before?" Sipping at his brandy, his eyes grew wide while never leaving her for a single moment.

"The universe is precise—it makes no mistakes." She spoke quietly, "Destiny and Fate place us into position to make the correct choices—our decisions dictate the final outcome."

"Allow me to ask you this?" Putting a finger to his lip in thought, he asked, "If the universe is really so precise—then why do bad things happen to decent people—and why do children and babies suffer and die without ever having had a chance?"

"The darkness knows no mercy—," She whispered, saying, "And it takes the greatest pleasure within the suffering and destruction of the innocent…"

"It's a shame that Rich has such a low opinion of the church--." Sighing deeply, I shrugged, "It seems that they've known about these things far longer than anyone else."

"And so they should--," She frowned, saying, "They were poisoned long ago, and tempted with carnal and monetary pleasures. Very few still share the true faith that once was…"

"I prefer to avoid topics of religion--," Tim scratched nervously at his nose, "And some even say that the Bible isn't even true to its original sources anymore?"

"Even through its many re-translations, it still stands as a book of knowledge, inspiration and morals." She looked between us and then sadly said, "But, like so many other doctrines and illuminated manuscripts, has fallen victim to misrepresentation by those who seek to use it to a means of their own ends."

"Our modern laws are based on the ten commandments--," Thinking aloud, I rubbed the sleep from my eyes, "And I couldn't imagine a world without ethics and order."

"Like the waters that flow with gravity—mankind will always take the simplest and most direct route." Tim swirled his glass and thoughtfully looked down into the slowly spiraling fluid, "We can only hope that one day, when all the books and belief systems finally fail, that the lessons learned will still remain…"

The clock suddenly chimed from behind us.

"It's getting late--," Reaching for my hand, she led me from off the couch, saying, "We should get what little rest we can."

"Sweet dreams, Caitlin." Waving, Tim settled back into the cushions, and looking to the hearth, said, "Oh—and I thought that you might like to know? I'll be making waffles with fruit, sausages and bacon in the morning."

Stopping quite suddenly as startling me, she had stared ravenously back at him! Her eyes shone with an eerie blue light as she had done this, and I felt her grip tighten upon my hand. He had jumped just a little when seeing this, and pulled a cushion to his breast in defense.

For all of her divine traits we were again reminded that there was still something terrifying lurking from just beneath the skin. The moment having passed, she smiled kindly and waving in parting, sweetly said, "I look forward to breakfast—pleasant dreams, friend Tim…"

Nodding and visibly unsettled, he silently watched as she followed me out into the hallway and then up the stairs.

Glancing back, I felt certain sympathy as while seeing the fear that still lingered in the shadow of his dark eyes… This strange and conflicting nature of Amica had both terrified and fascinated me. There was an excitement, an adrenaline surge that came with the thought of being in such close vicinity of such a creature. I could only wonder if swimmers had felt the same way moments before the shark had taken that first and potentially fatal bite. And then, I questioned my own sanity in having willingly swum so far out into that proverbial, deep water…

We had gone into the bedroom and neither of us had said anything while changing into evening attire. I suppose that to some extent, and due to her appearance, it had felt almost perfectly natural at the time. It was surprising as to how similar she had become to Caitlin, even in habits and the little things that she had done.

I was captivated in the moment, as she had taken pause before the mirror, and leaning down, began brushing the fiery curls from her hair. There was loveliness within longing and it brought a sweet-sorrow to my heart. In essence she had become my own dear Caitlin, and though my love remained true, the illusion had become so much more than mere dreams.

We had soon made our way into the office and to where she had taken her usual place in the chair beside the desk. Wrapping herself in a quilt and drawing her legs up, she rested her head upon the arm of the chair. With her fiery hair flowing from over the side, those green eyes lovingly gazed upward.

"Did you want a pillow or anything?"

"No—I'm fine just like this." She smiled sadly, "Thank you…"

Sensing that she needed more than mere words, I leaned down and gently kissing her brow, said, "Sweet dreams…"

The gesture had been accepted in the sweetest possible way, as smiling, she closed her eyes and whispered, "You are a sweet dream…"

Smiling and switching on the little lamp above my desk, I slumped back into the chair before the typewriter. She had fallen asleep in moments, but I kept glancing over at her. Even through the horror of it all, these little moments made it all worthwhile.

Turning back to the typewriter and looking anxiously down at the empty page, I drew a complete blank. Although I'd remembered to bring the notebook, fatigue seemed to have left me somewhat disenchanted. It was one of those evenings where nothing came to mind, and not even dreams could have drawn any inspiration. I knew that I had to make note of the current events, but something now halted all efforts. Perhaps, in some way I had not felt as though they had quite concluded, and was simply awaiting an ending?

Gathering what little enthusiasm that remained, I was about to attempt something when Amica had suddenly looked up from where she was curled in the blankets. She spoke as though dreaming, and as the heavy lids fluttered across the brilliant glow of her emerald eyes.

"Michael--," She asked in an almost daring manner, while whispering, "Do you fear my darkness?"

"I don't know the darkness within you—should I?"

"It exists as a bestial thing--," She spoke slowly and as though reaching out while attempting to define the true nature of her curse, "It is a growing hunger, a ravenous brute that is never satisfied, and an evil that I had become…"

"But—it isn't really who you are—or what you have become since."

"I feel it deep inside—a dark force that thrives for control--." She appeared in trance while speaking, her eyes closing as she said, "And once released, it shall bring chaos and death…"

"Then we won't release it--," Reaching over and gently taking her hand, I forced a smile, "One day soon you will be free—and the evil will no longer be a part of you."

Noticing Merlin's shadow in the open doorway, I was surprised as to his sudden and strange apprehension. Something glinted fearfully in his wide eyes, and then as swiftly as he had appeared, he had turned before vanishing into the shadows of the corridor.

"Soon, mortality shall free me of these terrible bonds--," She appeared barren of all expression, her eyes suddenly opening wide, "Hence, do you dare gaze upon that which remains in my stead?"

"Beware, Michael—for the beast seeks to overcome her--," Marlowe's wavering voice warned from the darkness, and he said, "Do not taunt or invite its wrath—for she is weak of the flesh and unable to control what she becomes…"

"How is this possible--," I had spoken to Marlowe in thought, "How can this evil exist on sanctified ground—communicate to me without the darkness sensing this?"

"It exists within—and as a part of her, and thus, is sheltered from hallowed ground. This demon is by far older than the darkness—and holds dominion over lesser of its kind—," His voice was a whisper, words spoken in fear of being overheard, "Whatever secrets it may hold remain as such, for there is a deep loathing, and inner hatred, even among their own hierarchy.."

"Marlowe—what do I do—what do I say?"

"Do nothing—and speak even less… Above all, do not dare look upon this evil—for it is beyond my power to protect you now. Seek only favor within its grace—such as it may be..."

At a loss for words and frightened out of my wits, I said, "Who am I that would dare invoke the wrath of a God? No, I would not dare gaze upon such dark majesty…"

"Invoke the wrath of a God—art thou truly so humble—or dost thou bow down before me in fear?" She spoke in a whisper, a diabolic tone that revealed an obvious amusement in my words, "Look upon me then, if thou dare, wanderer of the wasteland—gaze upon a God …"

Remembering Marlowe's warning, I struggled against my own fear and fascination to avoid looking. Then, leaning closer to the typewriter, I desperately attempted to focus upon filling the page. One letter at a time, I began typing out the events of the day. Each thought coming painfully slower as while becoming aware of something terrifying in the chair beside me!

The room grew ever darker as the breath escaped my lungs in icy gasps from before my face! In the edge of my eye I caught the distinct flash of a blue flame, and the world suddenly became deathly still.

The quilt had slipped to the floor, and as while avoiding turning to look, I knew that whatever watched from the chair beside me was no longer Amica… In the darkness and barely able to see by the paled glow of the still burning lamp, I stared intently upon the page in the typewriter. I could sense that whatever now occupied the chair beside the desk was patient, waiting and almost daring me to turn and take notice.

There was a presiding bitter cold that, utterly consuming, numbed, and penetrated through my entire being. Although resisting the terror and urge of just spinning and looking, I allowed a glimpse from out of my peripheral vision. Although unclear in the deep shadows, I could see that it was the pale and nude form of something that had once been human.

Fighting with every ounce of my will in aversion, it was still unavoidable. It somehow became clear in my thoughts even without having looked. It was a sixth and possibly some kind of seventh sense that now revealed the terror clearly in my mind.

Sitting upright and grasping the arm-rests tightly, she leaned forward while stretching outward and into the room. Barren of gender, her body had become hideously lengthened and slender, the ribs and bones protruding grotesquely from all angles. Leathery and glistening, the pallor of her skin had taken on a wet, waxen, and sickly green hue. From a neck extending several times its normal length now swung the leathery skull of an Elk or stag with savage tusks and razor sharp teeth. An ethereal blue fire burned from upon its massive horns, while flowing in a flaming mane that poured down its back. From behind unfolded immense and blackened, bat-like wings, as clawed and prehistoric reptilian feet tore at the floor.

Slowly turning, the eyes and gaping jaws were burning with all the blue blazing fury of the furnaces of hell. Desperately focussing entirely upon the typewriter, I tapped at the keys while writing nothing but gibberish. An icy breath rushed against the side of my face as something leaned closer, and I felt an icy claw clenching tightly about the wrist of my left arm.

Unable to detain the horror any longer, I spun toward the looming nightmare!

"Would you care for some tea?" Amica feigned a smile, "I couldn't sleep and, well, to be honest, you look very tired. I really don't mind running down for you?"

With my heart thundering and pulse racing, I had fought to catch my breath while just staring wide-eyed and terrified beyond words.

"Are you okay?" Placing a hand to my brow, she felt for my temperature, and then shaking her head, muttered, "You don't seem to have a fever—but you are a little warm." She gazed innocently back at me and I suddenly realized that she was oblivious to the events that had just taken place. Somehow she had been cast into some kind of altered state. It was a condition wherein, reaching from beyond the subconscious, the demon could peer out without her having known or suspected. Marlowe was right: It was growing stronger now with each passing day…

"Yes, I'm fine—just a little over-tired." Unwilling to discuss the matter for fear of causing another occurrence of the creature, I shrugged, "But, I would really love some tea."

Noticing Merlin wander back into the office, I felt sudden relief as he accepted a friendly scratch from Amica in passing.

"Um—how are you feeling?" I had looked to her as she stood in the doorway, "I mean—don't you feel tired—or anything?"

She hadn't replied immediately, but reaching up and taking hold of the frame with both hands, curiously glanced back. Her robe had slipped open, and the light in the hallway behind her shone through the light material of her gown.

"I am feeling much better—and how are you, my dearest?"

There was an awkward moment where my eyes had sought to travel where morality and loyalty swiftly forced me to look away. This had not been an aspect of Amica's previous, moral disposition or general character. In this sense, I could only assume that the demon had growing influence and had been instrumental in her actions.

"I'll feel a lot better once I get some hot tea--," I looked away, "Maybe, with a little lemon—if you wouldn't mind?"

"Of course--," She turned to leave, and hesitating, glanced back, "Are you certain that everything is alright?"

"I'm just very tired and have a lot on my mind."

"I'll fetch the tea."

Watching her move, I felt my imagination and emotions begin to run wild. When she had existed as the boy, she had been a terrifying, supernatural force compelled to evil by necessity, but was now something quite different. I felt as though I were experiencing the Garden of Eden and witnessing the birth of Eve. And yet, as a creature of flesh and possessed of the demon she was little more than a living puppet, and being played by the devil…

"She would never willingly harm you--," Marlowe whispered from out of the shadows of the room, "But the evil within her would seek to destroy you… Beware, for the flesh weakens her with the passing of time—and so does the dragon also grow…"

I could hear the old kettle whistle from downstairs and the blood ran cold in my veins. "If you knew this previously—then why didn't you warn me before we made this choice?"

"You also knew this soul—and of what had taken it long ago--," Marlowe spoke swiftly as I heard the feint creaking of footsteps upon the stairs, "For Michael—in doing so—have you not freed the soul from the demon—as you had so dearly wished before?"

"What happens to her—and all of us when she finally becomes a part of our reality?"

"She is unnatural to this dimension and therefore, cannot become complete to this world. Hence, rather than the two becoming separate entities, the demon shall cast her soul out and assume the physical form…a living nightmare born unto the flesh…"

"Oh—dear God…"

"Hot tea—with lemon slices." Amica happily announced, bringing the tray to my desk and setting out the cups, "I thought that you might like a few cookies—they are not enough to harm you." She had done a double-take and stepping back, asked, "Are you well—you seem a little pale, is something wrong?"

Slipping an arm about her waist, I gently pulled her close, and hugging her tightly, said with the utmost confidence, "I'll be just fine—and like I'd said earlier, I'm just feeling very tired. Thank you, my dear—for the tea and cookies."

At first she had seemed unsure of my reaction, and then leaning down and kissing my brow, said, "You are very welcome—now have some before it gets cold."

Something had already changed about her. It was warmth of humanity that had taken the place of the once predominant, cold logic. Marlowe had been right, the clock was ticking and soon our angel would become an abomination… Somehow I had to warn the others, but how could I do this without her discovering this curse? What would happen if she found out—and even worse, what would happen if I kept the terrible secret?

"Are you certain that nothing is bothering you?" Curiously leaning from across her seat, her eyes reached deeply into my soul, "You seem distant—and as though you were an eternity away."

She was asking too many questions to things that she had quite recently been able to sense. I knew that she was still capable of many things, but those powers came from the very same evil that we feared. I had to be careful not to alarm her any further. In the end, I knew that her redemption would come when the beast arrived—and hell would follow...

"It's just everything and nothing at the same time--," Smiling and gently running a hand through her silken hair, I sighed deeply, "I suppose that it's strange, unsettling to be surrounded by such extremes. Knowing the horror of what's waiting out there in the night—and then there's you? You are the fairest and finest of souls—and an unimaginable nightmare at the same time."

"The Babylonian culture believed that even the brightest light of the greatest god would always cast an equally long and dark shadow." Appearing as though having been awakened from a nightmare, she whispered, "As my light grows—so does the shadow..."

Bowing her head and attempting to conceal her eyes with a hand, I could still the reflection in her palms of an ethereal fire flashing from the depths of that emerald gaze. Whether it had been an epiphany or the blasphemous whispers of an evil within, it was apparent that she now knew...

"We are to lose one another again—," The words came through a pained whisper, "But I will do whatever I am able—before this life fails me."

"Have the fates and destiny truly betrayed us?" Swallowing hard with the realization that all had been revealed, I pleaded, "Is there no other means of escape from this damnation for you?"

A great sorrow now took her. It hurt to watch as I saw the first tears stream from those beautiful and brilliantly shining eyes. Slowly, she shook her head, as bowing and softly kissing my hand, whispered, "When the hour arrives you shall know, and you must destroy me by fire before the demon takes this vessel that we now share..."

"There must be some other way..."

"The body exists purely for the sake of mortal deeds—and it is the soul that holds true significance." Her eyes shone as the tears flowed, "This is the path that we have both chosen and shall travel together, until we are no longer able."

Falling to my knees and tightly embracing her, I prayed to all the angels and God above, pleaded that from somewhere, from anywhere, mercy would shine upon this selfless soul. I even dared beg the hosts of hell in the slightest hope of redemption! It seemed only moments, but as the fever of fatigue took me, I faded into the shadows and knew no more...

There was a thundering clamor from out of the blackness, the sounds of explosions and steel weapons clashing together! Flames lit the heavens, and a foul black and oily smoke trailed like immense serpents into a night sky! Covered in filth and crawling through mud and human remains, I winced to the sight of the dead and dying upon a field of battle. Gasping for breath, I struggled through the maggot and worm infested mire! Barely managing, I crawled atop a mound of weapons, indistinguishable rot and putrefying human remains. From there I stared out while cringing fearfully in the chaos, horrified at what I saw. Surrounded in blackened, charred and jagged mountain peaks, the heavens glowed in the reflection of the hellish inferno of war. To the one side stood a massive army of unspeakable horrors that crept, crawled and slithered across a field of bodies. As to the other, waged a hopeless battle fought by men in armour, spears, shields and swords. There were immense and hideous insects of all manner and shape, cutting, stinging and eating their way through the masses! I saw nightmares, that existing as some abominable conjunction between plant and animal, swung massive, crushing roots, and lashing tendrils that whipped outward at the human host!
My eyes burned and lungs were seared by the streaming smoke and embers of a hellish world lost to endless darkness. I struggled to make out any insignia or specific design that would identify the warriors, but nothing bore any semblance to the days of old. Then, and as while observing the strange and almost symmetrical formation of the mountains, it struck me... They were not distant peaks or cliff edges, but rather the remains of a modern and fallen city! I was not witnessing some battle from the ancient days of yore, but the last stand of mankind!
"These are the end of days—witness as mankind falls and darkness reigns once more." The demon that was patient 1366 stood mere yards away, while glaring in ghastly delight. There was a fire blazing within the empty sockets of his charred and torn features, as he spat while saying, "You will fall, Michael—you will all burn, and your bodies be torn asunder upon the bloodied and blackened battlefields before the hosts of hell."
I could only stare in utter horror and disbelief at the blazing nightmare of blood and death that surrounded us on all sides. Enormous dark and

crawling things crushed the life out of the opposing army, as hordes of corpses and unimaginable horrors flooded the enemy's gates! Bodies of men were torn and broken, only to be cast aside to become engulfed in some other nightmare, and fight again upon the side of Hell!

"And what of you—that would bow like a dog beneath a master that causes you eternal suffering and damnation." Terrified and desperate, I pointed an accusing finger at the demon, and said, "Why do you continue to fight against that which you know to be true? Though fallen—do you not still remain as one of the Elohim?"

Strangely amused, the demon now moved closer, and grinning through broken and razor sharp teeth, cried out hatefully, "And how does your master reward you? Look out upon these battlefields and the pitiful ending of your kind." A cruel smile twisted its already hideous countenance, as it said, "Your master disregards their pleas for mercy, and turns a blind eye to their suffering and pitiful ending." There was a moment of reflection, as though haunted by some bitter and distant memory, it looked back to me and spat, "I fight to spite this false god of whom you so blindly follow, and to watch his faithful grovel and lay dying in their own blood and filth. Cry out for mercy—if you will. But, you shall only fall, your entrails ripped out, the flesh stripped from your bones, and your soul sent to burn!"

"I pity you for the memory of what you once were and have since become." Upon gazing upon the fiend, it faltered briefly and seemed suddenly confused. A scorching wind blew across the plains of destiny and from somewhere an angel wept... Regaining its vile composure, it became infuriated, as pointing a trembling finger into my face, it hissed, "Cry out if you will—plead for your master to save you!" It grinned, spittle, filth and blood running from between its blackened teeth, "Breath wasted, and better used for the screams that will soon end your pathetic existence."

Utter madness burned in those eyes, evil purely for the sake of evil, and I finally understood. I had often wondered as to what sickness drove murderers into a mindless, blood-lust. It was never possession or even obsession, but the evil of personal desire. If the fall of mankind ever came to pass, through personal evil, we would have brought it down upon ourselves...

From out of the darkness a firm hand suddenly took me by the wrist, and drawing me upward, pulled me free of the filth and decay,

"Come—Michael--," Holding his staff high, Marlowe brightened the blackness while leading me away, "You have wandered too far and are required elsewhere in space and time..."

I awoke suddenly as Amica gently shook me from where we had lain together in the blankets upon the office floor, "Michael—something moves in the darkness of the attic."

I had rolled over in the blackness, and looked up while we listened in the stillness. The little lamp had been turned off, and through the blackness all things seemed that much more intense. At first there had been nothing but the steady beating of my own heart and Amica's gentle breathing as she pressed her face close to mine. Then, as the stillness slowly returned to the night, I heard it. It came as a feint scratching, a clicking sound, and then the unmistakeable squeaking of rusted and old bed springs bending beneath a large weight. We listened quietly for several moments as other sounds soon came. They were quiet little sounds, and quite similar to those that a curious baby playing within a crib might make.

"She really doesn't sound so dangerous?" I had looked to her for guidance, "What should we do?"

"If the guardian has permitted her here—," She thought for a moment as we listened to the tell-tale sounds of movements in the attic, "Perhaps we should do nothing at the moment."

"What about the others—shouldn't we warn them?"

Listening briefly, she looked back and said in whisper, "She has eaten and taken the shelter that was offered, and there is no threat to anyone on this night."

"And near the end of all things—she's finally come home."

"Not all that would seem evil are your enemies--," Gently pulling me back down into the blankets and drawing me close, she whispered, "All are safe tonight, close your eyes, dream and let go of this world for a while..."

Laying together and gazing into each other's eyes, I could feel the world slipping from all around me. A gentle calm slowly drifted from out of the night. Nothing else mattered at that moment, and the only awareness that I still had was for the comfort and warmth of her embrace.

"Caitlin--," Tenderly kissing her brow and closing my eyes, I whispered, "Follow me into the land of dreams—and stay there with me forever..."

"I might--," Kissing me softly, she quietly said, "If we are to ever become lost—look for me there—and I'll find you..."

Her words echoed in my thoughts as we closed our eyes and slipped away into the night together...

Deb Carlson was awakened suddenly and in the middle of the night. The room had been quiet, and with exception to the soft breathing of her husband, she couldn't imagine why. Other than the gentle ticking of the mantel clock that her mother had given them on their first anniversary, everything was absolutely still. Moving carefully as not to awaken her husband, she sat up in bed while looking toward the window.

The curtains had been left partially open, and something in the night now caused her to pause. Sleepily looking around the room while attempting to discover what might have disturbed her, she peered into the blackness of the window. It was shortly before the dawn when she thought to have seen something gazing back in at her. Her hand slipped to the charm that hung about her neck as she felt her heart skip. The clouds had parted ever so slightly and the dim moon light reflected in the chilled breath before her face.

Trembling, she had looked between her sleeping husband and the window several times, contemplating whether to wake him. In a moment of panic, she had held her breath, listening, watching in the darkness. Utter stillness...

Then there had been just the slightest sound, much like the pop and tick sound that fine crystal makes when cracking. It had been something very faint, but enough to draw her attention back to the bedroom window. It was the locking mechanism upon the window that now stood out to her, brighter and more vivid than ever before. The metal lock that by slight degrees, now appeared to have slowly been moving...

The only thought in that split-second had been to utter a silent prayer, her heart racing as something in the blackness halted, and the lock became absolutely still. She clung to the charm about her neck, her eyes fixed upon the lock and window. From somewhere in the darkness she thought to have heard someone speaking? As she listened, she heard what sounded like a multitude of voices whispering, fading until becoming the whistle of the wind in the distance.

Shivering, she rubbed at her arms while noticing the chill dissipating, and the darkness lightening by several degrees. Although she could never have proved it, all her instincts now told her that something had come for them in the night.

Slipping back down into bed, she drew the covers closely about her. Trembling violently, the hairs on the nape of her neck and forearms stood erect, as goose pimples tingled across her cold flesh. She would call and warn Michael and the others in the morning. Slipping up behind her still sleeping husband, she tightly closed her eyes while praying for the coming dawn...

Tanya sat awake long after the boys had gone to bed. Unable to sleep, she had made hot cocoa to calm her nerves, sitting at the large kitchen table, and listlessly gazed out the window. The heavens were heavy with clouds, but the moon's pale face peeked in from the blackness beyond.

Taking an oatmeal cookie from the plate in the center of the table, she nibbled at it. They weren't the best that she'd ever baked, but she was still getting used to the oven in Rich's house. The boys hadn't complained, in fact, they'd been delighted to have the fresh baked treats. Danny was growing up so fast, and as much as she hated to admit it, she feared losing him more than anything else. They may have been a broken family, according to the authorities that had shamed her when she'd asked for financial assistance, but she'd never regretted having him for a moment. Her greatest regret was never having enough money to provide the kind of a home that she felt he deserved....

Her eyes followed along the edges of the luxurious brown- and gold-trimmed draperies that lined all the windows in the enormous home. It must have cost a fortune to have all of that done. If she had only a fraction of the money that Rich so frivolously spent, she and Danny could have retired comfortably in a little house of their own.

A dark reflection in the window caught her eye. Taking a look, she saw the moon vanishing behind the blackened clouds again. The whirring and hum of the fridge caused her to jump as the pump started the cooling process all over again. Laughing at being startled by something so ridiculous, she rubbed at her brow and sighed deeply while looking around.

The floors were tiled in cream and chocolate brown designs, the cabinets were oak, the counters marble, and even the appliances were matched.

Moving from the chair and pausing before the fridge, she thought for a moment, and said, "Frigidaire—I didn't even know they came in this shade of brown?"

A sound had caused her to spin and she curiously gaze back toward the window, "It's your nerves—," She grumbled, saying, "Not that I have any left?"

The reflection in the large kitchen windows traveled as though the glass itself were being forced inward from beyond. Rubbing at her eyes, she looked twice, and then three times while slowly approaching the glass.

"Oh—you're starting to lose it, girl--," Whispering to herself, she swallowed hard while reaching out to touch the glass, "There's no way the wind is strong enough to budge this stuff." It was true: Rich had replaced all the windows with double panes of reinforced glass.

Stepping back, she turned to return to the table, but something had halted her. Was it just anxiety and paranoia —or was someone or something now watching her?

Slowly turning to look over her shoulder and back at the window, her blood suddenly ran cold... It wasn't something that she had seen or heard, but rather what she now sensed. Her eyes drifted into the darkness beyond the glass. In the dim light of the lamp posts she saw the swaying branches of the pines being tossed in a strong wind. And then, for no coherent reason, it had all just suddenly stopped. Absolute stillness as she stood there blinking and with her cup in her hand.

The lamp posts suddenly flashed from before the house, flickered, and then went out. Slowly backing away from the window, she felt suffocated with the absolute emptiness that seemed to be closing in from all about her!

There was a desperate sense of complete seclusion and vulnerability. Although they occupied a mansion in a highly regarded area, the large property spanned several acres and the nearest neighbor was well beyond sight or sound. She pondered, dared wonder whether anyone might even hear if she cried out for help? The sound of her heart pounding grew louder in her thoughts as her arties flooded with fear fueled adrenaline. Shaking, her eyes widened as she assumed to see something moving in the blackness beyond the window!

Startled as the fridge pump clicked loudly from behind her, she jumped, and spilling hot cocoa, hurried to the sink to clean up the mess.

No sooner had she done this, than did her skin crawl with the realization of having turned her back to the blackened glass... Her heart pounded furiously, as fearing to look back, she knew without a doubt that something was now there... Although she hadn't physically seen it, she sensed something infinitely old and colder than the grave...

A movement now came from behind her, as panicking, she prepared to scream! With wide eyes and trembling hands shoved before her mouth, she recognized the sound of soft footsteps in the dark hallway behind her. Too terrified to even move, much less look, she just stood there with her back to the dark corridor while paralyzed with fear!

They came ever so slowly and very softly, as cautiously entering into the kitchen from behind her... She screamed, spinning toward the source of the sound. The cup slipping from her trembling fingers smashed in an eruption of hot cocoa!

Danny jumped back in the hall when she shrieked. Then realizing to have frightened her, he swiftly raced into her open arms. She clung desperately to him, weeping hysterically as he gently rocked her in his arms.

"There was something in the window--," She gasped out the words, "And something was looking in at me when you came sneaking down the stairs…"

"I'm sorry for scaring you—but I wasn't sure if you were still awake?" Glancing back suspiciously, and seeing nothing there, he simply held her close while saying "It's okay now mom—if there was anything there—it's gone now."

Dennis rushed into the kitchen, his face flushed and eyes huge, "I heard a scream—what happened?" He looked fearfully between Danny and his mother, "Is everyone alright?"

"She saw something in the window?" Danny spun between the window and his friend, "But whatever it was—it seems to be gone now."

Holding her shaking hand before her eyes, Tanya discovered where the shattered mug had cut her right palm. The blood ran freely, dripping onto the floor and splattering her slippers. Shocked, she turned toward the boys.

"Oh damn--," Grabbing a roll of paper towel from off the kitchen counter, Danny looked to his friend, asking, "Could you please get the first aid kit—it's under the sink in the master bedroom."

Without question Dennis had just turned and swiftly hurried off.

Rinsing the wound in the sink, Danny gently bound it with paper towel, "Just hold that tight until Dennis gets back. It's not as serious as it looked—so we don't need to take you for stitches."

"That's a good thing--," She stared blankly, "Because nothing on earth could make me take either of you out there—nothing…"

Shuddering with the thought, he stared back at her defiantly, "If it ever came down to your life or going out there to save it? Then I'd take you and there'd be no damn argument, understand?"

"You're so much like your father--," The tears ran freely as she kissed his cheek, and said, "And he would've been so very proud of you."

"Watch where you step." Danny ignored the comment, busying himself with the broken shards of the mug, carefully picked up the shattered pieces, and dropped them on the counter.

His mother had used her good hand to retrieve a cloth and attempted to assist by wiping the spilled cocoa, but he had taken it from her, saying, "It's okay, mom, just keep pressure on that cut—and I'll deal with this."

"Danny, I couldn't see anything--," She struggled with the words, "But, I felt it out there…" Turning to peer back at the window, she whispered, "It was there—just watching me…"

"I've got the first aid kit." Dennis returned with the little box, and quickly providing Danny with gauze and tape, said, "It was buried behind some other things—sorry it took so long."

"I was thinking--," Danny nodded toward the window, informing his friend while he bandaged his mother's hand, "Maybe we'd better all stay together and down here tonight. It's almost morning anyway—what are a few hours just to be safe?"

"That's fine by me—I couldn't sleep anyway." Retrieving the broken pieces of the mug from the counter, he disposed of them into a trash can beneath the sink, "I'll bring some bedding down—and you get some lights on in this place."

"I'm sorry--," Tanya sniffled while wiping the tears from her eyes, "I suppose this whole thing is starting to really get to me."

"It's okay—it's getting to all of us--," Pulling the charm from beneath his red plaid pajama shirt, Danny said, "But we're together—and we have these."

"They've put symbols of protection around the doors and windows--," Tanya pointed to the windows, walls and ceiling, "They're all over and around this place. So we should be safe as long as we stay inside."

"Not from everything--," Shivering, he pointed toward the window while saying, "And not from those--…"

"Please, don't say it--," She interrupted him and pleadingly said, "Don't talk about those things in the darkness and not at night…"

Drifting slowly from out of the blackness, an enormous shadow passed from behind the window. It hung there unnoticed, as with tendrils of black smoke, tested each and every crack and crevice of the old sill. All of a sudden it whipped back as though having come into contact with a powerful electrical charge! With blinding speed it was repelled by sacred script and ornament, as receding, swiftly vanished into the surrounding blackness of the forest! There was a sudden sound of rising winds, and a howl of primal rage shrieked in the distance!

Horrified by the clearly undefinable and unnatural sound, Danny and his mother clung together as they spun toward the window in absolute terror!

Resounding through the dark forest, it howled like the winds of a hurricane in passing as it faded into the distant night. There was no sound similar and it would be indescribable to anyone unfamiliar with the nightmares that nature could release.

"That wasn't any wind--," Holding his mother tightly as they stared aghast, he whispered, "It was the devil at our window tonight..."

"Let's get into the main room—and get some light on in this place." She whispered as while half dragging him, they scrambled out of the kitchen and down the dark hall.

Entering into the enormous living room, they hurriedly went in different direction while turning on lights and stoking the huge hearth. The fire had been burning from earlier, but almost embers, Tanya piled the wood high.

Quickly switching on the large lamps that stood on the end tables, Danny dropped onto the couch while watching as his mother tightly closed the draperies. With his mind spinning, he attempted to focus upon anything but the horror of what had just happened. His eyes fell upon the lamps, which standing three feet tall and with cream shades, were unique in their design. They were a bizarre blend of faux wood and metal. The bases and tops were cylindrical in shape, ornate and brushed in a brass tone. A faux wood formed the middle of the lamp, and the central part was four metal-caged chambers. Each of the chambers contained candle-light bulbs, which operated as a tri-light when desiring subtle ambience. They were both rustic and gothic in appearance, and hadn't held his attention for nearly long enough...

"Your mom's right—there is something out there." Dennis dropped linens and blankets onto the two couches, startling his companions, as he said, "Did you hear that wind howling—it was like nothing on earth."

"It's still out there and watching us—I can feel it..." Dropping onto the couch between the boys, she spoke in a whisper, saying, "It's trying to find a way to get in..."

Looking to where the draperies had separated in the middle just slightly, they watched the darkness beyond... There was a sense of impending doom, a desperate urge to escape that place, and simply run as fast and far away as possible. But they all understood the consequences of succumbing, and what would certainly happen in the moment that they left that house....

"Let's make beds--," She struggled to retain what remained of her composure and support the two young men, "There's no point just sitting here and staring out there—we'll just fall apart that much faster before morning."

Drawing the leather couches closer and so that they faced one another, they sorted the sheets and blankets into beds for themselves. It was hard to remain calm, their eyes continually darting to the window and then back to where they worked.

It was a feeling that Tanya had known all too well and from when she and little Danny had first been alone. Broke and destitute, desperation had caused her to work as a waitress in a local night club. The hours had been long and the company poor, but she justified the effort as they had needed the money. Worst of all, she had been forced to walk a long alley between several old buildings and to a bus stop each night. It was before she had known anyone well enough to have been offered a lift home, and she remembered those long, cold and dark nights. Those moments where fearing every shadow, she had almost run the distance, watching, wondering who might be waiting for her in the dark. Often she had feared that some dark stranger would appear from behind a dumpster, and that she might never see little Danny again.

It all flooded back to her now as she fought back the tears, and the fear that caused her to tremble and stumble as she moved. Danny had caught her, and seeing her terror, hugged her close, "It's going to be okay—don't worry, mom, we won't let anything happen to you."

The wind had howled among the pines, rattling the window panes and their nerves along with it. Through the darkness and doubt something in their hearts spoke of an unnatural evil that they all knew now hunted them...

"What are we going to do?" Dennis whispered while they cringed among the blankets and between the couches.

"Nothing--," Tanya sniffled, "Michael said that no matter what happens—that we can't leave the house—and to never go into the darkness."

"Then we'll just stay close to the fire--," Dennis agreed. Tossing more wood into the large hearth, he said, "We have more than enough wood to last the night."

"It's just after five--," Danny motioned toward the antique cuckoo clock that hung from above the couch, "It should be light around seven."

"Should we call Michael and Rich? Maybe they'll--." Dennis paused as his mother shook her head without a moment's thought.

"They won't come," Danny whispered, "They can't—not in the dark..."

Tanya had pulled both of them close, as slipping deeper into the cushions of the couch, silently huddled together. The lights had flickered, the lamps flashed and then all had become dark. With the shadows of the flames dancing demonically from all about them, they silently clung to one another and prayed.

"Should we get flashlights?" Danny whispered, "There in the kitchen drawer, and it'll only take a second."

"I don't think that they'd do much good—," She argued, "Let's just stay here altogether—and keep the fire burning bright."

CHAPTER EIGHT

Monday, January 27th, 1975.

The morning had arrived in a deep gloom as heavy clouds once more darkened the shadow haunted skies. I had awakened in my bed, and was surprised to discover Amica resting beside me. We had fallen asleep together, as fully clothed and still atop the covers, still held onto one other. It had been the first true sleep that I had in months.

Moving quickly and quietly, I managed not to disturb her as while climbing from off the bed. Carefully closing the door behind me, I slipped into the hallway and hurriedly made my way into the office. I had listened for any signs of movement from the attic. After several moments of absolute silence, I had assumed that Trudy must have departed at first light. This bothered me considerably, as I could not imagine where something so large could conceal itself during the day. There was always the possibility of a nest—but I dreaded the thought. What if this creature was hermaphroditic like certain frogs or snails, and didn't require a mate to reproduce? The thought of destroying it prevailing over all others, I forced myself to remember Amica's words. Or had it been the influence of the demon over Amica, misleading us toward some imminent destruction?

"I am with you, have no fear, my friend--," Marlowe interrupted the thoughts, saying, "The creature is beyond a means of procreation and poses no threat to you or your companions."

"And—what about Amica, can I truly trust her counsel?"

"You possess the senses and sensibility to know the difference—and you become more aware of both as the time passes. You must not invoke the unclean spirit in questioning that which only the demon may know or hold dominion. For in doing so, with each effort the beast grows stronger within her."

"So, as long as I treat her as though she knows nothing—it won't possess her body as quickly." I had whispered the thought, but Marlowe had swiftly hushed me.

"Be wary, for though she no longer hears or senses all—the beast is always listening and aware…"

"Thank you--," Looking to the golden beryl, I sunk back into my chair, "I'll heed your warnings and as always, appreciate your guidance, Marlowe."

There hadn't been any reply in return and I simply moved from the chair and departed the office. I felt stale and my hair was stiff with the dry climate of the hot water heating.

Going into the washroom and locking the door, I intended to indulge a quick shower. Slipping out of my clothing and piling it neatly upon the hamper, I paused for some reason and stared into the far corner of the room. Drawn almost against my will, I slowly walked across the tiled floor and paused before the old mirror. Carefully testing the sheet to make certain that it was tightly covered, I stood as though mesmerized while caught in a thought.

"Caitlin really loves this old thing--," Sighing deeply, I contemplated, saying, "And I just know that it would break her heart if I dragged it out of here, and locked it away in the vault."

Running a hand the length of the frame, I could feel the smooth shapes of the intimate figures embraced beneath. In thought I had imagined Caitlin returning to find it missing, and the look of sadness and betrayal upon her face in my having removed it. Saddened and feeling guilt beyond words, I muttered in thought, "If it's covered and left in a corner, it should be just fine. Shouldn't it?"

It had always seemed to be a battle of conscience whenever I considered removing it. I knew the ever present danger and consequences, but with me, love had always prevailed over common sense. In truth, I could have kicked myself...

"Let's think this over--," Drawing my hand from the frame and walking back toward the sink, I looked into the bathroom mirror, "We still have time. They still have to come and get Pan and the Maiden."

After showering and slipping into my favorite black bath robe, I proceeded to brush my teeth. The mirror was still fogged by steam, and as I brushed a hand across it, was shocked to see Amica's reflection from behind me!

Waving the pointed end of a coat-hanger, she smiled, "Sorry—I need the bathroom and saw that this would fit into the lock-hole in the door to gain access."

"Don't you think that was rather inappropriate?"

"Only if you feel that soiling the hall carpet would be less inappropriate?" She gently shoved me out of the bathroom, and with a smile, closed the door

Standing in the hall with my tooth brush in hand and my mouth still hanging open, Merlin had slowly walked past the door, and having noticed, glanced up.

"Sure, go ahead and laugh—just wait until she takes over your litterbox…"

His ears had gone back as those golden eyed had become wide. For a moment it had seemed as though he had understood, but then yawning, he casually wandered into my office.

8:30 a.m.

Stumbling down the stairs, I caught the railing, as half-blind, was still attempting to wake up. I loathed the earliest part of the day, but circumstances being what they were, was required to take advantage of the daylight.

"I've already contacted the work crews—," Rich poured tea, "They started arriving a few minutes ago."

"The sooner they get this done, the better off we'll all be--," Thanking him for the tea, I rubbed sleep from my eyes, and said, "It's getting harder to get out of bed—I almost stayed there today."

"You look better rested than usual--," He remarked, shrugging, and admitted, "I was restless and didn't sleep a wink. I had the notion that someone or something was here in the house with us, last night…"

"You were right—Trudy was here sometime during the night."

Rich almost tipped over his juice glass while sitting straight up and staring, "What did you say?"

"Trudy was up in the attic last night--," I repeated, "Amica and I heard her moving about .The old floorboards and bed-springs make enough noise to wake the dead…"

"Why didn't you come and wake us?" Raymond and Tim appeared from out of the kitchen while bringing the breakfast.

"Well, to be honest, it seemed like a rather bad idea at the time. We might have either startled the creature or caused her to panic, and possibly attack us. Or she might have just flown off never to be seen again."

"He has a good point." Placing down the platters of food, Raymond looked to Rich, and said, "If you're trying to make it comfortable with humans—we should give it a chance to settle in here first."

"What happened to--," Tim gestures with both hands as though firing revolvers, and said, "Blowing it from here to eternity?"

"If it was in here with us last night and never tried anything funny--," Raymond replied with a thoughtful glance, "Then maybe it's worth giving Rich and this thing a chance?"

"Thank you--," The comment had come quickly, but was sincere. Looking to me, Rich asked, "I was thinking—maybe we could build her something better—something on the property?"

"Let's cross that bridge when we come to it--," I looked to Rich, "But for now, let's just refill her food dish and make her comfortable. Maybe she'll be calm enough to approach once she realizes that we've accepted her here?"

"That makes perfect sense—in a creepy, crawly kind of way." Raymond shuddered at the thought, "Still, the idea of living under a giant man-eating roach is just damn unsettling."

"Do you think that they'll get those gates in place before night-fall?" Tim came out of the kitchen with the previously promised waffles and fruit.

"Well, as long as the weather holds up—," Rich plucked several waffles from the plate, "They should have this together some time this afternoon."

"We also got a call from Deb Carlson this morning--," Tim's eyes seemed sunken due to the dark circles beneath them, "She said that they had a visitor in the night."

"The darkness is moving again--," Pouring tea, I shivered, saying, "I hope that you asked her to remind everyone at the office to wear those amulets at all times."

"I certainly did, and she sounded really scared--," Clasping his hands upon his breast as he leaned back into the chair, he frowned, "I've never heard her talk like that before. She sounded like the devil had paid her a personal visit and peeked in the window last night."

"That's because he did." Buttering his toast and grimacing, Rich leaned toward me, saying, "We need to make a move soon—I get the feeling that things are about to get real nasty again..."

"It's testing the boundaries—and trying to force us to make a mistake in the process." Squeezing lemon into my tea, I looked around the table, "We just need to secure those gates before we consider making a move of any kind."

"Well—they're already at it out there--," Raymond brought more toast to the table, saying, "I can hear them pounding away at those rails to seat the old gates—so it shouldn't be too much longer."

"I sure hope so--," Taking a swallow of orange juice, Tim glanced back at me, "Because it's already gone after Red Cloud, Deb, Carrie and Tanya— so who's next?"

"Things will come together--," I promised the impossible, "And somehow, we'll figure this out…"

"Simms's called to confirm his noon appointment." Raymond mentioned it while he remembered, saying, "He sounds pretty rattled about this investigation—I've never seen him like this before."

"Who can really blame him--," Scoffing at the thought, I said, "Could you even imagine what this must be doing to him? He spent his life chasing down bodies—and now they're chasing him…"

Amica had casually wandered into the room, and taking a seat beside me, had politely greeted everyone. She wore the black gown that we had previously purchased, and I noticed that she appeared rather concerned while looking to Rich, and asking, "Are you alright—you look a little rough?"

"I didn't sleep a single wink all night--," He sighed, looking up as Tim graciously served coffee, and he said, "I had the worst nightmares."

Oddly enough, his poor condition had previously evaded my notice. Whether it had been the dismal lighting, or simply some fault on my part, I was uncertain. But when looking again, I noticed his sickly pallor, and the darkness that hung all too deeply beneath his eyes. It seemed to have withered and aged him considerably, and almost over-night.

"Did you care to share the details of those nightmares?" I had shrugged, "Sometimes it helps to give up the ghost, so to speak."

It was the first time that I had ever seen him hesitate about sharing something as simple as a dream. Sipping at my tea, I motioned with a kindly gesture of my hand, urging that he share. He did this in a rather quiet manner, and in a nervous way completely foreign to his general character.

"I dreamed of a distant island—with foggy shores, and a dark lake on the edge of the dawn." He began, hesitating as appearing confused, rubbed at his sleep-filled eyes.

"It sounds almost darkly romantic--," It had been a futile attempt on my part to encourage him, as sighing, I said, "Please—continue."

"I couldn't see anything but walls of fog from all around, except from where dark hills seemed to peek out and rise in the distance." Stirring far too much cream and sugar into his coffee, he sipped at the hot fluids before continuing, "There were torches burning around a mansion on the island, but I didn't see anyone. Somehow, I sensed that there were people there, but they were hiding for whatever reason."

"That's symbolic of how we exist now." Waving his toast, Tim nodded, saying, "Or it might even be the way that the enemy sees us from the other side of the gates."

I took several waffles, and avoiding the syrup under Amica's ever watchful eye, nodded at Rich, "So, what happened next?"

"I saw an old man--," Rich poured syrup over his pancakes and drowned the pork sausages on his plate, "He wore a heavy and hooded, dark cloak. His beard was long and white, his hair was flowing behind him, and he walked with a staff. At first, I would've guessed that he was a mystic or Druid. But he was different in ways, and seemed both modern and ancient at the same time."

Raymond shoveled a heap of bacon onto his waffles, and neatly pouring syrup over everything, asked, "Could he have been this Marlowe character that we hear so much about?"

"It wasn't him—I'm sure of that." Shaking his head, Rich waved a fork in thought, saying,

"I felt that the old man lived in that place—or at least owned it. And as I watched him, he walked toward a stone gate that surrounded the castle. But just as he came to where he could've entered, he stopped suddenly. It was almost as though he'd encountered some kind of invisible wall or barrier. For some reason, I had the strongest desire to help him get into that place. I'm not sure why—I just knew that I had to get him in there no matter what happened."

"So, what did you do?" Tim's eyes were wide with anticipation.

"I wandered up the stone steps from out of that fog--," Rich explained, "But when I got to the top of that hill and reached the old fellow, he had gone all dark and solid as stone. I turned to look and see what had stopped him, but there was nothing there. There was an opening between the stone walls as wide as a car, and nothing blocking his passage. At that point, I could make out the forms and shape of the mansion from just above the drifting mist, and saw figures through a dimly lit window. They were on the main level, and seemed to be watching, beckoning for me to come to them."

The short hairs on the nape of my neck stood on end, and I sensed something bad on the horizon. I had looked to Amica, who slowly indulging her breakfast, had not removed her attention from Rich for a single moment.

"I walked through the passage between the walls and then out into a courtyard." He spoke slowly, and as though recounting the event through previous visitation rather than the recollection of a dream, "As I walked toward the place, I saw that it was more like a mansion, or an old English estate. I stopped at the foot of a wide, stone stairway that led to an alcove and the main doors."

At that point in the story, Amica had just peered up at me, and then looking down, focused her attention entirely upon her meal. The reaction had roused suspicion, and now caused me to place my fork down, and listen even closer as Rich continued.

"It was like everything had suddenly gone into slow motion." His features twisted with the memory, "The doors flew open, and from out of the darkness came these two figures. At first, I couldn't really make them out. But then, as they came down the stairs toward me, I recognized them both! It was Caitlin and Eva, and they were wearing what looked like old fashioned funeral gowns. They came at me with outstretched arms--," His features grew dark and sickened, as wincing, he looked to me and mumbled, "But as they came closer, I realized that they were dead and rotting corpses... I tried to run, but couldn't move my legs. I screamed, cried out for help—but they grabbed and pulled me down!" He began to visibly shake, his eyes huge and filled with horror, saying, "Then, something came out of the fog. It flew from over the lake and out of the mist. It was some kind of pale, hideous thing with dragon wings. It had the head of a ram, and there was some kind of a flame on its horns..."

Amica had dropped her fork onto the plate and we had all stopped and stared.

"I just woke up at that point—and was gasping for breath, and soaked in an icy sweat. I've been awake ever since—and that was around five this morning."

"That was a real whopper of a nightmare!" Raymond had taken a firm hold upon Rich's shoulder, attempting to make light of things, "You should write that down, maybe Michael can use it somewhere in his book?"

Raymond was closer to the truth than he might have imagined. Peering back at Amica, I suspected that she knew something that she now withheld...

"With everything that's happened, and with Eva's loss, this really isn't so surprising." Tossing down my napkin with a shrug, I said, "Stress related dreams are the worst—and I'm sure that we've all been experiencing our fair share."

"I really hope that you're right--," Rich had stared across the table at me, "Before I woke up from that dream, I heard your voice, Michael." His stare became so intense that I thought his eyes might explode from their sockets, "You told me that Caitlin and Eva were both dead, and that Scott, Carrie and Maya were trapped in that place..."

"Christ, have mercy." Raymond cursed, "It was just a dream, brother, lighten the hell up."

"He has experienced premonitions before--," I had spoken in Rich's defense, "So, I can understand why something this vivid might cause reason for concern."

"What--," Tim had just looked over to me as the eggs fell from his fork, "Are you saying that there might be a possibility that there's some fact to this dream?"

"I'm not entirely excluding the possibility." Returning my attention to Rich, I spoke in a low tone and calm manner, "It might be a good idea to call the girls this morning—a little reassurance never hurts."

There hadn't been any verbal reaction, but his expression had clearly revealed his thoughts. It was quite apparent that he was not expecting to reach them, not now or ever again. It was enough to force me to move from my seat, and politely insist that he join me in the kitchen. He had moved slowly at first, but then followed me out of the dining area.

"Please, make that telephone call." I had nodded to the phone resting upon the kitchen counter and patiently waited. Nervously looking at the telephone and then to where I sat across from him in the breakfast nook, he reluctantly groaned. Although apprehensive, he eventually took a firm hold of the receiver, and then slowly dialled the number.

His fingers had moved instinctively as he had dialled the number so often that it had been committed to memory. Slipping down into the nook, he had just stared blankly as the number rang. It had seemed an eternity as we had just sat there gazing upon one another, and then the call was answered.

"Hello--," His eyes widened as the receiver now visibly shook in his trembling hand, his features becoming pale as he slowly stared back at me, "It's good to hear from you, too."

There was something increasingly disturbing about the call as he stiffened in his seat, and holding the receiver away from his ear, stuttered as he spoke, "Eva said that she'll go out into the garden and fetch them."

Leaping forward and ripping the phone from his grasp, I slammed the receiver back down onto its base! We had both just sat there shaking for several moments, and then sliding the phone back toward my friend, I insisted, "Dial again."

He did this with the greatest of reluctance, but desperation forced his fingers. Once more he sat and waited as the number rang. The moments seemed to pass like hours as the silence became suffocating. He suddenly gasped, and I knew that the call had been answered. He turned to look back at me again, but this time he spoke with the greatest of surprise, "Maya—sweetheart, is that really you?" His expression twisted with fear, shock, and then sudden relief, "No, everything is just fine darling." He looked to me as he spoke, "We were just worried and wondering how you and Caitlin were doing—are you holding out okay? We've all been wrecks since we got the news about Eva."

Sinking back into the seat and covering my eyes with both hands, I could feel my heart pounding as the fear raced like fire through my veins. Moving from the nook, I made my way back out into the dining room, and raising a hand before my friends, said, "Everything is just fine—Rich is speaking with Maya right now. But, I'm feeling a little rough—and need to relax before our company arrives. I'm going up to my office, please let me know when our guests come calling."

"I'll knock on your door about fifteen minutes before we expect them." Tim volunteered, "That way you can freshen up a little."

With a wave and polite nod in parting I had left the breakfast table.

They had just watched as I went toward the stairs with Amica in swift pursuit. Her concern was obvious by her expression, but deep behind those emerald eyes, I sensed some element of dark mystery. It was a secret that I fully intended on finding out.

For the first time in many years I had closed the office door as she had followed. We had taken our usual places, and pausing in thought, I had curiously looked over at her, "Amica, what did you hide from the others while Rich shared the dream?"

Her eyes had flashed briefly, as bowing her head, she softly said, "You already know that this was not just some dream. In his mind he has seen the sanctuary—the demon, and through his fear, might reveal all to the enemy."

"Then he can't leave the estate--," The thoughts raced through my mind, "The darkness will see into his fears and give us all away. But, did it already discover this when he made the telephone call this morning?"

"No--," Slowly shaking her head, she brushed the hair from my eyes, "All that was revealed were voices in multiple streams of energy. As for Richard, all that it will take to preserve our secret is to provide him with a false image. You must show him a photograph of a distant place, something that he will focus upon rather than the dream."

"And what about the fiend that he saw in his dream?"

"We both already know the nature of the beast." She had looked away from me, saying, "And, I fear the part that it may play before the end of all things…"

Going to the window and looking out into the dull grays between the dark heavens, I peered down upon the frozen earth. Without any true light or dark in comparison, we now drifted through shades of gray in a land of shadows. It was a place where doubt would only lead to destruction, and necessity meant breaking physical and even moral boundaries… I would have preferred to explain the situation to Rich, but realized the significance of misleading him. It was the same reason that I had refused knowledge of their haven, or spoken to Caitlin. Some secrets had divine purpose, and regrettably some lies were designed to protect the innocent…

"Nothing is written in stone—maybe the fates will be merciful." Looking to where she now sat in the chair near my desk, I sighed deeply, "Maybe, there is still hope for you?"

"Our concern now is to shield Maya and the others--," She refused to continue the discussion any further, "Not waste precious time and harbor false hopes in the face of the inevitable…"

Sensing her darkness and remembering Marlowe's words of warning, I dropped the subject, saying, "I have some photographs of old mansions that I took a few years ago. I'm sure that there is something there that we can use for Richard."

Moving from the chair, she leaned down beside me in a gentle embrace, saying, "There is much beauty and wonder waiting beyond the horizon. All that we have to do is believe, and trust that we shall all meet there again, someday."

Gently stroking her long and soft hair, I had looked deeply into her eyes as through the depths of despair, and thought to have seen a fleeting hope? It was only a faint glimmer, but enough to carry me onward as even a slight chance was still far better than none.

We had held one another not as lovers, but as dear friends. There was a depth of emotion well beyond the carnal desires of the flesh. It was pure as the morning light and seemed to cast out all other fear and doubt. I had closed my eyes, remembering better times, and moments seeming forever lost…

"Yes—close your eyes—if but for even a single moment." She placed a palm across my face, the soothing warmth and darkness carrying all fear and doubt far away.

I had moved to speak, but she had only hushed me, and then gently forced me back down into the chair. The world grew absolutely still as the solace of the darkness carried my thoughts into utter nothingness. For a while it felt as though I were as light as a feather, and drifting, floating in the absence. Then, I became aware of warmth, and a light that shone from the distance. Drawn without thought or intention, I began slowly drifting toward the strange and brilliantly shining anomaly. A sound now followed the light: A soft whispering that seemed to come from all directions as while growing louder within approach. There was a strange recognition, as though following distant pathways to a familiar destination or source. Realizing to have been attracted by familiar polarities and a common destiny, I could only continue with burning desire and blind determination! Then, there was the steady and irrefutable echo of a heartbeat, one that I soon realized to have been my own. There was a benign presence, and an undeniable and overwhelming sense of love that now carried me safely through the darkness. A sudden and brilliant light shone as, being raised up, I was gently placed into the loving arms of my mother. It was my arrival into this world and the love and warmth had overwhelmed me...

Awakening suddenly, I discovered Amica fast asleep in the chair beside the desk. There had grown a type of vulnerability to the entity during her mortal change. She appeared so innocent, so foreign and lost in this world. It was so hard to even conceive of how such a gentle creature must suffer with the hidden horror that lay buried within her... There was a type of mystique that often left me spellbound in matters concerning Amica. As even though the horror of what would come, I loved this lost soul more dearly with each passing day. Still, there was a subtle beauty through ugliness, as within her final release from the demon in dying, I would willingly pay the penance in blood...

The clock chimed once, and realizing the hour, I had wondered if we had missed the appointment with Simms? Then smiling, I laughed while remembering that this clock was never adjusted in accord with day-light savings. It was the only time-piece in my home that was permitted this idiosyncrasy, and naturally the one that I depended upon the most.

Opening her eyes to the sounds of footsteps upon the stairs, she leapt up light as a feather, and swiftly opened the office door. Surprised with her swift reaction as he held his hand up to knock on the door, Tim gasped, "Our guests have arrived."

"Thanks for the warning—and I can't even see straight yet--," Patting his shoulder, I had curiously looked to Amica, and sighing deeply, asked, "Are you ready for this?"

"Just allow me a few moments to fix my hair and freshen up a little--," Politely acknowledging Tim, she promptly turned and hurrying toward the washroom, said, "Go ahead without me, and I'll be down to serve tea and coffee shortly."

Slowly shaking his head, Tim muttered, "If we can't tell the two apart--," He looked to me with a strange glint in his eye, "And believe me, I can't anymore. The authorities certainly won't know the difference."

"There is a definite resemblance--," I had admitted while receiving a questionable glance from my friend, and saying, "I'll admit that it's striking, but I can still tell them apart easily enough."

"Sweetheart--" Amica had called as she peeked out from the open bathroom door, "Do you have any idea of where my big hair-brush ended up?"

"It's in the top drawer of the bedroom bureau, honey—" I answered without thought, "And exactly where you left it after you and Eva went away…"

The words had caught in the back of my throat, as thanking me, she had quickly vanished back into the bathroom .Tim just stared. I had realized the mistake in the last moment and looked away in shame. Was it finally happening? Had she truly taken Caitlin's place in my thoughts, heart, and home? And then I remembered that it was the intention of the masquerade, and nothing more… Or was it?

"We shouldn't keep our guests waiting too long." Motioning with a nod for me to follow, Tim offered a subtle glance in warning, "You know what Rich can get like if you leave him alone with religious people or the authorities…"

"He should be alright—he has Raymond with him." Looking to Tim with little concern, I'd caught the questioning glint in his eye. Rather than debating the matter any longer, his concern had carried me out of the hall and down the stairs that much faster.

When we came into the living room we were surprised to discover that Detective Simms had brought a companion. There were all comfortably seated about the hearth, coffee had already been served, and Raymond offered pastry. It appeared to be a friendly gathering, although our previous encounter had left much to be desired.

"Welcome back detective." Extending a hand in greeting, I turned and looked to his guest.

Considerably younger and taller than his associate, he hair was black and trimmed very shortly and in military fashion. His features were noble, his eyes were blue, and he sported a neatly trimmed mustache. He wore plain clothes, spoke in a deep voice, and smiled pleasantly as we greeted one another,

"I'm Sergeant, Ian MacTavish, head of Missing Persons. I've heard quite a bit about you—and your organization."

"Well, I'm sure that you have--," Winking and grinning facetiously, Rich settled back into the couch while proudly saying, "We've been known to ruffle a few feathers at the department from time to time."

"If it was just a matter of a few ruffled feathers--," Distraught, Detective MacTavish frowned while saying, "Then we wouldn't be here today."

"Alright then, let's cut to the chase." Returning to his seat and waving at Simms, Raymond urged that he speak. It was obvious that the formalities had ended. Reaching for a black leather briefcase that rested beside him, Simms had emptied the contents, and placed the files and documents onto the coffee table before us.

"I'm assuming that Raymond's already given you the details as to why we're here—," Peering suspiciously around the house and then at me, he tapped a finger upon the heaped files, saying, "So here's the hard evidence, police reports, ballistics, and coroners results. Now, I didn't come here today to begin where we left off the last time." Looking to me and sighing deeply, he fidgeted with a pen and notepad, saying, "I'd like to start fresh—and leave anything that we said or did in the past. Now, I realize that we're dealing with some things here that go well beyond any rational explanation. That having been said, I would also like to clarify that anything shared here is strictly confidential."

"Now when you say confidential--," Looking curiously between the two officers, Rich squinted skeptically, asking, "Does that mean that it's confidential in the sense that only police records will reflect any shared information? Or that this is going to remain off the record and just between us?"

Sensing Rich's blatant disregard for law and authority, and obviously annoyed, Simms clasped his hands tightly before him, and staring intently upon Rich, said, "You tried to steal a candy bar from Becker's store on the west side when you were nine. At age twelve you were discovered drunk and urinating in the Principal's office at Princess Margaret Secondary, one of the few schools that would even have you. You were busted at sixteen in an uninsured vehicle with no driver's license or insurance, multiple times... Mr. MacDonald--," Unimpressed, Simms forced a toothy smile and spoke through it as though he might just draw a revolver and shoot Rich where he sat, "I would appreciate it very much if we could just cut with the bullshit—and proceed with the matters at hand..."

"Oh--," Brushing it off with a friendly smile and shrugging, Rich said, "By all means, carry on."

"Before we become any more involved--," Looking between Simms and his partner in dark warning, I said, "You should be aware that what happened to our friend Harry could and might just as easily happen to either of you..."

"Please, explain that so that we can both understand what you mean in saying that." Obviously intimidated, Simms was taking no chances and appeared threatened by the statement.

"Anyone who gets too close to this situation places themselves directly under threat of death—," Speaking slowly while gazing between them, I said, "Or quite possibly something far worse."

"I know how that may sound--," Rich defended the statement, "But you need to be aware that any information provided here will put you both in immediate danger. There's a good possibility that when you pass out of those gates today, neither of you might live through the night."

Apprehensive, Simms looked to his partner and glanced back to Rich in question. It was apparent just by his reactions that he was no longer the skeptical and arrogant individual I had previously encountered. I could see that he was far more cautious, paranoid and even frightened to some degree.

"Would you be kind enough to enlighten us as to the reasons why?"

"It's the same reason that people keep dying around us--," Rich thought for a moment, "As crazy as it may sound? Something is hunting all of us. And as we've already learned from previous experience, it doesn't like outside interference and never leaves witnesses..."

"Guessing from all the evidence--," Raymond motioned toward the accumulated files and documents, "And the fact that you're even here—you already have some idea of what he means..."

"I'm married and have a four year old daughter--," Swallowing hard, Sergeant McTavish turned to look at Simms, visibly unsettled, as he said, "I'm not sure about this—but will proceed at your discretion."

The comment had left Simms at something of a disadvantage and somewhat reluctant to reply. A distinct shadow of doubt and fear now reflected within his usually stern gaze, as looking between the piled documents and his fellow officer, he suddenly fell silent. It was obvious that he was weighing all the odds before speaking, and that the scales had not tipped in our favor...

"I'm alone in this world—and am only putting myself at risk." He looked to the young Sergeant, "If you'd prefer to avoid getting involved any further, I really wouldn't blame you."

Remaining silent as the younger officer contemplated the situation, I suddenly realized the full impact that the investigation had placed upon the two men. They were both visibly scared while still appearing determined to find the answers. I wasn't sure if they were truly heroes of society or simply brain-washed, government watch-dogs.

"I'll stay with the investigation--," Sergeant McTavish swallowed hard, his eyes glassy, "We don't really have much choice in the matter—and all roads seemed to lead here."

"I've seen what this thing can do--," Raymond looked to the Sergeant while expressing his sincerest concerns for the young man, and said, "And, we can't promise to be able to protect you or your family. So, please consider this further before making a final decision. Because, once you step into this circle there are only two ways out."

"Dead—in either case--," Rich nervously fingered at a cherry pastry, as slowly pulling it apart, he said in a sinister tone, "Except in one you rest peacefully—and in the other you become the devil's puppet ... and something too horrible to even describe."

"It seems to me that the world is involved whether they choose to be or not." The Sergeant solemnly replied, "And that we're all moving targets, and that it's just a matter of time... I'd rather have the opportunity to make a difference than hide while hoping that we're not noticed."

"I realize how insane this must sound--," I had attempted to offer some rational semblance of an explanation, "But, what we have encountered here is some darker aspect of the forces of nature. It's an elemental, a pure form of evil that has the ability to manipulate the dead, as well as summon forces beyond our understanding. I'm afraid, that for the most part we've become prisoners of our own home. We never leave the property between the hours after dusk or before the dawn."

Looking down and clasping his hands tightly, Simms had nodded knowingly, and said, "We were already aware of that. I've had your place watched since the homicide case with your friend Harry." He glanced back at me, "And, might I add, on a long list of spook-show stake-outs this place has top billing down at the precinct."

"I told you--," Tapping a finger against his coffee cup, Rich shot a cynical glance in my direction, "It was just a matter of time before the law became involved."

"What else do we know about this entity or whatever it is?" Sergeant McTavish was visibly scared, and with a family at home to worry about, I really couldn't blame him.

"We've discovered that while in its pure energy state--," I sipped at my tea, "That it's unable to pass onto hallowed ground, unless it uses the bodies of the dead. They form a type of protective shell or shield that it uses like armor."

"It can't harm us in its energy form as long as we wear these." Rich produced the charm that hung about his neck, "But, in physical form, the only way to stop it is to utterly destroy the corpse or corpses that it inhabits."

"Are you telling me that this thing can inhabit more than one corpse at a time?" Simms now appeared both frightened and fascinated.

"In a manner of speaking, I suppose." I thought before saying, "It has the ability to meld numerous decaying parts into a uniform creature or possess a group in one specific area. In one particular instance it utilized the corpse of a Grizzly and a number of other animals." The memory sent bitter chills through my entire being, and I said, "It was a horrific union of mangled and decaying carcases that became something too hideous to imagine…"

"I was there--," Shuddering with the thought, Raymond offered a wide-eyed stare with the recollection, as he said, "It was almost unstoppable and was nearly the end of us all…"

"Jesus…" Sergeant McTavish gasped, his eyes flitting from one face to another, "I can't even imagine anything like that."

"Just start hoping that you won't have to--," Raymond shivered, "The first might be your last…"

"Going back to my original question—," Simms fought to remain focused, asking, "Can this thing be in two places at once—or affect multiple groups of people in different places?"

"As an entity, it can influence many in a single place—but it can only manifest at one specific point at a time." Explaining to the best of my ability, I paused, saying, "It can travel as fast as thought—and can appear in any place at any time as long as it remains in darkness."

"This means that, if you get caught out somewhere after dark--," Rich peered between the two men, "Or in an underground parking lot, basement, or deep shadow anywhere, you're open season…"

"So, we're safe as long as we stay out of the dark?" The Sergeant rubbed at his eyes.

"Well, we're not absolutely sure about that either--," Raymond shrugged, "Not only can hide in corpses, but it can also influence and possess the living. This could be even worse that we've seen so far—but we just don't know the full extent of what it's capable of doing yet."

"If it's even remotely possible--," Simms looked among the group, "Could you simplify and sum up the total of your knowledge on this thing in a nutshell?"

"Now that's reaching--," Sinking deeper into the couch, Rich groaned, "We aren't even completely sure of all the angles on this yet?"

"Can you at least try to give me some idea about the whole ball of wax?" Simms looked desperate, as scratching at his brow, he said, "Where did it come from and and how can we possibly deal with it?"

Reaching to Marlowe in thought, I asked for guidance as while unable to answer such a thing myself. I could feel his presence opening my consciousness into the vastness of space and beyond. There was a sudden expansion of reality and all things were clarified in simpler terms.

"Imagine an ever expanding sphere--," I began while speaking slowly and looking between the two men, "From within exists a negative force which by degrees alters to become a positive power at the furthermost and outward regions." Thinking briefly and allowing the theory to settle among my companions, I continued, "This negative energy is a type of moral gravity. It exists primarily as an opportunity for mortal choice between right and wrong—good or evil. And, between the dimensions of higher enlightenment and those of primordial instinct, are entities that either guide or disrupt us upon our path. They travel through a multi-dimensional reality that exists through time and space. For each positive there exists an equal and opposing negative, challenges to overcome, and personal evils to defeat or hence be destroyed."

"So, ultimately--," The Sergeant dared theorize where Simms had become utterly lost, "The human spirit accumulates allies and enemies in the same way that people make friends and enemies in average life."

"All things in this reality and those beyond follow a similar course and order." Nodding, I continued, saying, "Polarities attract—souls are drawn together, and are born under certain signs in alignment to come together for whatever purpose. Life continues in this way from one reality into the next dimension, and beyond."

"You seem fairly certain of these theories." Simms paused in question, and asked, "Can I ask your sources?"

"Aside from corresponding literature--," I looked between the two police officers, "Let's just say that through the course of these events, we have made alliances, as well as enemies."

"And if this entity manages to destroy us here." Simms swallowed hard, "Then assumedly, it will continue to hunt and destroy us through time and space, forever."

"And- you should also keep in mind--," Raising a finger in thought, Rich said, "We have no idea if we'll ever come together like this again, or will ever be able to share the awareness that we have now. So, it could be a long, murderous and bloody journey until we have an opportunity like this again—if ever."

"Being an elemental, the evil is always consciously aware of this struggle--," I explained, "And, it bides the time until we stumble over it— or it finds us again."

"The biblical text says that we travel onward from here." The Sergeant thought aloud, "The heaven and hell theory."

"And to some extent that's the truth--," I agreed, "But, we must first overcome the challenges put before us here and then make the right choices to ascend to the next dimension."

"In which case, and if we should lose in this world--," The Sergeant reasoned it out to the best of his ability, "Then we'll just keep coming back here until we get it right."

"And until we do--," Rich shrugged, "We'll all just become an assortment of missing persons, freak accidents, and cases of human internal combustion for the next few thousand years. Or until we somehow figure this out again?"

"I knew that there were more sinister aspects involved in this case--," Appearing utterly astonished and horrified at the same time, Sergeant McTavish turned to me while quietly saying, "But never in my wildest nightmares would I have ever imagined that it was anything like this…"

"So, this is really just about the whole balance of polarities thing--," Assimilating the discussion, Simms put a finger to his chin in thought, saying, "And it'll stop at nothing to wipe you guys out, and anyone that gets in its path along the way."

"Which in turn disrupts the balance of things here--," Nodding, I spoke slowly as while he closely listened, and I said, "And creates a negative flux that ripples through dimensions through eternity."

"So, if these things want control over everything--," Simms shrugged, "Then what's stopping them from just doing that?"

"There are certain powers that govern all things--," Feeling even further unsettled with the striking revelation shared by Marlowe, I quietly said, "It's a hierarchy on both sides, and they allow things to sway only so far before intervening. It's not all strictly black and white like it might be presented in religions around the world, but shades of grey. Mankind isn't the only entity permitted to seek out redemption, or even change sides at any given point. And this, gentlemen, also includes the sources of which I previously spoken."

"I'd guess that it might work something like a casino--," Tim played with a deck of cards as he spoke, "They're all playing to win, some cheat and others continually lose, but keep coming back to try again. But at the end of the day and when the chips are counted—house rules always stand in the end."

"Okay then, simple enough--," Peering around at the little gathering, Simms nodded in silent resolve, saying, "We find this thing—and just destroy it."

"It's not that simple--," Staring in utter disbelief at the asinine suggestion, Rich cursed saying, "It can't just be killed or destroyed. If it was that easy—don't you think that we would've done it by now?"

"So what are you telling me?" Wide-eyed and appearing somewhat insulted by Rich's snide tone, Simms's scoffed, "That this thing is indestructible?"

"A life force, regardless of its magnetism in the universe, can never truly be destroyed..." Sipping at my tea and looking solemnly at the old Detective, I said, "Even organic matter never really dies, it just breaks down into chemical components and elements that return to be used again in some other way."

"So the logs that you have burning in that hearth aren't being reduced into nothing?" Posing a theoretical debate, Simms scratched at the stubble on his chin.

"The flame only alters the material into assorted elements as while leaving the carbon which is the basis of most living things."

"If this is all true, then why hasn't science become aware of this?" Asking politely, Sergeant McTavish looked to me in question, "I would think that the existence of multi-dimensional monsters would be something of a concern?"

"They know more than they'll ever tell us--," Rich sneered, "The public are just sheep that keep the financial wheels grinding so the rich can suck Champagne and eat *filet mignon.*"

"So, if we can't just destroy this thing--," Simms became obsessive, "Then what do we do—there must be some way that we can stop it—there must be..."

"Well, although energy can never be destroyed, only transmitted or transferred, "Rich explained while sipping at coffee, "We have reason to believe that we might be able to force it into a void, or a type of worm-hole into space."

"But if you do that--," Simms paused in thought, "Theoretically, won't it just be replaced by another one of those things?"

"Not for us in this lifetime, and that we're aware of--, "I spoke frankly, "All that we can do is hope that we can find the elements to open the portal that Rich mentioned—and dispose of our current demon—so to speak..."

"These won't protect you against the possessed--," Rich moved from his seat, and offering both officers protective charms, said, "But they'll keep the entity away in its raw energy form."

"How can a little thing like this protect us?" Simms fidgeted with the talisman.

"All shapes possess a frequency or power of their own." Scratching at my brow, I nodded in explanation, "I don't have the answers to everything—but we know from previous experiences that these do work. Sound alters forms, ultraviolet light affects all living things and therefore certain forms influence the elements. You'll see in ritualistic practices used throughout history that most cultures use sacred items and sounds to incur some kind of spontaneous reaction from the environment."

"It's no different than objects used in ceremonies of exorcism by the Catholic church--," Rich added, "Or the moonlight rituals of Pagan cultures. In one form or another they're all trying to illicit some kind of elemental or spiritual reaction."

"If it comes down to sacred symbols--," Sergeant McTavish paused in thought while examining the charm, "Then why aren't we using a cross or a crucifix?"

"It's not a question of faith--," Drawing the golden Celtic cross that Caitlin had given me from beneath my shirt, I held it before them and said, "It's a matter of knowing what works. And gentlemen, believe me, when the time comes neither of you will want to test that theory."

"Is there any reason that you would have your doubts about the crucifix or cross?" Once again Sergeant McTavish had approached the question respectfully and without intending insult.

"In the Lumberton house--," Recounting the events with s shudder, I looked at the two men, "I witnessed an elderly clergyman, a decent man with true faith—die for what he believed. Now, I'm not saying that Christian beliefs don't have their own power and place, because we've used them in the past as well. All that I'm telling you right now is that, for whatever reason, this symbol is tested and true."

Simms had picked up the talisman, closely observing the relic, and peered around the table. Instinctively, we had all produced the charms that we wore, and held them out for our guests to see.

"That's fair—and you're right, it's better to be safe than sorry." Slipping the charm about his neck, the sergeant watched as Simms followed by example. They both appeared increasingly perturbed. Awkwardly fidgeting with the charms, they now appeared as though dreading to have unwittingly joined some dark and exclusive cult. I had almost smiled while being amused with the thought, but then realized the insinuation been disturbingly close to the truth...

"These are for your wife and daughter--." Rich offered the sergeant two more charms, "Make sure that they wear them at all times..."

Accepting them, he had looked down into his palm, and inquiring with certain anxiety, asked, "And how will we know if this thing is near?"

"It's an instinct that we all have for self-preservation--," Toying with the golden cross, I peered blankly back at the two men, saying, "We all feel the things that pass in the night, and from the dawn of time, feared the dark because of it. You'll sense it—it's the cold chill that causes goose pimples or the hair to rise on the back of your neck and forearms."

"Have you ever seen it?" Simms just silent stared.

"It can come in the form of a strong wind or fog." Raymond gazed blindly while speaking in vivid recollection, and saying, "It can appear as a shadow deeper than the rest, a black and festering fungus, or even a brutal winter storm."

"The more that you tell me about this thing--," Simms looked between us, "The slimmer our chances of surviving this seems."

"Oh, we're all going to die--," Rich gazed intently, "It's just a matter of where or when?"

"And you think this thing has a long history here?" Sergeant McTavish asked, "And possibly even among you or distant relatives?"

"Without a single doubt in my mind--," Rich had immediately agreed, "And, I'm fairly sure that it was also responsible for an assortment of centuries old, inexplicable and horrific events. As a matter of fact, Michael first discovered it mentioned in historical documents that were found at the McCreary estate."

"What records were these?" Simms eyes bulged as he turned to me, "And do you still have them?"

"It happened when I was working on the manuscript for my first book--," There was remorse in my tone that echoed directly from out of my heart, as I said, "My wife, well, just Caitlin to me at the time, had offered me some old documents concerning her family and the estate It was just supposed to be material that I could use to loosely base my story around. It was mostly information about the family business, gem trade and antiques, and the building of the McCreary mansion." Pausing in thought, the recollection bothered me even more than ever before. Not just due to its sinister nature, but the fact that I had ignored all the warnings, and risked everything and everyone for the sake of that damned book...

"And--," Sergeant McTavish leaned closer, "What happened after that?"

"Sorry—just the memory of that place has a nasty effect on me--," Recounting to where I had left off, I promptly continued, saying, "After viewing the historical documents, and mentioning that there had been some juicy and dark details of which very little had been shared. She was kind enough to entrust me with the personal diaries of Sir Reginald McCreary. They dated back to a family mansion in Dublin Ireland, and sometime during the mid to late sixteenth century. Even then, there was mention of an evil presence that pursued the family, mysterious deaths, witchcraft, and human sacrifices. It was all considered nothing more than the fevered delusions of a man with a debilitation disease. Unfortunately, he suffered from Syphilis and it was eventually the end of him."

"They'd originally assumed the entity to have been some kind of a vampire--," Raising an eyebrow, Rich scrutinized the two men, "But what they didn't know is that there were two separate occurrences appearing at the same time. There was one that they brought onto themselves with back magic—and the other was the entity. It used the lesser demon as cover while it slowly wiped out their entire family..."

"Oh my God--," Apparently a sensitive and caring man, Sergeant McTavish was horrified, and asked, "So, I'm assuming that it obviously didn't end with them?"

"No, it was obviously dormant at the estate while Caitlin was there alone--," Rich motioned with a nod in my direction, and then said, "But when he showed up and started investigating the claims for his book—he woke something up…"

"You mentioned another demon at the estate?" Confused, Simms's shrugged, "What was that all about?"

"It was an attempt to resurrect a loved one who died in an unfortunate accident." Relating the series of dismal events, I felt something cold churn in my guts, "They didn't bring the girl back—but they managed to open a portal and allow something else to come through. It possessed the young woman, and of course matters only worsened from there. The Canadian line of McCreary was completely wiped out, with exception to my wife, of whom I later discovered to have been adopted into the family."

"Which would explain why she was spared--," Simms nodded, "And why she'd never encountered and problems while living there."

"We suspected that she was likely just used as bait." Chewing at a nail and wincing while drawing blood, Rich grumbled, saying, "By a particularly nasty spider that was just waiting for Michael to drop into its web."

"So, why hasn't anyone else ever come forward with this story?" It was the rational question, though Simms appeared well beyond the means of any feasible explanation.

"They used to institutionalize anyone who suffered from 'flights of fancy' or that appeared deluded." Tim tapped a finger against his tea cup, "What rational person would dare risk attempting to explain that situation to anyone?"

"It stands to reason that most of the evidence would've appeared in diaries and hidden documents." Simms agreed, "I'm just surprised that things like this could've ever existed without having been properly documented by someone, somewhere?"

"Throughout history we have legends and folklore that told stories of demons, undead, and monstrous things that haunt the dark places of the world." I poured more tea, and leaning back, said, "Modern science and psychiatry has explained away certain aspects, but a great deal still remains unexplained."

"We tend to make light of the past--," Rich frowned, "What we tend to forget is that some of our greatest scholars, men of science and philosophers came up out of those times. Many of them told stories of evil spirits, ghosts, and other horrors that plagued the countryside. And, you can't tell me that they were all hysterical and just imagining things."

"No, you're right about that--," Simms peered suspiciously around the room, "But, if all of these things were really happening—then why haven't we discovered a single shred of physical evidence? There should've been something left—bodies and bones don't just vanish. Someone somewhere must have saved or preserved some proof that these things really existed."

"It's like he told you earlier--," Raymond drained his coffee cup, "These things cover their tracks. Keep in mind that they've had an eternity to master their craft. The only reason that you were permitted to discover Harry, was so that you would split us all up and leave people vulnerable."

"Make no mistake about it--," Glaring and pointing a finger in warning, Rich said, "This thing doesn't make mistakes. Its moves are all well calculated and it works by one specific design. It eliminates all opposition and when methods become too extreme, it conceals all evidence in clever ways."

"With all the people who just seem to vanish into thin air each year who could argue that?" Sergeant McTavish sighed deeply, and looking to Raymond, said, "Please, feel free to call me Ian--," He looked around the group, "I think that we've surpassed formalities at this point."

"Just call me Gordon--," Simms slowly nodded, "Or plain crazy and possibly institutionalized by the time that this is over."

"If we survive this--," Rich frowned, "At least you'll have lots of company."

"Could you please continue with your story about the McCreary house?" Ian's sipped at his coffee, and holding the cup between both hands, looked back at me.

"It was where he first met me." Amica had appeared from behind us, and resting her hands upon my shoulders, said, "It was my ancestral home—and the beginning of something terrible..."

"Mrs. Schreiber--," Gordon had politely greeted her, as smiling, he politely bowed his head, saying, "It's a distinct pleasure to meet you again."

"Caitlin, please feel free to call me Caitlin," She looked down at me, "Since everyone else is on a first name basis, I'd feel terrible being left out."

"Certainly, Caitlin it is, ma'am." Gordon appeared fascinated with her, and waving a hand within introduction, said, "And this is my colleague, Sergeant Ian MacTavish."

Ian had stood and politely bowed, "It's a pleasure to meet you, Caitlin."

Bowing her head, she smiled, "It's a pleasure to meet you as well, but I'd best be leaving you gentlemen to your business. I'll see to fixing a little lunch for everyone."

"If you wouldn't mind terribly," Tim had looked to me, "Would it be alright if I helped Caitlin in the kitchen, I doubt that I'll be of much use here, anyway."

There was desperation in his eyes that touched me deeply. I knew that discussing Harry's death would have been too much for him, so I nodded, saying, "Of course, we can handle this from here, go right ahead."

He had hurried after her without as much as a single word or glance back. In all truth, I could hardly blame him. The sight of those large black and white photos of the death scenes in Harry's disclosure had left an icy lump in the pit of my stomach.

"Please continue—tell us what happened next." Gordon sipped at his coffee, and scrutinizing my every movement, slowly slipped back into his seat.

"Well, as Caitlin had just said--," The words came slowly as I licked at my lips, "We encountered something in that house. In the beginning I had assumed that it might have been a haunting, but soon realized that it was something far worse. In the end, we managed to dispose of the demon that had been summoned there accidentally and by the family. It was drawn into some kind of a void or portal into another dimension. Please, don't ask me to explain, because I really wouldn't know how?"

"So, this demon was active at the same time as the one that's coming after you now?" Ian appeared terribly confused, "Is it possible for multiple incidents to occur like that?"

"It's something like the insects and creatures that occur around decay--," Rich thought briefly, "As between the maggots, flies, and dermestid beetles, we suddenly find ourselves confronted with a vulture…"

"So, initially this thing was permitted to exist there for whatever reason--," Simms made a mental note, "But why didn't it just take you out the moment that it realized who you were?"

"It may have assumed that something lesser would have managed to destroy me. But, as fate would have it—luck and the powers that be were with me on that night."

"Why didn't you ever report any of these events to the police?" Ian asked.

"What you need to understand here is that I had lost all sense and sensibility. I was very sick due to a chill and the mold in that place and, at one point, even assumed that most of that experience had been some kind of fevered delirium. But then, my associate--," I had motioned with a hand toward Rich, "Had returned to the location and discovered a strange substance."

"I took it to the University lab and had it tested by an old friend." Rich explained while picking at a pastry, "It was organic matter which consisted of dried willow roots, human tissue, sulphur, and very high mercury content."

"This is beginning to sound like a lesson in alchemy." Ian poured more coffee from the urn for himself and the others, saying, "And strangely enough, and according to the coroner's report, Harry also had traces of sulphur and toxic levels of mercury in his tissue."

Rich had just looked across the table at me. I knew what he had been thinking. It concerned something that Dr. Edward Wong had mentioned after the incident with Dennis and the demon. On a whim, our dear doctor had done some private tests. The results had revealed unusually high traces of sulphur, and the presence of mercury in the stains left upon the sheets...

"After the incident at the Duff Glenn everything seemed fine--," Sipping at my tea and holding the cup close for warmth, I said, "And though we had experienced other phenomena during investigations, there hadn't been anything quite as prolific. Well, not until the incident at Harrison Mills. That was something that I couldn't even begin to describe. I'm still not completely sure as to how we made it out that night, but our client died during the attempt."

"Frank Jorgensen--," Gordon nodded, having obviously investigated all and any possible leads, and said, "He was under suspicion for the murder of a 15 year old girl who drowned during the mid-fifties. I did some checking up on that character—and he wasn't exactly *kosher*, if you catch my drift."

"He was far worse that you might imagine--," Cracking his knuckles, Rich stretched his arms before saying, "Then there was that incident at Woodlands." With all eyes upon Raymond, with a nod, Rich said, "We were confronted by a lunatic who, claiming to be a demon, almost got the better of us. But thankfully, Detective Emerson came to our assistance."

"I'm sure that you're both aware of the extenuating circumstances of the case involving patient 1366--," Glancing between the two men, Raymond suddenly appeared very uncomfortable, saying, "I filed a complete report based on what little information was available at the time."

Suddenly realizing that Rich had inadvertently placed our friend beneath the scrutiny of his peers on a potentially career threatening case, I gawked at my friend.

With his eyes bulging from behind his glasses as while realizing the mistake, he just gazed apologetically while sinking deeply into the couch.

"None of the events or claims on that night were ever clearly established. So no one really knows what happened." Attempting to draw the attention from off Raymond, I was halted as Gordon politely raised a hand, questioning our friend.

"And so, according to the paper you submitted that night--," Gordon looked through notes that he had scribbled into his little black book, "You believe that patient 1366 was likely possessed and under demonic influence, is that right?"

"And to the best of my knowledge--," Raymond looked back at them with a stern gaze and solemnly, said, "I wrote down exactly what I saw—and provided all documents to substantiate any claim that was made."

"And this concerns an individual--," Ian began putting it all together, "Whom being suspected to have occupied that same cell for almost one hundred years, attacked an intern, Dennis Monroe, before blinding and then crucifying himself with shattered fragments of his own broken rib bones."

"The evidence and coroner's report corroborate my findings--," Raymond looked between them, "It's no less believable than the files you left on our coffee table..."

"It's not that we don't believe you--," Gordon immediately corrected the misunderstanding, "There were eleven witnesses on that day. I'm just putting facts and evidence together on this whole affair."

"We believe that the person responsible for doing all of that--," I had intervened, saying, "Was just a messenger sent by the evil to confuse and bait us."

"What do you mean by bait you?" Gordon appeared increasingly agitated, "What could he have possibly done to bait you?"

"He told us things--," Raymond answered, "He provided information, intimate details of old crimes involving multiple murders, and exact locations where the evidence could be located."

"I spoke to the night duty doctor, Edward Wong." Gordon caught us all by surprise, and smiling, said, "You know, he denied having any knowledge of any interaction between you and a young man by the name of Dennis Monroe, but the night-shift doctors and staff insisted that you were there. They also told us that the kid was as good as dead before you guys showed up."

"Dr. Wong really didn't have any knowledge of what happened in that room." Defending Edward, I shrugged, "Yet, Raymond witnessed the event."

"It's true—I did--," He admitted, "When we entered the room that young man looked like death. I've never seen anything like that in my entire career. He was covered in huge welts and dripping with infection, he was literally rotting right in front of us."

"What did you do at this point?" Ian scribbled notes into his pad.

"I blocked the door while they performed an exorcism on the kid." Raymond admitted, "But, I met patient 1366 prior to this. And, what we saw lying on that hospital bed was definitely not Dennis Monroe. I saw it with my own eyes—and swear on my life and badge that it was patient 1366."

"And, according to what you witnessed, how would you describe what took place in that room, that night?" Ian's fascination caused him to write even faster.

"It's not easily described--," Raymond recollected the event with apparent loathing and fear, "I was told not to watch, but I did catch some fleeting glimpses of what happened."

"Why did you insist that Detective Emerson not watch?" Gordon appeared suspicious.

"The eyes are the windows to the soul." Rich stirred sugar and cream into his coffee, "We didn't want anything getting into him, and took every precaution that we could, under the circumstances."

"I was fighting to hold the door closed--," Raymond explained, "We couldn't risk anyone else and didn't want to lose the boy. All that I remember, quite honestly--, "He thought for a moment and looking to the officers, said, "They were reading a roman ritual from a prayer book, I could hear what sounded like patient 1366 threatening and cursing at them. There was a sudden hot gust in the room, darkness, and what seemed like a storm of shadows. There was a deafening screaming, I fell against the door and covered my ears, and then it was over. When I looked over at them, the boy was conscious, and except for being tired from the ordeal, appeared to be perfectly fine."

"And that's when the staff came in through the door and discovered the change in Mr. Monroe." Gordon scribbled notes and quickly dotted and crossed the letters.

I could see that he had been absorbing every detail and contemplating the substantiating stories and evidence. It would have been apparent to almost anyone that, even through the utter madness, it had a solid foundation of truth.

"So, you're telling me--," Gordon thought aloud, "That a man, who according to specialists was at death's door at one moment, was inexplicably cured, and then released in good health, only days later."

"It wasn't a medical condition--," Looking toward Gordon and Ian, I threw my arms up in frustration, saying, "It was a spiritual poisoning that was affecting the young man's body. Unfortunately, modern medicine couldn't have discovered a cure, because they would never have accepted the cause."

Ian had looked to Gordon and they had exchanged mutual nods in agreement.

"Not long after the incident at Woodlands--," Rich began unravelling and unveiling the entire ghastly affair, "We were called out to investigate a secluded old farm house--," Removing his glasses and rubbing his eyes with the recollection, he shuddered, "And, once again we were confronted by the entity that had been patient 1366."

"But I thought that you had exorcised that demon?" Pointing with his pen and realizing it, he apologized.

"We exorcised it out of Dennis--," Rich explained, "But not out of this dimension."

"In any event--," I had continued for him, saying, "We narrowly escaped with our lives. And although the demon that was patient 1366 was cast into the abyss, several members of the family, a local priest, and two of his companions were lost in the process. We managed to save the lives of our client's wife and one young daughter—but were forced to set fire to the place."

"Unfortunately, the evidence was burned and the fire and deaths were all reported as accidental—," Rich continued from where I had left off, saying, "But there was still some kind of ancient and dangerous presence in that place—a natural force that was somewhere attached to that property long before people had ever arrived. So, being as she was destitute with the little girl, I bought the property from the woman, and we funded her return home to family in England. I've had the property completely fenced, and it no longer accessible to anyone but us."

"That was a very expensive investment." Gordon's features had softened in that moment and especially after having heard about the woman and child. "It was a noble act, especially when you'd already known that the property was virtually worthless."

"It wasn't about the money--," Staring him straight in the eye, Rich had sadly said "It was about the victims, and sealing that place off before anyone else falls into that pit."

"So, you're saying that there's still something out there?" Gordon looked to Ian and then back at Rich, "Is it any relation to what we've been talking about here?"

"No—it's something very different." I had attempted to explain, "The world is filled with energies, elementals and different entities. Some just co-exist and others are dangerous. There's a type of balance to all things, and whatever exists in that place has been there long before us. Sure, it's definitely dangerous to livestock and people, but it isn't anything inherently evil. No more than a lion, crocodile or any other apex predator might be."

"The natives designated certain places as sacred grounds--," Rich scratched at his head, "While others were to be avoided at all costs. We might've avoided a lot of terrible things if we had regarded their beliefs with a little respect. Unfortunately, modern society doesn't accept the existence of anything beyond their belief systems."

"So, in buying the place, you have designated it off limits to protect others." Ian nodded as he scribbled down the thoughts, "But none of us live forever, so what's going to happen when we can't control it anymore?"

"We do have younger members of our society." Considering the question briefly, I looked back at him and said, "We can only hope that they'll continue from where we leave off. We will be leaving the business and finances to them when the time comes."

"So, what happens if we can't stop this thing--," Gordon played the devil's advocate, "What will happen to them and everyone else?"

"We can't fail--," Rich's entire demeanor became dark, even desperate, as he looked around the table, "No matter what happens..."

"You mentioned something to me about an incident in Hedley after that?" Gordon squinted while flipping to a new page in his pad and readying the pen.

"Yes--," Raymond remembered, saying, "After I heard about what happened at the farmhouse from Michael and Rich, there was concern for their friends Tim and Harry. It was late in the season and close to the holidays, so Michael and I took Rich's four wheel drive, custom Suburban, and made the trip to Hedley for Tim and Harry."

"And did you meet with them at that point?" Ian scribbled notes.

"Well, we found Tim alright—but never did see Harry." There was deep remorse in his expression, as continuing, he sadly said, "If we'd just been a little sooner we might've saved him."

Gently patting at his shoulder, Rich spoke compassionately, saying, "You were risking your life just going up there—and you still saved the lives of Tim and Michael when that thing came after all of you."

"This entity—it came after you at that point." Gordon continued to document the series of events in his pad.

"It showed up when we were at the funeral parlor and picking up Tim--," The vivid recollection caused a shudder to visibly pass through him, and he said, "We barely got out of there, and if it wasn't for two Native brothers running plows that night, we might not be sitting here and talking to you right now."

Still writing, Gordon had just nodded for him to continue.

"Well, we got out of the parlor—but the younger brother was killed when the monster shoved his snow plow off the right and down an incline."

Ian had suddenly looked up from his notepad, and staring between Gordon and Raymond, asked, "This shadow or ghost-like presence did that?"

"No--," Raymond slowly shook his head, and staring coldly back at them, said, "It had somehow gotten into a huge grizzly carcass that it must have found rotting and partially frozen in the woods. It brought this thing back, but along the way it collected all and any dead things that it could find."

Gordon and Ian were utterly horrified and just kept writing.

"Well, all those dead varmints were combined into that big old bear's corpse, and the whole frozen and rotting mess came after us... In the end, if it hadn't been for that Native brother taking that thing out by blowing the gas station at the cost of his own life, like I said before, we wouldn't be here."

"And at that point this entity had given up and you all came back here?" Ian halted, and chewing at the tip of his pen, raised an eyebrow.

"No, I'd used all my ammo--," He remembered, "And we'd gone back into town for more rounds. After the deal with that grizzly, there was no way that I was risking the highway home without some way of defending ourselves."

"And so you went to the Fish and Game supplies store." Gordon was already aware, and asked, "What happened there?"

"Well, I broke into the place, and while we were gathering supplies this woman had showed up. She looked really scared, and after identifying myself as an officer of the law, she had come into the store with her Great Dane. Apparently she had been out walking her dog when the blizzard picked up, and she'd panicked when she noticed us in the shop."

"And at that point everything was fine?" Gordon paused to glance over at Raymond.

"No—the darkness got into her and that damn dog, and possessing them both, forced them together." Raymond's eyes were huge while recollecting the vision of the horrid thing, and he gasped while saying, "It just crushed them together like clay, and claws and tentacles came out of it from everywhere. I had to blow up the store with gun power just so we could get out, but even that was enough to stop her."

Neither of the two men spoke as they hurriedly noted every last word that Raymond was speaking.

"It came after us in the blizzard and it took every last effort before we finally managed to completely incinerate that monster. It was the only way that we could stop her."

"It was the only way?" Ian appeared visibly horrified with the thought.

"She kept rejuvenating, no matter what we did." Gazing in shock with the memory, I shook my head while saying, "We had to find a way to incapacitate her long enough to completely incinerate the remains."

"Now, going back for just a moment--," Pausing him while holding his pen up, Gordon thought briefly before saying, "Now you claimed that this Native saved you. But the local cops called it a botched robbery. In their report it says that they found parts of the suspect all over that place, and a revolver resting right beside the head. Not to mention, the local coroner verified that the woman and her dog were blown to bits in an accident. They claimed that a freak fire caused the ammunition and gun-power to go off."

"And you never once questioned as to how conveniently that had all been placed?" Raymond scoffed at the thought, "We've all attended countless homicide and accident scenes. Can either one of you honestly tell me of a single case where everything had its ducks lined up in a row like that?"

"It's only happened a few times." Ian had agreed, "And now that I think about it, they were usually on the scene of freak accidents and unexplained deaths."

"And do you really think that was just coincidental?" Raymond dipped a pastry into his coffee, and waving the soggy remains at Ian, said, "They were cold and calculated murders, plain and simple."

"I just noticed that these are the same symbols that you've got all over your gates." Gordon paused to scrutinize the character on the talisman that he now wore.

"Yes they are--," Rich motioned toward the partially open draperies and the crews working beyond, "It's the only thing that keeps this place somewhat safe."

"Well, if what you're assuming about this entity is true, and it's made of pure energy--," Ian pondered while peering toward the window, and then said, "Then technically it should be able to short out electrical systems and open those gates easier than you?"

Becoming as pale as a sheet, Rich had just turned and gazed straight over at me. It was obvious for reasons beyond explanation, that none of us had even considered the possibility until now…

"Well—if we have everything now--," Gordon paused before closing his notepad, "Are there any other little surprises that we should know about?"

"We've made a big pot of cream tomato soup, and grilled ham and cheese sandwiches for everyone." Amica proudly announced as she and Tim entered the room carrying trays, and she said, "Would you all come to the table please, lunch is served!"

"No—no other surprises—at the moment." I watched as he promptly closed and tucked the pen and pad into his coat before following us over for lunch…

"You really didn't have to go through the trouble." Ian had thanked both Tim and Amica as they served the food. There was a gentle and decent manner about the man. So much in fact that I could never imagine him enduring the horrors of homicide and missing persons. In the end, I suppose that it made sense that only the most dedicated and caring individuals could undertake such a terrible task.

"It was no trouble at all--," Amica had pinched my cheek in parting, "I'll leave you to your lunch and discussion, sweetheart."

"Thank you, dear." I had watched as she made her way off and disappeared into the kitchen.

"Your wife is a very charming woman--," Gordon had winked at me, "If we could just clone her—the world would be a better place."

Almost spilling my soup, I choked at the comment and attempted to feign a laugh. It sounded and must have appeared absolutely ridiculous, but my nerves were swiftly reaching their end.

"Returning to where we had left off--," Ian had continued with his notes as we indulged lunch, "If you had to use such extreme measures, how are we expected to defend ourselves against them?"

"As I'd mentioned before--," Rich began explaining, "The only way to stop them is to burn them. I've devised a simple weapon that creates instantaneous and intense flames. It reacts through chemicals, so can't be extinguished in conventional ways. As a matter of fact, it is water that causes the reaction."

Gordon and Ian had immediately turned to Raymond, who quietly nodding, placed down his sandwich, and said, "I emptied both barrels of my twin 44's into one of those things and it just kept coming. Rich's chemical gun is the only way to really stop them."

"And how many of those chemical weapons do you have ready?" Gordon's attention returned to Rich.

"I have six ready to go now—and enough compounds to refuel them three times over, each."

"What makes you so certain that this thing will reappear?" Ian dipped his sandwich into his soup and looked over at me.

"Consider this a vendetta that transcends time and space. At some point, we have all been involved in a series of events involving this entity. Enough in fact, that it is solely dedicated to our destruction."

"What makes you so sure that it won't just wait until you're all too old to fight back—and just take you one by one, and at its convenience?" Gordon chewed at his sandwich.

"Because we've fought back—and made others aware of their existence." Raymond answered,

"They're greatest strength is public ignorance—can you imagine what would happen if we could convince and save even a few people?"

"It would tilt the balance of things drastically--," I had agreed, "And that's something that they would never allow."

"The facts remain the same--," Rich frowned, nervously toying with a spoon in his soup, "They don't like to leave witnesses alive, and we've definitely pissed this one off..."

"So, how would you suggest that we deal with this?" Gordon looked to me for an answer.

"Apparently there's a weapon of some kind--," I had spoken up, "It's a talisman or tool, and a way that we can open another portal. Once we find it—we might be able to force this thing into another dimension."

"Okay, where do we find this weapon?" Ian nervously tapped his fingers upon the table.

"Well, according to what we've been led to believe--," Rich cracked his knuckles and looked to Gordon, "it is possibly hidden in the home of that recently deceased east-side woman."

"And if we do manage to locate these items--," Ian frowned, "What then?"

"Our sources have suggested that we search for our demon at the McCreary estate." Sipping at my tea, I suddenly felt something stir in the depths of my stomach. It was greasy, cold, and I felt as though it might induce an immediate sickness. Swallowing back the bile, I leaned back in the chair, deciding that it was nothing more than an attack of nerves. As a child, this had been a common reaction when subjected to severe stress or suffering from anxiety.

"Assuming that we accept all of this as truth--," Gordon cleared his throat, and speaking in a rather reluctant manner, asked, "What are our odds of finding this weapon—and surviving this?"

"Not very good, I'm afraid." Speaking quite frankly, I had slumped back into my seat, and thought briefly, before saying, "Gentlemen, let me remind you that we are fighting against something ethereal, and a power beyond this world. It can penetrate our thoughts, use our own fear against us, possess anyone unprotected, and has the ability to animate the dead. It can never be killed or ultimately destroyed, and is only hindered by time and space. And, in the event that we should succeed, as you had previously mentioned, there is no guarantee that something else might not come after us...."

"It sounds as though we may be screwed either way." Ian slid his bowl away, and reaching for his coffee, sighed, "Can I ask you, why you're unwilling to reveal your sources?"

"Because, in this particular case, some things are best left unknown--," Clasping my hands together on the table before me, I spoke clearly, but quietly, "What you don't know—the evil can't sense and use against you— or by the same means, harm others who are involved."

"Of course--," Ian agreed, "You already mentioned that the entity can sense our thoughts—and could use information like that against us."

"I'm not going to say that any of this has been easy to swallow." Gordon slowly looked to each and every person at the table, "But neither was the incident with your friend Harry. So, ruling in order of the evidence, and as crazy as it may all sound, it makes sense."

"So, what's the verdict?" Raymond looked anxiously between the two officers.

"We'll work with you on this." Gordon agreed to the relief of all, "But, we need to keep this thing wide open. Which means, other than your sources, no secrets, and no-one moves a muscle on anything unless we all agree, do we have a deal?"

"That sounds fair enough." I had agreed without giving it much thought. After all, we had a better chance together than struggling from opposite ends.

"Alright then--," Gordon nodded, "I have permission from the Captain to organize a task force to investigate this situation. That means six extra men and more of these--," He tugged at the talisman about his neck, and pointing to Rich, added, "And, we'll need six more of your chemical weapons just to be sure. I'll brief the men, but this is all off the record, so we're on our own once this thing starts rolling."

"You do realize that we are likely condemning the men and families of anyone that we involve?" I had felt obligated to make it very clear before we began.

"In my mind we're condemning a lot more people by ignoring this threat." Gordon appeared both frightened and determined at the same time. He had nervously fidgeted with his tie, and then looking back at me, muttered, "I'll make sure that everyone involved are single, older members, and are made aware of the consequences—I'm not completely heartless."

"Alright then--," I had looked to my companions, "The rules are as follows: Never travel by night, wander into dark places, or go anywhere alone. You must wear your talismans at all times, and never speak of these matters to anyone beyond the group."

"That's perfectly clear." Ian politely excused himself from lunch, and gathering the files and documents from the coffee table, said, "Where do we continue from this point?"

"I think that we should start with the old lady's place." Gordon nodded toward me, "If that tool or key is there—and we find it, we can plan the next move after that point."

"I think that we can all agree on that." Rubbing at my eyes, I looked to my friends as the vote became unanimous, and I said, "If nothing should turn up in that location—we'll continue to the Duff Glenn."

"I'll admit that I don't like the sounds of that." Ian returned to the table, "But I'm almost willing to bet my bottom dollar, that we'll find our answers in the worst place imaginable."

"You learn fast--," Raymond frowned, "And in most cases around here, it's almost guaranteed."

"Well then--," Gordon moved from his seat, and thanking me for lunch, said, "We have a lot to do in a short time. I'll get things organized back at the office—and we'll be in touch in the next day or two. It'll take a little time to put the task force together. So, we'll be attending the old girl's place alone, but I'll make sure that we have back-up at the McCreary place."

"Seriously--," Raymond shook their hands as we all now moved from the table and followed them toward the front door, "You guys be careful out there. That thing will be onto you the minute that you go out of those gates. Please, don't remove those symbols, no matter what!"

Gordon had turned to look back at Raymond in the open doorway. The skepticism had completely faded from his gaze. Whether he had really believed a single word that we had told him mattered very little at this point. It was apparent that the detective in Gordon Simms was now hunting a monster...

"Once you pass through those gates—it's going to sense your thoughts, and become aware of our plans." I shook Gordon and Ian's hands as they prepared to depart, "No matter what happens—do not leave the safety of your homes—or go out into the night."

Gordon's fingers slipped down to where the talisman hung about his neck, "What should we be expecting to happen?"

"Hope for the best--," Rich muttered, "but plan for the worst..."

"We'll be in touch." Gordon spoke as though he now had his doubts, as turning, the two men hurried off.

"I really hope that they took us seriously--," Rich slowly shook his head, "I'd really hate to see anything happen to them—or their families."

"We have to put our trust in the powers that be—and hope..." I watched as they departed through the open gates, and the work crews scurried from all about them. I could see that the tracks had been laid, the mechanisms installed, and that the crews now struggled to set the heavy iron gates into place.

There was a strong and bitter wind, and though the heavens had darkened with heavy clouds, the weather had not failed us, yet...

"It looks as though the crews have almost gotten the gates together--," Rich closed the door, and parting the curtains, said, "The foreman said that we can expect the gates to be fully functional by three this afternoon."

"That's a relief--," Raymond sauntered into the living room, and dropping onto the couch, grumbled, "Because that weather doesn't look like it's going to hold out for much longer."

"Do you think that they really believe that Amica is Caitlin?" Rich whispered as we made our way toward the hearth.

"I certainly hope so—for the sake of Caitlin and Maya." Drawing a photograph from a shirt pocket beneath my suit vest, I placed it on the coffee table before my friend, "Oh, I thought that this might help to calm your nerves—after that nightmare of the previous night." I had not claimed the photograph to have been the actual location of our wives, but merely suggested the possibility. It was a simple black and white image of an old rectory that I had photographed several summers back. It had been well maintained, and being one of the lesser known locations, seemingly served its purpose. Glancing at it, he swiftly concealed it in a shirt pocket before the others might see it. With a nod, the topic had ended without as much as a second thought. I could only hope and pray that this ruse would succeed, for the sake of us all.

"You know, the world feels like it's getting smaller and darker all of the time." Rich had sighed deeply, and turning to tend to the hearth, paused in thought, "It's like the girls are getting further and further away from us with each passing moment. Hey, you know that old adage, about distance making the heart grow fonder? Well—I'm calling bullshit..."

"Everyone needs something to believe in—even if it's just to survive within the moment."

"I'm beginning to question a lot of things that I once felt and believed. It's amazing how, just when you think that you've got a grasp on things, life comes around and smacks you upside of the head." Tossing several more logs into the hearth, he glanced back at me, "I mean—if you'd tried to have told me any of this without my ever having witnessed anything, I would've thought that you'd lost your marbles."

"You did at one time—when we first met in the old store." I had reminded him, "That seems almost a lifetime ago now."

"Do you ever wonder--," He had returned to his seat on the couch, and pondered, "Whether it would've been better to just remain oblivious?"

"It still would have come for us—it's the grand design."

"But, what if we had never known about any of this—maybe it might've been different?"

"I think that—for me at least--," Looking into the hearth, the answer had come all too easily, "It was all worth it—because having the knowledge of something is still better than existing with expectations of nothing."

"Amen to that, brother." He had bowed his head and fallen into dark contemplation.

Moving to the window and parting the draperies, I stood and stared beyond the protective barrier of Sanctum Arcanum. There was a mind-numbing cold that seemed to be penetrating the glass, through my body and into my soul.

Silently, I watched as the workmen had finally managed to erect the gates into the tracks, and now slid them back into place. It had required modification to the bottom rails of the gates, but they now slid effortlessly back and forth upon the chain-driven gears. There was a clanging sound, and then completely automated, the workmen activated the fully functional gates. I would have felt far better under the circumstances, if not for Gordon's previous comment concerning electronics and the entity…

CHAPTER NINE

9:25 p.m.

Dinner had consisted of roasted chicken, mashed potatoes, green beans and freshly baked rolls. Although it was proper to share white wine with poultry, we had indulged another bottle of the fine Bordeaux that Amica had previously selected. I rarely drank, and even less now due to the medication, but had indulged a glass with my friends. It had been the first light-hearted moment that we had all shared in what seemed an eternity.

"Where did you learn to cook like this?" Rich had smacked his lips as he poured gravy over his potatoes, "This is absolutely fantastic!"

"It's amazing what one might learn given the time and opportunity." Amica had smiled, "Thank you kindly—I'm very pleased that you are enjoying it."

Rich had placed the gravy boat down and Amica had immediately moved it from out of my reach, coyly glancing back at me.

"She's getting as bad as old Rich--," Raymond had chuckled as he cut into his meal, and winking at me, said, "If you weren't already married— I'd be telling you to snap her up quick!"

It was apparent by the glances exchanged that neither Rich nor Tim had found amusement in the jest. As clearing his throat, Tim had quietly asked, "What will happen when Caitlin finally returns? I mean—how will she react to Amica?"

"I will cease to exist in this form and dimension—long before that," Amica spoke with a depth of sadness that now halted us all, and looking to Tim, had said in the sincerest of tones, "Forced to forfeit all for the sake of redemption—and at what cost to all of you."

There had been an emotional storm in my companions eyes, as looking between one another, they surmised a secret of which had not yet been revealed to any of them.

"You speak of redemption—at what cost to all of us?" Wiping at his goatee with a napkin, Rich squinted suspiciously, asking, "Would you be kind enough to explain that?"

"In assuming physical form—and having been previous possessed of a demon--," I had almost choked on my food while attempting to explain, "The two will separate—and as she is expelled from our reality—the demon will manifest in her place."

There were no words that could properly explain the shocked expressions of those gathered around the table. Although my greatest fear was invoking the demon through continued discussion on the matter, I forced out the few words that I could.

"It grows stronger with each and every time that we discuss this, or she invokes its power or preternatural knowledge. I plead with you all, having heard what has already been revealed, due not pursue this matter, please."

"It's coming to the point where I'm not even sure who or what you really are?" Tim spoke more out of thought than intending to utter the words, his startled expression revealing that almost immediately as he looked about the table.

"Regardless of what I may be—for the moment, I am of no threat to anyone here--," She looked down at her plate, her expression grieved beyond words, "Least of all Caitlin or Michael. Please, excuse me…" She had risen from her seat and departed before any of us could have moved to stop her.

Looking between my companions, I could only stare, my jaw still hanging open, "How could you…." Dropping my napkin down upon the table, I moved from my seat, swiftly following Amica upstairs and to where I found her in my office. She had dropped Caitlin's dress upon the floor and now wore the black gown which we had first purchased. She silently wept as she knelt with her head down in the old chair. The sight had broken my heart. I had always sensed her utter loneliness and knowing her fate, felt the heat of tears. Moving to where she knelt, I dropped down t my knees and pulled her close, gently embracing her.

"Please—forgive me--," She sniffled, her heated tears dampening my breast as she rested her head upon my chest, "I fear that at times I forget my proper place."

"My dearest Amica--," Gently stroking her hair and looking into the burning emerald pools of her eyes, I whispered, "You have done nothing wrong—but are the victim of a hell that we have shared too long. You are something far, far finer than any of us deserve. We are blessed to have you….."

There was a soft knock at my office door, and as we turned to look, discovered Tim in the open doorway, "I want to apologize." His voice was weak, his nerves shattered by all that had happened and continued around us, "Caitlin, please forgive me…."

We had slowly stood as he timidly entered the room. He hesitantly moved to where we stood, and opening his arms, said, "I don't know why I said what I did, it was wrong, insensitive and I am truly, very sorry."

Without a word she had hugged him, and kissing his cheek, said, "I forgive you, my friend. We are entering the darkest of times. The shadow of evil is heavy upon our hearts, fear and doubt often rule such moments."

"Will you please join us for dinner, dear lady?" Raymond asked as he and Rich appeared in the doorway behind us. They looked like two school boys who had been scolded by the head-master.

"It's really a wonderful meal—and one of the best that I ever had--," Rich fumbled with his words, "It would be a real shame if everything got cold...."

We had returned to dinner and rather than continue as they had, we had eaten swiftly, fearing to ruin the mood and a lovely meal. There had been dessert, though both Rich and Amica had swiftly removed it from my presence. To some degree they had developed a certain kinship. Although he had never completely accepted her in Caitlin's place, he had certainly acknowledged her as a unique presence. It was strange how after suddenly realizing her humanity and sensitivities, that the others had now seemingly adopted her. Whatever she had previously been or might become mattered little now, she had earned her place in our hearts, extended family and home.

11:15 a.m.

With the hearth well fueled and brandy glasses in hand, we had all gathered and quietly shared our thoughts and concerns. Amica had slipped in close beside me upon the couch, and with a woolen blanket upon her shoulders, silently gazed into the crackling flames. I had looked to her for several moments as she gazed into the hearth, her hair glowing brilliant red in the firelight as her eyes seemed to shine with a strange luminescence. At first, I had attributed an aspect of the supernatural to her appearance, but then it had faded as she looked back at me. It seemed that the longer that she existed in this world, the more she became a part of it.

"I'm really concerned about taking Gordon and Ian into the Duff Glenn." Rich had sipped at his brandy, and sinking deeper into the cushions of the chair nearest the hearth, said, "That place is a horror show, even without our current issues."

"I wouldn't worry too much--," Raymond grunted, and rubbing sleep from his eyes, said, "I'm willing to bet my badge that something will jump out the minute we enter that old lady's basement."

"It's hard to say--," Gently swirling my brandy glass, I glanced back at Raymond, "There's also a possibility that this might work to our benefit."

"Are you suggesting that she might have reached out to us from beyond the grave?" Tim appeared skeptical, frightened as he sipped at his drink.

Rich shrugged, "Not much would surprise me at this point."

"There are those beyond who would seek to guide and support our cause." Amica had looked to the others, "But there are no certain ways to distinguish them, and we must trust our instincts and intuition."

"Then how will we know who to trust?" Rich looked between Amica and where I sat in silent reflection

"The enemy smiles, as it slips the dagger between your ribs and into your heart." Amica's features grew long and dark, "None shall know friend from foe, until the fatal flash of the blade."

"Even if we do find this key--," Raymond drained his glass, "What guarantee do we have that it'll work?"

"Marlowe seems fairly confident that when we find the key element--," Placing down my empty brandy glass, I peered fearfully between my somber companions, "That the third component will be revealed to us—and that everything will fall into place."

"Third component--," Rich repeated the words as he thought aloud, "What was the first?"

"Amica was the first revelation--," Gently placing a hand about her shoulders as she leaned into my breast, I said, "She provided vital information—a key to the past, and shield against the darkness that will safeguard Caitlin and Maya."

"The photograph was not enough to completely convince him." Amica's voice echoed in my thoughts, "I still bare the gift of illusion—you must provide opportunity."

There had been an awkward moment, as looking between my friends, I had turned to Rich, and stuttering, said, "She is also the only one who knows the true location of our wives."

"I wish that I could've seen the place—at least once." Rich whispered as though speaking in thought, "But I know that it would risk everyone…"

"If you will allow me--," Amica moved from the couch toward my friend, "I am able to also share this mental image—while concealing it from the enemy."

"Is it safe?" Tim appeared terrified, "Will she invoke anything or suffer for this?"

The thought having frightened me as well, I had looked to her for an answer. The question forming in my thoughts, as she answered it for all to hear, "This is a natural ability, a sensitivity that is shared between mortals—there is nothing to fear."

Everyone had appeared startled as she had offered her hands, and accepting them, he had followed by example, closing his eyes, as he waited for a miracle. It had happened within the flash of the mind's eye, and a moment later she returned to me.

"Well, did you see anything?" Raymond gawked, "Did you see the place?"

"Yes—I did--," Removing his glasses to wipe the lenses, he peered over at me in the dim golden glow of the hearth, "I saw a rectory upon a hill, surrounded by cliffs and an endless emerald sea."

"What else?" Tim appeared utterly fascinated, but Rich did not reply, as scratching at his head, seemed suddenly confused. He had looked around at the group, and then to me, saying, "I don't know—the image seems to have vanished from my thoughts, and I can't remember a single, solid thing?"

"It was shared only for a moment—a moment now erased for the sake of all involved." She apologized to Rich, "I hope that you understand."

"Of course--," He thanked her, "It seemed like any number or places or pictures that I might've seen. I doubt that I would have remembered anyway."

Amica had gently taken my hand as she moved beneath the woolen blanket and rested her head upon my shoulder. In my mind I could hear her voice as clearly as though she had spoken aloud, "It is done—the others are safe...."

"Do you feel a little better?" Curiously looking to Rich as he slipped his glasses back on, I watched the flames reflection as it danced in his lenses. There was something in his expression that caused certain doubt, his features twisting in confusion as he spoke, "Yes, I do, but I'm not sure why—but when I think about Caitlin, all that I can see in my mind is the Duff Glenn."

Amica had reacted suddenly to this, her eyes becoming mere slits as she suspiciously observed our friend. He appeared more confused than anything else, and looking to Amica, shrugged, "I think that I had a little too much of that wonderful wine with dinner—and the brandy was over-kill. I'd better drag my sorry back-side to bed while I still can."

"That makes two of us--," Raymond placed down his glass, and patting at his swollen belly, said, "I feel like fifty pounds of crap in a ten pound bag. I might've eaten just a little too much?"

"I'm going to call it a night, too." Tim moved from the couch, and gathering the empty glasses, said, "I'll rinse these off before heading out."

"No--," Amica halted him in mid-step, "Please remain here with us on this night."

Tim had looked to me in question and I had nodded in agreement. It was unlike her to say anything without purpose, and I was certainly not about to chance it.

"I'll toss a few extra pillows and a blanket on the couch." Rich chuckled and waving at Tim, said, "It's our turn to make breakfast in the morning anyway—you might as well stick around, one more night."

"Well, knowing that giant insect of yours is somewhere out there--," Tim frowned as he looked between us, "I really don't feel safe at all."

Drawing his dual 44s from beneath his robe, Raymond's expression hardened, "If that thing makes a move on any of you—I'll blow it to kingdom come…"

It was apparent by Rich's expression that he dreaded the thought of an armed confrontation. Quite frankly, I couldn't blame him. After having witnessed the speed and ferocity of the infuriated insect, knew that the odds of survival were against us…

"Let's try to avoid any kind of aggravated confrontation--," I had placed a hand upon one of Raymond's revolvers, and gently forced it down, "Please, keep in mind that no matter how strange or terrifying, this creature is more sentient—than just some monster. It might be best—if you simply left it to us."

Raymond had lowered and replaced his revolvers into their holsters, his expression revealing obvious skepticism, "For your sakes—I sure hope that you're right about this thing. It still makes my skin crawl—just thinking about it…"

"If you knew what those creatures were really capable of--," Tim shuddered with the thought, "You wouldn't be in such a big hurry to pick a fight with this thing."

"Let's just worry about it when the time comes." Rich urged, "I need to lay down before I fall over. I'm totally beat, man."

The discussion had ended with that, but as they departed I couldn't help but feel an ominous sense of pending doom.

The old wall clock had chimed midnight as Merlin casually made his way past. He had glanced back briefly before disappearing into the shadows on his way down to the kitchen. I had returned with Amica to my office while allowing the others to retire for the evening. Although we had additional rooms, Rich had always preferred the couch, while Tim occupied the other. In some aspect, I suppose that it was close vicinity to the hearth that had provided some additional sense of security. Though I had never admitted it to anyone else, before my life with Caitlin, I had spent many nights on that very same couch before the hearth.

"I left some chicken in his bowl--," Amica had looked back at me with a sigh, "Just a little dark meat—his favorite bits."

"You really are so very kind--," Leaning back into my seat, I had looked to where she sat curled up in the chair, "I can tell that he's taken a real shine to you."

"He's a wonderful old soul." She had replied without a second thought, "And he loves you dearly."

"It's surprising how love can exist during such terrible times."

"Love shines brightest in the darkest moments." Her radiant emerald eyes fell upon me as utterly captivated in the moment, I had thought to profess my love for her. She must have sensed the weakness in that moment, and moving from her chair, said, "I'll fetch some tea—neither of us seems tired, and there is a slight chill in the air."

"That would be perfect—thank you!" Concealing my shame and riddled with guilt for having even considered such a thing, I turned my attention back to the desk. The double student lamp cast a radiant golden glow about that particular corner of my office, but the rest lay in long shadows. When she had departed I pretended to have busied myself with a book, but leaned back into the seat as I heard her descending the steps. Suffering in the depths of despair, loneliness and now guilt, I threw a remorseful hand to my face in utter shame. It was finally happening, my love and longing for Caitlin was drawing me ever closer to Amica.

"Do not punish your-self within matters of the heart—there is no guilt in the thought, only acting upon it." Marlowe whispered from out of the shadows, "All that occurs now is by grand design—and serves the greater purpose."

"I'm confused--," Swallowing hard and rubbing at my eyes, I whispered, "I don't know what I'm feeling or thinking anymore."

"Confusion is only denial of the truth--," Marlowe's tone was compassionate, though solemn, "You must stay focused and true to the quest—all else shall reveal itself in time…."

The telephone had suddenly rung out in the stillness and I fumbled to answer before it woke the entire house! Catching it upon the second ring, I was surprised to discover Ole Papra on the other end of the line.

"Michael—I'm sorry, did I get you at a bad time?"

"Ole, no, no trouble at all! It's good to hear from you!" Fumbling with the receiver as I settled back into the chair, I rubbed at my eyes, "It's just that I was sitting here reading and when you rang, it startled me."

"Alright then--," He sounded apprehensive and then said, "I had a few questions concerning some of the material in your book."

"Of course—what seems to be on your mind?"

"Well, it concerns the first chapter and mention of an incident in Harrison Mills. Were you aware that something quite similar occurred in a locale near this place?"

"In all honestly, I tend to loosely base my stories around actual events. It lends a kind of realism to things, and I feel it offers the reader something more tangible. Is there an issue with that?"

"Of course not--," His reply wasn't altogether convincing, "I was just curious about the series of events in connection. Also, there was a little matter of mentioning books, music and other materials. Have you written acknowledgements and properly accredited them?"

"I have everything completed and am just waiting for you to finish the editing. I'll submit the rest to you as soon as we have completed the manuscript."

"Fantastic--," He sounded more confident, "Also, I wanted to ask about this remark by Ted, who says: 'Geez Louise'. Was that a typo?"

"It's just old slang." Chuckling, I felt a little guilty knowing that English was his second language, "It's like saying 'oh wow', or 'holy smokes'."

"Thank you--," He took a moment to write something down, "I studied Linguistics, but am still learning slang terminology."

"Well, we seem to be a lot alike." Tapping a finger upon the desk, I smirked, "I studied philosophy and am still trying to learn how to write."

He had laughed heartily, and then asked, "One more thing and I'll let you get back to your evening. I noticed that you mention Deb Carlson had military background, and then you continue to say in a clerical position. How do you connect these two things? Is she military or involved with the church?"

"English is a little confusing--," I sighed, "A cleric is involved with the church, but a clerical position means office work."

"I should have known that--," He sounded a little annoyed with himself, "I'll keep my Webster dictionary close—and do you mind if I call to clarify things from time to time?"

"I welcome the assistance, my friend. Please, feel free to call anytime."

"Oh—and one more thing, now that I remember--," He flipped through pages, and paused to ask, "I noticed that you also own a magazine—by any chance, are you in need of additional editors or writers?"

The thought had been appealing, but the consequences too extreme. It was with great reluctance and disappointment that I had responded, "Not at the moment—but maybe in the near future?"

"I am very interested in the paranormal--," He explained, "If there is any opportunity for part-time work, please keep me in mind?"

"You can count on that."

"Then I wish you a good evening, Michael—talk again soon."

Amica had returned with tea, and curiously looked over while setting the tray down upon the little table, "Who would call at this hour?"

"That was my editor Ole--," I had promptly explained as she served the steaming cups, "He was just checking up on a few details. I told him to feel free to call anytime—so he wasn't being rude or intrusive."

She had placed our tea down upon plates at the edge of my desk, and gently running her fingers through my hair, said, "Alright. dear, I was just curious."

A sudden and chilling sensation ran the length of my spine, the sense of which now tingled like the legs of a spider that crept into my right ear. Amica had noticed as I had physically convulsed, as swiftly taking hold of my hand, leaned down to look directly into my face, "Is something the matter?"

There was an icy mass churning deep in the core of my being. It was a sensation that, causing sudden nausea, now left me almost speechless, "I'm not certain—I just feel bitterly cold...."

She had moved from the chair and retrieving the blanket, slung it about my shoulders as she gently rubbed at my arms. I had looked up at her and sensed a deep dread in those wide and brilliant green eyes.

The cold seemed to spread outward and into my limbs, creeping through arteries and flowing like ice through my veins, numbing and chilling me to the bone! Trembling uncontrollably, my jaw clattered as Amica now pulled me from the chair, and throwing the blanket about us both, attempted to warm me with her body. My flesh had become so cold that I could neither feel the blanket, nor any motion or movement that she made.

"What do you feel?" Brushing the hair from my eyes, she leaned close, her words barely above a whisper, "Michael--," She took hold of my face between both hands and forced my gaze into her own, "You must tell me—what do you feel."

"Terribly frightened--," The thoughts had seemingly come from out of nowhere, "Helpless, hopeless and desperate...."

She had immediately taken me into a tight embrace, shoving my face into her breast and covering me with the blanket. I'm not exactly certain as to how long she had silently just held me like that. It might have been moments or hours for all that it had mattered. All that I know for certain is that we had remained there until the chill had finally dissipated.

"What just happened?" I had looked to her for an answer that never came. She had only stared as while gently assisting me back into the chair, returned to her seat. The fact that the tea had grown cold was an indication of how long we had been embraced upon the floor. Noticing this, she had promptly taken my cup and gone into the bathroom to empty the contents. Returning a moment later, she poured a fresh cup. The hot tea had done me some good, but my thoughts were scrambled and the chill had left me buried in doubt.

"Nothing evil could have entered these grounds—or come into this place--," Amica spoke as though knowing my fear, "But something did come--," She stared upon me as though terrified, her eyes filling with tears as she quietly said, "A final farewell before departing this world...."

"A friend--," The horror now took hold of my heart as I leaned closer to Amica, "Was this some kind of a final visitation by a friend, or loved one?"

She only watched like one mesmerized or caught in some unspeakable nightmare. It was almost as though she refused or simply could not reveal the truth. This only served to terrify me even further, as I contemplated the possibilities, and feared the answer....

"Amica—please--," I had gently fallen before her upon my knees and taking hold of her hands, pleaded, "If you know something, anything, please tell me."

Slowly shaking her head, she had just sadly looked down at me. It was apparent that neither of us had even the slightest clue.

"Then, at least for mercy's sake—tell me that this had nothing to do with Caitlin."

"I cannot answer that--," She appeared even further distraught as a tear rolled down her cheek, "I am no longer able to see or sense her. My power fades with mortality—and I dare not inquire of other forces..."

"She remains secure--," Marlowe spoke from deep within, "As does the beloved of your companion. But beware—the power that Amica had is far less than it once was. Soon, you shall both be at the mercy of flesh and the coming darkness...."

"Marlowe, I'm afraid—for all of us." Pausing in thought, I gazed upon Amica as though for the last time, "I fear the darkness becoming aware—and finding others in distant places."

"Hold true to yourself and those who now depend upon you." Marlowe sounded confident, "The evil is far less intelligent than you perceive it to be. It functions upon lower levels, frequencies befitting things that creep in the damp earth, and dwell in ancient caverns. Though it might be crafty and deviant, it does not reason, and cannot fathom beyond its design."

"Are you telling me that this thing can be fooled?"

"It is a force of nature—a power and presence to be respected and feared—but is not among the enlightened of the Elohim."

I knew the word. It was the old Hebrew name for God. Marlowe was now referring to angelic beings. It had all begun to make sense. Amica altering her form to become a target, the darkness identifying individuals by energy rather than physical appearances. She had become Caitlin to draw our affections, and through that power, now hoped to deceive the horrors of the night. Our enemy had its faults, weaknesses of which I now knew that we could use against it.

"Be wary--," Marlowe warned, "For even a blind dog may bite and kill. All things shall soon come together—as we shall meet fate upon destinies path...."

She looked to me as though having heard his voice. It was more than I could bear.

Gently taking her hand, I whispered in promise, "I'll die first before I allow anything to happen to you, this time..."

A single tear rolled down her cheek as she looked back at me. I felt a timeless sorrow that echoed like a distant cry in the chambers of my aching heart. If this was going to end in darkness, then we would perish together upon oblivions pathway....

Wednesday, January 29, 1975.
3:35 p.m.
The morning had started with a fast breakfast, and then the departure of Raymond, Rich and Tim. Their intensions were to move Tanya and the boys from his home, and into an apartment near Red Cloud and the others. Once safely secured, they would retrieve the truck and return with Scott to move everything and anything of a questionable nature. It had been well over two hours before they had returned, and another several before the moving had finally been completed. This had consisted of items taken from the warehouse, Rich's private menagerie of horrors, and lastly, the figure of Pan and the maiden, as promised. By the time that all had been done and said, it was well after two in the afternoon and we were all exhausted. I had

wanted to introduce Amica to Scott, but she had refrained, insisting that it was not the proper time. Rather than argue the matter, she had just avoided being seen, and remained in the bedroom.

"What do you figure we should do about those noises we keep hearing on the roof?" Scott was visibly unsettled, as closing the rear doors of the moving truck, paused to look back at us.

"No matter what happens--," I had gently patted his shoulder, "Don't leave the house—or set foot anywhere in the darkness. The evil has awakened again. It's testing us, looking for a weak link."

"What happens if something else comes around--," Adjusting the collar of his coat in the frozen wind, Scott nervously looked around, "Something that charms and those runic symbols won't stop…"

Rich had reluctantly peered over at me. We both knew that it wasn't just a possibility, and that it was simply a matter of time. There were few choices and only one feasible answer to our friend's question. Rich had literally taken the thoughts out of my mind and spoken before I could answer.

"Scott—the safest option that we could offer would be for you to take Pam and your family, and move into the building with the others, for the time being. It's fortified against burglary, has steel gates, is alarmed, and has all the same symbols as Sanctum Arcanum."

"Everyone was talking back at the office this morning. Old Red, Deb and Tanya all got visits on the same night--," Scott frowned, as removing his glasses and wiping the fogged lenses, quietly said, "To tell you boys the truth, it scared the living day-lights out of me. Are any of us really safe anywhere from this thing anymore?"

"No—we really aren't," Tim swallowed hard, and looking between us, said, "I couldn't even begin to imagine what it must be like for you, going through this with a wife and child, but knowing what's out there—and what it's capable of doing, Rich is right: It's better to stay altogether."

"Please--," I looked to my old friend, "Take Carrie, Patrick and Pam, and relocate to the office apartments. It's just for the time being—and I agree with the others, it's the safest prospect at the moment."

"It's the best idea and only safe course of action at this point--," Raymond agreed, "I'll see what I can do about getting you some rifles—and a revolver or two, just in case."

"We're already licenced, and we've got our hunting rifles loaded, and out where we can reach them--," Scott thanked him, "Carrie's a dead-shot at a hundred yards—and I'm no slouch either."

"Please, ask Carrie to call Deb and her husband--," I followed as Scot began making his way back toward the cab of the truck, "Have them move into the building as well. I'd like to have everyone in one place as soon as possible. Would you be kind enough to give me a call, and let me know how soon they can get their things together? I really don't want anyone alone or out after dark, anymore."

"Sure thing, bro--," Scott climbed back into the truck, and grunting, glared back at me, "When will it be our turn to fight back against this thing—or is that even possible?"

"Well, we're working on it. We have police involvement now--," I had attempted to reassure him, "Detective Gordon Simms and Sergeant Ian MacTavish have joined the effort. Also, I'm working day and night on this, and I'm hoping to come up with some kind of an answer soon."

"Isn't that the same sour-puss that tossed you in jail?" Scott raised an eyebrow in question, "Can we even trust that turkey?"

"At this point—we need all the help that we can get." Rich shook his head, glancing up at Scott, and grumbled, "But still, and for what he did to us before? I'd still like to put a swift boot straight up that Detective's--."

"Gas--," Raymond pointed toward the fuel gauge as he climbed into the truck, "We're running low, and don't need to be taking any more chances than we have to."

"I'll call you when Carrie gets a hold of Deb." Scott promised as he slammed the cab door, and leaning out the window, added, "I'll see to it that we're moved into the building long before dark. Oh—and when the time comes, bro—you know that you can count on us to be there for you."

Reaching upward and taking a firm hold upon his hand, I smiled sadly while looking into my dear friend's eyes. I couldn't have possibly wished for a truer or greater friend. It hurt that he and his family had to suffer this nightmare. In the darkest of times, I had been surrounded in the most amazing, loyal and loving people. I would have done anything to spare them the hell to come...

"I know that—and never doubted it for a moment. Drive safely—give Carrie my best, and please—don't get caught outside after dark..."

"You got it--," Scott started the engine, and bringing up the revolutions, waved back at me, "Hang in there, bro—we'll get through this—we always do!"

He had always been a feisty and brave soul, and his words offered hope on that dismal and bitter cold afternoon. I had given him the 'thumbs-up' in gesture as they departed, and waved as they slowly pulled away. I stood silently and watched as they traveled down the long driveway and toward the gates. With the world in shades of black and white and shadows blending all in between, it seemed more like the ending of some timeless and frozen, bad dream. In passing, the shadow of their truck crossed the path of where Harry's sad ending still stained the snow. The crimson had faded into a deep brown, and though the boys had tried to remove and cover it, the memory still stained the frozen ground. Rubbing at my eyes, I couldn't help but squint and stare. Was the stain even truly still there—or was it an image that burned into memory, was a grim souvenir that now haunted my heart? Or perhaps, it was just Harry's restless soul, and where death and the devil had forever left their mark...

Rich had leaned close, and speaking quietly, asked, "You're not going to drag Scott and Carrie any further into this nightmare, are you?"

"Not on your life--," Glancing over at my friend, I shivered in the icy wind, "And not even to save my own..."

"Yeah, that's what I thought." He tugged at my sleeve, and motioning with a nod toward the house, said, "Let's get inside before we catch our death of cold out here..."

"The guest house is all locked up tight for the evening." Tim blew hot air into his hands with a shiver, "It looks like those work crews have almost finished with the gates."

We had all looked to where the men now struggled with the massive gates while attempting to fir them into the tracking. It appeared reassuring at first, but then someone shouted something about further modifications, and we all stepped back. It all meant more time, and with the tock ticking, we simply couldn't afford to wait much longer...

"They had a hell of a time modifying those old gates to fit onto modern tracking--," Rich explained, "We had to weld an additional support bar at the base—it's just a matter of grinding it until it drops into place on the carrier. We even used larger wheels so that they'd move in the snow. It should be okay—I hope..."

"With all the snow that we've been getting--," Tim groaned, "Maybe you should have installed a draw-bridge instead?"

I might have laughed, if I hadn't agreed with him. Usually our winters were fairly mild, but I now had concerns about becoming trapped in the snow, and by my own gates...

"In any case, I should get over to the guest house." Tim looked between us, "I need to warm up these old bones before I catch a nasty chill."

"Would you care for a nice hot cup of tea?" Sensing that he'd been awaiting an invitation, I smiled, "It's close to supper-time anyway—you might as well stick around."

"Well—I suppose, if it's no bother." He had appeared overjoyed at the prospect, and all things considered, who could have blamed him.

4:28 p.m.

Moving toward the living room and opening the draperies, I peered out at the gates. They had installed motorized tracks with wheels and securely mounted the gates upon them. Anxiously, I watched as they were finishing with the enormous chain-driven gear boxes that operated them from either side. Rich had even gone so far as to have them disguised as an extension of the brick-work pillars. It had taken several crews the better part of the day, but the results were astonishing!

Amica had taken my hand as we stood before the window. I felt her fingers tighten upon mine as she looked up at me. There was a mixture of relief and pending doom reflecting in those brilliant emerald eyes. I sensed it as well, but only smiled in return.

The clock chimed on the half hour from behind us and she turned to glance at the old mechanism. She had always had a strange fascination for clocks and the illusion that we knew as time. It had never troubled her before, but that was before she had experienced the fragile form of mortality.

Amica stood silently beside me, as observing the progress with the greatest of anticipation, cast suspicious glances into the high branches of the surrounding pines. At first, I had considered inquiring as to what had drawn her attention, but then decided against it. In any event, it was either the insect, or some undead nightmare awaiting darkness, before descending upon us.

At the moment, my greatest concern was for the fact that we had neither received a call from Scott, nor seen the return of Raymond. With the hour growing late and darkness soon approaching, my nerves were stretching to their ends.

"It appears as though they've finished with the gates." There was something victorious in her tone, but unsettling in her expression, "They're removing their tools and leaving."

"That's very reassuring, but I just wish that Raymond would get back soon."

Taking hold of my hand, she gently led me away from the window and to the couch, seating me before the hearth. Tending to the coals and adding another log, she glanced back from the fire, and quietly said, "He's likely gone off to help Scott and his family get moved. Or possibly, in a last moment's thought, decided to assist Deb and her husband."

"That's what I'm afraid of…"

Usually, the smell of spiced meats cooking and a warm hearth would have settled my soul, but not on this afternoon. All that it meant now was that evening approached and members of our extended family had not returned… Unable to just sit there, I went back to the window, and parting the curtains, looked out into the pale gloom. The work crews had now gathered, and moving to their trucks and assorted vehicles, began departing the property. Amica had returned to my side, and understanding my anxiety, stood silent.

I had followed every movement and each action taken until the last vehicle had passed through the gates. Then, with nothing left to see, I gazed somberly out and into the empty, snow-covered street.

"Hasn't he come back yet?" Rich startled us at the window, as curiously peering out from between us, frowned in the failing light, "He should've been back a while ago…"

"Amica felt that he might have gone to help the others get moved."

"If he did--," There was a hesitation in Rich's tone, "Then I sure hope that he stays with them tonight—and doesn't try to beat the clock back here…"

No sooner had the words passed his lips than did the telephone suddenly ring! I had raced to answer it and was relieved to finally hear my friend's voice, "Raymond—where are you—it's getting dark!"

"You're not going to believe this--," The desperation and anxiety caused him to stumble over his own words, "I was running late, because I helped Scott and the others get moved into the apartments—and I've got a freaking flat tire, not ten blocks away from home!"

"Oh—dear God…" Desperate, I looked back as the others gathered about me to listen, asking, "Where exactly are you—I'll come to get you."

"No—it's too late for that--," Raymond argued, "I'm in a telephone booth at the corner of Elm and nineteenth—you'd never make it here and back in time."

"A flat tire—and you're in a telephone booth at Elm and nineteenth." I repeated the words as though failing to have heard or even believed them, "Most of that district is all undeveloped—Raymond, for the love of god, get out of there. There must be houses within a few blocks…"

"I'm not bringing this into the home of some unsuspecting family--," He argued, and though I could hear the terror and despair in his words, he said, "I drove as far as I could before the rim cut through the tire—this is it…"

Having heard the call, Rich had turned and ran hysterically toward the door. Before anyone could have even said anything, he had thrown on his boots and coat and dashed out the door!

"Rich is coming for you—Raymond, please stay on the line."

"That crazy son of a bitch is going to get himself killed!"

"There's still time—you can make it--," I spoke calmly, assertively as I heard Rich's truck roaring as it sped down the driveway, "He's already off the property—just hold on—he'll be there shortly."

It had finally happened, the inevitable and desperate race against the one thing that there never seemed to be enough, time…

Tim had silently slipped down into a chair at the dining table, his face ashen and blank. In that moment, and through the terror, I had seen death in his dark eyes.

"I thought that I had enough time--," Raymond apologized, his voice becoming desperate as the darkness now descended, "This shouldn't have happened—those tires are brand-new!"

"Rich gave me this—before he left." Tim placed the large remote upon the table before me, tears welling in his eyes, as he whispered, "It's for the gates…"

"I'm sorry--," Raymond sounded distant, "I have to hang up now—it's getting dark. God bless and keep you all, my friend…"

"No—wait!" My plea had fallen upon deaf ears and to the sound of the dial tone, as the phone went dead in my cold and trembling hand…

The enormous truck slid dangerously as Rich maneuvered through the snow at hazardous speeds. He could see the end of the street, and to where the light of the little telephone booth stood against the darkening heavens. With all the flood-lamps, side-lights and head-lamps burning brightly, he slammed a fist down upon the air horns! Plowing like a locomotive down the empty street, he raced against time, the night, and the devil!

Raymond hung up the phone as the light began to fail from all about him. The shadows deepened, the wind grew stronger and the chill now bit deeply into the exposed flesh of his hands and face. Of all the places that he could have broken down, why on a long stretch of empty road, and surrounded in forested property? He suspected that it had not been a coincidence, and that their worst fear had finally come true…

Slowly drawing his revolvers, he prepared for the inevitable. It was something that he knew he wouldn't have to wait on for much longer. There was already movement in the deep shadows of the dense pine branches, and it had immediately caught his attention. It began to snow, light at first, and then became a steady flurry that covered all evidence of his ever having been there.

"Alright, you bastards--," He stepped out from the telephone booth, and raising his revolvers, cursed under his breath, "Come and get me—if you think that you can…"

The forest came to life from all around him, things creeping, crawling from the deep shadows as the final rays of light now faded from all around him. Firing blindly into the stumbling and lumbering horrors, he cried out in despair as the bullets were soon emptied from his prized revolvers!

The sound of thunder echoed from all around him and he spun into the flood of brilliant light that approached the street ahead. There was a sound like a train, which he suddenly realized to have been Rich's air horns! In a moment of desperation, he began running wildly toward the swiftly approaching vehicle, when unexpectedly, something came up from beneath the snow, and bowling him over, reared upward and from high above him!

In those final moments, and as he had spun to look upon the nightmare, he saw his own death approach in the form of a hideous, writhing mass of conjoined and decaying corpses.

"Get in the freaking truck!" Rich shrieked, as leaping from the vehicle, he threw a firebomb at the horror. There was a sudden eruption of flames, the inferno lighting the area as a mind-numbing shriek shattered the growing darkness!

From all about them came the horde, a crawling, and creeping mass of hideous decay. They had been waiting, watching for an opportunity, and now slithered and crept out from the dark and hidden places where they had been concealed.

Pulling at his fallen friend, Rich cried out as the deepening shadows reached out toward them! He knew that the talisman could not save them from the dead and that the light had no effect upon physical entities. Having been unprepared and only brought the single fire-bomb, their options and time was swiftly running out.

"You shouldn't have come out here!" Wailing as they struggled through the unnatural storm and toward the truck, Raymond cursed, "Those things are everywhere!"

"Well—I wasn't about to leave you out here! So, just shut up and run!"

They had narrowly escaped the tendrils of something indistinguishable, and slammed their doors as something immense slithered toward them from out of the forest! Comprised of animal and writhing, human remains, it moved like an immense and ghastly centipede, rearing up and towering over the vehicle!

"Drive—for the love of God—drive, man!" Raymond reloaded his revolvers and began firing blindly into the black and moldering hell that stood before them.

Shoving the shifter into reverse and slamming his foot down on the gas pedal, Rich sent the all-wheel drive truck sailing backward! It had been done not a moment too soon, as the horror crashed down into the very place where they had been parked only seconds before. The effort had been done with such force, that fragments and entire corpses were torn free and cast from all about. Then, the slippery and oozing parts had crawled through the deep snow, as gathering, conjoined once more with the seething mass. It would have been completely invisible to anyone passing, as shielded from view by the blizzard, continued its pursuit of the men.

In those few moments, Rich had managed to turn the truck around, and with horrors clambering and struggling all over the truck, sped back down the dark road.

"They're all over us!" Raymond grabbed spare rounds from the center console, and loading his revolvers, continued firing out the open window.

"I can't shake them!" Rich gawked, "You keep bullets in my truck?"

"They were still in there from the time that I took Michael up to Hedley. And you should be grateful—and not complaining about it!" Raymond fired into the face of something that crept over the cab and hung down into his open window, "Not that bullets make much of a difference against these damn things!"

"Just hold on—we're almost back to the house!"

"We're not going to make it—they're just too many of the damned things!"

Struggling to reload his revolvers again, Raymond cried out as something smashed the windshield! With shards of glass exploding inward, both men fought desperately against the rotting nightmares that now forced their way into the cab!

"We can't close the gates." Tim swallowed hard as we stood in the open doorway, "Not as long as there's even a slight chance for them."

Holding the remote in a trembling hand, I watched as the shadows ran deeper, the snow came, and night descended upon Sanctum Arcanum. Through the increasing flurries I could make out dark forms and twisted shapes that began gathering in the gloom at the gates. Whether they had only been shades or something far worse, I could only dare to imagine. All that I knew for certain is that I could not abandon my friends, or surrender while a single hope remained.

Amica had stood firm at my side, her tone cold and words calculated, "Gate-keeper—prepare to summon the guardian from the vaults. Something is coming..."

Drawing the golden key and placing the whistle end to his lips, he awaited final instructions.

"What about--," Fearing the guardian due to the demon within her, I had begun to speak, but she had hushed me by placing a finger to my lips. Her answer had been whispered, "Have no fear, I am sheltered between the key, Marlowe and our love."

Startled by a sudden sound of fluttering, the insect suddenly crashed to the frozen earth before us! Shielding Amica with my body, I had motioned for Tim to remain absolutely still. The creature righted itself and slowly turned to gaze upon us. She was the height of an average human being, but appeared taller due to her lean build and antennae. For all of her humanoid qualities, she was still very much an insect in appearance.

Those large and luminescent blue eyes piercing the shadows, she curiously examined us, and uttering a sound that was more inquisitive than threatening, drew our attention down to a lower pair of her arms. She held a piece of fruit in the claw of her right arm, and making a type of purring sound, looked back at us. Her antennae moved ever so slightly, it was an expression of understanding, and a gift in sharing. Making a soft mewling sound, she looked between us, and extending an arm, made the offering of the fruit to all of us.

"That's for you—Trudy." Smiling and speaking softly, I had knelt and gently touching the claw, moved it back toward her, "For you..."

There had been an almost immediate reaction, as the entire demeanour of the insect had become subdued and she moved closer. I was taken completely by surprise, as between her movements and the motions of her antennae, she was even capable of communicating through expression. Rich had been right, she truly understood, and for all of her differences, was a sentient being. I had attempted to communicate further with the creature, but a sudden and violent uproar at the gates sent us all sprawling backward. It was Rich! Accelerating and racing recklessly toward the open gates, he slid through while carrying a host of nightmares with him!

Seeing this, Trudy had screeched, and spreading her wings, leapt high into the air as she shot toward the approaching vehicle!

Pressing down upon the button, I gasped as the gates began closing. The truck had stopped only yards away from the garage, and as Raymond and

Rich struggled to escape, Trudy now desperately fought against the horde! I could see that my friends had both been terrified at first, but understood as Trudy had shielded them with her body. Then, slashing outward into the ghastly horde, she had provided them several moments and an opportunity for escape.

Blowing upon the ancient golden key, Tim now summoned the guardian! As through the gale force blizzard, I saw the insect as overwhelmed, in a last and desperate attempt, grabbed both men and flew off while carrying them!

In that same moment the keeper of the vaults had appeared. It appeared as an immense, formless and shining, green mist! A light of which, wherever coming into contact with one of those nightmares, caused them to burst into ethereal blue flame!

Trudy's fight had not ended, as watching from the doorway, we saw her battling against something near the rear of the property. With Raymond and Rich stumbling toward us, we had dropped everything else and rushed to their assistance.

They were both battered and bleeding and fell into our arms as we half-carried them from out of that chaos and into the house. We had all fallen into the main hall and slamming the door closed, locked and bolted it.

"You saved my life--," Raymond tightly grasped Rich's arm, "I owe you."

"And Trudy saved both of us—and she's still out there—alone," Rich stumbled to the window, and parting the curtains, gasped, "Oh my God, it's gone—everything has just vanished! The blizzard, those things and whatever you summoned from the vault!"

Rushing to the window, we had all stared in disbelief. With exception to the truck, which still sat running near the garage, it seemed like nothing had ever happened...

"What happened to Trudy—I don't see her out there anywhere?" Rich appeared more concerned than frightened, as opening the door, ran desperately out into the night. Oblivious of our own welfare, we had all quickly followed our friend out the door.

Blinded by the bright lights of the truck, which illuminated the entire driveway, we were forced to approach even slower. Ever so cautiously, we made our way to where we had last seen the creature, but there was nothing to be found. All trace of the horrors and ensuing battle had been erased as though it had all been some terrifying hallucination. It was apparent by their expressions that none could believe their eyes. Instinctively, I had turned and looked to the gates. As through the long shadows and from between the black iron bars, I could still make out the shadows and forms of things that still lurked there.

Raymond had followed Rich to where, moving the truck into the garage, they had slowly walked back toward us.

"It's like nothing ever happened here--," Raymond cursed under his breath, "No tracks in the snow—no blood, not a single damn thing."

"It's always this way--," Rich muttered, his eyes attempting to pierce the surrounding forest and shadows, "I don't see Trudy here anywhere—she must've taken off again."

"She was here before all hell broke loose--," I had informed him, and shivering in the icy gust, said, "She came to us while we waited for you at the door. She brought a piece of fruit—something that you had left for her. It was a gift—an offering of peace and friendship between us. You were right—she's just like a child—and was only trying to come home..."

"I knew that she wasn't just some experiment gone wrong." There was hope in his eyes again for the first time, "She's intelligent—and has feelings, like us..."

"She's nothing like the others--," Tim agreed, and drawing the collar of the coat closer about his ears, said, "But that's because, unlike them, she's always been a part of you."

There had been a moment of silence between us as the wind moaned mournfully through the tall pines. It was a journey of terror and confusion that had finally come to a conclusion, and an opportunity that we had all only previously dreamed.

"Maybe she's in the attic?" Rich appeared hopeful, as turning and looking into the dark window high above, he muttered, "It's her home—and makes sense."

I could see that he was becoming desperate and was grasping at straws. In fact, something now had my nerves on edge. Looking toward the dark attic window, I sensed that something was terribly wrong.

"Well, it's too damn cold and I've seen enough of the dark for one night--," Raymond reminded us, "Please—let's go back inside."

Rich was reluctant and became increasingly agitated while continually glancing back and into the dark forest. For reasons that I couldn't explain, I shared his apprehension with giving up the search, but Raymond had been right, we couldn't accomplish much more. The estate was quite large, it was freezing, and if she was out there somewhere, eventually she would come home.

"She'll come back, old buddy--," Raymond reassured him, "Now, let's get inside and warm up before we all end up as permanent fixtures out here."

We had all begun to turn and make our way back to the house when Amica had halted us, listening, and peering about suspiciously, "Did anyone else hear that?"

At first, all that I could make out was the whistle of the wind in the pines, but then it came.

It was a strange, though familiar, mewling. My heart ached as I sensed that it was the beckon call of something wounded, and suffering...

Rich had spun to look at me, and then rushed out while following the whimpers into a dense patch of thick pine branches. To our utter horror, Trudy lay upon her side, bleeding, twisted, battered and broken. With her wings and shell torn away in places, the life was seeping away into a dark stain in the deep snow.

She had looked up at Rich, a single remaining antenna rising hopefully as he fell to his knees beside her. There were tears in my eyes, for in that moment, we had all realized that this terrifying creature had in fact been little more than a child.

"Oh no—Trudy..." His whisper echoed in our aching hearts.

In the darkness of that desolate and cold place we had all gathered, watching as Rich knelt, and gently stroked the face of the dyeing creature. It was mortally wounded, having received injuries that would have easily killed a lesser being. Yet through it all, it had recognized Rich and gently touched his face as the father held his child in her final moments. She had mewled in affection, and then, as the blue faded from her eyes, slipped silently down onto the frozen earth.

"So alone in this world—so lost--," Amica had whispered through tears, "Her suffering has finally come to an end..."

"She came home to us--," Rich had trembled as he looked back at me, his lenses fogging as the tears flowed from his eyes, "She came home..."

Raymond had leaned down beside his friend, and placing a supportive arm around him, bowed his head. Looking to the heavens and then back down to the fallen creature, Rich cast a hand before his face and openly wept. I wept with him, not just for the loss, but because I knew that on that night, something truly special had died within my friend.

We had wrapped the body in canvas and laid her out upon a pyre of wood that we had built in the garden. Surrounded by stone angels, Rich had cast a flame in parting, and we had all bowed our heads in silent prayer. Not all the devils in hell or the things that walked by night could extinguish the love, or flames that now carried our lost child into the heavens. Never in my life had I regretted anything quite so much, as while considering how I had allowed fear to rule over my heart.

"Not all things that appear evil are your enemy." Marlowe's words echoed in my aching heart. We had all stood close together and supported one another as the flames reached high into the darkened heavens. There was a sudden stillness as the winds calmed and the night fell into utter silence. In the sanctity of the moment, and among the solemn gaze of stone angels, we bade farewell to Trudy, one last time...

CHAPTER TEN

Thursday, January 30, 1975.
10:25 a.m.
Dinner had been silent, and other than the complimentary small-talk, we had all retired early that night. I had made the necessary addition of the events of the evening to the manuscript, and soon after, fallen into dark and disturbed dreams. Amica had slept beside me on the bed, and when the morning came, I felt as though I hadn't slept in days. My dreams had been plagued with images of Hedley, the destruction of the nest, and possibility that we might have extinguished a possibly sentient species. Knowing that they had begun as a government experiment and that under improper conditions they could become a plague still did not justify our actions. What we had done was nothing short of genocide, regardless of intentions. It had become a moral battle of ethics in my mind. Could we justify the right to a creature's existence, simply by the means of having existed, regardless of the source?

"Nothing that exists has lived without purpose—or without right to the life that it was granted." Marlowe spoke among my thoughts, "The body is fleeting—and living energy eternal. None can truly extinguish that which is intended. Cease these thoughts—and do not punish yourself unjustly for actions taken in righteous intent."

"But, to be granted life artificially or by means other than naturally intended--," I had attempted a theoretical debate on the moral principle, but was swiftly intercepted.

"All things in creation bear life—none but the eternals may grant such a thing. Although, and by alchemical process, the seed or spark of life may be manipulated, all exist by design."

"Trudy was created in a lab--," I was interrupted again as Marlowe knew my thoughts long before they had even been properly expressed.

"The Corporeal—the physical manifestation of a thing means little. The homunculi can be created—and yet, without the spark of life, it exists only as flesh without vitality. Scripture speaks of revitalising the soul—but never of the man who might bring life to that which has never before existed."

"Then how is it possible for the darkness to animate the bodies of the dead?"

"Elementals possess and obsess the body—but can never bring soul or conscious life to decaying matter. They revel within such things, as this is blasphemy, and an evil that stands against the natural laws of all things in existence."

"Then I can consider myself admonished of all guilt in the matter."

"Are you awake?" Amica rolled over, and curiously drawing the blankets from where I had pulled them to shield them from the daylight, smiled, "Tim called us to breakfast earlier—but I thought to allow you a little extra rest."

Realizing to have drifted off, I rubbed the sleep from my eyes and glanced over at the clock. What I had presumed to have been a five minute discussion with Marlowe had actually been closer to two hours.

"That was very thoughtful of you, but you must be starving?"

Raising a dinner plate from where it had been concealed from sight on the floor, she grinned, "No, I went down and brought some back—while I waited for you." She thought for a moment, and then presenting a second, empty plate, added, "I brought some for you as well—but when you didn't wake, I was worried that it would become cold and be spoiled."

"I'm not really much for breakfast--," Climbing off the bed, I made my way to the door and looked back at her, "I'm going to have a quick shower—did you need the bathroom before I go?"

"Not at the moment--," She halted me with a finger raised in thought, saying, "But it's a woman's prerogative to change her mind—so don't be long."

I couldn't help but pause to smile back at her. She had taken on Caitlin's appearance, but her own personality had begun to shine through. It was like spending time with a twin who was just as endearing as her sister. In those moments, and in the absence of her dark counterpart, I knew that I truly loved her…

Noticing my expression, she had suddenly appeared concerned, asking, "Are you alright?"

"Yes--," I lied, "I was just remembering what happened with Trudy last night. I'd better go and have that shower before it gets any later…"

10:45.am.

Making my way down the stairs and into the kitchen, I was surprised to find Raymond sitting alone at the dining table, playing Solitaire.

"Is everything alright?" Pulling out a chair and joining him, I looked around the empty living room, "Didn't you have to work this morning?"

"Third game consecutive that I've lost--," He tossed down the cards, and leaning back in the seat, looked back at me, "I took light-duty all winter to avoid coming back in the dark, but after what happened last night? Well, I took a leave of absence for medical reasons—one month, pending return."

"I'm sorry to hear that—and at the same time, I feel a lot better that you won't be running that risk again."

He had noticed that I peered about inquisitively, and motioned toward the window, "Rich and Tim went out to run a few errands. Poor guy, he's still pretty shook up about what happened to his bug last night. He asked if I would go into the attic and remove the things that he'd placed there for her. I did that after they left—and I've been sitting here sucking back coffee and playing cards ever since."

"Has there been any word from Simms yet?"

"Not a peep—but if I know him, he's been putting something big together. He's known for organizing teams for manhunts and tracking down some of the worst characters that you can imagine. Under the circumstances, I'd sure hate to be him. Can you imagine what it might be like, recruiting a group of dependable and honest men, many of them friends, to possibly send to their deaths?"

It hadn't taken long to answer that one. He'd seen the look in my eyes and frowned, "I suppose that you might, but we all came willingly, it's not like we were recruited or forced by anyone." He suddenly stared past me and into the kitchen, and bursting into a grin, said, "Go right ahead, darling, it's all yours."

Turning in time to see Amica vanish into the kitchen with the remains of the previous night's pork roast dinner, I could only laugh. Merlin had been close on her heels, and meowing loudly as he knew that she would happily share the spoils.

"It's amazing, the way that lady eats--," He chuckled while scratching at his mustache, "It's a miracle that she doesn't just explode. I have no idea where she puts it all."

I had my suspicions, but said nothing.

The telephone rang and we were both startled. Hurrying into the kitchen to answer, I had smiled in recognition, "Carrie—How are things?"

Amica had been sitting across from me in the breakfast nook. Busily working her way through the last two pounds of pork roast, she paused to listen.

"We got everyone moved into apartments over here at the office--," She sighed deeply, "I can't say I'm thrilled about this—but it sure beats risking another night at the store."

"Did you hear about what happened here last night?"

"Yes--," She paused in thought, "You boys came really close to a bad ending. I was also sorry to hear about Rich's pet project. I always figured that there was more to that thing than any of us really knew. It's too bad that it had to end the way that it did."

"Rich hasn't been the same since it happened--," I nodded in thanks as Amica brought me a cup of tea, and I said, "This has all been getting more complicated, dangerous and confusing with every passing day. How are Tanya and the boys? Did Deb and her husband get settled in?"

"Tanya's still shaken up, but she's got the boys with her, so she'll manage. Not to mention, she has Jen, Red, and Pam for company. Deb and her old man are moving in as we speak. All that anyone brought were a few comforts from home and some personal things. So, moving really wasn't such a big effort. Red ordered a bunch of queen-size beds, and with everyone helping, we got things sorted out here pretty fast. The boys helped bring up whatever we needed from the warehouse, so furniture wasn't an issue either. These places aren't so bad. They're spacious, and all the plumbing and heating works just fine. All they really needed was to be vacuumed. Mind you, they could've used a little paint, but heck, they'll do the job for the time being."

"Is there anything that we can do to make things easier on everyone?"

"Well, we have a diner in the building, an anything that we might need down in the warehouse. Old Red has the cable hooked up, so we have television and most of the comforts of home, but maybe someone could do something about the laundry facilities? Red just takes his down to that old Chinese drycleaner down the street. I know this isn't going to be forever, but it would sure help for now."

"Alright—I don't really have the time to handle that, but if you don't mind managing the purchase and organizing everything—just put it on the company account. How many do you think that you'll need? Would three washers and three dryers do the trick?"

"Michael—you've got five women here and six men—it might be better to run six and six. Even then, we'll have to arrange for people laundering on certain days."

"Maybe we should start charging rent?"

"Don't you go and start getting cheeky with me--," She chuckled, "Because, I'll come right over there and slap you right upside the head."

"Alright then—six and six--," I laughed, and thinking for a moment, said, "And while you're dealing with appliances—could you please make sure that everyone's fridges are working properly? We might as well get this all done in one fell swoop."

"You really don't pay me enough for this--," She chortled, "Maybe I should start billing you extra?"

'Touché, you got me." Her endearing character and sharp wit had always warmed my heart, "Add a few cases of that beer that you and Scott like, and toss in some soda for Patrick."

"Are you sure that it's not going to break you?"

Amica had laughed while chewing, covering her mouth as the pork dinner had made a last attempt to escape. I'd forgotten how keen her hearing had been, and how loud Carries voice was over the phone.

"Okay, how about this?" I knew that Carrie was just having some fun with me, but it felt so good that I was obligated to sweeten the proverbial pie, "Being as this is everyone's official first night together, in the building: Arrange for an early dinner, gather everyone together, and order steak and lobster for everyone from Lester's down the street."

"Holy smokes, that'll cost a fortune!"

"Don't tell me that you're going to complain about that now, too?"

"No, I certainly will not—but don't come crying to me when you get the bill."

"No, not a single tear, I promise. Now, was there anything else that you can think of?"

"No—we've got everything else tied up here. Oh, but there's one thing that I think might make you smile?"

"Oh, and what might that be?"

"Well, you know those scary comics that you like so much? I noticed that Danny's started collecting them, too. I think that you've created a monster."

Laughing with the thought, it warmed my heart as I remembered the first time that I had seen his freckled face, peeking over the garden gate. Mortality had touched me at that moment, and all things considered, I made a decision.

"Could you do me a little favor?"

"What—on top of everything else?"

"Seriously—have Danny and Dennis stop here tomorrow, preferably sometime after breakfast. Does Scott still have the canopy on his pick-up truck?"

"He sure does—and I had a heck of a time getting him to do it. You know how much he hates working in the cold."

'Perfect, see to it that the boys use his truck—I'll explain later."

"Alright then--," Let me write this down--," She rummaged around for a pen and paper, "So, we have six and six, check fridges, steak and lobster for everyone from Lester's tonight—does that include wine?"

"Yes—include dessert as well, if you like."

"Alright—have Danny and Dennis drop over sometime after breakfast, and bring Scott's truck. Okay, we're good to go, any last thoughts?"

"Not unless you wanted a new television?"

"Well, now that you mention it? I did have my eye on one of those thirty-two inch screen, RCA color console televisions?"

"Do you hear that sound, Carrie?" I had warned with a chuckle, "It's me oiling the gate of the trap door on my basement alligator-moat."

"Oh come on—you know that I'd just come back out with matching alligator-luggage, and one between my teeth."

"More than likely--," Sighing deeply, I winked at Amica, saying, "Make sure that everyone is home before dark, and call me, if you need anything."

"You got it—and Michael?" She sounded somewhat distant, "You make sure and call us if you need us, okay?"

"Have a pleasant dinner—and stay safe…"

Looking to Amica who covered her mouth due to a surprisingly loud burp, I couldn't help but laugh. She had managed to finish off the roast, carrots and remaining potatoes, and still appeared willing and capable of dessert. I couldn't help but test the theory.

"If you have any room left—there are still two slices of that strawberry-rhubarb pie leftover from the night before."

Without hesitation, she had happily rinsed off the dinner dishes, and hurried to the fridge to fetch dessert. In some aspects she was eating like a woman expecting twins, and to a certain degree, she truly was…

Raymond had wandered into the kitchen for more coffee, and seeing Amica indulging the pie, laughed, "At least someone wanted to finish that one off. It seems like I'm the only one who cared for strawberry-rhubarb around here."

"Actually—I really like it, too." I had cringed with the glare that Amica had offered, as sniffing at her plate, I said, "I've lost my taste for it over the years…"

There was a sudden and frantic pounding upon the front door! Without a second thought, I had hurried to answer with Amica in close pursuit.

Drawing the door open, I stood in shock at what met my eyes: Gordon
Simms had turned from out of the bitter cold, and staring blindly, muttered
something incoherent. All previous perceptions of the detective now faded
as the stuttering and terrified man trembled violently.

Amica had immediately taken him by the arm and drawn him inside. It
was obvious that he was in shock, and we had to literally remove his coat,
muffler and hat before seating him near the hearth. I had poured him a
brandy and watched as struggling to hold the glass. He gobbled the drink
down in great gulps. His features registered obvious horror, his eyes
flashing wildly as he looked between the flames and to where we sat across
from him. He had soon finished the drink and clearing his throat, slid back
into the couch as he rubbed at his eyes. He appeared as though he were
attempting to speak without a voice. It was apparent that he had suffered
some terrible shock and now suffered from the trauma. In all truth, I was
amazed that he had even managed to find his way to the estate.

Amica had taken the glass from his trembling hand and hurried to the
liquor cabinet. I could only watch as he fought some inner demon while
attempting to regain his composure.

"Gordon—you're safe here with us." Amica had returned, and resting a
gentle hand upon his shoulder, offered him the glass, "Please—try to tell us
what has happened."

He had looked up at her and after a moment's thought, accepted the glass
of which he proceeded to gulp at. It had been during one of several
swallows that he had finally settled down enough to speak. As still
gripping the glass, he had looked to us as while sinking deeper into the
cushions.

"Something came to my window—late last night." Shaking his head in
disbelief, he pulled the talisman from beneath his shirt and tie, and said, "I
kept this on—like you asked me to. Sweet Mother of God—it was so cold,
it was horrible, I couldn't breathe and felt like I was going to die--," He
trembled violently, and looking into the hearth, whispered, "It was like
death was a winter night—and it was coming to take me…" He looked
back at us, "How can you fight something like that?"

"It's testing our boundaries--," Speaking calmly and as confidently as
possible, I said, "Several of our colleagues experienced the same thing that
you did. We've moved them all into a common place—a safe place."

Slowly shaking his head, he stared at us, "Is there really any safe place
from something like that?"

"It can't trespass on hallowed ground in spirit form—and the bodies can be burned. All that we have to do is stay together and work through this, one day at a time."

"Time is running out--," The words were weak as his eyes rolled between the flames and where we sat, "Ian's wife called this morning and told me about the accident."

Raymond almost dropped his coffee mug, gawking as he looked between us, "An accident—what accident?"

My heart had leapt into my throat, as looking between Amica and the detective, I waited for the explanation. Gordon sipped at his brandy, the flames reflecting in his wide and terrified eyes. At one point, it had seemed as though he had lost the thought, or drifted into some safe, inner-chamber while attempting to escape the moment. It was likely both as he just looked away, staring silently into the warm glow of the hearth…

"Gordon--," Speaking softly, I had leaned closer to our friend, "Can you tell us what happened?"

He had motioned as though to speak and then halted, slowly shaking his head in suspension of disbelief. Sipping at the brandy, he looked back at me, "Apparently, he'd been in the shower after dinner—when the power had suddenly gone out in his house."

The answer had become painfully clear before he had even finished, but I forced myself to listen. It took another mouthful of brandy before he continued, but his tone became clearer and more audible, "His wife said that he'd come out of the shower, and was still wet, and in his bath robe." Gordon pulled something out of his vest pocket and held up the talisman in a trembling hand, "She said that she found this on the bathroom sink counter."

Amica and Raymond had sadly looked away as there was little mystery as to what had happened.

"Apparently he'd gone to the fuse box—and tried to flip the breakers." Gordon swallowed hard, "The boys downtown said that he was burned beyond recognition." He looked back at me, "So bad in fact, that if it hadn't been for his wife, even dental records would've been useless. They said that his teeth exploded in his mouth like popcorn, and that there was virtually nothing left of the upper and lower mandible…"

"Is that even possible?" The thought had completely taken me off guard.

"According to the coroner it's highly improbable, especially in this situation." Gordon's expression revealed utter and complete terror, "Especially since the fire department didn't find any evidence to substantiate the cause. Not even a burned fuse or damn flash-point."

"So, how on earth will they validate what happened?" Raymond could only stare.

"Spontaneous human combustion." The words soured Gordon's features even further as he spit them out like poison, "They're calling this a freak accident...."

"And what are your thoughts on the matter?" Amica had quietly asked.

He had simply loosened his tie, and drawing the charm from about his neck, solemnly said, "I never took mine off—and I'm still here. I don't know what the hell that thing was—but I do know that somehow it killed him..."

"Are you still willing to risk involving a task force?" The thought had bothered me from the moment that he had first mentioned it, so I felt compelled to ask. He had paused briefly before looking back at me, and saying, quite sadly, "After what just happened to Ian, there's no way in hell that I'd be willing to chance it with anyone else. I've known most of those guys for years. They're friends and have families, little kids and babies...."

"So, where do we go from here?" Raymond appeared even more determined.

Draining his glass and placing it down on an end table, he stared back. The fear had faded from his features, as he spoke with a sudden and fierce resolve, "There isn't going to be a task force—but I'm sticking with you people. I spoke to the Captain this morning, I've got clearance with the department for any weapons that we might need, and any warrants or classified information, access unlimited." His eyes narrowed, becoming black slits as the flames reflected darkly, and he said, "This isn't just an investigation any more—now it's personal..."

"It might not be a good idea for you to stay alone anymore." Raymond scowled, his eyes flitting about the group before returning to the older detective, "It's obviously aware of you now—and knows where to find and get at you."

"I've got this--," Gordon had tapped a finger upon the talisman about his neck, but was interrupted by Raymond before he could continue.

"The charm only works on the entity in spirit form." He nervously tapped a finger against his coffee mug, and said, "This time—it might come back in a solid form, and trust me, you don't want to encounter that alone, and in the dark..."

"We do have a spare room." Amica politely offered, "You would be more than welcome to remain here with us, rather than risk being alone."

"I wouldn't want to be any more trouble than I've already been." Reluctantly, he had looked to me as though requiring additional permissions. I could see the fear and desperation reflecting in his glassy eyes, but knew that he would not accept the offer without further invite.

"Honestly, I would prefer to have everyone closer together." I had looked to our friend, "We can't guarantee you absolute safety—but it's a far cry from being out there alone."

"I live in a furnished room in North Vancouver--," He shrugged, and contemplating the thought aloud, looked between us, "Everything that I own would go into a couple of suitcases."

"Then let's stop wasting daylight—and do this--," Raymond insisted, "Don't make me freaking beg you."

Gordon had nodded after a moment's thought, and sighing deeply, said, "You're all very kind—I'll accept that offer just as long as it takes to clear this nightmare up."

"There is strength in numbers--,"Amica looked curiously between the two men, "None of us should ever be caught alone."

"I'll tag along." Raymond moved from the couch, and checking his revolvers, said, "I need some air anyway." He paused in thought, appearing strangely confused, and then saying, "You know, when I was coming home the other day, I saw a guy sitting alone at a bus stop in the middle of nowhere." His eyes became huge as he now seemed startled, "For the rest of my days—I don't think that I could ever do something like that again?"

"Let's hope that we never need to." Slipping an arm about Amica's waist, we followed him and Gordon as they moved toward the front door. They had quickly adorned boots, coats, hats and gloves. I had watched curiously as Gordon had fumbled with his scarf, stepped back as Raymond had noticed this also, and said, "I'll drive."

There hadn't been any argument from the older man, as he had willingly given up the car keys.

"We can discuss things over dinner this evening, and when everyone is here." I had halted before opening the front door, "Once again, I'm terribly sorry about Ian…"

He hadn't answered, but instead looked down as though half-expecting to see his friend's reflection in the highly polished tiles. I had regretted mentioning the name again, but felt obligated for decency's sake.

"He knew the risks—and was warned about taking off that charm." The words came in a low and remorseful tone as he looked back at me, "And, if it's the last thing that I ever do in this life—I'll get even…"

"Drive carefully--," Amica gently petted Gordon's shoulder, "And please be back soon—we close the gates at dusk."

"You can count on it." Raymond's eyes flashed with the fearful memory of his recent experience, "I'll call when we're leaving his place—just to touch base."

"We'll be waiting--," Startled as snow fell from the awning behind us, I gasped, "Please, avoid going anyplace without light. No basements, underground garages, or storage rooms."

"Stay safe—we'll be back as soon as possible." Gordon motioned with a nod for Raymond to follow, and the two men departed.

We had stood in the open doorway and watched them for several moments. He no longer appeared as the skeptical detective, just a lonely old man, caught on the edge of a nightmare. I'm not sure whether it had just been pity or something else, but I welcomed his presence in our home, such as it was. They climbed into the unmarked Dodge police-cruiser, and with a parting wave, Raymond took his leave. I could only hope and pray that there wouldn't be any more flat tires or unexpected car problems…

"When do we expect Tim and Rich to return?" Amica had stepped inside as I slowly closed the door.

"Raymond never mentioned that—only that they've gone off to run some errands. Please, don't mind me, my thoughts are scrambled, and I can't seem to focus at the moment."

"Ian's death--," She acknowledged and sadly nodded in agreement, "My heart mourns for his wife and child."

"I'll see to it that they receive an anonymous gift—enough money to carry them both safely for years to come. I know that Rich will also want to donate to this cause."

Amica has placed a hand upon my cheek, and gazing into my eyes, whispered, "So much kindness and compassion—someday you will make a wonderful father to someone."

"You know—I once dreamed that my mother came back to me, as a daughter." The words were caught in my throat as the emotions cut into my heart, "in the dream, I named her Annaliese—after my mother's grandmother."

"It's an old and very beautiful name--," She smiled, and looking down, thought briefly, before saying, "Who is to say what path destiny may take us—or what fate decides?

I had dreamed of having a child since the loss of our baby. All things considered, it would likely never happen now—and it was sadly for the best. It hurt to even think about it, and I had to force the thoughts from my mind.

"We should get dinner started." I led her into the kitchen, and feigning a smile, said, "I was thinking about something simple. How would you feel about a nice beef stew?"

"That would be wonderful—and I can bake some fresh rolls--," She grinned from cheek to cheek, "And apple pies for dessert." She thought briefly, and putting a finger to her lips, said, "If you're very good, I might even allow you a small slice?"

"That's very sweet of you, but I'm not so sure that we could slip that past mother Rich?"

"Let's cross that bridge when we come to it." She winked, "You sear the meat and I'll chop the vegetables—off we go!" She slapped my back-side and I yelped. There were times when we might just as easily been mistaken for a couple, and in some aspects we truly were. That was the moment when I had realized why some mysteries were necessary, and that those left behind in our wake were best forgotten. It was hard to even imagine a memory of one dearly loved and lost, and then, being consciously aware of their returning during another lifetime. It would be unfair to those having hopefully and lovingly returned, and turmoil to those we currently loved. Yet, how could we not love both, or lose one for the other? I suspect that this was the purpose in reincarnation, reuniting and rejuvenating old bonds without destroying current ones. Life had its purpose, and mortality was a necessary illusion. I would keep its secrets, as enduring this knowledge, protect the unwary and thereby preserve the innocent...

"Come along now!" She insisted with a chuckle, and taking me by the hand, pulled me toward the counter, "We have a lot to do and little time to do it!"

In my life, this had always seemed to have been the problem. There had never been enough time, not for my parents, loved ones, or friends. I had often wondered why bad things seemed to happen to some of the kindest people. In the end, my mother had been right when she had said: The devil always works hardest against good people—because the rest already belong to him...

"Michael! Come quickly!" Rich had called from the front door.

Without hesitation, both Amica and I had dropped everything and rushed to the door!

"Something's happened—," He gasped, "you need to see this..."

We had slipped into boots and coats, and quickly followed as he led us across the drive and toward the garage.

"I don't know why I never noticed this before--," He appeared devastated, opening the side door and leading us to where Tim still stood in shock, "I don't even know how they got in here…"

Caitlin's beautiful Imperial and the wondrous Challenger convertible that Rich had bought me sat in complete ruin. The quarter panels were torn, front fenders crushed inward, and the rims rested upon ripped and flattened tires. The floor was covered in glass, oil, and running with transmission and brake fluid. Speechless, I had turned to Rich whose eyes widened as we had shared the same thought in that moment.

"Oh God, what about the other garage—the one connected to the house?" He swallowed hard, raising both hands in a gesture of utter shock and bewilderment, "Wait here—I'll go look."

Tim had rushed after him as Amica and I had looked to one another. There were few words that could have expressed the shock and terror that I now felt.

"How is this possible? How—could anything manage to get past the gates, onto the property and into here without being noticed?"

"Maybe, it was something that was already here—and that we were not aware of?"

"Trudy would never have done this—and if she had, there would've been prints somewhere among all these spilled fluids and loose parts."

"Whatever it was—it got into the other garage as well." Rich suddenly returned his features pale and drawn as he stared in wide-eyed disbelief, "Your 300 is finished— and beyond repair…"

"It must have happened while we were fighting off those things last night." Tim looked between us, "Otherwise your truck would have been trashed too. We just didn't notice it in the dark and with everything else that was happening."

"That's the only thing that would make sense here--," Rubbing at my eyes, I couldn't help but stare in shock at the absolute destruction, "It's trying to cut off our resources—and eliminate any opportunity for escape."

"It's an old and common strategy—we just didn't expect this." Tim swallowed hard, his eyes growing large as he turned to Rich with the sudden realization, "Oh, no… has anyone looked into your place?"

There hadn't even been time to exchange words as Rich bolted from the garage. Tim had followed in close pursuit, as climbing into the truck, moments later, they roared down the driveway. Without a windshield and the truck having been far worse for the wear, I could only hope that they would be alright.

Examining the chaos that surrounded us, Amica had slowly turned to look at me. Suspicion now glinted in her heavy-lidded eyes, as speaking in low tones, she had leaned close, and asked, "Have you considered that whatever might have done this might still be here?"

My blood ran cold while staring into the long shadows of the large garage. As surrounded in tall shelving, work benches and an unfinished ceiling, anything could have remained concealed in the shadows. Realizing to have come mid-way into the garage, some twelve feet in distance, the door suddenly felt all too far away. Moving ever so slowly, I put a finger to my lips, and backing out of the place with Amica behind me, gently forced her toward the door. Nervously watching each and every space and dark corner, I felt a cold lump form in the pit of my stomach. I knew that the guardian would have sought out and destroyed anything of a malign nature, but there were other things not so easily identified. Old, unexpected and unknown beings and creatures that could be manipulated without revealing themselves… My thoughts raced to the beast at the Dayment farmhouse, and the immense turtle at the Waldense bog. All living things of which, acting upon animal instincts, would not stand out until the darkness took them… We had no idea of what might be lurking in the shadows of that garage—and might reveal itself at any given moment. Ever so slowly we moved backward, until finally reaching the open doorway, both leapt out together and into the light of day!

"Did you feel or sense anything in there?"

"No--," She appeared utterly distraught, "I can't sense things as I once did. I only know that something bad has happened, and I'm afraid of whatever might have done this."

"It's alright—," Fearing to draw upon her darker nature, I took her by the hand and began leading her back toward the house, "We don't need extra-sensory perception to know that we're in trouble here."

Hurriedly going inside and closing the door, we had made our way into the kitchen, and dropping into the breakfast nook, looked to one another as though lost.

"If something can do that—and enter into a garage that's directly connected to the house." I slid closer to her and took hold of her hand, "Then what security do we really have here?"

Amica leapt forward, and embracing me tightly, fearfully peered around the large kitchen, "Inquire of the one who will know—summon Marlowe…"

The mere thought having led to the action, our answer came in the form of a whisper, "The perpetrators of this violation entered the breach with your companions in the night. The guardian has sought out and taken them—you have nothing to fear…"

"Marlowe—how was it that they could enter the property with Rich—but otherwise, the dead stand blind beyond the gates?"

"The evil remains blinded upon hallowed ground—and the dead are hindered by the presence of the sacred seal and guardian. None shall enter—if not through carelessness…"

"And when they did enter—why didn't the guardian appear? Why were we forced to summon it in our defense? I thought that it wandered these grounds by night?"

"When the key-master is no longer present in the keep—the guardian remains bound within the vaults. Hence, no shadow may see or pass beyond the seal, but a thing obsessing the flesh may enter the breach…"

"Dear God—so all these nights that Tim has been staying in the house with us?"

"That which walks within the dead—has wandered these grounds…"

"Why didn't you explain this to me before—warn me about what was happening?"

"Need I remind you that we are now in constant peril from within—and that such great and evil power causes the lesser to vanish from the sight and senses?"

Remembering that Amica unwillingly hosted a demon, I realized Marlowe's inability to sense beyond that darkest of powers.

"How is the guardian guided? How does it know which ones to take?"

"The guardian senses its master's desires and acts upon them. In this way—it devours only that which is undesired, or considered a threat. For not all things considered evil—are our enemies."

Amica had held me close, and I could feel her violently trembling in my firm but gentle embrace. I knew that, although she could not hear or sense what was being said, she had somehow suspected and understood... We both knew that one day the evil growing in her would attract the guardian's attention, and both feared the consequences.

The telephone rang behind us and I felt my heart leap into my throat. Grabbing the receiver from off the base, I placed it to my ear and just listened. It was Rich. At first, I could barely understand him through the hysterics, and knew that something had gone terribly wrong.

"I'm calling from the neighbors' place—," He gasped for a breath after some immense physical exertion, "They were kind enough to let me use their phone. Mine weren't working."

"Good Lord--," At a loss for words, I stuttered, "What's happened—are you and Tim alright?"

"No, my house and everything inside of it's been trashed and totally torn to pieces. The drywalls ripped out, the electrical is everywhere, and even the plumbing was gutted. It's a virtual lake in there—Michael, nothing's even salvageable."

"Once this thing is all over, we can rebuild—start again."

"There's nothing left that's even worth rebuilding--," He cursed, "Michael—these things even destroyed my garage. NR002 is nothing but scrap now—Maya's Mustang, the old Thunderbird, all of them are complete write-offs. There's not even a single straight hub-cap between them…"

"What are we going to do?"

"Well—I'll tell you that the guys down at the insurance company are going to have a stroke when they see this. I'm not going to tell Maya anything about this, for now. It'd break whatever spirit that she might have left. Promise me, this stays between us."

"Who would I tell? You're the only one that speaks to them." Putting a hand to my face, I felt my knees almost give way, "Thank God that Tanya and the boys weren't there when it happened."

There was silence at the end of the line as the realization took him. I could hear Tim ask what was wrong, but he had never answered.

"I don't even want to think about that--," Rich sounded emotionally and utterly physically spent, as coughing, he said, "Listen, I'm taking NR001 to the glass shop—I called and they had the right windshield, and the time to get it done."

"But Rich—the time, it's getting too late in the afternoon--."

"Michael—this thing is knocking out all of our resources. We don't have a choice right now--," He argued, "This is our only vehicle at the moment—and could be a last chance to get out if things go wrong over there."

As much as I didn't like it, he was absolutely right. Instead of arguing, I quietly conceded, adding in thought, "Marlowe informed me that this all happened last night, and when those things were dragged onto the property with you. He said that the guardian took them all—but not before they destroyed our cars. So, we're safe here, for the moment, anyway…"

"How did they even get past the guardian—isn't that thing supposed to be night security on the grounds?"

"Apparently, and according to Marlowe, when Tim is not in the keep as he referred to it, the guardian is unable to leave the vaults—it's some kind of unspoken law."

"Oh great—just another one of those insignificant, little details that wasn't mentioned to the rest of us. Listen, we need to run—I'll explain everything to Tim while we're at the glass shop."

"Oh, Simms was here earlier--," I swallowed hard, peering back at Amica before saying, "Ian was killed in a freak accident last night. Raymond went with Simms to get his luggage. We've invited him to stay with us here."

"Sweet Jesus—what about his family? He had a wife and kid..."

"They seem to be fine for the moment—but I'm going to arrange a fund for them."

"Count me in—listen—I'll be back soon... we can talk then."

"You better both be very careful—anything could happen, anywhere... till then."

"You too—till then, brother..." The phone went dead in my hand, and placing it down, I looked over at Amica. She just stood there, twisting at the ends of an apron that she had intended to put on while helping me with dinner. She looked so innocent, so vulnerable and lost. In some respect she reminded me of Trudy, who, having only wanted to come home, had lost everything in the end. I couldn't have imagined ever harming her, much less burning her as she had requested. In a second thought, I had asked myself what would happen to her soul if her physical body was destroyed before the demon had completely taken control.

"She would become possessed of the demon once more—and suffer servitude in darkness...A being forgotten to the light—and forever lost..." Marlowe replied, but I had already assumed the worst, and understood why she had requested that I do this. Once again, she had intended to sacrifice herself to protect me...

"Amica—I love you dearly..." Taking hold of her in gentle embrace, I softly kissed her brow, "I will never abandon you—no matter what may come..."

CHAPTER ELEVEN

4:25 p.m.

Gordon and Raymond had returned with two large suitcases and a hand-bag. With a stew simmering and the bread and pies in the oven, Amica had happily shown him to his room. It was the one located directly beside Raymond on the main floor, and was nearest the front door. It had once been Eva's room, and the one area of the house that I had completely avoided. Although Amica had shared the dear woman's final sentiments in parting, Eva's loss had still weighed heavily upon my soul. There had been so many things that I had wanted to say and apologize for. It was all now meaningless as Eva had been lost in time, and the empty room had been a constant reminder.

Wearied from a sleepless night and long day, Gordon had simply left his suitcases in the room to be dealt with later, and followed Amica back into the dining area. She had served coffee and tea, and we had all sat down to wait for the others.

"They did a fabulous job with the gates." Gordon had broken the silence, and looking to me, sipped at his coffee, "From the outside—you can hardly tell that they're mechanized."

"Well, we really have Rich and Raymond to thank for that--," I swallowed back a mouthful of Earl Gray, "They did most of the design and ground-work."

"Rich did most of it--," Raymond's modesty was showing through again, as he said, "All that I was doing was following his direction."

"That stew sure smells terrific--," Gordon sunk back into his seat, as closing his eyes for a moment, he smiled sadly, "Reminds me of home."

"Where was home?" Amica had politely inquired.

"Home was the spring of 1964--," He sighed while pouring more coffee from an urn, "With my wife Edith, and a little apartment that we shared on the North shore. God—just thinking back, it was a terrific little place. We had a gorgeous view over the bay, and loved to watch the tide go in and out on those hot summer nights." Staring into silent reflection, the shadow of some bitter memory had soon wiped the smile from his face.

"Raymond had mentioned that working on the police force was very hard on relationships." I kept looking toward the window, and dreading the steadily growing darkness, said, "He went through a divorce as well, sadly."

"Divorce—no, not us." Gordon gazed down into his coffee cup, "I lost her to lung cancer in the winter of 1970. She'd been complaining about being short of breath, but we'd never expected anything like that. Neither one of us had ever smoked in our lives, but they told us that it was likely caused by asbestos. A lot of the old houses and schools were insulated with the stuff, and there just wasn't anything that they could do for her." He forced back the emotions, and breathing in deeply, said, "I spent the last two years with her, helpless and just watching her fade away...." In that moment he had just bowed his head, looking down to where he clasped his hands in his lap, "Come to think of it—it's probably the reason that I've been such a miserable old bugger."

Reaching out and taking one of his hands, Amica had sweetly said, "I believe that love is one of the greatest powers in the universe, and that it binds—and brings us altogether again, one day. Even with all the evil that's happening around us—there's still love enough to share, dear friend. You aren't truly alone in this world—you still have us."

I knew that she had somehow reached into his heart and soul, and touching the darkness, brought light into the depths of his despair. His features had softened and the light returned to his eyes, as gently patting her hand, he looked across at me, and said, "You're wife is such a sweet soul—and I can see why you fell in love with her. You should both feel blessed to have each other, because no matter how many people we may meet or care for in this world, true love only comes around once in a lifetime."

She had paused to gaze back at me, and I saw the longing that reflected in those eyes. It was sorrow for a love already known to be soon lost. It hurt even further as looking upon the face of my own beloved, Caitlin, the thought of losing either one of them utterly broke my heart.

"You know—you have quite a place here." Gordon had thanked Amica, as pouring more coffee, she offered him shortbread cookies from a jar on the table, "But, I have to admit—it reminds me a little of those old horror films that we saw at the bijou as kids. No offense."

"None taken—in fact, I'm flattered to be honest." The comment had left me grinning devilishly, "As an author of horror and lifelong fan of those old horror films, I consider that a compliment."

"Do you ever wonder?" He contemplated before curiously glancing back at me, "If we draw things to ourselves by creating these types of environments. Or whether—they influence us into doing it?"

"It's likely to be both--," Amica had replied swifter than I could contemplate the question, "All things happen by design between destiny and fate—we simply accommodate and choose from whatever options remain to us."

"Wow, that's some pretty heavy stuff--," He chuckled, looking between us, and said, "I was raised Lutheran, and prefer to believe that there's a God watching over us all."

"Well, I was raised Catholic—so we share the same belief system," Sipping at my tea and shrugging, I sighed deeply, saying, "But, what I once referred to as God, seems more like a collective consciousness and type of life-giving, positive energy that we are all spiritually connected to, through space and time."

"A mosquito likely sees us the same way." He winked, "And, maybe we should be grateful that God never swats back."

He reminded me very much of a Pastor I had once known as a boy and truly admired. Pulling the pen and notepad from a breast pocket of my blue plaid shirt, I scribbled down the thoughts. It wasn't that we had shared anything prolific, but the smile in the moment was worth the effort.

"Are you quoting me there?" Chuckling, he nibbled at a cookie, and said, "I doubt that I've ever said anything memorable in this life, as of yet."

"You'll get used to that—he's always doing it," Raymond observed my efforts, "He's worse than us for taking notes."

"I wouldn't go as far as to say that, but in this case, most of what we say becomes significant to our story." Closing the pad and placing it back into my pocket, I said, "As you might have already assumed, I use a lot of this random material in my books."

"In fact--," Raymond stirred cream and sugar into his coffee, "You could use those books as evidence in most cases."

It was apparent by the glances exchanged that Gordon had long suspected this, but said nothing.

"I'm not a big reader--," He admitted, "And I can't say that I would read your books, even if I had them. Now, don't take me wrong, they're probably great for what they are, but I'm not much of a horror fan, anymore."

"No one would blame you there. I've read a few of them--," Raymond admitted, "But now, all they do is give me nightmares."

"I can imagine why." Gordon grimaced, and tapping his fingers on the table, said thoughtfully, "I wonder how many other people lay awake at night, wondering about the things you wrote?"

"I doubt that many would be interested in my work. It's more of a personal account, a legacy to anyone who might follow in our tracks…"

"Don't say things like that!" Amica took immediate offense to the statement, "I think your work is wonderful—and that there are things to be learned, for those with the wisdom and awareness to understand."

"These are great--," Gordon waved a cookie, "Did you bake them?"

Admiring the skillful way in which he had cleverly changed the subject, I could only look away and smile, as beaming, she had said, "Yes—I baked them a few days ago. Do you really like them?"

Making a yummy sound, he nodded, "I do believe that they're the best that I've ever had."

The front door had suddenly flown open as Rich and Tim returned. The clock chimed five behind us, and I knew that they had beaten the darkness, but not a moment too soon.

"We're back—and barely by the skin of our teeth." Rich wandered into the dining room, and seeing Gordon, nodded, "Gordon, Michael told me that you'd be joining us here—it's good to have you, welcome aboard."

Gordon had reacted to this almost tearfully, as patting Rich's hand, nodded in thanks.

"I was beginning to worry--," I had welcomed my friends home as they all took seats around the table, "How did everything go with the windshield?"

"They managed to get everything done--," Tim shivered with the thought, "But we were cutting it very close in the end."

"I'm parked at the front door now--," Rich poured coffee for himself, "The truck still needs some work—but being as I no longer have a shop, I'll had to run it over to a garage in the morning."

"What's happened?" Gordon asked, as Raymond turned in question.

"Whatever got through the gates here last night trashed our cars--," Nodding toward my disgruntled friend, I said, "And then proceeded to make a disaster area out of Rich's house, garage, and the remaining vehicles."

"Sweet Jesus--," Raymond cursed and looked to Rich, "What are you going to do now?"

"Insurance will cover all the costs—but I'm not going to be moving back onto the property. It's just never going to feel the same."

Tim swallowed back his tea, coughing as he did this too fast, and choking, asked, "Does Maya know about this yet?"

"Not yet—and I'd prefer it that no one said anything about to anyone else, for the moment."

"Also, in case anyone didn't already know--," Sighing deeply, I looked around the group, "We lost Sergeant Ian McTavish in the night to a supposed accident. I also wanted to inform you--," I spoke calmly and quietly, but with certain resolve, "He has left behind a wife and child, and I'm going to arrange a fund for the family. I'll be going to the bank in the morning, so if anyone else is interested in contributing, please let me know after dinner."

"I realize that it's a sensitive subject--," Rich nervously looked between Gordon and me, "But, what were the circumstances surrounding this supposed accident?"

The room had become deathly silent as everyone stiffened in their seats and just stared in horror. The tension was so thick in that moment that you could've cut the air with a butter knife.

"Apparently, sometime after supper, and just after he had gotten out of the shower, the power went out in his home--," Gordon swallowed hard, as volunteering the information, he looked to Rich, and said, "His wife said that he had gone down to the basement in his bathrobe to check the fuses. Somehow, there was a fire… One that was so bad, it left the remains unidentifiable—even by dental records."

"What was the cause of the fire?" Pouring tea for himself, Tim courteously topped mine.

"The fire department couldn't establish the source of the ignition. It's still under investigation, but the cause of death has been documented as spontaneous human combustion."

"Oh, dear God…" Tim appeared paler than usual, "But how could this have happened?"

"It seems that during his shower--," Gordon drew the amulet from a shirt pocket and held it out for all to see, "Ian had taken this off, and then forgotten it on the bathroom counter."

"In lieu of this incident—I have asked Gordon to stay here with us. It's also the reason that we won't be involving a task force. The risk to everyone and their families is just too high…"

"We still have the complete support of the department." Gordon explained, "I can provide whatever weapons or written permissions that we might require to attend private locations. All that this really means—is that we've become the unofficial task force."

"So, we've been granted full authority--," Raymond appeared almost pleased with the idea, "Does that mean that we'll be held liable for damages to property—or anything else?"

"It's all going to remain classified--," Gordon shrugged it off with little concern, "So, there really isn't any need for concern of liability, especially under the circumstances. We will be expected to file reports, and record dates and events, but it's all off the general record."

"It may not be used to incriminate and incarcerate us--," Contemplating, Rich struggled with the idea, "But it's enough to put someone in the looney-bin for life."

"If we live long enough, at least we'll have lots of company." Raymond nervously tugged at his mustache.

"Now, did you want to write me a list of things that we might need?" Gordon looked curiously between Rich and Raymond, "We have access to some fairly impressive firepower."

"Conventional weapons are pretty much useless." Rich drained his coffee cup, and then thinking briefly, said, "I would've suggested that we get some protective gear—but the less attention we attract—the better off the general public will be."

"Body armor won't do anyone a bit of good anyway--," I thought aloud, "It will only serve to slow us down. We're better off packing light—and moving as quickly and quietly as possible."

"Alright then--," Gordon nodded, "That makes things a lot less complicated. Let's put this together as fast as possible and make our move while we still can…"

Deb Carlson and her husband Ray had just settled down for the evening. The move into the building hadn't been so bad, but with the elevator out of service, the four flights of stairs had been murder on them both. If it hadn't been for everyone else helping, the several suitcases, bedding, and three totes would have been abandoned at the foot of the stairs for the evening. The single-bedroom, fourth-floor apartment that they now occupied wasn't small, but it left them feeling somewhat smothered. It had a large balcony that provided a lovely view of the North Shore Mountains and the little book store on the street below. The living room was quite large, and Red had already placed a new queen-size bed in their bedroom. On the lower end of the spectrum, the paint was old and yellowed, it was baseboard heating, and everything needed a thorough cleaning. But having been previously abandoned, it had to be expected.

Her husband Ray was a big man with a heart to match. She had attempted to clean the bathroom, but he had quickly accepted responsibility for the chore, insisting that she rest before dinner. Needless to say, with so much to be done and having a stubborn streak, she had soon busied herself with cleaning the fridge and little kitchen.

"It's a darn good thing that we brought those old drapes of your mother's-," Ray had called to her as having finished in the bathroom, he now tended to the large windows, "They fit perfectly on these rods—it's almost like it was meant to be."

Having completed the cleaning of the fridge, kitchen sinks and counters, Deb wandered out to look. The drapes were a sullen cream color and evenly matched the fading paint. It wasn't a great surprise to her, as her mother's tastes and the building were likely close to the same age.

"As long as the windows are all covered—I don't care what color they are." She had good reason for having felt this way, and dreaded what lay beyond.

There was a knock at the open door, and Carrie casually sauntered into the room, "Knock-knock—anybody home?"

"If you can call it that--" Deb snickered, "It's more like a four story ghost town."

"I'd agree with that--," Carrie pulled out a pen and paper, "How's the fridge working?"

"I just cleaned it—and it seems fine, for the moment anyway?"

"Dinner's going to arrive shortly--," Carrie scoffed at the drapes, "Sweet Jesus—my mom had a set just like those."

"Well, you can have these when we leave." Ray laughed, as admiring his handy-work, he said, "I think they were a slightly darker color when we first got them?"

"They can stay here--," Carrie waved them off, and laughing, said, "It took me almost ten years to get rid of my mom's. I had to fight her for them."

"One day our kid's will be saying the same thing about us." Deb put a finger to her cheek in thought, "I don't even have any yet, and I'm already reconsidering."

"What do you mean, one day? My kid's already telling us what to keep and what to ditch." Carrie shook her head, and examining the baseboards, asked, "You guys warm enough up here? These things seem to be working okay?"

"Oh—everything seems to be fine—I mean, it's not forever, right?" Deb smirked, but there was doubt in her eyes.

"We're getting brand new washers and dryers--," Carrie raised an eyebrow, and adjusting her glasses, sighed, "So, if we have to suffer here, at least we can do it in comfort."

"You should have gotten into politics--," Ray grinned, "Because you sure know how to make a silk purse out of a sow's ear."

"That's me—the good-cheer lady." She made her way back toward the apartment door, and glancing back, said, "Everyone's gathering for dinner down in the diner. There were bigger tables, and we had everything that we needed down there. Don't be late!"

"Steak and lobster--," Ray beamed, "Late—now I know that you're kidding!"

Pam Montgomery had hurried Jen Valdez out of her apartment and then pounded on the door to the adjoining one, which belonged to Red Cloud.

"What is wrong with that man?" Jen had put a hand to her hip and frowned, "The only time we get steak and lobster, and he's fussing around in there!"

"Red—it's Pam and Jen--," She had called at the door, knocking again and appearing strangely unsettled, "It's dinner time—let's go before it gets cold!"

"Will you finish up powdering that big nose of yours—and get your old, making-me-starve butt out here!" Jen growled, "If we didn't love the old fart so much, I'd say leave him be…"

"This isn't like him at all…" Pam bit down on her lower lip, and knocking again, called, "Red—is everything okay in there?"

"What's happening, ladies?" Scott passed in the hall with Patrick and halted immediately after having noticed their distressed expressions, asking, "Is everything okay?"

"Red isn't answering his door," Pam explained, "And, he's been here all day—and knows we're having dinner altogether. Scott—I've got the worst feeling that something's wrong…"

"I saw him earlier in the warehouse—and he seemed tired, but fine?" Scott placed an ear against the door, and listening, knocked and shouted, "Red—we're all out here waiting on you, buddy. Are you okay in there?"

Without a single sound in reply, Scott now became seriously concerned.

"Dad, I say you bust down the door--." Patrick frowned, "It isn't like Grampa Red not to answer. Aunty Pam's right—something must be seriously wrong."

"Stand back." It hadn't taken much to confirm his own fears, Scott wasn't waiting any longer, as putting his shoulder into it, he now slammed his full body weight against the door! The entire frame shook, but the door hardly moved! A second attempt and the lock split in the door frame! A third and Scott exploded inward, sprawling on the floor in the little hallway!

"Oh my God--," Pam wailed, as finding Red Cloud face down on the floor near the balcony window, she spun in terror, "Call an ambulance!"

6:45 p.m.

The call had arrived just as we had all sat down to supper. I had answered, and stood speechless as Carrie had informed me of what had happened.

"He's had a heart attack--," She wept, "The ambulance took him away—oh God, what are we going to do?"

"Stay calm--," I had looked among my friends as they all sat and stared from around the dinner table, "Which hospital was he taken to?"

Having heard this, Rich had leapt from his seat, "Hospital—but it's already dark, what's happened?"

"It's Red Cloud—," Explaining while Carrie informed me, I said, "He's suffered a heart attack and has been taken to Vancouver General."

"Oh no—this can't be happening—not now!" Rich panicked as Raymond and Tim attended to him in a futile attempt to calm him down.

"Carrie--," I spoke assertively and was terrified for the safety of my friends, "Under no circumstances is anyone to leave the building in the dark, do you understand?"

"But Michael—we can't just leave Red like that. He's helpless and all alone out there…"

"I'll call the hospital right now--," I promised, "Maybe Eddy Wong is working the night-shift, let me call you right back."

"I'll be here waiting-," She sniffled, "Oh please, do something… save Red…"

"I'll do what I can—but I need to go right away." Hanging up, I ran for a telephone book, and locating the number, called the hospital emergency ward. Unlike many people, I had the direct line codes and soon reached Dr. Edward Wong. It had also been fortunate for us that he had been on call that night and that I'd caught him on his last shift.

"Ed—it's Michael, I'm sorry to bother you at work, but this is a matter of the utmost urgency."

"Of course—what can I do to be of assistance?"

"One of our friends just suffered a heart attack, his name is Robert Farley, and he sometimes goes by the names Bob, or Red Cloud. He was just brought in by ambulance."

"Yes, I see him here on the chart—he's in the cardiac unit, stable, but pending further examination."

"Ed, please listen to me--," I swallowed hard, already fearing the worst, "He's wearing a pendant around his neck, a round charm with a symbol in the center. It's a matter of life and death, that they do not remove that talisman."

"I'll call you right back—I'll run over to his room right now." The phone went dead in my hand and my heart began racing as the moments passed.

Everyone had become deathly silent, sitting absolutely still, as we anticipated the call to come. The minutes seemed like hours, the sweat beading on my brow as we helplessly sat and waited. When the call finally did arrive, we had almost all jumped out of our skins, as answering, I listened intently.

"Michael—it's Edward--," He had spoken in a low tone which now troubled me, saying, "I'm in your friend's room right now. He's sleeping. I checked his vitals, his oxygen is low, and he has an irregular heartbeat, but appears stable. As for the amulet that you mentioned, it doesn't seem to be here, or in his personal things. I checked with the night staff and they said that all of his personal things should have been in the room with him. I checked the bag, and even went through his vest and pants pockets, but found nothing. What do you want me to do?"

"Maybe it's somehow fallen on the floor or into his bedding when they moved him?" I was desperate, and grasping at ideas, "Could it have possibly been caught in his hair?"

"Let me look—one moment."

"Michael, be careful—you're involving him too much--," Tim warned, his eyes huge and fearful, "it's dark and if he interferes too much—it might come for him…"

"He's in Red Cloud's room and can't find the pendant." Attempting to explain, a sound suddenly caused my blood to run cold, "Eddy—what's happening?"

"Oh—there's a bird or something at the window—hold on, I'll draw the curtains and look."

Before I could even utter a word in warning, he was gone. Horrified and staring, I heard the rest happen in a matter of a few seconds. The sounds of Edward opening the blinds, the terrible screams, and then the explosion of something shattering the glass! The phone had slipped from between my trembling fingers as I felt my knees give way, and fell to the ground without any further recollection…

Tuesday, February 5, 1975.

In the end, I had simply fainted, and awoke to the evidence of what had happened. In the days to come, the newspaper headlines, television and radio had been alive with the reports. It had been a story about a delirious trauma patient, who having lost all faculties, cast himself and the doctor in attendance from out a fourth story window of his room, to their deaths. We had all known that it hadn't been Red Cloud who had done this, but rather the nightmare that had possessed him as he lay helpless. Unable to accept what had happened, I had gone out of my way to avoid seeing or listening to any of the reports…

There hadn't been any need to inform the others, as very few people had not seen or already heard the news. It had been Scott who had discovered the pendant that had been dropped in the hallway. Apparently, it had fallen off as the ambulance attendants had taken the old man away. The morning had been further worsened, as Rich had contacted Maya to inform her of the loss of their house and her Uncles passing. It was another call that I couldn't bear to witness…

We had even received a telephone call from Edwards's widow, Kim, who was in absolute shock. She hadn't outwardly blamed anyone, but I could sense by the tone of her voice that she had held us all responsible, and rightly so…

We had attended two funerals that week, and due to the severe circumstances of their deaths, they had both been closed-casket services. I remember the horror that I had felt when standing near the caskets, and the fear that I had experienced when wondering what was really laying inside those oak boxes. Had the evil truly surrendered the bodies of our friends, or was it just waiting until the darkness came before sending them after us, like it did with Harry? I had gone long before anyone else had arrived at the funeral parlor, and with Rich watching the doorway, had ever so cautiously unlatched and opened the caskets. Refusing to look upon the contents, I slipped an amulet and silver crucifix in through the partially open lids and hesitated as a strange noise caused me to dare gaze within. It had been a strange and hollow 'plunk' sound of which I could not understand, but the answer came soon enough, and as I stared inside. The circumstances of their deaths having been so extreme, the parlor had placed the broken bodies into their caskets while still in the white plastic bags from the morgue. Trembling uncontrollably, I had heard Rich usher a quick hiss in warning, and hurriedly dropped the talismans onto the bags and resealed the casket lids. We could only hope and pray that even unto the grave, these symbols would offer divine protection, for the sake of all involved.

There were no words that could have expressed the remorse I had felt for Edwards's death, or Red Cloud's loss. Kim had watched me from beneath a black veil through the entire ceremony, and I knew that she had silently and secretly hated me.

With Maya indisposed, Jen had attended the service for Red Cloud with Rich. She was a strong and determined young woman, and her courage and support had carried him through. Pam had stood by Raymond, Tanya with Tim and Amica held my hand tightly as the last rites were read. Carrie and Scott had stood silently, as young Patrick stared blindly, in utter disbelief. None of us would ever have expected this, as we had all felt in some sense that Red Cloud was immortal. We had provided a proper Catholic service, as though he was Cree, he had always stood by the belief of his father. There had been a stranger among us and in attendance that day. He was an elderly native, who, attired in ritual Cree robes, had waited for the Priest to depart before saying a prayer in his own language. We had all remained for this, and as he turned to leave, I had inquired of his name. The old man had just looked at me as though I had committed some great offense. Then, waving a hand in my face, he released red sands that drifted upon the icy wind and vanished without ever having touched the snow at our feet.

In my thoughts, this had been symbolic of the blood that had been spilled, and when I looked up, the old man was gone. I had suspected to have known him, but my soul spoke of Red Cloud's grandfather, an ancestral wraith returning for his spirit. I prayed for the soul of my dear friend and asked for peace, but found none…

It was while turning, when I thought to have seen or sensed another shadow or shape. It stood near an old oak and among the ancient rows of stones that marked that frozen place. There had been something familiar about this shape, as through the bitter cold tears, I knew to have seen Red Cloud, one last time. Attired in customary Cree garments, he had stood proud beneath the dismal heavens. We had looked to one another, his features softening, raising a hand in parting, as he slowly nodded before fading into the realm of memory and dreams.

3:45 p.m.
We had all returned to the house for the reception, but few words had been exchanged between anyone. In the end, Carrie had taken the others back to the building and to where they held a candle-light vigil in

memorial. Afterwards, they had sealed Red Cloud`s apartment, and then given the key to Rich, pending Maya's return.

All that I really remembered from those few days were the endless tears and bitter suffering of my friends. Marlowe had remained silent throughout these events, and Amica had sought only to comfort me in the darkest moments. We had lost people before, but never one so near and precious to us all…

"There wasn't anything that anyone could've done--, Rich gazed sadly from across the dinner table, "You did everything that you could…"

There were no words to offer in comfort, or even a thought to share in condolences. It was probably the first time in my life that I was absolutely and utterly speechless. In response, I had only looked away and toward the partially drawn draperies. The sun had peeked between the clouds in that moment, casting a beam of light into the dining area, which touched my face and heart. There may not have been anything significant in the moment, but for me it was sublime and meant everything. I knew that Rich had sympathized with my position involving Edward and Red Clouds deaths, but to some extent, I would forever feel responsible.

We had sat alone, as Amica had gone into the kitchen to assist Raymond and Gordon with the evening meal. Tim was sound asleep on the couch, there was a comforting fire burning in the hearth, and the smell of roasted chicken filled the house. At any other time this would have been a pleasant evening and well worthy of sharing with good friends. Unfortunately, after having already lost Trudy, Ian, Edward and Red Cloud, I knew that the body count would rise if we didn't act swiftly.

"Michael--," Raymond had called my attention into the kitchen, "There's a telephone call for you."

Moving without thought, I had answered, and was surprised to hear from Carrie so soon.

"Michael—can you take this call somewhere private?"

"Of course—one moment--," Turning to Amica, I had said, "I'm going to take this call in my office—would you be kind enough to hang up once I grab it upstairs?"

"She had complied without question, and I had hurried to answer the phone in my office.

Rushing up the stairs and partially closing the door, I slumped into the chair and answered. "Thank you, I have it—you can hang up now, Amica." I listened as she hung up, and then asked, "Carrie, how have you been managing through everything that's happened?"

"Well—as you know, we've all been better," She thought briefly, as speaking in low tones, and said, "After we had the service for Red, me and Scott got talking, about everything that's been going on."

"Alright--," I was already dreading the possibilities, but asked anyway, "So, what did you conclude?"

"The bottom line of the matter—is that none of us are really safe. That this thing is just going to pick us all off, one by one."

"If you just stay in the building--,"I had attempted to intercede, but she had immediately cut me off, saying, "Michael stop—we both know that it's just a matter of time—and we also know that it's likely that none of us are getting out of this alive…"

"Carrie—you can't just give up hope, what other choice do we have?"

"We have the right to choose our own time and place. It's a chance to try to make some kind of a difference somewhere and somehow. Even if it just means buying you a little more time to try and stop this thing—it's better than just waiting for the inevitable. Either way, I can't just sit here and wait anymore."

"I understand, but what about Patrick, Scott and all of the others? They need you, Carrie—I need you…"

"We're sending Pam to my dad's with Patrick on the bus, first thing in the morning. They'll be safe over there with him—and away from all of us."

"And Pam just agreed to this?"

"Oh hell, no—," Carrie scoffed, "You know her—she argued until she was almost blue in the face. But when all was said and done—she knew that I was right. We've already told the others—we talked this over while we had dinner the other night."

"And what was the general consensus?"

"Deb, her husband and Jen agreed to stay here with Tanya and the boys. I hired a new guy—he's really nice and can manage the warehouse. Jay Leonard is his name—he should be fine, he's one of those motorcycle-riding tough sorts, with a big heart and great smile. He was a truck-driver for years and has lots of warehouse experience."

"That's terrific—but then what? You can't just go running off into the wild blue yonder—that would be nothing short of suicide…"

"Well, we already know that you'd never involve Scott or me any more than you already have, bless your sweet, stubborn heart," She sniffled, and I knew that she had wiped tears away, "So, since we can't do anything against this thing—we've decided to do the only thing that we have left."

Fearing the words before she had even uttered them, I felt my heart sink as clearing her throat, she said, ""I've already booked the flight—we're leaving for Ireland in the morning."

"Carrie—what have you done?"

"If we can't be of any use here—then we're going to go where we're needed. I called Maya earlier—they're alone and we all need to stick together now. No matter what happens to us—or what comes of it."

"But you can't do this--," I struggled with the words, and fearing the consequences of all concerned, said, "None of us even know their exact location. Carrie, the demon sees into our thoughts, it will follow you and find them—and take you all..."

"She didn't give us the exact location over the phone. We're going to a hotel—and they'll come to get us during the day and take us back with them. Don't you see—we're doing this for you, for Caitlin and Maya, our family. Michael—I can't lose any more of you—and won't go down without a fight. So, please—don't try to talk me out of this. I love all of you—and this is how it's going down, because it's who we are..."

Already knowing that the conversation concerning the decision had ended, I swallowed back the emotions and cast a trembling hand before my eyes.

"You know that during a big part of that flight—that you'll be in darkness..."

"Yes I do—but we already know that thing can't be in two places at once. Which means that if it's following us—that it's not watching you. I'm willing to bet that it won't leave your gates for long."

"Are you willing to bet your life on that?"

"You know that Maya and Caitlin need us now—more than ever. And besides, it might just buy you enough time to make some kind of a difference..."

My heart was broken with her selfless sacrifice.

"Is Scott there with you?"

"One second--," She called to him, and said, "Here he is—I'll finish talking to you when you guys are done."

"Of course..."

"Hey, bro--," His voice sounded weary but determined, "How're you holding up?"

"Scott--," I swallowed hard, fearing this may be the last time that we might ever speak again, "Are you absolutely sure about doing this?"

"Yes, sir—we are, come hell or high water."

"You know—that for Patrick's sake—and all of you, that I didn't want you any more involved."

There had been a moment of silence as he held back the emotions, and then said, "Bro, we're family—and you just don't get any more involved than that. You must've known that we could never have just let you do this alone…"

Realizing that there hadn't been even the slightest chance of discouraging this desperate attempt, I swallowed back the tears and nodded, "I really love you guys."

"And, we love you too, bro. So, no matter what comes of this—we'll see you again, somewhere, someday…"

"God bless and keep you—please put Carrie back on the line…"

"Till then—God bless and keep you, too."

"Till then…"

When Carrie had answered, I felt as though the whole world had dropped out from beneath me. My thoughts were racing, and the only things that came to mind were pieces of advice that Marlowe had given me.

"Listen—this darkness isn't intelligent—just sneaky—and crafty. It has the hunting instincts of a rodent, and if you're very careful, you might be able to fool it—and escape."

"And how exactly would we go about doing that?"

"It doesn't track us by sight or sound—it hunts by sense. It feels its way around, seeks us out by our fear and thoughts, so to speak."

"So, if other people are scared for some reason—it might cloud the trail?"

"In dreams none can be pursued--," Marlowe whispered, "Only between waking and dreaming are we truly vulnerable…"

"Is there some way that you and Scott can medicate yourselves enough to sleep through most of the flight?"

"I've got enough sleeping pills to knock out a horse—sure, why?"

"According to Marlowe, you should be safe as long as you're wearing your amulets—and sound asleep."

"Alright, I'll make sure that we leave some kind of false trail, somehow. And, not to worry—I'm sure that we'd rather be out cold for most of the flight anyway. Scott hates planes—and to be honest, we can both use the sleep."

"Carrie is there is anything that I can do for either of you? Just ask and I'll do whatever I can."

"Well, there's one thing—," Her words were now whispered, "Michael, if we don't make it--," She stuttered in the thought, "Would you, could you please see after Patrick?"

There had been a soft knocking at the office door, and Amica reluctantly made her way to the chair. Having seen my expression, she had immediately panicked, taking hold of my free hand, and assuming the worst.

"You have my promise—but I want yours --," Swallowing hard, I was unable to see through the tears, "Promise me that you'll both come back to us…"

"Michael, you know that I can't promise that…"

"Then, please tell Caitlin that I love her with all of my heart—and that, when this is over, I'll be coming back for her… and for all of you. I love you, Carrie…"

"God bless and keep you--," The words came harder as she held back the tears, "I promise that we'll do everything that we can—and, I love you too, my dear friend, till then…"

"Till then…"

It was almost impossible to place down the telephone receiver. It was like releasing the hand of a dear friend during some long and terrifying fall…

Amica had moved closer and held me tightly as the phone went dead in my hand. Although she hadn't heard the complete content of the call, my reactions had made it obvious that something was terribly wrong.

"They go to your beloved--," She had gathered from my words, "And so, into the breach we must also now go…"

We had gazed deeply into one another's eyes, and there had been a singular truth residing in the darkness that existed there. For better or worse, our last stand was only a heartbeat away…

"What will you tell the others?"

"Only what the darkness will discover for itself—and what I absolutely need to."

"You do realize that once the generality is revealed—that the evil will seek them out."

"You're companions' hearts and actions stand true--," Marlowe whispered from out of the shadows, "For the darkness has already discovered the locale, yet not the exact place. Immediate assistance is duly required—as without it… I fear that things do not bode well…"

"But I thought that they were safe in a hallowed and secret place?"

"Hallowed indeed—but I fear, secret no more…"

"What do we do now—Marlowe—I beg of you—please tell me?"

"There are no more steps to be taken back—all now move forward, and into uncertain darkness… Make haste, you must seek out the pathways into oblivion before all is lost…"

6:35 p.m.

The shadow of Red Cloud and Edward's deaths still hanging heavy, there was little discussion over dinner beyond common courtesies. On several occasions I had considered bringing up the most recent developments, but then decided to wait. It wasn't until after dessert, and when we had all gathered around the hearth, that I finally spoke. Clasping my hands tightly together, I sighed deeply while attempting to gather the proper words.

"I spoke to Carrie on the telephone earlier--," I had announced, "And it seems that she and Scott have arrived at a conclusion, not that I agreed."

"What kind of a conclusion?" Rich nervously scratched at his goatee, and looking around at the others, focused upon me, "Are they leaving?"

"Something like that--," The words came hard as they ached in my heart, "They're sending Patrick away with Pam, and having been aware that I had no intention of involving them any further, have gone off in defense of Maya and Caitlin..."

Rich had almost leapt off the couch as he gawked in wide-eyed terror, "They can't do that! They'll give the location away—and likely get themselves killed in the process!"

"Marlowe has informed me that the evil has already discovered the locale—but hasn't found their exact location. It's just a matter of time, and this might be our only hope of saving Caitlin and Maya..."

"Caitlin--," Gordon almost spilled his coffee, and pointing to Amica, said, "But she's right here."

"It's all rather complicated--," Tim had nervously looked between us, and said, "It's likely better that you don't ask—or know any more than you should, please trust me..."

Although Gordon looked absolutely perplexed, he had accepted Tim's advice, and simply did not pursue the matter.

"I had a feeling that something might've been going on--," Rich sipped at his coffee and frowned, "Last week, Carrie hired a new guy to work the counter at the warehouse. He was only supposed to take a few shifts to give Red and Scott a little more time off. His name's Jay Leonard."

"She told me—and mentioned that he'd come highly recommended."

"He's a really nice guy--," Rich shrugged, "But I should've known that she had something up her sleeve."

"Did you guys know that she also made Deb manager at the office--," Slowly shaking his head, Tim stared over at me, "And put Jen in charge of the magazine?"

"She's an intelligent and stubborn lady—," I had agreed, "It's more than likely that they've both been thinking about doing this for a while. Red Cloud's death was likely the straw that broke the proverbial camel's back."

"So, what do you propose that we do now?" Gordon nervously fidgeted with his coffee cup.

"Well, they're taking a huge risk, and hoping to buy us some time by occupying this thing—so we should take advantage of the opportunity. I say that we make our move in the morning—and look into that old woman's house, as we agreed before."

"Forensics is done with the place." He shrugged, "So, I should be able to get clearance from the office, first thing in the morning. It's just a matter of a piece of paper with a signature—and just insurance so the family doesn't come back on us later. Worst case scenario—we can go over there some time before noon?"

"I'll go with him--," Raymond volunteered, "I need to pick up a few more cases of rounds."

"It's better that we always work in pairs." Rich had agreed, "One person might notice something that the other didn't." He snapped his fingers with a sudden recollection, adding, "I have to meet with the insurance clowns at the house at ten in the morning."

"That works out just fine—I promised to meet Danny and Dennis here after breakfast."

"Okay, I'll tag along with Rich--," Tim motioned to Amica, and said, "And the two of you can watch out for each other until everyone gets back."

"Alright—let's plan to leave here at noon--," Gordon stared into the bottom of his brandy glass, "God have mercy on Scott and Carrie—let's not waste their sacrifice in the cause…"

It was almost as though everyone had slipped into a cataleptic state. There wasn't a single sound or movement for what seemed many minutes. The fire had crackled, and the flames danced in the long shadows from all about us. It was a somber moment, a time of reflection, as we gazed almost blindly upon one another. Most of all, it was apparent that we had all realized that this was truly the beginning of the end…

"We should all try to get some rest--," Amica had broken us from the trance, and said, "We will need it in the days to come."

"I'm tired, but scared out of my wits." Drowsy and rubbing at his eyes, Tim looked over at her, "I doubt that I could sleep even if I wanted to."

"Anyone who wouldn't be scared of this would have to be insane--," Rich moved from the couch, and standing, said in quiet reflection, "What Scott and Carrie are doing took true guts."

"I'd say true heart--," Looking up at my friend, I dreaded the thought before having even expressed it, "Because, all other things aside, they both know they might not even survive the flight."

"If any of you have ever believed in anything in your life--," Raymond stood, and making his way into the hallway, paused to look back at us from the shadows, and said, "Start praying now—because we're all going to need it..."

CHAPTER TWELVE

Wednesday, February 6, 1975.
8:40 a.m.
It had been a very long and restless night. Although we had gone to bed at a reasonable time, I hadn't slept a single, straight hour. Haunted by Red and Ian's deaths, and reliving Trudy's final moments, I had visions of fiery plane crashes and losing Scott and Carrie. Weak and worn, I was awakened and blinded by the sunlight that now crept in from between the draperies.

Amica had stood at the window, as showered in the mornings shimmering rays, she had appeared as an angel before the golden gates. I hadn't said a word or done anything to interrupt the moment. She had slipped into one of Caitlin's white and flowing gowns during the night and the veil shone with an unearthly brilliance. Although she had first come to me in the form of a demon, I now only saw an angel.

"The morning has arrived as a blessing--," She glanced over at me and beckoning with a hand, said, "Come, warm yourself in the sun's rays."

Without so much as a word, I had climbed from the bed and contentedly joined her before the window. She had thrown the draperies wide open and the light had warmed our bodies and hearts. I had breathed deeply in its comforting glow while the shadows were chased from my thoughts and soul. Amica's skin was pale and radiant, her hair like the torches of Mount Olympus and her eyes like emerald pools. They glistened, shimmered with a light all of their own as she had turned to look at me. I became instantly and utterly lost while captivated within those greenest and most brilliant of gems. In every sense, the experience might have been very similar to that of having wandered one's own gardens, and discovered a unicorn.

"We should prepare for the day--," The light seemed to fade from the heavens as she turned from the window, "The others will be returning soon."

Making my way toward the large bureau, I had retrieved two towels and politely offered her the larger of the two, "Ladies first, I can be ready in fifteen minutes."

Dawning Caitlin's emerald bath robe, she had accepted the towel, and putting a finger to her lip, paused in thought, "It might serve you best to wear black today."

Realizing that she still retained certain aspects of her previous abilities, I had only nodded in agreement. In truth, almost everything that I owned was either black or shades of blue. I had never really given it much thought. I suppose that subconsciously, it had just reflected the bruised and battered soul that lay beneath. I could only scoff at my own melodramatic contemplations. In the end I had always loved the long black trench coats worn by television detectives and mysterious villains. Admittedly, I had always felt caught somewhere in between...

9:27 a.m.

Carrie had hurried Scott along as they made their way through the Vancouver airport and into the passenger waiting room. They had spent very little time with customs, traffic had been lighter than usual, and their flight would be leaving in less than forty minutes.

There were about thirty people waiting, and Carrie made a mental note that most were older and that none had children. For some reason, this lessened the fear and guilt that now haunted her. She knew that that they might be solely responsible for the crash of this plane and the deaths of all aboard.

"At least they didn't take our candy bars away." Scott grumbled while searching through their carry-on bag, "I'm surprised that they didn't toss us out of the airport, the way that you were carrying on out there."

"Well—Michael said to cause a little distraction."

"Going around asking folks if they're scared of flying and ending up in crashes isn't a distraction--," he groaned, "It's called causing a panic. I mean, geez—you must've scared the heck out of half the airport?"

"Do you really think so?" She smirked, elbowing him and hushing him as she said, "Keep it down, we don't want to scare anyone on our flight."

Utterly shocked and amazed, he just stared at her.

"Have a candy bar, sweetheart." She winked, gently patting him on the shoulder.

10:25 a.m.

Gordon had called shortly after ten. At first, I had been terribly nervous, but then he had reassured me that he had secured the necessary permissions. Apparently, the old lady's only living relative was a distant and wealthy niece, whose only interest in the matter was to sell the property with as little effort as possible. It seemed that this happened all too often among the old and wealthy.

Amica had attended to a knock at the front door, and quickly welcomed Danny and Dennis who had arrived as agreed. They had brought Scott's truck, and although shocked and surprised with my gesture, soon loaded my entire comic and magazine collection into the back.

"Are you sure about this?" Danny had stood and stared in the open doorway, still dumbfounded.

"I couldn't think of anyone else I'd rather give them to." He had always been like the son that I'd never had, and this was the least that I could do.

He had looked to Dennis, and stepping forward, looked at me before hugging me tightly.

"Michael—I don't want anything to happen to you."

"This isn't my way of surrendering--," Taking him firmly by the shoulders, I forced a smile, and said, "I'm just making room for other old junk—and books…"

"If you need us--," Dennis moved forward, and taking a firm grip on my hand, said with the utmost determination, "You just call us—and we'll be here."

"All that I really need--," Looking between them, I felt proud of them both, and said, "Is for you to take care of each other—and the others."

"You can count on us—no matter what." Danny's eyes revealed a depth of emotion that caused me to look away and into the tall pines. I knew that he was terrified of losing us all, and struggled with the fear and doubt.

"The only advice that my father ever gave me--," I looked back at Danny, "Was that no matter whatever happens—to always carry on. I guess that it was good advice—because I've been doing it ever since."

Neither one of them had said another word. They had just looked solemnly down, and then with a grimace that revealed a certain courage of conviction, carried on.

I had stood and watched as they pulled out through the gates, and without so much as a glance back, drove down the street. The sun had warmed the earth that morning, and as the wind played in the tree-tops, the snow had begun to melt. Turning to depart, I had hesitated, curiously peering back toward the gates. It was still there. That dark patch which still spoke of Harry's horrific ending… The days were slowly growing warmer and soon the snow would disappear. But I knew that long after the shadow of death had gone, it would forever remain a scar upon my heart and soul. So much had happened in this place that I had once called home. I knew that, even if we managed to overcome the evil, it would never be the same.

Closing my eyes, I had breathed deeply, soothed by the sun and warming wind. Through the chilling gust I could smell a silent promise of spring, the scent of pine and damp earth. The distant call of a raven caused me to stir from that peaceful dream, and look high into the branches of the surrounding pines. In that moment, the sunlight poured down from the heavens, as breaching the shadows, it cast illumination and life upon the pale and frozen earth. I had imagined things as they had once been. Dreaming of the long and warm summer nights, I remembered sharing tea with Eva and Caitlin in our lovely gardens. It was a moment that I now held dear, while turning and slowly walking back toward the house.

Rich and Tim had returned just before ten as promised. With all things moving along according to plan, we had quickly turned our attention to the matter at hand.

"Are you sure that these things won't blow up in our hands?" Tim cautiously inspected the darts before carefully laying them out on the table.

"They can't go off without leaking and being exposed to fluids--," Rich sipped at a mug of steaming coffee, "And besides, right now, I'd be more concerned about what might be waiting for us out there…"

Tim shuddered with the thought, receiving a dirty look from Rich as he muttered from under his breath, "I'm beginning to wonder which one of you is more dangerous."

At that moment the front door had opened and Gordon and Raymond hurried into the house. Quickly removing their boots, they came into the dining room, still wearing their coats.

"We have all the legal angles covered--," Raymond announced, "So, we can get this show on the road whenever everyone's ready."

"I'm just finishing up." Rich explained, offering holsters and weapons to our friends, "Like I was just telling Tim, I can't guarantee them—but it's the best that I could manage."

"You won't hear me complain--,"Raymond slipped into the shoulder holster and delicately dropped the weapon into place, "I'd rather go up in flames than end up being a part of one of those things."

"Just hearing that was enough to put a crease in my shorts." Gordon secured his weapon, and noticing Rich tuck a large plastic cylinder into a side pouch, asked, "What's in that thing?"

"Its extra water--," He replied while motioning with hid bow, "Just in case we need it. I'm not taking any chances."

"What about the other one?" Raymond noticed the concealed cylinder in Rich's military vest.

"Extra chemicals—," He bowed his head for a moment, and then looking about the group, said, "In the event that we're not going to make it out— we'll take them all down with us."

"Fair enough--," Gordon agreed, "But—for the love of Christ—be careful with that thing. We don't need any accidents."

"Okay--," Raymond searched for a pouch of darts, "Who is going to be carrying loaded darts, and who will the water guys be?"

"For safety sake--," Rich strapped several pouches on either side of his belt, "And since I'm already a walking bomb, I'll be carrying the loaded darts and hand them out when needed."

"I'll take the water darts--," Tim volunteered, "We can work from either side of the team, just to play it safe."

"Give me one of those fire-bombs--," Gordon insisted, "Just in case something happens to you—we need a back-up man to pull the pin for all of us."

"He's right--," Raymond looked to Rich, "We need to hope for the best— but should plan for the worst…"

Rich had carefully removed and offered a pouch and bomb to Gordon, swallowing hard as he watched the old detective clasp the pouch to his belt. None of us really felt any safer for it, but worst case scenario, at least we had options.

"What are you doing?" Turning from the table, Tim followed Amica into the kitchen.

"I'm getting ready to go with you." She buckled the belt that secured her blue-jeans, and tucking in the black turtle-neck sweater, made her way toward the hall closet.

"Where is she going?" Rich had taken notice as she slipped into one of Caitlin's fur collared, down-filled vests and wandered back into the dining room.

"She's coming with us." I shrugged, "You all knew that she was traveling as part of the group."

"That was when she could defend herself." Rich argued, his eyes wide as he looked to me in sudden shock, "Seriously brother, you can't put her in the middle of this now. You know what we're up against here."

"My place is with all of you." She said in a calm and complacent tone, and turning to look upon him, said, "It's our destiny…"

There was a moment of utter silence, stillness as they all gazed in horror upon Amica. She had changed so much, appearing and seeming so much like Caitlin that none could fathom such a risk. In the end, realizing what she had truly been beneath the flesh, Rich had slowly nodded. Tim had just stared at me as though the illusion had carried him so far that he doubted his own senses and my sanity.

"If you don't mind me saying it--," Raymond interjected, "Wouldn't it be better if she maintained security here? I mean—hell, in case anyone forgot, this is ground zero. If anything manages to destroy this place like they did with Rich's property, we'd all be screwed by nightfall."

There was a part of me that wished to agree and desired nothing more than to protect her, but something from deep inside warned me. It happened instantaneously, the words forming upon my lips without as much as a second thought, "And then what--," I looked into the frightened faces of my companions, "She would be here alone, and with whatever managed to get inside…"

"An evil grows within me--," She stared solemnly into their faces, an eerie green light burning in her eyes, "A dark power that will defend this form in the hopes of soon possessing it. So, if we should encounter anything threatening—it might be best if you stand clear when it appears."

With his suspicions established, Rich had sadly looked away. The others had been speechless, as caught in the moment and without any other recourse, I felt obligated to explain.

"She was never truly the demon incarnate, but a soul possessed. The two now occupy a single body—one that the demon intends to eventually take from her…"

"And what will happen then?" The look on Tim's face said it all. He was terrified for all of us.

"She will ascend, and finally be free of the demon--," I looked among them with certain guilt for having kept such a diabolical secret, "And we will be faced with the creature—in the flesh…"

"And, how much longer until this happens—do we even know?" Raymond swallowed hard, his eyes wide and focused upon Amica.

"You will witness the changes—they will be gradual," She appeared frightened and even ashamed, looking away as she said, "It will alter this flesh according to its own design and desires."

"Well, so much for remaining incognito--," Rich shrugged, "But with everything else happening—I suppose that doesn't really matter anymore, anyway."

"I'm not really sure what the hell is even going on here, but we're wasting precious time and daylight." Gordon reminded us, "Let's worry about everything else when the time comes. At least we know that she has some form of defense other than us."

"Here's the remote to your gates." Rich handed me the control mechanism as we all made our way toward the front door and he halted in thought, "Are you sure that we shouldn't leave someone here? Seriously, Raymond has a valid point—look what happened to my place…"

The decision had been swift as without a second thought, I had looked to Tim, "He right—Tim, you would be the best man for the job." He had attempted to argue, but I had raised a hand in gesture, saying, "You control the keeper of the vault—and I'd rather leave this with you."

Accepting the gate remote, he had slowly and quietly bowed his head as though shamed with the decision.

"If we need to trust someone with our home—and our lives--," Placing a supportive hand upon his shoulder, I quietly said, "I can't think of anyone better."

There was a moment as he had looked back that I thought he might still argue, but he didn't. Instead, he had removed his weapons and handing them to Raymond, looked among us, and sadly said, "May God go with you and return you safely, I'll be here waiting, my friends."

Firmly shaking his hand and at a total loss for words, I had only nodded in parting. We had watched for only a moment as he hurried back to the house and stood waving in the open doorway. Hurrying toward the truck, Rich looked to where Gordon's police cruiser sat parked nearby, "Maybe we should all just take my truck?"

"No, you mustn't." Amica had interrupted as we moved toward the parked vehicles, "We should never travel in a single vehicle, if it can be avoided."

"She's right--," Raymond reminded us, "One flat tire could be the end of us all. It might not make much of a difference in the end—but we shouldn't make this too easy for that thing."

"Alright, I'll take her with me." I had turned to move as Gordon tossed me his car keys, saying, "You're better off in my car—it's had a recent tune-up and has new snow tires."

"Michael--," Rich had paused at his truck door to look back at me, "Do not go into that place until we get there, please…"

His expression was desperate, his features pale as he stared while awaiting an answer. An icy gust had whipped the hair across my brow, as licking at parched lips, I had muttered, "I promise, not a single step until we're all together…"

The roads had been cleared fairly recently, but the journey had still been treacherous due to icy conditions. Avoiding the highway, I had taken more central routes and roads often travelled. After what had happened to Raymond I wasn't risking getting stranded alone on some barren stretch of highway or back road. This had made the journey considerably longer, but offered opportunity for escape in the event of a possible "freak accident."

Peering suspiciously into the distant clouds and then back at me, Amica hadn't said anything. In truth, she didn't have to, as I could see it plainly enough for myself. There wasn't any mention about bad weather over the radio, but something was definitely brooding on the horizon...

Pulling in before the old mansion, I had slowly climbed out of the car and just looked at it. This was certainly nothing like what I had been expecting. Overlooking and surrounded by dilapidated houses and old apartment complexes, the place was a diamond in the rough. Hailing from a time before the modern luxuries of motor cars and television, it stood like a giant upon the hill. A short stone wall encircled the several acres where it rested, and stone steps led to a large and surrounding veranda. Barren of trees, the grass was overgrown and the tall hedges blocked view of the neighbors from all sides.

The house stood three stories tall and, with towers upon either side, revealed a central balcony upon the second floor. There was a widow's peak, ornate moldings and large windows that gazed darkly upon the empty street. It was obvious by the peeling blue paint and white trim that it had been long neglected. There had been evidence that someone had attempted to maintain the old structure, but the efforts had been futile in the end. The veranda wasn't cluttered with junk like so many others, but contained a white wooden swing, and matching table and chairs. It had a stately presence, and though located in a less than desirable area, still held potential for the right owner.

"Oh dear, it's another enormous and creepy looking old house." Amica stood beside me and sighing deeply, said, "Oddly, I was expecting far worse..."

"Just give it a chance—I have a feeling that it might not disappoint you..."

"Where are the others?" She looked up the empty street behind us, "We took the grand tour, and they should have been here before us."

We had stood in the snow covered street and looked down at the crumbling asphalt. There was a growing tension, an anxiety that now caused a deepening pressure in my breast. I had tried to shake it off but feared irregular pains and pressures due to my heart issues.

"There they are--," She flung her arms in the air as they pulled in behind us, "At least we can all be thankful for having made it this far...."

A raven called in the distance and it sent an icy shudder up my spine. It had been the mournful cry that warned of death and disaster all of my life.

Rich and Raymond had removed lanterns from the truck, offering them to each of us before turning our attention toward the house. We had been armed with the crossbows, but the thought of an incident in confined quarters could only spell a fiery ending for all. I had looked down upon the weapon in a mixture of fear and fascination, and while realizing that death was the least of our worries. Gripping the old cane, my knuckles became white as my fingers clasped tightly about the form of the silver hell-hound.

We were gathered like old gunfighters before the steps of that place and shivered in the growing cold. The North wind had begun blowing again, and the skies were growing dark with heavy clouds.

"Let's get inside before we attract attention." Gordon reluctantly moved up the steps, and fumbling in his pocket, pulled out the keys. It had only taken a moment to unlock the front door, but had felt like an eternity before we finally stood inside. When Gordon had closed and locked the door behind us, I had felt completely trapped. The air was stagnant, as the place had been shut tight for many weeks, and the dust seemed to drift in the air from all about us. It was apparent that the poor old woman had lived alone, and the poor state of the place reflected that.

The windows were covered in long, yellowed draperies, which had been tightly drawn. There was a pale glow peeking from around them in places, but from beneath they cast shadows that grew long and wide.

Amica and Rich had hurried about, as swiftly opening them, allowed the dim light to stream into the large rooms. In the glow of day, it wasn't such a frightening or unpleasant place. Aside from purveying an attitude of disrepair, it appeared quite pleasant. The furniture represented the accumulation of several generations, and though nothing drew any immediate attention, revealed a modest though respectable lifestyle. The floors were polished hardwood, and there were cream colored carpets in the halls and main living areas. The walls all about were pale and bare, and it seemed quite obvious that the previous owners had cared little for art or anything considered fanciful.

At first, I had assumed that relatives might have already taken items of interest. But then, and after closer examination of the walls, I found no evidence of the usual staining that time left in the removal of such things.

"It's just like a hundred other places along this street." Gordon had remarked while taking notice of my investigations, "Old and run down, but nothing seems out of the ordinary."

"And that's all the more reason to exercise even greater caution." I had warned, "It's usually in the least likely places where you'll find the unexpected. But then again, you already know that, don't you, detective?"

"So where do we start?" Raymond had peered around the gloomy corridor, and then looked toward the staircase, "This place is bigger than we expected…"

"According to what Red Cloud told me, the old girl was concerned about the basement." Swallowing back the emotions in his memory, I directed their attention to the floor with a nod, saying, "So, as much as none of you wanted to hear this? If there is anything of significance here, I'd expect to find it down there."

"He's right." Rich cursed under his breath, "No one ever hides or leaves anything important somewhere easy to find. But why—why do they always have put it in the freaking basement!"

"Because, anything important enough to hide--," Raymond slipped an arrow into his crossbow, and said, "Would be put into the least likely and last place that anyone would want to go."

"The door to the basement is in the kitchen--," Gordon grumbled, and with a nod, led us down the corridor, "And the kitchen is at the very back of the house. The windows face out into an enormous yard. As you saw from the front, the hedge is very tall and overgrown. So no matter what happens, don't run out there—because you won't be able to get out."

Halting the group, Raymond went into several rooms on either side of us, and looking out the windows, cursed. Obviously not pleased with his discovery, he returned, saying, "The damn hedge has grown tight against the house—and well over twelve feet high. So if anyone thinks they can get out of a side window—guess again."

It suddenly felt as though the house was growing smaller from all about me, and the fear became suffocating. The thought of an impenetrable wall of roots and vines enclosing everything now gave off the impression that we had entered into a grave. There was a sudden, cold and greasy lump forming in my bowels. It was a bitter reminder of the old woman who had been found dead in that very same basement only weeks before…

"My Seiko has an alarm." Raymond announced as he promptly set the wrist watch, "I'll set it for three—that should give us plenty of time to get back before dark."

Rich had looked to his own watch and then withdrawn and examined his gold pocket watch, "They're all still showing the same time—so we should be fine."

"Don't put your faith in electronics--," Feeling obligated to remind them, I said, "Keep in mind that batteries tend to die very fast in the presence of ethereal beings."

"Oh, so that's why we're using oil lanterns." Gordon nodded, "I was going to ask you about that."

"We learned about not using battery operated lanterns the hard way." Rich quietly informed Gordon, "It was another close call—I'll tell you about it sometime…"

""No offense--," There was obvious fear in Gordon's eyes as he replied, "But if we somehow manage to survive all of this, I'd really rather not know. As it stands, I'll likely never sleep through another night again…"

The hardwood floors creaked loudly beneath our combined weight, and our footsteps echoed like thunder throughout the place. If anything lurked in the darkness beneath, our presence had long been given away.

"It's just over this way--," Gordon guided us into the large kitchen and then toward the back of the room, "Damn place sure is chilly." He rubbed at his arms with a shudder.

"I guess they turned off the power when the old girl passed." Raymond tapped a finger at an old thermostat while passing through the corridor, "It's a good thing that we brought the lanterns--," He glanced over at me, "There'll be no lights when we go down into the basement…"

The kitchen was large, and an era-typical robin's egg blue with white trim and matching cabinets. An oak table with six chairs rested beneath a large window, and upon the large black and white tiles of a checkered floor. An antique cabinet proudly displayed assorted Pinwheel crystal and Royal Daulton China. There were a few ornate figures and a pair of silver candelabra, all likely family heirlooms and some of the few treasures to be found in the place.

"The poor old girl shouldn't have been left here alone." Rich peered into the cabinet, and catching his reflection in the dusty glass, turned to look back at me, "This should never have happened."

"Time can be cruel--," Amica frowned at him, "And leaves little for those left in the wake of love and loss."

"Isn't that the truth--," Gordon had halted before the basement entrance and motioning with a finger, drew out attention to the large crucifix that had been firmly fastened upon the door, "Now that's a little unsettling. Anyone else get the impressions she had some concerns about the basement?"

"Only if you believe in monsters" Swallowing hard, Rich's hand slipped to the amulet about his neck, "And I do…"

"Alright then--," Raymond took hold of a lantern, and lighting the wick, growled, "Let's see what's going on down there."

Gordon had reached for the door handle, and flipping the little hook-latch, had slowly drawn it open. It was an old and heavy oak door and squeaked loudly upon hinges long neglected of oil. The sound gnawed at my nerves, as shoving it wide open, Gordon paused at the foot of the steps to look down. A cold draft issued from out of the darkness, as hurriedly lighting the remaining lanterns, we followed close... There had been a moment's hesitation before nervously peering back at me, Gordon had drawn his revolver, and cautiously led the way.

It had felt completely different than what we had previously experienced with the house. Not just because we were unnerved by the deep shadows, but the sense that we were no longer alone. I knew that it was far more than just a general suspicion or anxiety, because I could not fight off the feeling. It was a distinct impression that we had either found something, or that it had most assuredly found us…

As we neared the bottom of the steps, I had remembered the vision in the golden beryl, and seen the ghost of the old woman. It hadn't been an actual presence, but a memory of having previously seen the place before.

"This is the place that I saw in the stone." Informing my companions, "I motioned to the bottom of the stairs, saying, "The old woman had something hidden down here, I'm absolutely sure."

The short hairs on the nape of my neck and forearms had stood on end. It was apparent in the unsettling glances shared by my companions that I was not experiencing these things alone. The steps creaked and groaned as we slowly made our way down to the cold stone of the basement floor.

The room appeared enormous, as with few windows and baring very little light, much was concealed by clutter and darkness. Sturdy beams held the old house aloft, as shelving bore dust covered preserves from a bygone age. Old furniture littered one corner to the far side of the room, and laundry facilities occupied the area to the immediate opposite. There was a smell of detergent, mildew and ancient wood that caught me sneezing almost immediately.

"They found the poor old girl over there." Gordon had motioned with his revolver, "On the floor near the washing machine."

"What a dark, miserable and lonely place to die." Rich had spoken out of thought rather than intending to have said anything aloud, "It feels completely different down here than in the rest of the house."

"That's because they removed the body--," Raymond's eyes flashed in the lanterns glow, "But they couldn't take away that feeling of unnatural death. All homicide scenes feel like this—it's as though something or someone was still here..."

"And now that you've successfully scared the living crap out of me--," Gordon angrily turned back to look at Raymond, and said, "Can we please just get this done and get the hell out of here?"

Without another word we had moved toward the place where the body had been discovered. The lanterns flickered and shone upon the stone floor, which was still darkly stained where she had been found. None of us had said anything, having already assumed the reason. Amica had been cautious to avoid stepping anywhere near the splayed darkness, her eyes glistening suspiciously as she followed.

"Alright, so what exactly are we looking for down here?" Raymond had already become anxious, the fear vivid in his taught jaw and drawn features.

"I'm not exactly sure—but we'll know it when we see it." Raising my lantern and peering around into the shelving and heaped boxes, I swallowed hard, "But it looks like we're going to have our hands full--this place is a hoarder's paradise."

"Didn't the demon have special skills for things exactly like this--," Rich reminded me while glancing curiously at Amica, "Wasn't it a gift of sight, knowledge of secret places and hidden things?"

Looking to him in warning, I feared that his curiosity might invoke the evil within her, but it was already too late. She had uttered a strange sound, a whisper that carried like distant thunder throughout the place. Speechless and terrified, we could only all stand and watch. Her eyes flashed in the long shadows, as she moved around from between streams of gloom and lanterns light. Her form and features altered ever so slightly, as between a subtle blend of the devil and herself, she glared with diabolical delight, "What you seek is near--," Her voice was familiar and yet cold, deeper as it echoed in that dark place, "A gift of eternal damnation—and what offering do you make to me in its place?"

"Silentium daemonium derelinquas nos in pace--," Marlowe's voice whispered like an echo through a dream, "Silence demon, leave us in peace..."

Horrified, I had wondered if I had been the only witness to this hideous vision and looked to my friends. They had all appeared rather confused, though calm and unaware.

"Be still, Michael--," Marlowe had warned, "For only you can see the shadow of the beast—and even now it passes back into the realm of troubled dreams…"

As the words had been spoken, I dared to look back upon the nightmare that had been Amica, as changing, she became herself once again. I stood in utter astonishment as the shadow of evil had faded like a ghost that existed just beneath her skin. The moment and image passing from all thoughts, she blinked as though oblivious and curiously looked around, "Is something the matter?"

Something heavy suddenly fell in the darkness somewhere behind us and we all leapt back! Staring, listening, we watched the shadows for even the slightest hint of movement. I watched in disbelief as a large, old and rusted tomato juice can rolled from out and stopped merely several inches from where we stood. We had all looked to one another, realizing fully that something so heavy could never have just fallen of its own accord.

Gordon shone his lantern into the direction from where it had come, noticing several old steamer trunks to the rear of the room. They were far older than most of the other items in the basement and bore markings in a foreign language. Had it not been for the uncanny powers of the cane, this might have presented something of an issue. Fortunately, gripping the cane tightly and staring for a moment, I read them quite clearly, "Property of Bratislava expedition, and its dated 1926."

"Bratislava--," Rich thought aloud, "That's the capital of Slovakia, and it rests along the Danube River along the border with Austria and Hungary. I recently read something about the region."

"Yes--," I recollected stories of European travels that my mother had shared with me as a boy, "My mother was all through there as a young girl. It's mainly vineyards and stands in the shadow of what they call the 'Little Carpathian Mountains'."

"So, we know that someone in the old lady's family was a traveler." Raymond cautiously moved toward the trunks, and glancing back, asked, "Should we take a look inside?"

The old steamer trunks had been familiar, as my mother had owned a similar set. They were deep blue, with shiny brass hinges and a large, central lock that required a key. There was a larger trunk on the bottom used for clothing, and the smaller one of which resting on top, usually contained hygiene and other personal items. With exception to several inches of dust, they appeared in excellent condition.

"The family doesn't have any interest in the contents of the house, or any of these old things--," Gordon sadly informed us, and said with a deep sigh, "So, it's not like anyone's going to notice or even care…"

I had just stood back and watched as Raymond, using a screwdriver that he had found on a nearby shelf, made short work of the old lock. It was a shame to see it ruined in such a way, but time was short and we had other concerns.

Amica and Rich had begun sorting through the items in the smaller trunk as Raymond opened the others. I had felt deeply disturbed, not through our obvious intrusion, but with the deepening shadows. The windows were small and dirty and allowed only the faintest of the afternoon gloom to enter into the enormous and cluttered room. The tall shelving was filled with all manner of treasure and trash and presented a threat in every dark crevice, corner and ancient crack. The light streamed through the dust that we had disturbed, as creating pale beams, it reached out like the fingers of hope into the all-consuming darkness beyond.

"Let's have a look through this one." Raymond had insisted while opening the large clothing trunk. Moving closer and holding a lantern high, I had observed as he rummaged through the sheet-covered contents. Reaching down and pulling the sheet away, he dropped it on a shelf behind him and called out to our friends, "Let's get through this as quickly as possible—we don't want to stay any longer than we have to."

Amica and Rich had sorted through the smaller trunks, while Gordon kept looking to the windows and his wrist-watch. The tension was intense, and the minutes seemed to pass like hours as we rifled through the contents of the trunks. There were books, old clothing, assorted post cards and other travel memorabilia, but nothing of any real substance. Quickly shoving everything back into them, we had made short work of both trunks and soon stepped back in utter frustration.

"Well—that would've been far too easy--," Discouraged, Rich had dusted himself off , and standing up, looked around, "If there is something down here—I get the feeling that we're going to have to really dig…"

"Then we'd better get serious about searching this place--," Raymond reminded us while tapping at his wrist watch, "It's already after two and you all know how time flies."

"Let's work in teams--," I pointed to Rich and Amica, "You two cover the boxes under the stairs, and Raymond and Gordon can search this side of the basement." I looked to the far end of the room and shuddered with the thought, "I'll deal with the far end."

"No--," Amica argued without a second thought, "Rich can assist the others, and I'm coming with you."

It was apparent from her determined expression that any argument would have just wasted our time, so l simply agreed. I would have been lying if I had said that I didn't appreciate the company. What little courage remained to me was quickly fading into steadily growing fear and desperation.

We had all parted and began a frantic search of the place. In an effort to provide better lighting, we had placed the lanterns in such a way that they offered a large circle of light that surrounded our work areas. There had been little concern for causing a mess, and we simply began dropping things into boxes rather than returning them to shelves. In some sense, we were simply packing and simplifying the job for those who would eventually empty the old place. Oddly enough, there were a number of neatly stacked boxes as though someone had already anticipated the effort. Admittedly, I had felt a little guilty when tearing them open and turning everything upside-down. We worked swiftly and carefully, saying very little, as we desperately searched through the heaped shelves, litter-covered counters and cluttered cupboards.

I found myself continually looking over at Amica, only to discover that she had been doing the same thing. There was a growing paranoia of what she had become, and a fear of the demons approach and inevitable return, I began looking to where the others now worked across the room. It was something that started as a tingle at the base of my spine, and ran like a chill while numbing my mind. Every thought became harder as my focus fell drifted into the growing shadows, and I had soon slipped away from what we were doing.

"Michael—what's wrong?" She had spoken quietly and to avoid alarming the others, whispered, "Are you going to be okay?"

"I don't know--," It was an honest answer and the only words that came to mind, "I'm feeling dizzy, nauseated and feel like someone has pulled the world out from under me."

She had suspiciously looked about the room and then nodding, quietly said, "We have been here long enough." She motioned with a nod toward the windows as dusk darkened the skies, "There is no need to remain here—we can return with the daylight and search another time."

"Michael!" Rich leapt up from where he was sorting through a large and old wooden crate, "I think that I might've found something, come and check this out!"

We had immediately dropped what we were doing, and hurried to where he promptly dropped a large stone into my open hands, "It was in a strange box and at the bottom of that old crate."

The stone was bitterly cold and as black as night. It was oval in shape and about the size of a grapefruit, and felt polished and was perfectly smooth. At first, I had assumed it to be smoky quartz, but then realized that it was some type of volcanic glass.

"It looks like obsidian--," Rich gasped, "But there's some kind of transparency, a strange luminescence glowing from within."

He had been right, although I hadn't noticed it at first. Through the mirrored blackness of its polished surface, I could see the rainbows of some dark and distant dream. Unlike Labradorite with its layers of refracting quartz light, this one appeared to have some inner life, a cold and shimmering light all of its own. I had suddenly looked down, and taken notice of the wooden box resting in the crate. It was undoubtedly ancient, worn and was scrawled with numerous, but unrecognizable, ancient symbols. Astonished, I gripped the cane tightly, but was distraught as the script even managed to betray the deciphering power of the cane.

"What does it say?" Rich had looked to me with the greatest of anticipation.

"I don't know--," Feeling absolutely startled by this, I had turned to Amica, "Is this text anything that you recognize?"

No sooner had she seen the inscriptions than did she rip the stone from my hands, and placing it back into the box, sealed it tightly! Clenching it tightly to her breast, her eyes became huge and features wild, "This is forbidden—and an evil above all others! Hurry—we must leave this place, now!"

I could feel the temperature rapidly dropping, the room growing darker as the air became an icy vapor before our faces! It was that same terrifying experience that I had first encountered at the McCreary estate, the opening of a portal as something entered into our reality and now came for us!

"Don't you understand?" Rich wailed, "That's why it came to this place and murdered that old woman—it was after the stone!"

"Run—," The house now shook from all about us as Gordon gasped, "Run for your damn lives!"

Leaving our lanterns behind, we all dashed madly toward the stairway! I had kept Amica ahead, as shoving her along from behind, raced across the cluttered basement. The room grew black behind us, the lanterns extinguished, and the light fading from the windows. Stumbling, we almost fell backward as something now violently shook the earth!

"It's coming!" Rich wailed, as racing up the steps from behind me, was still tightly gripping the little wooden crate of which he had refused to leave behind.

We had barely reached the top of the steps when a thunderous howl echoed from the blackness below! It resounded through the entire house and shook the boards beneath us as we desperately scrambled from out of the basement door. Gordon and Raymond had struggled with their footing, but managed to slam closed and lock the door. We had all fallen inward and crashing heavily to the kitchen floor, gathered ourselves in sheer panic.

"We definitely pissed something off!" Raymond choked, staring wide-eyed as he looked to Amica, who still fearfully clung to the box and stone.

"This is a stone of invocation--," She gasped, "It summons and binds the darkness when removed from its entombment.

"Entombment--," Rich moved closer and stared at the box between her trembling hands, "It's just an odd looking wooden box—what do you mean?"

"It conceals itself from mortal eyes--," She appeared terrified, and holding it up for all to see, whispered, "Many lives were spent in its creation, and souls lost within its binding. Their bones were weaved and their blood used for sealing the stone inside this cursed sarcophagus."

Upon closer examination, what had first appeared as little more than a wooden case in the shadows now revealed itself in the light of day. Roughly the size of a large cigar box, it was a finely crafted network of splintered, interwoven bone and script written in blood. I dared not guess at what foul substance had been used to hold those fragments together, but recoiled at the sight of the thing.

"It has the power to both draw—and hold the evil in one place--," She looked between us, "It is a powerful weapon in the right hands—and a terrible weapon against mankind should it fall into darkness. The evil would summon an even greater darkness from the void, and cast human-kind into endless night…"

"What in blazing hell is wrong with you people--," Raymond bellowed as the foundations shook beneath us, "We need to get out of here, right now!"

The house rumbled again and we scrambled to our feet, hurrying into the corridor and toward the front door. It was at that point that I suddenly felt disoriented, stumbling and noticing that the others appeared almost as though they were intoxicated. All of us were desperately clinging to the walls for support, and fought to maintain our composure.

"Hurry--," Amica forced us along as seemingly unaffected by the strange euphoria, guided us like blind men into the main hall, and then toward the front door, "The evil is beneath us—its sickness seeks to poison your minds! It desires the stone—and will stop at nothing to get it!"

Rushing ahead of us, she unlocked, and desperately tugged at the door handle! Falling to my knees from behind her, my mind swam in a dark and dizzying haze. I felt the pressure building in my chest, and the horror of what was happening drawing the breath from out of my lungs.

"Don't do it!" Rich wailed as Gordon had considered his crossbow and aimed toward the door, "We'll all burn to death in this place—we can't get out!"

"Back off, little lady—make way!" Raymond had howled, as crawling on his knees, drew and unsteadily aiming both forty-fours, and blasted the door lock right out of the frame! Still, it refused to give way, as using the wall for support and climbing to his feet, he threw his full weight against the door.

At that moment, and with my mind in a fog, I had seen something strange come over Amica. She had stood before the door, and slowly turning to look back at me, her features and form altered as though a ghostly apparition now took hold. Unclear as to whether it was just some effect of a delusional mind, I gasped with the sudden horror and realization! It was the ghost of a demon manifesting, and the haunter of her soul had come...

The answer had not come in words, but in warning, as crawling blindly, I managed to pull Raymond out of the way. Not a moment too soon, as spinning in a blind fury, Amica had howled in rage. Her body enveloped in the demons shadow, she lashed out with a blackened claw and through a mindless hate! The front door exploded from off its hinges, and splintering into a thousand wooden shards, was blown outward and into the front yard. The light flowing inward as sobering us in that moment, we all desperately scrambled out and into the late afternoon glow.

Amica, having been completely restored to her previous form, gripped the box tightly as she took me firmly by the hand. She was quickly developing a strength and stamina well beyond any mortal being. I was terrified in the knowledge that these abilities were not just supernatural benefits, but subsequent to her becoming the demon.

Frantic, we had all staggered off the veranda and down the steps, and fallen to our knees in the deep snow. The cold air sobering our clouded minds, as we all turned back toward the house and stared. The door had somehow returned to its proper place, as undamaged and sealed tightly, the blackness now gazed out through the shadow-haunted window panes.

"We need to get away from this place." Rich gasped, as still clinging to the wooden crate, he climbed unsteadily to his feet, "I can still feel its power—it's like it's trying to drain away my life..."

"We have further angered the evil--," Amica clung to the box containing the mystic stone, "We have taken the key-element to controlling this elemental, and summoning its dark masters from the beyond."

"I'm not sure why?" Gordon fought to regain his composure, "But for some reason, that doesn't make me feel any better."

"Let's get out of here while we still can." Taking hold of Rich's arm, Raymond guided him back toward the truck.

Apparently unaffected by the strange and mesmerizing spell, Amica had assisted Gordon as I followed at an unsteady, but reasonable pace. Never before had I experienced such a completely debilitating force. It had left most of us stunned for a considerable time, and until we were a substantial distance away from the house.

"The stars are aligning—as all things will now come to pass," Marlowe whispered from the depths of my mind, "The powers grow within the darkness—make haste, you must now discover the key to opening oblivions path..."

Amica had assisted Gordon into the backseat and swiftly hopping in beside me, leaned and placed her head against my shoulder, "It's better that he remain with us--," She spoke softly, "I'm concerned that this has all been far too much for him."

Glancing into the rearview mirror I saw that he had slumped over, and utterly fatigued, apparently fallen asleep. Pulling away from the curb, I had responded with a nod, and following Rich and Raymond, asked, "Are you feeling okay? Do you remember anything of what happened just before we all managed to break free of the house?"

"The demon did not assist us, but fled before our destroyer--," Amica spoke as though recounting a dream, "It would appear that we share a common and powerful enemy among the hierarchy of hell."

"Why would the darkness want to destroy its own kind?"

"Evil simply for the sake of evil--," She glanced up at me, "A destructive force with a desire to overcome any and all."

Realizing that her own evil would never succumb to bargains or mortal will, I couldn't help but wonder, and then ask, "Is there any chance that one might cancel out the other? What I mean to say is—would the darkness destroy your demon, given the chance?"

"What you seem to forget—sweet Michael--," She placed a cold hand against my cheek, "Is that under the circumstances—the demon may hold me for as long as this mortal body lasts. As through our affiliation—it too has become a target for the darkness. In the end, rather than parting, we might become spiritually bound and physically intertwined when it manifests…"

"But, that's not the bargain that was made with destiny when we first agreed to this path."

"Destiny may have granted the opportunity—but our decisions leave the ending to the fates."

"So, you're going to turn into some kind of a monster?" Gordon was wide awake and now staring from where he clung from between the front seats.

"That all depends on the greater will—," Amica wiped a tear from her eye, "And what happens to all of us in the end…"

He had slowly sunk back into the seat, his eyes unblinking as he stared as though blind. I had watched him for just a moment in the rearview mirror, and saw that he truly suffered with the horrendous thought. Things were getting uglier by the moment and I was terrified with the possibilities.

Quietly resting her head in my lap, I felt the warmth of her tears while gently stroking her hair. The heavens had grown darker and as the flurries came harder, I wondered if any of us would survive this almost unbearable nightmare.

CHAPTER THIRTEEN

As they soared across the clouds and into the heavens, Scott had gazed solemnly out the window and into the distant setting sun. He sighed deeply, watching as the flight carried them across an ocean and into darkness, and ever further away from home.

"I love you--," Carrie had whispered while tightly taking a hold of his hand, "And always will—no matter what happens…"

It was as though she had sensed his loss and needs in that moment, and fulfilled them as she always had. He had leaned over in the seat they shared, tenderly kissing her, and quietly said, "I love you too—and as long as we have each other, nothing else really matters…"

"It's getting dark--," She nodded out the window and into a deep mauve and crimson sunset, "And it's still four hours before we set down and have to exchange flights."

"Michael said that we might be safer if we're far away--," He swallowed hard with the thought, "There's also a chance that it might not even notice us with everything else that's going on."

"As long as Patrick is safe with gramps and Pam--," She responded quietly and after much thought, "I can live with whatever happens—and as long I'm with you. We just couldn't leave those poor girls all alone out there—not with what's going on…"

"I feel the same way, sweetheart--," He scratched thoughtfully at his beard, and looked down, "I just hope that we can make a difference to someone somewhere and help end this thing."

"We all have our parts to play—and I'm glad that whatever comes of it, mine will end with you."

Blinded as the sun peeked out from behind the clouds, he had watched as it slowly set. The brilliant orb casting smoky hues of smoldering orange and gold, as infused with deep purple, the world began drifting into a peacock, pastel dream. He had always loved sunsets and they reminded him of the greatest miracles and blessings of his life.

"Do you remember when we first met--," He looked to her and smiled sadly, "You were working at that bowling alley part-time, and I used to come in and just sit?"

"I sure do--," She fondly recollected, and smiling back at him, said, "I was beginning to wonder if you were ever going to ask me out?"

Swallowing back the emotions, he looked to her, and his blue eyes seemed to shine, "I loved you from the first time that I ever set eyes on you. And, I knew, that you were the person that I wanted to spend the rest of my life with."

"Oh crap--," Removing her glasses, she used a napkin to wipe at the fogged lenses, and then at her eyes, "Now you've gone and made me cry."

"As long as those tears say I love you--," He sniffled, and gently leaned his head down against hers, "Then it can rain in our hearts forever, for all I care..."

In that moment she had grabbed hold, and held him tight, as blinded by tears she had looked out and into the failing light. Ever downward they now soared and into the dense clouds, drifting through a dream as they slowly vanished from sight.

Wednesday, February 6, 1975.

5:22 p.m.

We had arrived home as the final rays of the setting sun faded from behind heavy clouds. It had been a race against time and the weather as an expected blizzard now ensued. We had all known the dark origin of that unnatural storm; it was an evil that even now had followed us home...

Hurrying into the house and closing the door, fatigued beyond rational explanation, we had literally all slipped down and sat staring from upon the floor.

"What happened?" Tim gasped as he began helping us with our gear and clothing.

"We found something--," Raymond explained while slowly moving to his feet, "And something else found us—we barely got out!"

"That was too close for comfort--," Rich had placed down the wooden crate, and kicking off his boots, looked to Gordon, and said, "You did the right thing in listening to me. If you'd fired that thing off in the house—we would've all been burned up in there."

"I was so scared--," He admitted, "That I didn't know what to do, and I couldn't even think. It was like a hard night of whiskey, and the morning after."

"That was the effects of whatever was in that place--," I coughed while still shivering with that unnatural chill, "It was trying to weaken and disorient us—and almost succeeded."

"What happened in the end—and how did that door finally give way?" Raymond slid along the wall for support while he regained his composure, "I blasted the crap out of it—and it wouldn't open, no matter what."

"It was Marlowe--," I had admitted, "I called and he came just before the end."

"I didn't know that he could do things like that?" Tim appeared confused as he assisted Gordon with his coat and hat.

"I suppose that he works through us to some extent—we're like a direct connection to the physical world."

"I still have it--," Rich grinned devilishly while retrieving the wooden crate, and then confused, examined it closer, and muttered, "I'm not sure why—but I got it?"

"Let's take everything to the table for a closer look." Urging them all out of the hallway, I followed close behind, "If you wouldn't mind, Tim, could you help out with some hot drinks?"

"Of course--," He saw that we were utterly spent and in sorry shape, "I have dinner almost ready—I'll bring out some tea and coffee right away."

There was a sense of relief from everyone except Amica. She had removed her boots and coat while refusing to place down the box that was still held tightly in her grasp.

"If that contains something dangerous--," Tim had curiously asked in passing, "Then shouldn't we be putting it into the vaults rather than keeping it here?"

"No—Michael must keep it near and safe. It must never be out of our sight."

It was the first time I had ever seen her so frightened, and it bothered me.

"Would it be safe in the office—and just for a little while?" I had moved to say something else, but she had been gone before I could utter another word.

"I'm going to assume that we found what we were looking for?" Gordon led the way as we converged in the dining room and immediately took our seats.

"Judging from the way that she was acting--," Raymond withdrew and reloaded his revolvers at the table, "We found a lot more than we expected."

Rich piled kindling into the hearth, and putting flame to the gathered paper, looked back and said, "Apparently, it's a stone of invocation, and a way that we can summon or lure the darkness out."

"That sure beats waving a flag and hoping that it'll show up." Gordon rubbed at his eyes, "But what the heck are we going to do when it does?"

"That's the hard part." Raymond slipped the revolvers back into their appropriate holsters, and clasping his hands together on the table, looked to me, "We still need to figure that last part out…"

"The stone is the second part of the puzzle--;" Shivering, I fought to escape a chill that simply would not fade, saying, "Marlowe said that the third element would appear once we discovered the second."

"If that stone summons the darkness, what makes us so sure that it can't get to us here?" Gordon asked the obvious question, "I mean, seriously, aren't we inviting that thing in by having the stone in the house with us?"

"It is safe as long as none remove it from its sarcophagus." Amica came back into the room, and taking the seat beside me, looked to Gordon, "The souls of the dead guard over the stone."

"That's reassuring." Raymond swallowed hard, and scratching at his mustache, looked to Rich, "And now that we're all safe for the moment, why the hell did you risk your butt to drag that old crate out of the house?"

Raising a finger in recollection, he hurried from the room and swiftly returned with the item in question. We had all watched, as dropping it before his feet, he rummaged through the contents, producing a letter of which he had handed to me.

"At first, I had no idea of why I even did it?" He shrugged, "It was like some subconscious thought had just forced me to act without really thinking. But then, I remembered seeing this."

Looking at the yellowed parchment in my hands, I was cautious while unfolding the delicate and crumbling page. At first I had assumed the archaic penmanship to have been written in a foreign language, but soon realized that it was simply poorly written, old English.

"Well—what does it say?" Rich became impatient, and clasping his hands together, anxiously awaited a reply.

I had barely managed to read through the first paragraph, and shrugging, said, "So far, it speaks about a family expedition, and three brothers on route to Hungary. The author talks about the train ride and a friend awaiting them in Debrecen. He goes on to explain how they plan to visit the Deri museum and have an appointment with the curator."

"Sounds like more treasure hunters." Raymond tapped his nails nervously upon the end table, "I wonder what they were up to?"

"There is mention of something that was found—an object of interest." I briefly fell silent while reading down the page, "It talks about a cathedral in France, Our Lady of Assumption in Clermont-Ferrand in the Auvergne."

"It was first opened in 1248 and comprised entirely of volcanic rock--," Tim returned with hot drinks, and placing down the tray, said, "It's the seat of the Archbishops. My father loved old churches and cathedrals--," He shrugged, "And especially stories of mystery and intrigue."

"It's kind of a coincidence that our stone just happens to be made of obsidian too, huh?" Gordon looked around the group before focusing upon me, "What else does that thing say?"

"It talks about something that was removed or stolen from the cathedral by rivals in the early part of the sixteenth century. Then explains how this item, I'm assuming our stone, spent several centuries concealed in the possession of dark magicians and was protected by gypsies. Somehow, it was lost again, there's a mystery surrounding that, and it was then discovered during an archaeological expedition to an old burial site near the Carpathian Mountains, which is how it had naturally fallen into the hands of the curator of the Deri museum in Debrecen."

"Talk about finding the proverbial jack-in-the-box--." Gordon warmed his hands around his steaming coffee cup, "I wouldn't have wanted to be there when he opened that one..."

I had returned to the reading and felt my heart sink as I continued. Being so nearly done, I had simply finished the letter before looking back to my friends, "Apparently, things were never carried that far—and the curator was spared. The final part of the story tells of one of the brothers stealing the box from the museum, and realizing what they had done, how he attempted to return it to the curator."

"Obviously something had to have gone wrong--." Rich appeared strangely amused, and grinning nervously, said, "Or it would've still been locked in some display case in that museum."

"It was the eldest brother, Stephan, who had initially tried to return the box and then simply vanished in the night." Shuddering uncontrollably, I leaned back as Amica gently took hold and embraced me.

"Are you alright?"

"I picked up a nasty chill back at that house--," Accepting a cup of tea from Tim, I wearily forced a smile, and said, "It's nothing that a nice cup of tea and a hot meal can't fix."

"Is there anything else?" Rich had curiously looked at the page that still hung from my trembling hand.

"The youngest brother, Andreas, had been killed by wild dogs while on route to the train station. The middle brother, Peter, had been the only survivor of that journey, and the box had come back in that crate that Rich found. I'm assuming that he was the old woman's father, and that either he or she must have hidden it beneath the stairs."

"What else was in that crate?" Raymond leaned closer as Rich examined the contents.

"It's full of old books, a bible and these." Rich presented a large, hand-carved crucifix, "It's Roman Catholic."

"It might be best to keep all of those things together." Amica had suggested, "And with the stone…"

"By all means—we're done with it anyway." Rich offered her the crate, which she promptly accepted and carried off.

"I wonder how Scott, Carrie and the others are all doing." Rich stirred cream and sugar into his coffee while shooting a nervous glance my way, "Maya promised to call me from the hotel where they're going to meet with Scott and Carrie…"

My hand had instinctively moved to my throat and the golden cross that Caitlin had given me. She seemed so far away and my heart ached while feeling as though our love was long lost. "Let's just keep our fingers crossed that we're keeping that thing busy." Raymond had raised his mug in a toast of good faith, "Maybe it'll be too occupied chasing us and they'll pass safely through the night."

"Amen to that." Still shivering, I sipped at the tea, soothed as I felt the warmth.

"Maybe we should've burned that old house to the ground." Gordon had pondered, and looking to me, said, "Before anyone else buys it and ends up like that poor old woman."

"The darkness will pass from that place now that we have removed the stone." Amica answered, "Elementals are drawn to certain shapes, sounds and energies, and have no purpose in a place without them."

Gordon almost spilled his coffee, looking to her and asking, "How can you be so sure of that?"

"Shared thoughts accrue a similar frequency and become an energy that is like a signal which can be followed--," Amica explained, "Our removal of the stone from that place has altered the energies and changed that frequency."

"So, instead of following that family--," Raymond sat and stared, "It's going to follow that frequency straight back to us…"

"Welcome to station NITRLM--," Rich played announcer, and speaking in calm and relaxing tones, said, "Your easy listening, all night frequency, guaranteed to take you straight to hell."

"Does he always do that--," Gordon appeared horrified.

"Only when something really freaks him out--," Raymond glared at Rich, "Would you please refrain from doing that, for all of our sakes?"

Obviously feeling remorseful for the jest, Rich had wandered into the living room and turned on the television. At first it had been somewhat disruptive, but then something on the six-o-clock news had caught all of our attention. It was another update on a recent series of missing young women and murders that had occurred across the Western United States.

"The King County Police are still searching for clues--," Shaking his head, Gordon cursed, "All that they know so far is that his name is Ted and that he owns a Volkswagen beetle."

"Evil walks this earth in many forms," Amica had nervously looked over at me, "He is the demon behind a smile. His eyes will betray him as he cannot hide what lurks within."

"They have missing women in Utah now as well," Raymond grumbled, "It's like they just vanish into thin air. Whoever this creep is—he's a monster..."

"I should see to dinner—," Amica moved from the chair, "It's getting late and I'm certain that you are all hungry."

"It won't take long--," Tim announced, "I marinated some chicken breast, peeled potatoes and shucked the corn. Everything is all cooked and ready to go—all that we have to do is serve it."

"You really are amazing--," I thanked him, "I don't know what we would do without you."

"It's the least that I could do--," He paused before going into the kitchen, "You didn't just expect me to sit around the place while you were gone."

He had always amazed me, and as he winked and vanished into the kitchen I sunk back into the chair. The bitter chill had numbed my thoughts and caused my whole body to feel like lead. Every thought and each movement required far more effort than it seemed worth. I just wanted to close my eyes and let go of everything, just for a little while.

"So, what do we do now?" Rich had interrupted the moment. I could see by his expression that his concern was still with Maya and the others, and understood his impatience.

"All that we have to do now—is live long enough to find the final piece to this puzzle, and end it all..."

7:25 p.m.
Danny and Dennis had surprised Tanya with a home-cooked meal. It was meat loaf, mashed potatoes, green beans, and they'd even brought an apple-crumble for dessert. It was the special of the day down at the diner, and as close to a kitchen as either of them had intended on getting.

Regardless, they had enjoyed the meal together and settled down on the floor with dessert and hot drinks.

"I still can't believe that Michael just gave you his whole comic book collection." Tanya sipped at her hot cocoa as they stared at the walls, "He really loved those things—I hope that you'll take care of them."

"I know he did—and it meant a lot to me. Of course I'll take care of them, sheesh mom, I'm not a little kid," He had rolled his eyes at Dennis, who sat in a chair across from him and wisely refused to become involved.

"I know that you're not a little kid—and I really don't mean to treat you that way." She gave him that motherly look, "But no matter how old we both may get—in my heart, you'll always be my little boy."

Her expression bordered on tears and they had both known that her words had come directly from the heart. All the same, Danny felt uncomfortable with the sentiments and quickly changed the subject, "Once we get back into a real place of our own, I'll get a sturdy shelf to keep the collection safe. Everything is safe enough over at the old book store for now."

"Maybe you should've brought them here--," Dennis shrugged, "It would've given you something to do."

Suspicion and doubt had caused Danny to pause, thinking briefly before he disagreed, "No, we barely have enough room for our beds in that room, and besides, this place just doesn't feel safe."

His comment had drawn Tanya's attention immediately. It wasn't the same fear that she had experienced at Rich's estate, but a sense of pending doom that crept into the shadows of her heart.

It had been dark for some time and they could see the flurries from beyond the partially drawn drapes. Danny had argued when his mother had first discovered them in a large box in the warehouse. They were clean and appeared almost new, but the mauve and light blue, purple paisley had driven both boys half out of their minds! To make matters even worse, she had singularly selected all of the furniture from the antique store downstairs. It hadn't been easy to match those drapes, but she had come fairly close. Their new warehouse manager, Jay Leonard, had happily offered to deliver everything. It would have been a nightmare for most, but the freight elevator from the warehouse adjoined the building, having once been part of the same business. Due to extenuating circumstances, and her complete bliss, Rich and Michael had provided everything free of charge. In fact, should she desire it, she had been told that she was even welcome to keep the mauve, velveteen furniture and enormous, pink and crystalline lamps.

"How much longer are we going to be sitting on the floor?" He had sighed and looked to his mother.

"Everything takes time, sweetheart--," Looking toward the window, she grinned happily, and said, "It was just a stroke of good luck that helped me discover those wonderful drapes."

"Oh goody--," Danny leapt up to a loud rapping upon the apartment door.

The boys had both been horrified, but Tanya had just calmly gone down the hall with them in close pursuit.

"What are you doing--," He attempted to stop his mother, 'You have no idea of what might be on the other side of that door!"

"Will you both please just calm down--," She unlocked the door, and reaching for the handle, said, "We are perfectly safe here—and besides, I'm expecting someone."

Flinging the door wide open, they all stood and just stared as something moved inward from out of the dimly lit hall. It darkened the doorway and caused them all to leap back, as someone shouted from behind the massive form, "It's just Jay with your furniture—sorry I'm late, watch out—coming through!"

He wasn't a large man by any stretch of the imagination, but he had the heart and determination of someone as big as a bear. Just a little over five feet tall and one hundred and sixty five pounds, he huffed and puffed as he dragged the love seat in. He was dressed in blue jeans, motorcycle boots and a black leather jacket. Unloading the large love seat from the dolly, he had stopped to look between Tanya and the boys. His long black hair was tied into a pony-tail from beneath his black baseball cap. With dark eyes that peered inquisitively from beneath large brows, he appeared somewhat sinister. It was a moment that hadn't lasted though, as thoughtfully tugging at his long beard, he grinned wide and said, "If I'd known that you boys were here—I could've gotten a little help."

Having already been familiar with his cheerful manner from work, they had all laughed.

"Thank you for the giant purple furniture--," Danny patted the loveseat, and glared at his mom, 'She has such amazing taste—doesn't she?"

"Oh sure--," Jay winked, "But it's nothing that a can of gas and a match couldn't fix."

"Oh be nice--," She scoffed at them, "I happen to love this stuff—and was lucky to find a whole set."

"This isn't a whole set—is it?" Danny fearfully peered out and into the hall.

"It sure is—and according to the documents, we've had it for months." Jay strolled back out the door, and scratching under his black ball cap, said, "I got a couch, matching chair, two end tables and pink lamps, and three dressers still in the freight elevator down the hall."

"Just give us a second to get some shoes on --," Danny sighed, and rolling his eyes at his mother, mumbled, "We'll give you a hand with this stuff. I know that you probably want to get home."

Laughing aloud, Jay had looked between her and the boys, and shrugging said, "I rented a place on the second floor—so I'm already there, I mean here, home. Oh, I'm also the part-time handy-man—plumbing, small repairs, that sort of thing."

"That's fabulous—," She thought briefly, and then pointing, smiled and said, "I noticed that the faucet in the kitchen sink leaks a little. Maybe you could take a look over a cup of coffee, sometime?" She was relieved to have another male presence in the building. Red Cloud's death had left a hole in their hearts and a definite sense of vulnerability.

"Who could turn down an offer like that?" Jay chuckled, and winking at Danny, said, "I think that I'm going to like living here." In that same moment he had noticed the drapes, and placing a finger to his chin, thoughtfully said, "Geez, aren't those terrific? I'm glad that they're in your place and not mine."

"Why does everyone pick on my draperies?" She playfully slapped at his shoulder and grinned, "I'll have you know that it took hours of rummaging through boxes downstairs for me to find those."

"If I'd known that, I would have hidden them better." He winked.

"We're going to get along just fine." Danny chuckled, as slipping into his shoes, nodded, "Now let's get the purple stuff in here before mom freaks."

"Do you have time for coffee?" Tanya asked before he could leave, "Maybe even a little dinner? We had a ton of leftovers tonight."

"You had me when you said coffee--," He licked at his lips, "And a little dinner sounds really nice. I didn't have time to eat yet, so it was going to be peanut butter and jam."

"Well, I think that we can do a little better than that—I'll heat some food while you finish the job."

Tanya could sense that he was a good man and it showed clearly in his manner and tone. She had been a little unsettled by the motorcycle jacket and his general attire, but it was like her mother had always said: 'It's not about the wrapping, but what's inside that counts'. Smiling to the sounds of the laughter down the hall, a tear found its way to her cheek. It had seemed a lifetime since she had heard anything cheerful come out of the boys, and she blessed the arrival of their new friend.

With the furniture in place and everything settled for the evening, she had served Jay a late night meal. He had happily indulged the leftovers, and then shared apple-crumble and coffee with Tanya when the boys had gone off to bed.

"So, if you don't mind me asking--," She asked as they sat on the couch beside each other, and she dusted at the purple, velveteen armrest with a hand, "Are you originally from Vancouver—and have you lived here a long time?"

Sipping at his coffee, he shrugged, and playing at the tips of his beard, reluctantly said, "Well, I'm originally from Ontario—and inherited my grandfather's home. It was a big, old beautiful place. I grew up there and ended up restoring most of it myself."

"So—what happened?" She raised a hand as though having carried things too far, and apologized, "I hope that I'm not prying too much?"

"Oh, it's fine, and I don't have anything to hide. It's just the same old story—the kind that you hear over and over again." He drained the cup, and brushing a few droplets from his beard, grinned foolishly, "I fell in love with someone who seemed too good to be true. And, to tell you the truth—in the end, I was happy to see her go. She left me after six months and took half of everything—I even had to sell the house. She ran off with some other poor sap—but she'll be robbing him in no time, too. I was so pissed about losing everything, that I took the money that I had left and came to Vancouver to start a new life."

"My husband—Danny's father--," She began, "Was talked by his dad into volunteering for Vietnam." She struggled with the emotions, "The old man wasn't a bad person—he just had certain beliefs that in the end cost my husband his life. We never received any positive confirmation—or even remains for a proper service. The military just told us that he was what they called an M.I.A." She swallowed hard with the recollection, "That's missing in action in military lingo. They just said that he vanished somewhere out in that jungle—and I've been alone with Danny, and hoping that he might just show up one day. I've heard stories of that happening--," She looked desperate but hopeful, and looked down, fidgeting nervously as she quietly said, "I suppose that none of it seems real without a body—and no closure, because we never had a chance to say goodbye."

"I'm sorry to hear that--," He placed the cup down and rubbed at his eyes, "Most people don't even realize how many Canadian volunteers died and are still suffering from the consequences of that war."

"I used to have nightmares of seeing him alone--," She shuddered with the thought and rubbed at her arms, "Out in that jungle in the darkness, injured and dying. It woke me in cold sweats for years—and sometimes even now, I wake up crying."

"Real love hurts forever--," He gently patted her hand, "My grandmother lost a child in a farming accident, and according to grandpa, she was never the same."

"We've been alone for almost ten years now--," She sipped at her coffee, "We lost contact with Danny's father's family after his grandmother died. She had a heart attack, and Danny's grandfather fell apart after he lost her. They never had any other children—and most of the relatives were so distant, they were strangers at best. So, I was working odd jobs just to stay afloat. Well, that was until Michael found us—or Danny found him, I was never really sure? He and Rich have been like uncles to him, and everyone else like the family that we never had. They were all a Godsend, really, a chance for a good job and a decent home."

"What about your side of the family? Don't they ever get involved or help out?"

"Oh, no, my parents thought that I was just the worst thing—unmarried and living alone with a young boy. At first, my mother tried to help out with money, food and clothing for Danny when he was little, but pops wouldn't have any part of that. He said that I should give up my son—and go back to school."

"You have my respect there—standing for what you thought was right. Um, can I ask about the other guy?" Jay pondered, "Dennis—yeah, that's his name. I'm better with faces than names--," He apologized, "Too many bumps on the noggin' playing ball as a kid."

"Dennis came to us when he lost his job at an asylum some time ago. He was friends with Rich and Michael, and helped us here at the warehouse and became friends with Danny over time. We just adopted him—he's older than Danny, but I still treat him like he's one of mine. Like I was saying, we all tend to stick together around here."

"Well, my folks and family are all back in Ontario—so I'm here alone as well. Who knows?" He grinned and winked at her, "Maybe I'll end up being Cousin Jay or Uncle something to someone around here?"

She laughed, as thanking her for the hospitality, he had moved from off the couch, "So hey, I hate to say this, but I'd better drag my butt down to bed. The morning comes much too early for me—I'd better get going before I pass out on your couch. Thanks again for the great meal, coffee and conversation, we should do it again, real soon."

Extending a hand and thanking him, she followed him toward the door, "I would really like that. And thanks again for helping with the furniture, and bringing a little light into our lives."

"Well--," He paused in the open doorway and looked back with a mischievous smile, "I've never been accused of that before, but if it's a compliment, I'll take all that I can get."

"Good night, new friend Jay." She waved as he had winked, and whistling cheerfully, rolled the furniture dolly back down the hall. She had watched as he disappeared around the corridor, and then listened until she heard the doors on the freight elevator close. In the distance she heard the little bell ring as the doors closed, and the rattling as it creaked on its way down. Then, slowly closing the door, she had stood in the dim hallway and cried. It wasn't because of this chance meeting, but due to the love that had been forever lost in time. She had covered her mouth to smother the tears, but the sniffling was impossible to hide.

"Oh, Barry—I miss you so very much--," She whispered, and forcing herself upright, wiped the tears from her eyes, "We'll be together again one day—and until then, my sweet love, I'll forever wait..." It was something that he had always said and promised her, and that she still held dear. One true love forever and none other would ever be near...

Jay rolled the dolly back into the warehouse and slowly closed and locked the door. It had been a strict security measure to make certain that all doors and windows remained sealed and secured at all times through the night. He had agreed to act as a security guard and handyman in exchange for the free apartment. It really hadn't bothered him, as living alone for a considerable time and unable to sleep on most nights, it gave him something to do. Rich had expressed a great concern for disturbances and possible break-in attempts during the night. This hadn't disturbed Jay in the least as, between the baseball bat and loaded twelve-gauge shotgun provided, he knew that he could handle anything.

Returning to the elevator and second floor, he wandered through the dimly lit hallway past the offices and down the long hall. The building was far larger than it may have seemed. It was an older structure designed for business, so the suites were considerably large. As he entered his suite, he hadn't bothered turning on the lamp that sat on a table next to his reclining chair. He navigated through the dark apartment with the utmost of ease.

There wasn't much to speak of, but he took pride in what he owned. Unlike all the other tenants, he had bought new furnishing to fill his home. It was a minimalist existence that he now comfortably occupied. He kept it simple and had never cared for unnecessary furniture or ridiculous décor. He had once been a collector of science fiction toys and film nostalgia, but that had been far away and long ago. All lost when that special someone had betrayed him and walked out the door with most of his life…

He chuckled while remembering Tanya's paisley and purple suite, and wandering to the window, paused to gaze out. The snow came in heavy flurries and he could barely make out the dim yellow haze of the street lights. It was nothing new in his life, as growing up in Ontario he was well seasoned when it came to the snow. He remembered being a boy and growing up in his grandfather's elegant old house. He had often stood in the window as a child and watched as the snow buried the wondrous gardens. The endless summers of gardening and many winters when he had helped his grandfather shovel the walks. As much as he loved his parents, it had been the kindly old man who had inspired his collector's spirit and passion for science fiction memorabilia. Sadly, the dear old man, his house and everything that Jay had collected over the years was now gone…

The darkness of the apartment seemed even deeper as he stood almost hidden behind his average and cream-colored drapes. In that moment a shadow fell upon him and he slowly stepped back from the large window pane. It was the immense shadow of something from outside. Failing to notice him, it cautiously and quietly crept past. His heart leapt into his throat, his eyes growing huge as he breathlessly stared! The hideous thing clawing and creeping ever upward, while leaving a ghastly trail of smeared and oozing decay…

Sitting alone with her final cup of coffee for the night, Tanya silently admired her purple velveteen dream. She knew that Danny hadn't liked any of it, but was it too much to ask? It was one of those quirky creature-comforts that she simply couldn't resist. It would be fine for the time being and until when they could afford their own little home. Well, maybe she would keep the furniture and just leave the drapes? As a child, purple had always been her favorite color, but she had never seen or been able to afford such luxurious things.

The hair on her forearms suddenly stood on end, as looking around, she rubbed at her arms. Moving toward the window, she leaned down and ran a hand over the metal covers while testing the baseboard heaters. They were working fine and there hadn't been a draft, but something now caused her skin to creep and her flesh to crawl. She felt something cold stir from deep within. It was a bitter sensation that, causing her to shudder, now forced her to slowly turn and to look toward the drapes. They hung long and deep, a mauve and paisley dream that would have otherwise lulled her to sleep. Shaking off the chill and returning to her seat upon the couch, she sipped at her coffee and slumped back. She closed her eyes and sighed deeply, weary, but still not tired enough to go to bed.

"My darling dearest, for mercy's sake—open your eyes… Save yourself and our boy…"

She leapt to her feet in utter bewilderment, as recognizing the voice, threw a hand before her mouth as her eyes filled with tears.

"Barry—where are you?" It was the sound of her own dearly departed husband that had whispered to her from out of time. She had stood there staring, blinded by tears as she gawked with a hand still covering her mouth. The sound of his voice still echoing in her thoughts, something drew her attention back toward the drapes. Was that a shadow from just behind the glass? She watched in awe, pondering as to the shape of something that appeared to be crossing the window pane? She moved, testing the forms that danced against her figure in the dim light. All things appeared as they should have, except for that strange darkness that came drifting, creeping from out of the frozen night…

In that moment, a desperate scream from the corridor had sent her reeling back! Danny and Dennis appeared in their pajamas and robes, and without another thought, the three of them dashed out the apartment door and down the hall!

Jen Valdez ran out of her apartment and crashed head-long into the group. Tanya had caught her in a gentle embrace, and frightened, attempted to calm the hysterical girl.

"Something was at my window!" Jen fearfully stuttered out the words, "And it sure as hell wasn't some ghost or a shadow—it was as solid as one of you!"

"Stay right here--," Dennis had volunteered, "I'll go and have a look."

With Danny in close pursuit, the two had entered Jen's apartment through the still partially open door. All had been in darkness with exception to a small, antique coffee table lamp. It cast just enough light to see a small and central portion of the living area, but nothing beyond that.

"Look at that--," Danny whispered as they approached the large panes, "What is it—that smear—just at the bottom of the glass?"

"It's some kind of grease or slimy stuff--," Dennis swallowed hard as he looked back, 'Jesus Christ—those are fingerprints —on the outside of the fourth floor…"

"And whatever it was--," Danny concluded while slowly turning and pointing, and said, "It was making its way toward the balcony doors."

"That isn't grease--," Dennis raised an arm protectively and gently forced Danny away from the window, "It's where something that was dead and rotting rubbed up against the glass…"

"Oh my God—we need to get mom and Jen out of here…"

The glass suddenly erupted in front of them, sending them tumbling backward in a shower of crystalline shards! The women screamed in the hallway and both of them ran toward the open door! From out of the darkness something now swiftly followed! It was an immense, hopping and spider-like nightmare that scuttled along on multiple limbs! The sickly stench of death was overwhelming, as they retched, staggering as they fled out and into the hall.

Danny ran for all that he was worth, dragging his mother and Jen swiftly along! They raced madly down the long corridor and toward the stairs with the horror in swift pursuit! A combination of multiple corpses combined, the numerous jaws of several heads clacked and snapped!

"Get to the door and down the stairs—," Danny wailed, "It's our only chance!"

"We're never going to make it!" Dennis shrieked as the horror came thundering down the hall directly behind them, "It's too damn far! Keep going—"I'll try to buy you some time!"

Using an elbow to smash the glass of the fire display box, Dennis ripped out the pick head axe. Cursing aloud and terrified, he forced them onward and turned to face the monster!

Danny forced the women ahead, his heart torn as they abandoned his friend. A moment later they heard his pitiful screams, as he was torn limb from limb!

They had just made it past the adjoining corridor when they heard it coming after them again: The hideous sounds of gurgling death and the pounding of numerous claws across the carpeted floor. The foul odor became so extreme, that Jen had become sick as they ran. Danny struggled to pull her along, but they stumbled and fell to the floor. Exhausted and terrified, they had all clung together, turning in horror as the monster appeared, the shock and revulsion of what they now saw leaving them helpless as they cried out in horror!

It was almost upon them as they held each other close and prepared for a horrific end, when the sound of a bell had caused them to look behind them as the freight-elevator doors opened.

There was a sudden explosion and blinding smoke as Jay leapt out and into the hall! He held a sawed-off pump action shotgun with a pistol grip, and emptied several rounds into the nightmarish ghoul!

"Get into the elevator!" He cried out, "Hurry—I can't hold it back!"

Danny shoved the women forward without a thought, leading them to the back of the steel and wood carriage. Noticing some tools that stood in a large old wooden box, he discovered a fire-axe among the items and hurriedly pulled it out.

Jay had leapt back into the elevator, still firing into the flailing creature. He had attempted to pull the doors closed, but the horror had been there right away. Danny lashed out with the axe, his efforts rewarded as several of the claws had been cut from out of the way. Jay had narrowly avoided the creatures grasp, quickly drawing closed and slamming the doors. The creeping death began pounding furiously as the women screamed, the elevator lurching and squealing as they began to slowly descend.

"How did you know—and why did you come back with a gun?" Danny choked while leaning back for support against the padded wall.

"The damn thing went past my window first--," Jay cursed, staring in utter disbelief, "And scared the living shit out of me. What the hell was that—and what's going on around here?"

"There's no time to explain--," Tanya wept hysterically, "Just imagine your worst nightmare—because it's coming after us right now."

There was a loud hammering as something broke through the elevator doors and now frantically scrambled down the cables in the shaft, the scraping of bone against steel and the stench of rotting death growing ever closer!

"Then what do we do—and how do we kill that thing?" Jay rushed them, as they reached the main floor and the doors opened into the mall.

"Rich said that fire was the only thing that works--," Tanya gasped, realizing Jay didn't have an amulet, "Oh no—the talisman, no one has given you one!"

"Never mind any of that. Let's just get out of here--," He pulled a set of keys from his jeans pocket and began running for the main doors, "My car is just right outside—and it's still warm and ready to go from earlier tonight."

"No!" Tanya cried out as he halted suddenly before the doors and looked back, "We can't leave the building or go into the dark—it's full of those things!"

The thundering of the thing pounding at the elevator doors sent them all into a sudden panic again. Looking around, Jay pointed and rushed passed the terrified trio.

"Get into the warehouse—hurry!" He shoved them down the hallway and toward the back of the store, "I've got something in the shop that just might do the job!"

They had barely reached the back of the corridor when the elevator doors finally gave way, the beast tearing its way through and pursuing even faster than before! They raced through the double doors and into the back room, where Jay fumbled with the keys. It took several attempts with violently shaking hands before he finally threw open the main door. In a mindless fear they all flooded into the warehouse as he slammed and locked the steel door. No sooner had he done this, than did the nightmare begin smashing its way through an echoing assault of numerous limbs as they pounded and thundered against the slowly failing door!

"This way--hurry!" He led them past immense shelves and around tall and stacked pallets, swiftly arriving at the private office at the back of the building. There, he unlocked another pair of steel doors, and hurriedly ushered them all in! A sudden and thunderous crash of a steel door behind them spoke of the nightmare's success, as it followed once more!

"Where are we going--," Danny gasped, "There's no other way out of here!"

"This might be the worst idea in history—but trust me kid—it's the only way!" Jay forced them onward and through another door, which he hurriedly locked as they'd all passed through. Speechless and terrified, Danny had watched as Jay opened the valves on an oxygen and acetylene tank, and quickly lit the torch. Waving frantically at the women, he said, "Get to the back of the room and behind something, and as low to the floor as you can! This'll get ugly real fast—so be ready to run like hell when I tell you to!"

What Danny hadn't known, was that some changes had occurred while he was gone. After Rich had moved offices into his home, Red Cloud had used the old quarters for the storage of flammable and dangerous goods. Ventilation fans ran from both sides, but he could still smell the surrounding fumes. There were forty gallon drums of chemicals, paints and even spare cans of diesel and other fuels. They were literally sitting in the middle of a bomb, and Jay was holding the lit fuse...

"Grab that can of gas!" Jay shouted as the monstrous thing now battered its way through the steel double-doors, "Splash it all around the door, but don't get any on yourself! Then run a trail from the front of that door to the far side wall where you're going to be standing. Then stay there until I tell you to move!"

Without question Danny had done as instructed, terrified as he ran to the far side, placed down the can, and pressed his back against the wall. It all happened so fast that there hadn't even been time to think! The doors exploding into the room, and the screaming of the women as it scurried in while sliding through the leaked fuels! It had not seen the women hiding behind the desk on the far side, and avoiding Jay's torch, howled as it went after young Danny!

"Run Danny--," Jay shrieked, as touching the torch to the gas trail, it became a ribbon of flame that raced to the far wall! Danny had leapt from out of the way not a moment too soon, as the can exploded and the monster had burst into flame! Not a sound came out from the monstrosity as it had already been long dead. It had just struggled while being charred, its muscle, tissue and tendons shriveling with the intense heat. Unable to even move or escape the flames, it fell to the floor, an inferno of flailing death. With billowing and black clouds of smoke blinding everyone, Jay had hurriedly forced them all back out of the room.

To their utter horror and complete dismay, another monster appeared in the open doorway! Terrified, Jen had had retrieved and flung another can of gas., the trailing fuel spilling and catching fire as it slammed into the nightmares chest. With arms flailing as it grasped blindly at them, they narrowly managed to escape its reach and swiftly slipped past. In passing last, Jay grabbed a long pry bar and managed to impale the nightmare against the wall.

"Let's go, we don't have much time—", he wailed while urging them forward. "This whole place is going to go up!" They ran hysterically from the inferno that now filled the rear storage rooms, choking and gasping for air as the smoke swiftly overcame everything, as they staggered out and through the main doors.

"Call the fire department--," Jay pointed into the diner, "You can use the phone in there—but be quick! We don't know if they're any more of those things around here?"

"We are so screwed--," Jen spun to look through the double glass doors, "We can't leave the building because of the darkness—but can't stay in here because of the fire and those damned dead things..."

"If we can last long enough for the fire department to get here—," Jay was desperate, his eyes darting into the darkness all about, "Maybe we can get out of here in a big group—and confuse anything that might be coming after us out there."

Danny swiftly returned from the diner, and looking reluctantly at the destroyed freight-elevator doors, said, "Red Cloud kept weapons—just in case. If we can get to his apartment, I know where everything is."

With the smoke billowing through the hallway and the power failing, the emergency lights flashed and came on. They had all panicked for a moment, and then slowly nodding, Jay had looked to Tanya. "I'll go up there with your son and see what we can find. It might be best for the two of you to stay down here until the fire department comes."

"Not on your life!" Jen answered before Tanya could say a word, "You're not leaving our butts down here with those monsters—I'd rather take my chances with you."

An explosion rocked the structure as the chemicals ignited, the impact sending them all sprawling as the windows exploded from all around!

"This whole place is going to be a barbecue pit in no time--," Jay choked on the fumes and rubbed at his eyes, "So, if we're going—we'll have to do it now!"

A blizzard raged beyond the building as something now caused them all too slowly turn and look. The shadows gathered swiftly and came from out of the storm, the darkness manifesting into an impenetrable blackness that now focused upon Jay.

"Sweet mother of God—what now…" He swallowed hard as they all stepped back.

"It's the darkness—the evil--," Danny looked at Jay, "You're not wearing an amulet—it's coming for you…"

Tanya and Jen hugged close to Jay, drawing and holding out their charms, a desperate move in the hopes of protecting him. To their shock and amazement he had reached beneath his black t-shirt and produced a large crucifix, which he defiantly held out before the beast.

"The Lord is my shepherd; I shall not want. He maketh me to lie down in green pastures; he leadeth me beside the still waters. He restoreth my soul; he leadeth me in the paths of righteousness for his name's sake--," He spoke in a loud and confident tone, the crucifix catching the light of the growing flames from behind them, "Yea, though I walk through the valley of the shadow of death, I will fear no evil: for thou art with me…"

Whether it had been some power of the cross, prayer, or simply Jay's faith, none of them had truly known. But the darkness waivered, the shadow failing as it drew back and then vanished into the frozen storm.

They had all looked to him in the streaming smoke and reflection of the growing flames; he appeared confident, and even stronger than before.

"I don't need any symbols except this--," He patted the large and ornate crucifix," It's been with me since my grandfather gave it to me as a kid—and it'll be here until I'm gone."

"The place is really going up--," Danny panicked and pointed to the rear doors, "Do we take our chances going out there now—or still try going up to Red Cloud's place for guns?"

"Whatever that shadow was, it's gone for now--," Jay looked between the flames and the night, "But I don't think we should go out there, in case we run into more of those dead things."

"Oh my God--," Jen put her hands to her mouth in shock, "We forgot about Deb and her husband, they're still up there."

Reloading the shot-gun with shells that he pulled from a vest pocket, Jay nodded at Tanya and Jen, "Then I really don't have any other choice—because there's no way that I'm leaving them behind. None of you have to come with me—but if you are—you better come now."

Another explosion rocked the building as chemicals in the warehouse went off.

"It's better that we stay altogether—let's go." Tanya took hold of Danny and Jen's hands as they hurriedly followed Jay toward the stairs.

Deb had just finished with the dinner dishes and wandered out to join Ray on the couch. They had settled in for the evening with the old black and white television, and watched a favorite sitcom. She hadn't been feeling right during supper, and sipped at a glass of Ginger Ale hoping that it might calm her stomach.

Ray was a large and athletic man, and had worked most of his life driving truck. They hadn't had much time together over the past few months due to long distance trips that often ran over a period of weeks. He was glad to finally be home, and didn't mind the old apartment as long as he shared it with her.

They had both showered previously and were attired in flannel pajamas and plush robes. They had never been the types to enjoy fancy or fleeting things, but had always been firm believers in the creature comforts of life.

"Did you hear that?" She asked curiously, attempting to listen through the loud television show.

Ray had paused thoughtfully for a moment, and listening, just shrugged, "No, darling—but it's a nasty night out there--," He looked toward the window and scoffed, "It might've just been the wind?"

Placing her glass down upon the coffee table, Deb moved to the television and turned off the sound. She had stood there looking between Ray and the window, both of them appearing befuddled.

"What was that?" Ray acknowledged something, and moving to stand next to his wife, scratched at his clean-shaven head, "It almost sounded like a thumping—or bumping, was it coming from the front door?"

Deb had quickly taken hold of his arm, and halted him before he could make any motion to look. For reasons beyond rational explanation, she was terrified with the thought of him opening the door.

"What's wrong, honey--," His expression grew dark, it was obvious that something was also bothering him, but he refused to frighten her by admitting it, "It's nothing to be concerned about—just wait here and I'll go have a look."

"No!" Her features twisted with sudden panic as she peered fearfully back at the door, "Don't go out there Ray, please—I know that something terrible will happen if you do."

A sudden shrieking from out in the hallway sent them both stumbling back! As briefly looking to one another, Ray ran into the bedroom, and quickly returned with a baseball bat.

"That sounded like one of the girls--," He pulled free of her grasp and hurried toward the door, "If something's going on out there—we can't just stand around and ignore it."

Deb had fully agreed, but was terrified beyond words. She swiftly followed her husband to the door and stood back as he pulled it wide open.

Recoiling to the sudden sound of shot gun blasts that tore through the halls, they spun away from the sound and covered their ears with both hands!

Slamming and locking the door, Ray gasped as he looked to Deb, "I don't know what the hell is going on—but I don't think that we're safe here, anymore."

"Red Cloud had weapons in his apartment--," She blurted, "If we could make it there, I know that we'd find something that we could use."

"But that's all the way down at the other end of the hall--," Ray thought quickly, "And these doors are fairly solid—and especially with deadbolts."

"Carrie made me manager, remember?" She hurried into the kitchen and returned with a large ring of keys, "I've got the keys to every place in this building—including spares for all of the suites."

Attempting to take them from her hand, Ray paused as she shook her head, "But if you think that you're going anywhere without me—you've got another thing coming."

"Alright then--," He grumbled, "But we'd better hurry and get dressed. We can't run around like this, and who knows what might happen next?"

The hallway had smelled of smoke and something sickly when they had finally crept out of the door. Ray had taken the lead while wielding the baseball bat, with Deb following very close. Swiftly and quietly they had moved through the dim corridor, each step carrying them further from the apartment. They had dressed warmly, and she had insisted that they take their coats and be prepared for the worst. Deb had a feeling that her fears were justified, as they usually were.

"What the hell is that stink?" Ray winced, noticing filth covered stains on the carpeted floor, "It looks like someone walked through sewerage and dragged it all through the place."

"That isn't sewerage--," Deb trembled, "Those prints were made by something that's rotting, and long dead…"

"Oh Jesus--," Ray pointed to something that lay sprawled and torn, "What the hell is that?"

Deb fought the tears with immediate recognition, forcing her eyes away, "It's what left of that poor Dennis, something must've gotten to him…"

Finding a large fragment of the lad's bath robe, Ray gently covered what remained of the face. The corpse was barely recognizable. It was just a mangled sack of flesh in a gore imbued lake of spilled innards, and shattered bones.

"I hope that the others made it out--," Deb held back the bitter taste of bile, and in a second thought, asked, "I wonder where they all are?"

Ray had not responded, but their movements had become more desperate as they hastened their pace. They moved swiftly and steadily down the hallway, and then suddenly paused when they came upon the partially open freight elevator doors. The steel doors were torn outward and smeared with blackened ooze that caused them to both retch.

"Whatever happened here--," Ray muttered from under his breath, "I'm glad that it wasn't us…"

"It might come back?" She urged him onward in barely a whisper, "We need to keep moving."

Fearfully taking her by the hand, he hurriedly pulled her along as they raced down the hall.

Jay slowly led the group up the stairs and through the blinding smoke. They had reached the fourth floor as gasping for breath, Jay had held open the door as the others hurried through,

"Please hurry, the smoke is getting worse and I don't know how much longer we have."

"It's just over here--," Tanya directed them toward a bend in a corridor, panicking as she was confronted by something in the shadow-filled smoke and screamed!

"Don't shoot!" Ray hollered, dropping the bat and raising both hands, "It's just us—me and Deb!"

Relieved, Deb and Tanya hugged as they had all fallen together as a group before Red Cloud's apartment door.

"The warehouse is burning—and soon the whole place will be on fire." Jay warned Deb and Ray, "Something came after us—I really can't explain. We need to get into this apartment and get some weapons fast if we expect to make it out of here alive."

"We knew that something must've gone very wrong--," Ray cursed, and coughing on the smoke, nodded back down the corridor, and said, "We found what was left of that poor Dennis guy—I couldn't believe my eyes…"

Danny looked away and Tanya pulled him close, neither of them able to find any words.

"Will someone please just open this door--," Jen choked, "It's getting harder to breathe!"

Quickly fumbling through the ring of keys, Deb located the one marked appropriately, and hurriedly unlocked the door. They had all rushed inside and Danny raced into the bedroom. It took less than a few moments when he returned with two rifles, boxes of rounds, and a hand gun.

"Leave the rifle and just bring that shotgun." Jay blurted as Danny and Ray took the rifles, and Deb grabbed the old .38 caliber Police revolver, "Give me some rounds for my custom pump and let's get the hell out of here."

"I did some time in the military—," Deb looked to Tanya as she loaded the revolver, "So I'm fairly handy with rifles and guns."

"What about me?" Tanya appeared terrified.

"Use this--," Ray handed her the baseball bat, saying, "And keep Jen in the middle of the group when we leave this place."

The sounds of sirens now howled from outside as the smoke billowed through the halls. They had all turned and without another word, hurriedly and quietly made their way out of the place.

"Stay as low as you can, hold hands, but keep moving as fast as you can," Jay took the lead with Deb and Ray at the end of the line. They travelled in single file, and moved almost blindly, trusting in Jay's swift guidance. Hurriedly, they moved back down the hallway until finding their way out and onto the stairs. It was becoming increasingly harder to breathe and almost impossible to see. Jen had staggered and fallen, but Danny and Tanya had carried her along. Jay feared the worst as they hurried down the steps, unable to see five feet ahead in the blinding haze. There were sounds of movement from all around them, the smoke concealing everything from sight. They raced madly down the steps, each turn becoming increasingly more terrifying as they reached the second floor!

"Keep moving—," Jay shouted, "We're almost there!"

A movement in the corridor behind them had caused Ray to halt, but Deb had just pulled him after her, as he almost tumbled down the steps. In that moment, she had silently blessed Jay for insisting that they all held hands. For in that blinding smoke and panic, she might never have noticed that her husband had stopped.

When they came to the main floor and attempted to leave, something suddenly burst through the doors! Jay had aimed and halted his weapon, realizing not a moment too soon that it was the fire department!

"Everybody out—hurry!" One of the three rescuers shouted, "The warehouse and antique store are ablaze—it's almost impossible to make it to the main doors!"

Ray had dropped the rifle behind him, obviously unwilling to attempt explaining its presence to authorities. Deb had concealed the revolver in her purse, and stayed hidden among the group. Hiding the custom pump beneath his leather jacket, Jay had made certain that all had gone before him, following closely from behind.

CHAPTER FOURTEEN

9:55 p.m.

Rich had answered the telephone as we were all gathered for evening tea around the hearth. It had been apparent by his panic and the way that he slammed the phone down that something had gone terribly wrong.

"There's been a fire--," He gasped, his eyes huge as he spoke, "The warehouse and our building are gone. Michael--," He gasped, "We lost Dennis tonight, he's dead—and Jay and the others are stuck."

"Oh dear God--," Tim leapt up from the couch and stood before the hearth, "What are we going to do?"

"They're all standing with officials near a pay phone--," Rich looked to me, "Someone needs to go after them—or they'll all be done for sure..."

"He's right, because once it gets quiet--," Raymond agreed, "They won't have a hope in hell."

"It now seeks to force you through desperation to enter into its domain--," Marlowe warned from the depths of my soul, "To even consider such a thing might cost more dearly than you might ever imagine..."

"To pass through those gates after nightfall is no better than suicide." The words hurt to even attempt to express, as looking among my friends, I said, "The evil is trying to force us out—it senses that we're close to an ending now."

"Then let me go--," Amica pleaded, "The evil grows stronger within me—and I am certain to soon be lost."

There was a moment when I had attempted to argue, but Marlowe spoke once again, "The demon within her loathes the darkness, they are archetypal enemies within their hierarchy—hence she is the only one among you with even the slightest chance for success..."

"No way--," Rich argued immediately, "If anyone goes out there, it's me."

"No, not this time, Rich--," It broke my heart as I stood and looked back at Amica, "Marlowe feels that he demon within gives her an advantage out there."

"Well, what if he's wrong?" Raymond was angered with the mere thought, "Do you even think or have feelings of your own anymore?"

"He's right--," Amica turned to the others, "There is simply no other possible means or feasible way. If any of you go out through those gates on this night—you will likely never return…"

"Dear God--," Tim through his hands up in utter despair, then turned to look at me, "What are we supposed to do?"

"Everyone get dressed and ready--," Making the final and bitter decision, I looked to the group, "Amica will go after them with NR001. Tim, get ready to summon the vault keeper, gentlemen get your weapons—let's open the gates…"

11:25 p.m.

Tanya wept as the flurries worsened and the inferno consumed their homes and all hope. She had never felt this terrified or completely helpless in her entire life. Jen and Danny had held her hands tightly as they sat in the ambulance and watched helplessly through the open rear doors. The emergency vehicles were parked close together and stood beneath a street lamp, surrounded in flood lamps and flashing lights. The blaze lit and heated the entire area like an immense furnace as Jay watched his life seemingly crumble before him. He had declined medical attention, as tightly gripping the concealed weapon beneath his coat, closely guarded over his friends. The police had arrived fairly quickly, and he had already given a statement, excluding the inexplicable. Their stories would all remain consistent. A tale of a daring escape while denying any knowledge of the possible source of the fire. At the moment he cared very little for the loss of personal property. His fear and true concern was entirely focused upon his friends, and how to safely get them away from there. Regardless of the storm and bitter cold, an enormous crowd had gathered in the streets to watch. But he knew that once the lights and people were gone, something concealed in that icy blackness would return for all of them. He had looked to where his 1972 Oldsmobile Vista Cruiser Station Wagon had been parked at the sidewalk, and less than fifty paces away. His eyes narrowing in the deep shadows as inexplicably, all four brand new snow tires were undoubtedly absolutely flat. Something was anticipating his thoughts, and though he could not be absolutely certain, this terrified him beyond words. He had to find some way of getting them all away from there before the crowds and emergency crews departed and the lights went out.

His attention returned into the crowd, as squinting in the wind and ice, he noticed movement in the blackness beyond. Were those people gathering from just beyond sight, or was it possibly something else? In the darkness he could barely make out the pale faces behind the swaying masses and the white, staring, dead eyes…

"So, that's the game--," He whispered while speaking to himself, "You're willing to come and take us—but not as long as there's witnesses. You don't want to be seen or found out. So, the question then is, how do we draw a ton of attention without being noticed trying to bail out of here?" He peered through the crowds and flurries, watching as the pale faces of the undead now faded and disappeared. His free hand instinctively slipped to the large crucifix that hung about his neck, "I could take them to a church or cathedral—but there are just too many windows."

"You must bring everyone to Michael—my Cree brother," A tall and elderly native man spoke to him from out of the darkness. Then reaching out and touching his shoulder with a firm but cold hand, he said, "It is the only place of sanctuary from this darkness…"

Unable to make out the old man's features, Jay shuddered to his icy touch, "Who are you—how do you know Michael, and how did you know that I'm part Cree?"

"Do not waste what you do not have—the time now runs short--," The phantom began to fade, "You must meet those who now come for you on the road back—or you will fail and all perish here on this night."

Jay fell back against the ambulance doors as the dark stranger vanished into the frozen blackness. Staring blindly, he attempted to gather his wits as he now desperately looked around. Had this truly been some kind of divine, spiritual intervention, or some emissary of darkness attempting to lead him astray? Looking to where the stranger had stood only moments before, he saw that there hadn't been a single print left in the snow. It had not taken the years of hunting and tracking experience that he had shared with his grandfather to realize what he had just seen. The trouble now was deciding upon what he had seen and heard, his sanity, and gut instincts.

A television crew was attempting to gather the story, as a young woman shoved a microphone in front of Ray and Deb. They looked utterly bewildered, clinging together before the open rear doors of an ambulance, where Jay silently stood. Deb had felt a sudden and familiar sensation, as though an old friend had mysteriously appeared. It caused an eerie tingling that traveled the length of her spine and caused her to look back at Jay. Although her eyes betrayed her in the confusion of the fire and flashing lights, something touched her deeply in that moment, and she whispered, "Red Cloud?"

"Can you tell us anything about what might have started the blaze?" The young reporter brushed the hair from her eyes in the strong wind, and stared anxiously between Deb and Ray.

"We really have no idea of what might've happened--," Deb wiped away tears as a paramedic wrapped a blanket around her shoulders, "All that I know—is that if it weren't for Jay and the others—we might've still been up there…" She burst into tears as Ray took her into his arms and looked back at the reporter, "I'm sorry, but this has all been so much to deal with. We lost a dear friend tonight, a young man named Dennis Monroe. He was overcome by smoke while helping the others escape, and his body is still up there on the fourth floor…"

Jay had appeared from out of nowhere, and placing an arm about Ray's shoulders, led them away from the camera crew, "I'm sorry gentlemen— that's the best that we can do for now. I need to get them somewhere safe—and out of this weather before they all catch their death of cold."

"Did you have anything to add before you go—anything significant to the fire?" The lead reporter shoved a microphone in front of Jay's face, and he gently shoved it away, "No one knows anything more than what you were already told—and we're just glad to have escaped…"

"What's the plan?" Ray shuddered as the storm blew hard and Jay led them back toward the ambulances.

"Somehow, the new snow tires that I put on two months ago are all now flat--," He was desperate, freezing and grasping at straws, "I can't explain it—or the reasons why. All that I know right now is that we need to try to make it to Michael's estate right away."

"Rich said not to move--," Danny overheard them as they approached, "I think that they're going to come and get us."

"Oh my God--," Tanya wept as Jay took hold of her in a gentle but firm embrace, "Don't you all see what happening here? That darkness, the evil that we were told about—it's forcing everyone out into the night, where we're vulnerable."

"Then the way that I see it, we have two choices here, people--," Jay looked around into their terrified faces, "We can either get taken one by one as victims—or all go down in a fight…"

The group had looked to Deb for an answer, and she stared in utter confusion, unable to reply. Removing her glasses, she wiped at the fogged lenses, then thinking briefly, placed them back on as she looked into the faces of her terrified friends, "If this has to happen—then I say that we go down in the same way that we've lived—as a family…"

"Okay, now we just need to find some way out of here--," Jay swallowed hard as he glanced back into the shadow of the frozen storm, "Nobody move—I'll see if I can find us a car."

"No wait—you can't go wandering around out there alone." Tanya grabbed at his arm and pleading fearfully, said, "We have no idea of what might already be waiting out there."

"She's right--," Ray squinted in reflection as he arrived at some dark conclusion, and said, "I think that I can do better—honey give me that revolver," Ray took the gun from Deb and peered suspiciously around, "Everyone stay close—and follow me."

"What do you think you're doing?" I grabbed at Rich and Ray as they hurriedly followed Amica toward the door.

"We're going to run cover for Caitlin --," Rich argued adamantly, a rage burning in his stare, "I've had enough of this crap—and we need to do something right now!"

"You, Gordon and Tim just keep those gates open--," Ray barked, "We'll be back with the others as fast as we can."

"I'll go with Raymond--," Gordon grabbed at Rich's shoulder and spun him around, 'Michael needs you here and I can handle this—please, let me go…"

Rich had looked between Raymond and Gordon and something had halted his step. I'm not certain whether it was respect for the older man, or simply common sense. Slowly nodding, he calmly handed the crossbow to Gordon, and gently patted his arm, "Godspeed my friend—we'll be waiting at the gates when you come back…"

"God Bless and keep you all." Gordon turned and hurriedly followed Raymond and Amica out the door. My heart was broken for allowing them to leave but I was faced with no other choice. It was a game of wits and desperation that I now prayed that we would not lose…

"There will be nothing to fear at the gates on this night--," Marlowe spoke, "Not so long as the evil is occupied and hunting your companions…"

Taking hold of Amica and kissing her brow, I watched as without a second look or word, they hurried toward the truck.

"I have a very bad feeling about all of this." Rich shivered in the bitter wind, and pulling the fur collar closely about his ears, quietly said, "You know, I really wasn't expecting to make it back, but just couldn't let her go alone…"

"That's why Gordon insisted on going—he must have sensed that as well." Tim muttered from where he stood on the front step behind us, "I mean, seriously gentlemen, we all know that this is a trap according to the design of the darkness, and that any who leave here now should not be expected to return--," He motioned to where NR001 now drove toward the main gates, and almost whispered as he said, "May goodness and mercy follow them always—the last charge of the light brigade…"

I had wanted to stop them with all of my heart, but realized that without them none of the others would have even the slightest chance. Pressing down upon the remote, I swallowed my heart back down as the gates widened to allow them passage through. I felt as though I was condemning them all by allowing this, and to some extent knew that it was true…

Ray apologized while he finished tying up the last ambulance attendant, and then leapt into the driver's seat, "Hang onto your asses everyone—this is going to be one hell of a nasty ride."

With lights flashing and the siren howling they took off and sped into the night. The utter chaos and blizzard covered all suspicion as while making their desperate escape.

"Are we going to jail for doing this?" Danny leaned forward and into the front seat.

"No--," Jay shrugged, "I whacked those guys hard enough that they didn't even get a good look. But try not to touch anything kid—if we manage to survive this you don't want to leave prints."

Danny quietly slipped into the back of the van, and using alcohol swabs that he found in a drawer, began wiping anything that he might've touched.

"Please stop that, sweetheart--," Tanya sniffled, "It makes you look like a criminal."

"Excuse me, girl--," Jen gently took hold of her friend's shoulder and pulled her close, "We're speeding in a stolen ambulance and left the attendants back there, with nasty ass headaches and tied up. In case you didn't notice? We are all criminals at this point."

"Give me some of those--," Tanya grabbed a handful of wipes from Danny and began feverishly scouring everything that anyone might have touched.

"I'm going to avoid any back streets or highway routes--," Ray informed the group, "That way we won't get caught anywhere completely alone or in the pitch dark."

"Is it just me--," Jay squinted out the windshield, "Or is it getting darker out there?"

Through the blinding flurries and flashing lights it seemed as though a dark haze now formed. It wasn't the usual shadow that occurred on a particularly dark night, but a fog of blackness that became denser with each moment.

"Something's happening—you're right--," Ray agreed as slowing down, he cursed, "It's getting harder to see anything. It's slowing us down—I don't know how much further we'll get?"

The buildings and street lights seemed to just fade as though having never existed. The blinding flurries began merging with the darkness and became a bitter cold and impenetrable shadow that now forced them to stop.

"What's happening--," Deb shouted from the back, "And why the hell did we stop?"

"I can't see a damn thing!" Ray began to panic, "Everything's just gone completely black!"

"It's an illusion of some kind, I'm sure of it—streets and buildings don't just vanish," Jay muttered, as taking hold of his crucifix, suspiciously said, "Something is messing with our minds—I'm almost sure of it…"

"What are we going to do?" Tanya cried out, "We can't just sit here and wait!"

"Let me drive—I can do this," Jay insisted, as suddenly becoming aware of the shimmering forms of buildings and hazed lights, they switched seats. No sooner had he done this, than did the ambulance suddenly and violently shake! There were sounds of something enormous that was now battering its way in through the back doors!

"Hold on!" Jay accelerated suddenly and they lurched ahead. Bodies were flying everywhere in the back as they scrambled to regain their balance and seats!

"I still can't see a damn thing!" Ray tightly gripped onto his seat.

"I can't explain it--," Jay drove madly as the ice storm continued to rage, "But to me, aside from all this snow, everything else is as clear as a bell."

"Thank God for that--," Deb leaned in from the back, "Because I can't see a damn thing either—everything is all just pitch black."

"Oh Sweet Jesus, have mercy--," Jay's eyes bulged in the last moment as he swung the wheel and the ambulance swerved out of control! A monstrosity as tall as a three story building now reared up from out of the darkness ahead! They slid sideways and slammed into several parked cars before tipping and dropping onto their side. The internal lights flashed and sparks erupted from inside the flickering chaos of the cab. Ray had struggled to get out of his seatbelt, and then desperately scrambled into the back.

"There was something enormous on the road ahead--," Jay gasped, as suffering a deep gash to his left brow, he wiped the blood away and clambered out of his seat, "It was huge—and there was no damn way to get past—is everyone okay?"

Deb wept as she hung over the twisted body of Danny's mother, "It's Tanya--," She turned and grabbed hold of Danny as he crawled over to see, "She's gone…"

"No, please—not my mom!" He cried out and struggled to break free of Deb's grasp.

"I'm sorry, buddy!" Ray took firm hold of the boy and stared straight into his eyes, "But I need you to keep it together until we can all get out of here. We all need you—do you understand?"

"Can't you see that he's in shock--," Jen hugged Danny close and fearfully stared around at the group, "He just lost his best friend and his mother tonight…"

Covering Tanya with a sheet that he pulled from a gurney, Jay took hold of his gun, "Well people—we're not out of this yet, so I suggest that we get out of here as fast as we can."

There was a distant and shrieking howl that grew steadily as though it were carried upon the wind. It caused them all to fall utterly silent and sit still as they looked and listened. The sound grew by degrees in volume that began to shake and rumble through the entire cab. It was an earthquake of utter terror, as something enormous smashed against the ambulance and sent them all sprawling as they spun out of control!

"Everyone get out!" Jay wailed as he gathered himself, "We don't have a choice—we can't stay in here!" He aimed his shot-gun and blew out the windshield, hollering, "Follow me—hurry!"

They did exactly as instructed, as something now pounded the back doors with such fury that they began to bend inward. Jay had been the first out and then assisted Ray as he climbed through. Then stepping back from the vehicle, Jay stared aghast at the horror that towered above him. It stood well over twenty five feet and possibly thirty odd long. He could see its body in the flashing lights and the sheer horror of it stole his breath! It was the bones of some prehistoric monstrosity that had been covered in putrid and pulsating, reanimated death…

Hiding before it noticed him, Jay had assisted with pulling everyone out through the broken glass. But as they prepared to make an escape toward the sidewalk, the monster had caught sight of the group. As lumbering unsteadily upon clawed reptilian feet, the enormous thing now pursued as they ran down the street.

"Make for cover--," Jay cried out as the monster swiftly caught up, "In here—hurry!" He shot the door glass out of a grocery store window, and then rushed everybody inside! With the burglar alarms ringing and lights flashing, it became even more surreal, the entire building drifting in twilight shadows with strobes flashing from all sides.

"What's it doing?" Jen halted the group as the nightmare crashed heavily downward, the bones shattering and crumbling as it fell to the street. The enormous thing began disintegrating as the moldering death devoured all evidence of it having ever existed. Then, creeping and slithering with a life all of its own, the putrid fungi entered in through the broken glass.

"Oh my God—that stuff is alive--," Ray gasped, "What in hell do we do now?"

"It looks like it's avoiding the bright lights--," Deb pointed to the strobes, and said, "Maybe it's photosensitive like other molds and fungi?"

"It's just like the stuff in Michael's first book--," Danny gasped, "It can't handle alcohol, bright light or heat of any kind."

"Burn everything and anything that you can find!" Jay shouted, grabbing a lighter from a display on the counter, and quickly setting a flame to a stack of boxes in the aisle. They had all imitated what he had done, and were soon surrounded in a wall of flame. The hideous moldering nightmare had resisted coming any nearer, while obviously wary of the light.

"What now?" Deb drew her revolver and fired into the gruesome mass that hung from the ceiling and slowly covered the walls.

"There's no way we're getting past that stuff--," Jay fearfully looked around, "Just keep burning stuff and backing up until we find some other way out."

"The police will be here in no time--," Ray set an aisle of bedding aflame, "What's going to happen when they find us on the scene of another fire, and on the same night?"

"Trust me—that's the least of our worries right now--," Jen pointed as the fungus now slid from the ceiling and walls, "I think that it's up to something." She suddenly stared down and looking to her feet, gasped, "Oh no—it's going under the floor."

"Let's ventilate this place people!" Jay began blasting holes through the floor before them.

"What if we hit a gas line?" Ray spun in terror, "This whole place might go up!"

"Believe me, friend—if that stuff gets to us." Jay fired again and again, "You'll be wishing that we had!"

Raymond drove slowly through an impenetrable blackness as Amica now guided him by senses alone. They had managed to make it to the building without encountering anything, but now blinded, back-tracked to an over-turned ambulance in the snow.

"They are close--," Her eyes shone with an unearthly and sinister light, "There!" She pointed to a grocery store window and the beginning of another four alarm fire! It appeared like some insidious burning oasis from out of the blackness that surrounded them all.

"Let's go--," Raymond drew his revolvers and Amica swiftly took hold of his arm.

"The darkness is with them in this place--," She whispered, "It might be best if the two of you waited here."

"Not on your life, sister—we're in this together and until the bitter end--," He gently pulled free and made for the door.

"God have mercy on us all." Gordon drew his revolver, and leaping out of the truck, quickly followed them down the street.

As they approached they could see two police cruisers sitting empty before the main doors. The lights were flashing and the radios were crackling as dispatch desperately called for updated reports.

"Judging by the fresh snow in their footprints they couldn't have been here long." Gordon grimaced, then looking to Raymond in question, asked, "Do we call for back-up?"

"No—we're already up to our asses in trouble. Let's see if we can get our own people out first--," Raymond swallowed hard, "Then we'll radio for assistance once we're all clear."

"This way—we need to hurry." Amica moved quickly and with a fearless determination that neither of them had seen before. It was almost as though she knew the place intimately, effortlessly leaping over and around things of which others would never have seen. Raymond's heart beat furiously as he raced madly after her with Gordon following close from behind.

As they came to the rear of the structure, Amica had instinctively directed them into a large loading bay, both men panicking as they could clearly hear a desperate shouting and pounding coming from behind the huge metal gate!

"How the hell do we get that open?" Raymond gasped as they reached the heavy metal door.

"What about the other door--," Gordon pointed, "We could shoot the lock out!"

"Something is blocking their escape--," Amica warned, "This is the only way out!"

Raymond pounded and shouted upon the gates, warning everyone to get back. Then in a desperate effort, attempted to shoot his way through the latch and locking mechanism.

"Caitlin—Oh my God—look out!" Gordon leapt forward and shoved her out of the way. Then staring upward in utter terror, he began firing blindly into the darkness above.

Raymond and Amica had spun toward their friend, gasping in horror as something now slipped down from the roof. It was like a river of flowing decay that descending in a large mass, fell upon the terrified man. In that moment, they had witnessed the black and oozing filth that covered and consumed their flailing. The flesh swiftly melting away from his bones as he reached out, and screaming, died horribly while pleading for help.

Raymond had fumbled to reload his revolvers as Amica shrieked in a fury that sent him reeling back. He fell against the frozen brickwork of the building, staring as she defiantly howled into the night. Her form began glowing and altering as a demonic phantasm enveloped her. Then raising hands that became long claws, she uttered a mind-shattering and terrifying roar. Once more Ray had fired, emptying both revolvers into the swiftly approaching mass. Hopelessly lost, he fell backward as his futile effort hadn't affected the slithering nightmare in the least. It was all happening so fast that he hadn't even had time to recover as the horror now slithered forward as it came for him. Amica now stood taller and shone brightly, as though caught within the spirit of another entity or ghost. A massive and demonic presence that leapt forward and standing between Raymond and the horror, fearlessly confronted the moldering death. A wall of blue flame appeared from between them, and erupted from all around the pulsating filth. It was an ethereal fire, which, burning brightly, now began utterly consuming the crawling and slithering fiend.

Horrified with Gordon's loss and Amica's insidious change, Raymond stumbled to his feet from behind her and backed up against the gates. Sensing the movement, she had turned and looked upon him. Her eyes burning with that same blue fire as she stood within the shimmering form of an unspeakable horror, blackened wings unfolding as a horned nightmare grew from all about her. Then, spinning toward the gate, she leapt up and swung out with a long and razor sharp claw, the steel door ripping like paper as she tore an enormous and gaping hole.

Through a billowing cloud of streaming smoke he had seen her suddenly change. As still shocked and amazed as she returned to her previous form, he hurriedly assisted her with rescuing their friends from out of the growing flames.

"Thank God—we need to get the hell out of here before that thing figures out something else!" Jay grabbed Raymond by the wrist, "Where did you park—hurry—we don't have much time!"

Ray and Deb pulled Jen and Danny after them, with Amica following swiftly from behind. They raced frantically through the alley, stumbling and gasping in the steadily growing flames and blinding smoke.

"Where are Tanya and Dennis?" Raymond halted suddenly while noticing them absent from the group.

"I'm sorry, brother--," Jay's eyes reflected his sadness as they raced toward the awaiting truck, "But they didn't make it."

"We lost Gordon back there--," Ray felt his heart break, "And likely any officers that attended the scene."

They scrambled desperately past the empty police cruisers and hurriedly piled into the truck. Jay had made certain that everyone else had been safe before he had climbed in and slammed the door.

"I still can't see anything--," Raymond panicked as he stared out the windshield and fearfully gripped the wheel.

"I can do this—quickly, change places with me!" Amica volunteered as she leapt from the seat and into his lap as he was attempting to slide away. He was barely into the passenger's seat when she had taken the wheel, and accelerating, sent the tires spinning as the vehicle turned around. With the horror of what had just happened still filling him with doubt, Raymond had just closed his eyes tightly and hung on for dear life. They sped dangerously through the blinding flurries in a desperate attempt to reach the safety of the estate. The wind howled and the darkness gathered as the evil pursued them through the empty streets. It was a blinding storm of sleet and utter blackness from which only Amica's inner demon was completely immune. She had feared her own evil, and the demonic thing that had surprisingly fought upon their side. She knew that it was certainly no bond of familiarity or strange kinship, but the discovery of a common enemy.

The lights suddenly exploded from the roof as the racks containing instruments and additional gear was torn free! The truck almost sliding out of control with the destructive force, as Amica struggled with the wheel.

"It's using chunks of ice against us now!" Ray shouted from out of the back, "It's trying to stop us from making it back to the estate!"

"Hold on—we're almost there!" Raymond cried out, "If any of you have ever believed in anything—now is the time to start praying!"

His words had been answered by a sudden shower of exploding glass and ice! The shards erupting inward as a frozen hurricane now howled through the truck!

It had been well over an hour as we had waited on the front steps, freezing and staring beyond the gates. Rich and Tim had stood on either side of me, desperate as we prayed for any sign of our friends. There hadn't been any movement or presence of the usual shadows and things that lurked at the gates. It was the irrefutable evidence that the evil was obviously preoccupied with matters somewhere else. As I stood there staring, I feared the evil that had most certainly befallen and possibly already taken our friends...

"When you see the lights coming--," Rich muttered as his words were all but lost in the whispering wind, "Be ready to close those gates fast."

"It's so silent--." Tim shivered while looking around as the world fell into a deathly lull, "And like the stillness that one senses before an open grave."

"The darkness is coming--," I spoke while feeling Marlowe's thoughts from deep within, "Be ready to summon the thing from the vaults—," I motioned to Tim in warning, "But only on my word..."

The wind suddenly howled as a storm of darkness and ice wailed while almost knocking us down! We had all stepped back and leaning against the house for support, watched as the night erupted as though all Hell had broken loose!

At that moment we heard the roar of NR001 as it plowed its way down the street, the lights shining like beacons from out of the blackness as it sped toward the estate. The truck swerved suddenly as they slid sideways, narrowly avoiding a headlong crash as they lurched forward, and sped through the open gates! Everything appeared to have now passed in slow motion as our friends roared toward the house. I had pressed the remote and stood in horror at the gathering darkness, watching silently as the gates began to close. It swirled like a blackness that could only have come from another dimension or from the depths of outer space. It was a formless but potent evil so vile, that it chilled my heart and froze the blood within my veins. I could feel it trying to reach me, blinded and infuriated while yielding before the power that protected the estate. It was a seething mass of perpetual hate, that bound by sacred spells of sanctuary, now dissipated back into the shadows of the fading storm. In a moment of absence I sensed something resembling an instinct or primal thought. This moment formed a vivid image in my mind, and revealed a strange place and persons unknown. It was a distinct impression of which I now perceived to have been a premonition, and vision of the next to fall victim of the foul thing...

"Michael—we need to get inside--," Rich had broken the spell, as looking into my face and taking me by the arm, asked, "Are you okay?"

"I don't know--," I followed feebly along as he led me back to the door, "I had a vision of sorts before the darkness vanished. I think that I might have sensed or seen something through the entity's thoughts."

Fear now halted his movements and filled his eyes, as halting, he questioned the moment, "What have you seen?"

"It was a place that I have never seen—or been to before. A modest house in the country-side, covered in snow." The vision still lurid, I swallowed hard, and looking to him fearfully, said, "There were several people that were either unknown, or too distant to be recognized in that moment."

"Let's get inside with everyone else first. We can discuss it once we get warm" Tugging at my arm, he rushed me inside, hurriedly closing and bolting the door.

CHAPTER FIFTEEN

Thursday, February 7, 1975.
1:28 a.m.
Terribly shaken and utterly distraught, we had all gathered with hot drinks about the hearth while sharing the horrors of the night. A great stillness had fallen upon us all with the losses of Tanya, Dennis and dear old Gordon.

"I'd like to say something--," Jay broke the silence from where he was seated on the couch beside Ray and Deb, "Now, I didn't know anything about any of this until tonight, but if I were you folks, before I considered doing anything else, you should get the women and young folks the hell out of here."

"We tried doing that already--," Rich had informed him while tossing another log into the hearth, "The building was supposed to have provided the same security as this estate. The reason that you were never informed about any of this—was because as far as we understood the threat—what you didn't know truly wouldn't have killed you. But obviously, our assuming that was a very big mistake."

"Then what makes you all so sure that we're safe here?" Ray sipped at his hot cocoa as Deb hugged him close, and he fearfully said, "What happens to us if they get into the estate?"

"We are better prepared and have far greater protection in this place." Amica leaned closer to me, and looking to Ray, said, "Which is why the darkness could not pursue us through the gates."

"It's pushing us to the absolute limits--," Tim intervened, "It's no longer just testing the boundaries, we are being hunted, my friends."

"I'll write a report on the evening's events--," Raymond swallowed back a mouthful of coffee, "Then submit it to department in the morning."

"Department--," Deb appeared astonished, "Are you telling us that the police are aware of these things and have never warned the public?"

"What would you suggest--," Rich shrugged, "That they inform an already fearful and unsteady society that there really are monsters, boogey-men and things that go bump in the night?"

Jay poured himself more coffee from an urn on the coffee table, and asked, "Well, what are they doing to help?"

"They opened a special division, of which our friend Detective Gordon Simms was made head," Raymond explained, "But due to the fact that these things generally only kill those who are already on their proverbial hit list, or become aware of them, the idea was scrapped."

"So, what kind of protection or assistance are we getting from the police?" Deb hugged closer to her husband, and looking between us, said, "Is there a special police department that we can contact when things happen?"

"Not really--," Rich swallowed fearfully with the thought, "And the only reason that we're even involved, is because we were already on one of those demonic hit lists, anyway."

"So why the hell did those things come after us?" Ray pulled Deb even closer as he looked around the group.

"I would assume that you would all be considered accessories to the fact--," Rubbing at my eyes, I shivered as some faction of the previous chill still attempted to take hold of my heart, "It's either that or it simply used you for bait—knowing that we would come."

'What are we actually dealing with here—does anyone really know?" Jay moved from the couch, and kneeling, warmed his hands by the hearth.

"It's an evil entity that we have struggled with through multiple dimensions and countless lifetimes." Attempting to offer some feasible sense to our dilemma, I shook my head and looked to our friend, "They exist throughout eternity, and are continually trying to shift the balances of what we consider to be good and evil."

"Something happened out there tonight--," Raymond spoke as though revealing some terrible secret, 'When we lost Gordon, a terrible change came over Caitlin."

His eyes were wide and filled with an unspeakable fear. I could tell by her composure, that Amica had suspected and dreaded that he might reveal this in front of the others. She hadn't attempted to argue the matter, but quietly looked down as though having been punished.

"The demon grows stronger with each conflict and passing day--," She admitted, "Though it seems somewhat subdued, as we now share a common enemy."

"Did she say demon--," Jay's eyes widened as they reflected both the fire and his utter dismay, "Are you saying that this thing already has some kind of hold on her, and if so, why is she here?"

"Oh no, it's nothing like that." Rich scoffed and waved his hands to suggest there was little concern, "She's an entity from another dimension—and shares this temporary body with a demon that once possessed her soul."

The entire room fell absolutely silent as all eyes fell upon Rich. He appeared rather undisturbed by the entire matter, as biting into a cookie, he asked, "What?"

"Just so that I understand a little bit more--," Jay directed his full attention back to me, "What's the difference between the demon in here--," He pointed to Amica, "And the devil out there?"

"It seems that demons, being fallen angels--," Tim sipped at his tea, "Have a natural hatred for everything—even one another. It's a control issues really, they loathe competition and, like pit-hounds, willingly destroy one another."

"So, the demon in her will destroy the monster out there--," Jay returned to the couch and sat back comfortably, appearing strangely relieved in some way, "All that we have to do is wait until it escapes your friend here—and it'll set everything right."

"Oh no, I'm afraid not--," Rich peered at Amica, the shadows making him appear quite sinister in the firelight, "Once that thing takes over completely—it's going to come after and kill us all…."

Ray was obviously lost in the conversation as well and looked between Rich and me, "I thought that we just agreed that it was on our side— and that it was going to kill that other thing?"

"My dear friend--," The words formed like a fire in my parched throat, and I feared to be coming down with a bad chill, "What we have here is not a truce, but a symbiotic relationship and the means to an end. Rest assured, if we should manage to overcome this evil—the demon within her has the full intention of destroying us as well."

"So, is there really any way for us to survive or win here at all?" Ray's eyes were huge in the long shadows of the Livingroom and the flames danced demonically across his face.

"We already know that the entity can't exist in more than once place at a time--," Sipping at my tea and finding it painful to swallow, I slowly leaned back into my seat, "It's possible that, if the lesser involved members here were to leave the group—that they might escape for a short time."

"What happens then?" Deb looked between Jay and her husband, "We'll all get taken out one at a time…"

"Not exactly--," I looked between Rich and Amica and then back at our friends, "We do have a way of forcing and summoning it back here—and trapping it at the gates."

"No--," Terror now darkened Amica's features as she spun and stared back at me, "You should not use the devil stone in such a way. Michael, you cannot even fathom the evil that you would summon through such an act."

"If it saves the lives of our loved ones, or even gives them a fighting chance--," Taking hold of her hand, I saw the fear and sorrow darken her face, "It's worth the risk, in my opinion—we really don't have any other choice."

"But, we can't trust telephones--," Rich reminded me, "And we really have no other way of staying in touch. So what good is using the summoning stone against the evil—when we wouldn't even know when to use it?"

"Why don't we just stay here altogether--," Deb spoke calmly and rationally, "The way that I see this—we're all up shit creek without a paddle anyway."

"If this has to get ugly--," Ray agreed, "I'd rather stick around and go down in a fight, rather than take it in the back, and while running away."

"Well, there's plenty of room on the spare couch--," Rich glanced over at Jay, "And, you're welcome to it if you want to stay."

"Consider it done--," Jay shrugged and looked to me, "I just to pick up my Oldsmobile from what's left of the apartment building—it's sitting on four flats."

"I'll send a tow truck to take it to a shop and have that taken care of for you." Rich shrugged, "All things considered, it's the very least that I can do."

"I'm good in this loveseat, if no one minds--," Jen fluffed the cushions from where she sat across from us, "I'm shorter than all the rest of you—and at the moment, I don't give a damn about privacy."

"Deb and Ray could take Gordon's old room--," Raymond suggested, "It's not very big, but it's good enough for now."

"I'd rather not go back to our old house yet--," Deb looked at me, 'We would really appreciate you putting us up."

It felt as though Sanctum Arcanum had become death's hotel, as without mercy or remorse, it had recently developed a swiftly revolving door. All things considered, there had been little choice left, so I had welcomed them all with open arms.

"There is also the matter of clothing and personal things--," Glancing over, I had looked to Rich, "I really don't feel that your truck will last much longer, what are your thoughts?"

"We can take my wagon when it's done at the shop--," Jay volunteered, "I'll take everyone shopping for clothes and necessities, it's probably better if we don't split up."

"After that last run--," Sadly shaking his head, Rich sighed, "I wouldn't trust NR001 for anything else again. I'll have her hauled away in the morning, then run over to a dealership to see what I can find for us."

"Count me in—none of us should go anywhere alone," Tim raised a finger and thoughtfully said, "And, you'll need an extra driver anyway."

"Now that we have an agenda for the morning--," Raymond glanced over suspiciously, "What's our next step with dealing with this thing—are we still heading to the old McCreary place?"

"I do have some thoughts--," Pondering briefly, I looked among our friends, "Tim needs to remain on the estate." I tapped to the charm and cross that hung from my neck and he immediately understood, "I would also feel better if Jen, Deb and Ray stayed here too. That way the estate is occupied, and we know that there are two men to stay with the women in our group."

Jay squinted suspiciously while up from the shadows, his features shimmering in the dancing flames, "So, it sounds like I get voted in to do whatever it is that you guys have planned?"

"No one here is ever left without a personal choice." I had replied, and nervously cracking my knuckles, looked back and quietly said, "It could easily be the last one that you ever make."

"I'll take my chances and come with you--," Jay agreed, "But it's like you said, I just prefer the opportunity of making up my own mind."

The old wall clock chimed twice from behind us and I wearily rubbed at my eyes, "Morning will come all too fast—we should all get whatever rest we can."

There had been no purpose in saying it twice. They had all been utterly exhausted, and though moving tediously, made bedding arrangements almost immediately.

"Do you have a few minutes?" Rich had swiftly followed and caught me on the stairs, as Amica and I had moved to depart the room.

"Of course—let's talk in the office so that the others might get settled in."

Sensing his urgency, Amica had gone into the bedroom and allowed us the time alone. I had switched on the little lamp beside my desk, and turned as he had slumped into Amica's chair

"I wasn't going to bother you with this tonight--," He had begun, "But I think that I'm slowly slipping—I'm feeling utterly lost, and I'm not sure what to do anymore?"

"My dear friend--," Placing a reassuring hand upon the wrist that he had rested upon my desk, I stared sincerely into his eyes, "Your wife is in foreign lands, and you have just recently lost your business and home. We are being hunted by an abomination—and you wonder why you're not feeling quite right?"

It was the first time in what seemed ages that I had seen him suddenly burst out with a boisterous laugh. But even through the humor of the moment, there was a great sadness reflecting within the deep blue of his shadow-haunted eyes. And then, in a somber moment, he had looked back, and quietly said, "What if for some reason—we can't defeat this thing?"

"Then I suppose that we'll all have to meet back here again, someday--," Attempting to make light of the moment, I grinned and winking, said, "For round six hundred and sixty six."

"I wish that I had your heart--," He clenched his hands tightly together and peered down into his lap briefly before looking back, "But I feel like we're losing everything and everyone, one miserable day at a time."

"It's really not a matter of heart--," The laughter had departed my thoughts, "It's more than likely that I'm just suffering from some kind of temporary insanity, and it's just how I have managed to cope. Nothing really seems real to me anymore—not of this world or the next. I feel caught and somehow lost in between, if that makes any sense at all?"

"It reminds me of the Greek legends and how Juno struck Tiresias blind, so that he might truly see and prophesize." Rich had dreamed in that moment as he always had, reciting a memory from the pages of some ancient book, "Paracelsus mentions this as well, with a warning of how to share in the beyond—is to also lose some aspects of reality in this world."

"Well, it only stands to reason--," I shared his theoretical moment, "That if you are told throughout your life about five senses and denied the existence of anything else. That when the proverbial rug is pulled out from beneath you, the foundations of reality tend to crumble as well."

"Promise me something." He sighed deeply and with some sense of momentary relief.

"Under the present circumstances I couldn't honestly guarantee anything."

"Then just humor me in the moment--," Rich appeared more confident again, "When this is all finally over—and everything is said and done. Let's both move far away from this place—and retire in some little town by the sea with our wives."

His pleasant daydream had suddenly brought back the recollection of a premonition that I had experienced earlier that day. As sitting up quite suddenly, I had looked to him in a semblance of sincere concern, "When we were at the gates earlier tonight—I told you that I had sensed something from the entity, a desire or some dark thought."

"Sorry, with everything else that happened—it completely slipped my mind."

"From above it seemed, I saw an old rustic, two-story house with a thatched roof--," I recollected the strange premonition and slowly repeated the details of what remained, "There were three people out in the snow—and an old green tractor resting beside a big, red barn."

Something in the description now caught his attention, as his eyes narrowed and he sat forward in the chair to listen.

"The trees were tall, but not pines—they were quite possibly birch and even old willows? I sensed that I was surrounded in rolling fields, and somewhere in the foothills near the mountains."

"And these three people that you saw--," He swallowed hard while having obviously derived some dark answer to his rising suspicions, "Can you describe them at all?"

"All that I can say for certain--," Reaching into the depths of my mind, I sought out the forms and faces in what seemed less than a lingering, and fading dream, "There was a man and woman—and possibly a young boy?"

"I remember the place—the house, barn and the tractor--," Rich's features became drawn and increasingly pale, "We had to leave NR001 there after the incident on the mountain with Scott and Carrie."

"Oh dear God--," I suddenly remembered, as astonished, looked back at my friend, "Carrie's father's house—it's going after little Patrick and Pamela..." Reaching for the telephone on my desk, I had attempted to dial out when Rich had stopped me. He slammed his hand down upon the base, and taking the receiver from my hand, quietly hung up.

"How do we know that it wasn't just baiting you? And maybe, possibly waiting for you to dial out to reveal their location, like it did when it used Harry?"

Amica appeared in the doorway behind us carrying a tray with hot tea, honey and lemon, "I'm sorry for intruding—is the meeting still in order?"

"It's nothing that we couldn't have shared--," Rich waved for her to enter, as moving from the chair, he nodded to me, "Let's sleep on things for now—and deal with what we can in the morning."

The telephone suddenly rang, causing him to leap back and bump Amica, who almost spilled the tea. I had grabbed for it immediately and before it woke everyone else in the house. But when I had replied and no answer came in response, I sat there staring as while listening to static on the other end of the line.

Amica had quietly taken the phone from my hand, and peering suspiciously between us, slowly hung it up, "There is a game of wits being played--," She spoke in a low tone, "Do not allow yourselves to manipulated or misdirected by trusting to assumptions, suspicions, or ill-gained thoughts. Need I remind you both, that what we are dealing with here has had an eternity to become a master of its craft? It will use all of your fears, paranoia and emotions against you in each, every, and any way possible. You must close your minds to all things with exception to the task at hand, regardless of loss or consequence..."

"And, to whom are we speaking right now--," Rich had stared at her blankly, "That has no care or concern for any others?"

Something flashed in her eyes and the answer came as silent and cold as death. Not a word had she uttered, but she instead poured tea and ignored Rich's question without a second thought.

"The truth is often uglier than we might imagine—and the greatest generals were considered butchers, but always won the wars," I had attempted to take off the edge, "It's not the messenger that we should judge, but the reason that we are forced to take such actions."

It was apparent by her reaction that the demon had taken compliment to the statement and faded away, as she now appeared whole again.

"I would have to agree--," He surrendered after sensing what had just occurred, "But that doesn't mean that we have to become as ugly and cold as the enemy in the process..."

"If history has taught us anything--," I slumped back into my seat, "It's that a man who forgets is condemned to repeat it. In this case—we have to learn and evolve to defeat the enemy, by whatever methods or means possible. It's not a matter or question of having to like it..."

"What was it that you told me that your mother used to say?" He thought briefly, and putting a finger to his lip, slowly nodded as he looked back to me, and said, "Never touch dire and you won't get dirty. Don't forget, my friend, all that this thing can do is destroy our bodies. Don't let it darken your soul—or all that's really worth fighting for is already lost..."

He was absolutely right, and it terrified me as to how quickly I sided with the darkness of which I had once so desperately fought. Was this battle occurring in our world—or was the war an internal struggle for our souls?

"Sleep will do you both some good--," Amica spoke softly as she looked between us, and said, "There really isn't any winning over debates of that which will truly never make sense. Evil suffers a voracious appetite of which can never be quenched, or understood by any beyond their own..."

This explanation had satisfied my needs for the moment, and I leaned over to mix honey and lemon into my tea.

Rich hadn't been quite so pleased, and it was obvious that the trust between them was swiftly fading again. Nodding politely to both of us, he had bid us a good evening, and quietly taken his leave.

Drawing a notepad from my robe pocket, I began recounting the events of the evening that I had taken down earlier from everyone else. It had added a whole new perspective to the work, as experienced by my companions, they were events previously unknown to me. The typing had gone quite quickly, which was surprising in my frightened and fatigued state. Amica had remained silent, as just watching me, seemed both distraught and unusually impatient. Ordinarily, I would have paused to question her, but was determined to finish my addition to the manuscript while still rational and reasonably awake.

These events had carried me some thirty seven pages, almost three chapters and two hours later. When utterly spent, I had concluded the efforts when running out of notes. Slipping the completed pages into the metal basket beside my desk, I looked to Amica as she still silently watched, "Are you going to be alright? I know that your experience this evening and moment with Rich was unpleasant, to say the least."

"I wonder--," She began in a tearful manner, "Whether I am truly a victim—or meant to be part of this unholy union, by the fates and destiny?"

Slipping from off my chair, I knelt before her and gently took her into my arms, "What would make you even assume such a thing, my dear, dear friend?"

"When confronted by the enemy tonight—and after witnessing poor Gordon's death--," She spoke with great conviction, though visibly struggling with the truth, "A rage and vengeance filled my heart—and brought the demon forth."

"We were warned by Marlowe—and knew of what might occur if you summoned its power. You can't blame yourself for having felt or done that."

"It filled my flesh with a power, a dark majesty beyond any you might imagine--," Her eyes filled with tears as she apologetically shook her head, "I'm sorry Michael—but I liked it—and desired nothing more in that moment than to remain that way, forever..."

"Temptation--," The horror of what was happening chilled me to the very bone, "It's trying to lure you into the darkness and tempt you, rather than possess you by force."

It was apparent by her distraught expression that her humanity had now become a weakness in a war that she was quickly losing. Then, in a moment of silent contemplation, I had seen something change in the depths of her emerald eyes. Her features grew taught, as a dim glow now shone in her stare and she gazed blankly down upon me.

"You could possess all that you have ever dreamed or desired--," Amica's lips moved, but the demon whispered through her, "This flesh, eternal devotion and endless power, in exchange for that which you shall certainly lose, anyway..."

"These things cannot be offered—or accepted as they remain properties of fate and destiny." Marlowe had answered in my voice before I had even realized it, "But, a pact could be struck between us and against a common enemy..."

"What need have I in the service of humanity—what gains are offered in trade?"

"You desire to rule above all others—and yet your rival still betters you." Marlowe rationalized with the demon, "It is a darkness even greater than you—oh, mighty one." He soothed its battered ego and avoided the beasts wrath, saying, "Seek now for the truth in the heart of your host—see the mystery, a secret that must be kept for the power to be offered unto you."

Still kneeling, I had noticed the claws that now held me, the hooved legs at my sides and immense, blackened wings. It was completely unintentional, but helplessly peering upward, I gazed into the dreaming face of the demon. Terrifying to behold, its icy touch held me firm as through seemingly blind and staring eyes, its thoughts drifted somewhere in time. In that moment, I saw my ending in a vision so horrendous that I bowed in terror, while tightly closing my eyes.

"I know not why thou dost provide such a dark and powerful secret in offering--," The demon awakened and cast its burning gaze down upon me, "But know this--," It reached out and gently caressed my face with its long and razor sharp claws, "When mine enemy is cast down into utter ruin, our pact ends, and I shall claim all that is indebted to me..."

Marlowe had faded as the conversation ended, and I knelt in horror as the beast held my face. Its eyes burned with an unholy light, and the mantle between its enormous horns blazed. Speechless and unwilling to utter a sound, I had simply closed my eyes and prayed.

"You need to lay down, my dear, "Amica had said quietly, as I opened my eyes and just stared. She had appeared basically the same, but some dark semblance of the beast had remained. It was like some kind of sinister shadow that hardened and altered her features to some degree. Most might never have noticed this, but I knew that face better than any other and could see the demon lurking from just beneath.

"Yes—I'd best be lying down. And, to be honest, after that biter chill, I'm feeling pretty rough…"

I had still been kneeling between her legs, and with her hand holding my face. As even through the terrifying encounter, I had never even moved my arms form that gentle embrace.

"It's after four now--," She took notice of the mantel clock, "It's going to be a busy morning for the others—but I'll see to it that you get some proper rest."

It was as she climbed from the chair and I gotten to my feet, that I took notice of her build and stance, and realized something distinctly different. She appeared altogether leaner, her fingers, toes, and neck were longer, and there was something in the way that she moved. It was subtle enough, but as previously mentioned, immediately came to my attention. Saying nothing, I had quietly followed her and hurriedly climbed into bed. In the early morning darkness and as she slipped beneath the covers, I felt a sudden chill, and knew that I now slept with a devil…

Thursday, February 7, 1975.

12:05 p.m.

The early morning hours had passed all too quickly, as I was haunted with all manner of horrific nightmares, When Amica had finally awakened me, insisting that we share lunch, the house was already devoid of all other life. Merlin had all but vanished, and with the others out on the morning's business, we had found ourselves completely alone.

She had heated some tinned chicken-noodle-soup, and made toasted ham and cheese sandwiches, of which we shared with tea. My throat felt better and the chill seemed to have vanished, but the incident with the demon was still prevalent. I'm not certain as to whether she had suspected anything, but assuming from the nervous little side-glances, it was quite possible.

"How are you feeling today?" She asked while stirring honey and lemon into her tea, "Is that chill any better than it was?"

She still appeared slightly different as I observed every detail of her face and hands. It wasn't that she was becoming hideous by any stretch of the imagination, but rather as though the demon wanted to remind me of its presence in some sinister way.

"The cough is completely gone--," I had replied with a smile, "And my throat seems to be feeling just fine. By the way, thank you for the wonderful lunch! I'm sure that the hot chicken soup will help chase off this ridiculous chill."

"A hot bath might do you a world of good—and maybe I could wash your back?"

It had seemed innocent enough, but by her sly smile I suspected that the demon was testing my faith and moral boundaries. Sooner than make an issue of the thing, I brushed it off jokingly, and said, "Oh come now, Amica. You know that I'm shy, and besides that, I'm a married man."

"Don't be silly--," She winked, "There isn't anyone around—and I won't tell if you don't."

"Really, you are much too sweet, but thank you anyway, I've already showered."

"Suit yourself--," She appeared somewhat disappointed, and returning to her meal, just shrugged, "I was just trying to ease the pain of being alone so long—not trying to become a bother to you."

It was just the kind of devious and manipulative behavior that I would have expected from a narcissistic presence, and nothing like the Amica that I knew. It was apparent that the demon had more influence upon her general being than I had originally anticipated. I had read something on the subject of abnormal psychology while researching the haunting of Woodlands Asylum. Thus, feeling it best not to pursue the matter, I disguised my anxiety for concern.

"The others should be coming back soon--," Looking to the clock I paused in thought, asking, "Do you have any idea of how long ago they left?"

It would be foolish of me to ever conceive that a mere human might ever deceive a demon. All the same, whatever control remained to Amica seemed to accept my reaction, and consider it to have been little more than a fear of being discovered in a compromising situation.

"Rich took Jay to the shop to wait for his car—that was shortly after nine. Then, he returned for Tim and they left to go car-hunting sometime after ten," Thinking for a moment she raised a finger, and smiling, said, "Jay returned for Ray, Deb and Jen, and they went off just before I woke you."

"And what became of Raymond?"

"Oh yes--," She sighed deeply, "A policeman came for him just after ten. Apparently, they will provide him with a new police cruiser since his last one broke down."

"Thank you—I really don't know what I would do without you--," I stirred more lemon into my tea, "It seems that I have my head up my back-side most of the time."

"Well—at least you'll always know what you had for dinner on the previous night."

There had been laughter, but I had glanced back at her several times. After having previously known of her slightly evil disposition, it was the first time that I'd ever felt uncomfortable with her while being alone. Not in the fact that I feared for my fidelity, but that in her absence, it caused me to mourn my beloved Caitlin that much more. Was this some darker intent upon the demon's design, or simply a flawed and unforeseen circumstance of destiny upon oblivions path? Even through the shadow that now haunted Amica's heart and form, I knew that I loved her dearly, regardless of what may come...

1:45 p.m.

The telephone's ringing had awakened me after having passed out while sitting at my desk. With a heavy head I had answered, still dizzy and feeling as though I'd never even slept.

"Michael, hello, I heard about the fire and your loss--," Ole spoke calmly and quietly, "If there is anything that I might do to assist you, please don't hesitate to ask."

"Thank you—it was all so unexpected--," I looked at the clock and rubbed the sleep from my eyes, "It's been a shock to everyone—especially with the loss of our friends."

"I thought that it was just the young man—that Dennis Monroe on the fourth floor?"

He had caught me as I accidentally revealed more than I should, "There was also an accident last night. We lost a dear friend, an office girl by the name of Tanya, and a detective that we knew in unrelated events."

"I realize that this is a bad time to ask--," I had almost guessed at what he was going to say as he said it, "But, it seems that the people around you have an exceedingly high mortality rate."

"It's the price of knowing so many people in life. It just can't be avoided."

"And, while we are on the subject--," He sighed deeply, and sounding reluctant, said, 'It's about Ted—they admitted him to the hospital this morning. He collapsed in the office—but no one really knows what's going on. He asked for you..."

It was all becoming far too much, as feeling the sting of tears in my eyes, I swallowed hard, "Ole, can I trust you with something that can't get out to anyone else?"

"Of course--," He sounded insulted, saying, "I'm your editor—if you can't trust me, then you are really lost."

"Ted has lung cancer--," The words spilled out before I had even given it much thought, "He's terminal and doesn't have much time left, but he didn't want anyone else to know."

"Oh God—I'm so sorry to hear that. I was wondering why he took on business partners just out of the blue like that." Ole closed a book in the background, and speaking quietly, asked, "Is there anything that I can do to help either one of you?"

"As a matter of fact—there is." Wiping the tears from my eyes with a sleeve, I cleared my throat, and looking past the open draperies, stared out the office window, "Could you go to the hospital and find out how he's making out? I would do it myself, but with everything happening right now."

"I completely understand--," There was a determination in his tone, "I will go there today, right this minute—and call you when I know something of his condition."

"You are truly a special person, my friend—and I would've been lost without you."

"That's what editors are for--," It sounded as though he tried to shed a little light in that dark moment, "Please be well, and don't worry, I will see to this matter immediately. Talk soon."

Amica had entered the room as I had hung up the phone, and looking very concerned, asked, "What's going on?"

"It's my publisher, Ted--," It became harder to discuss it while aware of the inevitable, as sniffling, I said, "He collapsed and was taken to the hospital today. He has lung cancer—and the doctors said that he's quickly running out of time…"

Amica gently embraced me and pressed her cheek close against mine, "My dearest Michael—this is something that you must learn to suffer—as you will live, love and lose many others in your time."

The words had sounded soothing, but had torn deeply into my heart, "My time? I have a bad heart; I'm in my forties, and have an evil entity from another dimension that's hell-bent on my demise. How long can I possibly last?"

"Some have greater purpose than others—souls that are stronger than many of the rest. You are no longer simply a part of this world—but through divine and darker intervention, both blessed and cursed to be lost somewhere in between."

"What are you telling me?"

"That you are blessed with longevity—and cursed while existing far beyond those you love."

"My greatest fear wasn't dying--," The words brought tears back to my ears, "But seeing those that I loved pass away and be lost in time."

The demon has grinned facetiously through Amica, its eyes wide and brilliantly aflame, "An eternity to consider all things, above all, those of whom you have loved and forever lost..."

"None ever truly die or are ever lost--," Marlowe whispered, counteracting the demons vile promise, and reawakening me from the dark dream, "Be wary young master—for the beast tests your boundaries while seeking a weakness, of which to orchestrate your demise..."

When I had looked back up I had only seen Amica standing there. She appeared so meek, lost and beautiful beyond anything conceived within the mortal realm. As surrounded in mortality and unspeakable loss, I questioned my sanity and true purpose in that moment.

"Have you ever considered the possibility--," Something muttered from out of the shadows of the room, "That perhaps you have succumbed to insanity long ago, and what you think, feel and seem to hear, are merely the echoes of madness whispering into your ear?"

I knew the voice, but couldn't quite place it. My eyes darting about the room in a panic as Amica watched my every movement. Had I truly begun to lose all sense of reality? For in that final moment, I realized the voice to have been that of my own...

A loud honking from the gates below snapped me out of that suspension of disbelief, and I moved from the office with Amica close behind.

CHAPTER SIXTEEN

3:25 p.m.

Rich had waved and hollered as he and Tim now pulled in through the gates. He drove a bright, red GMC Suburban, and Tim followed in a 1975 class 'A' Diplomat motorhome. It certainly wasn't what I had been expecting, but knowing Rich, I suspected that there was more to come.

"We're just dropping these off—I have to run back to the dealership to pick up one more," Rich shouted as Tim parked the motorhome beside the house, and ran back to where Rich was parked.

"Watch the time!" I pointed to my wrist, "You're already running a little late!"

"Back soon!" He shouted as they roared down the driveway and quickly vanished up the street.

We had stood in the cold wind and gazed up and into the bright and cloudless heavens. The sun was shining and just for a moment, I thought that the world had returned to what it had once been.

"Here they come--," Amica stood and pointed as we lingered near the open door, "That's Jay's station wagon—I remember seeing it before."

She had been correct as the car-load of people and supplies now quickly pulled through the gates. Jay had waved, and then cautiously pulling in as close to the back door as possible, parked as they all hurried out.

"We have a ton of stuff--," He announced, "So we'll work in two teams passing stuff into the house to avoid tracking mud through the place."

"Who brought the house on wheels?" Deb pointed as she approached the front door.

"It's something that Rich picked up." Shivering, I rubbed at my arms, "He was just here a few minutes ago. They went back to the dealership for something else."

"Has anyone gone to get Raymond?" Jay began unloading shopping bags from the wagon and curiously looked around, "He was supposed to pick up another cruiser and then come straight back."

"He took Gordon's belongings with him when he left." Amica informed me, "He mentioned stopping somewhere and giving them to charity."

Her words had brought little comfort as I looked out toward the far side of the fence and to where he used to park. That was when I first noticed that Gordon's car was been missing, and curiously turned to my friends.

"What has happened to Gordon's car—does anybody know?"

"Someone came by from the department just after Raymond left--," Deb began assisting Jay with unloading the car, "They came to the door with identification."

The sun had indeed begun melting the snow. It appeared flatter and had disappeared in places, but the dark stain at the gates still carried a shadow of Harry's memory. Rich had been right about one thing. If ever we managed to survive and overcome this, I could never again call Sanctum Arcanum a home. In the end, I had recreated the horror of the Duff Glenn, and within doing so, brought death and the devil home.

"What are you thinking about?" Amica sensed my growing distance and brought me back.

"I was just reminiscing--," I had looked to where our friends busily carried their bags into the house, and remorsefully said, "And realizing how much I wish that I could just run away..."

"Maybe you should burn the place down, collect the insurance money, and leave town?" Jay passed with several bags and noticing my pained reaction, apologized, "Sorry—..." He paused to look to the tallest peaks, then into the surrounding stone gardens, and remarked, "It's beautiful— and the architecture is really second to none. But with all due respect, it feels more like a mausoleum than a home."

"Oh for crying out loud--," Jen shoved Jay toward the house with a bump of her hip, "Leave the poor man alone, he has enough to deal with already."

"I was just offering some constructive criticism--," He defended himself and shrugged, "Some places aren't homes anymore—just houses filled with bad memories."

"So, you're telling him to burn down his home?" She rolled her eyes and kept pushing him along, "I'm sure that was real helpful! Come on, Jay..."

"He's right about that--," I had glanced at Deb as she assisted Ray with the last few bags, "This hasn't been a home since Caitlin left—and with all that's happened here, I doubt that it will ever be again..."

"Don't give up hope, friend, "Ray sighed deeply, "Home is where the heart is—and as long as you have each other that can be anywhere..."

"And after all of this--," Jay muttered as he casually wandered past, "I'd still consider torching the old place, and sewing the earth with salt."

Amica gently took hold of my arm, her eyes growing incredibly wide. I could see the desperation, loneliness and longing there, but we both knew that it could never be.

"And could you remain with a monster in this house of horrors and broken dreams?" She whispered so that none of the others would overhear.

"I already have for far too long--," The sadness took my heart as I whispered with the realization, "And that monster is me…"

The red Suburban appeared at the gates once more, as Tim was now driving and honked. Amica and I had turned to look, and what met my eyes now caused me to step several paces back! Rich had waved happily while pulling into the driveway with the triple black 1972 Cadillac Eldorado convertible. It shone like volcanic glass in the sunlight and I felt as though the ghost of my beloved Eldorado had returned.

"I ordered this from the dealership some time ago--," He pulled in close to the house, "I was going to surprise you with it on your birthday, but it seems that you need it more now."

Stunned and rubbing at my eyes, it felt as though time had somehow wound itself back. I was speechless as I walked around the beautiful black car and ran a hand gently across its sleek hood.

"It's all yours—," Rich jumped out and tossed me the keys, "The papers are in the glovebox—you'll need to sign those, and I'll run you over to the insurance company to finalize the deal."

To many it might have just been another car, but to me it was a perpetual magic that carried endless and amazing memories. It held recollections of first meetings, great adventures and was a mirror of all and everything that I had ever truly loved. The nostalgia warmed my heart and left me speechless as I just stared, and then tightly embraced my dear friend.

"Oh, don't worry, old boy--," Rich attempted to offer a little humor in the moment, "You'll still be getting a cake and birthday card."

"Rich--," I slowly climbed into the driver's seat and looked up at him, "I don't even know what to say."

"Then just consider it life's way of returning an old friend--," He thought for a moment, "I knew how much you loved that car, and to be honest, without it you just weren't you."

Jay and the others had noticed the commotion and now all stood on the front steps and quietly watched. Tim had removed his fogging glasses as he shed a tear and forced a smile. As from somewhere upon the winds breath on that sunny late afternoon, I had felt a familiar presence in the passenger seat. A whisper within memory as glancing over, I had thought for just a moment to have seen our dear old friend Harry…

The strangest thing in that moment was when I had looked back to Rich and Tim, and realized that I had not been alone. They stood and gazed almost blindly into the seat beside me, as though having seen a ghost.

"You'd better get it parked somewhere safe for the night--," Amica urged as she motioned for permission before climbing into the seat beside me, and saying, "That's odd—this seat feels warm?"

Rich had followed alongside as I slowly drove toward the garage that was attached to the house. The wreckage of the previous vehicles having long since been removed, he opened the gate with a remote and stood away as I carefully backed in. I sighed deeply while noticing that Danny's 1969 Super bee now occupied the stall where my old hearse had once been. After the recent loss of his home, best friend and mother, I hadn't had the heart to ask him to leave it behind.

The lights flickered as Rich swiftly followed into the garage, and closing the gate, handed me the remote.

"I've alarmed this garage after that last incident--," He informed me, directing my attention to a small mechanism with a red flashing light on the wall, "If anything tries to enter this building, alarms will go off, as well as a series of large, internal and external spotlights."

"That's far more reassuring than the way that we had things before."

"We never had the issues that we have now--," He frowned, "And after seeing what happened at the building and my place—I never make the same mistake twice…"

"I know—it seems that we keep making new one's all of the time."

"If it's true that we learn from our mistakes--," He tapped thoughtfully at his brow, "Then soon I'll be the smartest guy in the world."

"Thank you again, Rich, for everything—you have no idea of how much this really means to me,"

"Yes I do--," He winked as he walked toward the internal house door, and looking back, said, "That's why I did it…"

Raising the electric top and rolling up the windows, I felt as though I had finally come home.

5:15 p.m.

Ray had returned just before dusk, but in a taxi that brought him straight to the front door. I had been watching by the window with the remote in my hand, but refused to risk closing the gates until he came home.

"What happened?" Tim had approached Raymond as he entered the front door and with a solemn glance and hung up his coat.

"Things really didn't go well today." He wandered into the living room and warmed himself by the hearth, "There were a lot of questions and complications at the department—and things that I just couldn't explain."

Amica, Deb and Jen were working on supper in the kitchen, and all of the others were sitting near the hearth while awaiting the evening meal. There had been reasonable purpose for concern, but it was young Danny that had moved closer, and timidly asked, "And what about Dennis, Gordon and my mother? Was there any news about when we can make funeral arrangements for everyone?"

Raymond's expression had twisted painfully as he looked back at the lad, and my worst fears were confirmed as he spoke.

"I'm so sorry, Danny--," He almost choked on his own words, his eyes speaking volumes in sympathy, "But part of the problem at the office today was, that they never recovered bodies from any of the scenes…"

"But—how on earth is that even possible?' Jay was shocked and outraged, "I mean, they didn't just get up and walk off by themselves?"

He had no idea of how hideously possible his comment had actually been. Having overheard the conversation, Deb had hurried out of the kitchen and now held Danny close, "You said that thing always covers its tracks and never leaves evidence—could it have done the same with the remains?"

"It's quite possible--," Rich gazed sadly at Danny, and said, "When this has all ended—and things return to normal—we should have a personal service for all of those dear whom we have lost."

"But, how can she just be gone?" Danny's eyes welled with tears as the boy looked to all of us in question and partial blame, "And why isn't anyone doing anything—what's going to happen now?"

"We are doing something--," Having intervened, I drew all attention upon me, "We just needed time to prepare for a final strike—and it's going to happen in just a few days."

"What the deal with the motorhome?" Jay asked while looking over at Rich.

"It's a 1975 Diplomat two--," Rich explained, "It has all the modern luxuries and comfort, shower and toilet, light build, but super strong, collateral construction. Instead of bringing a bunch of vehicles to the McCreary House, I thought that we'd just take the Suburban and the motorhome."

"Will there be enough space for the gear that we'll need to bring?" Tim appeared concerned.

"It has internal and external storage compartments--," Rich nodded, "I'd already thought of that too. Someone else will have to drive the motorhome—I'll be bringing the flammables and explosives in the Suburban."

"You're all going to die--," Danny began falling apart and turning into an emotional wreck, "This thing is going to kill everyone—and there'll be no one left!" He tore free of Deb's hold, and running across the room, stormed out the door.

"I'll go after him!" Jay leapt up and ran from the room.

"He's just a kid—," Raymond blurted, "He shouldn't be mixed up in this living hell…"

"Believe me, if there had been any other choice--," I put a hand before my eyes, "I would've made certain that he and Tanya were a thousand miles away from here…"

Danny had run through the twilight of dusk and straight into the dense and snow-covered trees. It was bitter cold, his heart ached and the tears had all but frozen to his cheeks. When he stopped he had arrived in a clearing and to where the stone angels had silently stood. It was a place that he had known all too well, as he had gardened there with Caitlin and dear old Eva.

There was stillness in that place and a sorrow that reflected in the solemn faces that surrounded him. The once beautiful gardens and angelic figures now appeared as little more than marble ghosts in some frozen graveyard. The heavens were darkening swiftly as the shadows grew long among the old stones. Danny suddenly felt the presence of something, but nothing could be seen… The wind whistled through the tall pines as he slowly began backing away. Had there been a movement among those pale angels, or were the shadows haunting his troubled mind?

Terrified as the darkness reached out from behind wood and weathered stone, his heart began pounding furiously as he felt distant, but no longer alone.

"Danny--," The wind whispered, calling from somewhere beyond the tall and spiked iron fence, "I'm here, sweetheart—please let me in…"

"Mom--," Doubt now rocked the foundations of all that he'd ever known. Without a body there had been no evidence that she was truly dead, and maybe she was really coming home? Turning toward the sound, he slowly began making his way through the dense thicket and wood.

"It's me, sweetheart—," The voice called again, sounding more desperate each time, "Hurry, open the gates and let me in before it's too late…"

There had been a small and separate entrance to the property, an iron gate that was locked only by a latch and skeleton key. Eva had shown him the hiding place, a little metal box that was hung from a tall pine tree. He had gone to this place and removing the key, turned with the intent of opening the gate.

A sudden movement from the shadows behind, and he was tackled and dragged to the ground!

"Don't do it, kid--," Jay held him close and brushed the snow from off the lad, "It's just something out there that's messing with your mind."

"You came after me? Danny was startled, his eyes wide with wonder and unspoken fear.

"Of course I did, buddy." Jay brushed the snow from the boy's face and hair, "I'd never let anything happen to you—we're friends."

Looking to where he had first heard the strange whisper, Danny paused while noticing it to have vanished.

"I thought that I heard mom out there--," He glanced suspiciously back at Jay, "She was asking for me to open the gates and let her come in..." Tears of horror and confusion now took the young man, and he dropped the key into the snow while covering his face with both hands.

Jay took a firm hold of Danny and hugged him close, "I'm here for you, kid—I'm sorry, but your mom's gone."

Danny wept while releasing all the grief, which he had previously managed to withhold. They sat there holding one another like father and son, as looking up, Jay had said, "She's finally back with your father—I know how dearly she loved you both. And no matter what happens, I promise, I'll try my best to never let you down."

Danny had looked up and into Jay's eyes and saw the sincerity and determination that burned there. It was courage of conviction that now offered strength and solace from the growing nightmare.

"Danny!" I stumbled out through the bush, with Rich and Amica following close behind, "Thank God—it's getting dark—we all need to get inside!"

"You've got more family now than you ever knew." Rich nodded toward the three of us, as panicking, we frantically motioned for them to follow, "Count your blessings, kid—now let's get the hell out of here."

We had shared a dinner of oven roasted chicken, mashed potatoes and green beans. The meal had passed quite quickly, without much conversation beyond common courtesy. We had all fallen deathly silent. Through it all, I had noticed a distinct change in Danny and the way that he now looked upon us all. It was apparent that he still mourned his mother, but rather than being mere friends, he acted as though we had grown far closer and truly become family. Silently blessing Jay for his unselfish act of sincere kindness, I could only be grateful for what still remained.

Indulging tea and a fresh fruit dessert by the hearth, we had continued the previous conversation about the Duff Glenn.

"I'll have the motorhome loaded by afternoon--," Rich munched at a large pear, "And we can have the weapons and other gear in the Suburban well before dark."

""So, we're doing this McCreary House thing on Saturday morning?" Raymond appeared seriously concerned.

"Well, that's where we're going to run into a real problem--," Rich reminded me as he looked around the room, "No matter how we play this—we either leave in the dark or arrive there at night, it's not a quick trip."

"I thought that it was just five or six hours--," Raymond looked between us while peeling an orange, "It's just out past the Fraser Canyon, right?"

"You have to take into consideration that we'll be doing this with a motorhome and Suburban loaded with gear--," Tim nervously picked at a platter with grapes, "Through the snow, on icy roads and along a steep canyon highway."

"Why couldn't they have just built there place closer to town." Jay grumbled before biting into an apple, and munching aloud, said, "There's a lot to be said about crazy rich people. Present company excluded—of course." He waved the apple at Rich.

"Maybe they knew what was coming--," Deb thought aloud, "And did this to protect other people."

"Well, whatever the case may be--," I nibbled at a pear and looked to my friends, "We don't have time to wait any longer. The evil must have sensed that we are getting closer to possibly defeating it. It's becoming desperate, and that's why it started hunting us all, one by one. If we don't make a move right away—there's no way of being certain of whom or what it might do next..."

"Then Saturday morning it is--," Raymond agreed, and peering over at Tim, said, "You're the guardian's keeper, so you'll have to stay here."

It was apparent that he had intended to argue, but glancing at me, he quietly nodded while bowing his head. It was a bitter pill to swallow, but responsibility and protection of the estate and all within had to come first.

"We'll next an extra man to stay here as well--," Rich leaned over and looked to Ray, "You're a married man anyway, and I'd feel better knowing that you were here watching the women and the estate."

"Please--," Deb tightly grabbed her husband's wrist before he could speak, "For once in your life—just don't say anything and just stay here with me."

There had been a moment of eye contact between them that had spoken more than any words could have ever done. To this he had quietly just agreed with Rich and then moved closer to his wife. There hadn't been any secret to the matter, and we all realized that it was unlikely any of us would return from this trip.

"Danny--," I looked to the lad, and quietly said, "I would like you to remain here with the others as well. Maybe everyone could work together while we're gone—and try to clear away a little of this snow?"

"I should be coming with you--," He courageously volunteered, "No offense, but I'm younger and faster than most of you guys."

"You are right--," Nodding slowly and fidgeting nervously with my fingers for a moment, I looked back at him, and quietly said, "But for that same reason, I need you here…"

"Okay then--," Raymond intervened while conveniently ending our somewhat, awkward conversation, "That leaves Michael, Amica, Rich, Jay and myself to make the trip--," He looked to Jay in question, "There's no shame if you'd prefer to remain behind."

"No way, Jose'--," Jay had just laughed at the suggestion, and then smiling, slowly shook his head, "Someone has to go along to make sure that you guy's all make it back."

Although terrified, Danny had looked to Jay with the greatest of admiration and growing respect.

"Alright, gentlemen--," Rich addressed the group, "If anyone here has any personal affairs or final documents that they need settled, it's probably best that you do it in the morning."

"I don't have anyone to leave anything to—and even if I did." Jay peered over at Danny, and smirking, said, "I'll leave a signed transfer of ownership and my car keys with you."

Danny's features paled as the horror of sudden loss once more took hold of his heart. Jay had seen this immediately, and pointing an authoritative finger at the boy, said, "But don't you go cruising around in it and wasting my gas. Or when I get back here on Sunday—I'll kick your scrawny little--."

"Gas--," Rich snapped his fingers in thought as Danny and Jay chuckled, "We'll need to fill some spare cans tomorrow to take along on the trip. It's freezing out there—and we might need to leave the motorhome running all night to stay warm."

"I'll fix you all some sandwiches and things--," Deb volunteered, "I also noticed a bunch of thermoses for soup and coffee under the kitchen sink."

"You can count me in, too--," Jen raised her hand and waved to Deb, "I'll help make coffee, tea and soup—and we can make up a basket that'll last the boys a few days. Well, long enough to make it there and back again, and without having to stop for anything but gas."

"Can I ask?" Deb tightly held onto her husband as she reluctantly looked up from the couch, "What exactly are you planning to do—once you get there?"

Rich had glanced over at me, his eyes expressing an emotional storm and obvious loss for words. At that moment, I had suddenly realized that we were flying on a distant hope and fleeting dream.

"The plan--," I had begun while attempting to explain the impossible, "Is to use a special stone that we recently acquired to summon the darkness out, and to where it might possibly manifest into a physical form."

"You mean like that weird, flesh-eating fungus crap?" Jen pointed.

"Yes--," Looking back to Deb, I had grimaced with the thought, and said, "And then, when it has become tangible, and solid mass or form, open a pathway into oblivion and somehow force it into the void."

"What if it doesn't work?" Jen's eyes became huge with fear as the thought chilled her heart.

"Well--," Peering over at Rich before looking back to our friends, I said, "Then this will all end for our part anyway, and the rest of you will be free…"

"This just isn't fair--," Deb wiped tears of frustration from behind her fogging lenses, "If all this evil really exists—then there must also be a God. Where is he now—when we need him the most?"

"There are already angels among you--," Amica finally spoke, "And wherever there is love, goodness shall prevail! Do not give up all hope, dear friends…"

A silence fell upon our home as the shadows danced frantically beyond the firelight, the hearth casting demonic shapes upon the ceiling and walls, which seemed to frolic in devilish delight…

11:45 p.m.

The tall pines creaked and groaned along the mountainside, swaying in the winds bitter embrace. It blew the snow from the jagged peaks and cast enormous rivers of cascading ice down the steep and blackened cliffs.

The enormous beast moved cautiously through the darkness, navigating a path between the dense pines. Awakened from its slumber far too early and by forces unknown, hibernation had left it withered, wounded and ravenous. It bellowed through an infernal suffering, of which only beasts in their autumn of life had known. Roaring through abscessed gums and broken teeth, blood and froth erupted from its mouth. A blind rage which, fueled by pain and starvation, now drove it faster and ever faster, as it steadily made its way down.

The wind howled and the trees moaned as they were tossed and almost torn from their roots. There was an echo of madness on the mountain, the enraged cries of the grizzly as hell now most certainly followed from behind.

The old man had gone off to bed long ago. It was customary for him after many years to take supper, listen to the news on the radio and then retire shortly after seven. This hadn't bothered Pamela so much, but being in such close vicinity of the mountain and being a city person, the sounds kept her awake long into the night. Carrie's father had shown them nothing but the utmost kindness, but she couldn't help but feel homesick. Patrick had gone off to bed around nine, and with school first thing in the morning, she sat alone while listening in the night. The branches scratched at her window pane and the wind howled as though the devil were there. She wondered as to how the others were doing, and now wished for nothing more than to be able to return home.

She sat quietly on the edge of the bed and near the little lamp of her main floor room. During the day the large window offered an astonishing view of the mountain—but in the evening, all was pitch-black. Preferring to avoid that blackness, she had moved her bed away from beneath the window and across to the other side of the room. For reasons that she could not quite explain, that dark window had frightened her in the darkest hours, just before the dawn.

To remedy the dread and discomforts of country life, she tried to take her mind from things by accessorizing. Tonight, she wore her favorite pink gown, pink robe and matching, fluffy slippers. After making hot cocoa, she had settled down in her room and listened to the farm report on an antique, cathedral-style radio.

"I can see why people loved these old radios back in their day." She closely examined the beautiful woodwork and polished veneer, "On these dark and cold nights—it's sure nice to have some company."

Curiosity having gotten the better of her, she moved the radio around on the shelf to have a better view of its rear side.

"Atwater Kent, 206, cathedral, 1934--," She whistled while gently putting it back into place, "You're an oldie but a goody, I wonder if Carrie's dad would sell you to me."

"Are you still awake?" Patrick appeared in her partially open door.

"Aren't you supposed to be asleep?" She gathered her robe about her and gave him a motherly look.

"I couldn't sleep--," He wandered into the room and dropped down on the far end of her bed, "The wind is howling something fierce—and it's giving me the creeps."

"That makes two of us--," She rubbed the chill from her arms and looked across the room and out the window, as the beast stared back!

The glass exploded as they both cried out in utter terror! The bear began clawing its way inward, as Pamela took Patrick by the arm and shoved him out the bedroom door.

"Run!" She shrieked, "Get into the attic and lock the door!"

"What about you?" He panicked while pausing at the foot of the stairs.

"Just listen when I tell you, dammit!" She screamed as the Grizzly crashed through the window behind her, and roaring, fell heavily to the floor.

Patrick vanished into the darkness of the staircase in that moment, as she desperately slammed closed the bedroom door. It had been a futile attempt, as turning to run, she had been bowled over as it ripped the door from the hinges and charged into the hall!

"Shit—shit—shit-shit!" She dashed madly through the dining area and into the kitchen. Thinking briefly, she hurriedly took hold of the fridge and shoved it over, dropping it onto the floor! The door blew open and the roast from the previous night was thrown out. Condiments and assorted food spilled out everywhere, as leaping back, she hid in the mud room near the back door. The beast thundered into the kitchen, its snout and gaping jaws soaked in its own blood. At first glance it had immediately noticed the food, but something else now drew it away, as it pursued more desirable prey.

With each step sounding like thunder upon the creaking and splintering boards, Pamela heard the monster coming for her. She desperately looked from side to side, but soon realized that there wasn't any escape. Although they lived close to town, it was still dark and the nearest neighbor was over a mile away. Even should she manage to make it out the back door, it was nothing but blackness on an open highway, and primal forest on both sides.

Ripping a cane from a bucket containing umbrellas and other walking sticks, she clutched it tightly while forcing her back against the wall. As with her heart thundering furiously, and her breath coming in short gasps, she prepared to face what would inevitably become her murderer....

The monstrous thing bellowed as while snorting blood, and frothing with infection as it thundered into the kitchen through the open hall! Enraged and almost utterly insane with suffering, it was in a state of being almost blind. With the stench of its own infection filling its sinuses, it stepped toward her as she stood back and screamed! A blinding flash took them both by surprise, as she cringed, staring in utter disbelief. There was an apparition, a shining visage of Red Cloud standing between her and the beast. With outstretched arms he now beckoned into the heavens, calling out a Cree prayer that sounded like a song. He stood tall and proud as without fear, blinded the Grizzly as it stood frightened before the brightly shining apparition. A gun shot rang out through the madness, hot lead flying through a cloud of Sulphur and smoke. It came again and again in a deafening blast, as covering both ears with her hands, she fell to her knees. The beast turned and roared, until a lucky shot through an eye scattered the bear's blood, bone and brains against the opposing wall! The floor shook beneath them as the enormous animal fell heavily, convulsing and kicking violently as death came for the beast.

When Pamela finally looked up, the bear lay silent, and less than several feet's distance from where she knelt. There was a crimson river flowing from beneath its head as what remained of its life slowly spilled away. Red Cloud had vanished, and as she slowly turned toward the kitchen doorway, Carrie's father slowly lowered the rifle. Patrick ran out from behind the old man, and rushing around the bear, fell to the floor beside her, tightly hugging Pam.

"I thought that he got you--," He wept as while tightly clutching the young woman, he gasped, "I went for grandpa and his rifle, right away. I'm sorry that I didn't listen when you told me to go to the attic and hide."

"Knowing both of your parents--, "She took his face in both hands and softly kissed his brow, "I should've known better than to expect a Dayment to ever run away from anything. Patrick—God bless you..."

"Just look at that miserable son of a bitch--," The old man cursed while scratching at his head, "Laying there and messing up the place. How the hell did he get in?"

"Oh my God--," She leapt up and rushing over, threw her arms up while hugging the elderly man, "It came in through my bedroom window—and I didn't know what to do?"

"Well, you did the right thing, because you're still alive." The old man put a finger to his chin and peered up suspiciously, "What I can't figure out—is what stopped the old bugger long enough for me to get a clear shot?"

"It was Red Cloud--," Patrick took hold of Pam's hand as he stood beside her and they all turned to peer back at the dead bear, "He came back when we needed him most, just like he always said that he would…"

A strange shadow had crept in from out of the night, and slipping to the floor, now made its way toward the animal's corpse. Like tendrils of blackened smoke it crept, halted only as coming within inches of the beast, it now encountered a shimmering light. The crouching form was barely visible to the naked eye, but the impenetrable light had a protective aura all of its own. The darkness had refrained from traveling any closer, as the tendrils that attempted to approach would wither and fade. It knew this power, which was now far greater than it had once been in life. It had an ancestry of divine intervention spanning dimensions and was a keeper of the sacred light. Had it not been for the convenience of opportunity and the inevitable, the darkness would have certainly allowed it to remain in this realm.

The form moved, and a hand began gently stoking the enormous head, as the light whispered into the bear's single and remaining ear.

"Sleep, my brother--," Red Cloud spoke in between words of a prayer, "Let no other thing come into you—rest now and be troubled no more…"

A faint shudder had convulsed through the grizzly as though something were passing through, and had been forced out and finally set free. Neither had been noticed by those who still stood and watched, but a demon now exorcised, slipped silently back out the window and into the night…

"What are we going to do now?" Still tightly gripping Pamela's hand, Patrick looked up.

"We're going to a damn hotel—that's what." The old man cursed while shaking his head, "It's the damnedest thing that I've ever seen. Now I'll have to contact Fish and Wildlife and deal with this mess in the morning."

"I have a strong feeling that this was just the beginning--," Pamela gawked at the nightmare that lay sprawled in the middle of the kitchen floor, "Call it women's intuition, if you want to--," She looked between the old man and boy, "But we all know that bears don't do things like this…"

"What the hell's my daughter gotten herself mixed up with now?" He grumbled, and prodding at the bear's corpse with the end of his rifle, grumbled, "As if a werewolf on the mountain wasn't enough."

"Grandpa--," Patrick stared wide-eyed, "You really don't want to know…"

CHAPTER SEVENTEEN

10:40 p.m.

It had taken me well over two hours to account for the events of the day. The typing went surprisingly faster than I'd expected, especially since I was so fatigued that I could barely see. It was a strange tale of monsters, a dark treasure and murders where the bodies were never found. Had it not all been true, I might have found some amusement in what I had done.

Amica had sat quietly as while closely observing every motion and word that I had written while completing the work. There were several instances, where pointing out certain details, she had insisted upon correcting the work. Unlike previously in years and where something like this would have certainly offended me, I appreciated the assistance. What had begun as a writing adventure into the supernatural, had left me as little more than a narrator of the consequences of having gone much too far.

The telephone had startled us both, and as answering swiftly, I was surprised to hear the voice of Pamela Montgomery on the end of the line

"I'm sorry to have called you so late--," She spoke in something of a panic, her voice crumbing through a field of static, "There was an incident at the house this evening, but I wanted to let you know that we are all okay."

"What's happened? Could you please speak up—I can barely hear you—we seem to have a bad connection."

"It's just the weather--," She reassured me, "You probably won't believe this—but we had a grizzly come right through my bedroom window and into the house."

"Were any of you hurt? And where are you now—you didn't stay in the house—did you?"

"Carrie's dad insisted that we get into a hotel for the night. He said that he'd take care of everything in the morning."

"Oh thank God--," Rubbing the sleep from my eyes and glancing over at the clock, I quietly asked, "Do you feel that you might be safer, if you take Patrick and go somewhere further away? I can send money—it's completely up to you."

"To tell you the truth--," She thought briefly, "I really don't think that any of us will be safe anywhere, at least not until this is done and finally over."

"Um--," Realizing that she hadn't been notified of recent events, I felt it my responsibility to inform her, "There was a fire at the office—and we have lost everything."

"Oh dear God—was anyone hurt?"

"We lost Tanya, Dennis and poor old Gordon--," I swallowed back the emotions, and looking to Amica, said, "But they were taken by the darkness—and their bodies were never found…"

"What about the others—are they okay?" She spoke through tears and while fighting a field of static.

"The building and business were all completely gutted, according to what Rich told me—," Sipping at a cup of cold tea, I cleared my throat, saying, "And I've brought everyone else back to the estate, they'll stay here for the time being."

"Michael, I thought that I something at the last moment—", " She sounded reluctant to finish the statement, but then finally said, "It was Red Cloud—he saved me in the last moment, and distracted the bear long enough for Carrie's dad to get a clear shot."

The words cut deeply as I nodded, and understood, "I placed his charms into the casket before the service—it must have offered some kind of a reprieve from the darkness and finally allowed him to rest in peace. Of all the people that we have lost through this—I still can't believe that he's gone…"

"Michael--," She whispered, "He's never left us—none who love or are loved ever really do. Isn't that what you always tell us—because after what's happened here tonight—it's what I truly believe."

"Sometimes—it's just so hard to be mortal—this world is so full of illusions and tells so many lies…"

"It's not the world, my dear friend—but the evil in people that does… So, what's happening now—have you made any new plans?"

There was a moment of hesitation on my part, as I truly dreaded information passed through phones. There was a fine line between precautionary methods and paranoia. It was one that I had likely crossed many times, and suffered to venture even now.

"Well, we've made all necessary arrangements—and will be leaving for the McCreary house this coming Saturday. And, to be quite frank, I'm not exactly certain of how long this will take—or what might even happen."

"If you need me to come back--," She swallowed hard with the thought, and then said, "Patrick would be safe with his grandfather, the old boy has nerves of steel, and he's quick with a rifle."

"Pam, all that you have to do right now, is stay there with Patrick, hold on and keep hope. One way or another, I can assure you that this will all soon be over…"

"That's what scares me—I don't want to lose any more of you. You're like family to me—and if you need me to be there, all that you have to do is ask."

"Pam, you really are such a blessing and I could never begin to tell you exactly how much your friendship has meant to me. But things should be okay, and either way, someone will contact you by the end of the weekend."

"I wish that you wouldn't say it like that—but I feel blessed to know you as well…"

"We plan for the worst with intentions for the best—it's the only honest way to get through life. Be well my dear friend, and with a little luck and a lot of prayer, hopefully we'll talk again soon."

"I can't say goodbye--," I heard the tears in her voice as she said; "I'll just say this and hang up--till then, my dear friend…"

Hanging up without hesitation, I felt terrible for having been unable to listen anymore. Noticing this, Amica had taken hold of my hand and held it firmly between both of her own.

"She said that she saw Red Cloud--," Speaking quietly, I slowly closed my eyes, "And, that he saved her life in the last moment, when she was being attacked by a bear…"

"Even from beyond—those who loved us in life will continue the fight--," Amica kissed my hand as a single tear rolled down her cheek, "And so shall I when my time comes, when all other hope seems to fail…"

"And what of the demon, my dearest--," I fought back the fear while looking straight into her eyes, "Will it allow you to make that choice in the end of all ends, and when forced to take sides?"

"Do not underestimate the strength of the spirit—simply because the flesh is weak…" She pressed her cheek down against my hand, and sniffling, looked away.

A wind at the window caused me to turn, as Merlin crept out from beneath the desk. He had paused to curiously glance up at us, but then something had caused him to suddenly start. It had been the moment when he had made eye contact with Amica and most likely seen or sensed something else. Hurrying from the room, he swiftly disappeared into the shadows of the hallway, as I looked back toward the drapes. Half expecting to have seen Marlowe or some distant shadow standing there, I sighed while realizing it to have just been the heat. The curtains moved ever so slightly while dancing gently from above the vent. It sent my mind drifting, as with heavy eyes closing, quite unwillingly, I slipped silently into the night.

Friday, February 8, 1975.
10:22 a.m.
Rich and the others had made off together in the new Suburban, as I stood quietly watching from the open door. They had managed to load the motorhome quite quickly, and gathering things such as they would need, hurriedly rushed out to sort their personal affairs. It would be our last day spent altogether, as the forthcoming adventure would likely carry us all to our doom. The sun was warm that morning and I breathed deeply while sensing the promise of spring in the air. With the snow slowly melting, and the sounds of ice dripping, I couldn't help but feel sad for all involved.

"I would come with you no matter what happened--, "Danny appeared from out of the open doorway behind me, and said, "If you asked."

Placing an arm around his shoulder, I had smiled warmly while pulling him closer, and said, "I know—and thank you from the bottom of my heart, but wouldn't even dream of doing that."

"I'm not a little kid--," He appeared offended and spoke as though having to defend himself, "I'm old enough to manage a rifle—and can do just about anything that anyone else can."

"I need you for something far more important," I curiously glanced back at him, "But I need to ask first, can I trust you with all of my affairs, and Sanctum Arcanum?"

His jaw had dropped open, as taking his hand, I shoved the entire ring of keys into his palm.

"In the event that for whatever reason I do not return--," I spoke solemnly and while gazing out and over the property toward the gates, "I need you to pass a message to Caitlin—and present her with the keys and papers to our home."

Realizing this to have been of singular importance, he had nodded and changed his tone, "I'll do whatever you need, and you know that you can count on me, as always."

"In that case—would you consider staying here from now on, not as a groundskeeper or servant, but my heir and adopted son?"

There were no words that would form upon his lips, just a stutter as he stared in a manner of wide-eyed, suspension of disbelief.

"I realize that this place is a candidate for a Halloween-horror weekend-special." I mumbled while staring sadly upon the gardens and then at the shadow before my gates, "But, I'm going to be asking Tim to be staying on—and Caitlin will need you more than ever before."

"I don't want you to go--," He whispered as the tears formed in his eyes, "I've lost almost everyone, and you're all that I've got left..."

"Which makes us so very much alike--," I brushed the curls from his tear-filled eyes, while struggling to hold back the emotions that now welled within, "And, the very reason that I know that you will make it—and someday be an amazing success. I know that I've never said it nearly enough, but Danny, I am so very, very proud of you."

"You're one of the greatest and kindest people that I've ever known--," He choked back the tears, and looking straight into my eyes, said, "If my dad was even half as good as you, I would've been the proudest person on earth."

Without another word he had just hugged me tightly as we stood upon the doorstep, and where all that I had ever loved through life had been lost. In that moment, I had sensed what my mother might have felt, each and every time that we had parted in the same way...

"I'm sorry if I seem like I'm giving in to this nightmare—or falling apart..." Despair had found me as I was forced to look away and into the distant mist of the frozen mountains beyond.

"You're not frightened or weak--," Danny argued, as appearing strangely encouraged, he looked up at me and determinedly said, "You're like King Arthur and his knights—going off to slay the dragon... I'll bet that most of them were shaking so bad, they were rattling in their armor, but writers of legends never tell us about that."

"Or maybe Merlin was simply too polite?" We had shared that little laugh as the darkness slowly faded from where it had been lurking in my heart and mind. Then, from the corner of my eye, I had suddenly become aware that Amica had stood silently watching, unmoving, as while remaining concealed in the shadows of the corridor. Blindly staring, she appeared mesmerized or lost in some distant and dismaying thought. Sympathy tore into my heart as while considering the vile wretch that was slithering, winding, and thereby anchored tightly about her soul. Frustrated, I felt utterly helpless while realizing to have become utterly consumed and lost within the entire dismal and seemingly hopeless affair

"Well, I should really get back inside--," Danny paused to glance over at me, and said, "I promised that I'd help Deb with making lunch, and the dessert for tonight. "

"Thank you, Danny—for everything." I gently slapped his shoulder, and smiled, "Try not to eat too much of it before your finished making it—or you'll end up like me when you get old."

"Getting old isn't the worst thing that could happen to a person—and from where I stand, it's still better than the alternative."

"Danny—I was just wondering about what happened to you last night at the fence?"

"I know, according to what you said—there was no way that anything could've been really talking to me." It was apparent that he was both frightened and confused, as putting a finger to his lip, he suspiciously peered back at me, "But I swear to God that I heard it, a voice that sounded exactly like my mother…"

"I believe you—but I just can't understand how." Looking toward the gates, it bothered me even more with each passing moment of doubt.

"I suppose that some things just don't have answers--," The sadness returning, now reflected in his pale face and blank eyes, "Maybe it's just better that sometimes we never find out."

"You are wise beyond your years. I wish that I'd had half of your common sense, even now."

He nodded, and saluting, turned and slowly made his way back inside of the house. In that moment, I had seen that Amica had vanished and took advantage of the private moment alone.

"Marlowe—I need your counsel—are you there?" The matter seriously bothered me, I just had to know…

"I am here, always—ask whatever you dare." Marlowe's faint reply came from the depths of my mind and soul.

"How was it that the darkness could reach Danny through the gates—but never touched anyone else?"

"Had you previously considered this—you might have realized that it was not the darkness, but a lost soul merely attempting to return to her child. None among the spirit realm may pass the gates without permissions—thus stands the law of the guardian…"

"I thought that the darkness had claimed her—how is this possible?"

"Only the earth-bound remains—and not the eternal soul…"

"There are so many things that I still don't know or understand—how is it even possible to tell the difference at times?"

"Remember this--," Marlowe warned, "All realms contain boundaries—and not all that seem allies or enemies are truly what they may seem… Trust in the wisdom of your heart—and regardless of all else, always remain true to yourself…"

"I'm putting some lunch together, if you're interested." Deb poked her head out of the door, "Geez, it sure is beautiful today." She breathed in deeply, and then gazing into the crystal clear blue heavens, said, "You could never imagine anything bad happening on a day like this…"

"And while we're enjoying this wonderful moment in the sun--," I had glanced back at her, and quietly said, "Loved ones may be fighting for their lives, half-way across the world…"

She had just looked at me as a gentle breeze tossed the hair about her face. It was apparent that I had taken the proverbial 'wind from her sails' in that moment, but shared a mutual understanding as to the reason.

"I hope that they're all going to be okay." Adjusting her glasses, she sighed, "Now get in here and eat some lunch—you're going to need your strength tomorrow…"

1:46 p.m.

After lunch, Tim had asked to speak privately and we had gone out to the garage for a walk. I had invited him to sit in the Eldorado, and with the garage door wide open, lowered the windows and top.

"So, what seems to be on your mind?" Leaning back into the seat, I had placed my arms behind my head.

"Several things actually, "He began, "First of all, in the event that something should go wrong?" His dark eyes flashed fearfully, "What will happen to this place, the vault and Caitlin?"

"I've already asked Danny to stay here as my heir, to assist Caitlin. I intend to write a letter to her and then give it to him in the morning before we leave."

"Okay, that soothes the mind just a little--," He nervously chewed at a fingernail, "Is it really all over now, the books, the magazine, the offices and the antique business as well?"

"That's what I wanted to talk to you about—but you beat me to it." Sighing deeply, I crossed my arms over my breast and glancing over at my friend, said, "I realize that once this ends, that none of this is your responsibility."

"Don't say it that way." He scratched at the stubble on his chin, and briefly looking away, said, "We're all scared, but I need to believe that there's hope." His eyes were desperate, a concern derived only through the truest of friendships, "And, that no matter whatever happens—you will always be my family…"

"Alright, so you'll understand when I ask, that in the event of my not returning, that you just abandon this place. Seal up and leave Sanctum

Arcanum and all of her horrors behind. Take Danny and Caitlin far away from here. Start a new life in some nice new house and forget all of this…"

"When you come back from the McCreary place--," He trembled, and staring without as much as even blinking, said, "We can discuss this again."

"Tim, please--," I swallowed hard while taking hold of the steering wheel with both hands, and unable to look at my friend through the grief, gazed out the windshield, "I need to know that I can trust you with the only things that I still hold dear in this life."

"You know that you can--," He swallowed hard, "But what about the vault keeper? We can't leave something like that for others to stumble into?"

"I'll arrange something with Marlowe--," Tightly gripping the wheel until my knuckles whitened, I thought before looking to Tim, and saying, "Leave the keys in a metal box and bury it at the foot of the lead angel in the gardens."

"Even if you survive this ordeal--," Tim's features paled with the sudden realization, "You don't intend to return to any of us—do you?"

"I'm just preparing for the absolute worst—while still hoping for the best. If for some reason I'm delayed, and you depart before I'm able to make it back, I'll still have access to the estate."

"In that case, I'll make sure to leave the key to the private gate taped to the rear side of the bottom hinge, for easy access." His eyes narrowed, as pointing an accusing finger into my face, he said, "But promise me, promise me that if you do make it, that you'll send a message to me, somehow."

"I don't have any plans to abandon all of you in the end. I'm just insuring that in the event that things should go terribly wrong, I still have access to the estate."

"Just promise me…" It was as though my words had fallen upon deaf ears.

"I promise…"

7:30 p.m.
When Rich and the others had returned, they had provided numerous documents into the care of Tim and Ray. Little had been said beyond muttered instruction and the envelopes were swiftly filed away. Danny had assisted Deb in preparing an absolutely amazing roast beef dinner. It had become something of an event, as to some extent, it felt like a last meal.

Not a word had been uttered when we had shared dessert, a peach and pear cobbler a la mode. All things considered, my diet had been forfeit on that evening, and I even had a second helping. We had gathered around the hearth for tea and brandy as always, and reflected upon the day to come.

"The motorhome is a virtual, rolling fire-bomb—and we're armed to the teeth," Rich had warned, adding in thought, "And we have enough supplies to last three days, thanks to Jen, Caitlin, Danny and Deb."

"Better too much than not enough--," Deb saluted Rich, and said, "But knowing you boys—you'll be out of coffee, tea, and snacks before anything else."

"We made roast beef sandwiches from tonight's dinner--," Jen announced, "That should keep you busy for a while."

It was almost as though they had all pursued matters of food rather than facing the reality of the journey ahead. I could hardly blame them, as the mere thought now chilled my blood. It hadn't taken much to notice the tension that now hung like a suffocating cloud about my friends. It seemed that the conversation had soon dwindled into nothing more than unsettling glances and nervous fidgeting of fingers.

"Well, I need a shower before bed." Rich politely excused himself from the growing apprehension that now stifled the room, yawning and stretching as he glanced back, and said, "Morning comes all too early still…"

"I'll see to the dessert dishes--," Jen volunteered, "Would anyone care for more coffee or tea?"

After glimpsing into each and every face individually, Tim looked back to her with a smile, "It looks as though we've all had our fill for the evening, thank you kindly."

"I'll help her--," Danny acted the gentleman, "I know a damsel in distress with dishes when I see one."

"We should call it an early night too." Ray tickled Deb's ribs playfully and caused her to jump. She slapped at his hands, and blushing, looked around while moving from the couch, "I'd better get this clown out of your hair before he starts poking at the rest of you, too."

"Pleasant dreams, my friends." I had waved as they turned to leave, and Deb had paused to look back at me, "Are you going to want breakfast in the morning—and what time were you planning on leaving?"

"We can just eat what was packed for us when we get hungry--," Looking up at her with a smile, I added in thought, "There's no need for you to be up early—we'll see you when we come back."

There was a sudden fear, distance and sadness in her wide stare, "You'd better come back—or we'll come looking for you…"

The tension between us all had become ominous

"God bless and keep you all—we'll see you when you come home." Ray looked into the faces of all around him, "This is going to work out—just keep the faith." It sounded more hopeful than anything else, but at this point we needed all the optimism that we could find. They had taken each other by the hand, and with a nod in parting, vanished into the shadows of the hall.

When I turned back toward the hearth, Tim, Raymond, Jay and Amica had just sat, staring back at me. It was the edge of the emotional razor that we were all beginning to finally share. It felt like the hours were passing even faster, and as the old clock chimed behind us, we were drawing that much closer to leaving…

"This room is feeling so much emptier than when we'd all first started out." Raymond swallowed hard, and sipping at his brandy, looked back at me, "So, what's the plan—once we get to the Duff Glenn?"

"Well, it seems to me that where a portal occurred once before—it might happen again." Nervously playing with my tea cup, I looked back at him, "I'd really like to start by destroying the mansion—and then using the stone to confront the darkness at the mausoleums."

"That makes us sound like God's demolition team." Jay fidgeted with his crucifix, "You can count on me for that…"

"The sound of it all scares the living daylights out of me." Tim cursed from under his breath, "The thought of going down into those dark tunnels under the old place, and setting charges."

"You're not alone." Rich grumbled as he re-entered, and drawing his dark blue robe about his flannel pajamas, sat in the chair nearest the hearth, "But after everything, I have to admit that the thought of blowing the living hell out of that place really turns me on."

"In essence, we'll be destroying its lair, so to speak." Scratching at my nose, I peered back at my friends, "You have to keep in mind that for centuries, possibly even longer, the darkness has remained connected to this family and their people. The McCreary house is the very root of its connection to this world and how it's managed to remain here all of these years."

"It exists in that place the same way that I've managed to manifest within this body." Amica agreed, "To destroy the form is to disconnect the spirit or energy from a person or place."

"In the same way that we have to burn the bodies to ultimately cast out whatever might remain." Rich removed his glasses, and wiping the lenses, looked up in thought, "But, once we do manage to break its physical bonds—where will the energy go?"

"I'm hoping that given no other choice--," The thought terrified me even as I spoke it, "That it will come after us and into the pentagram at the mausoleums…"

"And, that where you plan to use the devil stone--," Rich slowly nodded, "To force it into the center of the pentagram, thereby breaching the physical laws of this world—and being drawn back into the ensuing void."

"Why couldn't you just do the same thing here?" Tim nervously scratched at his ends of his mustache, "We can use the vault keeper and trap the darkness inside the gates."

"The keeper is a neutral force—like a guard dog watching the grounds--," Amica quietly explained, "It will repel a demonic presence or evil spirit, but could never truly defeat a power of this magnitude."

"Not to mention--," Raymond drained the little that remained in his glass, "If we bring it in here and breach all boundaries—what will happen to the others, if our plan doesn't work?"

"They would be open season—and lost without any other hope." Tim agreed, "It was a bad idea, I suppose that I'm just grasping at straws."

"Besides--," Rich shrugged, "We only have the vault keeper and the blessings that made this sacred ground. Michael is right about the Duff Glenn, if the vortex appeared when the evil crossed onto sanctified ground, the vortex might open there again."

"That's the answer—why didn't I realize it sooner?" With my mouth hanging agape, I stared in utter astonishment, "It was never a third person, thing or an object. It was knowledge that we needed, and that became apparent once we had the Diabolus Lapis."

"What do you mean?" Jay now listened with the greatest of enthusiasm, "Are you saying that we need to trick this thing into trespassing to open a dimensional gate?"

"That makes sense—breaking natural laws--," Rich swallowed hard and curiously looked back at me, "But it doesn't explain the warehouse and the old woman, and that incident in North Vancouver."

"Yes it does--," The memory flashed vividly as though having happened only moments ago, "Red Cloud sanctified a circle of protection just before the evil appeared. In breaking that circle while attacking us—it was torn from our reality for doing so."

"So, whoever designed the mausoleums at the Duff Glenn must've known about all of this long ago." Tim accepted a glass of Brandy from Amica as she refilled my mine.

"The formulating of symmetrical designs--," Rich slowly nodded, "And rituals of sound and elements that affect time and space. It's perfectly harmless in its separate components."

"But becomes a power to control dimensional doorways--," Looking between Rich and Raymond, I said, "And to summon or expel whatever exists between realities."

"All through history, we have records of rituals practiced by ancient cultures--," Rich tapped a finger in thought to his chin, "All of them include sacred design and ornament, sounds or songs, minerals, certain roots and sometimes blood."

"And the white man has been laughing at the ancient people for centuries--," Tim appeared pale and terrified with the thought, "And calling them primitive and savages, while they knew more than we might have ever imagined."

"It makes sense that the people closest to the origins of all things would have a better understanding of how it works." Raymond appeared utterly lost, "How in our infinite wisdom and vanity, we would complicate and confuse everything."

"Does this mean that we can travel into different dimensions when you open these supposed gates?" With the fascination shining brightly in his wide eyes, Jay had looked between Rich and me for answers.

"Nothing physical may pass from one dimension into another." Amica quietly explained, "But spirits travel between worlds and can inhabit the bodies of others."

"Haitian rituals--," Jay agreed, "Voodoo, altered states and possession."

Surprised at his arcane knowledge, Rich had just stared at him.

"I'm Catholic--," He shrugged, "Curiosity about good and evil had me reading some pretty dark things."

At that point, Jen and Danny had wandered out of the kitchen. They appeared emotionally spent and utterly exhausted with the doubts and fear of the coming day.

"If I don't see you all before you leave--," Jen came over and proceeded to offer everyone enormous hugs and kisses upon the cheek, "Just remember that I'll be praying and waiting for you to come home."

In turn, Danny had gone from one to the other, and firmly shaken their hands. When he came to Rich, the emotions had just been too much, leaping from the chair, Rich had tightly hugged him, saying, "You take care of the house and everyone else while we're gone." He stepped back, and taking Danny by the shoulders with both hands, added, "We'll be back before you know it."

Having stood as he came before me, I had just opened my arms and embraced the young man. It brought back a painful moment that had returned from my youth. It was a memory of bidding my father a final farewell on that fateful day when the mine had taken his life.

"Take this—for good luck--," He held out a little keychain with a red rabbit's foot, "Mom gave it to me when you and Uncle Rich bought me that Super Bee. I'd like you to take it for good luck—and until you can give it back, when you come home."

Without a word I had just nodded, and shoving it into my pants pocket, smiled and said, "And what will you do for good luck while we're gone?"

"I just won't drive the car--," He shrugged, and smiling sadly, said, "Or you can catch the speeding tickets when you come back?"

"It's not nice enough weather to drive a car like that." Raymond raised a glass in toast to Danny, "And besides, I've added your name to the members list of our team. As long as you don't do anything too drastic, the police won't be bothering you."

There was a sudden, mischievous and wild light in Danny's eyes, as pointing a finger in warning, I said, "Don't push your luck while we're gone—remember--," I reached into my pocket and pulling out the rabbit's foot, waved it before his face, "I've got this…"

"Raymond's right anyway--," He sighed, "I wouldn't want to drive her around on the ice. Some new driver, foreigner, or woman might hit me, and I'd never forgive myself."

"A woman, are you serious?" Jen put an arm around the boy's shoulder, and pulling him close, looked straight into his eyes, "Are you implying that we can't drive?"

"No--," He shrugged with a wink, "I'm just saying that you shouldn't."

Obviously taking the comment for the joke that it had been intended, she just gawked around the group, "I can see that the boy's been hanging around with some male, chauvinist pigs."

"And an oink, oink to you as well--," Raymond laughed with a wave, "We'll see you both soon again…."

For all of the smiles that his comment had generated, the final thought hadn't sounded convincing at all. All the same, Jen and Danny had waved, as bidding a final good night, hurried off and down the hall.

"He sure is a great kid--," Raymond contemplated rather sadly while still watching the deep shadows in the corridor, "Can you imagine what a terrific family we might've all been, if it wasn't for this nightmare?"

"Actually—and if you consider it for a moment," Tim interrupted the thought, "It was the evil that brought most of us together to begin with."

There was bitter finality in his words that now caused us all to pause in reflection. It was a stillness that was only interrupted and broken when the telephone suddenly rang.

I hurried into the kitchen, and dropping into the nook, grabbed at the phone.

"Michael—it's Carrie." She sounded terrified, "We've landed in Dublin, and are going to take a local flight on a small plane into Killkenny."

"Thank God--," Relieved to hear her voice, paranoia suddenly caught me off guard, and I asked, "Are you, Tanya and Gordon alright?" She was unaware of their recent deaths, so if she said too much, I would certainly know...

"What? Are you feeling alright?" She sounded utterly confused, "You know that it's just me and Scott that flew out here. Everyone else stayed there with you. Have you been dipping too deep into the brandy jug tonight?"

"No—thank God, "I sighed with the relief of knowing that I had actually been speaking to Carrie and not some disembodied voice, "I was just testing the waters to make sure that this was actually you."

"Well that's reassuring--," She cursed from under her breath, "I can't talk long—we're at this little airport, and the private plane is leaving very soon."

"Please call when you reach Killkenny--," My throat was dry and I struggled with the words, "I'll be awake and waiting for you to land."

"Okay—we just got called--," She sounded panicked through the engine sounds of a plane in the background, "I'll call just as soon as we land, they said it shouldn't take more than half an hour."

"Godspeed—," I licked at parched lips, "I'll be waiting, remember to call before you do anything else, till then..."

When she hung up a shudder coursed through my entire being. It wasn't a chill caused due to weather or some inexplicable cold breeze, but the thought of after everything, losing Scott and Carrie along with Maya and Caitlin.

"Is there news?" Raymond asked as I slowly returned to my friends, and they anxiously looked up for the reply. Dropping back onto the couch near Amica, I had taken up my glass and finished the brandy in a single gulp.

My head felt warm and eyes grew heavy, but I simply could not escape that bitter chill. Peering about the group, I had swallowed the itch that now tickled at the back of my throat, saying, "They've landed safely in Dublin—and have chartered a small plane to carry them the rest of the way into Killkenny. She said that the trip shouldn't take any longer than half an hour and I've asked that she call when they land."

"I'll be sweating bullets until we get that call." Raymond thought aloud, "And why Killkenny, I thought her family was from Killybegs Harbor, county Donegal?"

"They shipped out of there--," I replied with some hesitation, and suddenly feeling less informed than I could have been, said, "But the business being long defunct—Eva and her companions travelled to stay in an old family estate, an Abbey where an Uncle had served as Pastor."

"I realize the reason why none of us could be informed of the exact location--," Rich nervously fidgeted with his coffee mug, "And why Maya wasn't given an address or directions beyond the airport, but this whole thing is really starting to freak me out. I mean—why couldn't they have just gone to some other Province—none of us would've known. And let's be honest here—that thing can travel anywhere in the blink of an eye, distance means nothing in the spirit realm."

"Well, I wasn't given any say in the matter." I felt drawn toward anger, "They just went off without even informing me of their plans..."

"I'm sorry—I didn't mean anything by that." Removing his glasses and wearily rubbing at his eyes, Rich slowly shook his head, "This just all feels so very wrong..."

"Does anyone want any hot cocoa?" Tim interrupted, and looking around the group, said, "We need to hold ourselves together—and not allow fear and doubt to tear us apart."

"I'll take you up on that--," Raymond waved like a high-school boy, "But could you make mine in that giant mug that Rich got me for Christmas?"

"That's not a mug, it's a bucket." Rich chuckled with the memory, "With that much sugar you won't sleep for weeks."

"I really didn't have any plans to anyway." The comment was predictable and the complete truth for most involved.

"I'll be glad to have one of those too--," Jay waved, "My sweet tooth's been acting up and that'll fit the bill nicely."

Killkenny Airport.

The little plane had experienced complications when attempting to land. The fog had rolled in from off the sea, and was now as thick as pea soup. If not for the experience of a seasoned pilot, things may not have gone quite so well.

They had departed the plane, shivering in the damp mist as they hurried toward a little red brick building while looking for a telephone. Scott had carried their baggage. Weary of each and every shadow, they soon stood beneath the pale glow of a little lamp post.

"Can I be of service?" An old man asked from behind them in a heavy Irish lilt.

Carrie had spun in horror, shocked and dreading what might appear from out of that fog and darkness. He was little more than a deep shadow among the others, but smiled kindly as his eyes glistened from behind glasses in the dim light. He was a short and stout fellow, mid to late fifties, glasses, and with wild hair that stood out from beneath the sides of his cap. He smoked a pipe and watched intently while waiting for their reply.

"I've got a cab--," He gestured into the dense fog, "I'd be happy to give you folks a ride into town. It's only a ten minute trip—but I can't promise that it'll be quite as fast in all of this fog."

Scott had appeared nervous almost right away, but nodding at Carrie, pushed her along as they followed the old man.

"Watch your step, my friends--," He had warned as they made their way blindly through the cold mist, "Stay close—you don't want to go wandering around in this…"

"Do you always sit around out here in the middle of nowhere all night—do you?" Scott had inquired somewhat fearfully, and while suspicious of the old man.

"Only when me radio tells me there's a flight coming into town." He turned with a smile while opening the rear door of his cab, "Not much happens around here—and I can use all the fares that I can get."

"Sorry, if we seem a little edgy--," Carrie had apologized, while patting the old fellows arm, "But' we're very tired—and had a hair-rising flight coming in."

"No need to say it, sweet lady--," He smiled kindly and winked, "I completely understand. What you both need is a whiskey by the hearth, and a good night's rest."

"Now that sounds super--," Scott sighed deeply, "My whole body hurts right now and my brain feels like a sponge."

"It's the damp and chill--," The old fellow shrugged while assisting Scott with the baggage, "This fog would take the life from right out of the stoutest man."

Climbing into the cab, Carrie had watched as Scott hurriedly loaded their luggage into the trunk. The fog shone an eerie red in the tail-lights, and for an instant, she had thought to have seen something move in the darkness...

"Jumping Jesus—it's a frosty one out there tonight." The old fellow hopped into the cab as Scott climbed in beside Carrie, quickly closing and locking both of their doors.

"Do you know where to find St. Francis Abbey?" Carrie curiously asked while receiving a nervous glance from Scott.

"I certainly do--," The cabbie thought for a moment, "But, you really don't want to be poking around there in the dark—do you?"

"Honey—he's right. This can wait until morning--," Scott raised an eyebrow, "And besides, we should get settled in somewhere before we do anything else."

"Can you take us to the Abbey first please?" Carrie became adamant, as glancing back at Scott, she said, "I just want to have a look since it's on the way."

"The Abbey's are all located in town--," The cabbie reassured them, "And the one that you're asking about, it is just a minute down the street from the hotel."

"Well, if it's that near to the hotel?" He put a protective arm around her shoulders, and pulling her close, said, "I suppose that it wouldn't hurt to have a quick look..."

The little yellow Checker cab bounced down the old country road, tossing its occupants about as they travelled along through the night. It had been an expensive trip from the airport due to the fog, but the least of Carrie's worries as she gazed out into the fog.

"It's going to be okay, sweetheart." Scott had taken her hand as they rode together in the back seat, "If something was going to happen to us—it would've happened already."

Her eyes stung with tears as she dropped her head down upon his broad chest and clung for dear life. They had endured so much together, lost almost everything, and her only thought now was for young Patrick.

"Do you think that Patrick's okay?" She sniffled, frightened and frustrated as she looked desperately into his eyes.

"He's safe with Pam and you're old man--," Scott scoffed at the thought, "Are you kidding-- that old grouch is tougher than nails. I'd be willing to bet that he'd bite the head off an alligator if it looked at him the wrong way."

He always seemed to know what to say. It was one of the reasons that she had loved him more than anything else in life. Taking notice of her tearful reflection in the darkness of the glass, she watched the image of her husband as he held her tight. It never ceased to amaze her as through everything, he remained a constant pillar of love, hope, and strength.

"You can see the lights of town from here--," The old gentleman had puffed at his pipe, "Far be it from me to go asking people about their private affairs. But why on God's green earth might you be sight-seeing in the dark?"

"We were invited to stay with friends--," Scott had answered without a second thought, "They had family that once worked or owned an old Abbey somewhere around here."

"Do you have many Abbeys in the county Killkenny?" Carrie inquired while moving closer, tightly embracing Scott.

"Well, there's St. Francis Abbey, or the Killkenny Grey Friary as we like to call it, which is located in town." He thought while puffing at his pipe, "The Black Abbey, a Catholic priory of the Dominican order, also in town. And then, there's Canice's Cathedral, which is right across from the Killkenny hotel. And of course, Jerpoint Abbey--," The old fellow sighed, and adjusting his cap, said, "Which was a Cistercian abbey founded in the second half of the twelfth century, but it's just a ruin now. Not many folks visit there, except for tourists. There's likely more that I don't know about, but I didn't grow up here. I'm originally from Wexford, grew up in a fishing village."

"Does it always get this foggy here?" Scott reluctantly gazed out into the blackness.

"So much that you'll hardly notice--," The cabby chuckled, "But, it's not too bad in the warmer months."

"You remind me of my Uncle, Irwin McIntyre--," Carrie smiled, "He was always quick with a joke, and a smile."

"Well, bless my soul--," The cabbie laughed, "He wasn't from Donegal, was he?"

"Yes, my whole family lived there until my parents immigrated to Canada in 1936."

"I knew an Irwin McIntyre—a truly fine gent." He reminisced, "We lost track of each other after the war. It's a pleasure and an honor to meet you, Miss McIntyre."

"That would be Dayment now." Scott reminded them both.

"Oh my, you're a Scott."

"In more ways than one--," He replied, "And proud of it too."

"We're not so different lad--," The old fellow glanced into the rearview mirror and winked, "We love a good Whiskey and cheery song, and all still hate the English."

"Aye—aye--," Scott whole heartedly agreed with a smile, "Some things will never change."

The cab suddenly crashed against something on the way and lurched violently to the side! The driver struggled desperately with the wheel, but the cab slid and dropped into a shallow ditch at the road-side.

"Holy Mother of God--," The old man groaned as he wiped at a bloody scrape upon his left brow, and squinted while peering into the back seat, "Are you folks alright?"

"Yes—we seem to be?" Carrie looked between Scott and herself, before addressing the old man's injury, "You're hurt!" She drew a small packet of Kleenex from her purse and leaned forward to attend the wound, "You're lucky, you won't need stitches. It looks much worse than it is because of all the blood."

"Don't worry, darling--," The kindly old man chuckled, "It'll take a lot more than a little bump on the noggin' to take me down."

"She always worries—she was a nurse--," Scott explained while gathering himself in the back seat and looking out the window, "What the hell did we hit?"

"I'm not sure?" The cabbie thanked Carrie, and turning back, slumped down into the front seat, "When I looked there wasn't anything there, and then a moment later, it just came from out of nowhere."

He had been halted by Carrie as he reached to open the door, and she grabbed at his arm, "Maybe it's a big animal—and it might still be out there…"

"Not to worry, my dear--," He looked out and into the complete darkness beyond the headlights, "The engine's still running fine and there's no steam from the radiator—so whatever it was, it didn't harm the car and likely didn't injure itself too badly in the process." He leaned over in the seat and grabbed a gnarled walking stick, looking back at her with a smile, as he said, "And if it were something nasty, then by God, I'll give it a good whack on the skull with my Shillelagh."

He had slipped out the door before they could do anything else to stall the man, and vanished into the night.

"He shouldn't have gone out there." Carrie hissed as she watched the windows for any sign of movement.

"You try telling him that…"

"We should go out there—we can't just leave him alone."

"No—I'll go, you wait here--," Scott moved to climb from the car, but she tightly grasped his wrist. Her face became white as a sheet as her eyes grew wide, "Like hell I'm staying here alone or letting you go out there by yourself!"

The door suddenly flew open and the old fellow reappeared, "We've gone and run down a stupid sheep. The bloody thing's gone and wandered out of the field and onto the road."

"So what do we do now?" Carrie watched as climbing back into his seat, the old fellow shrugged, "Leave it to whatever will find it in the night—or the farmer by day. I dragged it off to the side of the road so no one else shares our misfortune."

"What about this ditch?" Scott leaned over the seat and through the windshield.

"We got lucky—it's shallow and not full of water like most of them this time of year."

The cab had rocked back and forth as accelerating forward and backward, the rear wheels finally caught and they slipped free. Carrie had been watching fearfully, as half-expecting a nightmare, took a deep breath with the sudden relief. When they had cleared the damp grass and slid back onto the road, she had affectionately petted the cabbie on the back.

"It's just a little Irish off-road adventure--," The old man had mischievously grinned, "And nothing to write home about. You can't see much at the moment--," He advised them, "But we're just a hop, skip and jump out of town."

"The sooner we get off of this lonely, old road--," Scott's eyes scrutinized the stifling darkness beyond, "The better I'll feel…"

They had soon entered into the town of Killkenny, turning off to the right, and traveling along a cobblestone path. They were surrounded closely on both sides by old homes, well-kept buildings, and beautiful architecture that remained from a bygone age. Through the dense fog it appeared as though it had drifted back through time: Lights glimmered in the windows from time to time, and street lamps broke the darkness as they navigated the narrow roads.

"Here she is--," The old fellow slowed, and pulling off the road, finally parked in a large lot, "St. Francis—not that there's much to see, especially in the dark."

Carrie stared out the windshield and through the headlights into the drifting fog. It seemed to slowly part like phantasmal draperies, while revealing the pale ruin of something that stood silently within.

"This can't be right?" Carrie squinted, as through the headlights she saw the roofless ruin of the old Abbey.

"This is St. Francis without doubt." The cabbie peered over his shoulder and back at her, "And there isn't another one by this name in this county."

Unlocking the door and climbing out, Carrie hurried toward the structure with Scott and the cabbie in swift pursuit.

It was a small building of graying brick and stone, and gaping holes where beautiful stained- glass windows had once been. The door had been taken long ago, and the entrance lay wide open before them. They had all just stopped and stood staring up at the dark tower, a castle parapet now barren of its cross or bell.

"Our friends were supposed to be staying here..." She whispered while still staring upward in utter disbelief.

"I'm sorry, my friend--," The cabbie urged that they return to the cab, "But no one's stayed here for almost a hundred years. It's nothing more than a landmark now, and tourist attraction."

"Maybe we mixed up the name?" Scott slowly led her back toward the car.

"No--," She climbed back into the cab, and looking back at him, said, "I wrote it down—and double-checked before we left the plane..."

"It must've been some kind of misunderstanding--," The cabbie attempted to comfort her, winking as he smiled and cheerfully said, "It happens all the time around here. Ireland is full of different counties that give some places the same names. Don't worry, little darling, it'll all work itself out in the morning, you just watch and see."

"Speaking of names—I never did catch yours?" Scott held Carrie close again while watching the old fellow's eyes in the rearview mirror.

"Lawrence Handley--," He offered a hand over the seat, "But my friends just call me, crazy Larry or duck. On account of the fact that I used to race stock cars—and on occasion, have been known to treat my cab like one."

"Okay then, Mr. Crazy Larry or duck, can we get your card?" Carrie felt an immediate endearment to the old man, "I think that we'll need your services again, soon."

"Why would anyone call you, duck?" Over-tired and appearing oblivious, Scott raised an eyebrow.

"On account of the fact that I waddle when I walks—and don't have any teeth." He pulled out his dentures and grinned huge.

"I had to ask…"

Vancouver, British Columbia, Canada.
Saturday, February 8, 1975.
12:01 a.m.

We were all wearied and worried well beyond words. Unnerved, I had glanced between my companions as they quietly stared into the hearth, slurping at hot cocoa and anxiously waiting for the telephone call. The half hour had long passed, and I had even moved to check the receiver and make certain that the plug was properly connected into the wall. The stillness becoming ominous, we were startled with each sudden crackling and leaping ember that danced within the flame. The ticking of the mantel clock seemed to become louder with each stroke. As with every progression of the minute hand, I noticed that the others also kept glancing over at the clock. Through the growing tension of waiting, this had become something of an odd and grim game. As while peering between one another to see who looked next, we soon did nothing more than just stare at the old clock. It was odd while caught in such moments, as the loudest sounds always occurred when least expected. Which is why the ringing of the telephone had sent us all lurching, as leaping from off the couch, I ran to answer!

"Carrie--," I felt relieved to hear her voice, "How are you—is everything alright?"

"That's the last time that we fly in a little plane at night--," She coughed in a chill gust, "We're in Killkenny now—and sorry it took so long, but it's very foggy and we had to get a cab into town."

"Are you alright—and have you found a place to stay?"

"We're in town now—and will be getting a room at the Killkenny Inn. I just had to call you first, and before we did anything else."

"Okay then—get some rest and try to reach Caitlin and Maya in the morning."

"Um, Michael, about that--," She stuttered in explanation, "The Abbey where she said that they were staying? It was on-route to our hotel—so we had the cabbie take us there first."

"Oh—so then you're with them now?"

"No—when we arrived there, the first thing we noticed was that the roof and windows are gone—and that the place is nothing but a ruin… and Michael, the cab driver told us that there hasn't been anyone there for almost a hundred years…"

The blood ran cold in my veins as I looked into the living room to where Rich suddenly turned and stared back at me. His eyes were wide, dark and empty as though he had instinctively sensed that something had gone terribly wrong.

"But, that's simply not possible--," Arguing more out of denial and fear than actual disagreement, I gasped, "Rich has been talking to them for months now, and Maya…"

"Michael--," Carrie pleaded with me as the distant rain caused the phone line to crackle, "The place is empty—and has been for a very long, long time…"

"Get to the hotel," I had snapped back into reality, my only concern now revolving around them, "Call me when you're both locked away for the night, I'll be waiting to hear from you."

"The Killkenny Inn is in the middle of town and it's always busy. We're at a pay phone just down the street and I can see the steeple of St. Canice's cathedral from here. The cabbie told us its right across from the hotel."

"Perfect—just get there safe, and call when you do."

"I'm so sorry--," Carrie wept, "We love you—talk soon, till then." The line went dead in my hand, and placing down the receiver, I stumbled back out and into the living room. No sooner had I done this than did Rich peer up at me, the lenses of his glasses fogging with the heat of tears. It had always seemed as though we had shared thoughts, and often knew in advance before the other had even spoken. I'm not certain as to whether he had read my thoughts, or my expression had revealed all, but he knew…

"Something's wrong--," He whispered in utter dismay, "What's happened to Maya and Caitlin?"

"Scott and Carrie took a cab from the airport to the Abbey—apparently it's somewhere in town." I looked between my friends, "That's what took so long and why they didn't call sooner."

"Thank God they're okay--," Jay used a finger to form the symbol of the cross over his brow and breast, "What about the others?"

"Well--," The words refused to form while looking to Rich and then Raymond, "Scott and Carrie went there—and she told me that it was nothing more than a roofless brick-ruin, and abandoned for almost a hundred years."

"But, that's not possible! I just talked to Maya two nights ago." Attempting to swallow back the tears, Rich trembled violently as he looked between us, "If they were never there—then who—or what have I been talking to? And where are they?"

"They might've hidden someplace else--," Raymond took Rich firmly by the arm and stared straight into his face, "And the number that you're calling could be some kind of party-line."

"Or maybe Rich is right--," Becoming as pale as a sheet, Tim gripped the armrests of the chair until his knuckles turned white. "Maybe it predicted our actions and used this opportunity to separate us."

"So, what will we do now?" Jay moved to add another log to the hearth.

"No matter what happens--," Raymond cursed angrily, "We need to stay focused and stick to the plan."

"He's right—there really isn't any other choice. And either way—there's nothing that we can do for anyone else now, anyway." Attempting to calm my friends, I stood up and began pacing the room, "If there are any answers to be found in that place—you can be sure that Scott and Carrie will find them."

"You must not lose hope--," Amica spoke sympathetically, but with determination, "The enemy is moving against us, because it becomes desperate. Perhaps it senses that the tides now change in our favor?"

"How can this possibly be to our advantage?" Rich gasped, his features becoming a mask of sorrow that cruelly twisted his features, "Our whole reason, our purpose in fighting, was to find some kind of happiness in this world again. A chance to live and share what was left of this life with the ones we love. What good is any of that—if we lose everyone and everything?"

"What we do not know, the enemy cannot see either." Amica spoke solemnly as the tears welled in her large and luminous eyes, "We fight so that even at the end of all things—that something better remains for those who survive, and shall follow."

"Hail-hail--," Raymond raised his cocoa mug, and sternly gazing around at the floundering group, said, "To salvation or death—and to whatever ends this may take us, we go together."

Mugs were raised and the challenge accepted, but darkness had grown around our hearts. It was a reminder that being mortal meant that winning was fleeting, and life just a flash in the pool of eternity.

The hearth crackled behind us and my heart sank into the depths of despair. I had never considered the possibility of ever having truly lost Caitlin, much less Maya in the process. There were no words of comfort to be offered in that moment.

"We couldn't sleep." Deb and Ray had returned, and wandering back into the living room, looked around and asked, "Did we miss something?"

"Carrie and Scott made it safely into Killkenny." Tim had quietly explained, "They called on the telephone just a few minutes ago, and informed us that the Abbey where Caitlin and Maya were supposedly staying, has been abandoned for almost a century."

"What?" Ray moved closer and taking the seat across from me, said, "Maybe they had to relocate for some reason, maybe…"

"Or maybe, the place was never occupied?" I looked to our friends who just stared in utter dismay, and I said, "Carrie had to use a payphone to call back. They're taking a cab to the hotel, and I'm just waiting for the confirmation call now."

"Speaking of calls--," Raymond rubbed the sleep from his eyes, "I'll call the office first thing in the morning and get a trace on that number. I'll make sure that they contact someone here to pass the information onto Scott and Carrie. We need to keep open lines of communication and one way or another we'll get to the bottom of this thing…"

"Eva might be the answer to this--," Tim waved a finger in thought, "If she really died there, then there will be a death certificate, or burial record. Sorry--," Having startled everyone with his sudden outburst, he said, "If nothing else—it's a place to start."

"He's right about that." Raymond went back into Detective mode while attempting to rationalize things, "It's also quite possible for security reasons, and their own protection, that they might never have been there in the first place. You did say that this evil presence can sense our thoughts outside of the estate."

"Then how would Maya have found them?" Rich asked the obvious question.

"They could've easily sent someone to meet her there." Raymond shrugged, "All things considered, that would've made perfect sense."

"I'd much rather believe that than the alternative--," Rubbing at my chin and looking between my friends, I sighed deeply, "It's getting so hard to tell the difference between nightmares and reality…"

"I didn't know that there was one at this point." Deb frowned, "Let's just take this one step at a time. The first thing that we should do is to make sure that Scott and Carrie are safe, before anything else."

"They're only down the street from the hotel." Rubbing at the sleep in my eyes, I fought back the nauseating haze of fatigue, "They should be calling any minute…"

"Ireland is five hours ahead of Ottawa on the time schedule." Raymond sighed, "I checked into that earlier."

"Which means that they're seven hours ahead of us--," Rich frowned while looking down at his wrist watch, and saying, "It's just after nine for us—so its four in the morning for them."

"Oh, dear God--," Gripping his mug tightly, Raymond peered over at me, "They're traveling in the dark..."

"It's morning there now--," Rich looked at the clock and back at me, "Let's hope that it gets light there faster than it does here..."

Killkenny, Ireland.
Killkenny Inn
7:55 a.m.
The cab pulled in before the hotel and like a dream drifting out of the fog. Scott and Carrie had hurried out, and retrieving their luggage from the trunk, paid and bid their new friend farewell.

"You'd be best to double-check first before you allow me to go running off." Lawrence had called after them, saying, "Something tells me this place is fully booked."

"Hold that thought!" Carrie had waved back at him, as leaving Scott with their luggage at the front doors, she hurried inside. She had not been gone longer than a moment when she rushed poor Scott and their luggage back to the cab.

"You were right—they're booked full--," They wandered out to where Lawrence stood waiting, and loaded everything back into the trunk, "So what do we do now?"

"If you're not too superstitious and fancy antiquity--," Lawrence peered thoughtfully into the back seat, "I know just the place."

"I need a shower and a warm bed--," Carrie groaned, "I'm just about ready to sleep in a barn."

"Kyteler's Inn always has rooms—and the building has been there since 1639."

"That sounds terrific--," Scott nodded while fighting to keep his eyes open, "But what did you mean about us not being too superstitious?"

"The place was associated to the Kyteler family—," Lawrence shrugged, "And Dame Alice Kyteler was a woman rumored to have been a witch."

"Is there anything nice to say about the place?" Scott grumbled while struggling to stay awake.

"It's been recently restored from medieval times—," Lawrence pointed as they pulled in before the long stone building, and he cheerfully said, "And it has a lovely restaurant and pub."

"I'm sold—just point me in the right direction." Carrie patted Lawrence on the back as they parked before the main doors.

Vancouver, British Columbia, Canada.
Saturday, February 8, 1975.
12:59 a.m.
The old mantel clock was chiming midnight as I had raced into the kitchen and swiftly answered the phone.

"Michael--," Carrie had gasped, her voice sounding raspy, "We're safe, we've booked a room at the Kyteler's Inn, the other place was full."

"Thank God." Placing a hand to my pounding heart, I listened closely, asking, "I'm not familiar with the country or any of the locations, but would it be hard to make a return trip to the airport, first thing in the morning?"

"It's just a day-trip by car from Killkenny back to the Dublin airport." She thought for a moment, grumbling as she said, "I'm not getting back onto that stinking little plane. And, need I remind you, that here it's already first thing in the morning."

"I'd like you both to take a flight out of Killkenny as soon as possible—and sometime today. And yes, Carrie—I know you hate little planes, but it's the fastest way back to the airport."

"Michael, first of all, we're just too beat to do anything right now. And secondly, if you think that we're going to give up without any answers and just turn around now, I'm sorry, but you're sadly mistaken. We came a long way—and I'm not going anywhere until we get to the bottom of this…"

"Carrie--," I had known that there was little hope in arguing with her, but was terrified for their well-being, "The risk is just too high."

"I've already discussed this with Scott on the way to the hotel--," Her resolve bordered defiance, but I could hear the tears as she spoke, "And I'm sorry, but we're not coming back home without Caitlin and Maya."

I had attempted to dissuade her, but she had just passed the phone to Scott. His voice was solemn and he sounded a million miles away, "Bro, there just isn't any two ways about this. We're staying until we find the girls, no matter what. We've come too far and through too much to just give up and leave now."

At that point I knew that it had already gone well beyond discussion, and slowly nodded as my heart sank, "Scott--," I swallowed back the emotions, "I don't want to lose you and Carrie, too."

"And you won't—at least not without one hell of a fight." Scott attempted to comfort me, although I could hear the doubt and fear in his tone, "We'll check in with you when we wake up. Neither one of us can hardly even see straight right now."

"Okay then, if you're staying, Raymond and Tim came up with something that might help--," I had remembered the suggestion, "Maybe you could visit the local funeral homes and find out who took care of Eva's service. The documents and waiver should contain names, numbers and an address."

"You got it—we'll get on that after we get a little sleep. We're both bagged from the flight and cab ride. We kept the taxi drivers card—he knows everything about this place—you'd be amazed."

"That's great—at least we have a contact for you in case something happens on either side."

"I've got his card right here—did you want the number?"

"Yes, just a second, I'll write it down." I had scribbled down the name and number as Scott read it aloud. As odd as it seemed, it sounded appropriate for the situation that now confronted us. After all, who would be better than a crazy cab driver when everyone else began losing their minds...?

"Scott—we're all loaded here and will be making the trip to the Duff Glenn in the morning."

"Oh God, bro--," At a loss for words, he stood silent for several moments, before quietly saying, "You know that you can count on us to do whatever we can from our end. Please, watch your back..."

"And we'll be doing everything that we can from our side of Hell--," Swallowing hard and turning to look into the darkness beyond the window, I swallowed back the grief, "Please watch over Carrie and yourself, and never lose hope. Things will come together for all of us, very soon."

"We'll meet again—one way or another, I love you, bro, till then...." At that point he had passed the telephone back to Carrie, who spoke before I could utter a single word. "Don't you worry, we're going to find Caitlin and Maya—and then all come home together, real soon."

"I just told Scott that we're making a stand at the Duff Glenn—first thing in the morning," I swallowed back the emotions, "When you see Caitlin, please tell her that I love her more than anything in this world, and always will..."

"You can tell her that yourself--," She sniffled, "When we're all back home together again."

"Tim and some of the others will be staying behind at the estate—please keep them updated as often as possible."

She paused as though pained, and quietly asked, "Of all the worst possible places that you could go—why the Duff Glenn?"

"That's exactly why—we're going to turn over a nasty old rock, and see what comes crawling out..."

"And what then—," A stillness fell between us, "And what if it does?"

"We'll do everything within our ability and even beyond to put an end to this thing."

It sounded like a desperate hope, but it was the truth and all that now remained. She had fallen into silent contemplation for several moments, and then said, "I'll call every night—and until I hear you tell me that you're home, and safe and sound."

"I love you both with all of my heart—please take good care of each other, till then..."

"We love you too—and don't you ever forget that, dammit—," She wept, "Till then..."

I sat there for several moments with the phone in my trembling hand. It had all been so very much, and now I struggled with the distinct possibility of losing Scott and Carrie as well.

"Are you okay in there?" Raymond leaned backward and over the couch to peer at me through the hall.

"Scott and Carrie made it safely into Killkenny and are staying at the Kyteler's Inn. They're going to look into the local funeral homes later today—and then call here to report what they find out." I had moved out of the kitchen, and nodding at Raymond, dropped onto the couch next to Amica, "I told them that we're going to the Duff Glenn in the morning—so they know they'll have to speak with Tim or one of the others if—until we return."

"You're not sounding so confident." Tim swallowed hard, his eyes widening as he curiously looked over at me. "You seem to be forgetting that you're travelling in exceptionally brave and blessed company."

Taking a firm hold of Amica's hand and looking among my friends, I nodded, "I haven't forgotten—I'm just concerned..."

"And I'm scared for Scott and Carrie." Rich had slowly raised his head from where he had sat in silent refrain, "They should've come back when you asked them to. They're sitting ducks out there, and all alone."

"Well, you all know Carrie and Scott--," Tightly clasping my hands together, I had looked around the group, "They're as stubborn as the day is long, but together, they're a mountain that few could ever move."

"What's going to happen if they do find the girls?" Raymond appeared white as a sheet, "That thing will just take them all out."

"Not if we get to it before it finds them." Rich growled, a fire of desperation burning in his somber stare, "You said that it can't be in two places at once--," He directed all attention upon me, "So as long as its busy with us—it can't get to them."

"That's exactly what I was thinking…" Grimacing with the thought, I said, "We have to keep it occupied—one way or another."

"We will overcome this evil--," Amica spoke with the utmost confidence, as looking among us, said, "We do not wander alone into this wasteland— we are accompanied by both angels and devils, and are blessed and cursed by the same means…"

"To freedom from this terror—and to those that will remain--," Rich raised his mug, "May we all find favor among the fates and destiny…"

"Amen…" The word was whispered as Amica's grip tightened upon my hand…

Saturday, February 8, 1975.
9:15 a.m.
We had awakened at first light, and were all stumbling around blindly while still weary from a long and restless night. Breakfast had been fast, consisting of hot drinks, muffins, toast and assorted fruit. There was crispness to the air that still warned of snow, but clarity that spoke of spring. The heavens were clear as the darkness receded, and I thought that I could see eternity within the glow of the growing dawn.

Amica and I had joined Jay, who commandeered the Suburban, while Rich had followed with Raymond in the motorhome. Our companions had all been awake that morning, and stood waving in the twilight before the doors of Sanctum Arcanum. As the iron gates parted and we pulled out and onto the street, the sun peeked from over the horizon and cast a shimmering glimmer of hope upon our procession.

The roads were far clearer than ever before, and the warm morning sun now shone down and melted it even further, as we traveled onward. There was hope in the light that seemed to brighten all of our hearts. I remember silently praying as we departed the main road, and swiftly followed eastward on the Trans-Canada highway.

Jay had switched on the power and now gripped the microphone of a CB radio, "Breaker two one—this is Red's Spirit—do you copy, Fire-Heart."

"It was Rich's way of keeping Red Cloud close--," Amica explained, "And reminding all of us why we fight."

"Ten-four on that--," Raymond replied, "We hear you loud and clear, Red's Spirit. Onward and upward my friend, put the pedal down, clear."

"Ten four—dropping the hammer now, I'm out, clear." Jay hung up the microphone, and grinning devilishly, accelerated, sending our convoy roaring down the highway.

There had been a strange mixture of fear and adrenaline that now surged through my heart and soul. I shuddered to the sound of the howling tires and engine roaring as we sped onward and into oblivion's embrace. We were no longer frightened children in death's shadow, but warriors willing to give all in the name of those we loved. Even if it all ended in that dark and dreadful place, I knew as the sun had shone upon my companions that I was both cursed and blessed. It was an adventure beyond any ever imagined, and friendships, and loves that had existed through all time. In that moment I had accepted all things, and as all fear departed, only love and courage had remained.

Amica has seemed to sense the change as she looked to me and smiled in the suns warming rays. Her eyes appeared larger and greener than ever before. Smiling softly, she slowly rested her head down upon my breast.

Kyteler's Inn, Killkenny Ireland.
2:15 p.m.
Scott and Carrie had awakened later than anticipated, but hadn't wasted any time in getting ready and calling dear old Lawrence for a cab. They had spent the better part of the early afternoon calling local funeral homes, and been utterly dismayed as none had known of whom they had inquired.

"This doesn't make any sense at all." Carrie slammed down the phone and spun toward Scott, "They were either never here—or Eva isn't dead."

"Maybe the answer is both?" Scott grabbed his coat and scarf as they hurried toward the room door, "Maybe this was all pure crap just to confuse everything and lead everyone astray?"

"Well, somehow Maya managed to find them--," Carrie hurried Scott out the door and down the dimly lit corridor, "And if she can do it—you can bet your bottom dollar that we will!"

Lawrence had arrived at almost the same moment that they had rushed out of the Inn, and been a little startled with their first request.

"A dark haired Canadian girl about three months ago--," He rubbed thoughtfully at his stubbly chin, "Come to think of it—I do remember, because she wanted a trip to St. Francis as well."

"Where did you take her--," Carrie was desperate, "Her name was Maya, a dear friend of ours, and we really need to know."

There was a terrified look of recollection in the old man's eyes, as he turned to peer back at them, and said, "I can take you to her…"

St. Canice's Hospital, Killkenny Ireland.
2:35 p.m.

The immense and old stone building stood like a gray giant beneath the clouding heavens. It was long and resting upon immense grounds, was hidden behind only a few sparsely scattered trees. With its pointed peaks and long rectangular windows it had all the appearance of an early eighteenth century castle.

When they had pulled in before the main doors Carrie had just stared upon noticing and reading the sign, "A psychiatric hospital--," She gasped, "What's going on here?"

"She asked that I bring her to St. Francis and be left there to meet friends." Lawrence followed as she hurried out of the car and toward the door, "The last that I heard of the poor girl—she was found without identification, and suffering from amnesia."

Scott and Carrie hurried in through the main doors with the old fellow in close pursuit. They had found their way to a nurses' station in the main entrance, and flagged down an old woman who had been searching through a cabinet of old files.

"I'm looking for a young woman that was brought here several months ago--," Carrie produced a photograph of Maya and Rich, "She's the wife of a dear friend—and went missing somewhere around here."

"Let me see what I can do for you dear—I know someone that might be able to help, just a moment, please," The elderly woman raised a finger before turning and making her way into the back. She had returned with a younger lady within a moment, who closely examining the photograph, asked, "Are you family?"

"We're representatives of her husband--," Scott interrupted, "And would really appreciate your help, please…"

The younger nurse had looked between them, and then returning the photo to Carrie, waved for them to follow, "She's on the second floor, please follow me."

Carries heart pounded furiously as they followed along through the tall and dismal corridors. The walls were all painted in pale colors, which were hard to distinguish in the pale light. There was a strong scent of antiseptic, moldering wood, and something else that now caused her stomach to slightly turn.

"This way, please." The nurse opened a door before them, and followed as they entered into the large room.

"Maya—oh my God--," Carrie ran to the young woman's bedside, and sitting upon the edge, took hold of her hand, "What's happened, sweetheart—talk to me, please!"

Maya had slowly turned to look upon her with heavy-lidded eyes. At first glance, Carrie had assumed this to have been an effect of medication, but soon realized that something was terribly wrong.

Drawing the talisman from beneath her shirt, she held it before Maya's suddenly wide and terrified eyes, "Come back to us, Maya, please."

"When she first came to us she was incoherent--," The nurse quietly explained, "She didn't have any identification, and only had the clothes that she was wearing."

Scott and old Lawrence had stood at the foot of the bed as the nurse watched in utter disbelief.

"Maya—Rich needs you—and we all love you--," Carrie held the talisman before the young woman's face, and then gently touched her brow, "Come back..."

Maya now stared as though having seen some light from a great distance, but resisting the affects. With tears in her eyes, Carrie continued in loving defiance, and speaking as one to a spirit long departed, "I know that you're in there—I feel you, please, oh please come back to us..."

Maya's eyes filled with tears as she suddenly convulsed! The nurse had attempted to intervene, but Scott and Lawrence had interceded, the three of them just staring in utter horror! Carrie had gently held Maya shoulder's down as the young woman fought against some unspeakable thing that now attempted to maintain its hold!

"For the love of God--," Carrie wept, "Come back to us Maya—come back..."

Maya suddenly screamed, her entire body convulsing as the windows shattered, and a great darkness passed out and into the gloom of the late afternoon sky!

There was a moment of absolute stillness as everyone had just gawked at the young woman, who now fell into Carrie's loving embrace.

"I'll get the mother superior." The nurse wiped tears from her eyes and rushed from the room.

"Maya—oh Maya--," Carrie held her close, "We thought that we'd lost you."

"Carrie—Scott—oh God--," She wept hysterically, "I thought that I would never see any of you again."

"What happened?" Scott took to the other side of the bed and rested a supportive hand upon the woman's still trembling shoulder.

"I went to St. Francis too meet with Caitlin and Eva--," She sniffled, running a hand through the wild curls of her hair, and looking between the couple, "It was just before dark—when I saw her." Her eyes reflected the horror as she looked among her dear friends, "But it wasn't Caitlin..." She shuddered uncontrollably, and noticing the old cabbie, suddenly pointed as she wept, "I remember you—I should've listened when you didn't want to leave me there."

"It's okay now, dear child--," He came to her side and gently patted her arm, "You're among friends and safe now."

The door opened behind them and the nurse returned with an elderly nun who stood and simply gazed upon them all.

"It was a miracle--," The young nurse could hardly keep her breath, "I saw her cast the devil from out of this young woman."

The nun slowly walked over, and gently taking hold of Carrie's hand, placed a large silver crucifix into the palm, "I don't know what evil has befallen you—but know in your hearts that should you need us, we are always here for you."

"There were two others—that came before her--," Carrie took the Mother Superior's hands into her own and looked desperately into the steel-blue of the older woman's eyes, "Caitlin McCreary and her elderly friend, Eva."

There was a slight hesitation as looking to the nurse, and then swallowing hard, the Mother Superior asked, "Surely you don't mean Catherine McCreary and her maid's hand, Eva?"

"We've only ever known her as Caitlin." Scott shrugged.

"Catherine is the Irish form of Caitlin--," Carrie remembered, as turning a suspicious eye back upon the Mother Superior, asked, "Why do you ask?"

"They couldn't possibly be one and the same--," The Mother Superior replied, as looking to the nurse and then back at Carrie, and quietly said, "I know where you might find the both of them..."

"With all due respect--," Lawrence interrupted, "If you'll just say it, I'll take them to their friends."

"My dear man--," She politely addressed him, "That would require a lengthy drive into Dublin, and a visit to the Christ Church Cathedral."

"I knew it—they're not even in Killkenny." Scott grumbled, "They're at a completely different cathedral."

"The only thing that remains of Catherine McCreary and her lady Eva, are contained in the archives at Christ Church Cathedral. Unlike most of the McCreary family—their deaths were never recorded, and bodies never found." The Mother Superior looked between the astonished group, "I know this, because when I served there as a young woman, I had an interest in the history of the shipping trade. Of which the McCreary family were well renowned."

"They obviously had birth records, if you had information on them." Carrie clasped the crucifix in both hands before her breast, "Do you remember when they lived?"

"It was some time during the early eighteen hundreds--," She thought briefly and shaking her head, said, "I'm sorry if I don't remember correctly, but I recollect that the family emigrated to Canada at the latter part of the nineteenth century. No other records exist for them here beyond that."

"That would make them well over a hundred and fifty years old." Maya gasped while slipping behind a screen with the nurse's assistance, and quickly getting changed into her street clothes.

"Well, that's just simply impossible--," Scott shrugged it off, "Our Caitlin and Eva were alive and well when we saw them a few months ago."

"I'm sorry that I can't be of any further assistance--," The Mother Superior moved to where Maya stepped out from behind the blind and gently hugged the younger woman, saying, "I pray that you will all find safe passage and God's guidance, wherever your journey takes you."

"It looks like the wild goose chase ends here?" Appearing utterly dismayed, Scott slumped down into a chair that stood near the bed.

"No, it's just beginning--," Carrie turned toward the old gentleman, "Lawrence, how would you feel about joining a crazy and very dangerous cross-country tour?"

Removing his cap and bowing, he winked back at her. As peering out from beneath those bushy eyebrows with a smile, he said, "It'd be an honor, dear lady."

Looking back to the Mother Superior, Carrie politely asked, "Would you be kind enough to give us an address, and maybe the name of someone who could provide us with some information about the McCreary family?"

"Certainly--," The Mother Superior motioned for them to all follow, "I'll do whatever I can."

"I get the feeling that we might just be chasing down some ghosts?" Lawrence spoke quietly as he followed from close behind the group.

"More than you know..." Scott glanced back at him as they all hurried down the long corridor, "More than you know..."

CHAPTER EIGHTEEN

Vancouver, British Columbia, Canada.
Saturday, February 8, 1975.
11:45 a.m.
We had long passed through the little town of Hope, and now sped
dangerously through the Frazer Canyon. With sheer frozen cliffs to one
side and a sudden icy drop to the other, we navigated the snow-covered
and serpentine road. The world all about us was silent, frozen and
seemingly lifeless. I had looked about, dismayed to discover that we were
also the only travelers on that lonely stretch of road. The highway that had
once been an old friend had now become a bitter pathway into oblivion.

For what little chance that we had to listen to the radio before we
encountered the mountainous terrain, there had been nothing good. The
forecast had warned of possible flurries somewhere just beyond the town
of Hope. But in all truth, we had all suspected something far worse.

"So, now that we have a chance to talk alone--," Jay had politely
acknowledged Amica with a nod before continuing, "I still really don't
know a lot about any of this—how the hell did it all start, and what was
your part in this to begin with?"

"All things in creation belong to an intricately weaved game of good and
evil," I sipped at tea from a thermos that Amica had given me, and said,
"It's a constant battle for a balance between negative and positive.
Somewhere along that path, I pissed off something really bad, and through
time and space, it's hunted us down and we all came together here."

"Okay, that's cool." Jay shrugged, and sipping at a mug of coffee,
smirked sarcastically, "I was just a little confused about it all, before…"

We sped along the highway as the light seemed to fade with the gathering
clouds. The long shadows of the cliffs and snow-tipped trees leaving us in
partial darkness as we swiftly passed from beneath.

Vancouver, British Columbia, Canada.
Sanctum Arcanum
12:10 p.m.

"I don't think it's going to ring just because you keep staring at it." Jen patted Tim on the back as she passed him in the kitchen with a tray of sandwiches.

"I can't help it--," He moved to help Deb as she followed with urns containing tea and coffee, "I feel so damn useless—helpless to do anything."

"We all feel the same way--," Ray assisted with the cutlery as they all sat down to share lunch, "I just wish that someone would call—or that we could somehow make a difference, somewhere."

"Michael said that we should all just stay right here--, Danny sighed deeply, as dropping into his seat at the table, poured grape soda into his glass, "I'd rather have gone with them…"

"I know you would've, kiddo." Tim gently patted Danny on the back, "But someone had to stay behind to guard the fort."

"You know that he only said that to protect us." Danny's eyes narrowed as shame filled his young face, "Without Caitlin, none of this means anything to him—and all he has left is us…"

They had all just sat between their soup and sandwiches and quietly stared. If there had been any words of comfort to have been spoken in that moment, it would have been lost among their grim expressions.

It was the ringing of the telephone that had broken the moment, and Tim's rushing to answer it had drawn all attention.

"Carrie—oh, we've been so worried!" He gasped in relief, and shoving a hand to his brow, asked, "How are you and Scott, what's happened, is everything alright?"

"We've found Maya--," Carrie sniffled as she turned to look back at the cab from the little telephone booth, "She alright—and here with us now."

"They have Maya!" Tim reported to the others, throwing a thumb high into the air, "She's with them now and they're all safe."

"Listen--," Carrie's tone became alarming, "Don't say anything about this out loud, but we've run into some trouble where Caitlin and Eva are concerned."

"Oh?" He felt a tremble course through his entire being, "In what way?"

"I can't go into a lot of detail over the phone--," She explained, "But we're taking a cab, it's our friend Lawrence, and going with Maya into Dublin, right now. I'll call when we get settled into a hotel. Please, let Michael know about this as soon as possible."

"Tell me why—I know that something is very wrong here. Carrie—I can feel it from the depths of my soul."

"We found Maya in a psychiatric hospital after something got a hold of her at St. Francis. I managed to break her out of it with the talisman, but Carrie and Eva were never even here. The Mother Superior used to practice out of Christ Church Cathedral in Dublin, and she remembered an old history of a family that once shipped out of there. Tim, she told us that Caitlin and Eva lived there over one hundred and fifty years ago. I don't know what the hell is going on—but we're going there right now to try and get to the bottom of this."

"Oh, dear God in heaven…" Tim stared out the window and into the heavens through tear-filled eyes, "What devilry is at work here now?"

"Please tell Michael everything that I've told you--," She sniffled, "May God be with all of you—I need to go now, good luck and till then, my friend."

"Till then—God bless and bring you all home safely…"

"What's going on?" Deb and the others now all stood behind him.

Tim slowly turned to look at his friends, his voice a trembling whisper, "I'm afraid that the devil may have been among us the entire time?"

Rocky Mountains, British Columbia, Canada.
2:45 p.m.

"It's our last chance to stop--," Jay directed our attention to a small service station along the road-side, "Just give the word, nay or yay."

The service station had been an oasis among the endless snow-covered trees and cascading mountains that now surrounded us on both sides. It had come and gone in the short time that I had watched, tongue-tied as we roared past.

"I'm guessing that was a no--," Jay slowly nodded, "All the same, we're making pretty good time according to your directions. We should be at this place in less than an hour."

"This still doesn't leave us very much time to work before dusk." The thought of being there now sent chills that danced like icy fingers along the length of my spine.

"It matters very little--," Amica gently stroked my hand and spoke as though day-dreaming, "Because the vaults lay in perpetual darkness anyway…"

"This place sounds like Fort Knox--," Jay groaned, shooting a nervous glance at me while asking, "Are we even going to have enough explosives to bring this place down?"

"Knowing Rich--," Tapping a finger nervously upon the dash pad, I peered back at him, "He'll be more than prepared…"

The motorhome shuddered violently as Rich followed closely from behind the Suburban. The road had been more forgiving due to the tightly packed snow, but every ridge and bump rocked them dangerously along the passage.

"This stuff won't just go off over a few bumps—will it?" Raymond sipped nervously at his coffee and peered into the back.

"No—it's not activated like that. The elements have to be mixed to become dangerous."

"As in an accident--," Raymond frowned, "And the stuff spilling out and into the snow?"

"Now that you mention it--," Slowly nodding, Rich chuckled as his knuckles whitened upon the wheel, "That might just do it?"

"Drive carefully--," Raymond warned, "There's no point rushing, if we're not even going to make it there."

"Don't worry--," Rich sighed, "There's far worse things to die from—trust me…"

"You know--," Raymond settled back into his seat, "I've honestly never been this shit-scared in my entire life."

Laughing Rich had happily agreed, saying, "But at least we're travelling in true luxury!"

"How can you think about something like that—at a time like this?"

"Because sometimes it's just better not to think about things so much—it only makes them worse…"

Nodding, Raymond looked around the cab and curiously asked, "So tell me about this thing? Is it fully loaded—and does it have every modern option and new technology available?"

"Since you asked—we are currently travelling in the new 1975 Diplomat II built by Executive Industries. It has deluxe bucket seats, as you've already noticed, built-in kitchen, modern bath, retractable bunk, temperature control, unrestricted interior mobility. "

"Unrestricted interior mobility--," Raymond appeared to have had trouble grasping the concept. "That sounds very technical."

"It just means that we have an open cab rather than the van style." Rich winked, "Which makes it easier to hop back and forth inside without having to leave the vehicle first."

"Is that it?"

"No--," Rich grabbed the sales brochure from off the dash, and reading aloud, said, "It also has super-strong collateral construction, and super-light sandwich construction of brawny steel, and genuine Styrofoam!"

"Geez--," Raymond admired the vehicle with a new perspective, "It'll be a real shame if we have to blow it up..."

Rich glared at Raymond briefly, and then stared intently out the windshield while tightly gripping the wheel.

Carlow, Ireland.
3:45 p.m.
Carrie had quietly watched from the front passenger seat as they traveled westward along the M9 toward Dublin. They had passed the exits to Goresbridge, Ballon, Tullow, and had now sped past the little town of Carlow. The gently rolling hills and endless pastures stood like emerald shores beneath a bright blue sky. They had been travelling for an hour and twenty minutes, and Lawrence had attempted to keep them entertained by playing an eight-track of Irish drinking songs.

"Oh—I just love that Finnegan's Wake--," He chortled while puffing upon his pipe, "It reminds me of my youth and some of the fights that we used to get into."

"What I'd give for a ham sandwich and cold mug of beer right now." Scott groaned as Maya affectionately leaned over in the seat and patted his shoulder.

"Don't you worry--," She motioned toward Lawrence, "I'm sure that he can find us all a lovely place to stop for lunch."

"Stop--," Carrie peered fearfully from over the front seat, "No, we can't be doing that. We still have a long way to go and it'll be dark again soon."

"Not that far now, my dear--," Lawrence motioned to the windshield with his pipe. "I'll wager a beer and lunch that we'll be in Dublin within just over an hour."

"And if you can pull that off--," Scott slapped the old man's shoulder and laughed, "I'll happily lose to you on that!"

"I don't think that I've even seen more sheep in my life than I have here." Carrie watched closely as they passed another field full of the quietly grazing beasts.

"Well then--," Lawrence sighed, "They're cuddly and cute—produce wool, and make a lovely stew."

"I never cared for the taste of mutton." Carrie shuddered at the thought, "I always thought that it tasted a little too gamey."

"My mother used to soak it in buttermilk over-night." Lawrence advised while smacking his lips, "It does away with that strong, nasty bite, and leaves nothing but the finest taste. A little mint jelly—nice roasted taters, carrots, turnip, rosemary and herbs, and pure paradise, my girl! We'll have to treat you to some before you leave."

"She's always liked the local venison from where we came from--," Scott informed his older friend, "But never been much for foreign flavors, I guess we're just too old fashioned."

"She's an Irish girl--," Lawrence insisted while taping the ashes from out of his pipe, "The least that she can do is to give her heritage a little try?"

"Alright then, if it'll make you clowns happy--," She grumbled, "When we finally have dinner, I'll give mutton a second chance..."

"You won't regret it!" Lawrence beamed, "It's a taste like no other—it's like coming home..."

Vancouver, British Columbia, Canada.
Sanctum Arcanum
1:15 p.m.
The Eldorado slowly rumbled from out of the garage as Tim carefully pulled in before the main door.

"This is insane--," Deb pleaded with him as Danny and the others silently watched, "If you go after them now—it'll be dark before you can even catch up!"

"He has to know about Caitlin and Eva--," Tim shivered in the bitter gust, "It might make a world of a difference to them—and for all of us."

"Or it might just get you killed trying." Danny stepped toward the car, and pleading, said, "They're likely already close—or already at that old place. And besides, I thought that you had to stay here—aren't you the keeper of whatever that thing is in the vaults?"

Remembering the golden whistle in the last moment, Tim removed it from around his neck, "Deb—please take this--," She leaned down and he placed it about her neck, "If you blow that whistle—it will summon the thing from the crypt. But, no matter what, no one is to ever enter that building without you and that key—or they'll never be seen again. Do you understand?" He looked to the remaining members of the group, and gently patting Deb's shoulder, said, "I know that this may seem crazy—but I need to do this..."

"Then I'm going with you." Danny hopped into the car, and glaring defiantly at anyone who might disagree, said, "My place is with my family—and Michael's all I have left..."

Deb and Ray had stepped forward, but Jen had reached out and halted them, "Let him make this decision—no matter how much it hurts... He has the right..."

A cold wind whipped Danny's hair about his stern and steel blue eyes. They could all see that the decision had been made, and slowly stepped away.

"Please keep communications open between Carrie from here--," Tim saluted them all as he began rolling forward, "And I'll try to stay in contact with you from the road."

"Godspeed--," Deb stood within solemn refrain, though her heart ached, "I'll be waiting to hear from you—till then..."

Accelerating, they lurched forward as the enormous engine howled. The powerful front wheel drive swiftly carrying down the long drive and through the open gates, and they sped off beneath the darkening skies.

Pressing the remote, Deb stood silently watching as the gates slowly rolled closed. She had looked fearfully into the cloud-filled heavens, turning to look as Ray and Jen moved closer to her from behind. Her hand had slipped to the golden key that now hung about her neck, and she whispered in silent prayer to the unforgiving wind, "Oh please, if there's really is someone listening up there—bring them safely back..."

Ray had moved in from behind her, and taking her into a gentle embrace, hugged her close. Jen moved closer, and as they all stood together, the wind howled and the snow began to fall...

British Columbia, Canada.
The House of McCreary
4:15 p.m.

Rich had parked the motorhome near the immense stone fountain that stood before the house. It was only a few yards distance from the main doors, which would make unloading the equipment far easier. Taking greater precautions, Jay had distanced the Suburban from the motorhome in case of an unforeseen accident. I don't believe that anyone had felt entirely secure about the highly volatile nature of its cargo. It was apparent just in the side-glances and nervous fidgeting that could be seen as we unloaded the supplies.

"The damn weather didn't waste any time getting ugly." Jay cursed as he slammed and locked the truck door.

The wind had picked up considerably, and from out of the once blue sky now formed dense clouds, and the flurries had soon followed. There was a darkness approaching long before dusk, and I knew the nature of this beast all too well.

"Don't bother yourself with the weather--," I had led them both to where Raymond and Rich unloaded our gear, and glancing up and into the dark windows of the house of McCreary, said, "I'm sure that this place has a lot more in store for us than a little wind and snow…"

Loading duffel bags filled with explosives from out of the motorhome, Rich distributed everything equally among us, including his 'chemical fire' crossbows.

"Alright--," Rich pointed between us, "Listen up, because this is where it gets really dangerous. These bags--," He pointed down at them, "Are filled with a mixture of my home-made fire-bombs and dynamite. So when they go off—this whole place is going down."

"Why is Raymond wearing a backpack?" I suddenly noticed the difference in gear.

"I volunteered to run through the basement--," He winked, "And to leave a few presents along the way."

"No, he doesn't even know his way around down there—let me do that!" I panicked realizing what was about to occur.

"I can manage it just like I've done a thousand other things before." Raymond physically restrained me, taking hold of my shoulders with both hands, his eyes pleading as he said, "And let's be honest here, your health just isn't what it used to be."

Both he and Rich were obviously concerned about my heart condition, their eyes meeting several times as they glanced between one another and then focused upon me.

"We don't have time for this--," Rich cursed as he waved toward the house, "Let's just do this as fast as possible. We're already running out of time, and daylight."

Frustrated beyond words and terrified for my friend, I had conceded, but never agreed. Amica had shot a sly glance in my direction as we now moved toward the house. It had roused my suspicions and I had the distinct impression that she was analyzing things, and scheming…

The wind howled and the resounding echo from somewhere in the shadows sent us all back. We had looked to the stone face of the beastly place, as through the blackened ports of cathedral sized windows, it solemnly stared back. The manor seemed far larger and even darker than ever before. It stood in defiance against the heavens with its rising, pointed peaks and menacing gargoyles. It was a majestic monstrosity that now sent shudders down my spine and caused every molecule within my being to tremble with sheer terror. There had been a time not so long ago when I had been captivated, and even admired the old place. But now, it left nothing more than a deep inner loathing, shattered nerves, and even sickened me within approach.

We ascended the steps quickly and carefully while carrying our deadly cargo. If anyone had ever told me that this day would have arrived, I would have thought them to have been utterly insane. All the same, we soon arrived in that corridor where I had first stood so long ago, and knocked upon the front doors. The mere memory sent chills that gnawed and tore at my already seared nerves. Then, gathering what wits remained to me, I moved forward and slowly pushed upon the heavy oak doors. There was a deep groan and I stepped back, as squealing loudly upon rusted hinges, the doors slowly parted and swung wide open.

"I feel like I'm stepping into the mouth of some monster." Visibly shuddering with the thought, Jay looked between us, "This place makes my skin crawl…"

"That's because you are--," Rich motioned for us to follow as he now hurriedly led the way, "Amica, you go with Michael, and Jay, please come with me." Rich halted in the grand entrance and turned to face us, speaking swiftly as he explained, "You all have bags containing six pre-made packages. Just go to the far end of your wing, and start leaving one in every room. Light the fuses as you go—and keep moving as fast as you can. You'll have approximately sixty seconds between each explosion. So whatever you do, never put down the duffel bag—and never slow down. This is going to be a little hair-raising, as once the first one's go off, this whole place will go up."

"What affect will this stuff have on stone?" Raymond jabbed a thumb to the pack that he wore.

"You're carrying enough dynamite to level some of the foundations--," Rich now appeared extremely concerned, "The idea is to drop the place down and in on itself—and leave nothing but rubble. Purification by fire— we can deal with having the ground sanctified later."

"Alright then--," Raymond heartily slapped Rich on the back and took one last look at us, "Good luck, my friends—and see you on the other side."

"No--," Amica rushed forward and ripping the pack from off Raymond, spun to look back at us, "Michael and Jay take the west wing, and

Raymond and Rich can handle the east. I'm faster than all of you—I know this place, and will deal with the basement and vaults."

She was gone before there had even been an opportunity to disagree, and I stood speechless.

"You heard the lady, gentlemen." Raymond waved while tugging at Rich's arm, "Let's send this place back to hell—where it belongs."

What began with hesitation now turned into a desperate race for time against the failing light. Jay had followed closely as I ran down the long corridors past the main hall, dining room and enormous stairways. There was a permeating scent of moldering wood, decay, and something sickly sweet that I couldn't quite define. It was carried to the senses much like the aroma of a perfume, as through sweet scented promise, it bore some ghastly secret while becoming sour and suffocating. We had quickly turned, and passing into a long corridor, entered into the east wing. The ceilings were high, and leaves had drifted in upon the wind over the fall and through many a broken window. By this same means did the snow now blow inward, heaping against the far wall and causing the floor to become even more slippery. The empty halls echoed like thunder beneath each and every footfall as we desperately hurried along. The shadows gathered as they always had, the wallpaper peeled, and the wooden panels moldered away with time. As we rushed past, the old draperies that remained before broken windows, danced like pale phantoms in the wild and icy gusts.

Gasping for breath, we reached the corridor's end and hurriedly scrambled into the room at the end of the hall. Jay ripped a package out of his duffel bag, and fumbling with a lighter, nervously proceeded to light the long wick.

"In a world full of crazy—and I just had to say it," He cast it down into the middle of the floor, "This is the stupidest and most dangerous thing that I've ever done--," His eyes were huge as he looked back at me, "Run!"

I'm not exactly sure as to when the first explosion occurred. It might have been as we lit another fuse in the third or fourth room? In any event, the violence of the eruption had shaken the very foundation of the place and sent us stumbling back out into the hall! We hadn't exchanged a single word, but the shocked and terrified expressions we exchanged said enough. Immense flames and black smoke billowed through the corridor as we paused just long enough to drop another package and light the wick. Another eruption left us deafened as we fell to our knees while covering our ears with both hands.

"Keep moving--," Jay bellowed as he took hold of my arm and now pulled me along, "They're doing the same thing in the west wing—if we don't hurry, we'll get caught in the middle!"

The final light of day shone in through the enormous windows as the snow poured in through the broken glass. The wind howled like the devil through the corridors as we ran, and the belching flames began consuming the ancient manor house. At this point, Jay had empties his cache and now removed the packages from mine. He wasted no time as he had previously, just lighting the packages and then sliding them into the rooms.

Finally, falling half-blinded and choking back out into the main hall, we had rushed back toward the staircase. It had only been a moment before our companions had arrived, pursued by belching flames and billowing clouds of black oily smoke.

"We need to get out of here!" Rich wailed as another explosion rocked the mansion and we all fell to the floor.

"Where's Caitlin?" Raymond threw a hand before his eyes as he fought to peer back through the growing smoke and flames. Windows exploded and a hot wind howled through the corridors as the inferno became an all-consuming beast! It became blinding from behind us, and followed closer and ever faster with each and every passing moment.

"She should've been back here by now." Rich gasped, as spinning to look back down the hallway behind us, said, "If she doesn't get out of there soon—this whole place is going to collapse!"

"I'll go after her--," I shouted, "The rest of you get out!"

"Like hell you will--," Raymond bellowed, and running back into the smoke and flames, shouted back, "Get out of here—I'll bring her out!"

Jay and Rich had taken hold of either of my arms and dragged me struggling and fighting as we hurried down the corridor and into the main hall.

"There's no sense in getting us all killed!" Rich pleaded while fighting back the emotions, "Please—we need to get the hell out of here!"

Another explosion sent us downward as the roar of bending and breaking beams splintering, burning, now echoed thunderously as part of a celling somewhere crashed heavily down!

Without another word I had just followed my friends, as scrambling to our feet amongst the blazing chaos, we raced madly through the hallway and toward the main doors.

The inferno roared in defiance from behind us as the east and west wings had succumbed to the flames. There was a mighty groan from the ancient manor as beams and floors began to give way, stone cracked, and it began collapsing unto itself.

We stumbled down the stone steps and out into the blizzard, the explosions sending us forward and into the deepening snow.

"Oh God--," Rich gasped as he looked back into the inferno that was now the house, "They're never going to get out of there!"

The heat had become so intense that the stones supporting the structure were cracking from all sides. The windows were belching flames, billowing smoke and roaring like the furnaces of hell. The main portion of the entrance still stood unscathed, but bore a steadily growing crown of flames. As we had watched, the intense heat had caused all the remaining windows to explode, casting down a crystalline shower of shattered and shimmering death. We had narrowly evaded the scathing hail by dropping down and rolling beneath the motorhome!

"We need to move this thing before the heat gets any worse!" Rich wailed as we slid out from beneath the vehicle, and he ran for the driver's door, "I'll park beside the Suburban, and meet you there!"

Hurriedly pulling away from before the mansion, Rich sped off while Jay and I stood alone before the blazing carnage. The main portion of the building was now brightly alit from above, and the empty windows were blazing, as from a charred brickwork face, they gazed furiously down. The main doors hung agape as the smoke poured out, as within that moment, the entire mansion appeared as some monstrous and hellish thing.

"There's just no way that they're getting out of there--," Jay had turned sadly and slowly shaking his head, put a firm hand upon my shoulder as he quietly said, "I'm sorry, but we'd better get going."

Looking toward the door in utter desperation and despair, I suddenly gasped as through the smoke I saw them suddenly appear! Raymond had obviously succumbed and fallen, but Amica, ever resourceful, immortal, now carried him out. She hadn't succumbed entirely to the demon, but was now something that appeared caught in between. As with a horned mane and outspread dragon's wings, like a dark angel, she now bore Raymond from out of the smoke and flames!

"What in God's name is that?" Jay choked and made the symbol of the cross upon his breast.

"Hope---," I gasped, "Where no other exists…"

Amica had suddenly brightened and we were all blinded while caught in a brilliant light. She vanished into the brilliance for only a moment, and then returned to her previous form. There was fear and fascination in the faces of all who had witnessed her terrifying but miraculous change, but none had said anything.

"Raymond!" Jay slapped at our friends face as we half carried him away from the inferno and back toward the motorhome, "Speak to me, buddy!"

"Raymond—oh my god, no-," Rich had stumbled while running toward us as we had all crumpled into a heap with our fallen friend into the snow.

"He's not breathing--," Rich's lenses steamed as looking up at me, the tears welled within his eyes, "I can't feel any breath."

Kneeling down, Amica had gently touched the side of Raymond's face with a pale hand, and then whispered, "Raymond—your time here is not yet spent, return to us—dear friend..."

Speechless, we had all just watched in the wind and snow as his eyelids had flickered, his eyes opened and then flashed back to life. He choked and vomited bile as he coughed out blackened phlegm and cleared his lungs of the smoke. Rich and I had held him close, as choking and fighting for breath, he struggled for life while returning to the physical world.

"I couldn't see anything—and then I couldn't breathe--," He coughed while sitting up in the snow, "I remember falling down the stone steps into the vaults, how did I get out?"

Amica had wiped the tearful smoke from his eyes and face and quietly said, "That was very brave—and foolish of you to come back for me."

"Well, I wasn't about to leave you in there alone, sweet lady--," He coughed and wiped at his mouth, and then suddenly looking astonished, glanced up at her, "Are you the one that pulled me out?"

"Something did--," Jay swallowed hard, "All that matters is that you're still with us."

"That's the end of the house of McCreary--," The flames danced in the lenses of Rich's glasses as we watched the place burn, "But what I don't understand—is why the darkness never tried to stop us when we were doing this?"

"Maybe it isn't here?" Jay swallowed hard as we moved from out of the snow and began making our way over toward the vehicles.

"Well—if it isn't here--," Raymond regained his composure and fearfully looked over at me, "Then where the hell is it?"

"It doesn't really matter at this point," Looking among my friends, I blew hot air into my freezing and trembling hands, "Because no matter where it might be—once we get to the mausoleums, the stone will force it to come straight back here..."

"But Michael—you seem to be forgetting--," Rich reminded me, "If it's isn't here with us—then where, and who is it after..."

A thunderous crash and resounding moan echoed through the Duff Glenn, as the house of McCreary crashed to the earth and was consumed by fire. In that moment, I had imagined to have heard the cries of the dead once trapped there, finally being released from that accursed old prison...

CHAPTER NINETEEN

Dublin Ireland
Christ Church Cathedral
5:25 p.m.

The little cab had long parted the M9 from Killkenny, entered onto the M7 and sped westbound on route into Dublin. The countryside had been a scattered mixture of rustic farms, quaint little towns, and the beautiful and forever gently rolling hills. Had it not been for the urgency of their journey and the forthcoming darkness, Carrie would have truly enjoyed the visit.

"They say that Christ Church Cathedral is the seat of the conjoined Diocese of Ireland--," Lawrence glanced over at Carrie while puffing at his pipe, "But the plain fact is that it's only ever been the seat of the Archbishop of Dublin, and church of Ireland since the English reformation." It was apparent that Lawrence had become increasingly nervous since their experience at the hospital, and it showed in his fidgeting and stuttering explanations.

"How much further is it from the cathedral now?" Carrie rubbed at her eyes beneath her glasses, and quickly covered her mouth with a hand while politely concealing a yawn.

"As long as the traffic isn't too bad--," Lawrence glanced down at the pocket watch that hung from his vest, "It shouldn't be more than a few minutes."

Scott had quietly watched as Maya softly snored while nestled against his broad shoulder in the back seat. His heart was broken as he looked upon her wearied countenance, and the long shadows that now welled beneath her sunken eyes. It was obvious that the horrific experience had aged her prematurely, as this once beautiful young woman now appeared thin and quite ill.

"How is she doing?" Carrie spoke softly as she reached back and affectionately stroked the side of her husband's bearded face.

"She passed out some time ago--," He sighed deeply and with the greatest of remorse, "The poor thing looks like she's been through hell. We really need to get her home..."

"Now, mind you--," Lawrence raised a finger while interrupting, "Far be it from me to stick my nose where it doesn't belong, but might I ask exactly what's happening around here, and between all of you?"

"Lawrence, are you a religious man?" Scott stared solemnly into the older man's eyes.

"I'm Catholic born--," Lawrence appeared startled by the comment, and slowly nodding, said, "And although I may bend the rules just a wee bit here and there, I try to stay true to form."

"Well, then I'm not going to beat around the bush--," Looking reluctantly between Carrie and the older man, he swallowed hard before saying, "We belong to an organization known as Nightrealm, and study and investigate paranormal activity. Our founder, Michael Schreiber, accidentally stumbled on something during one of those investigations and it opened a literal can of worms."

"What's he trying to say--," Reaching into the back seat and affectionately clutching at her husband's hand, "Is that we're being followed by some kind of an evil entity—and that we came here to try to find our friends before it gets to all of them."

"I was afraid that I'd seen the devil in that young woman's eyes." The old man muttered as though speaking to himself, "And after that thing back at the hospital, not much would surprise me now…"

"I hate to disagree with you on that--," Frightened and realizing the predicament of which they had unwittingly involved the old man, Carrie gently took hold of his arm, "But, we're all in serious danger. This thing that's coming after us has already murdered several of our friends—and once it figures out that we're here and what we're doing—it's going to find us too…"

"It can't touch is during the daylight ours--," Scott informed the old man, "But once it gets dark, not even these charms--," He pulled his out from beneath his shirt to inspect it, before saying, "Not even these charms can protect us from the possessed…"

Lawrence had just glanced curiously between them while slowly shaking his head. They were uncertain as to whether he had accepted a single word in explanation, or simply considered them both utterly insane.

"I know how crazy this must all sound--," Carrie pleaded, "But you have to believe us—it's a matter of life and death, for all of us now…"

"My dear lady, need I remind you that you're in Ireland--, "He raised a bushy eyebrow in question, "The land of ghost stories, family curses and the darkest tales of evil that you'll ever hear. " Puffing at his pipe, he raised an eyebrow, and asked, "What I'd really like to know is what in the name of Jesus, Mary and Joseph are you planning to do about it?"

"We're going to Christ Church to meet with father Donoghue--," Scott volunteered the information, "The mother Superior told us that he has parish records that might help us. She contacted him already, so we're expected."

"What exactly do you hope to find in parish records that might help you with this—evil thing?"

"We need to find out about the McCreary family--," Carrie swallowed hard, "And any surviving heirs."

"Sweet mother of God—I might've known," The old man cursed under his breath while glancing into the rearview mirror at Scott, "They were a wealthy and well-known family in the shipping industry, some hundred years ago. Of all the shippers in Dublin, they seemed plagued with accidents at sea, unexplained deaths, and folks just going missing."

"How do you know about them?" Carrie was utterly astounded.

"When I was a wee lad I lived near Dublin Bay, and my grandfather used to tell me stories about fishing, the sea, and that bloody McCreary family."

"So they were notorious for having bad luck--" Scott almost climbed into the front seat, "Is that what you're talking about?"

"I'm talking about hauntings and evil things that befall anyone that commits terrible acts--," The old fellow shuddered at the thought, "And none of that had anything to do with luck."

"What kind of terrible acts might you be referring to?" Carrie's eyes flitted nervously between the darkening horizon and the smoky haze drifting between her and the old man.

"Now, I can't say it's all for certain as stories tend to grow longer over time." He spoke with certain reluctance, having been a very profound old man, "But, my grandfather made mention of witch craft, demons and even human sacrifice. It was even whispered, that one of their relatives had given his soul up to the devil, in exchange for the family wealth."

"You might be surprised just how much of that might actually be true." Carrie glanced back at Scott as they pulled in before the cathedral and parked.

"This is the place--," Lawrence announced, "Christ Church Cathedral. But after all that's been said, I'm not waiting around here for the dark, I'm coming with you, and might I also suggest that you wake and bring the girl."

"I was going to ask you to come along anyway." Carrie gently patted the old fellow's shoulder, "I would dream of taking the risk of seeing anything happen to you."

As Scott awakened Maya, Carrie had hurriedly climbed out of the cab and looked over at the church. Located from just off the main street and resting upon gated and well-kept grounds, it stood as an archaic work of architectural genius and great beauty. Consisting of two immense Gothic structures on either side of the street, they were connected by a beautiful stone bridge. With its ornate stone-work, pointed peaks and main tower, it stood majestically against the pink and greying clouds of the horizon.

Directly from off the sidewalk there was a series of wide stone steps. Carrie and the others had wasted no time in ascending these, and hurriedly entered into the tall archway of the cathedrals main doors. The light was already fading in the heavens from behind them as the cerulean hues now cast long and reaching shadows upon the buildings. The sun was quickly setting, as just for a moment, it had peeked out from behind the dense clouds.

There had been a moment as they entered the cathedral that they had all paused, stepping back in awe. From the beautiful brown mosaics and red-cushioned benches of the aisle floor, they gazed upward past the enormous arches on either side, to the ornate buttresses of the ceilings high above. The failing light cast golden, pink and orange hues through the enormous stained-glass windows that stood above and below and upon on either side. There was an overwhelming and humbling sense of majesty that thrilled and inspired all who now stood gazing into the fading light.

"Welcome, I'm father Donoghue--," A tall, middle-aged man had approached them from out of an adjoining corridor and from beyond the arches to the right, "Are you the people that the Mother Superior sent?"

"I'm Carrie Dayment--," She introduced the group while accepting the father's hand, "Yes we are—we're desperately in need of your help and really appreciate your time."

He was lean with dark hair and deep brown eyes that revealed a gentle disposition, but disciplined lifestyle. His hand was soft, but grip firm as he looked into her eyes, and nodding knowingly, said, "I've already located the documents that you wanted to see--," He waved a hand in gesture and hurriedly led the way, "I've put them out in the library—if you'll please just follow me."

They had quickly followed him down the aisle toward the altar and made a sharp left through a doorway and into a large room. They passed through this one quickly and through another door leading into what was obviously the library. The room was lined on either side with shelves and bookcases stood symmetrically the length of the room, while the center was occupied by a series of long tables with lamps.

"The material that you requested is here--," Father Donoghue led them to a central table, and switched on extra lamps, "Please feel free to take all the time that you need."

"My cab--" Lawrence remembered, slapping a hand to his brow, "I've left it parked out front."

"I would be glad to move it to the rear parking lot of the building for you—if you'd like?" The father smiled sincerely and Lawrence happily handed him the keys.

"Thank you kindly, father—I really wasn't relishing the thought of going back out there, just yet."

"So, what do we have here?" Scott and Maya took seats on either side of Carrie as she carefully opened the books and found the page markers that the priest had left.

"It's the birth and death records of the McCreary family--," Carrie ran a finger down the length of the family tree, "Not that this'll likely help us that much—it's missing any documents relating to relatives after 1893."

"What's that--," Scott had noticed an old, gold-framed painting on one of the library walls, "Isn't that the picture that Mother Superior mentioned seeing?"

They had moved as a group, and standing before the large and antique oil painting, quietly stared at the images of the group gathered there. It was a depiction of Dublin Bay with the old ships returning from sea, and happy onlookers upon the docks. Among those who had been gathered there were an old woman, and a fair skinned, red haired girl...

"If I didn't know better--," Scott muttered while glancing between Maya and Carrie, "I'd almost swear that was Caitlin and Eva."

"You mean Catherine and Eva--," Father Donoghue returned with the car keys, and handing them to Lawrence, paused to admire the painting, "They went with the last of the McCreary family when they left the shipping industry and departed Dublin Bay."

"When was this painted?" Maya looked closer at the little brass plaque before staring in astonishment, "It says 1883."

"It couldn't be them--," Scott nervously tugged at his beard, "That would've made Eva over one hundred and forty years old."

"I'm certain that they would have long passed into the good grace of the Lord." Father Donoghue sighed, "Ireland has a long line of fine folks by the name of McCreary, but none that were ever likened to that unfortunate lot."

"I've heard that they were notorious on the docks of Dublin--," Carrie peered over at the priest, and tilting her head thoughtfully, said, "Do you know much about their family history?"

"There are records of accidents, several unexplained deaths--," The father shuddered at the thought, "And people that just seemed to vanish into thin air. Unfortunately, most were impossible to investigate because these things happened either at sea, or to wandering sorts, sailors are a rather private lot, to say the least."

"Have you ever heard mention of the family participating, or being involved in extracurricular activities that would've been frowned upon by the church?" Scott caught the father's attention almost immediately with the comment, and the priest appeared suddenly distraught. At first he had said nothing, but simply looked around the room as though having become lost in another thought. The answer had come with some reluctance, and as father Donoghue solely addressed Carrie, "From what little I have gathered from previous parish records, in the beginning they were goodly and God-fearing people, but there were rumors, and mind you, they were never substantiated by the church. But the people of Dublin often spoke of them in whispers, and told tales of demons and witchcraft."

"So, they didn't leave here just to find a new home." Scott scratched at his cheek, "They were running away from their reputation, which would've ruined their business here anyway."

"I'm afraid that some might have suspected that they were running from far more than that." The priest turned and opening one of the larger and leather-bound volumes upon the table, pointed to an illustration, and said, "You might be interested in this paragraph and the illustration as well."

The image was a fourteenth century woodcut depicting a female demon seducing a falling man. A moment later, Carrie realized while reading, that the paragraph that father Donoghue had directed them to concerning night demons referred to as the Incubus or Succubi.

"Can I ask why you'd direct us to folklore when discussing the McCreary family?"

"Because all things of dreams and legends stem from origins in reality…" He seated himself upon the edge of the table, and thoughtfully looked up at the gathering of friends, "As a priest and believing in God—I also have to accept the existence of the devil. In all truth, and from what I do know of the McCreary family, if ever one existed in league with evil, it was most certainly them. Now, can I ask why you are all so interested in this family, and what possible connection you might have to them?"

"Father--," Carrie stared as her expression became pale and utterly blank, "Whatever evil or devil the McCreary family may have brought into our world—is now hunting us and our associates… We came here to find two missing friends, Caitlin McCreary and her lady servant, Eva, which is what finally brought us all here and to you…"

"And you are associates of Michael Schreiber and the organization known as Nightrealm." Father Donoghue clasped his hands together while scrutinizing them all with a sharp eye, "The church has been aware of your activities—and have been for quite some time. After I spoke with Mother Superior, I made some inquiries and received a return call within minutes, and from the highest order. How can I be of assistance to you, my friends?"

Hope, British Columbia, Canada.
5:25 p.m.
It had been fortunate that Danny had noticed that the fuel tank had been virtually empty, and prompted Tim to pull over long enough to get gas. The weather had not improved and as it grew dark, the snow came even harder.

"Are you sure about this?" Tim had climbed back into the car at the Husky service station, and offered Danny a cup of hot cocoa, "There's no shame in waiting here—just until I get back."

Danny had glanced over to where an old diner had once rested beside the service station, and swallowed hard while looking into the empty lot. The moment has passed as quickly as the thought, as shaking his head, he turned to Tim, and said, "I'm not staying here alone—and it wouldn't feel right to let you go off like that either. Let's get out of here."

Tim had never desired children in his life, but in that moment, had felt both sad and proud of Danny. Never before had he met anyone so determined, reckless, and defiant against all odds. With exception to Michael, the person of whom Danny so remarkably resembled more with each passing year. Tim had imagined that Danny's father may have shared many of the same qualities as well. The sandy curls, bright blue eyes, broad shoulders and slightly rough but friendly disposition. He felt horribly guilty for having permitted the lad to come along, but would have felt even worse just leaving him behind. There would be no guessing as to what horror might be awaiting the boy when night came, or what now awaited them both on the road ahead.

A snow plow startled them both as they approached the highway entrance and it suddenly roared passed! Tim had just watched as it cast massive rooster tails of snow upon either side, as it vanished up the highway and into the storm. Never before had he experienced such a strong impulse to just turn back and make for the safety of the estate as fast as possible. Was it just paranoia, and just some lingering fear? Or had something from deep inside, some primal instinct, now warned him that they were being hunted...

"Last chance, amigo." He peered over at the lad, "It's not too late to turn back."

"I'm scared shitless too--," Danny had looked to him with wide eyes, "But, it's like you said back at the house—this might make a world of a difference for them and all of us..."

Tim slowly pulled out onto the highway and accelerated through the deepening snow. The flurries had quickly filled in the plows tracks, as the Eldorado's tail lights disappeared into the swiftly coming night...

Vancouver, British Columbia, Canada.
3:15 p.m.
Deb had answered the phone before it had even reached the second ring. She and Jen had been preparing for an early dinner, while Ray read quietly in the breakfast nook.

"Carrie—it's good to hear your voice!" She gasped, "What's happening and where are you?"

"We're all at Church Christ cathedral in Dublin--," She replied, "Father Donoghue is putting us up for the night—it's too late to leave, and this is likely the safest place."

"Have you found Caitlin or Eva yet? And are there any plans as to when you're going to come back?"

"Listen--," Carrie swallowed hard, her hand trembling as she held the phone in the priests office, "We didn't find Caitlin and Eva, well, not in the sense of the term. And to be totally honest, I really don't think that we ever will."

"Oh no--," Deb had feared something like this, and turned to look at Ray and Jen as she said, "What did you find out?"

"There never was a funeral for Eva, not anywhere in Killkenny. And they were never at St. Francis where they lured poor Maya. The Mother Superior sent us to Christ Church to see father Donoghue—he showed us some old historical documents on the family, and told us a story about them. Deb—Caitlin and Eva were never real—they were some kind of creation like Amica, and made out of energy to begin with."

"So all of our suspicions were right--," Deb threw a hand before her eyes, "This is all just too horrible to even believe...."

"Is there any way that you can get a message to Michael and the others?" Carrie was desperate and grasping at straws.

"Tim and Danny already went after them--," Deb snapped her fingers, her heart sinking as she saw the flurries beyond the window, "They're going to try to reach them before it's too late."

"Why the hell did you let Danny go with him?" Carrie gasped, "He's only a kid!"

"It was his choice--," Deb had remained calm, although she too had initially disagreed, saying, "He wanted to be with Michael—and said that he was all that he had left. We couldn't just stop him—oh Carrie, please understand."

"I do--," The reply came quietly, but in sincerest regard, "I guess that I would've felt the same way if I'd been him—or been there..."

"What now—what are you going to do?"

"We've got Maya with us—she's safe." Carrie thought briefly, and then said, "We've done everything that we could here—and there's really nothing left to do. We'll catch a flight out of Dublin first thing tomorrow—and make our way home."

"Please be careful—this thing isn't even close to over yet."

"I know it—but we have to try to keep our wits about us—or things will get a whole lot worse."

"Call us when you make flight plans--," Deb wiped the tears from her eyes, "Let me know when you'll be arriving in Vancouver, and I'll make sure to be there to pick you all up."

"You just sit tight and wait for calls—we need open communications through this thing," Carrie insisted, "I'll keep you posted, and we can catch a cab back to the building."

"Um—Carrie--," Deb had forgotten to inform them of the recent situation, "The building, the warehouse and the business are all gone. We lost everything to a fire—along with Dennis, Tanya, and Gordon... I'm so sorry that I didn't tell you sooner, but I just couldn't."

Without the words to even express her grief, Carrie could only reply in a cry of utter despair, "Oh no—no, no no...."

"When you return--," Deb had trouble with the words while sharing Carrie's grief, "The last safe place that we have left now is Sanctum Arcanum..."

Scott had moved closer and gently embraced his wife as the others quietly watched. Removing her glasses and tossing them down upon the father's desk, she mournfully rubbed at her eyes, "Deb--," She sniffed while struggling with the words, "Don't any of you leave the estate, or go anywhere for any reason until we're back."

"But, what if--," Deb had intended to speak but was immediately cut off.

"Not for any reason--," Carrie demanded between tears, "Do you understand?"

"I promise--," She agreed, "We won't set foot outside of this place, no matter what."

"I love you guys--," Carrie sniffled, a dark determination filling her soul, "When we get back, we'll sort this out together, till then…"

"We love you too--," Deb gasped, "Till then…"

Ray slid across the seat and took hold of his wife, "Honey, what's happened, are you okay?"

"Caitlin and Eva weren't human--," She stared in utter disbelief, "They were homunculi and unnatural things, just like that Amica…"

"So we were right." Jen dropped the soup spoon into the pot, and leaning a hip against the stove for support, covered her mouth with a hand, as she said, "All that we can do now is pray that Tim and Danny reach Michael and the others in time…"

How is this even possible?" Ray stood in a state of suspension of disbelief, "Michael and Caitlin have been together for years. Eva has cooked meals for all of us, and we've shared holiday and birthdays for years." He shook his head and looked to Deb, asking, "Wasn't Caitlin even pregnant once?"

"We don't really know what was real or just lies and illusions--," Deb shrugged, "Keep in mind that just because they have physical form, it doesn't mean that they don't still have the ability to cloud our minds, and fool us into believing things that might never even have happened."

"This is going to destroy Michael--," Jen fought back the tears while looking between her companions, "She was his whole life…"

"Well, he has us now--," Deb growled, and looking defiantly between Jen and Ray, slammed a hand down upon the table, "So if that bitch thinks that she's going to take us down that easily, she has another thing coming."

"I just wish that there was something that we could do--," Ray cursed, "I feel so damn helpless and useless just sitting around here."

"But we aren't helpless or useless—don't you see?" Jen spoke with determination as tears of frustration filled her eyes, "We're the last line of communication between everyone—and the lighthouse keepers on the edge of hell…"

Deb and Ray hugged Jen close, huddling as the lights flickered, the storm raged, and shadows gathered about the gates of Sanctum Arcanum.

British Columbia, Canada.
The House of McCreary
6:24 p.m.

The flurries had soon become a blizzard, and as we drove the Suburban down the old cobblestone path, I wondered if we would even make it much further. Both Rich and I had known that it would only take us as far as the path leading to the pond, and that we would have to walk the rest of the way. Regrettably, this would most certainly leave us all stranded at the mausoleums after dark, and at the mercy of the storm. With the light fading fast and snow growing deeper by the moment, I shuddered within the glimmer of a faint hope.

"Don't you think that was just a little too easy?" Raymond leaned forward from the back seat and looked between us, "I mean—that thing didn't even try to stop us when we burned the place?"

"I sensed only the wandering souls of those who are lost in the vaults--," Amica agreed, "There was no other presence in the tombs or house…"

"Maybe it isn't here—could we have been wrong?" Jay's comment had been almost inaudible from where he sat beside Raymond. I had my own suspicions and doubts, but refrained from sharing them for fear of only worsening matters.

"Beware Michael—for the demon desires the stone," Marlowe whispered from somewhere out of the storm, "As once removed from its place of concealment—it becomes vulnerable to anyone or anything…"

"Amica's evil also desires it--," I glanced over at her while replying in thought, "And expects to claim it when all of this is done…"

"Not all that seem evil are your enemies--," Marlowe repeated the phrase, "And not all that appear as loved ones truly are…trust in your heart Michael—and stay true to yourself, or all is lost…"

"What exactly do you mean by—loved ones?" His words had caught me off guard, but he had fallen silent, and was seemingly gone. This had roused an immediate suspicion of Amica, but as I glanced over at her, she had smiled sweetly. There was an innocence that shone from those loving and trusting eyes. As, no matter how wild that green fire may have once been, I could not help but completely trust her. It was so hard to imagine that just beneath that beautiful and pale façade, a demon silently watched and waited…

"I don't know how much further the Suburban will take us--," Rich cursed as we ascended to the crest and struggled to continue, "Four wheel drive is great until you run out of road."

"That's the path that leads over the hill, and then to the pond where little Henry drowned--," I pointed out through the windshield, and into the swiftly fading light, "The mausoleums aren't far from here. We should be able to make it before dark, if we hurry."

We had hurried out of the Suburban and quickly grabbed weapons and gear. I had nervously and hurriedly shoved the box containing the devil stone inside of my jacket, pulling it tightly closed. Amica had glanced over in that moment and I thought to have caught a glint of ethereal blue burning from deep within her eyes. It had just been a flash, but enough for me to realize that something else now watched my every movement.

"Hurry—the storm's getting worse!" Rich led the way, as taking Amica by the hand, I had hurried after him. Jay and Raymond held lanterns, as holding their weapons in their free hands, were following closely from behind. It was almost impossible to see through the blizzard, and as the world slipped into the twilight of dusk, the cold and wind fought us every step of the way. We had clambered up the steep slope, slipping and sliding as we scrambled on hands and knees.

Ascending the ridge, we had made our way through the dense and snow-covered brush, gasping while finally reaching the top. Stumbling from out of the deep forest, we hurriedly made our way out and into the clearing. It would be ludicrous to say that I had felt any sense of relief with the sight of the place, because it still terrified me. Not so much in respect to the nearing of the mausoleums, but that gnarled and ghastly old Willow that still stood at the ponds edge. I remembered when I had tripped for some unexplained reason, and fallen into that foul and murky pond. I had almost become its next victim, as while tangled in the massive roots and blindly struggling, had narrowly escaped. The memory of that moment, and the lonesome death of poor little Henry now chilled my soul as we hurried along.

"I hate that damn thing too--," Glaring back at me as though having read my thoughts, Rich pointed a threatening finger at the tree, shouting, "And when we come back—I'm going to burn you down too!"

The world seemed to suddenly swim in a dizzying haze. Every movement and effort slowing as though time has slipped backward from all around us, and we now walked in space. As traveling through that terrifying moment that had seemingly taken forever, everything had halted as we had all stopped and just stared back. The storm had ceased from all about us, and the only sound to be heard was the crunching of the hard-packed snow beneath our boots.

"What just happened?" Raymond gasped, "Was that my imagination—or did everyone feel that?"

"Something just passed from out of one dimension and into another--," Amica's eyes became huge, "Something is coming…"

"Oh God--," Slowly turning and looking back toward the old Willow, Rich whispered, "Please tell me that this isn't really happening…"

It was almost as though something deep within the decaying soul of that horrible old tree had heard him, and to our horror, those enormous roots suddenly came to life! There was a roaring boom and the cracking sound of ancient wood bending, creaking and snapping, echoing like thunder as the thing moved. The limbs flailed and whipped like the tentacles of an enormous squid, as those mighty and ancient roots lifted the bulk from out of the pond, while showering us in frozen mud and decaying filth. The ground shook beneath us as it hauled its massive bulk across the cracking and crumbling cobblestone path, the slimy, immense and massive roots working altogether as it slithered and crawled after us!

"Shoot it—for the love of God—shoot it!" Rich cried out while firing blindly, his first arrow finding the base of one of the larger roots and exploding in a blinding flash! Raymond followed by example, aiming for the crawling thing as they now attempted to disable the massive and rotting hulk. Jay and I fired, our arrows striking the trunk neat the lowest part of the base. The flames now raged, smoke billowed, and the monster turned and cast itself back into the pond! There was an explosion of water, hissing flames, and foul smoke that now suffocated, and blinded us as we fell backward. As to our utmost horror, the nightmare had managed to smother the chemical fire, and the charred and smoldering thing now climbed back out again! Without having had time to reload our weapons, we were utterly helpless before the fiend.

"Everyone—run for the mausoleums--," I waved and shouted, "It's our only hope!"

"There's no way that water could have put that fire out!" Rich wailed as we now desperately raced through the deep snow.

"The darkness has possessed this form--," Amica screamed out, "But no fire or earthly weapon has hope of slowing, much less destroying such a thing!!"

The ground shook beneath us as we were deafened by the monsters approach. It moved almost effortlessly across the deep snow, a smoking and smoldering, charred horror that now swiftly came up from behind.

"It will not follow you upon hallowed ground so long as you possess the stone!" She shouted at me, "It knows the consequences of breaching the boundaries—run—it's your only hope!"

In that moment, she had stopped dead in her tracks, and standing alone, turned to face the fiend.

"No, don't--," I cried out, "You can't beat this thing!"

But it was too late, the horror was upon her! Grabbing at my collar, Rich had pulled me close, "We need to go—right now, or none of us are going to make it!"

In that instant I had looked back in time to see Amica, as with blackened wings unfolding, she flew upon the fiend with a howling and unearthly rage!

"Oh Jesus Christ--," Jay cried out--," What the hell is that?"

"Don't concern yourself--," Raymond shouted while dragging him along, "It's on our side—for the moment at least—run!"

We raced through the deep snow, choking on the bitter cold air as we fought for each and every breath! I could see the iron gates to the mausoleums in the distance, and from just between the tall pines. There hadn't even been time to look back. The shrieking wind numbed our senses, bit into our flesh, and we fought onward with every ounce of courage and strength that we could find. Ever onward we surged, struggling, stumbling as we grew closer to those black iron gates. I could feel my heart thundering within my breast, the blood racing like fire through each and every pulsing vein and pounding artery. And then, when I thought that I couldn't possibly manage another moment longer, Rich had cried out as we reached the gates.

"Go—keep going--," He pushed me ahead of the group, "It's just a little further!"

Almost tripping as we passed through and into the immense snow covered gardens, I had fallen against a large marble planter while struggling for support.

"Are you alright?" Rich had placed a hand upon my face and looked fearfully into my eyes, "It isn't your heart—is it?"

"No—I'm just winded—just give me a moment."

"We don't have a moment--," Still gasping from the effort himself, Raymond took hold of my left side, and nodding at Rich, said, "Give me a hand—we need to get him over to the mausoleums!"

They had attempted to half carry and drag me along, but I had resisted, saying, "I'll be okay to walk—really, I can make it just fine."

They had released me with some reluctance, forming a protective ring around me, as we stumbled in a tight group across the memorial gardens. The memory of having first seen that vile tomb had flashed vividly through my mind. There was a sudden guilt and insufferable remorse as I realized the full extent of the evil that I had unwittingly released from that place. The angels no longer stood guard in their protective pentacle, and the evils of the Duff Glenn were now the incarnation of Sanctum Arcanum. What had I done? I hadn't closed this evil chapter of the McCreary clan, but rather, brought its reincarnation to my own estate, and invited the devil home...

"What now?" Raymond spun in question, and I pointed to where I had once faced the demon Amelia, and said, "That's where the portal opened the last time. It might be our only chance!"

Without another word, we scrambled toward the largest and most central of the three. Not long ago it had once housed the corpse of the unfortunate Amelia. As brought down in her prime by a father suffering the evils of alcohol and jealousy, she was consigned to a demon by that same grieving and murderous hand.

Rich and I knew this place all too well, it had become a reoccurring nightmare for both of us, and one that I hoped and prayed would soon end. We had stumbled almost blindly to the far wall and to where I remembered the void to have first appeared. Then quickly removing the box from within my jacket, I hesitated while looking into the terrified faces of my friends. My hands were trembling uncontrollably and I could hardly feel the flesh of my face or fingers.

"Let's light this place up, boys!" Rich wailed as he fired an arrow against the far wall to provide some semblance of light, "It's almost dark—and this is likely going to be our last stand!"

Raymond and Jay had reacted without as much as a second thought. They fired arrows in a wide circle before us, creating an arc of flames that cast long shadows that danced demonically upon the pale marble walls.

"If you're going to do something--," Rich cried out while reloading his weapon, "It's now or never!"

Carefully opening the box, I reluctantly reached inside and gently plucked out the large and black stone. It felt frozen to the touch and smoother than glass. At first it seemed the same as any other, but then being upon sanctified ground, something completely unexpected now happened. There was a strange and ethereal fire burning from the blackness within. It shone like an ember that slowly grew brighter, but never became warmer in my hands.

In the distance the dismal heavens shone above the inferno that had once been the McCreary house. As within that abysmal glow, we heard distant thunder and suddenly saw the monstrous Willow approach!

"Oh Jesus—there it is, and it's got Caitlin--," Raymond pointed, "Or whatever the hell she's become?"

The Willow now appeared enormous, as branches became multiple arms and tendrils flailed from out of its back. From beneath, the massive roots still carried its bulk, and entwined within one of those long tendrils, it held the demon that was Amica. I could see that the ethereal flame still burned from about her horns and flowing mane. Her flesh still shone pale in the twilight of dusk, as her blackened arms and legs lolled from side to side as she was dragged from behind and through the deep snow. She was alive, or at least still existing in whatever semblance of energy that sustained such things might be called.

"You must force it to release her--," Marlowe insisted from out of the darkness of my soul, "For even now it drains the life force from out of her—and shall release the demon within her demise…"

Looking upon the horrendous fiend, I desperately sought some possible weakness, looking for an opportunity to strike a blow against the thing. Its head was a mass of gnarled and thrashing branches, and its gaping mouth was the rotting and darkened hollow of the old tree. There had to be something, somehow, some way to even distract it long enough to set her free!

"Oh God in heaven, have mercy!" Jay gaped in sheer horror as it lumbered toward us, "What do we do now? There's no place left to run— and no place to hide?"

"We force it to break the sacrament--," Realizing there was no other way, I held the stone above my head and turned toward the thing, "And when it comes onto hallowed ground—the dimensional border will be breached!"

The stone felt as though it was growing even colder, as if radiating like a beacon in the growing darkness. It was a pale blue fire that, burning brighter and ever brighter, almost blinded me! Yet the monster still swaying, it stood in silence while hesitating, and watching from before the mausoleum gates.

"What happening--," Rich cried out in dismay, "I thought that the stone had the power to summon and force the evil into itself!"

"I don't know?" Shouting through the rising winds, I stood within the protective circle of friends, saying, "But something has stopped it at the gates—and we all know that once protected inside a physical shell, it could've easily entered into this place!"

"Then why isn't it moving?" Tightly gripping his crossbow, Jay's features were wild and almost unearthly among the dancing flames, "And what's it going to take to piss the damn thing off enough to come and try getting us?" Aiming his crossbow high, he let fly an arrow that shot through the darkness and impacted the ground near the mausoleum gates. The explosion cast a fiery light upon the swaying nightmare that, standing silently, remained distanced from the hallowed boundaries while observing us.

"What's it waiting for?" Panicking, Raymond's eyes became huge, "It's got us trapped—there's no way out of here except past that damn thing."

"It's draining the life from out of Amica--," I had explained while staring at her limp form in the thing's grasp, saying, "And with her physical death, it will release the demon that's inside of her—and use it against us..."

"Michael—there's something else that we never thought about--," Rich spoke in an almost sinister tone, "Maybe the stone only works on raw energy--," He turned fearfully back to me, "And can't touch that thing while it's still manifested in physical form..."

"I thought that you sent the last thing back through a portal here--," Jay spun fearfully, "Are you telling me that we've just trapped ourselves out here, in the middle of freezing, fucking nowhere—with that?"

"When Michael faced the demon Amelia here--," Rich trembled uncontrollably as he spoke, "She'd already left her physical body—and was then sucked into the void!"

"And the reason that the demon in Amica wasn't affected by the stone--," It had finally occurred to me, and I said, "Is because of her physical form—it was shielded by her body—even from the stone..."

"So, if it didn't have any effect on Amica—," Raymond almost choked, stuttering upon his own words, "Then why would it have any power over the darkness in that thing?"

"Michael—," Rich slowly backed against the mausoleum wall, "We didn't have any idea of how this was supposed to work—or the time and opportunity to test the theory... Oh dear God—we may all be truly, and finally, totally screwed..." His face had become deathly pale as he shivered in the frozen wind, and we all became utterly still.

"So, what you're saying is that we're caught in a Mexican stand-off--," Raymond gasped, "And that thing has all the time in the world to wait..."

"Once Amica dies--," I swallowed back the fear and emotions, "The demon within her will breach the barrier trying to get to us—and be drawn into the portal when it opens."

"Oh my God--," Raymond finally realized the subsequence threat, "And it'll take as many of us with it as it can…"

"So all that thing has to do now is just wait." Rich agreed, "And the rest will happen as a consequence of us making this mistake…"

"Marlowe—if you are still with us--," I pleaded in a loud and clear voice, "I beg of you—please don't leave us to the darkness in our greatest moment of need…"

The wind howled, the monster stood waiting in the darkness, and not a single movement or sound was to be seen or heard. Yet, still I stood there with the stone held before me, silently praying for diving intervention of some kind.

"Why do you beckon to me in such a manner--," Marlowe replied while his voice echoed from the depths of my soul, "When I have ever left you…" A sudden and brilliant fire of courage now grew from within my soul, as raising the stone higher, I shouted into the night and before the monster, "Foul wretch that crawls in the bowels of the earth, and hides in the filth among shadows! Come forth and face thy foe—or be damned, and return forever into the darkness!"

The wind howled and the fires about us flashed and grew, the lumbering giant bellowing, as infuriated and echoing madness, it now thrashed and raged beyond the gates!

"Vile worm and unfaithful vermin that grovels in fear before the gates--," Crying out in a loud and clear voice, Marlowe spoke through me as I became the vessel of his wrath, "Bow down and tremble, I command thee, kneel before thy master!"

 The stone now shone like a beacon, its blue flame engulfing all and touching the horror that stood beyond.

"Give it everything that we've got left!" Raymond fired his bow as the others fell in beside him and let less loose a rain of hell-fire. Their bolts flew straight and as though guided and compelled by some greater force, exploded upon impacting upon the nightmares massive trunk!

This had only served to have further enraged the fiend, as suddenly becoming careless of all other things, it crashed through the mausoleum gates in a blind rage. I saw the demon that was Amica drop from its grasp, as helplessly falling, she crashed and crumpled into a heap upon the frozen earth.

And then it happened: The horrendous tree appeared to falter, stiffen, crumble and explode into a darkened storm that, dissipating, was scattered into the bitter cold wind!

"It's realized our trick--," Rich wailed, "The demon's backed off—it's up to something else!"

"It almost had us?" Raymond barked, "Why would it just give up?"

"It didn't give up--," I glanced suspiciously back at my friends, "It must have realized that it couldn't maintain that form for much longer. It's just changing strategy—it's still here, somewhere. I can feel it…"

"Oh, dear God--," A voice called out from behind us and we all turned. I stood and stared in utter disbelief, as dressed very warmly, Eva had appeared in the open doorway to the mausoleum, "We've finally found you!"

"Eva?" Rich almost stumbled as he moved toward her, and then halted, "Can it possibly—is it really, is that seriously you?"

"We've been hiding here--," She explained, "It was the only truly safe place, you see."

"Don't fall for it--," Jay growled in warning, "There's no way that anyone could've possibly been staying out in this cold, much less living in there."

The dismal entrance to the tomb behind Eva appeared even darker and colder than I had ever remembered. There was a strange sense of foreboding, an impression that now causing my senses to burn, screamed out within warning.

"Michael—is that you?" Caitlin appeared from out of the tomb with a lantern in one hand, and moving out of the shadows, paused to stand next to Eva. She was dressed in a green Parka with a fur-collared hood, but from within the dark opening, I could clearly see my beloved's beautiful, emerald eyes.

"Caitlin—but this can't be--," I struggled with the sight and emotions of those whom I was assuming to have seen, "It's not possible for either of you to really be here."

"What are you talking about?" Caitlin gasped, desperately attempting to reason with everyone, "We had no other place to go! There are tunnels—secret places that run beneath the mausoleums and back to the house. We were staying in the house until you burned it down, and we were forced to make our way out here—to find you." When she looked to me with those large and tearful eyes I had truly wanted to believe her, but fear and doubt kept holding me back.

"Don't come any closer--," Jay had readied his bow, and shooting a glance back at me, said, "Brother, you'd better get your head on straight. I don't know what you're thinking—but for crying out loud—these two just aren't right, and you know it."

Raymond had lowered his weapon and directed the arrow at Eva, but Rich had swiftly halted him, shrieking, "But what if we're wrong—and this is really them?" His eyes fell upon me, "Are you willing to take the chance of killing Eva, and murdering your own wife?"

"Michael—for God's sake--," Eva had begged, "Have you completely gone out of your mind?"

Gazing mournfully upon the two women, I struggled with fear and doubt. They shivered and appeared terrified while desperately attempting to resist the cold of the swelling storm. All of my instincts insisted that this might possibly be them, but something far deeper in my soul now warned of a possibly dire mistake...

"Stand away from them." Amica called from behind us, and we spun to gaze upon the pale woman. She was neither human nor completely demon, but a hideous union of both. With blackened bat-wings folded at her sides like some ghastly cloak, she pointed a long and clawed finger to Eva and Caitlin as she spoke, "The darkness seeks to betray you--," She turned her fiery blue gaze upon me, "It conceals and shelters itself within the living decay of this place..."

"What is that thing?" Caitlin shrieked while tightly clinging to the now terrified Eva, "And what's it talking about? Why is it trying to come between us?"

"But how could it possibly enter onto sanctified ground to even get into the bodies?" Rich began panicking, as his once secure grasp of reality now obviously failed, "It couldn't have trespassed onto hallowed ground in its energy form, or the stone would've drawn it into a void." He turned to look between Caitlin and Eva and then back at me, "Right?"

"You desecrated the sanctity of this place when you removed the keepers of the pentagram--," Amica pointed to Rich, "And now the evil has come for you all..."

Turning and looking back toward her, vivid visions of Caitlin danced like love's ghosts before my eyes. A life spent together, blissful moments, and loving memories. How could that have all just been an illusion? Utterly lost in that moment, I had searched my soul, pleading for Marlowe's guidance but found only darkness there.

"Will you all just come to your senses—look at that beast—that's the true evil here!" Eva had shouted as she hugged Caitlin closer, and looking angrily among us, said, "We can stand out here freezing to death all night—or be done with that devil and this place, forever..."

Rich had slowly lowered his crossbow and turned toward Amica, who had just stared. I could see from the desperation in his wide eyes that he intended to make a short end to things. Before I had even had the opportunity to move, Raymond had pulled the weapon from Rich's hands! "What are you doing--," He gasped, "Have you completely lost all common sense?"

"They do not truly live--," Amica warned, "But are only vessels that have remained in this place until required by the darkness..."

"If this isn't hallowed ground anymore--," Rich stuttered, shivering in the icy wind as he spoke, "Then we're all sitting ducks out here." His eyes bulged from behind the fogging lenses of his glasses, "So, what's stopping it from taking us all—right now..."

We had all stood there as though frozen in time. The flames danced, the wind howled, and no matter how hard I fought back the emotions, it was just simply impossible to decide. In that moment I had caught a faint shadow that had passed through Eva's once brilliant and bright blue eyes. There was a dark suspicion, a strange tingling tension that left me paralyzed where I stood. As like a cat, she had hunched as though about to pounce, and focusing intently upon me, her eyes became utterly soulless and black. There wasn't even time to react as shrieking hatefully, she launched herself with such force that she bowled me over with the attempt.

Her features twisted hideously and became grotesquely swollen, her entire body erupting as tendrils exploded from throughout the gruesome flesh, and she became an enormous and lumbering thing! I had heard the panicked screams of my friends, as fighting back desperately, I was swiftly overwhelmed.

"I can't get a clear shot--," Jay cried out while aiming his bow, "They're moving around too fast!"

"Get off of him!" Raymond leapt onto the horror that had once been Eva, and ripping her away, tumbled backward with the hideous fiend.

In the confusion, I felt a claw tightly grasping onto my left arm, as Amica pulled me out of the way. The effort had proven far greater than expected, as in the panic, she had sent me stumbling down the mausoleum stairs.

Having fallen, the stone had slipped free of my grasp and dropped into the snow just out of reach. In terror I had looked up as the demon within Amica had looked down and seen the stone lying at the foot of the steps! There had been a blue glimmer of greed in her emerald eyes, but then she had looked back. A sudden and terrifying expression having crossed the monsters face, she suddenly leapt forward and fell upon me!

I felt powerful wings closing from all about me as something crashed heavily against us, and she shielded me from whatever attacked. A moment later, the wings had parted to reveal the beastly thing that Eva had become, as it crawled up from where it had fallen away. Then, to my utter shock and terror, Amica had stooped down, and snatching the stone from the snow, offered it back to me. We had exchanged glances of desperation and struggles that waged from within souls that now fought for control! As grabbing it from out of her claw, and swiftly placing it into the box, I safely concealed them in my coat

"Hold on, Raymond—I'm coming!" Jay shouted as while attempting to aim at the horror that, lashing out, now cast him against the mausoleum wall. Stunned, he dropped the weapon while sliding helplessly to the cold, stone floor. It had all happened in the blink of an eye, and before anyone could have reacted, but the gruesome monster had fallen upon Raymond once more.

I had attempted to break free and rush to his assistance, but Amica had swiftly drawn me back. As folding a single wing closely about me, she left me standing in her dark embrace, while staring helplessly at my fallen friend.

"Die—why won't you just die?" Rich bellowed as the monster swung around to the sound of his voice, and he fired a bolt into its chest! Raymond had rolled away in the last moment as the horror exploded, erupting in a blinding white flash!

Having recovered, Jay had ripped Rich backward, saving him as the hideous and long tendrils had lashed out while attempting to snare him. Together, they had rolled away as the flailing, blazing nightmare now quickly followed in pursuit.

Rich and Jay had narrowly escaped, as while tumbling behind one of the mausoleum pillars, the monster crashed against it in a shower of molten ash. They had scrambled desperately around the second pillar and almost made the second building when it was upon them again! Unable to escape, and looking to where I stood, I witnessed their horrific ending to come.

But in that last moment and as all hope had faded, Raymond appeared from behind the horrendous fiend!

"Run—get out of here!" He cried out, as finding the strength, he ripped the remaining bolts and bombs from his belt. As he did this, the terror had turned upon him, and I saw the reflection of courage and desperation in his wide eyes, as he wailed, "Run!"

We had all turned and raced down the stone steps as Raymond smashed the explosives against the marble wall behind! When the crystalline shards and powder residue came into contact with that snow, it erupted in a blinding, white flash!

The thing that had been Eva had shrieked. It was an inhuman howling that echoed into a deafening and mind-numbing screech that faded into the frozen wind!

I had spun in time to see Caitlin, silently standing in the dark mouth of the mausoleum, as she glared back at me. Her eyes narrowing hatefully, a green fire shining as fading into the shadows, she hissed, "I will see an ending to you all—and you shall burn…"

Spreading her arms wide, a storm built from behind her and lightning flashed from all around! The winds howled as her garments thrashed, and we all felt back before the wrath of the growing storm!

Helpless before Caitlin's power, Amica had sought to cover and protect me, as the others cringed before the mausoleums stairs.

"You burn in hell!" Jay leapt upward, and firing a bolt into her, leapt back as it exploded against the marble wall. All at once there came a shrieking, a howling that left us all cowering and covering our ears as we fell to the frozen ground!

In that moment of confusion, Rich had taken the opportunity and thrown one of his bombs at Caitlin. It burst into a wall of all-consuming flame that sent her flying back into the darkness beyond! From within, I could see the shadow among the flames, as a figure flailed as it burned, floundering down into the blackness beneath the stairs.

In a moment of sudden fury, Amica had stepped back, and with wings spread wide, poised her arms at the door. There was a flash as ice formed upon the mausoleum, marble cracked and the stone structures crumbled, collapsing down upon themselves! As the smoke and debris cleared, we could all see in the firelight that the entire place had been reduced to rubble.

"It is over in this place--," Amica shouted as she took a firm hold upon my arm, and motioning with a nod to the others, said, "The darkness has departed —and now seeks out those more vulnerable."

Gazing down to where Raymond's bones and the monster had been reduced to little more than ashen embers, I threw a hand in grief before my face.

"There is no time for mourning--," She insisted, "The time grows shorter for the others the longer that we linger here."

"I can't even see things clearly--," Rich had fallen against me, and covering his face with both hands, wept, "I don't even know what's real anymore…"

"The darkness casts shadow into the hearts and thoughts of men." Shuddering, she put a hand to her brow as her body began altering, the wings and fiery horns vanishing, as she became slightly more human, and stumbling forward, said, "It creates doubt and fear—and none are sound within its presence…"

"I don't know what you are—," Jay gawked at Amica, and panicking, said, "All that I do know is that I'm not planning to stick around here to see what happens next…"

An explosion suddenly erupted in the distance and we all spun to look upon it with wide eyes and gaping mouths. It appeared to have originated in the vicinity of the inferno that had once been the McCreary house.

"Oh no--," Rich climbed to his feet, and looking between Jay and myself, said, "I sure hope that wasn't what I think it was—because if it is—we're all seriously screwed…" We had all looked over to Amica as her body had altered again, her pale flesh glowing in the firelight as she finally returned to human form.

"You're going to freeze to death like that." Revealing a sudden compassion, Jay removed his coat and hung it about her naked shoulders, saying, "You might have been better off staying in that other body until we got somewhere warm…"

"We'll have to make do in any way we can," Assisting Amica, I looked between my friends and into the darkness beyond the mausoleum gates, "And we're moving targets out here."

"We're playing with forces beyond our ability or knowledge to deal with." Rich took Amica's other side as we carried lanterns in our free hands, "I had no idea of what I was doing when I removed those five stone angels. They were part of a pentagram that was guarding and keeping that thing trapped in this place."

"We were all at fault in our best intentions--," I peered over at Rich while we carried Amica along, "But our biggest mistake as of yet--," I shivered in the bitter cold, "Was my decision to bring you all out here on a guess…"

"It's not your fault--," Jay cursed as he followed closely from behind with a bow in each hand, "None of us knew how that stone really worked—or what it would take to do this right. We just have to keep trying until we get that thing—or it gets us…"

"Why hasn't it come after us--," Rich gasped as we staggered through the deep snow, "We're out in the open and have nowhere else to go?"

"When you destroyed its physical forms by fire--," Amica explained, "You left it without the means. It must now seek out another vessel of which to possess—or is nothing but energy in this world."

"That's the answer--," Rich coughed as he spat out the words, "We need to bring the thing onto sanctified grounds, then burn the bastard—and use the stone to hold it until the portal appears."

"I should have thought of that--," Stumbling over a fallen branch in the deep snow, we narrowly escaped a nasty tumble, "We need to lure it into a secluded area and to where we can defend ourselves. It has to be a sanctified place that's away from the public, and where no one else will be harmed."

"Are you talking about luring that thing into a cemetery?" Jay followed in our tracks while nervously surveying our dark surroundings.

"No--," Rich shivered as he peered back at Jay, "He's talking about inviting the devil into his house…"

"That didn't go so well for us the last time." Jay reminded us of the apartments, "And I get the impression that this thing isn't exactly stupid."

"It's instinctively crafty--," Rich peered into the darkness of the surrounding pines, "It's patient, and it's had forever to refine its methods."

"Marlowe told me that it reacts recklessly when provoked." Assisting Amica, as while struggling to hold the lantern, I said, "That's why I was speaking to it the way that I was at the mausoleums."

"So, I guessed right on that one--," Jay scoffed at the thought and shook his head, "You were trying to piss it off into making a mistake."

"And, if the grounds had still been hallowed--," Rich cursed at himself, "It might've worked."

"Save your breath and stop blaming yourself--," Trembling uncontrollably, I looked over at my friend, "And let's just focus on trying to get out of here alive…"

CHAPTER TWENTY

Revelstoke, British Columbia, Canada.

7:26 p.m.

The little Greyhound bus station had been quiet as Pam and Patrick had hurriedly followed Carrie's father to the ticket booth.

"Are you sure that this is a good idea?" Patrick had adjusted his backpack while looking between Pam and his grandfather.

"Well--," The old man sighed deeply and patted the youth on the head, "It's a lot safer than driving alone through the mountains—or sitting around at my place waiting for something else to happen."

"Maybe we should call--," Pam thoughtfully put a finger to her lip, and scanning the room for a pay-phone, said, "Just to let them know that we're on our way back."

"The departure for Vancouver is leaving right away--," The clerk handed the old man the tickets, as she said, "Bay four—you'd better hurry."

They had all run through the hall and out into the bays, and the bus had already begun to close its door as they arrived in the last moment!

"Be careful, kiddo--," the old man hugged and kissed the boy's cheek, "You make sure to be good now, you hear? And make sure to call me the first chance you get, and the second that you make it back into town."

Patrick hugged the old fellow tightly, and then looking at him as though for the last time, mounted the steps into the bus.

"Thanks for everything--," Pam hugged and kissed the old man's cheek, as habitually straightening his shirt collar, she tearfully said, "Please be careful going back there—and take good care of your-self—okay?"

"You just watch over yourself and my grandson--," He slowly nodded, and sighing deeply, said, "He means the world to me."

"I'll be sure to call you the moment that we reach Vancouver--," She gently patted his shoulder, and looking away briefly, stared back at the man, "You know, you saved my life back there with the bear." She was at a total loss for words.

"You'd better get on that bus, sweet lady--," He waved with a wink, as he turned and slowly walked away, "You can thank me another time—I'm rather fond of apple pie and coffee--just keep it in mind..."

Ascending the steps onto the bus, she produced her ticket and handed it to the driver. As he stamped it and handed it back to her, she sadly watched the old man vanish into the shadows of the station.

"It's just about empty--," Patrick beamed from where he sat at the front of the bus, "We can have front row seats, two each, and see everything from here!"

"You got it, partner--," Pam dropped into the seats directly behind the driver, and shoved her bag down at her feet. If it had just been a matter of comfort she would have been greatly pleased, but the empty bus now left her feeling even more vulnerable.

"Were you out visiting your dad with your son?" The driver politely inquired as he switched off the interior lights, and backing out, guided the bus from the station and out onto the main street. He was a clean-shaven, middle-aged fellow with wavy brown hair, blue eyes, and a big cheerful smile. He wore his cap slightly off center, and she grinned as he reminded her of a young Ralph Kramden, from the Honeymooners.

"Oh no—just friends--," She replied, "And I'm taking care of young Patrick here, while his folks are away on vacation."

"You looked a little alike--," The driver looked at her in the rearview mirror, and smiling, said, "Just the blonde hair and blue eyes—sorry, it was a simple mistake."

"No insult taken--," She took an apple from out of her bag, and taking a bite from it, smiled as she said, "He's a good looking kid—I'd be proud to have him as a son."

Offering Patrick an apple from the bag, which he immediately accepted, she leaned back into her seat and looked to him in silent contemplation. She had always loved children, but being a free-spirit and never meeting the right guy, had left those thoughts long behind. Or at least, so she had assumed. She had thought back to Raymond and how he had so shyly offered to share dinner some time. Laughing, she pondered his rugged good looks, bashful and even sweet disposition whenever she came around... In that moment, and as while having been a confirmed bachelorette for some time, she decided to accept his offer the moment they returned home.

The road had opened up before them as the snow came in light flurries, the headlights piercing the darkness as the twin beams reached out into the deep forest and steeply ascending pine peaks.

"It looks like we might be in for a little rough weather--," The driver spoke reassuringly, "But have no fear--," He tapped at his nametag, "You're traveling with Rob Sampson, ace of the mountain highway route.

I've been navigating these roads for four years now—through all kinds of weather and all year round."

"Well, thank you--," She leaned back into the seat with a sigh, "I'm Pamela Montgomery—and that's very reassuring. I'm pleased to make your acquaintance, Robert."

"Just call me Rob--," He saluted her with a tip of his hat, "All my friends do."

Although his manner seemed quite comical, he had confidence and an undeniable sense of reliability that now comforted her. She stared into the blackness beyond the enormous windshield, watching as the snow became like streaming stars in the headlights before crashing into the glass. The steady rumble of the diesel engine had slowly numbed her mind, as the heating vent beside her slowly lulled her into a daze. Her eyes had suddenly become quite heavy, as blinking continually, she attempted to stay awake. The dimly lit cabin began slowly fading as her eye-lids kept dropping, until finally falling closed. She could hear Patrick's voice in the distance as he and Robert had begun quietly speaking. She had attempted to fight the exhaustion, but in the ensuing warmth and darkness, had soon quietly and quite helplessly slipped into a dream.

British Columbia, Canada.
The McCreary Estate
7:45 p.m.

Making our way back through the snow, we carried lanterns as the flurries had strangely faded and the wind had calmed down. Cold, I was so very bitterly cold! The pant legs were wet from where the snow had melted near the tops of my boots, and I could barely feel my face, hands or feet. Wearing only a scarf and heavy woolen sweater, Jay had stumbled while half-frozen and following blindly along. Still, he had never complained once about having surrendered his coat to the demon and woman, who shook and shuddered as the elements took their toll.

Walking while wearing Jay's coat, Amica had never allowed my hand to slip free for a moment. As continually glancing over at me, I saw the pain through the reflection of Caitlin's eyes. Had this all been some horrendous nightmare devised by the darkness to break our spirit? Or was this possibly the sinister revelation of what Caitlin had been all along? Had I finally and truly lost her? Had she just been some illusion, and demon acting from within as while destroying all that I had ever loved or known? Or truly, was she still missing, loving, and waiting for me in some sacred place upon distant shores? Surely, this must have been it. The evil was simply attempting to break my heart and spirit, and defeat my will to continue fighting... She was alive and well, I needed more than anything to believe this! Carrie and the others would return with my beloved, and life would continue once we beat this vile abomination!

"It can't be!" Rich directed his light toward the pond as we hurried back through our previous tracks. I had looked to where he had cast his beam and the breath had departed my lungs. The ghastly old Willow had returned to its silent and frozen sepulcher beside the pond. Its huge and gnarled roots deeply submerged, its withered and crooked mass bowed as though having never moved.

"Be still—and move quickly--," Amica warned while leading the way, "Do not disturb that which now silently slumbers within a frozen tomb..."

I had wanted nothing more than to see that horrendous old thing burned to ashes, and the earth about it sewn with salt. The thought of returning in the daylight had passed through my mind, but the sound of a creaking branch had sent me hurrying even faster along the way.

We had cautiously navigated the trail through the dark forest and then down the treacherous and icy hill. Slipping and sliding, we struggled through the dense brush in swift descent and until almost falling in a heap at the bottom. Then, struggling forward, we hurried to where the Suburban was parked in the deep snow.

Amica had finally collapsed, as her earthly form could no longer resist the elements. As falling forward with a gasp, I had caught and held her close, pleading, "We've made it—you can do this—it's just a few steps further."

Realizing that she had expended her last ounce of energy, I had leaned down, and lifting her from out of the snow, carried her toward the truck. Having seen this, Jay had come to my assistance, and taking hold of her legs, we bore her through the bitter cold of that blackest of nights. Rich had struggled onward and ahead of us with the truck keys in hand. In the stillness that now hung about us, I could hear his breath coming in short and desperate gasps, as the frozen air seared his lungs.

In those last few moments and as we neared the truck, I could see the courage and determination in Jay's eyes. He was colder than either Rich or myself after giving up his coat, but still valiantly carried on. Even while mourning poor Raymond, I blessed the day that they had both come into our lives. There was a beauty within terror, as it revealed the true character of people in ways that none other could. It always seemed that those who spoke loudest were always the first to break...

Carefully loading Amica into the front seat, I had slid in beside her. Then huddling close, rubbed at her arms and legs while attempting to increase circulation.

"Why won't the demon protect you?" Astounded in the moment, I had gazed into her heavy-lidded eyes, "It needs you alive as much as we do—what's happening here?"

"It feels no pain but revels within human suffering--," She whispered from trembling and icy lips, "I will not perish as easily as mortals—and it will only come in times of true threat…"

"What are you doing out there?" Jay had hurried back out to see what was keeping Rich, "We need to get this thing started and crank up the heat. Caitlin looks like she's going hypothermic!"

"Well, I really wish that I could help--," Rich shouted, cursing aloud while lowering his lantern and examining the broken grill, "But something's punched holes through the radiator—and this thing isn't going anywhere!"

"Screw that—it's going and right now!" Frustrated and utterly fatigued, Jay kicked angrily at the front tire, "I'd rather ruin the engine than freeze to death out here. All that we have to do is make it back to the motorhome!"

"Damn it all to hell--," Rich slammed down the hood and tossed his lantern aside, "Let's get this thing rolling—and see how far we get!"

Amazingly enough, the engine had started. As ever so slowly, Rich navigated through the deep snow and back toward the blazing house. The flames reached higher and ever higher, as through the billowing smoke, the radiating glow appeared to have scorched the dark heavens. We had travelled through our original tracks which offered less resistance on the journey back. Still, it was obvious by my friend's reactions that the over-heating engine wouldn't carry us much further.

Locating several woolen blankets among the remaining gear, I had covered Amica and attempted to keep her warm. She had become deathly cold and less responsive, and I suffered even seeing her like that. The ride had been rough and it hadn't taken long before the engine had begun to steam.

"You might as well gun it--," Jay cursed, as looking over at the engine temperature gauge, said, "This baby's going to blow pretty soon, anyway. Let's see how much closer we can get to the house!"

Rich had done exactly that, as slamming his foot down upon the accelerator pedal and tightly gripping onto the wheel, he shouted, "Everyone, hold on this is going to get ugly really fast!"

The truck had suddenly surged forward, releasing a stream of steam, which, erupting from beneath the hood and wheel-wells, became a trailing oil cloud behind us! We bounced and slid in a frantic race, each second counting as the temperature gauge now drifted hopelessly into the red! The distance between the path and the house closed rapidly, the engine roaring, overheating and finally exploding!

Holding Amica tightly, I gasped while hearing as the cam-shaft and lifters blew out through the bottom of the oil pan. It was an expulsion of hot steel and shrapnel that caused the truck to rattle and then sputter, as we rolled to a smoldering and steaming stop.

"That's the end of the Suburban--," Frustrated, Rich punched angrily at the dash and wheel, "Let's get out of here and make for the motorhome before the weather gets any worse!"

Recovering slightly, Amica had become strong enough to manage on her own. I had wrapped one of the blankets around her shoulders, and then she had used another to fold about her chest. This had created some protection from the elements, and she quickly offered Jay his coat back.

The chaotic ride had carried us a short distance from the rear gardens, and the southern-most tip of what remained of the house. It had become a roaring inferno of tall timbers, cracking stone, and embers that popped like thunder while exploding into the night. Its once majestic peaks had fallen into utter ruin as, consumed by the fire, they had become indistinguishable among the charred framework and burning rubble.

The heat was so extreme that the icy pines had been burned away in places. There were flaming limbs upon the nearest trees, burning bush and hedges. Hurrying along, we were forced to shield our faces while passing within fifty yards. Immense clouds of black an oily smoke billowed upward, as caught in bitter gusts, were carried off in the steadily growing winds.

"It's just a little further now--," Taking notice of Amica's weakening state, Rich offered a supportive hand, "I have a change of clothes and some spare boots in the RV—they won't fit very well, but they're clean and you're welcome to have them."

I could see that the darkness had been lifted from out of my friend's soul, the confusion had faded. Until that moment, I hadn't realized just how deadly the evil's influence had been upon our minds. It bothered me even further while realizing how easily it had blinded all of us, by using the simplest of emotions in a moment of doubt...

"Anything would be better than this." She tugged at the woolen blanket about her shoulders, and sighing deeply, said, "It seems that the demon leaves me at some disadvantage, whenever it departs."

"Yeah well—maybe you should carry a change of clothing?" Jay shivered in the frozen wind, "Or even a bathrobe—or in your case, a cape?"

There had been a curious exchange of glances with the suggestion of what might have been somewhat humorous, if not so closely resembling an insult. She had only nodded, as cautious to avoid a clump of burning rubbish on the path, carefully stepped off to the side. As she did this, Rich had suddenly leapt before her, and purposely knocking her to the ground, cried out!

"Get back—there's something in the hedge!"

In our haste to escape the freezing weather we had lowered our guard. As having become unwary due to frost and fatigue, we failed to notice what had pursued. In the brilliant glow of the inferno it glistened, wet and oozing, as it came out of the withered hedge.

At first glance my heart had been gripped with horror while recognizing what was left of Raymond! His charred bones combined among several others, while congealing within that bloated and repulsively festering flesh! Hideously re-animated, it moved like some enormous arachnoid, while scuttling upon multiple, bony limbs.

Rich and Jay had both fired their weapons, the missiles struck their target, and the nightmare burst into flames! Yet, it still kept coming, as oblivious of pain or suffering, the undead thing flailed while singling out and attacking me! No sooner had it done this, did the world suddenly erupt in a dizzying flash of movement, as my feet were swept off the ground. Helplessly caught in the claws of the demon, I felt the mighty wings thrashing as it carried me off and away from that place. Rising ever higher, we soared above the smoke and flames and into the frozen night.

My heart skipped, as looking down, I witnessed my companions fleeing while attempting to evade the ghastly and burning thing. Then, as swiftly as it had happened, Amica suddenly swooped downward while raising a brightly burning claw! I could clearly see where our friends had retreated, but become cornered between the dense forest and the ruins of the house. The desperate fiend, still burning brightly, had crept toward them even as its bulk was being consumed by the fire.

In a blinding blue flash, a spell had been cast, and the hideous and burning thing had stopped suddenly while becoming a block of solid ice! Still cringing, they had looked to where Amica now gathered her blankets.

Although neither had uttered a single word, their expressions had revealed their horror, and utmost gratitude.

Keeping a safe distance for fear of the hideous thing, we had all stood and stared at the nightmare captured in ice. Amica had kicked at the crystalline statue and it had shattered, the shards vanishing as they had fallen to the frozen earth.

"Merely a puppet of the devil--," She waved for all to follow as she led the way toward the road beyond, "And a desperate attempt to claim yet another before this night is through..."

"It went straight for you this time—," The terror burned in Rich's wide eyes as he followed from behind, "And I wouldn't have even noticed it, if it hadn't moved so soon..."

"Just keep your eyes open--," Jay reloaded his weapon, and said, "and walk wide around everything from now on..."

Cautiously making our way out and onto the main drive, we began circling the immense stone fountain. It had once been a thing of beauty, but had long since developed into something distinctly diabolical. Keeping a safe distance from the dark and icy filth of the fountains base, my attention travelled upward and into Poseidon's stern gaze. The ominous god held his trident high while striking out defiantly at the blackened heavens. As while cast in shadow and defined by the inferno, it became a vision of hell.

"Oh no--," Gasping, Rich had stumbled as he stopped, and just stood staring.

Having caught my immediate attention in his utter despair, I had turned to look at what he was seeing.

What remained of the motorhome lay upon its side and was burning at the end of the road. It was little more than the flaming fragments of the explosion that we had all witnessed from the mausoleum.

"Oh Jesus—what are we going to do now?" Rich clasped his hands about his face, and fell to his knees in the deep snow, "Once the fires die down and the temperature drops—all they'll find is our frozen bodies..."

"You haven't won, you filthy bastard--," Jay howled out in rage, and waving a fist toward the burning house, wailed, "We still beat you—we beat you—burn in hell!"

Even through our ultimate failure, there had been some semblance of victory within his statement, as the house of McCreary was no more...

"Do not despair--," Amica encouraged the others, as taking hold of my hand, pointed toward the end of the drive, "For hope remains—and approaches even now..."

A sudden light shone through the darkness upon the road ahead, stunned, we all stood and watched as my Eldorado slowly pulled down the long drive.

"You have got to be kidding me--," Jay gasped, as pulling Rich back to his feet, laughed and said, "It's Tim and he's got Danny with him—God bless them, they came after us!"

"Quick--," I waved for everyone to follow, "Let's get out of here while we still have a chance."

Danny had leapt from the car before Tim had even had the opportunity to pull over or park. He ran toward the group, and throwing his arms about me, hugged tightly while saying, "We thought that we'd lost you when we saw the fire."

"What are you doing here?" Shocked with the sudden realization, I looked at Tim through the windshield and then back at the lad, "You knew the risks of leaving the estate, especially in the dark?"

"Carrie called us--," He almost choked while stuttering out the words, "They have Maya with them and she's safe--," He hesitated while looking back at Rich, who almost collapsed with the news, and then back at me, before saying, "But Caitlin and Eva--," He shook his head, "Carrie said they never went to Killkenny, and there was never any funeral. They found Maya in some mental hospital—something got to her at St. Francis—and Michael, Carrie went to Christ Church cathedral, and the priest there told them that Eva and Caitlin McCreary died over a hundred years ago… So you see—we just had to come…"

Amica had taken hold of my hand, her eyes wide and as empty as the dark heavens. There hadn't been any need to say anything as we had shared the same thought in that moment. With the bitter winds that carried the smoke and flames away from the house of McCreary, so also died the dreams in memory of my beloved Caitlin.

With eyes that were partially frozen with tears, Rich had bowed his head while silently standing beside me. There were no words in that moment that would have made any difference at all.

Jay could only turn and look away, and then kicked in frustration at the frozen earth.

"Not all is what it may seem--," Amica's eyes shimmered like emeralds in the firelight as she took hold of my hand, "And not all is lost…"

Rich and Jay had stayed close, nervously watching the dark forest, as they awaited my word on departure. Unwilling to waste any more time or keep them standing in the icy darkness, I turned to look back at Danny, "Thank you, that was very brave—but we're not out of the hot water yet. Let's get out of here…"

Hurrying toward the car, Jay and Rich had taken the back seat with Danny, while Amica followed me into the front seat.

"You're the captain--," Tim slid over and offered me the wheel, "And I'm here for you, brother, no matter what happens…"

Gently patting my shoulder, I could see the pain in his eyes. He knew that my heart had been utterly broken and that the true nightmare had just begun.

Driving toward the burning carnage, I carefully navigated around the immense stone fountain while turning the car in the drive. It felt good to be back behind the wheel of the black Eldorado, and I pondered while gazing into the flames reflection upon the midnight hood. It was the car that had first started the adventure with me, and then thought to have been forever lost. But in the fire's light, it was like the phoenix, that rising from its own ashes, had returned to save us that night. A blackened steed before the gates of hell, I pressed hard and long upon the horn, a cry of defiance! A tear found its way down my cheek within memory, and I whispered, "We lost Raymond here tonight."

Pulling out and parking between the stone gates, I looked to Tim, "He gave his life while saving ours—it's a debt that I can never repay…"

"We all came with the knowledge of what might happen--," Looking back remorsefully, he sadly said, "It's not how we started or even ended. But that we could make some difference to someone, somewhere, while we were still here."

Swallowing hard, I had looked into the rear-view mirror and into the sorrowful faces of my friends. Amica had been the only one who seemed barren of expression and lost within contemplation.

Slowly pulling onto the open road, I peered back at the flames between the tall pines. It wasn't a prayer that now touched my heart, but a curse within final parting of the ruin of the house of McCreary…

Christ Church Cathedral, Dublin, Ireland.
4:25 a.m.
Awakened by an unfamiliar sound, Carrie had opened her eyes to peek about the little room. It was a modest space occupied by an antique desk, small table, dresser and double bed. A lantern had been left burning upon the table-top at her request, and the drapes had been pulled tight. Father

Donoghue had provided them with the best at his disposal and even made arrangements to assist them in the morning.

"Is something wrong?" Scott whispered, raising his head from the pillow and peering suspiciously around the room.

"I thought that I heard something--," She reached for her glasses on the little night table and quietly sat up in bed, "It sounded like something at the window—or possibly footsteps from just outside of the door?"

Knowing fully that his wife had never been the nervous type, Scott swiftly moved from the bed and quickly got dressed.

"Where are you going?" She followed him, fumbling while slipping into her clothes.

"If you said you heard something—then I'm not taking any chances, sweetheart."

They had both walked very softly to where pausing, ever so gently unlocked, and slowly slipped open the door. The hallways had been pitch-dark with exception to a glow coming from beneath a door some distance down the hall. They had looked to one another, and deciding to investigate, slipped out the doorway and crept ever so cautiously toward the lighted room.

The ancient boards creaked beneath their weight and they halted, fearing that the squeaking might have given them away. But no further sound was heard from beyond where they now stood, holding their breaths while they listened in the dark hall.

Placing a finger before her lips, Carrie waved for Scott to follow as they continued forward, one slow step at a time. It was cold in the corridor and they heard a faint whispering as though the wind had entered through some hidden crack or crevice. Halting to consider this, she wondered if the sound had possibly come through a window, from beneath a door, or through the ancient brickwork of the wall. Scott had urged her onward, hushing her as they approached the lighted room and gently pressed their ears against the old wooden door.

"You'll not hear nothing--," Lawrence startled them as he crept up behind them from out of the darkened hall, "Because, I'm not in there--," He pointed curiously behind him and into the empty corridor, "I was following that young lady friend of yours--," He spoke in a whisper, "I think she's off sleep-walking, I lost her somewhere in the cathedral, not two minutes ago."

"I thought that I heard something--," Carrie said apologetically for having invaded the old fellow's privacy, "So we'd come out to investigate the sound."

"Then you'd do well to follow me--," He motioned with a wave as he turned in the deep shadows and began making his way back down the hall, "We'd best be finding her before she falls into some kind of trouble. I wouldn't recommend wandering about here in the dark…"

"Why didn't you call on us when you first noticed?" Carrie followed while speaking in low tones, "She could have gone anywhere in this place—it's enormous, and we don't even know our way around."

"I didn't think to trouble you over something that I wasn't sure about myself?"

They hurried down the long corridor, and swiftly descending a set of steps, soon found themselves in the main aisle of the cathedral. The lights that were still burning cast an orange and golden hue about certain doorways, figures, archways, and pillars in the halls. All the rest lay in the long shadows of the early morning hours, as not even the slightest light now shone through the stained glass windows from high above.

"She was just here—not a few moments ago--," The old man pondered the possible directions, and finally guessing, pointed a finger and said, "I think that she was going that way—but I can't really be sure?"

They had followed without question, as pausing across the aisles and into a dark archway, made their way down another dimly lit hall. They moved quickly across the mosaic floors until, reaching the halls end, they came upon a large and partially open door. Darkness within, as Lawrence turned back to peer at them, and quietly said, "I think that she might've gone down there?"

Scott had looked to Carrie as both of them hesitated, looking nervously into the blackness of the basement door and beyond. A cold gust issued from out of the blackness, sending shudders that chilled them both to the very bone.

"Where does that lead?" Carrie asked, as reaching out, gently shoved the door a little further open.

"It looks like some kind of basement?" Scott moved slightly forward and paused as though to look for a light-switch or lamp.

"If she's down there, I hope nothing's happened to her--," Lawrence's eyes grew wide as he shoved a hand before his mouth, and muttered, "I hope that she hasn't fallen…"

This had been enough to panic Carrie, who stepping forward, thrust her hand into the darkness while feeling around upon the wall for a light switch. The door had creaked open ever slightly, as moving ever forward, she became braver with Scott standing close at her side. Her hand touched the cold stone of the brickwork within, but as she slid her hand about, she could find nothing resembling a button or switch.

"We should've brought that lantern--," She grumbled, "I had a feeling that we might encounter something like this."

"Maya—are you down there?" Scott had called softly, hushed by Carrie, who pointed into his face and whispered, "Don't you know how dangerous it is to wake a sleep-walker? For all that we know, she might be sitting, or even standing in the darkness down there somewhere, and still on the stairs?!"

The door had slowly swung wide open as they stood there still fumbling for a light switch on the inner wall. A movement in the shadows of the hall behind them had caused them both to stop and suddenly turn and stare.

"What's going on here—is everyone alright?" Lawrence asked while standing with Maya and Father Donoghue in the hall behind them.

Scott and Carrie had spun toward the dark figure that had led them down there, and both suddenly gasped! The shadow that they had assumed to have been Lawrence had begun to hideously contort. It grew taller, the arms lengthening as long claws sprouted from the hands and feet. The head swelled, the eyes shone pale, and the jaw dropped open to reveal a blackened tongue and rows of long and razor sharp teeth.

Screaming, Carrie pulled Scott away as the ghoul lurched forward, and lashing out, attempted to drag them down the stairs. It had spun back to make a second attempt, but Scott had grabbed a small table from out of the hall and smashed the creatures over the head as it tried to ascend the steps. Roaring, it fell backward as the shining eyes of others like it now appeared in the darkness below. The reactions had been purely instinctive, as slamming the door closed behind it, Carrie had panicked as she and Scott now followed the others. Terrified out of their wits, they hysterically raced back down the dark corridor!

There was a thunder of fists hammering against the old door, and the sound of splintering wood as the frame about it undoubtedly broke beneath the immense force. As they ran they could hear the pattering of bare feet from behind them, as a horde now pursued across the highly polished, mosaic-tiled floor.

"This way--hurry!" Father Donoghue led them out of the archway of the corridor, and across the aisles toward an adjoining hall, "My office is in here—we'll be safe in there!"

They ran for everything that they were worth, as coming to a locked door, the priest now fumbled with trembling hands through a ring of keys. The sounds of the approaching fiends behind them grew steadily as they were pursued. Maya had burst into tears of terror as Carrie, turning and gazing into the darkness behind them, saw the first of the monsters to appear. They came charging like bull-apes, their limbs swinging low to the floor. Hundreds of shining eyes within a mass of blackened fury, hell-bent upon catching them!

"For the love of God--," Lawrence gasped, "Father—please!"

Whether it had been divine intervention or simply the luck of the Irish, frantically fumbling, he finally found the right key and quickly unlocked the door! Scott had literally shoved everyone forward, and as they fell into the room, he slammed and locked the ancient oak door! No sooner had he done this, than did the horde start hammering and pounding from the other side.

"Help me with this!" The father struggled while attempting to shove the enormous executive desk across the room, "Let's use it to bar the door!"

Working together, they had managed to move the massive desk, and with the greatest of effort, slammed it tightly up against the door. The door thundered with the brutal assault from beyond, but held fast within its reinforced steel frame.

"Get that hearth going--," Carrie took immediate notice, "When nothing else works—our last hope is light and fire!"

Working swiftly, old Lawrence and the father had heaped logs, and hurriedly touched a flame to the pile. The kindling erupted quite quickly, as opening the flue, the priest stepped back while turning fearfully toward the thundering door.

"It seems to be holding--," scot stepped back without removing his attention from the desk and door, "But I don't know for how long—it's really taking a pounding from those damn things."

"What in the name of all that is holy--," Father Donoghue asked, "Are those hideous things?"

"In short--," Carrie had joined the others as they stood with their backs against the far wall while watching the door, "It's the work of pure evil— an unrelenting force that will stop at nothing to try and keep us from escaping this place."

"May the good Lord grant us all strength--," He gasped, as kissing his crucifix, stared in utter terror and disbelief, "But how can it be possible that the devil may walk in the house of the Lord?"

"Evil exists in every moldering brick and decaying element upon the face of the earth." Carrie slumped into one of the several chairs that stood in the corner, "It can't enter on sanctified ground in its pure energy form—but you can guarantee that it'll form out of the rot if it can."

"What are you saying?" The priest still appeared utterly lost, "And, how is that even possible?"

"Nothing evil can enter this place in spirit--," Scott fearfully rubbed at his eyes, "But if it can hide inside something or someone, then it's safe inside a physical shell."

"May God have mercy upon all of us--," Lawrence made the symbol of the cross as the door was brutally hammered, but still refused to give way, "And hold back whatever's behind that door...."

"Prayer soothes and protects the soul--," Father Donoghue swallowed hard, and licking at dry lips, leapt back with the echoing pounding of the door, "But what defense have we against a menace such as this?"

"Only fire and daylight will destroy it when it manifests like that." Scott paced nervously back and forth while considering their options, and then looking up toward the stained glass window, asked, "How much longer until the dawn?"

Father Donoghue looked at his wrist watch, the sweat beading upon his brow as he looked back, and said, "Possibly an hour—maybe more. What would you suggest that we do now—call out for assistance?"

"No--," Maya panicked, "You'll just get a lot more people killed."

"Keep the fire burning bright—and keep an eye out for anything that might try creeping out from under that door," Carrie tossed another log into the huge hearth, and looking between her friends, muttered, "And start praying that we make it until dawn..."

"I don't think that Michael and the others made it--," Scott swallowed back the emotions as he glanced back at his wife, "If he had—this whole nightmare would've ended by now."

Moving across the room and tightly embracing her husband, Carrie sniffled back a tear, "All that we can do now is pray that they've somehow survived, and that we can figure this out, if and when we make it back home."

"Is there anyone else in this building right now?" The thought now terrified Scott, "Clergy or even janitorial staff?"

"No—thank God." Father Donoghue clasped his hands tightly together as though in prayer and quietly said, "The diocese is away on vacation right now, and I am the only one present until the morning..."

"Are you absolutely sure that there isn't anyone else in the building--," Carrie looked between the father and Scott, "Anyone else at all?"

"No—the grounds-keeping staff no longer reside on the property--," The father thought briefly before saying, "And the janitorial responsibilities are managed by the hired help. Why do you ask?"

"Because--," She slowly turned, and looking suspiciously back at the door, muttered, "Those things don't like to leave any witnesses—and people just vanish when they're around...."

The pounding upon the door had suddenly stopped, as the world fell into utter stillness. They had all looked to one another in question, but hadn't dared moving a muscle or making any sound. The hearth had crackled, and as the ember spat, Maya had rushed into old Lawrence's arms. He held the young woman, as placing a finger before his lips, peered fearfully about at his friends. Taking a hot poker from out of the hearth, Scott had quietly walked closer to the desk and door, and watched for any movement from the shadows beneath.

There was a muffled shuffling, like the sound that slippers make while being dragged across a polished floor.

"What's happening out there—can you hear anything?" Carrie whispered while reaching for Scoots arm, cautiously pulling her husband away from the door. At first he had said nothing, but as they approached the others to the rear of the room, he had quietly said, "If I had to guess—I'd say that it's figured out that it's not getting through--," He looked back, and swallowing hard, muttered, "So it's changing into something that can slide under the door..."

The priest gawked, his eyes growing huge as he stared into the shadows beneath the desk and before the door. "But what could possibly slip through from under there--," He whispered as he glanced back at Scott.

"Trust me father--," The reply came in a deathly cold tone, "You better pray that we don't find out..."

Kamloops, British Columbia, Canada.

Jarred awake as the bus slowed on bumpy terrain, Pam stretched out while curiously looking around. They were on a slow and steady decent from high among the hills, approaching the lights of the little city far below.

"The snow stopped a while ago--," Robert eagerly reported as while speaking quietly to avoid disturbing the now sleeping Patrick, "But it left a few rough, icy patches. Nothing of any great concern, I've driven on far worse."

Leaning forward from out of her seat, she rubbed sleep from her eyes and blinked while staring ahead. Descending steeply, the highway slowly weaved ever downward, as with a cement barrier upon the ridges edge, the dark hills climbed out of view from the other side. A slight slip had jolted her as the bus slid ever so slightly, and Robert winked while regaining control, "Easy does it—and we'll be just fine…"

Patrick had slept soundly, and Robert, although the friendly sort, had been grateful when the lad had finally drifted off. It seemed that the moment Pam was sleeping, the boy had become an endless stream of guessing games and questions, most of which Robert had no interest in sharing. He was a confirmed bachelor and travelled nights because he preferred the peace of mind that was offered by the empty road.

"Was he really annoying?" Pam had winked while gesturing with a nod and raising an eyebrow as she smiled.

"Oh no--," Robert grinned gleefully as he politely lied, "The little guy wasn't awake much later than you." Nervously, Robert shot a glance at the still sleeping boy.

"Is anything going to be open--," She pointed toward the approaching lights as they descended the lower portion of the hill, "I need to use a telephone."

"There's a pay phone in the station--," He shrugged, "But, I can let you use the one in the office while we're waiting to be refueled?"

"Well, its long distance into Vancouver--," She appeared reluctant, "I wouldn't want to be a bother or get you into any trouble."

"We dropped our last passenger in Salmon Arm—and aren't doing any other pick-ops until Chilliwack," He shrugged, "So it's just the three of us on this trip, it's no trouble at all."

"Thank you—I really appreciate this." She settled back into her seat.

When they had pulled into the little depot and parked, Patrick had accompanied her as the bus was taken to be refueled. Kamloops had always been the mid-way fuel stop for departures travelling between Vancouver and Edmonton.

It was bitterly cold as they left the bus and followed Robert through the frosted, double glass doors into the building. There was a small diner that was closed at night, a ticket booth, and the little office to the right where they joined their driver.

"It's not much—and there's the telephone," He offered them both seats before the desk, and said, "But please, get comfortable—we'll be here for a little while." Moving to leave the office, he had paused, and snapping his fingers, looked back, "Can I get you coffee, tea, or maybe some nice hot cocoa?"

"Cocoa for both, please." Pam had smiled and waved as she hurriedly dialed out on the phone.

Ringing several times before Deb had finally caught it, she answered drowsily while looking at the time, "Hello?"

"Deb—it's me Pam--," She informed her, "I've got Patrick with me in Kamloops, and we're taking the bus home."

"Oh no--," Deb was sobered with the thought, and immediately wide-awake, "Pam, you shouldn't have done that… Things aren't right around here—and we haven't heard from anyone else for some time."

"Things were wrong at the farm house, too--," She spoke quietly while anxiously peering around, "A bear came through my bedroom window, and if it wasn't for Carrie's old man, I wouldn't even be talking to you right now."

"Oh sweet Jesus--," Deb swallowed hard while slapping a hand to her face, "What time is your estimated arrival in Vancouver?"

"Depending on the weather—give or take, just over five hours."

"Call me when you get into town—and whatever you do, do not leave the bus station."

"You got it--," Pam thanked Robert as he returned with hot cocoa for all of them, and then said, "I'll call as soon as we arrive—till then."

Deb has slowly hung up the phone, glancing over to the couches where Ray and Jen peacefully snored. They had all been so exhausted that not even the telephone had bothered either of them. No sooner had she moved, than did the phone ring again and she snatched it up quick as a whip.

"Hello—it's Ole, the editor—Michael—did I get you at a bad time?"

"This is Deb--," She replied as somewhat confused, suddenly realizing who he was, "Michael had to go out of town, and I'm not exactly sure when to expect him back. Can I pass on a message?"

"Hello, Deb, it's a pleasure to make your acquaintance--," He sounded reluctant, "I'm sorry to have bothered you at this time of the night, but is he in some kind of trouble?"

Unaware of how much they might have shared, she had still approached the question with caution, "Has he spoken to you about anything in particular?"

"I know about the evil that you call the darkness—if that's what you are referring to--," Ole bluffed her while suspicious of everything, and saying, "And if there is any way that I might be of service, please don't hesitate to ask."

"The team is scattered--," Deb looked up as Ray had awoken, and wandering into the kitchen, sat in the nook beside her. He had leaned over, and gently resting his head upon her shoulder, swiftly fallen back to sleep.

"Carrie and Scott travelled to Ireland to look for Caitlin and Eva. They found Maya in some old psychiatric hospital, in a catatonic state." She quietly explained while attempting not to bother her sleeping husband, "Apparently, she never met with the others—and something had gotten to her out there."

"So, what has happened to her?" Ole felt his stomach drop as his worst fears were confirmed, "Is she alright?"

"Carrie managed to exorcise the darkness—and break her out of that hypnotic state. They've got her with them now, but the Mother Superior sent them off to Christ Church cathedral in Dublin, to speak to a priest about parish records."

"And did they discover anything?"

"Yes--," The words came harder with the realization of what was happening, "They found out that Eva and Caitlin McCreary have both been dead for almost a hundred years. And that the thing had just been using them like puppets to get to all of us..."

"So then--," Ole fought to decipher everything that he'd already read of the manuscript, and said, "As we suspected, they were actually part of the original darkness to begin with."

"Yes--," She sniffled, and wiping the tears from her eyes, said, "Which explains why this thing was always a few steps ahead of us—and managed to get to Red Cloud and the others the way that it did. You see, Rich was communicating with them on the telephone the whole time that they were supposedly away, and it used the information against us."

"What's happened to Michael and the others?" His hands trembled so badly that he almost spilled the mug of coffee that sat on his desk.

"They've gone off to try to make a stand against this thing--," She felt confident in his soothing manner and apparent understanding, "They have the Diabolus Lapis, but, things have gone very badly—and there's only a few of us left."

"The devil stone--," Ole felt the excitement of terror within its translation, "Where do you feel that they might be at this very moment—and should I go out and try to find them?"

"We can't leave the estate in the darkness—as you know, that's no better than suicide," She explained, "If Michael managed to survive the event at the Duff Glenn, then he should already be on his way back. Tim and Danny went after them—hopefully they've reached them safely and warned them about Caitlin and Eva in time..."

"What can I do to be of assistance?" He swallowed hard as a cold sweat now beaded his brow.

"Ole, listen to me. If you get any further involved--," She warned, "This thing will come after you and murder anyone that you've ever loved."

"I am alone in this world and without family--," Ole looked to the parting letter that his wife had left upon the fridge door earlier that night, and quietly said, "And am responsible only for myself. Now—tell me what I can do to help…"

CHAPTER TWENTY ONE

Hope, British Columbia, Canada,
Sunday, February 9, 1975.
1:45 a.m.

Between the distance, weight and poor road conditions, we had gone through far more gas than expected. It had been nothing short of a miracle that we had even made it into the little Husky service station in Hope.

"I'll volunteer to get the gas--," Tim shoved the passenger door open, and hurriedly climbing out, said, "If you get the coffee and something to eat—I'm starving."

"Count me in there, too--," Jay tapped me on the shoulder, and jabbing a thumb into the back seat, said, "And pick up a few Twinkies and a hot cocoa for the kid. It's going to be a long night…"

"Consider it done." I had moved to leave, and Amica had swiftly followed as I made for the service station door. It hadn't been immediately noticeable, but as we entered into the lit station, I saw that she appeared strangely different and more human than even before.

"Are you feeling okay, Amica?" Gently placing a hand upon her shoulder, we stood at the counter awaiting the attendant who had been busy with something in the back.

"Please, call me Caitlin--," Her eyes glinted like emeralds beneath the fluorescent lights, as gently brushing the hair from my eyes, she whispered, "For what time that we have left."

"You had a chance to take the stone--," Looking deeply into her eyes, I was both confused and terrified, "But you didn't—can I ask why?"

"Because love is stronger than any power in the universe--," The answer came, as gently caressing my face, she gazed deeply into my eyes, "And not all the evil in eternity could ever force me to ever harm you…"

It was true that I had loved her dearly, but within Caitlin's shadow, my heart had succumbed to emptiness and I was without words to offer in response. Instead, only the doubt grew, and glancing down at her, I quietly asked, "Did you know about her and Eva the entire time?"

"The demon did—," A depth of despair now filled her pleasant features as she sadly shook her head, "But, I simply could not bring myself to tell you—instead--," She raised her arms pleadingly before me, "I took the form of that which was dearest to your heart."

"So—now you have taken the form of two demons—and the face of the devil that stole my heart."

"But Michael—I was never the imposter--," She spoke sincerely while softly caressing my face, "Don't you see—it was the demon that took this memory of who we once were, and I am the true Caitlin…"

"If this is true--," My heart leapt into my throat, "Then why have you never spoken to me about this—or revealed her true identity to me before?"

"Not all that appears evil is your enemy--," Marlowe whispered, "And not all that seems dear is true… you were warned, many times…"

It was true, the words had been uttered in warning, but I had never heeded them, simply existing within blatant denial of the truth. Amica had committed no crime against me while withholding what would have certainly destroyed me at a weaker time. I had grown stronger through these experiences and been tempered through the mystery and mind-shattering horror of it all…

Her eyes shone like diamonds and she wore her heart upon her sleeve. Even the demon that still possessed her could not breach the bonds that we shared. It had all suddenly made terrifying and twisted sense. The reason that the vision of Caitlin had so deeply captivated me when we had first met was because of the love and distant memory that had already existed from deep within me. The darkness had stolen these moments, and manifesting, used this form against us all in the end. And yet, this brave and terrifying creature that now stood before me, so desperate and lovingly, had suffered in silence with the knowledge of the truth…

"Michael—I traversed time and space--,"She whispered through tears, "And endured the unspeakable just to stand by your side—and just to be with you, even one last time…"

"Demon—angel—none of it really matters anymore--," I felt my heart breaking as I pulled her close, and kissing her sweetly, whispered, "Whatever may come to us now, you are and have always been my one true, my beloved, Caitlin." There had been magic in that moment as we stood in that lonely service station in the middle of nowhere. It was an eternity spent together beyond all other evils or darkness that had passed within the blink of an eye. It happened in a little town that was nestled in the frozen foothills to the mountains, and aptly named, Hope.

"Sorry about that--," A young man hurried from out of the back while adjusting his tie, "I had to finish loading the cooler, it'll get busy in the morning."

"No trouble--," Clearing my throat and the fog from my mind, I looked over my shoulder and out to where Tim waved at the gas pump, "I think that's he's just about done out there?"

"You almost forgot--," Caitlin had rushed off, "The coffee, hot cocoa, sandwiches and Twinkies—I'll be back in a flash!"

"You've got one terrific lady there--," The service attendant smiled, "If I asked my wife for anything—she'd just tell me to get off my lazy butt and go get it myself."

"I'll consider myself blessed--," Glancing back as she loaded a tray with hot drinks and assorted snacks, I sighed deeply, and said, "It's amazing how in the darkest moments—the light always seems so much brighter."

"Tell me about it--," The clerk pointed beneath his eyes, "See these dark circles? These stupid night shifts are making me go half blind."

Caitlin had placed the tray down upon the counter and standing close beside me, quietly watched as he typed the prices into the till, and hurriedly bagged everything. She seemed so different in so many ways. Not just within this recent awareness of her true identity, but her having become so very human in the process. It was the change that Marlowe had previously warned would come. The day when having realized her true humanity, the demon would soon claim her earth-bound form. We had witnessed the change over time, and even experienced the power of both, but soon the separation of the two would come. In that moment, I had fully realized the insufferable consequences of what Marlowe had meant.

Paying for the gasoline and supplies, I had taken the bag as she followed with the tray of drinks.

"It looks like we've got clear skies for the drive home--," Jay pointed out the windshield as we passed out the snacks and drinks, "It's about time that luck played a little on our side."

"Luck has nothing to do with it--," Tim sipped at his hot cocoa, and turning, looked into the back seat at Jay, "The devil must be on a coffee break—let's hope that it lasts long enough for us to get home…"

It hadn't taken any convincing to get me motivated, I was already experiencing far worse fears. What the others seemed to have forgotten in their fatigued state, was that if the evil wasn't hunting us, that it was most certainly stalking someone else… It was patient and playing with us like a cat would with a mouse. Relishing the moment as stalking and murdering the innocent and unsuspecting, it would return for revenge upon us all…

Pulling away from the service station, I had looked to where the old diner had once been. It was nothing but a vacant parking lot now, and the memory of Peggy and the old place forgotten in time. I had noticed Rich's eyes in the rearview mirror as we had both silently shared that solemn moment. Then, pulling out and onto the dark and icy highway, I was sincerely remorseful while leaving Hope behind…

Christ Church Cathedral, Dublin Ireland,
6:15 a.m.
They all stood huddled closely and with their backs pressed tightly against the wall. The hearth burned brightly, as staring silently, they all watched as something pressed heavily against the outer door. The hinges creaked, and frame groaned, while something slowly bent the door even inward with each effort. But the ancient oak door and its reinforced steel frame hindered the evil that persisted from beyond.

"What's stopping it?" Maya whispered while struggling to withhold a hysterical scream.

"I'm guessing that it's the light from the fire." Scott held Carrie tightly, as he looked between the priest and the office door, "Is there any other way out of here—these old places are usually full of secret passages and trap doors?"

"Only from behind the altar, several places that I am forbidden to reveal, and the library--," Father Donoghue whispered, "This office is rather insignificant and only used by members of the general clergy."

"There's something moving--," Lawrence's eyes bulged as he stared down and beneath the office door, "It's crawling under and through the cracks…"

Realizing in the last moment that they had no other escape, Carrie had pulled free of her husband, and rushing to the hearth, had taken up a log of which she frantically waved at the door! Smoke and flying embers dropped everywhere, and the filth that had attempted to enter, now swiftly withdrew.

"It's the light--," Scott and Lawrence had followed Carrie's example as the three of them stood defensively before the desk and door, "That filth can't take the light."

"The minute that sun rises--," Maya gasped, "We should all make a run for the airport while we still have a chance."

"What will happen here—once you have all left?" The father peered fearfully about the little group, "Will this foul thing follow—or remain in the shadows of this cathedral?"

"The devil has always been on the doorstep of any decent human being—or good church--," Carrie had turned to the frightened priest, "I can't promise you anything…"

"Once you're aware of the evil—and it knows you are--," Scott whispered while nervously watching the shadows beneath the door, "You're really not safe anywhere, anymore."

"So be it--," Clutching at the large crucifix that hung from about his neck, the father slowly nodded, and said, "I place my soul in the hands of the Lord, and will accept whatever fate comes to me, in his good grace."

"The good Lord brought us altogether for a reason--," Lawrence spoke respectively while looking to father Donoghue, "And in my mind—it was to help these good people. I don't think he would just forsake us all in that case—so let's not give up hope…"

Hugging the old man tightly, Maya sniffled while wiping away a tear, "I just want to be back home, and in the arms of my sweet husband, Rich."

"And you will be, my darling--," Lawrence gently stroked her hair, "Even if I have to carry you all the way back on my own two shoulders."

"You know?" Scott's attention had become fixed upon the large stained glass window directly above them, as he thought aloud, "That isn't just a way out of here—it's also a way in…"

His words had barely been uttered when the glass had exploded from above. They had all scattered, as screaming, fell forward into the center of the room beneath a hail of glass! As brushing crystalline shards out of their hair and clothing, they had swiftly gathered closely about the hearth.

"Are you okay?" Scott kissed his wife while checking to make certain that she hadn't been injured in some way.

"Yes fine—just a little shaken up-how about everyone else?"

Old Lawrence had suffered only a few minor cuts, but still protectively watched over Maya who nodded in response.

"Get back—unclean spirit!" Father Donoghue shielded the group as he stood valiantly before the thing that had entered through the broken window, "You are not welcome in the house of the Lord!" Extending a trembling hand, he held the crucifix before the ghastly thing, and cried out, "In the name of all that is sacred—be gone from this place!"

It had first appeared as a blackened and decaying mockery of something resembling a large simian or ape. A form that it had obviously utilized while scaling the wall and breaking through the glass. Carrie and Scott had held the group back as the priest remained defensively poised before them. As with their backs to the immense hearth, they all stood staring in absolute horror.

In a loud and confident tone, Father Donoghue had begun reciting the 23rd Psalm. Then, to the astonishment of the others, the horrid creature began dissolving! A sickly stench began filling the room as the putrid mass seethed and mutated. Pooling as it thrashed, and then becoming something entirely different, it suddenly charged the unsuspecting father.

There was an explosion of flying furniture and breaking objects as the room became utter chaos! They had all scrambled to escape the violence of the moment, and then, everything had fallen deathly silent. The room lay in ruins as Carrie slowly stood up from where they had all been huddled. Splintered furniture had been sent flying everywhere, and broken religious artifacts lay smashed and broken from all about them.

"Where's father Donoghue?" Carrie suddenly looked up and into the darkness of the high ceiling above the broken window, "Oh—dear God..."

Hanging suspended from within the clawed limbs of what appeared to have been a giant, moldering spider, his head drooped upon a broken neck, as he blindly stared down. In some hideous manner, he resembled a crucifixion, and the mere sight of this had stopped everyone dead in their tracks.

"Sweet Saints preserve us..." Lawrence whimpered as Maya screamed in utter terror. Scott had looked desperately around, as still gripping the poker, stood defensively before the little group. He knew that they had reached a finale to this horrendous waiting game, but was defiant to the bitter end. Carrie had taken hold of a log that was only burning upon one end, and brandishing it like a club, stepped beside her husband.

"If this is where it's going to end for us--," She looked tearfully upon her beloved, "Then let's not make this easy for the rotten bastard!"

Lawrence had leapt up from behind them, and finding a flaming log, joined the trio in defense of the terrified Maya.

"Well, come on, you filthy bugger--," He called to the nightmare above, "Come and try to take us—if you think that you can!"

Dropping the priest's bloody and torn corpse, it sent it crashing heavily down upon the glass covered floor. As seemingly accepting the old man's challenge, it slowly began scaling down! The long legs clicked and clattered as it punched holes through the wall in descent. Carrie had gasped while realizing the monster was entirely comprised of that hideous fungus and human bones. The mass of its body glistened in a blackened and sickly seething ooze. A living and moving filth that, binding several corpses into that single and hideous form, now began to separate and slide apart.

Dropping heavily to the floor, the nightmarish parts gathered and began absorbing the priest's body before their terrified eyes! Within moments the corpse had vanished and the pulsating mass now turned back upon them. It surged, stretched and altered while becoming something larger and even more hideous than before! With multiple heads that snapped with razor sharp teeth, it became the ghastly semblance of an ogre. As smashing the lamp from off the side table, it extinguished all light beyond that of the hearth!

With all of his strength, Lawrence had heaved the burning log directly at the thing, and it had retreated into the far corner to avoid the fire. Seeing this, Carrie had done the same as they both returned to the hearth for another log.

"Keep it in that corner!" Scott bellowed, as following their example, he swiftly did the same. Within moments the horrid fiend had been surrounded in a blazing barrier, as the carpet suddenly burst aflame! It made no sound beyond the sucking and slurping noises of its oozing and gruesome flesh. But it recoiled from the fire, and having been cornered, now dissolved while creeping up the face of the far wall!

"We can't stop it!" Maya shrieked as it flowed like a river of oozing death across the ceiling, and then ran down into the darkness before the door and behind the old desk. Lawrence had moved to cast another blazing log at the thing beneath the desk, but Carrie had swiftly halted him, saying, "We can't start a fire there—it's our only way out!"

"The carpet's already burning--," Scott choked as the smoke began filling the room, "And that thing's just waiting until we get desperate and try to make it out that door!"

"What's that sound?" Maya wept, directing all of their attention to the broken window. The smoke billowed out and blinded them, but something could now clearly be heard. As bursting into tears with the slowly growing light, Lawrence gasped, "It's a piper—a piper playing for the coming dawn!"

As the light brightened, they had all stared up with the glow of the swiftly rising sun. The warming rays flooding in through the window as it chased the evil back into the shadows. Carrie had fallen into her husband's arms and then looked to where the priest's body had once lain. As slowly making her way over, she caught the glimmer of his crucifix in the morning light. Leaning down and retrieving it from the floor, she had held it close to her breast. It was all that now remained of the young priest, a memory of his courage that she decided to keep. Lawrence had assisted Maya to her feet, as from out of the glowing distance they heard the sound of the dawn piper, playing *Amazing Grace...*

"May the good Lord watch over and keep father Donoghue in his good grace." Lawrence formed the symbol of the cross before him, and bowing his head, whispered, "And be praised for saving us from sharing the same fate."

"We need to get out of here--," Carrie spoke softly while taking Scott by the hand, "Once we're at the airport, I'll make some telephone calls to inform the clergy of what's happened here."

"I'll go start the cab--," Sighing deeply, Lawrence peered sadly around the room, "I never thought that the closest that I would ever get to hell, would be in one of our own cathedrals…"

"We'll be right behind you, my friend--," Carrie hugged the dear old man, "Stay clear of any open doorways, and walk wide when you leave this place. We're not safe anywhere in the darkness—not even during the day…"

"I'll be waiting, dear lady--," He moved toward the immense desk that was blocking the door, and paused to look back, "Once someone gives me a hand with this bloody thing."

CHAPTER TWENTY TWO

Vancouver, British Columbia, Canada.
Sunday, February 8, 1975.
2:15 a.m.
The flurries had ceased well over an hour ago and the wind now howled across the rolling dunes. It was late, and Ole had spent well over thirty five minutes attempting to reach his wife at her mother's home. He knew that she would still be awake, but was simply refusing to answer the phone. In her very brief letter, which he had read over many times now, she had stated they just needed some time apart. But under the circumstance, and fearing of what he might have unwittingly become involved within, his fear was now for her…

"Maybe I should just drive over there—and knock on her window as I had done as a boy?" They had been teen sweethearts, and having known one another for most of their lives, could predict each other's actions without much thought at all. In fact, it had been this very reason that after having taken each other for granted, they now suffered marital problems.

"Okay, so maybe I should have bought her flowers more often--," He scolded himself while slipping into his coat and boots, and grabbing his favorite scarf, "But then again?" He paused while reaching for the door handle, "When was the last time that she made a special dinner, or treated my special?" His hand slowly slipped away from the door.

"Maybe I should just let her sweat a little? I know that she's probably just sitting there, and watching the phone ring while she laughs, knowing that I am trying to call." And with that, he removed his coat and began kicking off his boots.

"But, then again--," He put a finger to his cheek thoughtfully, "What if something has really gone wrong? I can just hear Anna now—," He imitated her speaking in a high and whiny tone, "If you really cared about me—you would have come calling, just to make certain that I was alright" He thought it over for a moment, "And to be honest—she would be right…"

Shrugging, he slipped back into his boots, and wrapping the scarf about his neck, made his way back to the door. But something had caused him to pause again, and he turned to look back into the dark house. They lived in a modest two bedroom apartment, of which they shared interests in art, music and theater. The furniture reflected their minimalist lifestyle, but the clutter revealed their passion for life. It was tidy, comfortable, and the second bedroom contained his musical instruments and her art materials. But in the long shadows of her absence, it meant absolutely nothing to him.

"That's it—I'm going to go right over there and tell her it's time to come home."

Yet still something hindered him, some lingering shadow of doubt. The conversation with Michael's friend Deb was still fresh on his mind, and it had truly bothered him that she insisted that he avoid going out in the dark. Had it just been his own stubborn streak that had prevented him from leaving the house? Or was it possibly something in the back of his mind, some sense of pending disaster that hindered him now? There was an aspect of curiosity, a deviant tendency to push the limits, which now tempted him to simply walk out the door. But in the same token, his primal instinct had now spoken of a devil waiting in the darkness beyond...

"And, that's what you get for editing horror novels--," He anxiously turned and curiously looked back at the door, "But what is Anna is perfectly fine—and Deb was telling the truth? What if I should go out there and encounter some kind of devil, and find my own bitter ending in the darkness, just outside of that door?" He thought it over again, the contemplation only worsening matters, as he now became visibly nervous and fidgeted with his car keys.

"If you should go out there--," He spoke to himself slowly, and with great reluctance, moved closer to the door, "Something very bad is likely going to happen—because you were warned and knew better, long before you even left..."

There had been a moment of indecision, but then removing his coat and boots, he grumbled, "Good going, Ole. You've managed to scare yourself now. Sometimes I could just kick myself..."

Closing the little closet door, he turned out the light, and walking through the dimly lit living room, decided to just go to bed. Wandering into the lonely bedroom, he had paused to look to where his wife had lain beside him for so many years.

"Okay, so no farting or cold feet on my back for one night—I might survive this, for one day..." And with that, he dropped onto the covers, and reaching over, switched off the lamp on the night stand beside the bed.

From beyond the long shadows of the window, the wind moaned softly as while dragging at the drifting snow. Through the blackness, all was within stillness, except where something far darker now crouched from just beyond view. It moved silently, as creeping behind the garage, slipped into the alley while passing behind Anna's car...

Summerland, British Columbia, Canada
Greyhound Depot
3:15 a.m.

The bus station had been little more than a tiny depot, which stood in the shadow of the Giant's Head. In years long before, the Kettle Valley Railroad had once travelled to that very same little mountain that Pam now stared upon.

"This is just a parcel stop more than anything--," Robert had spoken quietly while moving from his seat, "This is a retirement community—and hey--," He stopped on the step to look back at her with a smirk, "The kids around here refer to it as the town of the newly wed and nearly dead. There's probably cemetery's that have more action than this place." He shook his head with a chuckle, and hurriedly departed the bus.

Pam had forced a smile, but hadn't appreciated his little joke in the least. She had looked out the window and into the darkness, noticing the steeple of a tiny church. It stood against the mountain, and peeking from behind tall hedges, she could barely make it out. There was something unsettling about the place. Not in appearance, but the complete and utter stillness that hung in the cold night air.

The door had suddenly opened and she had been jolted as Robert peeked over and smiled, "Nothing for pick-up this morning--," He shrugged while closing the door and returning to his seat.

"Doesn't this place give you the willies?" She shivered while having been caught in the breeze that had entered before he closed the door.

"They're in bed by nine in this town--," He slowly pulled out and shrugging, glanced back at her, "It's only creepy when I pass through here at night, alone."

They had turned and slowly driven through the main street of the sleepy little town, and then entered the highway again. It ran alongside the Okanagan Lake, as traveling westward, she could see the reflection of the little lights of Penticton in the distance. An avid traveler, she had often passed on this route and truly enjoyed it on the previous adventures before. As a teen she had visited the little towns along this stretch and tanned and swam in the crystal blue lake. But now, as she gazed out into the utterly black waters, something cold and wet had tugged at her heart...

"Do you have another apple?" Patrick had startled her as he leaned across the dark aisle between the seats and curiously smiled.

"Sure, dear—just a moment." She had shivered, shaking off the fright as she reached down into the bag at her feet and passed him some fruit. She had felt somewhat bad as he thanked her, and promptly chewed at it while smiling at the anxious driver.

Deciding to close her eyes, she had peered out at the lake one last time, and suddenly froze at what she had thought to have seen. Had that been her own reflection in the window, or was something else out there, gazing back at her? Shaking her head and blinking, she turned her attention elsewhere while fearing her own fatigued and over-active mind.

"So--," Patrick looked to the driver, "Are you married—and do you have any kids?"

"No—I never settled down." Robert was leery of the young lad while having previously encountered his unique line of questioning.

"Why—don't you like girls?"

Pam was forced to cover her mouth with a hand as she snickered, and rolling over, covered herself with a coat as she attempted to rest. Within doing so, she had glanced back at the window before laying her head down, and once again, thought to have seen a pale figure there? Unable to distinguish anything beyond her own wide-eyed reflection, she stubbornly closed her eyes. "I will not look--," She had insisted while arguing with herself in thought, "I will not open my eyes, or look into that window again." The moment had come and gone, and she resisted the temptation, but then curiously looked. A pale and gaunt face had stared back at her from the blackness beyond the window. She had almost screamed, but throwing a hand before her mouth, turned to see if she had startled young Patrick. Unaware of her discontent, he had busied himself with a book on fishing lures that he had brought from his grandfather's house.

Swallowing back the cold terror, she had leaned forward and gazed through the windshield and out onto the empty road. The flurries had long vanished, and as they ascended from out of the valley, they had already passed through Penticton and left the Okanagan Lake behind. She knew the route without having to even guess, as having traveled by bus, could have called all the stops out by heart. For reasons that she could not explain, she suddenly thought of Raymond and simply could not get him from off her mind. Perhaps, it had been the security that she had always felt in his presence? Of course, that had to have been it. She had simply suffered from nervous tension which had brought his memory to her attention, due to stress.

"Now that's odd?" Robert had scratched under his cap, and squinting, slowed the bus while peering into the night, "I could've sworn that I saw someone or something just ahead on the side of the road?"

Pam felt a sudden jolt, as though experiencing a flash of electricity that tingled through every nerve of her body and mind. As leaning forward, she shrugged while fearing seeing anyone or anything out on that frozen and empty road.

"No—not a single living thing--," She shuddered, and peering over at the driver, said, "I doubt that we'd see much out here—especially in the winter, we're nowhere near a town."

"Oh, you might be surprised--," He sighed while still appearing unsettled by having seen something that wasn't there, "This stretch of highway gets pretty lonely, especially in the winter and dead of night. But still, I've picked a few folks up from around here—mainly hitch-hikers that didn't want to get caught out here alone, at night."

"I can imagine--," She settled back into the seat, and swallowed back her heart, "No one wants to end up alone on an empty highway through a deep forest, especially at night."

"Except maybe for a bear with some mustard and two slices of bread?" Robert chuckled while glancing into the rearview mirror, and saying, "Nothing like a hitch-hiker sandwich, midnight snack."

Her heart was pounding furiously as his words brought back visions of the murderous bear at the farm. He had taken immediate notice of her paled expression, and apologizing, said, "I'm sorry—the joke was in poor taste."

"Not really--," Patrick replied quite calmly as he pointed to her, and said, "It's just that she was almost eaten by a killer bear at my grandfather's farmhouse."

"Please forgive me--," The driver was absolutely horrified, as failing to notice the thing on the road, passed it as he looked in the rearview mirror at her, "That must have been terrifying—thank God that you're safe."

In that moment, Pam saw the shadow that had wandered out, and would have likely stopped the bus. It had looked like a large man from a distance, but as while nearing, she saw that it was a hideous and rotting mass.

"Oh God--," She gasped, realizing that neither Robert or Patrick had seen it, and nodded while fanning her face with a hand, "I'll be alright—it's no problem—I'm just recovering from the experience, that's all…"

Robert had politely nodded, and tipping his hat, turned his focus back onto the road. It had only been an instant, but in that moment, Pam realized that something was now hunting them on that desolate and frozen stretch of road…

Hope, British Columbia, Canada.
Sunday, February 9, 1975.
2:35 a.m.
It had all happened so fast that I hadn't even had a chance to react. Caitlin had suddenly panicked, and forcing me to pull over on the side of the Trans-Canada Highway, slipped over Tim and climbed out of the car.

"What are you doing? I jumped out and had attempted to pursue her, but she suddenly became a semblance of the demon and pointed back in warning.

"Quickly, take the others to safety—, "The massive bat wings unfolded from behind her, "There is something that I must do—now go while you still can!" The dark wings flapped and she suddenly leapt upward, vanishing into the night.

Hurrying back into the car, I had received startled and even horrified glances from those who had witnessed the departure.

"What just happened?" Danny whispered from the back seat, his eyes bulging from their sockets.

"To be honest--," I had glanced at him in the rearview mirror, and said, "At times I'm not even sure myself…"

Pulling back out on the dark and empty highway, I looked back for only a moment. Although I had not completely understood, that inner sense that Marlowe had spoken about now opened a window into my mind. As seeing Caitlin as the demon, and speeding across the darkened heavens, I somehow knew that she had undertaken a mission of mercy.

"Pam--," I had spoken her name more out of thought than intentionally meaning to say it.

"What about her?" Leaning over the seat, Rich had curiously inquired, "Is something wrong?"

They came like images that flashed into my mind, scenes that, revealing people, places and things, were like lighting interrupting a pleasant afternoon. It was hard to focus upon the current reality while experiencing this multitude of perceptions, and I was forced to slow down and pull over to the side of the road.

"Are you alright?" Tim panicked as Rich slid over the bench seat, and dropping down beside me, took hold of my face between his hands, and stared. Our eyes met, and from somewhere deep within the darkness of his pupils there was a light. Not a shining or earthly light, but a sentient presence, and the life that burned within him. In that instant, there had been contact beyond the physical reality. A sense of intimate and ultimate awareness that had revealed all to him within that exact moment.

"Slide over--," He understood without us having even exchanged a single word, and said, "I'll drive."

"I'm sorry—I just need a moment--," I had apologized to the others. They had been concerned, but Jay had patted my shoulder and simply nodded, "Do what you need to, brother."

Moving from out of the driver's seat, I climbed out of the car, and breathing deeply, attempted to shake all thoughts from my mind. The cold night air had not dulled the senses, but seemingly only made them sharper. The world as I knew it appeared to slightly fade, and my thoughts drifted into the surrounding fields and the heavens. I touched everything in a manner of which I could never have imagined. I could feel the power flowing through all things, and sense even the slightest movement and shift in gravity. Overwhelmed, I became unsteady and leaned back against the car for support. It wasn't just Caitlin who was changing, it was also happening to me. Realizing that I had closed my eyes and could still sense as strong as my sight had ever been, I reached upward and out into the darkness.

"And so, within losing everything--," Marlowe whispered upon the icy wind, "You come to realize that nothing was ever truly lost,"

"What's happening to me--," I spoke in thought, "I feel like I'm dreaming while still awake in the real world."

"You must discipline your mind--," He instructed, "When you sense the perception of your inner eye—cease all other thought and open your mind—and focus…"

"How will I know the difference between these perception and simple dreams?"

"Dreams--," He whispered, "Are only reflections of a most turbulent life—physical fears and earthly desires. Your perception reaches beyond the human condition—and into the psyche of all living things. But be warned, Michael—for should you ever gaze into the void, be most assured that something will be looking back…"

In that moment, and before I could even utter words in reassurance to him upon that matter, my thoughts flashed back. Images of a different time not long ago, and as while still visiting the house of McCreary, and peering into an old mirror… The glass of which had been pitch-black, and of which I had assumed to have opened before me to reveal another world. A shudder coursed through my entire being as Marlowe whispered, "Beware of gazing into the void…beware of that what which looks back and waits…"

"Michael—are you going to be okay?" Rich had climbed out of the car to check on me, and stood frightened as he gently took hold of my wrist, "Do you need to go to a hospital?"

Realizing by his fleeting glances that he was concerned about my heart, I had shaken my head and just sighed, "No—it's nothing like that. I'm just completely fatigued…"

Following as he led me back into my seat, I had smiled up at him as he closed the door. We had always had a sentient connection that had gone well beyond mortal speech or simple thought. At times, I had wondered who he had once been in a previous existence. It mattered very little in truth, because I was eternally grateful for what he was to me in this one.

Pulling back out and onto the dark highway, Rich had glanced over at me for a single moment, and then sped off into the night.

Princeton, British Columbia, Canada.
4:25 a.m.

Robert had eased the bus gently down the steeply descending, two-lane highway along the cliff's edge. The mountainous and rocky terrain had been treacherous enough, but the snow and ice now posed an even deadlier threat. It had always bothered him that the only thing preventing them from plummeting from off that cliff into the rocks far below, was a tiny cement barrier…

The city of Princeton rested among those rocky peaks. It was primarily a mining community, and produced a vast amount of copper. Robert had friends that had worked at the Copper Mountain mine. Sadly, it had been this very same stretch of serpentine highway that had claimed their lives two years ago…

"How are you holding out there, partner?" Pam had been watching his pale expression in the dim glow of the rearview mirror.

"Oh—I'm fine--," Smiling, he shot a quick glance back at her without taking his attention from upon the road before them, "This is the last patch of nasty road—then Merritt, Hope, and then we're home free." It almost sounded like he was trying to convince himself. It was apparent that he was a safe, confident, and very skilled driver, but these roads could curl the toes of any seasoned professional. They were responsible for countless deaths over the years, and most due to weather and falling rock and ice.

She noticed that Patrick was fast asleep again, and something inside of her was grateful that he was. Not because of his inquisitive and talkative nature, but due to the fact that she now feared the worst. She had felt the bus slip ever so slightly on some of the sharper turns, and was relieved that he would not bear witness to what might be the end of them all. There had been something building inside of her since having seen the thing on the road. Her previous experience with the bear had taught her to expect anything, anytime, and from anywhere. But out here and in the middle of nowhere, the stillness of the winter had a lulling effect that dulled the senses… She knew that it would be detrimental to all involved if she allowed herself to reveal this growing tension. So smiling, she made polite conversation instead. It was mainly small-talk, but offered a little comfort, as they slowly crossed the jagged cliff faces and crept ever downward into the valley. Her eyes had followed over the cement barrier beyond the little two lane highway and down into the darkness of the sudden drop beyond. The gorge opened up between the two mountains like the mouth of some gigantic and sleeping ogre with immense and jagged teeth. They were the type that chewed entire families, and swallowed all, never to be seen again. It was beautiful during the day, but by night, it was truly a place of monsters… Her eyes kept following along the little cement barricade that stood between the headlights and that steep drop. It was such a dark and desolate place. With exception to a breach in that barrier, no one would even notice if they slid from off that edge…

Princeton, British Columbia, Canada.
4:37 a.m.
Gerald Bonchek leaned lower over his plate as he shoveled the remainder of the mashed potatoes and gravy into his mouth. He snorted and grunted while eating, as suffering from respiratory problem due to his obesity, wiped a hand at the gravy running down his bloated face. The diner had been almost empty, and as he shoved his second dinner aside, he reached for the apple pie with extra whipped cream.

"Did you need anything else?" An older waitress came out from the kitchen and looked upon him in utter disgust.

"No—just a bill--," He grunted while forking great hunks of the pie into his gravy smeared mouth, "I'm in a hurry…"

Shaking her head, she moved toward the till, and glancing back at him, felt her previous meal attempting to vacate her stomach. He wore lace-less shoes, black track pants, and a black t-shirt from where his immense belly sagged grotesquely out. His hair was white and cut short, and his head appeared like a half-filled sack of potatoes that spilled over his bulk. He smelled atrocious, as between sweating and poor hygiene, his lack of exercise had caused his blocked intestines to omit an endless, continual stream of flatulence. It was for this very reason that he now cast a hand upon his bloated guts, as burbling and groaning warned of yet another diarrheic explosion. Dragging his bulk from off the chair, he winced, groaning as his feet and legs bent beneath the massive weight.

"I need a bathroom--," He cursed as she returned with the check, and waving her away, waddled toward the stalls at the back of the store, "Just another brainless woman--," He grunted, gasping for breath, as he made his way in through the bathroom door.

With his stomach growling and uttering guttural sounds, he slowly turned and intending to sit on the tiny toilet with his huge derriere, passed gas, and erupted like a fecal Mount Vesuvius. Beating a hand against the stall, he angrily cursed the owners for being inconsiderate wherein the installation of the facilities was concerned.

"These things are built for skinny people--," He struggled while attempting to avoid falling from off the toilet due to his disgusting mass, "No one has any consideration for husky guys, the ignorant bastards."

Having finally finished with the entire ghastly affair, he passed gas several times, as satisfied he was done, and unable to reach behind himself to properly clean, pulled up his pants. Leaving the stall in a hideous state, he slammed the door closed, and shaking his head, muttered, 'It's their own faults for making these things so small—screw them…"

Wobbling back down the aisle and between the tables, he dropped the money on the counter in passing, and said, "That should cover everything—I left your tip in the bathroom…"

Making his way out the front door, he struggled to where his truck and trailer were parked. He had departed Vancouver and was bound for Edmonton with a load of assorted alcohol and spirits. Already running late and suffering from a number of weight-related issues, he lit a cigarette before pulling the truck slowly out of the lot.

Looking toward the diner in passing, he had chuckled while seeing the waitress departing the fouled bathrooms. She had waved her hands wildly, as having suffered his sickness, appeared as though she were going to be ill.

"Serves you right—bitch--," He scoffed while pulling out and onto the highway leaving town. The cab was filled with six-packs of soda, assorted candy bars, chips, and the remains of assorted take-out. Aside from being filthy and smelling atrocious, it was dangerously cluttered as things that he had dropped and could not reach, rolled about the foot pedals.

"Oh shit--," I forgot to take my diabetic medication again--," He rubbed at his face, and putting his glasses on, squinted while suffering with failing visibility. Reaching over and digging through the assorted trash on the seat beside him, he located a pill container. Struggling with the bottle, it slipped from his fat fingers and dropped into the rubbish around his feet.

"I'll get it later--," He grunted, "I'll be fine for a while. I can't pull over right now anyway—I need to make up for lost time—and make that damn hill." Going through the gears he began bringing the Kenworth up to speed, the immense and sheer cliffs rising high before him as he sped dangerously up the dark highway.

Princeton, British Columbia, Canada.
5:05 a.m.
Pam had sat quietly listening to the straining of the diesel engine and hiss of the air brakes. She had decided to leave the driver to his hair-raising task, and start silently praying. They had navigated through what seemed the worst of the canyon route, and having passed the little city of Princeton, now made the final descent.

"There's a little diner and service station at the bottom of this hill--," Robert quietly announced, "It's not a regular stop—but after this ride, I think that we could all use a ten-minute break."

"I'm with you there--," She tensed in her seat, as restless, attempted to conceal her concern with a smile, "A hot coffee and a snack would go down real nice, right about now."

"Snack--," Patrick had awakened to the promise, and smiled, "I'm starving."

"We'll get something nice at the diner--," She winked, "How much longer will it take to get there?" She had remembered seeing it before in passing, but never stopped before.

Looking to his watch, Robert had smiled, "Oh—I'd guess about fifteen minutes at this speed."

"It looks like there's less snow down here?" Patrick took notice of the darkening patches on the highway.

"It always warms up a little when you come down into a valley--," Robert explained while accelerating into a turn, "The roads are safer here as well, so we can pick up the pace."

The sound of the engine roaring and force of the gravitational pull on the corner now sent Pam's stomach into a spin. There was a tingling that ringing like alarm bells, screamed, echoing through her body and mind. Her body tensed as the road became slowly straighter, and the bus accelerated, sending them speeding down the hill.

Princeton, British Columbia, Canada.
5:10 a.m.
Smoke billowed from the twin stacks of the enormous red Kenworth as Gerald dangerously sped through the canyon while making his way upward. The flaming boar on the driver's door flashing as it read boldly in black and gold custom letters: Road Hog.

"Come on, baby—," He snorted while shoving chips into his mouth, and chewing loudly, "Get rolling, we need a good run to make that hill!"

He was a resident of Edmonton, Alberta, and running empty due to a mistake at the depot, was hurrying back for a load to make up for his losses. As angry as this had made him, the empty trailer made the journey through the mountains a lot faster, as long as he didn't encounter any strong winds.

The night had become deathly still as the roar of his engine echoed through the valley. Like a big red freight-train, he high-balled, swerving dangerously into the oncoming lane while navigating the turns. He drove with a distinct air of over-confidence, a delusional narcissist that lacked a single ounce of common sense.

Fumbling with a bottle of soda, he spilled while struggling to keep a firm grip upon the steering wheel. Cursing and wiping at his wet shirt, he tossed the bottle from out his open window. It was an old habit of which he considered a 'make-work' project for the less fortunate. As loathsome and disgusting as he had always been, he looked down upon the poor and sickly, referring to them simply as 'street scum.'

"There's another one for the street scum to pick up--," He laughed while shoving a candy bar into his mouth, and dropping the wrapper in the cab, "I should pick up one of those lot lizards from the truck stop, and have her haul my ashes and clean up this cab."

His mouth has always been far larger than his means, and if he'd ever had an erection in twenty years, he could never have found it anyway. At fifty three years of age, he was nothing more than a foul-mouthed, degenerate, and loathsome waste of human skin. But he knew all of this and in spite of the facts treated others like garbage. Continually condescending, he had a sense of entitlement, and was vulgar and ignorant to everyone around him. The few that remained had either taken sympathy upon him and tolerated his abuse, or had simply been victims their entire lives. It was a sickness of the soul that all who exist in personal failure are condemned to become... It was for this exact reason that the darkness had only lingered like a shadow from out of his dimly lit cab. It was an infinite evil that, sensing the vile nature of this lost cause, now simply watched and awaited the inevitable

Princeton, British Columbia, Canada.
5:21 a.m.
Noticing that something had troubled Robert, Pam leaned out of her seat and into the aisle, quietly asking, "Is something the natter?"

At first he had been reluctant to respond, as peering into the darkness beyond the windshield, he shook his head, "I was sure that I saw oncoming headlights on the road below, but it would've been impossible for anything so big to be moving that fast up here."

"Could it have possibly been a reflection from off flowing water, or maybe an icy cliff?" The hair stood on end at the nape of her neck and forearms as she patiently awaited an answer.

"I don't think so—but it's late and these old roads can play tricks on a person at night. We'll be just fine." He winked while offering a reassuring smile.

Pam's heart was racing, the blood thundering in her mind like a hammer as her eyes remained fixed on the black and serpentine road ahead. She knew that area quite well, and had driven it herself during the summer. They had reached the three quarter mark to the bottom of the canyon, and had less than a few hundred yards to travel.

As they rounded a steep cliff face and Robert swerved into the turn, they were suddenly blinded by the high beams of an oncoming truck!

"What the fuck are you doing, you idiot!" Gerald screamed in a high-pitched, squealing tone, and applying the air-horns, refused to slow down! There had simply not been enough clearance for both vehicles. The little two lane highway had curved wide around the cliff face, but due to Gerald's speed, had left no room for either to make the pass.

It had all occurred within a flash, and without ever having the time or opportunity to even think. As the front of Gerald's red Kenworth had appeared on the bend before them, something had dropped from out of the cliffs high above. It moved with the speed of lightning, as crashing through the trucks windshield, sent the eighteen-wheeler across the lanes and into the cement barrier! The barrier had exploded into dust beneath the trucks weight, as shrieking and throwing his arms before his face, Gerald felt the truck dropping out from beneath him! In the seconds that it had taken, the Road Hog slipped over the edge and dropped down into the canyon. From out of the blackness the diesel tanks ignited from the rocky crags far below. An explosion rocked the soaring cliffs and brought down tons of debris, while crushing and completely burying Gerald and his old Kenworth.

Through the entire affair, Robert hadn't lost control of the bus for even a single moment. As expertly steering out of a slide, he skidded past the broken barrier and navigated the wide turn. With nerves of steel and skill accrued through many years of traveling the mountains, he ever so carefully regained control of the bus and returned to normal cruising speed.

"Holy shit…" Patrick gasped while sitting straight up in his seat.

Bursting into tears, Pam had leapt from out of her seat and tightly embraced the boy. She had looked over to where Robert, still maintaining his reserved demeanor, had cast a nervous glance, "I'll call for assistance when we reach the diner." He swallowed hard while steering with white knuckles, "It's not safe to stop up here anyway—and there wasn't anything that anyone could have done for that driver."

"God bless you--," She wept openly while tightly gripping onto the traumatized Patrick, "Robert—you just saved all of our lives…"

"There was something—I saw it in the headlights just before the accident--," He now appeared disoriented and suddenly frightened, "It came out of the sky—or maybe from off the cliffs?" He shot her a fearful glance, "I think that it was some kind of huge bird?"

"Well whatever it was--," She stuttered through the tears, "Thank God that it was there…"

"You folks just sit tight--," Robert motioned for them to remain calm, "Everything is perfectly fine now—we're all okay, and I'll have you sitting safely in that diner in no time…"

Deep at the bottom of that black gorge something now moved among the burning debris. It was a pale and lone figure, which, crawling out from between the rubble, slowly stood up and spread its immense bat-wings. The demon within Caitlin had slowly turned to look back, knowing the grisly ending that had come to Gerald Bonchek. Forever trapped in what remained of his cab, he had been crushed into a gruesome, fleshy and fatty paste by thousands of tons of rock. Although she felt remorse for having caused the death, the demon reveled within the victory and shared its insight of the dead man. Images of Gerald's life flashed before her eyes, as disgusted and angered with the atrocities that she witnessed, she had conceded to the demon. It had previously made her aware of the darkness and what was to befall Pam and little Patrick, and was the primary reason that they now still lived...

As having sensed the darkness, Caitlin had concealed her intention while silently waiting upon the dark cliffs. She had waited until the very last moment before casting herself into the path of imminent destruction. The darkness had never become aware of her presence due to the demon, and therefore been unable to intervene. The evil had shielded her and they had acted in unison, but for entirely different reasons. Where she sought to spare lives, the demon conspired to take one. In the end, the results were for the best of everyone involved...

"Caitlin--," The demon whispered as she stood among the scattered flames and icy, jagged rock, "Though your will be great—thou can never hope to defeat me... I am your undoing—and your time here grows short."

"I am aware of these things and more--," She replied as tears ran from the monster's burning eyes, "What would you have of me?"

"Only that of which has already been done--," It hissed, "Murderess..."

"I had no intention of taking lives on this night--," She argued, "Only sparing those of the woman and young boy."

"And yet, thou still committed murder—and are damned by thine own hand..."

"If you would take me--," She lashed out, smashing and shattering great slabs of stone with her bare fists, "Then do so now and be done with it!"

There was a sudden stillness among the rubble and flames, and then it spoke, whispering as it said, "Thou hast become little more than a spoiled child within thy master's protective embrace... Thou did once plead—and vow eternal service unto me in exchange for that, which thou dost now possess..."

"All that I have become is a monster!" She cried out, and falling to her knees, covered her hideous face with long and clawed hands, "An evil and accursed thing! I have become you! If it is your will, then be damned, and take me now!"

There was a cold, sinister and echoing laughter throughout the canyon, and then, in a quiet and calm manner, it hissed, "Be warned—and know this. For it is far better to rein as the destroyer—than be taken by one... A lesson of which thou hast long forgotten... So be it—thou art granted—freedom..."

Caitlin felt her entire body begin to burn, as shrieking in pain, she felt the demon slip from out of her as though it burst from beneath her skin! A moment later and she lay naked, shivering and trapped among the jagged rocks in the frozen night. She wept while suddenly feeling the bite of the bitter wind upon her flesh and becoming vulnerable before all the elements. Trembling uncontrollably, she slowly climbed to her feet, and shielding her eyes from the wind, peered out and into the distance. Nothing but blackness with exception to the tiny lights of the copper mine in the distance.

The wind blew and she stumbled, scraping her knee and crying out as she bled from a nasty gash on her leg. In the fires light she could see the great distance that she would have to climb to escape, and in her current condition, knew it to be impossible.

"What have you done—it's so cold..," She made her way toward one of the fires, stubbing a toe and wincing as she fell. Another terrible gash, except now her ankle bled as she wept while huddling near the flames.

It was only moments before she saw the first glint of the fire's reflection in its eyes. A low growl emanating from out of the shadows as the cries and yelps of the pack now echoed through the enormous and surrounding forest. Pressing her back against the rocks, she realized this had been no place to run, and no chance for shelter of any kind. She was caught out in the open and without a weapon of any kind, was left totally helpless.

The growl became an angered snarl and the snapping and gnashing of savage teeth. The sound now terrified her, as having never before encountered such a thing, she climbed unsteadily to her feet. She could see the bright reflections of many more pairs of eyes, all of them watching her from out of the blackness of the forest, and not fifty feet away. In that moment she realized that what the demon had meant by freedom, was a swift means to a bitter and terrifying end...

The eyes came closer and ever closer, the snarls and gnashing of teeth growing louder as, becoming bolder, they now approached.

Her heart pounded furiously, the blood rushing through her veins and arteries so fast that it pounded like hammers within her head! She was so cold, so terribly, terribly cold! The wind moaned, and the first of the wolves appeared as it crept from out of the shadows. Its large yellow eyes burning in the fire's glow as it snarled. It was an enormous gray wolf. It was the alpha male, and as leader of the pack, was the first to approach as it prepared for the kill.

She saw the others forming a circle from all about her, and all that she could do was stand there in absolute horror, petrified and unable to even move. Alone in the darkness and surrounded by a most brutal death, she felt her heart sink as the beast came within pouncing distance.

It growled, and no sooner than did it utter the first roaring snarl, than did it leap at her, and the rest of the pack charge in for the kill! Time seemed to stand suddenly still, as from out of the chaos, she heard that familiar voice once more, "I would see mine enemy cast down before me into utter ruin--," It hissed, "I would demand mortal sacrifice—and willing servitude. In exchange do I grant thee mortal rein—and the dark gift of which you wished to be released? If thou dost seek shelter within dark embrace—accept thy master's pact..."

"If I am to leave this world now—I go without you--," She cried out in defiance.

A brilliant blue flash erupted before her and the demon stood upon the rocks gazing down, "What would you have of me?"

The wolves stood frozen, as while caught in time, and the demons eyes burned as it stared, asking again, "What would you have of me..."

"Release Marlowe—," She pleaded, 'Allow his soul freedom—and I will willingly serve you... I ask only this and will submit..."

"Marlowe..." The eyes blazed as blue hellfire escaped with each breath as it spoke, "Marlowe..."

"Set him free--," Shivering uncontrollably, she whispered through the tears, "And I will forever serve you, master..."

The world stood absolutely still in the moment as the demon contemplated, and then looking up, hissed, "So be it—I release him.... What say thee?"

"I accept your terms--," She wept bitterly, shrieking, "I accept!"

The demon vanished as the night all around her came to life with the enraged and wild snarls of the ravenous beasts! She stood back, becoming suddenly calm, as her wounds healed and a blue fire flashed in the depths of her eyes.

The wolves lunged and she shrieked, an echoing sound of horror and madness that caused the cliffs to tremble, and send rock crumbling and tumbling down!

Her terror had suddenly turned to absolute and blind rage, as lashing out, her huge claws eviscerated and immediately killed the Alpha male, its torn and bloodied body crashing so hard against the rocks that it exploded, its corpse little more than an unrecognizable sack of broken bones, steaming entrails, and mangled flesh!

Moving with an unearthly speed, she spread immense bat-wings and flew directly into the attacking beasts! With savage claws she ravaged the now shrieking and terrified animals, dismembering, beheading, and ripping the life from out of them! It all happened in moments, and none had even had an opportunity to retreat. The rocks ran red with their blood, and silence once more fell in that dark and dismal place. As among the bloodied and still twitching remains, Caitlin the monster stood silent. The fire crackled, and the icy wind moaned as it swept bitterly down from the dark mountain high above. There was no other sound as the last breath was ushered from out of the mouth of the last dying wolf…

"It is far better to rein as the monster--," She whispered into the icy gust, "Than to be taken by one…"

Walking away from that dismal and blood-soaked grave, she leapt upward and swiftly vanished into the black heavens.

Dublin, Ireland.
Dublin International Airport
Sunday, February 9, 1975.
12:05 p.m.

"Patrick--," Carrie had suddenly gasped, as turning to look into the heavens, leaned back against old Lawrence's cab. Throwing a hand before her mouth, she felt something deep in her heart crying out.

"What's wrong, sweetheart?" Scott had rushed forward, and taking her into his arms, asked, "What's the matter—did you see something?"

"No—but I felt it--," Her eyes filled with tears as she hugged him close, "It's Patrick—I know that something's wrong."

"Our flight leaves in thirty minutes--," Maya hurried to their sides, "I can make a quick call and check in with things back home?"

"No—let's just stay altogether--," Carrie took hold of Maya's hand, and sniffling said, "Let's just try to make it back home."

"I'm so sorry that I won't be going with you--," Old Lawrence removed his hat and sadly looked around, "But Ireland's been my home forever— and it's where I want them to lay me to rest, when my time comes. Besides—I don't think that I could handle playing tag with the devil—I'm just too bloody old…"

Maya has stepped forward, and kissing the old man's cheek, adjusted the collar of his shirt, "I've got your telephone number— and I'll be calling to check in on you as well. You take care of yourself, Duck. And please remember what we told you…"

"I'll be praying for the lot of you--," He glanced fearfully between them, and quietly said, "And I'll also be expecting that telephone call, just to let me know that you all made it safely home."

Extending a hand, Scott had just hugged the old man and given him a hearty slap on the back, "You know?" He thought briefly, and then looking back at the old fellow, smiled, "I suppose that you Irishmen are okay?"

"We're all Scots at heart--," Lawrence waved as they turned to leave, "It's those bloody Englishmen that are no good!"

Carrie had turned and running back, threw her arms around the old man's neck. Kissing his cheek, she had brushed the white curls out of his eyes from under his cap. At a loss for words, she had just stared at him, as smiling, he had secretly understood.

"The world and life are full of partings—and most of them bitter-sweet--," He gently brushed an old hand against her cheek, "You just never know—we might yet see each other again, someday?"

And with that she had slowly turned and walking up beside Scott, taken her husband's hand as they hurried away. Scott had looked back one final time, as the old man just stood next to his cab and waved. A chill gust had blown at his silvery hair, as the smoke from his pipe was carried away. The clouds had lazily drifted, the rolling hills flowed, and somewhere in the distance, a piper played...

Vancouver, British Columbia, Canada.
Sanctum Arcanum
Sunday, February 9, 1975.
5:25 a.m.

It was still dark when Rich had pulled in before the black iron gates of home. We had hesitated for a moment, scanning the area for anything unusual before using the remote. The gates had slowly parted, and as we had pulled into the long drive, I suddenly felt like a stranger in a foreign land. There had been lights in the windows of the main floor as our friends took immediate notice of our return. Yet, the only thing on my mind now was the loss of Raymond and the growing concern for Caitlin. It was almost as though I could sense her, and feel the demon within her at the same time.

In some odd fashion, I suspected that they now shared a symbiotic relationship, rather than what had been originally anticipated. The demon's once ravenous appetite had somehow been satiated in some manner, as though feeding the evil in some way? I say that I could sense her, but not in the aspect that usual senses might be considered. It was more like feeling her through all of my five senses, and then communicating through a sixth, and possibly more? This still could not entirely satisfy me, as the human condition demanded physical evidence to gratify a troubled mind. Yet still, I felt a cold lump form in the pit of my bowels, and the suspicion that something terrifying and truly terrible had happened.

Sheltered behind the massive gates and once more upon sanctified ground, we had departed the car, and all hurriedly gone into the house. There had been expressions of relief and then tears of remorse when they had noticed that Raymond had been absent from among us.

We had barely had time to remove our soaked clothing and boots when there came a loud and abrupt knocking upon the front door. They had all turned, and looking to me, had then been utterly shocked, as hurrying to answer it, I had welcomed Caitlin back home.

"Where were you—and what's happened?" Noticing that she had used a small tarp to cover herself, I had quickly slipped her into my overcoat and hurried her away from the others.

"It was my intention to prevent the loss of others in a terrible accident—of which the darkness was partially instrumental." Swiftly ascending the stairs, I had followed her into the bedroom, where dropping the coat, she slipped into a bath robe.

"An accident--," I had previously seen something in the back of my mind and the pieces now fell together, "What exactly do you mean?"

She had led me into the bathroom, where running the water for a shower, she said, "You almost lost two others from among you on this night." Dropping the robe, she hopped into the shower, and still speaking, explained as she washed the grime from herself, "There was an accident between a long distance bus and a big truck upon the cliffs surrounding Princeton." She peeked around the curtain, a blue flash sparking from deep within her emerald eyes, "But there is no reason to be concerned—your companions were not among the dead…"

"But, who was killed—and what friends are you talking about?"

"They're alright, the woman Pamela—and the young son of Carrie and Scott." She replied from behind the curtain, "And the one who died--," She drew the curtain back ever so slightly, and stared as though looking from a million miles away, "Was a worthless plague upon mankind and no loss anyway…"

"I have never known a sentient being to speak of anything living in that way." A dark suspicion now took hold of my heart as I peered back at her beneath the running water, "And I have never known you to find satisfaction in the death of another…"

Slowly she turned off the water, and slipping back into the robe, reached for a towel and quietly began drying her long red hair. There had been moments, where as she had moved, I caught glimpses of blackened fingertips and toes which had almost appeared like claws. It wasn't that she had actually been physically changing, but the fact that I had started sensing and seeing the demon within her.

"You took the life of that truck driver tonight--," The words had slipped out before I had even been aware, "And somehow—formed a pact, a relationship with your demon…"

She had just glanced over at me, and then reaching for a brush, sat upon the edge of the tub while dragging it through her hair. It wasn't that I had intended to become judge, jury and executioner, but I had a burning desire to understand how this had come about.

"Caitlin—sweetheart--," I had leaned closer and gazed deeply into her eyes, "Please, help me understand."

Without the utterance of a single word, she had calmly placed down the brush, and taking my face into her hands, gazed back as a blue fire burned in her eyes. The light became all-consuming, as feeling as though I were falling into those fiery Sapphires, I sensed images forming within my mind. There was a pale green bathroom stall, a grotesque figure of a man, and an absolutely disgusting act. Then, I saw a dark and frozen highway and a bus that slowly descended from among the sheer and jagged cliffs. There was a flash, a flaming image of a boar and a red Freightliner racing madly upward from the bottom of a hill.

"Pam--," I had whispered as while looking from out of the darkness and into the window upon her pale and terrified face, "Oh dear God…"

Still, Caitlin held me firmly between her hands and forced me to gaze upon the truth that now burned in my mind. As through the pitch-dark of the blackened heavens, I saw a dark angel appear from out of nowhere! From high above the jagged peaks in the distance, I saw the headlights of both vehicles as the truck was swiftly approaching the bus. And then, as that disgusting and vile driver cursed and blasted the horn, I saw the end coming for the occupants of the bus! In a blinding flash the dark angel dropped from out of the heavens and sent the Freightliner and its darkness from over the cliff! Shivering in the blinding vision of the ensuing explosion and rock-slide, I saw Caitlin standing in the dark canyon alone. There had been a dark submission to a necessary evil, a silent promise of an eternity in exchange for wicked lives…

"So, rather than bow before a master in hell--," I had realized the consequences of her decision, "You shall reign together in this world…"

"It no longer possesses me--," She whispered as though sharing some unspeakable secret, "But exists and shares as Marlowe also does with you. Don't you see Michael—there was just no other way…"

It would have been impossible to judge her for having committed to such a thing, as in all truth, I was honestly and exactly the same.

"So what happens now?"

"We fight as we always have--," She replied without a second thought, "And remain together, always…" Kissing me softly, her eyes glistened as the stars returned to the emeralds that so lovingly watched me now. Marlowe had been exactly right from the very beginning, although I had never truly understood until now.

"Not all things that seem evil are your enemy—and not all that are near are true…"

"Did you finally have that mirror moved?" She took immediate notice of its absence.

"I did mention it to Rich--," I looked into the empty corner at the back of the bathroom, "But he never said anything to me about already having moved it."

There was a soft knock at the bathroom door, and Rich politely spoke from beyond, "Carrie just called from Dublin International Airport--," there was a stutter and sudden excitement to his voice, "They have Maya with them—she's safe--," He spoke as though he truly could not believe it, "And they're all coming home."

Moving from where I had been kneeling before Caitlin, I hurriedly went over, and opened the door. "Thank God—my dear friend." I hugged and held him tightly as he fought back the tears of joy. It had all been so terrible, and though they were returning, I had still feared the worst. I had kept this to myself in that moment, and permitted him the luxury of a distant hope.

"Oh, and by the way?" Changing the subject, I directed his attention into the far corner, "Did you already move that mirror that I'd mentioned."

Appearing somewhat confused, he had looked past me and slowly shaken his head, "No, but it's possible that one of the others might've done it. I'll ask Tim when I go back downstairs—he'll know for sure."

Thanking him, I kept looking back to where the mirror had stood, and felt unsettled with its mysterious disappearance. If it had just been an ordinary piece of glass, it wouldn't have been a bother, but I knew better…

"You know what?" I spoke more to myself than anyone else, "I can ask him myself."

Following Rich and Caitlin, I soon found myself gathered with the others about the hearth. I hadn't wasted any time, and attracting his attention with a gesture of my hand, asked, "Tim, I was just wondering? Did you move that old mirror out of the bathroom upstairs?"

"No—to be honest with everything else happening—it slipped my mind. Why—what's wrong?"

"Well, as odd as this may seem—it's gone."

There had been some confused expressions from around the group, but most of them had never even seen it because it was in my private bathroom.

"Maybe Scott or Raymond moved it down into the basement?" Rich had suggested, "One second—I'll run down and have a quick look."

The room had become absolutely quiet as he had hurried off, and not another word had been said until he returned moments later.

"No—it's not down there either--," He shrugged, "I don't have the slightest clue as to what might've happened to it."

"Is this thing important?" Jay tossed another log into the hearth.

"It might be--," dropping onto the couch beside Caitlin, I shrugged, "I suppose that we'll find out sooner or later."

"So what are we going to do now?" Fatigued from the long night, Deb could barely see as she wearily rubbed at her eyes.

"None of us are in any condition to do anything right now--," Jay peered about into the exhausted and worn features of his friends, "If I can make a suggestion—I'd say that we should all get rested up before we even consider trying anything else."

"We should wait until all the others get back--," Jen agreed, "There's no point in spreading ourselves this thin again, the cost of mistakes are just too high."

"At least we still have Ole--," Deb sighed deeply and slumping back against her husband on the couch, groaned, "I sure hope that he's going to be alright."

"Ole--," It had caught me completely off-guard, and I sat straight up off the couch, "What do you mean?"

"Well, he called last night and was concerned about all of you--," She explained, "I filled him in on everything—and he said that he'll do anything that he can to help out."

"And, what did you tell him?" Realizing what had happened, I swallowed hard with the growing concern.

"To avoid leaving his place at night--," She replied, "And that he should wait until he hears from you before doing anything."

"Thank you—I'll call him this afternoon…" Unwilling to pursue the matter in my over-tired and somewhat irrational state, I simply sank back down into the couch.

"Pam and Patrick are supposed to be arriving this morning from Revelstoke." Deb raised a finger in thought, and yawning as she looked to me, said, "They're going to be waiting for someone to pick them up."

"I'll do it--," Jen volunteered, "I managed to get a little more sleep than anyone else around here. Not that I really feel that great or anything."

"The only vehicle that we still have is the Eldorado--," Rich reminded us about the Suburban and RV, saying, "Unless you're willing to drive Raymond's car?"

"That's fine by me—I really loved that guy…" Jen covered her face with a hand and quietly wept. Deb had leaned closer, and taking the younger woman under her arm, held her into a gentle embrace.

"I'll get to a car lot later this afternoon--," Rich informed everyone, "And we'll arrange for everyone to get mobile again."

"I'll give you a hand with that--," Jay raised a hand, and said, "I still have my Olds Vista Cruiser. So, it's not like we can't get around."

"In all the confusion I completely forgot about that." I slowly moved from the couch as Caitlin followed, and pausing in the hall, looked back from the bottom of the stairs, "I need to rest for a few hours—please call on me if you hear anything from Carrie and the others before I wake up."

"Are we really safe here--," Jay had halted me as I had attempted to ascend the steps, asking, "Will anything be able to attack us here?"

Remembering the golden key, Deb had removed it from around her neck and tossed it back to Tim. He caught it from out of the air, and slipping it around his neck, winked at Jay, "Don't worry—we've got the ultimate grounds-keeper and a watch-dog from hell."

"Please--," I had looked back from where I stood at the steps, "Everyone try to get as much rest as you can. We can't allow ourselves to be run down any further; we need clear minds and strong bodies if we hope to get through this thing."

"I'll wait for Pam's call--," Jen caught Rich by the sleeve as he had turned to depart, "Just please leave me that remote so we can get back in when I come back."

Pulling it from his pocket, Rich placed the remote on the table before her, saying, "Raymond's car keys are in the bowl on the kitchen counter. You can't miss them; they're the only ones with a big golden tab that says, Raymond."

Jen had looked down, and sensing her grief, Rich had placed a reassuring hand upon her shoulder, "We all loved him—," He said softly, "And he'll be truly missed…

Moving from the couch, she took a firm hold upon him and hugged him tightly, "I don't know how much more of this I'm going to be able to take—," She sobbed, as looking up at him with tearful eyes, whispered, "I can't handle losing everyone like this—and not knowing what's going to happen from one day to the next."

"Something happened last night—and out at those old mausoleums of the McCreary place." He spoke softly and swallowed hard while looking down at the trembling woman in his arms, "I think that thing—the darkness, might have felt fear for the first time. Because when we challenged the thing--," Raising an eyebrow with the thought, his eyes reflected hope, "It wouldn't cross the boundaries—and then retreated."

"Are you saying that it might just back off?"

"No—I doubt that very much, but what I am saying is that together we've become much stronger. And if we can cause it to make that one mistake, and enter onto sanctified ground as an energy form, then we've got a good chance of sending it into the void."

She hugged him while accepting what little hope remained, "Thank you for that—it's not much—but it's a chance… and better than no hope at all."

She had watched as he had slowly walked into the long shadows of the corridor. She knew in her heart that she could never leave any of them, and would not abandon Sanctum Arcanum out of fear. In the end of all ends, and regardless of anything, she honestly and truly loved them all.

"He's right—we may not have won the war—but we took the battle last night." Jay sighed deeply while peering between Tim and Jen, "I thought that it was all over at those old mausoleums—we were trapped with nowhere left to run or hide."

Wrapping a woolen blanket about her shoulders in the morning chill, she had turned to Jay, and asked, "What happened—and what made the difference in the end?"

"I'm not exactly sure--," He thought for a moment, and then said, "It had something to do with that devil stone, and the way that Michael stood up in front of that thing. It's like it wasn't expecting a challenge, and that was the moment when everything changed."

"What's the deal with Amica--," Deb curiously asked, "Michael must be utterly broken, knowing that Caitlin was never truly real and is now gone forever."

Tim had sniffled while holding back the emotions. He had always been a man of 'strong intestinal fortitude' as his grandfather had always said, but so much had happened since. "Well that's where this story takes another turn--," Clasping his hands tightly together, he had looked back at Jen from where he sat on the couch across from her, and said, "It seems that the darkness had assumed that shape when he had first entered the McCreary house. He told us in the car—that it had manifested in the same way that Amica had."

"But why would it do that?" Jen appeared confused.

"Because of the image of the true Caitlin that still existed deep within his soul's memory. The darkness sensed this and used the shadow of that memory to captivate and hold him."

"So now that the identity of the darkness has been unveiled--," Jen looked between the two men, "Caitlin is gone forever."

"No—she isn't--," Tim's eyes had followed to the stairs as they all slowly turned and looked up, "She's been with him from the very beginning…"

There was a moment of stillness between them as they had all looked to one another in complete and utter astonishment.

"There are forces at work here that none of could even begin to imagine--," Speaking quietly, he continued to explain, "But now that they're united—I've seen some changes come over the both of them."

"I saw what she changed into--," Jay shook his head while reaching for the crucifix that hung from about his neck, and nervously said, "And I'm not so sure it's a good thing?"

"It's a good thing as long as she stays on our side." Rich raised an eyebrow in question, "Let's just hope for the best."

"Amen to that." Jay scratched at his beard, "I just wish that this was all a bad dream and that I'd wake up…"

"Another concern--," Deb raised a finger in thought, "I'm not sure about any of you. But have you noticed that Michael hasn't been taking his heart medication?"

"That's right." Ray looked around the little gathering, "I saw the almost full bottle in the bathroom cabinet just last night."

"And that's not all--," There was a dark suspicion reflecting in Jen's big brown eyes, as she swallowed back the anxiety and quietly said, "Even though we're all stressed out and not getting any sleep—has anyone else noticed that he seems to look younger?"

"He's always seemed younger than his years--," Rich shrugged, and looking to Jen, said, "And the grey doesn't look so obvious in sandy brown hair."

"What if this Marlowe entity is having some kind of diverse effect on him?" Deb asked, "What if, through possession, it's slowly taking him over?"

"Nothing in this nightmare really makes much sense." Staring blindly into the hearth, Jay fidgeted nervously with the crucifix around his neck, "But Michael saved my life out there—and I'm staying to make up that debt, come hell or high water…"

"None of us will know the truth until the time comes." Slapping at his face with both hands, Tim shook his head while trying to shake off the fatigue, "And for better or worse—we'll either win—or go down trying, together…"

"Amen to that, brother." Jay sighed deeply as the cold and exhaustion finally caught up to him, and he slipped even deeper into the couch.

"You boys get some sleep--," Jen moved off the couch, and waving toward the front door said, "I really can't just sit around here by the telephone. I'm going to go down to the bus depot and wait for them."

"She should be calling soon--," Deb led her husband out of the main room, and peering back from the shadows of the hall, said, "Even if the weather was a little nasty—they should already be in Chilliwack or somewhere close-by."

"It's okay—I'd rather drive down now. I can get a coffee and muffin along the way. See you soon--," Jen waved as though possibly for the last time, "Till then…"

It was obvious that farewells in any form had become too much for Deb. She had become acquainted with many new friends, and recently lost several to the darkness. She had just thoughtfully looked back, a shadow falling across her features as she frowned, and said, "Just get back here altogether, and in one piece…"

Ray had waved, taking his wife by the hand, as he turned and quickly vanished into the hall.

The hearth crackled, embers popped and those who were gathered around it, silently slipped into dark and troubled slumber…

CHAPTER TWENTY THREE

Vancouver, British Columbia, Canada.
Greyhound Bus Terminal
6:35 a.m.

It was a cold and clear morning as the bus carrying Pam and young Patrick had finally entered the West end depot. They were running far later than scheduled due to the accident and arrived hours later than expected. Robert had bought them both dinner in the little diner, and as they gave statements to the police, Pam could only be grateful for having survived the ordeal. Although it had been very early in the morning, insurance representatives from Greyhound had also arrived to speak to them. There were documents to be read and waivers to be signed, and the company assured her that there would be compensation due to the incident. She had politely declined, insisting that the driver had not been at fault, and hence the company was not liable. The two gentlemen had looked across the diner at Robert, who sitting alone and drinking coffee, stared out the window upon the dark mountain. They had closed their briefcases, and offering her a business card, thanked her for her time and swiftly departed.

It all seemed to happen in slow-motion as they shared those final moments in the little truck-stop diner. She could only stare as though having watched through some terrible dream. She trembled with the sight of the immense, jagged and misty mountain beyond the large windows, the rolling fog pouring down from the frozen peaks, as the blackened stone stood majestically beneath a dark and cloud-filled sky. And then, sitting quietly and appearing so very small beneath the window and mountain, Robert had slowly turned to look over at her. His features were stern and his bright blue eyes shone with a kindness that cleared the darkness from out of her heart and soul. Another unsung hero of the highways, she would remember him forever...

As the bus rolled to a stop and parked in the bay, Robert climbed from his seat and paused to look back at them, "Usually, I would thank the passengers for riding with Greyhound. " He shrugged at a total loss while sympathetically looking down at them, "But, I really don't know what to say?"

Moving from her seat, Pam rightly embraced the startled man, and hugging him closely, said, "If it wasn't for Greyhound and you, Robert--," She swallowed hard and sniffled back a tear, "None of us would be here today."

"It might've been an act of God out there on the mountain last night, or just kismet." Looking sadly between them, he patted Patrick on the head, saying, "Either way—good luck to you both, and God bless."

"Thank you, Robert--," She stepped back, and sighing deeply, said, "God bless and keep you safe, always. And thank you for everything…"

Nodding slowly, he picked up his briefcase from behind the driver's seat, and saluting them, quietly went on his way.

The baggage staff had already unloaded their suitcases, and as they picked them up, Pam was startled by a voice from behind them. Jen ran through the open doors and into the bay, as accidentally dropping the little Styrofoam cup full of coffee, she threw her arms wide open! They grasped each other tightly and hugged as though it were the end of the world.

"I was waiting for you--," Jen gasped with eyes bulging in fear, "I heard about the accident on the news while I was sitting in the arrivals bay."

Unable to even speak of the event without tears, Pam had only nodded as she took hold of Patrick's arm and they hurried toward the doors.

"I was never more scared in my life." Patrick looked to Jen thoughtfully, and sighing deeply, said, "I think that God saved us out there—the driver said that he saw a big bird, but I think it was an angel…"

"A dark angel—I think that I've seen one too..," Jen nodded with the sudden realization, and with-holding a tear, took hold of Patrick's hand as they hurried out and toward the car.

Vancouver, British Columbia, Canada.

8:45 a.m.

Awakened by the telephone ringing and still dressed, Ole drowsily rolled over to answer it and fell with a cry from off the bed. Having been restless and entirely upset with his situation with Anna and the events of Michael's life, he had slept very little. What little rest he had managed to get, was filled with creeping shadows and nightmares that had unrelentingly pursued him and his wife.

"Papra residence--," He had answered, and clearing his throat, said, "Ole speaking."

"Good morning, Mr. Papra--," A female voice calmly and quietly said, "This is Nurse Morris calling from Vancouver General, you left your number with us in reference to a Mr. Ted Cowan?"

"Oh yes--,: He remembered, "He doesn't have any immediate family and asked that I be listed as next of kin in the event of any issues, how is he doing?"

"Well sir--," There was a reluctance in her voice that spoke of sorrow, as she said, "That's why I was calling—I'm terribly sorry to inform you that Mr. Cowan passed away this morning. He succumbed in his sleep…"

Ole's hand trembled as he stared into the clouded heavens beyond the window, "I will stop by later this morning—and see to whatever arrangements are necessary."

"Well, sir--," She flipped through several pages and sorted files as she spoke, "What you really need to do, is contact the funeral home of your choice, and they'll take care of all your personal needs."

"Thank you for calling--," He was utterly stunned, "I'll see to things, immediately…"

Long after she had hung up, he still held the phone as though hoping in some way, that it had just been some kind of terrible and waking dream. Slowly, he placed the receiver back down upon its base and cast a sorrowful hand before his eyes.

The clouds slowly drifted across the dismal heavens from between the parted curtains behind him, and all time seemed to stand still. Although having been aware of the dear old man's condition, his sudden loss came as a complete shock. Only the day before, Ole had visited with him and he had been talkative and appeared in good spirits. How could this have possibly happened so quickly, and almost over-night?

The sound of a key in the lock of a door behind him caused him to turn and suddenly stare. There was movement in the apartment, and then Anna appeared in her coat in the open bedroom doorway. Her blonde hair was wild and tossed in the cold wind, and her bright blue eyes were full of tears. They had just looked to one another for an instant, and then she had rushed forward, hugging and holding him tightly.

Dublin Ireland
1:45 p.m.

After the long and terrible night, Lawrence had even been too tired to drive the several hours back to Killkenny. Rather than nap in his cab as he did during the warmer months, he had found a cozy hotel between St,

Stephens Green and the Gallery Theater. It was a small stone cottage that was run by an elderly couple, but had tidy rooms and plenty of hot running water. The shower had done his aching bones a world of good, and the steam soothed and cast away the troubles of the night before.

He had settled down at the little table beneath the window with a hot cup of tea and quietly puffed at his pipe. As the smoke drifted, blending like a dream into the drifting clouds that streamed across a crystal blue sky, his thoughts wandered. It seemed a lifetime ago, that his dear wife Julie had passed away from complication due to pneumonia. It had only been several years, but sorrow and loneliness had driven him to drinking, and then he'd lost their home to the bank. Gazing sadly out of the window and onto the street, he sighed deeply while realizing that the cab had become his entire world. The world was full of lonely people and he was most certainly one of them. Reaching into a vest pocket and producing a golden pocket-watch on a chain, he flipped open the cover to admire the little picture within. It was faded and yellowed with time, but the smiling face of his raven-haired Julie still looked lovingly back through bright blue eyes.

"Oh Julie—my sweetheart—what I wouldn't give just to sit and talk with you one last time."

What the old fellow hadn't told Carrie was that his wife had been a McIntyre before marriage, and that's how he had known her uncle in the first place. There had admittedly been a faint resemblance, but it was mainly due to the small nose, sharp eyes, and long upper lip. Closing the cover, he slipped the watch back into the vest pocket and stared out over the grounds of St. Stephens Green. The sun had travelled from behind his side of the hotel, and even during the day, it was drawn in deep shadows. It was a quaint little kitchenette with its own bathroom and a small, windowless bedroom at the back. It had the scent of fresh linens, wood and stone, but he hadn't minded, as it now smelled like pipe.

"Maybe I'll just open the window a little bit—and for a breath of fresh air?"

Moving from the chair before the little table, he took a firm hold upon the old window and grunted while raising it half-way. The cold wind had blown in, drawing the pale sheers aside while caressing and chilling his face. Breathing deeply, he had coughed suddenly, and grumbled, "What the hell was I thinking? I'll catch my bloody cold of death."

He had risen to close it again, and in his wearied state thought to have seen something in the corner of his eye. Pausing, he adjusted his glasses while slowly turning to peer back into the darkened bedroom. As his eyes had adjusted to the presiding gloom, he noticed a movement from the darkness beneath the bed. Unnerved and rubbing the sleep from his eyes, he ever so slowly stood up from the chair. Squinting, struggling to see what that shadow deeper than all the others might have been? There was a sudden chill that sent his nerves tingling, as the hair upon his forearms and back of his neck stood on end. And then he heard it, the faint shuffling of something rustling from beneath the blankets that hung down from the bed.

"Sweet Saints, preserve me--," He slowly pressed his back against the window and stared in wide-eyed disbelief, "But it's day-time, there can't possibly be anything there..." Remembering Scott and Carrie's warning in parting, he suddenly swallowed hard with the realization, and whispered, "Oh yes—but there certainly can...They exist in the shadows and the darkness that gathers anywhere beyond the reach of the sun."

Beneath the bed he now caught the slight reflection of something wet and glistening, as it crept out and slithered into the room. In that moment, he had leapt from out the window with such speed and agility, that it had even surprised him! His feet had already been moving, and he set of running the split-second that he hit the ground! It had only been a short distance, as with adrenaline flowing, he swiftly hopped into his cab. Looking back briefly as he began pulling away, he saw the hideous things rising from behind the shadows of the window. Weary and terrified out of his wits, he made a last minute decision and began driving back toward the airport. Over the past few years and having given up drinking, he had managed to save a pretty good sum. He knew that it would not do him an ounce of good if he never lived to spend it, so he convinced himself of a course of action along the way.

"Well look out, Canada—and hello, Carrie--," He swallowed hard as he pulled back into the airport parking lot, and gazing out at the planes, muttered, "Old Duck will be seeing you sooner than you thought..."

Somewhere over the North Atlantic Ocean
3:50 p.m.

The plane had been almost empty. Fortunately, and due to this fact, Carrie had managed to reserve seats close together. Completely exhausted, Maya had already fallen fast asleep in the seat directly in front of them. Holding one another close, Scott and Carrie silently looked out the window and over the sea.

"This time difference stuff is driving me crazy." Groaning, Scott looked to his watch, "It's a twelve hour flight from Dublin to Vancouver, and we left just before 1 p.m. Our flight is due to arrive in Vancouver International around 6 p.m. So, in effect, we travelled seven hours back in time." For a moment he had appeared pleased with the thought, but then the smile faded and he said, "Which means that we'll be landing in the dark."

"I hope that sweet old man is going to be okay." She tightly grasped her husband's hand and nervously looked over at him, "I hope to God that the evil will just leave him in peace," She fidgeted with father Donoghue's crucifix in her other hand, and sighed deeply, "It seems that no matter where we go in this world, that we leave a trail of dead friends along the way..."

"Don't say that, sweetheart." Scott kissed her cheek and ran a hand softly along her cheek, "If all things really happen for a reason, then maybe these people were meant to come to us, and served their purpose in this world?"

'And, what happens we serve ours--," She whispered while gazing solemnly into her husband's eyes, "What then?"

"Then we'll go onward together--," He held her hand tightly, and whispering, said, "Because wherever you go—I'll always follow..."

Quietly placing her head down upon his broad chest, she closed her eyes while taking comfort in his words. She knew that, no matter what happened, she would rather die with him than ever go on alone...

Scott began quietly humming an old Scot's tune that she's heard once played upon the pipes. It was a song of legends and great battles won among the ancient kings and clans of old. Her thoughts faded as the sound carried her safely into the highlands of her dreams. A lone piper stood boldly playing among the shadows of the mountains, and she knew that it was her own beloved Scott...

Vancouver, British Columbia, Canada.
Sanctum Arcanum
2:35 p.m.
Caitlin had gently awakened me from out of a dead-sleep with a solemn message concerning a telephone call. Still utterly exhausted, I had stumbled into my office, and slumping into the chair, answered the phone. As Deb placed down the party-line from downstairs, I heard the somber tone of Ole as he called out to me.

"Michael—I'm sorry for the deception of last night on the telephone with Deb--," He stumbled over his own words, "But, I knew that something was terribly wrong—and I wanted to be of some service to you."

"It's a nightmare that I wouldn't have even brought upon my own worst enemy--," I had replied calmly while rubbing at my eyes, "All that I can really do, my friend, is thank you for caring enough to become involved."

There was a deep sigh of relief from the other end of the phone, and then hesitating, he quietly said, "There was also another reason for my calling. I don't even know how to tell you this—but Vancouver General Hospital called me this morning—and we lost Ted last night... I'm so sorry..."

Almost dropping the phone, I sat straight up in my chair, the grievous news tearing through my heart and soul. Without the words to reply, I had mournfully looked up at Caitlin, as having entered my office, she now knelt down before me and held me tight.

"Michael—my dear friend... I am so very, very sorry..." The sympathy of his voice had torn into my heart as the heated tears flowed, once again. Images of moments shared together flashed like a dream before my eyes. The times that he'd teased me, supported, and shoved me along through the adventure of publishing and daily life. I saw the last moments that we had laughed in his office, and then Ted's smiling face slowly vanished into a cloud of streaming cigar smoke.

Caitlin slowly stood, and gently drawing me from the chair, embraced me as I struggled with the words to speak to Ole.

"What—can we do for him now..." I swallowed back the tears as half-blinded with the grief, slowly made my way toward the window and stared out.

"I haven't done anything as of yet--," He solemnly explained, "I have been listed as his next of kin—but prefer that you would assist with the arrangements, if you are able?"

"Thank you—that would mean more to me than you might ever know." I felt Caitlin come up behind me at the window, and gently rest her head upon my shoulder as we embraced.

"Please take some time to allow this matter to settle--," Ole stumbled while trying to find the words, "If there is a funeral service or cemetery of preference, please let me know, when you are ready."

"There is a place--," My heart traveled out to a lone tree upon a hill where my mother forever lay, and I whispered, "That I would like to have a service and burial."

"If you'll give me the name—I'll see to the details--," he scribbled on a pad and paper, "And wait for you on the final arrangements."

"It's a plot in Mountain View Cemetery that was intended for me--," I had looked to Caitlin, and sorrowfully said, "It's directly beside my mother—and I feel, an appropriate final resting place for a man that was more of a father to me than anyone else..."

The words had left Ole in tears as he struggled with the emotions, and said, "I'll contact a director at Mountain View and see to this immediately.

And Michael—I will do anything in my ability to help you—please don't hesitate to ask…"

"I'm going to send someone to meet with you—right now--," I turned toward the door as Rich stood staring, "It's of the utmost important that you follow his directions implicitly, it's a matter of life and death."

"I understand—and will be waiting." Clearing his throat, he thought briefly, and said, "I will be waiting for your call before doing anything else."

"Thank you—and till then…"

"Till then, my friend," Ole slowly hung up.

"Rich—can I ask you to do something?" Turning to look back at him, he had only nodded.

"We lost Ted last night--," I found the words unbelievable even as I had reluctantly uttered them, saying, "I'm going to have him interred beside my mother."

Her memory had flashed painfully in his eyes, as removing his glasses and wiping the lenses with a corner of his blue plaid shirt, he said, "I completely understand."

"I know that you and Jay are going to the car lot right away--," I had removed the charm from about my neck, and handing it to him, said, "Would you be kind enough to bring this to Ole, and explain everything. His life may likely depend upon it…"

"Keep it—you're going to need it," Rich dropped it back into my hand, "I made several more, "I'll take two for him and his wife. If I remember correctly—his apartment was just ten minutes away from the lot that I was planning to go to anyway. So it's not like we're really deviating from the plan."

Gently patting him on the back, we walked out and into the hall together, and pausing at the top of the stairs, he looked to me and said, "It's a twelve hour flight over the North Atlantic—I hope that they're going to make it."

I could see the desperation and doubt in his eyes. And furthermore, it sent my thoughts into flight and I thought to have seen or sensed the evil occupied elsewhere. It was like a growing signal that, filling my every thought and functions, caused me to lean against the wall for support.

"Are you okay?" He had taken a firm hold upon me, as faltering near the steps, I nodded, saying, "The shadow is distracted elsewhere—and while pursuing someone else…"

Caitlin had slowly stepped down before me, and turning, gently presented an obstacle in the event that I might fall. She sensed the power that now flowed through me and understood that mortal vessels required discipline and synchronization to attune to such things. Like a young dog learning to cope with large paws, I still stumbled while attempting to adjust to the intensity of this sudden, mental acuity.

"How can you know this?" He appeared deeply disturbed while peering suspiciously between us, "Is it Marlowe—or something else that you haven't told me about before?"

It wasn't that he had been oblivious as he had preciously sensed it, but that he now wanted confirmation of his doubts. We had never before hidden or betrayed one another concerning the facts of anything, much less something so significant. But, still uncertain and unsteady of the world beyond, or the one around me, I shook my head and denied that anything had changed, "I'm not sure if it's just Marlowe's influence—or some other sense or power that's awakened within me?" Truly uncertain of the facts, I sighed in solemn refrain, "But, if and when I finally understand this—I promise, you'll be the second to know."

"I'll get over to Ole's and get this sorted out--," He paused to look at me, "Are you sure that you're going to be alright?"

"I'm just exhausted and the news about Ted was a shock--," Sighing and rubbing at my eyes, I shuddered with fatigue, saying, "I'll be fine once I get a little more rest."

"Well, you better go lie down until we get back--," He looked to Caitlin, "Please, drag him back to bed and make him sleep."

"That isn't as easy as it might seem—even in his current state--,"Grabbing at my hand, she pulled me back toward the bedroom, and peering back at Rich, said, "You might consider buying another motorhome, we might all need it before this ends…"

There was something resembling a warning or threat within the statement, and judging by the solemn stare that he returned within reply, he had taken it to heart. With a nod, he turned and quietly and quickly made his way back down the stairs.

"What are you doing?" I was surprised, as shoving me down onto the bed, she began removing my shoes, socks and then went after my pants.

"You need some decent rest—and will not be getting it while you're fully dressed."

Previously and as while still disillusioned by the darkness, I would most certainly have resisted, but not any longer.

"Are we really alone—or is it also here with us?" The thought of the demon participating in anything of a personal nature sent icy shudders through my entire being.

'No more than Marlowe may be--," She smiled coyly while removing my tie and unbuttoning my shirt, "Why do you ask? Were you just concerned or considering something shameful?"

Moving into the bed and beneath the blankets, I had just looked up at her as while she curiously gazed down. Her true beauty had filled my every sense, from the curls of her fiery and flowing red hair to the shimmering of her emerald eyes. She had obviously sensed and shared the attraction, as allowing her gown to slip to the floor, stood utterly naked before the bed.

Unlike the Caitlin that I had previously known in such intimate matters, she differed in certain features and form. They had both been lean and athletic, but she now appeared taught and toned in ways that suggested something superior to that of mere mortals. Or perhaps it was a reflection of what lay just beneath that pale and exotically freckled skin... There was an excitement that exceeded all others, as bearing the mark of the demon, temptation extruded from the very essence of her being.

She had reacted to this by slipping beneath the covers, passionately embracing and kissing me. Although she had been an entity comprised of the ether and existing between realities, her touch exceeded all boundaries of physical experience. As like someone caught within the carnal throws of a most passionate dream, we lovingly indulged one another to the absolute extremes. Never before had I felt so utterly consumed, so entirely devoted, body and soul. Where once the passions of my Caitlin had seemed little more than a passing fantasy, I felt every movement, every muscle, and knew undoubtedly that this was truly real.

When our passion had found its release, we had fallen together in loving embrace. Through the dreams and the seemingly endless nightmares of a life I had once known, through complete bodily and spiritual connection, I was finally complete. In those loving moments and as we tightly held one another, all thought has passed from out of me, and I drifted into the stillness of dreams...

The world swam in long shadows as I walked through a twilight garden. I could see tall and rolling hills in the distance. Coming to a crest, I had stopped to look down. There was a long stretch of peach orchards on either side of me and the fruit shone like pale lanterns. From below the moon and stars reflected in the waters of an immense and slow flowing lake. It was warm and the peacock hues of the heavens promised of a dawn that lay but moments away.

Slowly making my way down the slightly sloping hill and among the orchards, I took notice of a dim golden light slightly brighter than all the others. Unable to quite make it out from between the trees, I felt drawn toward it and followed the glow until coming into a little clearing, and discovering a small table and chairs overlooking the lake, where my mother sat, taking tea…

"Son--," She had turned to look back at me from where she had been watching the waves of the lake, and smiling, motioned for me to join her, "Please—I was expecting you."

Slipping down into the large, white lawn chair, I could only stare. She shone ever so slightly, not in an unnatural way, but as though the sun still found and reflected upon her through the twilight.

"Mom…" I swallowed back the tears, "Is it really you?"

"There is no need for tears--," She sadly smiled, and shaking her head, reached across the table and took hold of my hand, "All is well in this place—and with those who manage to find their way here."

"What is this place?"

"It's a world between worlds--," She waved a hand toward the distant mountains, "And, is one among many of which grow more beautiful within ascension."

"So, then it must be one of the heavens--" I had gazed into the skies, "And a dimension away from our own."

"There are many realms and realities in between, back and beyond." She had looked to me curiously, and lowering her glasses as she always had while speaking of serious matters, said, "My dearest Michael, do you see how as while caught between planes, one must alter their own reality to right things again?"

"I don't understand…" Still holding her hand, I gazed into the depths of her deep brown eyes, and asked, "Do you mean as while passing from one life into another?"

"No, son--," Ted suddenly walked from out of the orchard, and taking the third chair at the table, puffed at a cigar as he looked over at me, and said, "What's she's trying to tell you—is that you need to close that can of worms that you opened. In short—undo everything that you did right from the beginning—in your current life."

"Ted--," I had attempted to move from my chair, but he had gestured with a hand for me to remain seated, saying, "It's not us that you should be worried about—but everyone that you left back there, in the world…"

"Undo everything that I did--," Glancing between them, the sudden realization finally struck me like a hammer upon the head, "Of course—undo what we have done… We brought all those evils home with us—and unwittingly built a monument to the darkness…Sanctum Arcanum must fall to end this…"

"The void exists within your reach--," Marlowe appeared from behind them, his pale eyes now shining with a living, golden light, "It was a reflection of evil that you had recognized from the very beginning—and was brought into your home…" He drew back his hood to reveal his face, the dark cloak dropping to the ground as he too shone with the same light as the others, "I have passed from out of your realm now, and exist only within waking dreams."

"Redemption—you have finally been released from the servitude of shadows."

"At a price to great to even speak of--," He slowly and sadly shook his head, "Your own beloved Caitlin—has given up her immortal soul in my place. Never again shall she be released from out of the darkness—her soul is forever damned…"

"So, evil has claimed all that I have ever known or loved--," I felt my heart sink into the depths of utter despair while looking among them, "And now, at the end of all things, I must destroy all that remains to me in this world—if there is any hope to restore the lives of the others."

"I can't do this without you--," I looked to the old sorcerer, "I can't…"

"Michael--," He raised his hands before me, and quietly said, "All that I have ever done was offer you guidance that already existed within you—and awakened the power that was always there. No, Michael—you do not require my services—for all the power and knowledge that you shall ever need, already exists within you…"

"Trust in your heart--," My mother clasped her hands together, "And always stay true to yourself. And remember, where there is love, there is always hope, my son…"

There had been tears in my mother's eyes, as Ted puffed upon his cigar and they all faded into the rolling mist that now drifted through the orchards.

"Sanctum Arcanum must fall." I kept repeating it as the world grew dark from all about me, and I struggled with the thought, "The mirror—that damned mirror is the key to it all!"

"Michael--," Caitlin firmly held both of my wrists as I awoke to her concerned stare, "What are you saying?"

Settling back down into the sweat covered sheets and damp pillow, I wiped a hand across my brow, "I had a dream that my mother, Ted, and Marlowe were in an orchard by a lake. Marlowe told me that I had to destroy Sanctum Arcanum, and that the mirror had some key part in this, and something to do with the void."

She appeared suddenly confused, as looking around into the early morning shadows, peered suspiciously back at me, "I do not sense the old sorcerer's presence any longer..."

"In the dream--," I could only gaze mournfully upon her while whispering, "He said that he had been released out of servitude to the darkness—because of the pact that you made with the demon..."

A single tear rolled down her pale cheek and she understood.

"I love you—and will never forsake you--," I took a firm hold upon her, and kissing her, held her close, "I will not lose you again, my love—not to fate or destiny, and even to death or the devil... Even at the cost of my own immortal soul..."

"Don't say such things--," She wept, as kissing me sweetly, gazed down with those beautiful emerald eyes, and whispered, "Together we will cast this darkness out—even if it means raising hell on earth..."

"Amen." I held her close in the darkness before the dawn...

"Where should this all begin?" She brushed the hair from my brow.

"We have to release the vault keeper—and send it away," Whispering so as not to be overheard, I said, "And remove all symbols of protection from the gates and grounds."

"In Marlowe's passage from out of this realm his spells are broken--," Caitlin's eyes burned with an eerie blue glow, "All that he has done is now unmade and passes into time with his fading memory in this place."

I had no need to question her knowledge or understanding of such things, as I knew that it came from a dark, though reliable source.

"I'll need to find that mirror--," Looking to her, I knew that I now spoke with the demon, "Would you possibly have any idea of where it might be found?"

A strange change came over her, like something from within now gazed out. Her fingers lengthened and cold claws slowly caressed my face as she drifted in thought. A blue flame burned from the depths of her emerald eyes, and she became the demon Caitlin as we lay there upon the bed. With large and blackened bat wings unfolding ever so slightly, she raised herself upon me, and stared down with a skeletal doe's face and burning horns.

"I will never submit to you—oh mighty one--," I now realized what was happening and although terrified, refused to succumb to its will, "But would willingly stand at your side and see our enemy destroyed..."

The creature altered even further, the neck extending and the body lengthening as all resemblance to Caitlin faded. The huge Elk skull with its massive jaws, tusks, and razor sharp teeth lowered within inches of my face. The blackened claws gently brushed against the side of my cheek. Then, it tilted its head ever so slightly to examine me closer with a singular and huge burning eye. It had become like ice upon my entire body, its touch bitter and deathly cold as we simply looked upon one another.

"Dost thou willingly offer thy services unto me?" It whispered while still baring Caitlin's voice. Then, a long black and forked tongue slipped out from between those razor sharp teeth, and sliding the length of my neck, slipped across my left cheek. The icy cold saliva almost burning to the touch, I shuddered and trembled violently from beneath the beast. Appearing almost pleased with the loathsome act, it leaned even closer, and licking at the other side of my neck and face in the same fashion, asked, "Dost thou offer terms in pact?"

"I offer only terms of a bond in the face of our enemy—and nothing more."

Its pale flesh was slippery and pressed tightly against me in places, and the frozen touch seemed to be draining the life from out of me. I had encountered this terror before, in a bath during an attempted possession at the McCreary estate. Horrified, I had attempted to struggle out from beneath the thing, but it had only forced me down ever harder, and asked again, "Dost thou accept terms in pact?"

"I offer a pact friendship--," I felt the breath being forced out of my lungs from under its muscular and tensing body, and gasping, said, "A bond of loyalty—and love for what you have become, my beloved, Caitlin…"

"Thou dare speak unto me of friendship, loyalty and love…" The words were spoken like a poison, "Of what use are such things beyond pathetic, human emotion?"

"They are power--," Closing my eyes and reaching upward, I gently caressed the leathery, icy skull of the thing, and whispered with my failing breath, "When all other hope fails…" I could feel the constrictive force crushing down upon me, the pressure building in my temples, and then suddenly, it eased back. I felt the huge head gently resting upon my shoulder as it took me into an icy embrace. I succumbed to its hold and returned the sentiment, holding it firmly but gently. I could feel the tension fading from its muscles, and the body altering, slowly returning to a human form. Moments later, I opened my eyes to find Caitlin lying upon me, and apparently sound asleep.

Gently stroking her hair, I carefully covered her and lay there quietly while still holding her. Realizing that she would forever be damned by the beast, I also knew that I never abandon her, regardless of how terrifying and loathsome the experience had been.

"I love you--," Whispering as I gently stroked her long red hair, a single tear ran down my cheek, "No matter what comes to us—or lurks in the depths of your soul…"

She moved ever so slightly and then lifting her head, opened her brightly burning blue eyes, "I accept thy terms—and thus, shall favor thee above all others…"

Slipping her arms tightly about me, the demon softly kissed my lips, and gazing with empty eyes, appeared saddened for but a single moment. Something from deep within me awakened, and I knew, that even among the greatest hosts of hell, even a demon desired acceptance… Gently taking the fallen angel into my arms, I joined my beloved and her lost soul in the realm of deep and darkened dreams…

CHAPTER TWENTY FOUR

Dublin International Airport
Sunday, February 9, 1975.
4:15 p.m.
Lawrence had seated himself near the brightest lit window in the airport waiting room. His flight had been booked over two hours ago, and as the plane was being refueled and serviced from a previous flight, he now waited for the boarding signal. The afternoon had cleared up considerably, and as he looked into the bright blue skies, he dreamed of home and his wife. When he boarded that flight, he would be leaving Ireland and his beloved forever.

Reaching into a vest pocket, he pulled out the little watch, and flipping the cover open with a thumb, paused to reflect upon the picture within.

"I'll be taking you with me when I go, sweetheart." His heart ached as he looked out the window at the city and the gently rolling hills of home.

"You know—it's a good thing that we caught a later flight--," An elderly woman nodded as she sat with her knitting across from him, "The plane that went off before us is caught in a blizzard, and some kind of trouble."

"Oh sweet mother of God--," Lawrence climbed out of his seat and turned toward the ocean, "Carrie and the others are in trouble--," He whispered while speaking to himself, "That bloody thing must've caught up to them…" His thoughts raced as he remembered their faces and the things that had been said during their time together.

"It can't be in two places at once--," Carrie had said to him, "That's why we're safe when it's after someone else."

"Sweet lass--," Tears came into his eyes as he looked toward the plane as the boarding signal was given, and then back into the heavens above the ocean, "I'll not let that thing take you—not as long as there's breath left in this body." And with that he took his bag and made his way out of the waiting room.

"It's boarding time--," The old woman had waved after him, and gathering her things, muttered, "I shouldn't have told him about that troubled flight—it must've put the fear into him."

Rushing out of the airport, he hurried down the walkway and to where he had left the cab parked, awaiting anyone that might claim it. Leaning down and taking the keys from off the top of the driver's front tire, he hurriedly climbed into the car.

"Now how the hell do I get the bloody thing's attention?" He snapped his fingers and sped down the street. He drove recklessly, a man on a mission and determined to get there as fast as possible. Honking, he ran through red lights and drove through back streets and alleys to avoid traffic. It had only taken him minutes, but he soon he pulled in before Christ Church cathedral, and rushing out of the car, hurried up the stone steps.

It was Sunday and a service was in progress, so hardly anyone noticed him slip past the crowds and make his way down a dimly lit corridor and toward the basement door. His hand had been trembling as he reached for the handle, and drawing the door open, stared into the blackness before him. Swallowing hard, he took out the pocket watch and his crucifix and slowly stepped down onto the first step. The blackness opened up beneath him and he felt his heart leapt into his throat. He knew what nightmares lurked in those shadows, and now trembled as he forced himself onward.

"Lord—give me strength—and save that sweet lady and the others, please..."

The old wooden stairs creaked beneath him, as moving with determination, he went ever downward. A cold gust issued from out of somewhere, and as the light from the open door began fading, he paused near the bottom of the stairs.

Grasping the pocket watch tightly, he pressed it to his heart, and called out, "Where the devil are you—you rotten son of a bitch! Come and get me if you think that you can!"

In his blind fumbling's he discovered a flashlight on a ledge, and turning it on, was relieved as it cast a string beam before him.

He looked to the cracked and ancient stone walls that surrounded him, and cursing, said, "By all the Saints in heaven—I knew that you were nothing but a bloody coward!"

The door suddenly slammed closed from above him, and throwing his back against the wall, he heard the sound of shuffling in the blackness from all about him. The light now trembled violently in his shaking hand as in wide-eyed terror, he swallowed back his fear, and called out, "You're bloody weak—and not worth a pail of sheep shit, come on out you filthy bastard!"

There was a sudden sound of movement, of doors banging and something coming up a corridor that he could not quite make out. Then, to his utter astonishment, a light shone from beneath a doorway, and it flew open as someone rushed out and came toward him with a lantern.

"What in the name of all that is holy are you doing down here--," The old priest held his lantern higher to better observe Lawrence, and squinting, said, "And why are you shouting profanities in the house of the Lord, and on a Sunday?"

"Forgive me, father--," He had begun to apologize, but his blood suddenly ran cold. As slowly looking upward, he saw something glistening in the lantern's glow from upon the ceiling. Pulsating, it gathered into a seething and ghastly mass, as reflecting ever so slightly, it slowly hung down while dangling from just above the old priest.

Pointing upward as the words froze in his throat, Lawrence attempted to warn the old priest. "What are you going on about now, man?" Angrily shaking his head and placing his hands upon his hips, he had curiously looked up, "Oh, my God!"

Like an immense hand comprised of bony spider's legs, it had reached down and snatched up the old man in the blink of an eye! He shrieked and struggled, but the vile filth extruded thick and yellow ooze that began dissolving the flailing man.

"God help us!" Lawrence spun on his heel and raced madly back up the stairs! There were sounds of movement behind him on the stairs, and he knew that it would be upon him in moments. With his heart pounding furiously, he reached the uppermost steps and the landing and flung himself at the door!

It was sealed tightly and felt as though it had been bolted from the other side. He pounded desperately upon the heavy oak door and spun back to look down the stairs. The hideous fiend crept ever so slowly as it approached him from only several steps away. Unlike the trolls and other ape-like horrors that he had seen before, this was something entirely different. He shivered so hard now that he almost dropped the flashlight, and stumbling, almost fell down the stairs.

Moving upon numerous, oozing and slimy tentacles, immense bony and spider-like legs stood like spines from out of its back. There hadn't been a head, just a mass with a wide and yawning mouth that vomited out filth with each and every movement.

Throwing his back against the door, he cast and arm before his face, and desperately cried out, "For the love of God! Somebody help me!" In that moment of utter panic the flashlight had fallen from his hand! It bounced down the steps and slipping from off the edge vanished into the blackness below...

Somewhere over the North Atlantic Ocean
12:15 a.m.

"Hold on, sweetheart—it's going to be alright!" Scott had clung to his wife as he tightened her seat-belt, and the plane was tossed in the frozen hurricane winds.

"This isn't just any freak storm--," She gripped him tightly and stared deeply into his eyes, "It's come after us—this is it…"

"I love you so very much--," He grabbed her and kissed her, holding her tight, "I'll never let go of you, no matter what."

"This isn't normal—is it?" Maya looked up as a stewardess struggled to make it through the aisle, and asked, "Are we anywhere close to land?"

"No, ma'am--," The young woman replied, "But the Captain and crew are doing everything that they can. Please just remain in your seat—and we will inform you of any necessary emergency procedures in just a few moments."

The Lockheed L-1011 Tristar roared across the dark heavens through the blizzard, as lightning struck from somewhere in the night, and the instrument panels flashed.

Captain Harold C. Black had turned to look over at the copilot, and desperate, said, "I can't see a damn thing—check in with Vancouver ATC and get a clearance for a course change. We need to ascend."

"Yes, sir--," First officer Wayne Marshall replied while tapping a finger at a gauge light that continued to flash, "I'm not sure if this bulb is faulty—or if the storm is affecting the onboard computers?"

"Sparky--," Captain Black shouted to the engineer who sat behind them, "How are the things looking back there—and what's the ETA to shore?"

Engineer Neil "Sparky" Dobson adjusted his glasses, and stuttering in reply, said, "We're showing increasing drag, and if we don't ascend immediately, we run the risk of ice building in the engines. At four hundred and seventy five miles per hour, our current ETA to shore is five hours and eighteen minutes."

"Wayne--," Captain Black looked to the copilot, "Any word on that clearance to ascend?"

"The storm is causing too much interference—I can't get through--," Wayne tapped at his headset, and looking utterly distraught, said, "And we have multiple failures occurring on control panels."

"We still have the autopilot, if everything else fails--," Captain Black assured them, "This technology was designed for emergency situations."

"With all due respect--," Sparky called to them, "We're showing system failures all over the ship—it might not be advisable to trust automated flight equipment."

"We're also running the risk of having the flaps, elevators, stabilizers and rudder freezing." Wayne's features paled, "And as you both know, if that happens, we won't have any control of the ship…"

"Dear God--," Captain Black stared out into the raging blizzard, "Wayne—would you be kind enough to advise the staff to notify the passengers of emergency procedures…"

"Yes, sir." Moving from his seat, Wayne hurried out of the cockpit.

"What happens if we don't receive clearance?" Sparky just stared.

Captain Black thought briefly, and then peering over his shoulder and back at the engineer, said, "Let's try to remain optimistic—the lives of everyone on board depend upon it…

Carrie pressed her face into Scott's breast as they tightly held one another, and the jet engines began issuing sounds of imminent failure. Maya had panicked while hearing the distinct howling and moaning as the plane lurched. Unbuckling her seatbelt and turning to look back at Scott and Carrie, she whimpered, "I just want to see my Rich and hold him one last time."

"Please, ma'am, get back into your seat and buckle up--," Marie Fischer, head stewardess, politely assisted her, saying, "I realize how terrifying this must be for you, but your safety depends upon following strict emergency producers."

Maya had fallen utterly silent, as taking a firm hold upon the cross that Rich had bought her the previous Christmas, she closed her eyes and began praying.

Adjusting her blonde hair from beneath the flight attendant's cap, Marie poised herself in the center of the aisle, "Can I please have everyone's attention--," Directing with her hands, she began reciting the emergency precautions that she had prayed she would never be forced to repeat. She was an average build, attractive young woman with big brown eyes, and a contagious smile. This had only been her sixth flight in the service and she was already beginning to regret it. At twenty five years of age, her life now flashed before her eyes…

Scott and Carrie had looked to one another as the stewardess struggled to maintain her footing. They had travelled on the Lockheed L-1011 TriStar many times before. It was legendary for its comfort, smooth ride, and considerably quiet cabins. In fact, it was often referred to as the

"Whisperjet" for this exact reason and was preferred by most. With state of the art computer systems and continually advancing technology, it could have almost landed itself. But none of that had mattered to Scott in that moment. All that he now imagined was the great steel bird plummeting from the heavens and into the depths of the ocean, and carrying them all to a dark, cold, and watery grave...

Carrie had turned toward the window, and looking into the storm, saw something pale staring back. She had leapt back at the sight, and then realized it had just been the reflection of her own terrified face.

"Hang on, sweetheart--," Scott kissed and held her tight, "I've got you."

"What's stopping it from taking us right out of the air?" Maya wept.

Pulling the talisman out from of her sweater, Carrie held father Donoghues crucifix in her other hand. She contemplated briefly, and realizing the reason, stared aghast, "Because it's methodical, and this has to look like an accident.... It's using the storm to bring us down..."

One of the engines suddenly howled, and whining, slowed to a screeching stall! The plane dipped suddenly and Marie tripped, landing in the laps of Scott and Carrie. Passengers screamed, oxygen masks were deployed, and luggage was strewn throughout the cabin.

"We've lost the starboard engine--," Sparky gasped, "And the port is showing signs of increasing drag." Lights flashed and warning beacons resounded through the cabin as they fought to maintain their calm.

"It's the ice--," Wayne returned to his seat and slipping back into his headset, looked to Captain Black, "I'll keep trying to reach Vancouver ATC."

"We're fine as long as the remaining two engines don't freeze up--," Gripping the wheel tightly, Captain Black stared out into the icy oblivion, "God help us all..."

"We just lost the Port engine!" Sparky looked to the others, "And the stern engine is starting to fail."

"Prepare to ascend--," Captain Black looked to Wayne, "We can't afford to lose that tail engine..."

"Captain, we run the risk of a mid-air collision--," Having never contradicted a senior officer in his life, his heart leapt into his throat, "Might I suggest a forced landing?"

"Any survivors would be dead of hypothermia within minutes of hitting that water--," Captain Black scowled, "We might have no other choice soon—and be forced to attempt a dead-stick landing if that last engine goes. But in the mean-time, I refuse to lose the ship—and everyone onboard. Prepare to ascend to twenty two thousand feet. That should take us clear of the weather."

"Captain--," Wayne's eyes bulged as he suddenly pointed to the windscreen, "Look…"

The heavens had suddenly parted before them, as soaring from out of the blizzard and into a clear, star-filled night, they could only stare.

"What happened?" Scott gasped as they all turned toward the window to look.

"It's gone--," Startled and amazed, Marie looked between the two of them, and gasped, "The storm just completely vanished like it was never even there?"

Tightly gripping Scott's hand, Carrie gazed out the window and into the endless blackness from above and below. As she had just sat silently and stared, something touched her from deep within. It was a familiar sensation, a comforting notion that for some reason had reminded her of a dear old friend.

"Lawrence--," She slipped a hand before her mouth as the sting of tears filled her eyes, "Oh no—not you…"

"What was that sweetheart?" Scott leaned closer.

"Nothing—I just need a moment." She fought back the sense of emptiness and loss while realizing why they had all survived…

Dublin Ireland
Christ Church Cathedral
It had never happened during a sermon before, but Father Brian Mullholland's bladder had refused to wait any longer. Pardoning himself, he had rushed from the altar, and hurriedly made his way down the corridor. There had been some humor in the incident, as the topic of his sermon had involved Noah's Flood. He could only hope that he reached the end of the hallway before he suffered one of his own. A sudden and furious pounding and shouting had almost caused him to fall as he had passed one of the cellar doors. And though his need was great, he had hurried over, and unbolting it, threw open the door.

Lawrence had fallen backward and from out of the darkness, scrambling desperately away and throwing his back against the far wall. "Get away from that door, father!" He pointed and cried out in terror, "There's something down there!"

"What on earth has happened, my friend?" The poor father had not even been aware of the thing as it lashed out, and grabbing him, drew him shrieking into the blackness.

Rushing to his feet, Lawrence had not even bothered attempting to close the door, but ran madly down the dim corridor.

"What has happened?" A young priest caught him by the arms in passing and stared into his face, "You look like you've seen the devil himself?"

"That's because I have—," He stuttered while trembling and hysterical with fear, "And it's down in your cellars and already killed two people, and almost got me!"

"I'm father Liam Grantham--," The priest placed an arm around Lawrence's shoulder and spirited him away through the hall as he spoke, "I'm here to investigate an incident that occurred here last night."

"Father Donoghue—I know, I was here and saw it all." Lawrence nodded as they went into an office, and the priest closed the door.

"If you wouldn't mind sparing a few moments of your time--," He motioned for Lawrence to take a seat while hurriedly sitting down at his desk, "We received a call from Carrie Dayment?"

"Yes—she was also there with her husband and another girl--," Lawrence nervously fidgeted with his car keys while peering into the shadows beneath doors, and under the large oak desk.

"Could you please describe the events of the evening in as much detail as possible?" Father Grantham produced a tape recorder, and slipping a cassette into the machine, placed it on the desk before Lawrence.

"I don't think you'd believe me, even if I tried."

"You might be surprised, my friend--," The priest motioned with a nod for him to continue, saying, "We're in the business of the supernatural— and have been for a very, very long time…"

Sanctum Arcanum
5:30 a.m.
Rich had been quietly slipping into his boots and coat with the intention of silently slipping off, when I had caught him at the door. Startled, he had just slowly turned within explanation, but none had been required.

"I know—and completely understand your reasons for going--," Hugging him as brothers do, I had gripped his shoulders with both hands, and asked, "But why didn't you think to ask me to come along?"

"Because you've already endured so much--," He appeared hung his head and sighing deeply said, "I'll be leaving before the morning light…"

"These are our last days in Sanctum Arcanum--," I whispered, as the words pained me deeply even within their utterance, "The mirror was the last key—and this is the final battleground…"

"But, this is all that we have left--," He appeared desperate, terrified as he pleaded, "Where will everyone go—and what will you do?"

"I'm planning to send everyone away on Monday morning--," Leaning to peer out from between the curtains at the door, I said, "And then I will remove the sacred seals and symbols of protection from this place—and leave the gates open…"

"You've gone mad--," He took hold of my wrist, his eyes begging as he appealed to my common sense, If you do that, you'll invite hell into this place…"

"My dear friend--," Turning back to him and resting a hand upon his shoulder, I said, "But it was already here, and we were just too blind to see it…"

"You don't have to do this—we can figure out some other way."

"No--," Unlocking and opening the door, I stood in the cold morning wind and stared out into the darkness beyond the gates, "Caitlin told me that they will all arrive this morning." Sadly looking back at my friend, I whispered, "It came at a high cost, a life sacrificed by a dear friend in the name of their safety…"

"The old cab driver--," It was as though he had picked the thoughts from out of my mind, and frowning, he said, "So many have already died over this damned thing…"

"Which is why I plan on ending this--," Determined, I motioned into the pale and distant dawn, "The light comes sooner with each passing day— but not soon enough for most."

"It's almost as though the sun knows the evils of a winter night--," He pondered in the blackness, "And that it moves slower in the hopes that the snow will bury the evidence that's left behind…"

My thoughts and focus had immediately traveled to those dark gates, and to where old Harry's body had been so hideously impaled. This was no home, it was a place filled with horrid memories of those who had died here, and was now haunted by those who remained…

"Let's be off--," Caitlin appeared from behind us, and hanging a scarf about my neck, offered me the black overcoat, saying, "If we encounter anything along the way I'll likely need this for the way back."

"Let's hope not--," Appearing increasingly unsettled, he followed us out the door, and pausing to close and lock it, turned and said, "Did you want me to drive? I brought a new Suburban back from the dealership with Jay this afternoon."

"No, let's take the Eldorado--," Breathing deeply and peering upward, I could see the pale forms of clouds slowly drifting through the dark heavens, "It seems that the devil has already taken its due on this night..."

There was a strange confidence among us while we marched to the garage, and opening the electric door, hurriedly climbed into the car. It had taken several minutes to warm the engine, and then slowly pulling out, I had activated the automatic gates. For a moment, I had feared that a horde of abominations might come flooding through those slowly parting gates. But there had been nothing there. Marlowe had been correct in assuming that my senses were heightening, as though my eyes could not pierce the deep shadows, my psyche perceived everything. Waiting on the road just beyond, I had watched them close, and driven away only after being certain that they were properly secured.

The roads had been clear for the most part, and what little snow remained had been melted and flattened by other vehicles. I was amazed to see other vehicles so early on a Sunday morning. In most cases they were janitorial staff, public servants, or simply some drunk that finally found his way home after an exceptionally long weekend. I had almost forgotten that people existed beyond our own personal nightmare...

"It's so hard to believe--," Rich had muttered as though speaking to himself, "That after everything that's happened, they're finally coming home."

"I told you before--," I had glanced over at him in the front seat, and said, "That Scott and Carrie would find her...and bring her back."

"I'm sorry—I can't even begin to imagine how you must be feeling--," He frowned and slowly turned away, "I'm still utterly lost and broken over Caitlin and Eva..."

"The darkness only used their memories to incarnate as a weapon to be used against us--," I spoke while attempting to force out the memories that we had all once shared, saying, "The true Caitlin had been with me always—and I just didn't realize it in time..."

She took hold of my hand, and leaning against my shoulder, said quietly, "It was the demon that had blinded us both—and love that revealed the truth and set us free..."

"And, are you?" Rich inquired quite innocently of her, "Are you truly free?"

"I have been granted mortality—and now share this form and world with the beast--," A strange confusion fell upon her, as pondering briefly, she looked back to him, and said, "But it is far better to rein a monster than to be taken by one…"

"And, while we're on the subject of monsters--," Rich stared out onto the road, "I heard on the news that they found the body of murdered woman in Colorado. She was a twenty three year old nurse—and they suspect that it's connected to a series of serial killings."

"We all have our demons--," Caitlin peered over at me, a blue flicker flashing in her eyes as she said, "Some seek greater sacrifice than others…"

"Well, I sure hope they get this animal before this gets any worse." Removing his glasses, he wiped the lenses with a hanky that he pulled from a coat pocket, and said, "They say the death toll has raised into the double digits."

"That would fathom the number to be far higher--," Caitlin cast an eerie smile in his direction, "Authorities should never assume anything upon their discoveries—but remain silent due to those of which they had not yet made…"

"You sound as though you have some insight into the natter?" Rich was both fascinated and frightened as leaning away from her, he asked, "Would you care to offer any information that we might use to assist the authorities?"

"And invoke the wrath of yet another fallen angel?" She scoffed at him, "Certainly not…"

The glances that I had exchanged with Rich in that moment were both expressions of shock and warning, as I urged that he not tempt whatever now spoke through her.

"The airport is just down that road--," He had changed the subject as planes approached from out of the distant heavens, and he pondered aloud, "I wonder which one they're arriving on."

"There--," She pointed to a plane that approached from a Northern route, and said, "They return from out of a storm with but with a single engine— and fortunately a skilled flight crew…"

There was little doubt between us that she now possessed insights to many things that were well beyond either of us. To some degree, I wondered just exactly how much and to what extent she might apply it? Aside from all other concerns was my desperate need to locate that insidious mirror. I decided that I would approach her with the dilemma, but only when we were alone. Rich's curiosity could get the better of him at the worst times, and I would do anything that I could to avoid any more unpleasant encounters with her demon...

Vancouver International Airport
6:47 a.m.

The flight had arrived rather late due to the circumstances of the storm, and then interviews that had been taken by airline authorities in the event of personal injury claims. When Carrie and Scott had first seen us, they had stopped dead while seeing Caitlin. Maya had dropped everything and blindly run into Rich's open arms. There had been tears and emotions that they needed to share in privacy, as I walked toward my awaiting friends.

"I know what she may seem--," I had said while introducing Caitlin to them all over again, "But, I can assure you that this is the real Caitlin—I'll explain everything on the way home..."

Carrie had fallen into my arms, and hugging me tightly, wept, "I don't even care what she is anymore—as long as you're okay."

"How do we know who you really are?" Scott had approached Caitlin, and appearing apologetic said, "We've been seeing a lot of strange things lately..."

"Because only I am capable of this--," Her eyes flashed with blue fire as she brushed his face with a blackened an icy claw, whispering, "And had I wished it, none would still live..."

"It's good to be back home—and see you again--," Scott had hugged her, and gently patting her on the back, reluctantly said, "Amica, Caitlin, or demon..."

"I never thought that we would see each other again." Maya had wept as Rich carried her luggage and she clung desperately to him as they walked.

"I've had some moments like that as well--," He had shot a nervous glance at me while loading the luggage into the trunk of my car, "But it's going to be okay now, let's just get home."

"I can't wait to take a hot bath—and sleep in our own bed again." She climbed into the back seat with Scott and Carrie.

"Oh, well about that?" Rich climbed into the front seat beside Caitlin and shut the door, "Our house is gone—and so is the business..."

"What?" She leaned between the seats, and looking between us, asked, "What happened?"

"While you were away the darkness has been hunting us—and destroying everything in its path," Rich struggled with the words, as I pulled away from the curb and began the drive home, "I'm afraid that we've lost everything with exception to Sanctum Arcanum and the little book store... It was all burned..."

Maya fell silent as she slowly slipped back into the seat, and Scott offered her a reassuring arm.

"And what about the others--," Suspicion and fear now darkened Carries drawn features, "Are they all at your estate?" She directed her attention upon me, "And where is Raymond? I know that he would never have let you come out here alone."

"We lost Tanya and Dennis at the apartments during the fire—and Gordon during a rescue attempt." I had spoken slowly and as while sounding out each syllable, "And Raymond died while saving my life at the mausoleum's..."

Throwing a hand before her mouth, Carrie fell silent while attempting to conceal the tears. Noticing a large silver crucifix in her hand, I swallowed hard, and asked, "A gift from a friend?"

"It belonged to a priest at Christ Church cathedral--," Scott answered as she clearly was unable, saying, "Father Donoghue, he saved our lives at the cost of his own, and she kept that in his memory."

"So, obviously things didn't go so well at the Duff Glenn?" Carrie sniffled as Maya offered her a tissue from her purse, and she blew her nose.

"No—and although the cost of that mistake came at a very high price--," Gripping the wheel until my knuckles whitened, I glanced into the rearview mirror and looked back at her, "I found out the reason that we could never find the darkness was, because it had been with us all along."

"We already know, bro--," Scott frowned, "Eva and Caitlin were puppets used by that thing to play us all, while it took us out, one by one."

"And that mirror--," I reminded Rich while explaining it to the others, "It's a window into another dimension, and it's gone missing."

"Missing--," Carrie looked curiously to Scott and Maya, "But wasn't that nasty thing in your private bathroom?"

"It was a few days ago--," Slowly pulling in before the estate, I used the remote to open the gates, saying, "I noticed it missing the morning that we returned from the Duff Glenn."

"So, who else could have gotten in there to move it?" Maya looked around as we pulled up the long drive and into the garage, "And where could they have possibly hidden it? You're house isn't that big that someone wouldn't have noticed it, somewhere."

"There is one place where no one would have looked--," Rich reminded me, "And no one's been up there since we lost Trudy..."

"The attic…"

Everyone had been awake to greet us upon our return, as through tears and loving embraces, we all settled down before the hearth. Caitlin had volunteered to check in on the mirror, and we had all awaited her before discussing anything of significance. She was back in moments, and seating herself upon the couch beside me, said, "It's not there…"

"With the keeper gone--," Tim had asked, "Maybe something carried it down into the vaults?"

"Caitlin--," I had turned to her, but she had already looked to me, and said, "The keeper may have gone—but something else exists there now…"

"What are we going to do?" Deb asked while holding her husband and Danny close.

"I say we burn this whole damn place down--,"Jen cursed, "And be done with everything--," She looked to me, "No offense…"

"None taken—and that's fairly close to what I already had in mind."

All eyes had fallen upon me with the comment, and I shrugged while quietly saying, "I want everyone packed and out of here on Monday morning."

There had been mixed emotions among the group, but none had argued, with exception to Danny.

"And what about you--," He looked among the gathering and then back at me, "You don't expect everyone to just turn tail and run now, and leave you to face this alone?"

"Caitlin will remain behind with me--," I spoke quietly and as calmly as possible, "We'll lure it back into this place—force it into the open, and using the stone and mirror, summon it into the portal."

"But you don't even know where the damn thing is now?" Jay argued, "And if you think that I'm bailing—you've got another thing coming, brother. I said that I'm staying until this is done, and that's the end of the conversation, period."

"I love all of you guys from the bottom of my heart--," Carrie hugged Patrick as she sat with Pam and Scott on the couch across from us, "But, I don't want to lose my son…"

"Then you should take him and Pam--," Scott sighed deeply, "And go somewhere safe…"

"No, Scott--," I slowly and sadly shook my head, "Your part in this is over now too, it's time that you take your family far away from us and this place."

Caught between friendship and family, he covered his face in sorrowful shame, and moving from the couch, stumbled into the kitchen. Carrie had looked to me, and understanding my intentions, whispered a blessing as she went after her husband.

"Well, we're staying too--," deb had attempted to speak, but I had interrupted, saying, "And I love you both for wanting to bear this burden—but you have suffered this long enough. Please, go with Scott and his family, and take Pam and Danny with you."

"No--," Danny leapt up and bellowed, "You brought us into this and my mother and best friend are dead, because of you! And now, you think that you can just toss everyone out like old news? How could you?" He ran from the room and Jen had looked to me before swiftly following after him.

"He doesn't mean what he's saying--," Deb sniffled and wiping away a tear, said, "It's just all been so very much for anyone to handle, and now here, and at the end of all things, we're parting ways..."

"He's trying to spare you all the nightmare of what's to come--," Tim threw another log into the hearth and looked to those who remained, "And don't fool yourselves--," His eyes reflected the firelight in the early morning gloom, "It's going to be hell on earth..."

"And what makes you think that we'll be any safer anywhere else?" Ray slipped an arm around his wife and pulled her closer, "That thing's been taking us all down—why would it suddenly just stop now?"

"Because it now has what it desired most--," Caitlin looked around the group as Carrie and the others slowly returned, "The reincarnation of the house of McCreary, Sanctum Arcanum—," She raised black claws before her as they all stared, and her eyes burned with blue hell-fire as she turned to me, and said, "And Michael..."

"Yeah—over my dead body--," Jay scoffed, "I'll shove one of those flaming arrows straight up its evil ass!"

"I'm staying as well--," Rich turned mournfully toward me, and said, "You'll need someone who can wire this place properly and make more weapons before this is over."

"No—not again--," Maya pleaded as she grabbed at his collar, "You can't do this to me."

"No—and you're right, sweetheart--," He looked to her, and wincing, said, "I should never have done any of this to you... It was my fight from the beginning as well—but I didn't realize what was happening until now..."

Moving from the couch, Maya had gone to Carrie who had taken her into a gentle embrace.

"Michael--," Tim had called softly from where he stood before the hearth, "I'm not going anywhere either. We started this together and, as God is my witness, we'll either finish it, or end together..."

"Amen to that--," Jay moved from his seat, and throwing an arm around Tim, grimaced as he said, "I'll give up my wagon to Deb and her husband." He pulled the keys from his pocket and tossed them to Ray, winked, saying, "But if I manage to come out of this—be expecting a call."

"Take the Suburban--," Rich pleaded with Maya, "Between the two vehicles, there's room enough for everyone, and luggage."

"And what then--," She stared back at him with large and tearful eyes, "What happens then?"

"When it's all over—I'll be coming home to you—and be done with all of this, I promise..."

I could only look away in shame and remorse for having involved him in the first place. Maya had seen this, and her features softened as looking back at her husband, she said, "Okay, but we'll be moving away from Vancouver when it's done and never returning..."

"I swear to you—on my life and soul." He gazed longingly into her eyes, and bursting into tears, she ran into his loving embrace. As they had silently just clung to one another, Caitlin had glanced over at me. I could see the love in her emerald gaze, as well as the blue fire that burned in constant reminder of the fiend within.

"I'm sorry for what I said--," Danny stood before me, "I didn't mean it—can you forgive me?"

Reaching upward and taking his hand, I pulled him down onto the couch and drew his head to my shoulder. He had not resisted, but rather fallen into place as though having intended to have always been there.

"I could never hate or be angry with you--," I had gently held the lad, and said, "I know you better than you may think—because you and I are very much alike. That's why I know that, regardless of what happens, you'll take care of the others, and make me proud."

"And what's going to happen to this place--," Jen asked, "And all that creepy-ass stuff you've collected in the building next door?"

"We're going to blow it all to the moon." Rich replied, "And hopefully send that thing with it."

"What if it doesn't work?" Deb played the devil's advocate.

"It shall work—," Caitlin spoke with a strange defiance, and looking back at me, the demon said, "The Beryllus was taken from this place in the night."

"What?" Staring in utter bewilderment, Rich gasped, "Something was in here with us?"

The demon had slowly turned to look at him, as realizing the mistake too late, he swiftly looked away. Rich was well aware from readings into occult matters, and knew that it was strictly forbidden to converse with a demon, unless authorized. He now became utterly still, as focused entirely upon Maya, no longer intruded. Having seen this, Danny had also turned away and allowed the strange and sinister beauty to speak.

"One might only guess as to what horrors crept through these very corridors—and spirited the mirror away as we all slept, unaware…" She looked among the members of our group and they recoiled at the sight of her burning stare.

"The question now isn't how it was taken--," Frightened Rich blurted, "But where it was taken to?"

"It now lays closely guarded and deep within the fortress of steel and stone that you so cleverly devised." She pointed a long and blackened claw at Tim, "A fiend from beyond this dimension now watches over it, from where the vault keeper once dwelled…"

"If we can find a way to get to the mirror--," I thought aloud, "I can use the stone to force the darkness into another dimension."

"The dead now wander the deep and dark halls of that place--," She warned, "It has become a tomb for all and any that dare enter into its shadow…"

None dared speak, as she suddenly became silent, and blinking as though blinded, looked around the room. Seeing this, they had all immediately realized that she had slipped into some kind of an altered state, and settled back in certain relief.

"The guest house has become the mausoleums." Carrie whispered.

"And this--," Scott stared in utter disbelief, "Is now the house of McCreary…"

"Maybe destroying that place wasn't such a good idea?" Ray looked to Deb and shrugged.

"Unknowingly, all that they really did was open a new venue for the evil--," Pam agreed, "And bring it all back here."

"What you all still don't seem to understand--," Rich removed his glasses and rubbed at his eyes, "Is that it wasn't the burning that created the transference of energy. It was when we brought all the damn antiques and marble statues to this property. We desecrated the sanctity by removing the objects that held the evil in the Duff Glenn."

"The McCreary family knew about this evil for generations--," Carrie explained, "That's why they built that mausoleum and situated the statues in the form of a pentagram."

"None of which anyone here could have possibly known about--," Tim defended us, "Much less expected or even believed possible at the time."

"No one's tossing blame here--," Jay interrupted, "We're just putting the puzzle together."

"But still, you might've thought that with all of our previous education in the occult and experience with the supernatural--," Appearing stunned with our blatant ignorance, he muttered, "That we would've know better than to remove haunted or possibly possessed items from that place—and brought them home…"

"Not all that seems evil is your enemy--," I repeated the words before my friends, "Most people are inherently good—but we only notice the truly bad ones, because they cause the biggest waves. If it comes down to collecting haunted objects—the reason that most things might be haunted, was because they were well-used or truly loved. That doesn't justify a haunted item as being evil, nor that which haunts it."

"This isn't a debate about whether we should have done it--," Jen looked around the group, "It's a discussion about what we're going to do about it now."

"Monday morning, I'll give you all an envelope with cash--," Rich looked around the group, "You'll travel as a group using the Suburban and Station Wagon, and find a very busy hotel in a crowded and well-lit area. You will not contact us—or your location might be given away. Do you understand?"

There had been a series of unspoken agreements made through gestures, as nodding, he said, "If and when we finally conclude this matter--," He looked to me before finishing the statement, "One of us will still be at the house and waiting for someone to contacts us. Now, it's very important that whoever calls waits a minimum of three days before trying."

"What if we don't hear from you?" Pale as a sheet, Pam just stared.

"Then there's a chance that you never will." The words had slipped out before I had even considered what I was saying. The reaction was what would have been expected. An absolutely silent room filled with expressions of utter dismay and wide-eyed horror.

"I've left your names with my lawyer--," Rich advised the group, "And have written his number upon the envelopes that I intend to pass out on

Monday morning. In the event of anything happening, you will all contact the lawyer, and he will see to everything."

"I have also done the same thing--," Looking among the sorrowful and terrified faces of my friends, I quietly said, "I leave Danny as my sole heir, and have made compensation for everyone here. The information will be included in the envelopes that Rich will be handing out."

"So, you guys have pretty much buried yourselves." Carrie sniffled as the lenses of her glasses fogged, "How is that supposed to make the rest of us feel?"

Scott had remained silent, but I could see the suffering that grew within him,

"It's supposed to make you feel truly loved—," Caitlin had appealed to them all, saying, "And cherished as friends and extended family. Look upon these men--," She waved toward the group, and speaking softly, said, "As even against such cruel odds—they consider your well-being above all else."

"Can I ask why you wanted the three days grace?" Deb looked between us.

"Because, I'm attending the funeral of my publisher and dear friend, Ted Cowan--," Bowing my head in his memory, the dream had come to mind, and I said, "I'm burying him next to my mother—on Tuesday morning…"

"I'm sorry--," Deb looked down, and thinking briefly, peered back as she said, "Oh, I almost forgot. Ole called again. He asked that you contact him as soon as possible."

"What about Merlin?" Tim had raised an eyebrow, as I had quite obviously forgotten the dear beast in the presiding chaos.

"No one has seen him in weeks--," Jen frowned, "I know that he's okay and just hiding, because he still empties his food dish and fills the litter box."

"I'll find him, my love--," Caitlin whispered in sweet promise, "And then you can see to his safety before anything else happens."

"If that thing is just next door--," Ken chewed at a fingernail, "Then how safe is this property now—or this house?"

"The sacred symbols still safeguard all windows and doors from the souls of the lost--," Rich directed her attention to the crown moldings and prayers etched into the wood, "And the cane that Michael usually carries, summons the hell-hound that comes for anything else…"

"It's the reason that I want everyone packed and ready to go first thing in the morning." Explaining myself, I appealed to their rational sense, saying,

"We can't guarantee your safety in this place—and the risks are just too high…"

"You possess such a weapon?" Caitlin's eyes flashed.

"I would not betray our trust--," Realizing the sudden concern, I whispered to her, "Or use such a weapon in your presence—I give you my word of honor."

"Honor means little among the desperate--," She spoke in words that only I could hear, saying, "Perhaps, you plan to betray me in the last moment?"

"My beloved exists as a part of you—and within your undoing I would most certainly lose her."

"In this singular thing I will trust far before any assumed honor among your kind." She slowly leaned back into the couch as the others had spoken from all about us, and failed to notice our discussion.

"Are there any other questions?" I had looked to my friends, and seen only the remorseful and somber faces that gazed back. "Then please get your things packed and get the vehicles loaded."

"If this is so dangerous--," Jen halted the group with the question, and asked, "Then why aren't we leaving right now?"

"She's right--," Tim glanced around the room, and then said, "It might be better if we clear this place out before anything else happens."

"I'll get those envelopes done right now--," Rich announced, saying, "Once you're all packed, we'll all help loading the cars."

"Bro--," Scott approached me and speaking softly, said, "I really don't want to leave you like this."

"But you aren't leaving--," Looking him straight in the eyes, I said softly, "You're taking our loved ones away—and keeping them safe. And Scott, there isn't anyone alive that I would trust more than you for something like this…"

There had been a silent moment as he contemplated my words, and then extending a hand in parting, we had hugged as family do.

"When this thing is over—we're going somewhere nice and barbecue until the cows can't come home, because they don't have any legs left." He forced a smile and we both laughed.

"I would really like that--," We had looked upon one another as though for the last time, and sighing deeply, I said, "You better help Carrie—you know how frustrated she gets with luggage."

Patting my shoulder, he had quietly turned, and without another word, hurried down the corridor.

"You should call Ole back--," Caitlin reminded me, "He might have something important to tell you."

"I have to sort some papers out first--," Kissing her and moving toward the stairs, I said, "I need to get them to Rich so he can finish with those envelopes."

"Ole and his wife are in danger--," She said without much thought, "They have been marked—and will not last through the coming night."

Her words had halted me in mid-step, and turning to look down at her, I said, "What would you suggest that we do?"

"Call Ole--," She followed closely after me, and said, "Have him pack a bag and bring his wife here. They can leave with the others…"

"That seems like the only option--," Making my way into the office, I searched for Merlin under the desk before sitting down, and asking her, "Would you please find Merlin, he seems to have completely vanished."

"He sleeps beneath your bed." She answered, "And in the last place that you should have looked first."

"I'll call Ole…"

Wandering into the bedroom, I had knelt down, and drawing the covers aside, looked into the shadows beneath. There had been a suspicious movement near the head end which stood against the wall, and then I saw the reflection of two eyes. They shimmered in the darkness where the light could not penetrate, and I sighed deeply, calling out, "Merlin—come here, old buddy."

It was apparent by his reluctance that he was terrified of something, as he had never avoided me before. Yet, there he sat in the blackness beyond reach and just stared back at me

"Come over here—it's going to be okay, old man--," I lay on my belly, and reaching beneath the bed, patted at the carpeted floor, "It's just me— let's go get a nice snack. I think that we still have some chicken leftovers from the other night?"

Ever so slowly he began moving toward me, each step taken with the greatest of caution as he peered from side to side. I had reached toward him, but still in the darkness and just beyond reach, he had hesitated. Something had not felt right. He was behaving in a manner unaccustomed to his general character and it now bothered me. Was I becoming so utterly paranoid that I had even become afraid of my own cat? Obviously, the poor thing was terrified beyond his own wits and with everything happening, he could hardly be blamed. Brushing off the sudden and strange paranoia, I continued attempting to coax him out.

"That's a boy—come into the light--," Lifting the covers just slightly, I had reached toward him, but he had backed off and just watched as I called, "Merlin—don't make this so hard—you're perfectly safe—just get over here."

"What are you doing?" Rich had appeared in the doorway behind me, and holding Merlin in his arms, gently stroked the big black cat.

The sudden realization had sent me backwards, as slamming with my back against a bureau, I just stared aghast.

"What happened?" Rich knelt down beside me, "Are you alright?"

"Rich--," I gawked while looking up at him, "I was just crawling under the bed while trying to reach what I thought to have been Merlin…"

"It was once welcomed here--," Caitlin appeared from behind Rich, and looking between us, quietly said, "And now it takes the forms of those familiar to us…"

"But, how will we know who is real?" His eyes widened, "And who to trust?"

"The amulets—the darkness can't reproduce or wear them." Taking hold of the talisman that hung about my neck, my heart sank as she slowly shook her head.

"Once within a shell such things cannot harm it--," She reminded us both, "Do not put your trust in physical manifestations of faith."

"Then how will we know the difference between real people and the darkness?"

Looking to Rich, she whispered, "Not by sight—only sense…"

"But—I didn't know that wasn't Merlin under there--," I had pointed to the bed, "I should have sensed something was wrong."

"You did--," Raising an eyebrow, she said, "You just chose to ignore the warning…"

"Please take him into my office." I petted Merlin while passing Rich and wandering out into the hall. Hurrying to my desk, I dropped into the chair and grabbed at the telephone. Dialing out, it had only been moments before Ole had answered, and I said, "This is Michael—it's urgent that you listen carefully to what I am about to tell you…"

10:35 a.m.

Ole rushed Anna as they hurriedly packed over-night bags and made for the front door.

"I don't understand this--," She argued, "Why are we leaving on vacation when I have to be at work?"

"Because your boss is an asshole--," Slamming and locking the door behind them, he rushed her out to the garage, saying, "And we need some time away to think things out. You always complain that we have no quality time alone."

"So where are we going?" She climbed into the car.

"To my friend's house—the author whose book I am now editing."

"What—that creepy old guy? How is that spending quality time alone?"

"He is not that old--," Ole dumped their bags into the back seat and climbed into the car, "And we are not staying with him—we are invited to travel with his friends and enjoy an all-expenses-paid week at some hotel and resort."

"You don't even know these people—or where we are going?"

"These are all just minor details. Why must you always argue with me, Anna? Why can't you just relax and have some fun for a change? You complain I am not spontaneous enough—so here I am." He backed out of the garage, and knocking over the neighbor's garbage cans, cursed while hurriedly pulling away.

"This is not spontaneous--," She scoffed, "I think that you have finally lost your mind!"

"Alright then, you want the truth?" He eyed her sarcastically while failing to halt for a stop sign and not even noticing the near collision, "Okay then—I will tell you." They ran a red light and sped toward the freeway on-ramp, "This author, or creepy old guy as you so eloquently described him, isn't actually writing fictional horror, but has discovered beings from other dimensions that hunt people. And during this experience, I have foolishly become involved simply by editing his work, and we are now marked by a demon for death."

She just stared as he raced down the on-ramp and lost a hub-cap, which was sent flying into a near-by ditch.

"Ole—," She ran a hand through her long blonde hair and stared at him as though he was a stranger, "Have you been smoking that stuff again?"

"I quit that weeks ago--," He became frustrated while passing others far too swiftly, and arguing, said, "See, you always do this when I try to speak with you. If I happen to say something that you do not like, or disagree with, you call me crazy, or accuse me of smoking funny stuff…" He thought briefly, and reaching down and fumbling through the glove box, produced a small plastic baggy, and smiling, said, "I forgot all about this?"

Snatching the bag from out of his hand, she rolled down the window and tossed it out.

"Oh, now that was real nice--," He shook his head, "Now some gopher or coyote will eat that, and because of you, likely get hit by a car."

"And now you make me feel rotten for trying to save you from your own bad habits," She sniffled and looked away.

"I was only joking--," Ole leaned over and kissed her cheek, "Gophers and coyotes would never even go near that stuff. It will likely be some low-life or homeless kid…"

She had just turned to glare at him, and he smiled, "What—now I can't even make a joke? Just shoot me and be done with it already…"

"Okay, now tell me the truth--," Crossing her arms before her angrily, she asked, "What are you really up to?"

"No kidding, my love--," He frowned and shook his head, "I have become involved in something really terrible—and we are in serious danger."

"You owe money to drug dealers?"

"No--," His eyes bulged, "When was the last time that you heard about guys gunning someone down over a joint? Never!"

"Someone is out for you?" She became more frustrated and confused by the moment.

"No—the devil is coming to get us, because I pissed him off by being involved with that creepy old guy."

"You should be writing this stuff not editing it." She laughed.

"And defense attorneys can't figure out why most divorces end in a cloud of gun powder…"

"What did you say?"

"Nothing, my love--," He turned off the highway and back into a main street, "I was just saying that I still can't figure out most of the turn-offs in Vancouver."

"I need to call work and explain--," She became utterly frustrated, "Or I won't have a job for much longer."

"You can do that from the hotel--," He promised, "Just tell them there was a death in the family. It would not be a complete lie with the recent passing of my boss, Ted Cowan."

"Are you sure about this—we have so much to do at home--," She puckered her lips, and flashed her beautiful blue eyes at him, "The dishes are still in the sink from last night's dinner—and there is laundry to do."

"And that's another thing--," He grimaced as his knuckles whitened upon the steering wheel, "I have an organization, a process in the way that I manage the laundry, and I wish that you would stop fooling about with things, because it messes everything up."

"Now don't you think that is just a little bit extreme?"

"Not if you want brighter whites--," He glared at her, "Sometimes I think you just don't care about things."

"Oh, I give up--," She flung her arms into the air, "Okay, let's just take a vacation before we both lose our minds."

"Now you see how easy that was, Anna?" He smiled sweetly, and sighing, said, "We should have more talks like this. I believe that it helps our relationship."

"As long as you have your way..."

"Don't be silly, light of my life--," He leaned over, and kissing her, said, "Things just work better when you finally realize that I know what is best for us."

She turned, and staring at him for several moments, laughed as she looked away and shaken her head. She knew that he had always loved her dearly and would never dream of ever leaving him, or looking at another man. What she did not know, is that his purpose in their immediate departure had likely saved both of their lives...

"My love--," He spoke in a sudden and serious note, as clearing his voice, turned to look over at her, "I need to speak to you about something quite serious, all nonsense aside."

"Ole--," Through all of their previous bantering she suddenly became terribly concerned, "Why do you look at me like that? Tell me what is really wrong..."

"I need you to follow me closely on this--," He swallowed hard, "As hard as this may be to accept or believe—we truly are in great danger from something that I do not really understand."

Unlike her previous reactions, she had known this rarely seen aspect of her husband, and respectively, silently listened.

"When I first came into the company of Michael Schreiber, we had been introduced through Ted Cowan, the publisher for whom we both worked." He licked at dry lips and spoke through a parched throat, "As you already know, he is an author of paranormal horror and fantasy, or so I had first thought."

"What do you mean by—first thought?"

"Well—after reading through his work, something from deep within had told me to do a little personal research." He looked in disbelief between his wife and the icy road as he spoke, "I discovered that, although some of the names of people and places were altered, many of the events portrayed as fictional had actually occurred."

"But many writers use some truth of which to base their stories upon."

"Not when those truths include multiple homicides, mysterious disappearances and police cover-ups." He slowly shook his head, saying, "Ted Cowan kept a scrapbook of newspaper articles—he had been following Michael's work from the beginning. It came into my hands just recently—and with his passing."

"Are you telling me that this Michael—is some kind of ghoul or monster hunter?"

"What I am telling you--," He frowned, "Is that he did find something out there—and now its hunting all of them, and killing anyone who becomes involved…"

At first she had questioned everything, but taking heed, stared in absolute horror.

"So what will we do now?" Speaking in a barely audible tone, she had whimpered, "And what will happen to us?"

"This is where it all becomes so much harder, love of my life--," He fought back the emotions as she sensed something was terribly wrong and clung to him, and he said, "They are sending away the women, children and families on this day—and only a few will remain to make a stand against this thing…"

"No--," Realizing his intention, Anna shook her head as the tears filled her eyes, "I don't understand any of this—it's just too horrible to believe—but you can't leave me… not now, please…"

"We must defeat this nightmare--," Ole took a firm hold upon her hand, and sniffling, said, "Or there will be no one left when it finishes with us…"

In those final moments as they drove up the street and toward Sanctum Arcanum, all the love, aspirations and hopes of a lifetime spilled out from between them…

11:36 a.m.

With the cars loaded with luggage and parked before the main door, we had all returned to the couches and the hearth. Rich had passed out the envelopes as promised, and we took the opportunity to spend a little more time together while awaiting the arrival of Ole and his wife.

"This is likely one of the hardest things that I have ever had to do--," I looked among the grim and dismayed faces of my friends, "But it's easier than attending any more funerals for loved ones…"

"I wish that I could say the same thing--," Danny's eyes were reddened with tears, as holding onto the kitty-carrier that contained Merlin, he said, "And I still wish that you would let me stay."

Pam and Jen had hugged Danny from either side, and I knew no matter what came now, that he would always be safe. I already knew that whether we survived the ordeal or not, nothing would ever truly be the same. It was also likely that, under threat of possible recourse for our actions and insuring their safety, I could never see any of them, ever again. There was a dark light reflecting in Rich's eyes, and I sensed that he had already suspected the same…

"I know how you feel, Danny--," Forcing a smile, I had looked down at the young man and quietly said, "I'll be back for Merlin—so you better take good care of him."

The words had offered a faint hope where none had really existed, but it had been better than nothing.

"None of this was every truly your fault--," Carrie frowned from where she sat nestled in her husband's arms, "Thank you for trying to protect us all—and being our family." I could see in her eyes that she had somehow already sensed or known my intention of just vanishing. There was a depth of emotion that ran well beyond the physical or rational. It was love of the truest kind.

"We will always be family—regardless of anything else…"

Maya had held Rich, Deb embraced Ray and the others had all fallen together in a moment of silence before a final parting.

There had been an abrupt knock at the door and Caitlin had hurried to answer it. Having previously opened the gates to allow them passage, I now turned to greet Ole and his wife.

They had entered the room rather hesitantly, and looking among our friends, politely introduced themselves. There were several moments of formal greetings and then everyone had begun gathering, and moving toward the front door.

"We have room for you and Anna in the Suburban." Pam offered.

"Thank you—we are indebted to you for this kindness." Ole had turned to his wife, and kissing her deeply, held her tightly as they seemed forever bound. A moment later, he had stepped back as she quietly turned and, halting but briefly, quietly followed the others out.

"They will be leaving right away--," I looked to Ole sadly, and resting a hand upon his shoulder, said, "May the good Lord watch over all of you, until next we meet." Extending a hand in parting, I sighed deeply, and said, "Till then.'

"Michael--," He paused to look up at me, "We're two old Germans—and maybe not so bright—but would never run away from a good fight."

"This isn't something that we can just fight--," Rich returned after bidding farewell to Maya at the car, "It's the wind and storm and can take the form of anyone or anything in your imagination…"

"I read about that--," Ole looked back at me, "But if imagination is detrimental, then you are all quite safe with me. Beyond my music and editing work, only my wife has ever occupied that place in my life."

"It will attempt to kill you--," Caitlin stood in solemn refrain, "And should you make the slightest mistake—it will succeed..."

"I know as much as you have shared in your previous books--," Ole bit down upon his lower lip, and looking among the remaining members, said, "Or more appropriately, your *grand grimoire*..."

Tim had looked over at me and I had remembered a conversation that we had shared concerning the books. This had been exactly the type of thing that we had both feared, and I felt mixed emotions, ending in remorse.

"Thank goodness that he published--," Tim had taken a firm hold upon my right arm, and slowly nodding, said, "Because without them, people would not be aware of this nightmare, and be utterly defenseless..."

Surprised with his reaction, I had peered over at him as he nodded approvingly.

"Either way--," Ole jabbed a thumb toward the open doorway, "It would appear that everyone has left—so you are stuck with me now."

"I can't be held responsible for what might happen here tonight--," I stared upon the somber and now silent man, "And can't guarantee your safety—or promise that you might even survive the night..."

"It was coming for my wife and I anyway--," Ole reasoned, "And there was no guarantee that we would have even lasted another night. Had it not been for your call, my friend..."

"Welcome to Sanctum Arcanum, my friend--," I had extended a hand, and said sadly, "And the beginning of its ending..."

12: 45 p.m.

Scott and Carrie drove Jay's Oldsmobile Station Wagon while carrying Patrick, Maya, Anna, and Danny, who clung to Merlin's kitty-carrier. Following closely from behind, Ray steered the Suburban as Deb, Pam and Jen sat amongst the accumulated luggage. There hadn't been much time to make previous arrangements for accommodations, but Scott's knowledge of the Lower Mainland was second to none. His experience with the railways had carried him clear across the country, as within the quiet moments, he had studied maps and located some of the finest places to stay.

Leading the group down the Trans-Canada highway eastward, he played the radio and listened to an old favorite. It was a haunting melody from 1961 done by 'Dick and Dee-Dee', entitled 'The Mountains High.'

"That song always gave me the willies for some reason." Maya rubbed at goose pimples that formed upon her arm, "It reminds me of death…"

Carrie had thought briefly, and then turning off the radio, looked to Scott, and asked, "Where exactly are we going?"

"Chilliwack--," He replied while shoving an eight track tape into the player, "They have some great truck-stop hotels and diners. Some even have swimming pools and arcades."

"That sounds self-contained and busy enough--," She agreed, as sighing deeply, gazed upon Scott, "You know, when we were coming back on that flight from Ireland—I never realized how much I really loved you, until we were in trouble…"

"Well—it seems that I'm always in trouble with you--," He forced a smile, "So I'm always reminded of how much you mean to me."

Leaning against his shoulder, she extended an arm, and pulling Maya close, said, "Rich sent that—and we love you too, my friend."

"I can't help but feel like we'll never see each other again." Maya's expression paled, her large brown eyes reddening, "We almost lost each other the last time… What are the odds of having that kind of luck twice in a single lifetime?"

"It's not about luck--," Scott glanced over at her and said, "What's meant to be is meant to be—and nothing in the universe can ever change that."

Closing her eyes, Maya quietly uttered a Cree prayer that she had learned from her uncle Red. Carrie and Scott had been unable to understand the words, but the sounds had deeply touched their hearts.

"Have faith--," Carrie hugged the younger woman close, and said, "He'll be home again before you know it."

Scott had heard his wife's words, but they had seemed hollow in retrospect. He knew the horrors that awaited his friends, and though he had wished to remain and fight, was ashamed with the relief of having finally departed that place. It was a guilt that also came with the knowledge of what would happen to all involved, should they fail…

1:14 p.m.

"You look like you're really enjoying that." Deb observed her husband as he followed along behind the Suburban with the semblance of something resembling a smile.

"You know, honey--," He shrugged, "This thing handles a lot better than I might've imagined." His blue eyes sparkled, and it was the first time that she had seen a genuine smile from him in what seemed forever. He had always been a good man, a strong and supportive husband, and in moments like this, a boy that she had always and truly loved.

"Sometimes you really crack me up, Ray." She leaned against his shoulder and laughed. Having been a military brat and something of a tomboy most of her life, it was her way of showing affection and appreciation. It was just one of the many things that he had always loved about her. Kissing her and pinching at her cheek, he said, "We should buy one of these for ourselves—what do you think?"

"This thing must be a real gas hog?" Jen had peeked over from the back seat, and pointing to the fuel gauge, said, "I mean—we've already used a quarter tank of fuel since we left the city."

"So what--," Pam pondered briefly, and then said, "Gas is cheap and in the end, it's all about the ride anyway, right?"

"I like the way that you think--," Ray winked, and smirking, said, "Now all that you have to do is convince my wife."

Deb slapped at his shoulder, and raising an eyebrow, said, "And since when did you start listening to anything I say?"

"Be fair now, honey--," He became suddenly serious. "I would never do anything without your approval first."

"I know--," She chuckled, "But I have to keep reminding you to make sure that it stays that way."

"Do you have a brother?" Jen looked between Deb and Ray, and laughing, said, "You just don't find good men like him anymore."

The sun had shone down through the parting clouds on that afternoon, and Pam had finally seen everyone for the happy and wonderful people they had really been. It was almost as though while imprisoned in the looming shadow of pending doom, Sanctum Arcanum had been draining the life and love from out of all of them. Her heart broke as she remembered Raymond and how he had so shyly and boyishly attempted to invite her to dinner. She wondered, as while looking around at the others who now laughed as the darkness departed their hearts and souls, what things might have been like in a different world...

"Well, the radio isn't picking up much—but I found this?" Ray had delighted within having found an eight track in the glove box, "It's a '50s and '60s hit parade—but better than nothing." Shoving the cassette into the player, they all settled back as 'Dick and Dee-Dee' sang, 'The Mountains High' and Pam stared out into the heavens...

CHAPTER TWENTY FIVE

Sanctum Arcanum
3:15 p.m.

Rich had taken Jay and Ole in my Eldorado and returned once more to the local car lots. I could only imagine the expressions that he might have received after having already purchased and destroyed so many. To avoid any further investigation by a multitude of insurance companies regarding this exact matter, Jay and Ole volunteered to assume liability for the new vehicles. The only one legally belonging to Rich now, would be the van carrying the explosives that he had purchased through black-market sources. These items also included the chemicals necessary for producing more of his explosive darts, and several bombs.

Caitlin served tea while we awaited our friends, and the three of us sat together in the little kitchen nook.

"I can't stop shaking--," Tim scoffed at the thought while holding his trembling hand before his eyes, and saying, "This has never happened to me before…"

"Don't trouble yourself about it too much--," I sipped at my Earl Grey tea and sighed, "We'll all likely be doing the same thing by nightfall."

Caitlin had slid a plate containing a large slice of apple pie across the table at me, and smiling, offered me a fork.

"Do you know something that I don't?"

"There are far worse things to die from--," She pulled her chair closer to me, and eyeing up the pie, said, "But I will share it with you—if that's okay?"

Just the thought of that sweet and delicious, plump apple pie had my mouth watering and senses running wild. I hadn't indulged anything like it in what seemed ages.

"Well, I suppose a little won't hurt?" Taking the fork, I had smiled like a mischievous child while cutting off a large portion, and offering her the first taste of it. She had smiled as while leaning forward, opened her mouth to accept the delectable morsel.

Tim had appeared dismayed with the whole affair and looked away. I knew that he was fearful of what might happen while breaking my diet, but it was just a little cheat. Cutting the next portion, I raised the fork to briefly observe that little bit of sweet paradise.

"Stop--do not eat that!" Caitlin shrieked while rushing down the stairs from my office!

Shocked at her sudden appearance on the stairs, I dropped the fork while turning to look at the Caitlin sitting beside me. The form of that which I had assumed to have been my beloved had suddenly erupted: Each and every molecule had separated and sought the darkness in every crack and crevice in the house!

Gasping, I had looked down at the table and recoiled at what I now saw. The fork had become charred by acid, and the pie dissolved into a seething, foul and blackened sludge.

"Oh—dear God--," Tim leapt back from the table, "What just happened?"

"The darkness grows stronger in this place." Caitlin snatched up the plate and swiftly vanished into the kitchen with it. I heard the tap water running, and looking to my terrified friend, reached out to him, "It's okay—we're safe..."

"But for how long?" He slowly slipped back down into his seat and watched intently as Caitlin returned, asking, "And where were you?"

"I took the opportunity for a quick shower--," She explained, as taking the seat directly beside me, appeared deeply concerned, asking, "Are you alright?"

"Yes—nothing happened—thanks to your instincts."

"How is this possible--," Tim spoke softly, as still shocked, he sounded as though he questioned his own sanity, "How is it possible for this thing to assume different identities? It seemed so real..."

"Reality is only what the physical mind perceives it to be--," Caitlin watched Tim with the intensity of a hawk, "And the eyes are easily deceived..."

"At least without having Merlin or any of the others here--,"I thought aloud, "It has fewer choices of forms to use and less opportunity."

"It just played us while using one out of three people--," Tim spoke in little more than a whisper, "We can't all stay in the same room together all of the time—and even if we try—if it even gets to one of us—we'll be wide open to be picked off, one by one..."

"Can you sense the darkness in people--," Taking hold of Caitlin's hand, I pleaded, "Can you identify the difference between us and it?"

Her features became suddenly blank, and slowly turning her head toward me, something else looked back, "The eyes reveal all—and it's just beneath the skin." It hissed, a blue flame dancing in the depths of her emerald gaze, "No soul exists there—and only darkness dwells within…"

The moment having passed, she looked up as though having awakened from a dark dream. Running a hand through her long and fiery red locks, she breathed deeply.

"I don't know if I want to get close enough to look into its eyes." Tim spoke quite honestly, as trembling while sipping at his tea, he struggled not to spill it.

"There are only six of us--," I thought it out, "If we work in teams of three, it'll be easier to remain together and keep track of each other."

"You must never separate--," She warned, "It can assume all of their identities and as while occupying a single space in time, return as all three…"

"That hadn't occurred to me--," Nodding at her, I sighed, "I should have known that. It did the same with multiple corpses and parts of itself when it attacked us before."

"You are tired, my love--," She gently caressed my face with a hand and frowned, "And sleep in this place comes at too high a price…"

"There are seven of us--," He pointed to Caitlin while correcting me, "She counts as two…"

"They exist together as one--," Sipping at my tea while looking over at her, I added in thought, "And from previous experience at the McCreary estate with that Willow—we already know that it's immune to the spells of the darkness…"

"Like some species of poisonous snakes that can resist the venom of their own kind." He seemed fascinated and spoke thoughtfully, rather than in a rude or insulting manner. Regardless, she had paid little attention and was instead occupied while closely observing me in every perspective. It resembled an odd type of confusion, which crossing between the skepticism of a cynical eye, stood upon the borders of admiration. There was something deeply unsettling about this sudden and strange fascination. As avoiding her strange glances, I suspected that something else now reached out and attempted to touch the depths of my soul.

It was a moment that, seeming to last an eternity, had left me doubting, wondering and fearing as to how much I had really shared with the demon? During those most passionate and loving of embraces, had I, had we become intertwined through body and soul even further than anticipated? A shudder of terror, revulsion and something that I dared deem excitement now coursed through my entire being.

When I had finally resolved to indulge those large and emerald eyes, I saw the demon's fire burning, watching from deep within. Had I truly seen or simply sensed it through everything that had occurred in that moment? As for reasons beyond my understanding, I no longer feared the evil that existed within my beloved Caitlin…

"Michael--," Tim had leaned across the table and gently tapped at my wrist, "Are you alright, brother? I was just asking you something—and you seemed to just vanish somewhere in thought?"

"I'm sorry--," Rubbing at my eyes while feeling Caitlin's warm hand upon my leg from beneath the table, I looked to my friend and apologized, "I think that everything is finally starting to catch up to me?"

"We're in the final stretch--," His eyes registered a depth of concern that I had never seen before, and he said, "It's just a few more days—and this will be over, one way or another."

"I'm sorry, Tim—what were you asking before I drifted off?"

"Well, it concerned what happened with you and Merlin earlier today--," His features became vividly pale and drawn, as he quietly asked, "If the shadows are moving in this house now—is the darkness also lurking beneath beds, in closets, and anywhere barren of light?"

"It's not the shadows that you need fear--," Caitlin replied, "But the physical forms that it manifests, and that are like the creature that were previously here…"

"But—that means that none of us are safe here now…" There was a terror in his tone that seemed to choke the words out as he attempted to speak them, "And that anyone who falls asleep in this house—might wake up as something else..."

"We will gather in a circle before the hearth--," Caitlin advised, "You shall remove all furnishing with exception to the lamps. There shall you create a pentagram, and remaining within its protective points, you shall sleep while I watch over all of you…"

"As much as I hate to see this happen--," Tim looked sadly to me and shrugged, "We should move the furniture outside, it's less area for the darkness to gather, and less obstacles for us to navigate when we're in a hurry to leave."

Tim had looked to me for approval, and nodding, I had immediately agreed, "I'm not taking anything out of this place but my typewriter, Marlowe's stones and the golden beryl sphere. Whatever is to be done with everything else really doesn't matter, because after tonight—I'm done here…"

"Then we should get started--," Tim had attempted to move, but Caitlin had caught his arm from across the table, and said, "I will see to this—but you must create the pentagram."

As she walked out with the first item of furniture, Tim had curiously looked at me, and said, "The pentagram is a Christian symbol of protection, isn't it?"

"It used to represent the five wounds of Jesus--," Thinking briefly, I shrugged, "But Satanists and Wiccans now use it as a symbol of protection in their own belief."

"Doesn't that seem a little backward to you?"

"Not if you just accept it for what it still is--," I shrugged, "It's still a symbol of protection, regardless of who's currently using it."

"One last thing--," He raised a finger in thought, asking, "What's the difference between sanctified ground and this pentagram, and tell me why she can't cross that boundary?"

"Sanctified ground is only as good as the faith of whoever blesses it--," Looking between my friend and the hearth, I frowned, "And the pentagram we use incorporates sacred symbols used by King Solomon, which somehow empowers it in ways that I still haven't quite figured out."

"I sure hope it works--," He shivered at the thought, "I'd rather not find out the hard way that it doesn't."

3:50 p.m.

Rich had walked out of the manager's office with several sets of documents and assorted keys. He hadn't looked impressed in the least as he left the GM dealership, and quickly made his way to where Jay and Ole had stood waiting.

"Alright then--," He offered Jay a set of keys, "You now own a brand new, black Pontiac Trans Am. It's a big block car with snow tires—but you might want to take it real easy on the way back."

"I'm used to big blocks--," Jay nodded, "I had a sixty nine GTO Judge—before the divorce. It was bright orange, with hide-away headlights, had the Ram Air IV 400, which was the best that you could get at the time. It was rated at 370 horse power. You would've loved it—I sure did. I should've kept the car and skipped the wife…"

"My heart goes out to you--," Rich patted him on the back, "Remind me about that again later—and we'll see what we can do about getting you another one."

Jay had just gawked at the statement, because it was apparent that Rich had been quite serious in doing exactly that.

"Ole--," He approached the younger man and handed him a set of keys, "You are now the proud owner of a new, white and brown, Chevrolet G30 Open Road camper van."

"A camper van--," Obviously not quite as excited, he looked to Jay, who grinned while holding the keys to his Trans Am, and said, "Why a camper van?"

"Well, you really don't expect me to load explosives into a car—do you?" Rich patted Ole on the shoulder as they departed for their vehicles.

Ole stopped suddenly, "Explosives?"

"Follow me—I need to meet with some guys." Rich paused in thought, "We can exchange vehicles when we get there."

"Explosives…" Ole followed after them across the parking lot.

4:10 p.m.

Rather than taking them any further, Scott had decided to pull off on the Sumas exit. It took them to an enormous truck-stop and hotel that was located directly off the highway. It looked older, but appeared well kept, and being occupied and busy all hours of the day and night, suited their purposes perfectly.

"We'll go get the rooms--," Carrie volunteered, "From the looks of things around here we should be able to get some close together."

"I'll help sort the luggage--," Ray volunteered, as Deb began unloading the vehicles and Scott and Carrie hurried off toward the main office.

The hotel was a two story structure and separated into four long blocks. Two of the buildings rested centrally, and there was one facing inward from either end. The diner had been located at the far end and nearest the highway, and this provided an immense parking lot for big trucks.

The structure itself was built of cement cinder blocks and painted in dull beige, as the sills, balconies and doors were done in a deep, reddish brown.

The office window had ages old cigarette smoke stains and a little neon sign that flashed 'open'. A little bell went off as they had entered, and Carrie frowned to the stale smell of cigarette smoke. It was common, and it seemed that everyone had started smoking after they had both quit.

The furniture was old, the plants yellowed, and Scott tripped over a curled rug while approaching the counter and slammed a hand down upon the service bell.

"Hold your horses--," An elderly woman came coughing from out of the back, "A person can only move so quickly, you know."

She was thin, sickly looking, and covered in far too much cheap makeup. Her eyes were almost black as she blinked at them with lashes more likely suited to that of a horse.

"We need a bunch of rooms, altogether—if that's possible?" Carrie announced, "We're traveling with family, and prefer to stay close."

"Well, rooms I got--," She looked to a board behind her, and selecting keys from main floor suites, was halted by Carrie, who said, "If possible we would prefer the second floor."

The old woman had hesitated as the ash fell from the tip of her cigarette, and she squinted, "Are you sure?"

"It's less noisy--," Carrie explained, "I never cared to have people stomping around above me while I'm trying to sleep."

"How many did you need, exactly?" The old girl butted the cigarette and immediately lit another, while accidentally dropping the match on the floor.

"Five should do just fine—we have a couple per room."

"You got any kids?" Something dark flashed in the old woman's eyes and Scott immediately found her unsettling. There was a strange reluctance in the way that she had asked, and it bothered him right away.

"Our son will be staying with us--," Carrie duly noted, "And Danny is almost an adult, so he'll be just fine on his own."

"I'm not much for renting to youngsters--," She appeared as though she might deny them the rooms, and turning to look back at them, asked, "Are you folks from around here?"

"We live in Vancouver--," Speaking quite honestly, Scott frowned while saying, "But we've all traveled a long way and could really use the rest."

"I completely understand—and don't get me wrong--," She scratched at a hair growing from out of her leathery chin, "I just don't care to rent to youngsters, and just had to make you aware."

"Our place won't be ready until Wednesday--," Carrie fabricated a white lie, "So we'll need those rooms for at least three days."

"Of course--," The old woman took five sets of keys down from the board, and laying them out on the counter before them, said, "B5 to B10 all in a row—," She jabbed a thumb to her right, and said, "Block B is just down from the office and it's easy enough to find, park anywhere you like. Five rooms at twenty five dollars a night each, you owe me three hundred and seventy five dollars for three days, cash money and up front, please..."

"No tax?" Scott was surprised.

"That's included in the price."

Digging through her purse, Carrie quickly found the envelope that Rich had given her. As hurriedly opening and thumbing through it, she was shocked to discover a thick wad of one hundred dollar bills. Concealing this from the hotel manager, she removed what she had required and dropped it on the counter before the old woman.

"Just a second and I'll fetch your change." She hobbled of hacking on her cigarette and Carrie had just shook her head as she looked to Scott, and whispering, said, "I don't care for her too much…"

"She's creepy--," Scott had leaned close and kissed his wife, whispering, "There's something just not right about her and the way she reacts to kids…"

"Alright then--," She returned with the change and counted it out in five dollar bills before them, saying, "I don't carry large amounts of cash or big bills around here, you just never know?" The way that she had eyed them had been a blunt insinuation and left them both insulted.

"Thank you--," Carrie snatched up the bills from off the counter, and nodding, sharply said, "You have yourself a good night…"

Hurrying out of the office she had followed her husband angrily across the frozen lot.

"Can you imagine the nerve of that old witch?" She spat, "After we leave this place, we're never setting foot in here again."

A shadow had been caught in the corner of Scott's eye from across the lot, and as he looked toward the buildings there had been nothing there. Usually he would have simply written this off as some kind of optical illusion caused by snow and direct sunlight, but this time it had bothered him.

"This place is huge--," Danny carried Merlin in his carrier and a large suitcase while looking to Pam, "You'd never think that truckers got to stay in cool places like this."

"They keep the world moving--," She had replied while unloading several duffel bags, and saying, "So they deserve all the comfort and loving that they can get."

"I used to be a trucker once." Ray had stood proud and smiled over at Pam.

"Yeah--," Deb smirked and smacked at his backside with a hand, "He trucks his ass to the kitchen and back to bed."

"No, seriously--," He helped his wife with several bags, "I drove my uncle's old Kenworth for a whole summer when I was nineteen."

"Oh—I remember that--," Deb had peered over at Pam with a sarcastic smile, "He had to quit, because he started a job at McDonald's."

"That's not funny, darling--," Ray shook his head, and rolling his eyes, said, "I didn't mean to run over those cows—I just didn't see them in time."

"You ran over a bunch of cows?" Jen eyed him up, "Seriously?"

"There weren't any guard rails--," He sighed, "And they just jumped out onto the road from out of nowhere."

"Talk about ground beef--," Jen shook her head with a chuckle, "You must've knocked them straight into their Big Mac boxes, boy!" Laughing she heartily slapped at his shoulder.

"All this talk about hamburgers is killing me--," Patrick rubbed at his stomach and looked over at Danny, "I'm starving."

"That diner looks fabulous--," Maya patted Patrick on the back, and smiling, said, "Once we get settled in, we'll all go over for dinner."

"That works just fine for us." Scott waved a fistful of keys, and winking, said, "We managed to get a bunch of rooms in a row and altogether on the second floor. Our luck, this time of the season they're almost empty."

"Almost empty…" Pam had repeated his words and Jen had looked back at her. The dread had been mutual, but there hadn't been any need to make things worse than they already were.

"We'll be just fine, sis--," Jen grabbed a bag in each hand, and forcing a huge smile, said, "So, let's just drag our tired butts up to our rooms before we all starve to death standing around here."

Carrie had been pleased to discover that their second level rooms faced the diner, and looked over the highway from off the balcony. They had parked the vehicles just beneath them and had unloaded everything within a short time

Scott and Carrie had taken a room with Patrick, Deb with Ray, Pam with Jen, Maya with Anna, and Danny shared with Merlin. It was a comfortable and close-knit arrangement, and they couldn't have possibly been happier.

"I know that it's not as big or nice as what you're used to." Speaking softly, Danny had gently stroked the terrified and trembling animal, "But it's going to be okay. I put your litterbox in our bathroom--," He carried Merlin over to show him, and then walking into the little kitchenette, said, "And your food and water dish are right there. Look on the bright side--,"

He scratched behind Merlin's ears and smiled, "The walk between meals and the toilet are a lot closer now."

The old cat had slowly settled down, as meowing and looking up at Danny who still held him, it obviously sensed the lad's kindness.

"Don't you worry about a thing--," He gently placed Merlin down upon the bed, "We're going to be good friends."

There was a knock at the door and a voice called from outside, "Hey—you decent in there?"

"Of course I am--," Danny blushed as he hurried over and opened the door to Jen, "I was just seeing to Merlin."

"Well lock it up, hot stuff--," She motioned for him to follow with a wave, "We're all waiting to get down to the diner for dinner, and your holding the party up."

Laughing, he grabbed his jacket from off the bed, and glancing over at Merlin, paused in thought. Making his way to the mat at the door, the old cat moved ever so slowly and as though treading upon broken glass. His ears were back and hair stiffened as he looked up at Danny with wide and fear-filled eyes.

"Oh—it's going to be okay, old boy." Danny went to the cat, and kneeling, affectionately scratched under his chin and behind his ears, "It's a strange place—I get it—but I'll be back soon and you'll be just fine."

Merlin hadn't moved a muscle, but just sat there silently watching as though he had seen or sensed something that none of the others had noticed. Danny had felt terrible for leaving him, but sighing deeply, petted the cat one last time and made his way out the door.

Merlin growled softly while observing the room from all around him, and then hissing, focused fearfully upon the shadows from under the bed…

There was still ice on the ground and a bitter chill in the air, but the sun had warmed their faces as they walked. Scott and Carrie had led the way, as the others all laughed and talked while following.

"That old broad in the office sure got under my skin--," Carrie informed the others, "She's a nasty character if I've ever seen one."

"Can you believe that she almost turned us down just because we had kids?" Shaking his head, Scott scoffed at the old woman, saying, "She's just bitter because her cherry went rotten, because no one wanted to get near her."

"Oh, Scott--," Carrie slapped at his shoulder with a laugh, "That was terrible!"

"And I was being nice that time--," He warned her with a wink, "I'm just getting warmed up."

"Maybe she actually loves kids?" Thoughtfully placing a finger to her lips, Deb said, "If they're properly cooked."

"I wouldn't put it past the old goat--," Scott glanced over his shoulder and back at Deb and Ray, who followed from close behind, "I'll bet she has a cauldron and pointy hat that she wears most nights."

"I wonder how the others are doing." Maya had thought aloud, "I hope that they're okay."

"A lot better now that they know that we're all safe--," Carrie had offered comfort from the emotional storm that she sensed was soon to come, "I'm sure that they can accomplish a lot more, and focus better without having to worry about us."

"Are we even sure about that?" Patrick had innocently asked, "I mean, about us being safe?"

"Look at that—they have turkey dinners on special with all the fixings--," Scott had pointed while attempting to change the subject, and smacking his lips, said, "That better come with pumpkin pie—or I'll want my money back."

"Just get in there--," Carrie had shoved him in through the open doorway, "You don't need the pie anyway as you've been rounding out over the winter."

"Rounding out?" He led the group into the diner and to where gathering around a long table, he slapped his belly proudly while exclaiming, "I'll have you know that's just winter muscle."

"Well, Christmas is over now--," She had the others laughing, "So you can just send that winter muscle back to Santa."

"Howdy, folks--," A young waitress had hurried over with a coffee carafe in one hand and a notepad in the other, "I'm Amy and I'll be serving you tonight. Can I start you out with some drinks?"

"Sure thing, Amy--," Ray cracked his knuckles in preparation of a big meal, "I'll take the biggest cup of coffee in the house, please."

"I'll just leave this--," Placing the carafe down upon the table, she looked to the others, "And what beverages can I get for everyone else?"

"Oh boy, are you in for a treat." Deb laughed while looking among her friends, "You're stuck with the wild bunch tonight--," She grabbed a mug from before her and holding it out, said, "You might want to bring a second carafe, dear, we're all avid coffee drinkers."

"Just sodas for the boys--," Carrie ordered for Patrick and Danny without thinking, and then threw a hand before her mouth while looking to Danny, "I'm sorry—you can have whatever you like."

"Soda is fine." He had smiled while feeling comfortable and among family, "But, I think that I'll look at a menu before I order, please."

"You got it, sunshine--," Amy placed menus before them, and smiling, said, "I'll be right back with those drinks, and to take your orders."

Leaning close to Danny, Patrick had winked and quietly said, "I think that she's got her eye on you."

"He sounds just like his father." Carrie snickered as Scott sighed and gave her the evil eye.

"Well, I'm doing the turkey dinner--," Ray proudly announced, "It's usually pretty darn good in these places."

"Well, why complicate things?" Deb smirked, "I'll have the same."

"Me too--," Jen looked to Pam who, hesitating but briefly, agreed with a smile, "We might as well gobble up every bird in town while we have the chance. I'm with you, sis!"

"It'll be like spending Christmas together all over again." Patrick smiled, "I'll have it to."

"Why not--," Maya smiled, "It'll probably taste a lot better, and be safer than anything I cooked."

Danny had remembered Christmas as the last cherished moments spent with his mother. Noticing his expression, Pam had slipped an arm around him, and quietly said, "Would you be my dinner date?"

Looking up at her as she did her best Groucho Marx, he laughed as she hugged him, and he said, "Sure thing—I'll have the turkey, too."

"You sure don't say much?" Scott glanced over at Anna, and said, "If you don't speak up, you might starve to death around here."

She had laughed, but in her heart she was terrified for Ole and a stranger among these people. They had all seemed very kind and supportive, but she was feeling lost and very alone.

"We don't bite, sunshine--," Carrie had given her a friendly little nudge and smiling, said, "Any idea of what you would like to have?"

"I'll have the turkey as well--," Shrugging, she looked to the others and said, "I might as well join the party and be a good dinner guest."

"Yee-haw—Anna's buying!" Scott joyously threw his arms into the air as Carrie gave him a gentle elbow in the ribs.

"You'll get used to us--," She winked at Anna, "Sooner or later."

She had liked Scott and Carrie since their first meeting at the house, and laughed as the couple suddenly poked and tickled at each other.

"Knock it off, you guys--," Patrick looked to Anna, and rolling his eyes, said, "And I thought that I was supposed to be the kid around here?"

"We're really not all that weird--," Deb had leaned closer to Anna, and winking, said, "Some of us are a lot worse."

The laughter lessened their troubles and, just for a moment, the darkness had faded from their hearts.

4:45 p.m.

The clouds had already begun to gather, as Rich had pulled off to the side of the road and hurriedly climbed out as the others parked behind him. Rushing back to where Jay was waiting behind Ole in the van, Rich leaned into the open window and quietly said, "Meet me back at the house—I don't want to involve either of you with these people."

"Are you sure about that?" Jay's concern for his friend was obvious.

"I've dealt with them before--," He reassured Jay with a wave, and said, "See you back at the estate."

Watching as Jay pulled out and roared up the street, he approached the driver's side of the van and opened the door, "Okay, Ole--," He offered him the keys to the Eldorado, "Please take Michael's car back to his place—I'll meet you both there when I finish with this meeting."

"Maybe I should stay?" Ole reflected the worry that Jay had shown, saying, "Not that going alone into a back alley with a large amount of money in this area is dangerous or anything?"

"I'll be fine—I know these guys--," Rich thought briefly, and appearing somewhat ashamed, said, "Not that I'm really proud to admit it."

"I'm in no position to judge--," Ole shrugged, "I get robbed on a regular basis and deal with a thief constantly. Have you met my wife?"

"Get back to the house--," Rich laughed while dropping the keys into Ole's open palm as they exchanged places, and Ole said, "Be careful on the way back with that stuff. I wouldn't want you to be the first unexpected mission to the moon…"

"You've got a good sense of humor--," Grinning and pointing as he pulled away with the van, Rich said, "That's a good thing, because you're really going to need it…"

Ole had paused beside the driver's door of the Eldorado as Rich drove away, and quietly said, "Not really—because I only start joking when I get nervous, or am afraid…"

Looking into the slowly darkening heavens he shuddered, and frowning, hurriedly climbed into the car.

Sanctum Arcanum
4:25 p.m.
We had watched in utter astonishment as Caitlin had removed the large couches and heavy furniture. She had insisted upon doing this alone, and accomplished the task with less trouble and in less time than a full crew of movers. Standing before the window, we stood speechless as she had effortlessly and neatly placed these items upon the porch. Although it really hadn't mattered at the moment, I felt some sense of relief knowing that they were covered and safe from the weather.

Tim had been very cautious while assisting me within creating the immense and white-painted pentagram. We had worked feverishly and with the greatest of precision while making the addition of all the necessary symbols. It spanned the full width of the living room floor, and its uppermost points stretched outward from the ends of the hearth.

While we had attended to the final details of the pentagram, Caitlin had brought several large loads of firewood from the garage and stacked it against the far wall. It broke my heart to see the once beloved home falling into utter disrepair in the face of inevitable destruction, but I had brought it all down upon myself and in the end, was the only one to blame...

"If you plan to keep anything when we leave--," Caitlin had come over to me and taken me by the hand, "We should go upstairs and gather what things will fit into your car. I have already placed a sturdy wooden crate in there for you."

"Thank you, sweetheart." I had kissed her, and sighing deeply, looked to my empty living room, and said, "None of this is going to be easy... I don't know what I would do without you."

"Then don't think about that--," Hugging me, she ran a pale hand against my cheek, "Just focus upon what must be done."

"I see cars coming through the gates--," Tim waved as he carefully finished detailing the outlines with a small paint brush, and said, "I think this thing is done—how does it look?"

"Very clean lines--," patting him on the shoulder, I said, "They have to be precise or the whole thing will be useless in our position."

"We should wait until they arrive--," She had warned me, "Just a few moments can make all the difference in the world, as you have both witnessed earlier."

"I'd better go out and tell them to park near the porch steps--," Tim motioned with a hand, "I'll just shout from the front door."

We had followed him regardless and watched as he did exactly that. Moments later, Jay and Ole had appeared in the doorway, and waving, announced their arrival.

"Where is Rich?" Concerned and stricken with paranoia, I had gone to the door, and noticing both my car and the black Trans Am, looked to Jay, "Wasn't he with you when you came back?"

"No—he took a van to meet some guys about some explosives--," Jay shrugged, "He said that he knew them and that he'd be fine."

"We have another problem--," Tim explained as both men came into the house, "There's something in here with us now—and it has the ability to appear as any one of us, at any time."

"What is he saying?" Ole's eyes became as wide as saucers.

"The darkness is no longer prohibited from this place--," I spoke reluctantly, as looking between them, said, "It can take any one of us at any time, and then appear as that person to the others."

"How do you know this?" Jay gasped.

"Because it imitated Caitlin earlier--," Tim explained, "And almost tricked Michael into eating…well, let's just say that if it wasn't for her quick instincts and reaction--," He nodded to Caitlin, "It could've been the end of him…"

"So, what are you saying—," Ole appeared stunned and absolutely terrified as looking between us, he said, "That we can't trust anyone or anything that we see anymore?"

"We need to always stay together—or at least work in pairs--," Leaning against the wall, my attention was drawn to the window as a van pulled into the yard. Watching as it parked before the guest house, I sighed with relief as Rich climbed out, and I said, "We can't let anyone be out of our sight or alone for even a moment. If it gets to them—it could be the end of us all…"

"So, it exists a pure energy--," Ole recounted what he had read, "It has influence over the elements, storms, blizzards--," He gazed fearfully between us, "It can possess human beings, animate corpses, and manifest unspeakable horrors from a combination of dead parts and moldering decay."

"It can also sense your thoughts--," Rich added as he came in through the door, "And scramble your brains so bad that you won't know what's real or fantasy anymore."

"And now it's manifesting as us--," My words had caused them all to just stare aghast, as I said, "From now on, none of us can be alone anywhere. If this entity gets to you—it will take you, and then come for the rest of us in your place…"

"Why didn't it do this before?" Tim appeared surprised.

"It did--," I reminded him, "As Caitlin and Eva—and who knows how many others?"

"It looks like you've been busy--," Rich peered into the living room, and then looking back at me, asked, "Can I ask why you've tossed the furniture out on the porch?" He pointed to the painted images on the floor, and shrugging, said, "And if nothing else will protect us now—what good is that?"

"The pentagram will protect any who remain within its lines—," Caitlin informed him, "And removing the furniture has diminished any opportunity of the darkness attacking us from within their shadow."

"And after all of the times I've slept on that couch--," Rich swallowed hard while peering back at me, "That had never occurred to me…"

"We need some guidelines here is we expect to survive this--," Pacing before the hearth, I stopped to look down at the huge pentagram, and then said, "Under no circumstances is anyone to be left alone—or wander off by themselves for any reason. And secondly, if you and your partner are approached by anyone who is alone—you are to burn them immediately and without question."

"Jesus--," Jay gasped, "Isn't that a little intense? I mean—what if someone gets separated by accident?"

"Then it's likely that they'll have already been taken--," Rich agreed, "Everyone should also keep in mind that if you should decide to go off alone, that you not only forfeit your life, but that of your partner's as well. Because, even if they haven't been taken, they're already as good as dead…"

"I don't know if I could just burn someone like that--," Horrified with the thought, Jay gazed about the group, "Especially not a friend…"

"Then you and whoever is working with you will die--," Caitlin spoke in a stern and solemn manner while addressing Jay, "Make no mistake about it—the evil is aware that this will either be its ending in this world—or ours. And it does not accept failure…"

"All that we have to do is last the night--," Pleading, I looked among my terrified friends, saying, "All that we have to do is stay together—it's that simple. And as long as it's occupied here and with us—the others are safe…"

"What makes you so certain of that?" Picking at an apple pastry, Ole nervously looked around the group, "How do we really know when it is here and when it isn't?"

"Because it's guarding the Beryllus--," Caitlin answered, "And will not chance losing it..."

"So, why couldn't you just run in there and get it?" Jay looked at her and shrugging, said, "No offense, but we saw what you're capable of doing. And if anyone could do it—it would definitely be you."

"And we also saw how the demon in the Willow took her down--," Rich disagreed, "It's obvious that this thing is bigger than any one of us."

"But together we have a chance." She placed a gentle hand upon Rich's back, and looking among the group, said, "This is a gathering of fate and destiny—and all of you were chosen by the powers that be. There is hope—as long as we remain strong, together."

"If it's just a mirror--," Ole curiously looked to Caitlin, "Can't it just be broken?"

"Powerful sorcery binds and protects it—and it is not so easily harmed--," She slowly shook her head, saying, "And any who dare destroy the Beryllus shall be lost within it, forever..."

"I feel that there's a serious need to discuss all of this further." Ole swallowed hard.

"Fair enough, we have all night to do that--," Rich looked to me, "What did you have in mind?"

"I need to pack a few things in my office and load them into the car. Caitlin will be coming with me, so I won't be alone up there. While we are doing that, I would like the rest of you to work together and help Rich get the weapons and explosive ready for the guest house."

"What if I need to use the bathroom?" Ole suddenly blurted out the thought, "You said that we can't be alone anywhere? I was just wondering."

"Then you leave the door open while someone stands outside and waits for you." Rich shrugged, "It may not be pleasant—but it'll keep us safe."

"Well, almost safe." Wiggling his eyebrows at Ole, Jay blew him a kiss and winked.

"What?" Ole cringed, "This is not funny..." It was obvious that in his current state, Ole had not realized that Jay had just intended to ease the tension with a joke. There had been awkward glances exchanged, and then catching the intent, Ole had smiled while shaking his head.

"We should make sure to refill all the oil in the lanterns--," Tim reminded us, "Just in case it takes the power out again."

"I'll make sure to bring everything into the living room before we finish up for the night." Jay slipped a bolt into his crossbow and peered over at me, "I'm ready when you are."

"Alright—everyone should meet back down here before it gets dark--," Peering between the draperies, I watched as the light had already begun fading from the heavens, "I'll be leaving the gates open from now on—and you should all be armed before you do anything else."

"I think we've got that covered--," Rich held the weapon before him, and said, "There's a bow for everyone—and I'll make up more bolts tonight."

"Remind me again why we're waiting until morning?" Jay peered suspiciously back at me.

"Mainly because we can't take the chance of doing anything at night—it's just too powerful in the dark," Looking between my friends and sighing deeply, I said, "We'll be attending a funeral in the morning. And when I come back, I'll bury what's left of my old life in this place…"

"Does it really matter how powerful it is at night--," Obviously terrified, Rich appealed to my common sense, "It could take us here just as easily as the vault."

"It merely toys with you at the moment--," Caitlin replied, "It has the Beryllus and knows that we require it. We are at a stalemate—it knows that we will come for it—and all that it has to do now is watch and wait…"

"So, what's stopping us from just blowing the hell out of the place?" Scratching at his beard, Jay shrugged, "It beats waiting until that thing sneaks up on us while we're asleep."

"Because we need to keep the Beryllus safe, that mirror is a gateway into another dimension." Frustrated with my own blatant disregard of the mystical mirror, I cursed, saying, "It's the only way that we can send that monster into the void—or none of us will ever be safe anywhere, ever again…"

"God only knows what's waiting down there in that vault for us--," Tim's eyes glistened fearfully, "It might have a few nasty tricks up its sleeve that we've never even seen before."

"We're not totally helpless--," Looking around at the motley group, Rich nodded respectfully, "We have Caitlin—and Michael has a cane that can summon a hound from hell…"

Caitlin shot me a nervous glance and I sensed that the demon suspected some form of future treachery. Putting an arm around her shoulder, I kissed her while brushing the long locks of red hair from her emerald eyes. It had been instinctive on my part, but the act had also somehow soothed the beast which grew restless at mere mention of the mystical cane.

"You will be safe within the pentagram and before the hearth—and I will watch over you in the night," Reassuring the others, she raised a finger in warning, "But should you wander alone into the shadows—it might very well be the last thing that you do in this world…"

Exchanging horrified glances, they were unnerved with her final words. Realizing this, I raised a finger in thought, and asked, "Is anyone opposed to urinating in a pail?"

"It beats wandering down those halls at night." Jay nodded in agreement, "That's a great idea."

"I'll do the honors--," Rich volunteered, "There's a few buckets just outside the back door."

"We can go together--," Ole offered, "I could use a little fresh air before dark…"

"Okay, gentlemen—," There was a shiver of excitement as adrenaline surged through my entire being, and I said, "Let's do this…"

It had only taken a few moments to gather my manuscript, typewriter, and writing materials. These were carefully packed into a large wooden crate that Caitlin had placed in the middle of my office. I had used stacks of newspaper that she had brought up from the kitchen, and continually wiped the transferred ink that blackened my fingers upon my pants.

Along with these things, I had kept the Labradorite globes that Rich had made from Marlowe's stones and the golden beryl sphere. Caitlin had just sat silently before my desk and watched while I had carefully packed everything away. She appeared utterly lost, as having finally become familiar with one place in this strange new world, watched as it now all fell apart.

Pulling the mystical cane from its place of concealment, I noticed that it had immediately drawn the demon's attention. Her eyes flashed as I carried it across the room, and pausing before the crate, looked back at her, "It's perfectly harmless—unless intentionally used." Carefully slipping it into the crate with the other items, I peered back at her, and smiling, said, "And as a point of fact, I find the beast absolutely terrifying, to say the least."

"As you rightfully should--," She thought briefly, and looking curiously up at me, said, "For the hound is neither demon nor angel, and abides only to the beckon call of its one, and true master…"

"Well, I'm not its master—just the one holding the stick when it's time to play fetch."

Amused with the statement, she had slipped out of the chair and followed me around the room. It seemed more often than not, that she was never entirely a single entity anymore, but a combination of both. Furthermore, I had realized that the trinity that had once included Marlowe had now incorporated the demon. It was also apparent that the once entirely vile entity, through its union with Caitlin on a mortal plane, had assumed aspects of her general character. Aside from being unsettling, this had also complicated matters considerably, as it became harder to distinguish one from the other while speaking. I had noticed that the once distinct 'old world' lingo of the beast had slowly been fading. Whether this has been due to its exposure to the modern world, or simply its melding with Caitlin, I was not absolutely certain. I could only hope that eventually, the demon might completely vanish into her psyche.

She followed with the wide-eyed curiosity of a child as we went from one end of the room to the other. From the bookcases I had selected a few cherished items and mainly gifts from loved ones. Among one the most precious was a little snow-globe, which, after carefully wrapping it in a wash cloth, I tucked into the crate.

"And what of the books--," Finally breaking her silence, she directed my attention toward them as I packed other things away, saying, "Or have they also lost their appeal?"

Moving to where a collection of lifetimes rested in the shelves before me, I sighed deeply, "The accumulated wisdom, theory and practice of mankind through the ages. The pursuits of mortals into night realms—and look where that gets us… It's hardly worth the bother, really…"

"All that you ever really need is someone to love--," She gazed deeply into my eyes, "And someone that truly loves you back."

The awareness of the demon had not hindered my desire, but only added an element of danger, excitement and temptation. It was this sense of morbid fascination and undying love that now fueled the fires of passion. Holding her close, I had kissed her deeply, and felt the warmth that was the fire of our love.

"Can you still love and desire me--," Her eyes glistened like jewels in the suns failing light, and she whispered, "Even knowing what lurks in the depths of my soul?"

"A monster exists within us all--," I held her close and felt the swift beating of her heart, "But if you choose to see only the love—then nothing else matters."

Through everything, I had never once considered her feelings concerning this sickness of the soul, as it could be called nothing less. It had festered deep within her, and now as she sadly looked upon me, I saw that she feared losing everything in the process.

"I may not have the answers—or the words to express them even if I did--," Embracing her tightly, I closed my eyes while smelling the lilac of her hair, and whispering, "But I would face a thousand hells if it meant spending eternity with you..."

"That night on the mountain--," She wept while attempting to find the worlds to explain, "When all was done and I stood upon the rock, which had buried the truck and that vile soul." She hesitated, and then speaking softly, said, "The demon set me free..."

"What happened?" Utterly astonished, my happiness had turned to darkness as her expression paled, and she said, "I stood alone and naked in the cold wilderness of the world—," She drifted in thought as words failed her, and a sudden remorse filled her eyes, as she whispered, "The wolves--," She whimpered while looking away, "The wolves came for me..."

Taking her gently by the shoulders, I forced her to gaze straight into my eyes, pleading while asking, "What happened—please, tell me..."

"It is far better to rein as a monster--," She stared blankly while uttering the words in barely a whisper, "Than to be taken by one..."

"A gift of damnation offered in exchange for escaping a terrifying death..." It hurt to even imagine her alone and so vulnerable out there, but now I completely understood. Although the deceit had filled me with an inconceivable rage, I withheld all emotion. It would not have been in our better interest to incur its wrath, especially under the circumstances. So, choosing to find the proverbial 'silver lining' upon the dark cloud, I quietly looked back at her and said, "In the end, all that demons really are is fallen angels—and now you have its protection. I can only bless this dark angel for an act of kindness in a cruel world."

"You forgot your iron clock--," Pointing, she had gone over to the desk, and removing it from the hutch, said, "And your doctor's bag."

Realizing that she had chosen to disregard the statement for the same reason that I had not pursued the matter, I had simply nodded, saying, "I think that there's still room in the crate."

Ever so carefully, she had slipped the clock into the crate, and handing me the bag, said, "Just use the bag to take anything else that you wanted to keep."

Remembering the loose board and Leigh's picture, I had hesitated while deciding to leave it behind. As much as it hurt, it was time to permit her to pass onward and allow the memory fade.

"This place has so many old and wonderful memories--," I had sighed while taking one last look around, "It's such a shame..."

"It's filled with the ghosts of broken hearts--," She crossed her arms before her, and tilting her head slightly, said, "And the shadows that you gathered while chasing the answers to a nightmare..."

"And I've found some of those answers—and learned that some things are just better left unknown..." Walking back to my desk with the doctor's bag, I took a last look through the drawers and little cabinets. I collected a few sentimental items. There was a gold pocket watch from the railroad, a magnifying glass, a large crucifix, and a ring of iron keys, which I quickly shoved into the bag. All of these items had sentimental value and were therefore priceless.

"The gifts from your uncle?" She went into my closet, and drawing out the crystal ball and old dragon chalice, asked, "Did you still want these?"

She had read my thoughts by the expression on my face, and quickly added them to the items in the large wooden crate. Last but not least, I had rescued the beautiful Fenton, cranberry double student lamp from my desk. The hanging crystals had jingled as I had crossed the room, and placing it down, I had paused to gaze upon its almost mystical opalescence.

"You might also want this?" She brought over a large, ten stick, Victorian candelabrum that had been one of my first acquisitions. As without a doubt carefully wrapping it in newspaper, she placed it among the other items in the crate. It was at that particular moment that I realized how large the wooden box actually was. Comprised of some kind of hardwood, it measured three feet in diameter, length, and two feet in height.

"That crate is going to weigh a ton--," I had thought aloud while carefully wrapping the separate parts of the old lamp, "I might have to get one of the guys up here to help carry it out to the car."

"I can manage--" Lifting it with little effort she smiled while gently placing it back down, "There are benefits to my condition—as you can see."

"As long as you're always aware of this strength when we're together--," I pondered the disastrous results of her forgetting in the heat of passion, and said, "I'll try not to be too concerned..."

A shadow had moved in the corner of my eye, and turning, I thought to have seen Merlin skulking beneath my desk. Caitlin had taken immediate notice, and rushing to my side, leaned down to peer into the shadows. Whatever had been there had now vanished, but she had sensed its presence, and unsettled, looked up at me, "We should finish this right away—and load the car--," She warned, and looking toward the parted draperies, said, "It's already getting dark."

The heater had caused the draperies to move ever so slightly, and leaping forward, Caitlin had torn them from off the wall! The change had been almost instinctive, and occurred in the blink of an eye. It seethed, the blue fires in its empty sockets burning brightly as spreading its wings, it gazed back at me.

"There was something in here with us—," I had spoken to the creature as though still communicating with my beloved, "I sensed it…"

"The enemy is among us--," The demon spoke in Caitlin's voice, taking me completely by surprise, as it curiously asked, "Did you truly mean what you said earlier? For, I have never known the man whom would dare offer blessings upon demon, devil, or angel."

"The one who is truly grateful would--," I thought for a moment while closer observing the creature, and then saying, "As even through your betrayal—you still safeguard the one most precious to him."

"Perhaps…" It took up the crate containing my possessions, and motioning toward the door with a blackened claw, swiftly followed me out of the room.

I shuddered as its long and hooked bat wings began folding inward, as while shielding me from anything that might approach from behind. There was a dark majesty to this devil that caused me to wonder, whether it had adopted certain aspects of Caitlin, or whether it bore some secret of its own? What had it been before it was cast down, and who would it be now if it hadn't? Was it possible that somewhere beneath that horrific exterior it might have been similar to Caitlin?

The creature had altered as we had gone out into the hallway and then slowly made our way toward the stairs. In the last moments I had gone into the bedroom with the beast, and slipped a robe over the naked form of my Caitlin…

CHAPTER TWENTY SIX

6:15 p.m.

Carrie and Scott had taken care of the bill as the others had gathered and patiently waited at the main doors. The once cheerful group had fallen silent as while solemnly gazing into the empty parking lot. It was the first time in many months that they had been beyond the protection of Sanctum Arcanum, and they dreaded the long walk back to their rooms.

"Off we go then!" Carrie had groaned while pushing the heavy door open, and taking Scott by the hand, hurriedly led the way.

It wasn't as cold as it had been earlier, as even with the dusk, the wind had almost completely vanished. The hard-packed snow crunched beneath their boots, and Carrie having thought to have heard a familiar voice, paused to look back.

"Is something wrong?" Scott still gripped her hand while gently pulling her along, "We should really hurry—it's starting to get dark."

His words had caused her to follow without question, but the sound of that voice still bothered her. It was distant enough to make it indiscernible, but clear enough that it had carried a familiar tone.

"You okay, mom?" Patrick hurried along beside her, "Or is something going on?"

"Nothing is wrong--," Attempting to appear unconcerned, she pinched at his cheek, and grabbing at his hand, pulled him after them, "I'm just hearing and seeing things as always—nothing unusual for me."

"I think that turkey's coming back with a vengeance." Ray slipped a hand to his belly, as he and Deb followed Scott and Carrie, and he said, "The only thing I hate about it—is that it just goes straight through me."

"And what I hate about it--," Deb agreed with a sarcastic grin, "Is how it always makes you gassy—especially at night…"

"Would it make you feel better, if I just tooted a happy tune?"

"I wouldn't be tooting, if I were you--," She winked as they held hands and walked along, "You might have water instead of wind—and have to swim back to our room."

"I'd laugh--," He groaned while rubbing at his belly and wincing, "But you're probably right."

"This might not be so bad for all of you?" Danny had looked to Pam, Jen and Maya, and said, "Since you're all sharing a room, you could have a pajama party."

"Oh yeah—because that's what girls do when we're all alone--," Jen laughed, "We get into our underwear and jump on beds while beating each other with pillows! Yippee!"

"Get those thoughts out of your head--," Pam jokingly clipped Danny in the back of the head after seeing his expression, and chuckling, said, "We most certainly do not do things like that."

"Speak for your-self, girl--," Jen winked at Danny, "I just can't wait to get these clothes off and bounce my booty all over that bed."

Anna laughed aloud, and embarrassed, had thrown a hand in shame before her mouth.

"No reason to feel bad for having fun--," Maya put an arm around Anna, and smiling, said, "The world needs a whole lot more of that, especially now."

"She's just kidding." Pam smiled at Danny.

"I'll bet you five bucks that she isn't." Maya laughed as she hurriedly followed from behind.

Danny had giggled mischievously while looking over at Jen. She was truly a beautiful young woman, and if he was older, he would have been proud to have asked her out. Unfortunately, there was almost ten years between him and all of the women that he knew. It left a lot of room for a young man's imagination, but that was the extent of it. At the moment it didn't really matter anyway, he just enjoyed their company, and managed to sneak a peek or two.

"Seriously—are you okay?" Scott paused as Carrie stopped at the foot of the stairs, and turned to look behind them again.

"I don't know--," She moved aside as the others climbed the steps, and gazing into the distance, muttered, "I just keep getting the feeling that someone is following us…"

He had looked to where she appeared to have focused, and seeing nothing in the lengthening shadows of dusk, shook his head, "I don't see anything, honey. But it's getting dark—we should be getting indoors."

Glancing between Scott and the empty parking lot, she slowly nodded and hurriedly followed her husband up the stairs.

"Is everything alright?" Deb had stood at the open door to her room as Ray had rushed inside.

"Oh—everything is just fine—I've just got the willies as usual." Carrie waved while unlocking her door, "I just need some sleep before my eyes fall out of my head."

"Good night, everyone—and pleasant dreams!" Pam had waved from her door

"Good night!" Jen waved and winked at Danny, whispering, "Pajama party time."

"Good night, John-boy--," Scott had mimicked a well-known television series and they had all laughed, as he said, "Now go to bed, people—we'll see you for breakfast."

With smiles and waves in departure, the doors had closed in unison, leaving Carrie standing there while still pondering unfamiliar sounds and distant shadows.

"I'm taking a shower--," Patrick called from inside the room, "Does anyone need the can?"

"No—go ahead--," Scott stood next to his wife before the open doorway, and whispered, "I thought that I saw something out there earlier, too..."

"What was it?"

"I don't know—it was like a shadow of a man standing between the buildings--," Slowly shaking his head and looking down at her, he said, "But when I looked it was gone."

"Have you ever stayed here before?" She shivered, "Or heard anything about the place from anyone?"

"No—I just saw it from the highway and figured that this would be perfect for what we needed."

A gently gust tossed the hair about her face, as looking to her husband, she whispered, "I'm not sure what it is—but something about this hotel is making my skin crawl."

Scott knew that his wife had never been easily unnerved and trusted in her intuition without question. Slipping an arm about her waist, he had pulled her close while peering suspiciously out among the lengthening shadows.

"Do you think that it's found us here?" Swallowing back the dread, he quietly looked back at her.

For several moments she pondered the possibility, but then slowly shaking her head, glanced back, "I don't know what it is—but I feel that something isn't quite right here. And Scott--," She slipped closer into the safety of her husband's arms, "I don't think that it's the same thing that was after us before..."

"Honey—you know me—if you told me to—I'd pack everything up and get everyone the hell out of here--," His features twisted fearfully as he looked into the darkening heavens, and said, "But we can't leave now— and not in the dark... All that we can do is watch over them all—and keep them safe until we talk to Michael."

"That's just it, Scott--," She frowned while still staring into oblivion, "I really don't know if we can..."

The old woman had peeked out from behind the blinds and sneered while looking into the empty lot. She hated the winter months. When things slowed down, she was alone in the old place. It had once belonged to her brother, a drunken pervert who had died several years ago in jail. She remembered how he would wander around on nights and peeked into people windows and rooms through secret peep-holes.

She had spent the last few years finding them all, as hidden behind pictures, false panels and mirrors, she had sealed them up. In her adventures into crawlspaces and attics, she had found far more than that. He had been imprisoned for sexual assaults on minors, and suspicion of murder in three cases. Unfortunately for the authorities at the time, they had never located the bodies.

She found the first one, an eleven year old girl, tightly wrapped in burlap and tucked deep into the attic insulation. The remains had been little more than bones, and she had secretly buried them to avoid further complications.

The second had been a thirteen year old girl who had gone missing from the diner across the lot. Her corpse had been rolled in sheets, and submerged in the mud of the unfinished basement of building block D. The third was a girl of twelve, whom he had bound in plastic bags and stuffed into a crawlspace. The remains had been concealed behind a wall for almost twenty years before she stumbled upon it, while searching for more peep-holes. They had all been buried in the thick mud to the rear of the property, and would likely remain there forever.

She had forever felt guilty for her part in concealing the bodies, but her brother had already been long dead by the time that she had discovered them. She had never been married, nor had children, but felt remorse every time that she saw them… She had often denied parents with young girls rentals while her brother lived, and just out of suspicion. There had always been some question as to his sanity, but she had never really been certain if he had done those terrible things. Not until long after, and when she had found the bodies.

She watched as the wind danced in the drifting snow. It cast tiny swirls, which spiraling, played in the lamp light's glow. Often she had wondered when it had just been the wind, or the lost souls of those little girls still wandering in that place…

"You were a no-good, rotten ghoul, Roy. And I hope that you're burning in hell for what you did…"

Tightly closing the blinds, she left the snow to dance alone in the glow of the empty parking lot...

Sanctum Arcanum
6:35 p.m.
It was already dark when we gathered in the living room and before the hearth. We had laid out sleeping blankets and supplies such as we might need for the night and made a ring of lanterns from all about us. Caitlin had helped me load the crate into the trunk of my car, and it had barely closed. In final preparation, and an emergency departure, we had parked all the vehicles near the front and back doors.

Although I offered an evening meal, none had felt any appetite. I couldn't really blame them. I had felt the same, and dreaded the thought of requiring the bathroom in the middle of the night. Rich had placed a large bucket in either corner of the front window, and a pail of clean water to wash up afterwards. It seemed rather barbaric, but in lieu of the consequences, a small price to pay. Switching on each and any light that was available, the manor shone like a beacon, as its glare brightly illuminated the driveway and surrounding pines.

Rich and Jay had busied themselves preparing addition arrows and bombs, while I sat with Caitlin, Ole and Tim before a blazing hearth while sharing tea.

"I never thought that I would live long enough to experience anything like this." Ole appeared utterly dismayed while observing the beautiful antiques that still surrounded us.

"Don't worry--," Tim sighed, "You might not."

"Thank you." Ole had groaned, "Has anyone ever told you that you have all the warmth and appeal of a funeral director?"

"Good call--," Grinning, Tim winked and said, "I've just recently retired."

"It's true--," I sighed as Ole had looked to me for confirmation and shrugging, I said, "If you have the time and interest you can find the details of his retirement in book four."

"No offense—but at the moment-," Ole nervously sipped at his tea while resting his back against the wall, "I am hoping to read about our success and survival in book five..."

"Well don't hold your breath--," Tim raised an eyebrow, "Because in case you haven't already noticed—the characters in his books don't seem to last long."

"I only record events—I'm not really a fatalist…" It was nothing new for me to have apologized for something beyond my control, and I was doing it again…

"In most horror films or television mysteries the new guy always gets it first." Ole appeared far paler than even before, and sighing, said, "And from what I've already read of your books, my odds are getting worse by the moment."

"Dear old Harry was with us from the beginning--," Tim gazed blankly into the hearth as he appeared to slip into a dream, "Red Cloud, Raymond, Gordon, Ian and so many other close friends were taken by this thing." Shaking his head, Tim had looked up from the fire and back to Ole, and quietly said, "Death isn't prejudice—it takes anyone that gets in the way…"

"If I could do it all over again--," I had thought aloud, "And could rewrite our own history through Nightrealm, I would have saved all of them…"

"You know—it's kind of funny." Thinking for a moment, Tim had looked over, and smirking, said, "An author has the power to create alternate realities and to give or take life, just like a God. I often wonder at times—whether writers are the true literary serial killers of the world?"

"I disagree--," Ole frowned, "I would say that it's the damned critics that are ruining the arts. Those eloquent yet vengeful assholes, who, having failed in their own literary attempts, take their frustrations out upon others."

"It sounds like you've had some experience in that field?" Jay scoffed.

"Well, yes--," Ole grinned mischievously, "I was a critic for our University magazine."

Laughing, Tim had slapped Ole on the back, "You're going to fit in around here just fine, my friend.

"I've watched Michael spend years alone at that typewriter--," Rich wandered into our circle, and dropping onto his bedding, said, "And after all the endless nights and devotion, this is what it's all amounted to. If someone asked me, I'd tell them that I'll be glad to see this place burn—and take all the bad memories and nightmares with it…"

"They never go away--," Caitlin quietly looked over at him, "They just haunt someone else…"

"Well once this is all over, I'm going somewhere nice--," Jay joined us before the hearth, "And maybe even meet a new misses 'I own half of your stuff and I'm leaving you' again."

"Optimism is important--," Tim winked, "I've always liked that about you."

"And what will you do?" Ole looked over at me, "Are you really walking away from all of this?"

Taking hold of Caitlin's hand, I had sighed deeply while looking at her. Before he had asked that question, I had never really considered anything beyond the moment. In fact, though I had kept a few mementos, I really did not expect to survive the final conflict.

"Well, I have my Eldorado and Caitlin--," Contemplating for a moment, and then looking to my friends, I had thoughtfully said, "Maybe once this is all over, and everyone is safe—I'll find others who need our help?"

A hellish blue fire shone in my beloved eyes as she suddenly smiled. Whether it had been the demon finding amusement in the statement, or the angel in Caitlin, I wasn't altogether certain.

"No, sir--," Rich had leaned over and resting a hand upon my shoulder, said, "You and Caitlin are coming with me and Maya, and we're going to retire in some tropical ocean paradise: Drinks with little umbrellas, hula-girls, and warm sandy beaches."

There was a light of love and hope shining in his eyes at that moment, and for a while it had chased out the darkness that still haunted my heart. The others had laughed as he leapt up and did a little hula dance, and as I watched, the world seemed to slow down from all about us.

Caitlin was staring blindly at me and as though we were utterly alone in that room. She appeared lost, though her eyes had all the seeming of one who was desperately dreaming of something better. We both knew that the world for us had forever changed, and that with this ending, we could never continue onward without each other. I knew in my heart that whatever happened, I could never abandon, or stop loving her...

"Just so that you know it--," Rich broke me from the spell of silence, saying, "I didn't trust all those explosive while we are staying in this place. So the wires aren't connected, yet."

"That was good thinking--," Ole agreed, "If they were, our nasty little friend could just make ends meet--," He snapped his fingers, "And then boom, we are all on the moon in this house."

"It would be more likely that this place will be blown to match-sticks--," Jay shuddered with the thought, "And we'll be the red jelly all over it..."

"Thank you for that colorful analogy--," Ole became as pale as a sheet as he looked to me, and said, "You should really be taking notes. From what I have already read, these anecdotes would make wonderful additions."

An abrupt knock at the front door sent us all scrambling, as we leapt to our feet and looked to one another. A moment later, we were armed and moved as a group toward the door. It was already dark, there were never visitors to my estate and we all now feared the worst.

"Let me do this—be ready…" I had moved forward and Caitlin had caught me by the arm.

"Whatever stands behind that door--," She whispered, "Is foreign to the darkness, and yet not alike to any of us…"

A thousand horrors flashed through my mind, as reaching for the door handle, I braced for the worst. In one swift movement, I had thrown open the door and leapt back with the bow in my hands! Everyone had suddenly moved forward together, as preparing to fire, now just stood and stared.

The young couple was well dressed and stood speechless and with open jaws as they held brochures advertising a religious service. We had all stood just looking at each other, neither of us knowing what to do.

"Um, pardon us--," The gentleman had said, "But have you heard the good news?"

"They'll never get off the property alive--," Rich looked to me, "What do we do?"

"But we can't have them here either--," Ole appeared terrified. "It's not safe."

"Please--," The woman now panicked, "Don't hurt us—we'll just leave."

"Ole's right—It's not safe--," Reaching out, Rich caught her by the arm, and pleading, said, "Just come inside, you'll be okay, I promise."

Caitlin had moved with lightning speed as the first tendrils erupted from out of the two strangers and lashed out at Rich! Pulling him out of the way and casting him down behind her, she slammed into them, shoving the already seething mass out of the doorway!

Ole had dropped his weapon in the chaos, and stumbling backward, fallen over Rich. Having become the demon, Caitlin struggled with the monstrosity as it fought to reach the open doorway! The foul thing lashed out with clawed tendrils, slashing and tearing at the demon as they came ever closer!

In the light I could see it clearly, and my heart pounded at the horrendous sight of the fiend. The two figures having melded together were a festering and fleshy mass of thorny tendrils, gaping mouths, and multiple clawed limbs! The entire thing absolutely oozed with decay and trailed filth with every motion.

"I can't get a clear shot without hitting Caitlin!" Jay cried out, "What do we do!"

Tim had fired his weapon, but the arrow sailed passed the monster and almost struck one of the cars. It had only been by sheer luck alone that it impacted into an old and frozen log, before bursting into flames. Struggling to reload, he had stepped back from the doorway as Jay leapt into his place. His eyes were filled with an unspeakable terror, but he courageously held his place beside me in the open door.

The demon fought valiantly, but the fiend was swiftly gaining ground and would soon be at the door! It was obvious that whatever effort the darkness was using in this attempt, that it was still far too powerful for her.

"Get everyone back—hurry!" Rich wailed as he ran out the door, and narrowly escaping the flailing tendrils, raced out behind the struggling pair. Seeing this, the horror had spun toward him and that was when he had fired. The dart sailed through the night and straight into the center of the hideous mass. Erupting in a blinding flash, the chemical fire spread swiftly as the horror burned! In the confusion Rich had stumbled, and as he fell, the blazing nightmare had surged toward him!

The demon grabbed Rich from off the ground, and lifting him bodily, leapt into the air as it flew straight in through the front door. We had all barely managed to get out of the way as it whipped past like a hurricane, and we almost lost our balance.

"Burn, you God-forsaken son of a bitch!" Jay fired into the festering and hideously bubbling mass, and the arrow exploded near what might have once been a head. The hideous and crawling inferno had suddenly spun toward me. Slamming the door, I locked and bolted it before leaping clear!

"It's melting into a lake of fire--," Jay shouted from where he now stood in the front window while watching the horrendous scene, "It's not moving anymore—I think that it's dead!"

"It never really dies--," Wiping the sweat from my brow, I looked back at my friend, "It just forms again somewhere else."

"You saved my life--," Rich gasped as the demon gently set him down, and bowing his head, he said, "I am in your debt..."

"You owe me nothing--," She began changing again, and grabbing at his blanket from off the floor, Rich had quickly covered her, and she said, "Alright I'll consider us even for the blanket."

"What in the name of God was that?" Ole was utterly shocked and trembling uncontrollably while cringing near the hearth.

"That, my friend--," Rich had gone over, and sitting down beside him, said, "Was what you can expect from strangers—or anyone that appears alone from now on..."

"And her--," Directing Rich's attention with a subtle nod, Ole quietly asked, "What is she?"

"Angel or demon--," Rich shrugged, "Pick one, none of us are really quite sure."

"I really wasn't expecting that--," Tim fearfully rubbed at his face, "They seemed so real?"

"At least we know that these arrows work--," Jay affectionately patted his crossbow, saying, "When you can get a clear shot."

"That's part of the problem with being in close quarters--," Sipping at what remained of his tea, Tim shivered with the thought, "We're likely to go up with whatever we're shooting at."

"Please, promise me something--," Ole looked between us, "If I ever get taken—burn me..."

"That goes for me to, brother." Jay sat down before the hearth, and placing his bow within reach, said, "I'd rather burn than become part of whatever the hell that thing was..."

"Let's all agree—right here and now--," Turning to my companions and extending a hand, I looked among them, and said, "If any of us are ever taken, no questions asked—whoever is left burns us ..."

"Amen—better by fire than like that..." Jay placed his hand atop mine as all the others had followed with exception to Caitlin. There hadn't been any question as to why she had not joined the circle, as the answer was quite obvious.

Ole moved closer to the fire, and appearing far calmer, looked back at me, "Is that what would have come after my wife and me if we had not come to you first?"

"I can't honestly tell you that--," Accepting a cup of tea from Caitlin, I shook my head, "It can appear in so many different ways, and kills according to opportunity."

"Like the way that it almost took down Scott and Carrie's plane--," Rich agreed, "And while using a freak storm that would have made the whole thing appear like an accident."

"Oh, it's just warming up—and you haven't seen anything yet--," Gazing toward the open draperies, Tim visibly shuddered with some vivid recollection, and muttered, "Just wait until it digs up something cold and wet—then things will get really disgusting..."

The horror in Ole's eyes had been indescribable, as swallowing hard, he had turned to me in question, "You do have some power over the dead—do you not?"

"Only this--," I had moved to where I had concealed the cane above the mantle place, and drawn it out, "But it only works on the souls of the lost, not on a reanimated corpse."

"How can you tell the difference?" Jabbing a poker into the hearth, Jay stabbed at the glowing coals while adding another log.

"Because souls appear as apparitions—or specters--," Rich answered while nibbling at a cookie, "And those other things are nothing but puppets made out of dead and rotting meat."

"We are not alone…" Leaping to her feet, Caitlin scanned the ceiling while listening for even the slightest indication of movement. Grabbing our weapons and scrambling from off the floor, we all stood while silently listening and watching.

The vision came to me in the form of a waking dream, or so I had first assumed? In fact, what I had actually been doing without being entirely aware of it, was sensing beyond the wood and stone, and seeing into the rooms above.

Jay suddenly moved, as producing a packet of matches from his shirt pocket, had quickly gone about while lighting the circle of lanterns that stood from all around us. At the moment it had made little sense as the house still shone like the rising sun. But then, we had all been entirely grateful as everything had suddenly fallen into utter blackness.

"Stay in the pentagram-," Caitlin stood defensively before us and warned, "And do not step out of the circle of light."

"We need to get out of this place." Ole's eyes were wide and glistened fearfully in the firelight, "If we are forced to use these weapons in such confined quarters, we will never get out of here alive."

"We'll just have to take our chances in here--," Rich choked, "And believe me—you don't want to get caught out in the open with those things."

The ceiling suddenly creaked loudly as though bending beneath an immense weight. The sound had been almost ear-splitting in the presiding stillness, and we had all moved back to avoid being directly beneath the movements. It came again, except slower as it now moved cautiously as though sensing where we stood from beneath it. Once more, we moved aside to avoid the possibility of having it come crashing down upon us.

Caitlin motioned for us to be still, and then waved within warning as she kept us from bunching up. In moments we spread out into a circle, and each stood before a lantern with his bow at the ready.

Concentrating upon the ceiling, I thought to have felt myself drifting upward and through the plaster and boards. My body became light as a feather as my thoughts traveled, and I could now see the thing in the darkness as though it was during the light of day. The huge fleshy mass hideously trembled, pulsating while expelling foul mucus and putrefying decay. It slithered about on countless and slippery tendrils, while apparently searching for something in my bedroom. It was while it had gathered its mass to turn around, when I saw the accumulated explosives within its tentacles and realized what it had done. If Rich had not disconnected that wiring, we would have all certainly already been dead…

Falling downward and drifting back through the ceiling, I had been restored to my body. The shock of what I had seen still burning like an image in my mind, I had whispered, "It's collecting all of the explosives—but why?"

"It intends to remain here--," Caitlin quietly said, "And will not allow us to destroy this place as we did with the house of McCreary…"

"But why this house--," Rich moved closer, "It can go anywhere—and there must be a thousand other places that would be far better to hide."

"Oh, but it doesn't' want to hide--," Slowly turning to look at my friends, my heart skipped a beat as I finally realized the truth, "It wants to inhabit this place like it did the Duff Glenn, and become us…"

"It must have done the same thing with the McCreary family in Ireland." Aiming his bow at the ceiling, Rich peered over at me, "Which would explain the stories that the sailors told about accidental deaths and missing people."

"And why they came here and built that mausoleum in an attempt to trap it--," The crossbow shook within Tim's trembling hands, "It's been playing us the whole time, and was just waiting for the right opportunity.…"

"We should just blow the hell out of this place right now--," Jay growled, "And go over there and deal with it while there's still a few of us left."

"If we go into that building at night—none of us will come back out." Motioning for everyone to maintain their positions, I whispered, "Our strength is the daylight—and it's our only hope of getting back out of there alive."

"I'm willing to bet odds that it's got that damn mirror in the old steel vault--," Rich cursed under his breath, "And it's always dark down there…"

"If I can get between the mirror and the entity with the stone--," I looked between Rich and Tim, "I'm sure that I can draw it into the void."

"But then it would drag you along with it--," Ole shook his head, and frowning, said, "There must be some other way."

The ceiling groaned again from just above us, and we had all fallen deathly silent as it moved. Ever so cautiously I took up a lantern, as listening, we followed the sounds as it made its way down the corridor and then toward the stairs. The weight upon the landing now caused the wood to split and crack, as hesitating briefly, it began making its way down the steps.

Caitlin had quietly forced us all backward into the pentagram and to where we all stood staring into the darkness at the foot of the stairs. The hearth suddenly snapped while spitting hot embers and my heart leapt into my throat!

Remaining absolutely calm and focused, Caitlin stood defensively before us, and a moment later, the demon's immense wings unfolded as it poised to strike.

"No one move a muscle--," I whispered while slipping in beside the demon, and looking into its burning gaze, said, "Tell me—what do we do?"

"Do nothing--," It peered back at me, and then quietly said, "All are safe within the pentagram…"

"You heard her--," Terrified almost beyond words, I looked to all of my friends and motioned for them to lower their weapons saying, "It can't reach anyone as long as we remain in the pentagram."

"Oh God…" Ole's eyes had reflected the horror even before we had seen the nightmare. Tim had raised his weapon, but Jay had halted him with a hand and slowly shaken his head.

A loud shuffling and scraping could be heard from out of the dark corridor. As even before having seen it, I could imagine how it dragged its immense bulk, as countless and clawed tendrils scraped along while slithering across the hardwood floor! In the moment that it had slipped from out of the long shadows, I realized that it had not been my imagination at all. I had sensed and somehow seen the nightmare through the eye of my mind. However, this had not lessened the terror of what now came into view before all!

It appeared in the form of a tall and grotesquely obese man. Bloated and festering, it hunched forward while dragging masses of its body from both sides and behind. Struggling to walk upon two legs, coils flailed from beneath, as it slid upon a trail of vile and decaying filth. The head was nothing more than a pale mass of blistering flesh, as barren of eyes, nose, or even ears, there gaped a mouth filled with twitching and trailing tentacles!

"Stand in the center of the pentagram while facing one other--," The demon ordered, "Take hold of each other's hands—close your eyes, and do not open them again until you are told."

Although terrified, they had all quickly done exactly as instructed, but I remained beside the demon. No words had been exchanged, but I felt a blackened wing embrace me as we turned to face the approaching fiend.

It came ever onward, the mouth gaping as a long, black and thorny tongue whipped about its bulbous head. I could see where the explosives had been gathered, and now dissolved into its hideous mass. It was protruding and being dragged in the folds of its stomach, as it was slowly consumed while vanishing into the rotting flesh.

"When you can no longer bear to gaze upon it--," The demon spoke in Caitlin's voice, "Trust within the pentagram—and choose to see only me..."

The stench had become unbearable as the loathsome thing approached. My senses burned and eyes watered, and the world swam from all about me. The putrid sweet odor of decay filled the room, and I fought to remain conscious. Still, ever closer it came, until mere inches from my face, its tendrils and tentacles whipped about frantically. An immense bat wing folded closer about me, and I felt myself being gently drawn backward and away from the fiend, the entire gruesome mass quivering, shuddering with anticipation while testing the boundaries of the pentagram!

The huge and ghastly mouth had parted ever wider, and as my eyes were drawn into the foul depths of its being, I felt my knees begin to give way beneath me. Unable to bear the sight of it any longer, I felt the cold and leathery wing shove me backward and into my friends, as the blackness took me...

CHAPTER TWENTY SEVEN

Monday, February 10, 1975.
8:15 a.m.
The morning sun had shone in through the parted draperies, awakening me from where I had slept on the floor. The memory of the previous night had flashed into my mind, and I sat up with a start.

"It's okay now—my love--," Caitlin had gently forced me back down, whispering, "The others still sleep—and the evil faded with the coming dawn."

"It stayed here all night—filthy bugger--," Ole drowsily muttered from where he sat while tending to the hearth, "All night—it kept trying to find some way to get to us…" Terrified and utterly exhausted, he mumbled as though speaking to himself, "And when the first light of day shone—it just melted into the floor… It's down there waiting—even now…"

"We need to get him away from here and somewhere safe--," Jay had whispered from where he had been lying and observing everything, "He's beat, and won't make it through another night."

"We should all attend that funeral--," Tim squinted, and rubbing at his eyes, groaned while sitting up, "It isn't even safe to leave anyone alone here during the day anymore."

"Where's Rich?" Panicking, I looked to the empty blanket where he had been sitting the night before.

"Making coffee--," Jay pointed to where Rich sat in plain view at the breakfast nook and waved back, "I've had my eye on him the whole time."

My head swam in a dizzying haze and my heart settled as I realized that everyone was safe. Caitlin had gently stroked my back as I sat up and winced with a stiff neck.

"I know--," Rich had brought coffee and tea into the room on a large silver tray, "My back feels like Fred Astaire was dancing on it all night."

"Hey, buddy--," Rich offered Ole coffee and gently patted him on the back, "How are you holding out?"

"After last night--," He carefully sipped at the steaming liquid, "I am just glad to still be alive."

"I would completely understand if you wanted to leave." Offering him the option, I wasn't really surprised when he had promptly declined.

"That thing would only come after me--," He shook his hand, and speaking in an adamant tone, said, "I just pray that my wife and the others are safe…"

"If it was occupied here with us, then we can be fairly certain that they're all safe." Stirring cream and sugar into his coffee, Rich added in thought, "She's in good company…"

Monday, February 10, 1975.
Sumas Inn
5:14 a.m.

It was still dark when a strange sound alerted Danny to someone testing the handle on the door to his room. He had slept with the bathroom light burning and left the door open just far enough to provide a sliver of light. He could see where the golden beam flowed from across the floor, and passing over his bed, nearly touched the far wall.

The sound came again, and as he peered out from beneath the covers, he saw that Merlin was nowhere to be found. The old cat fallen asleep in the old armchair the last time that he had looked, but it was dark and barren. Ever so slowly he slipped out from beneath the covers, and grabbing at a heavy flashlight that he had brought, crept toward the door.

The handle moved again, except with significantly more force. It twisted and was forced back and forth, and seemed as though it might just snap off. Gripping the flashlight in his right hand, he slowly reached for the door handle. With his heart pounding furiously, he held his breath in that moment, and then swiftly flung open the door!

The old man stumbled backward, as fumbling with a set of keys and bottle of whiskey, dropped straight onto his bottom! Startled, he raised a hand in apology as while slurring his words terribly, and said, "I'm sorry, young fellow—I must've gotten the wrong room?"

"Can I please see your keys, sir?" Danny held out a hand and the old fellow promptly dropped them into his open palm.

"That's why you got it mixed up--," Danny had chuckled, and looking back to the old man, said, "You wanted room C9 and this is B9—you should be at building C, which is further down."

When Danny looked back the old man was standing before him, and had a blank look in his face. His eyes were wide open, but it was as though he couldn't see anything.

"Are you okay mister?"

A cold gust tossed the hair before Danny's eyes, and he shivered as the old man just silently stood there.

"Well, I need to get back to bed—good luck--," He turned to go back into the room, but the old man had caught him by the wrist. His bony fingers were icy cold and his grip like steel cord. Unable to escape the old man's frozen grasp, he struggled, shouting, "Let go of me!"

"The devil waits for you in the darkness--," Still mesmerized the old man whispered, "And your dead mother weeps from your father's unknown grave. Soon—it will come for you and you shall all be together and burning in hell..."

Danny had suddenly ceased all efforts to escape and just stood in the darkness gawking.

With his wispy white hair blowing in the chill wind, the old man pointed as his eyes grew huge, and he whispered, "Ten have come to this place—but only eight shall leave..."

"Let go of him!" Bowling the man over, Pam grabbed and pulled Danny away!

Scott and Carrie had been right behind her, and restraining the old drunk, Carrie shouted, "What do you want with us—and what did you say to him!"

"I don't know what you're talking about?" The old fellow stumbled and slurred his words, "I was just trying to find my room and somehow ended up here?"

It was apparent that the man was intoxicated, but judging by his fearful and confused expression, he was obviously telling the truth. They had immediately released him as Deb and the others opened the doors to peek out.

"I'm telling you—I just got lost--," The old man pleaded while waving his keys, "I'm really sorry—and I won't bother you again."

"What did he say to you?" Scott turned to Danny, who replied through tears of disbelief.

"The devil waits for you all in the darkness--," He spoke slowly as while quoting the old man, "And your dead mother weeps from your father's unknown grave."

"You dirty old son of a bitch!" Jen had rushed toward the cringing old man as Carrie had caught and stopped her, gasping, "How could he have even known?"

"Ten have come to this place--," Danny stared through tears, "But only eight shall leave..."

"I swear to God--," The old man became hysterical as he fell to his knees and begged, "I really don't know what he's talking about?"

"Let him go--," Carrie took hold of Danny and hugged him close, "I believe him…"

Scott had done as she asked, and the old fellow had stumbled off and quickly vanished down the stairs.

"I'm not sure what happened here--," Carrie walked Danny toward his room, "But I think that someone should stay with him until morning."

"I'll do it--," Pam volunteered, "I can grab my blanket and sleep in the chair."

"Something was just trying to frighten us--," Carrie gazed deeply into the lad's eyes, "And nothing else. I need you to go back in there—and try to get some rest, okay?"

Nodding, he had swallowed back the tears, as trembling terribly, Carrie gently passed him into Pam's open arms.

"Don't answer that door again until daylight--," She warned, "We'll be watching and listening."

Nodding, Pam hurriedly led him back into the room, and swiftly closed and locked the door.

"Please--," Scott motioned with both hands while waving to their friends, "Everyone please go back into your rooms—and try to get some sleep while you can."

"What just happened here?" Maya chewed nervously at a fingernail while hugging Anna.

"Some old drunk got the wrong room--," Scott explained, "And he was jabbering off some mumbo jumbo that scared Danny, but he's gone now and everything is just fine."

It had been enough to soothe the group, but hadn't explained the content of what the old man had said. Deb and Ray had just looked to one another and decided to leave that conversation for the daylight.

"I say that we find that old bastard--," Jen cursed, "And kick his drunken ass into next week."

"Please--," Scot gently pushed her along, "Let's leave this until the morning."

"Hey, wait a minute?" She paused before her door, and turning looked back at him, said "I don't have a roommate now—Pam is with Danny?"

"Get your blankets and pillow--," Maya had paused before her door, and said, "You can stay with me and Anna."

Waiting until she had grabbed her personal possessions and bedding, Scott had watched as the three girls were locked away securely for the night. The balcony had been very dark, and shivering, he rushed back to his room.

"This was some kind of warning--," Carrie spoke quietly while looking to Scott, "Something is going on here—and it's not the same thing that's happening back at the house."

Closing and locking their door, Scott spoke quietly as not to awaken Patrick, saying, "If it was the darkness, Danny wouldn't still be here…"

Rubbing at her arms in an attempt to shake the chill, Carrie looked fearfully back at her husband, "This may be an entirely different kind of evil—oh God, what have we stumbled into?"

Pam had taken a spare blanket out of the little closet and made her-self comfortable in the armchair. Danny had turned on the little lamp on the night-stand and then gone into the kitchen.

"That guy was just a crazy old drunk--," Attempting to offer him words of comfort, she cursed, saying, "Sometimes nuts like that can pull things out of nowhere that sound true."

Without a single word in reply Danny had seemingly fallen silent, and she turned to see where he had gone. The young man knelt in the kitchen with his back toward her as he bowed over something he'd discovered on the floor.

"Danny?" Swiftly moving to where he knelt, her heart leapt into her throat, as looking down, she realized what was wrong.

"It's Merlin--," He sniffled while looking up at her and holding the old black cat close to his breast, "He was lying beside his cat dish—and it makes no sense, but he's dead…"

"Oh no--," She knelt down beside him, and gently stroking the old beasts thick fur, said, "Michael had him for years—and no one really knew how old he was."

"Don't you see? That old man was right--," Danny's eyes were wide and reddened with tears, "He said ten came—but only eight would leave, and now there are only nine of us left…"

An icy chill raced like frozen fingers up the length of her spine, and she swallowed back the growing dread with a shudder. The old man had known intimate details about Danny's mother and father, and predicted two deaths. There was no possible way that he might have just guessed at Merlin's demise, and the thought now haunted her. If he had known so much, was it possible that he may also know who was next?

"I can't tell Michael about this--," Danny held the cat close and slowly shook his head, "Merlin was all that he had left…"

Resting a reassuring hand upon Danny's shoulder, she said in a kindly whisper, "He still has us—and we have each other…"

Leaning toward her, he had gently rested his head against her shoulder and closed his eyes. She held him tightly as the world turned, and a shadow of sorrow crossed over their hearts in the memory of Merlin…

Mountain View Cemetery
Monday, February 10, 1975.
11:45 a.m.

The rays of the sun shone down from between the dark and drifting clouds, warming the faces of all who silently stood by as the priest read the 23rd Psalm. It was the second time that I had stood upon that lonesome hill and beneath the mighty oak that cast its shadow upon my mother's grave. Now Ted's remains would forever rest safely beside her in a grave that had been intended for me.

Caitlin had held my hand tightly as I looked among the large gathering. There had been some solace in knowing that Ted had been so dearly loved, and it was apparent in the expressions of the many, sorrowful faces. Dear old Ruth Sampson had been there, as with a bowed head, she spent most of her time brushing silent tears away.

Rich had stood next to Ole and Jay at Tim's side. There had been many familiar faces on that cold February morning, and then many more of which I didn't recognize. Ted would have been sincerely touched, if he'd known just how many people had really loved him and had come to pay their final respects. Appropriately, I had worn my dark grey suit, black overcoat, and dark sunglasses. We had been gathered at the foot of the casket, as representing immediate family, we were surrounded in friends. When the good father had finally finished his reading, he had closed the bible, and forming the cross before him, nodded toward the funerary attendants.

They had released the mechanism and the oak casket slowly drifted downward, as Ted's body was committed into final peace. There were tears from many in those final moments, and even more as the crowd began to dissipate. Caitlin had kept a firm hold upon my hand and rested her head upon my shoulder.

"I'm so sorry for your loss—my sincerest condolences--," An older gentleman approached with a tall blonde woman with bright blue eyes,

"This might be a terrible time for introductions--," extending a hand in greeting, he sighed deeply, and said, "I'm S.L. Kotar, but my friends just call me the Captain--," He gestured toward the lovely young woman beside him, and said, "And this is my sister, Amy Zimmerman, and we'll be working with you now."

"The new publishers--," Ole nudged me as I wasn't quite aware of what they had meant, and apologizing, said, "Please excuse me—I'm functioning on very little sleep, and with everything happening so suddenly."

"I completely understand." The Captain smiled sadly. He was tall, lean and clean-shaven, with short and greying hair. His features were kind and gentle, but his eyes were concealed behind large and dark sunglasses. Dressed entirely in black and walking with a fashionable cane, he appeared aristocratic, and as though having walked straight out of some bygone age.

Taking his hand into both of mine, I had been speechless in that moment, and stuttered in reply, "Michael Schreiber, it's an honor and a pleasure to meet both of you. I'm only sorry that we didn't have the opportunity of meeting sooner, and altogether."

"Once you have had some time--," The Captain gently patted my shoulder, and looking me straight in the eyes, said, "We'll arrange a dinner and proper introduction."

"It would be my pleasure—and I'll be looking forward to it." Slowly nodding, I watched as they turned and promptly departed. As the wind tossed his coat-tails and he cautiously escorted his sister safely among the headstones, I already knew that he was someone that I could respect.

A movement caused me to turn back, as dear Ruth Sampson stood before me with tears in her eyes, "He really loved you--," Using a handkerchief to dry her eyes, she sniffled, and said, "And, I just wanted to say that giving him a place here, and beside your mother, would have meant the world to him." The tears ran freely as looking up at me, she said, "If you ever need me, please feel to call anytime, I'm always around somewhere."

Leaning forward, I had gently taken her into my arms and hugged the dear old soul.

"Thank you, Ruth--," I swallowed back the tears, and said, "I really loved him too…"

Stepping back, a cold gust had tossed the white hair before her big blue, yet reddened eyes, and she said, "God bless and keep you, always." And with that, she had turned and followed the last of the attendants out of the graveyard.

"Are you going to be okay?" Rich had walked over, and looking between my mother's grave and Teds, anxiously turned toward me, "Because I'm not."

Hugging my dear friend, I felt him trembling and sensed the horror and sorrow that now haunted his soul. It was the memory of his parents' loss, attending the graves and the fear of the forthcoming night. Unlike previous experiences, I could distinctly feel what he was suffering from, and saw into his very soul. Stepping back, my gaze had passed between the faces of those who remained, and I assumed to have heard their thoughts as though they had spoken aloud for all to hear. It was a mixture of wild and terrifying emotions, as streaming between confusion, utter terror, and sincere concern, all remained loyal until the bitter end. It broke my heart as while realizing that they would risk everything, and even face death rather than abandoning Caitlin and I...

"None of you need to return to Sanctum Arcanum--," I had stood, and staring blindly, peered from one to another, "In the end—all that it really wants now is me..."

"Well, it's not getting you--," Rich glared, "Not without a fight..."

"My home and life as a funeral director is over, I'm just a drifter now--," Tim sighed sadly, and looking back at me, said, "And I may not have been able to help Harry, but I'll be damned if I turn my back on you now..."

"I'd rather go down fighting here and now-," Jay agreed, "Than live in fear for the rest of my life, or until it caught up to me somewhere alone, and in the dark..."

"This thing will never stop--," Ole looked among us all, "I would rather see an ending with all of you—than allow this nightmare to get to my wife..."

Bowing my head, as the emotions became overwhelming, I looked to my mother's headstone and thought to have seen Merlin sitting there. He had looked up to me as he always had and then vanished into the snow-covered headstones.

Gently squeezing my hand, Caitlin had frowned, and I knew that I had not been the only one who had sensed the dear old cat...

Adjusting his collar as his hair was tossed in a gentle gust, Rich gazed sternly into the faces of all, and said, "Let's go home—we have work to do..."

Without another word we had all turned from the graves, as bidding a final farewell, I departed that lonely hill for the last time...

10:45 a.m.

Scott had carefully lowered the little box containing Merlin into the grave that they had dug through the frozen earth. It was a peaceful place in Harrison hot springs that, resting in the shadows of the tall pines, overlooked the lake. It had only been a short drive, and having been there before with Michael and Rich, he felt a safety and serenity as he said a little prayer.

Pam had held Danny as the little group stood and said farewell to the dear old cat. There was a chill wind blowing from off the water and the wind softly whispered in the surrounding pines. Patrick had stepped out from between Carrie and Maya, and walking to the little grave, gently posted the tiny wooden cross that he'd made. It was just two pieces of wood that his father had bought when they passed a hardware store, and some wire to tightly bind them together. In black felt pen, Patrick had written, "Our beloved Merlin, R.I.P."

Carrie's sniffled as Scott walked back to where she stood, and placing an arm around her, paused to look back at the little grave overlooking the water.

"I wish things could be like they were when we all first met." Patrick stood beside his mother, and taking her hand, muttered, "And that we could have everyone back."

"Sometimes--," Scott looked into the clear heavens as the sun shone down through the dense pines, "The most that we can hope for is making the best of what we have left."

"We should get back--," Apprehensively peering into the forest and then out onto the lake, Jen shivered, and said, "The water over there looks so dark—it bothers me…"

Looking into the distance and toward Harrison Mills, he had felt something as well. They were nowhere near the old location, but he had to wonder, was it just paranoia, or the thing at the bottom of that lake…?

"What was that?" Maya moved to step down from the bank to explore the frozen and rocky shore, but Scott had gently caught her by the arm. His face revealed some kind of doubt, a sinister suspicion, as looking out and over the water, he said, "Jen's right—we should really be getting on back to the hotel. Besides--," He drew her attention to the snow and ice, "We don't need you slipping and injuring yourself—or worse…"

It hadn't taken any further coaxing, as just the insinuation had been enough to turn Maya around, and hurrying back toward the group.

"I'll keep this for Michael--," Danny held the little collar with the gold engraved tag that read 'Merlin', saying "I know that he'd want it."

"Okay, folks--," Scott picked up the little shovel, and said, "Let's head home and find some lunch."

There had been a slight hesitation as they had all taken a last look at the lonely little grave. Danny had felt horrible for leaving Merlin there, but understood that there was nothing else that could have been done...

"It will be okay--," Pam saw and immediately understood, as placing an arm around him, slowly led him away, "The part that we really loved about Merlin will always stay with us, in memory."

"Will they say the same about us?" Danny walked back toward the Suburban with her.

"If we're lucky--," She pondered briefly, and nodding, said, "People only remember you when you were truly loved..."

The sun had shone down and as he had looked into her face, he had seen his mother for but an instant. It was something that she might have once said to him, and hugging Pam, he whispered, "Thank you for being you, and being here for me..."

"You got it, sport." She hurt while knowing what the poor lad had gone through, but forced a smile, and shoving him along, said, "Now let's get going before Scott leaves us here..."

12:35 p.m.
The Best Western Hotel
Langley, British Columbia, Canada.

It had been at Caitlin's suggestion that we had left my belongings and the Eldorado at a hotel in a small town. The key would be left under the front bumper of the car, and would be retrieved by the survivors of the night to come. I had paid for the room a week in advance, and then we shared lunch at the adjoined diner, which was located downstairs. It was a convenient location, as it provided privacy, as well as having been converged upon by several main routes, and leading directly onto the highway. In the event of a necessary and swift retreat, few locations could have provided a better position.

Lunch had passed quickly, and though the food had been very good, little had been said. I had indulged the usual clubhouse sandwich, and avoiding greasy or fried foods, offered Rich the bacon. It had become a ritual of which he had quite happily accepted. The waitresses had always suggested that I order the turkey sandwich instead, but I liked the smoky essence left behind even after removing the bacon. It was just another one of those 'guilty pleasures'. Sometimes it simply amazed me that the little things in life seemed to make it all worthwhile.

As odd as it may have seemed to many, we had all used the bathroom before leaving, and had done so in pairs. Even during the daylight we knew that we weren't safe anywhere, and so, took no chances.

Leaving the diner, I longingly gazed upon my Eldorado in passing. It was parked directly beneath the room that I rented, and at the foot of the steps to the second floor. It was resting directly beside a tall lamp post and would be illuminated upon even the darkest night. In all truth, it could not really have been safer anywhere else, as small town hotels and diners in Langley were quite busy.

"You really love that thing—don't you?" Rich smiled through utter fatigue.

"Not just for what it represents—but who gave it to me." Patting him on the back, I added in thought, "It was there in the beginning and feels like it's returned in the end."

"Or possibly a sequel--," Ole raised an eyebrow, "The adventure continues…"

"I'll tell you a little secret--," Rich appeared suddenly guilty, and chuckling, said "It really is the same car. It cost me a fortune and took the shop forever—but they resurrected your old Eldorado."

"You must be pulling my leg—there wasn't anything left of that car…"

"It would've been cheaper to go to the States and get you another one in mint condition. But to be honest, I'd always thought that there was some kind of magic between you and the old machine. In the end, it saved your life in that accident, and who knows, it just might do it again?"

"Bless your heart--," Looking back, my heart warmed and I shook my head in disbelief, "And welcome back to the resurrected, ghostly midnight beauty."

"You are fortunate to have rich and crazy friends." Ole smiled, "It must have cost him three times what that car was new just to restore it."

"Eccentric--," Rich corrected him, "You're only crazy when you're poor."

"If we get through this one--," I smiled at Caitlin, "Maybe I'll just retire—and we'll take the convertible on vacation, and someplace warm."

Caitlin smiled, even as while knowing that I had only said it to increase the group moral. She knew the real reason that I had chosen to leave my car so far from home…

"I was considering buying another funeral home--," Walking close at my side, Tim had looked to the others, and shrugging, said, "But after everything that's happened—I think that I'm done in the business of death…"

"What about you?" Curiously addressing Jay, Rich had asked, "Did you have anything special in mind?"

"If I'm still in one piece--," He thought for a moment and then said, "I guess I'll have to start all over? But considering the odds at the moment—I'm not complaining."

"I just realized something--," Rich had halted us all near the end of the parking lot, "We all came down here in the Eldorado—how are we going to get back to the house?"

Utterly exhausted and emotionally drained, none of us had even considered the return trip.

Pointing to where the highways intersected, Ole brought our attention to a small car lot that was almost hidden among the industrial buildings, "How about Honest Al's Used Cars?"

"Unless you wanted to take public transit--," Jabbing a thumb toward a nearby bus stop, Jay sighed, "It's cheaper."

We all looked to where an elderly man slept peacefully sprawled upon the bench, and as while awaiting the next bus. In his restful state his hand had slipped away, as while revealing where he had soiled himself. The decision having being unanimous, we all turned and hurried toward the highway crossing.

Honest Al's Used Cars was an accumulation of derelicts, trade-ins and repainted taxis that had seen far better years. The lot was poorly kept, cluttered, and the streamers that lined the poles were torn and faded. It had all the appeal of a ghost-town automobile graveyard, and it certainly was…

Honest Al was a tall and gaunt man and wore a brown suede suit that was obviously several sizes too small. Rushing out of the little office, he frantically waved while skidding across the ice on his brown and weather-stained penny loafers. Balding, he had a bad comb-over, thin mustache, and wore cheap sunglasses while flashing a hungry smile.

"This should be an experience--," Ole spoke quietly while rolling his eyes, "He looks like he would sell his grandmother's wheelchair for a fast buck."

"We might be safer buying the wheelchair--," Jay commented from behind his hand, "Get a load of some of the classics that he's got parked around this dump."

The entire lot couldn't have been larger than an acre with the building included. Parked in three rows and circling the grounds, everything was tightly cluttered and uneven. Partially buried in snow, the vehicles ranged from the late 1930's to mid-60's, and were all well-used or long dead.

"Gentlemen--," Honest Al rushed over while extending a hand, "Welcome to honest Al's fine line of previously loved automobiles!"

"It's more like previously abused." Obviously unimpressed, Ole rolled his eyes while looking around at the dismal old wrecks.

"It's a pleasure to meet you, Al!" Rich had leapt before us and heartily shaking his hand, looked around and asked, "My name is Rich MacDonald, and we're looking for something that we can drive home today."

The statement had caused our host certain distress, as reluctantly looking amongst his clunkers, jalopies and wrecks, he coughed, and smiling, said, "Well, we have a fine selection—but let me show you something from out of our garage."

"Lead the way, my friend--," Rich gestured, and winking back at me, said, "Just let me do the talking and this shouldn't take too long."

We had all followed him to the back of the lot and to where, pausing before a pair of garage doors, he said, "I'll just be a moment, I have to open them from the inside."

Hurrying around and to the side of the building, he stumbled and cursed while tripping over something buried in the snow. A moment later and he had slipped inside a door, and then there was a grinding and screeching as he raised the garage door.

"It's just this way, gentlemen—and she's one of our finest--," He waved like a circus conductor, and guiding us toward the back of the garage, said, "It's a one owner car, and has new brakes, tires, starter, and battery. I have all the receipts in the glove box, and I believe that the owner recently replaced the mufflers and entire dual exhaust."

"A 1956 Cadillac series 62 convertible--," Rich had almost sung the words, as looking back at me, he said, "What do you think?"

The chrome flashed beneath the hum of the fluorescent lights, as even from beneath a layer of dust, the black paint was flawless. Moving toward the vehicle, I saw that the black top was perfect, and that the red leather interior still looked as if it had just rolled out of the showroom. Peering back at Rich, he had immediately seen my enthusiasm and obvious interest, as waving for me not to appear so anxious, turned to Al, and said, "Sure it looks terrific—but does it run?"

Grinning, Al had opened the driver's door, and reaching behind the visor, produced the keys of which he offered to Rich, "Why don't you have a look for yourself?"

Accepting the keys, he had casually strolled over, and hopping behind the wheel, shoved the keys into the ignition. It had started on the first attempt, and roaring to life through the new dual exhaust, idled nicely as the engine warmed. This had apparently surprised Rich, as his eyes bulged and he looked to the others who were nodding in approval.

"How much were you asking for this one?" Climbing from the car, he coughed in the exhaust fumes while approaching Al, and saying, "It could still use a decent tune-up—it's burning a little rich."

"That's not the only rich that will be burned here today." Ole mumbled to Jay who snickered, and said, "He can afford it…"

"Clark?" Al had wandered into the back of the garage and toward the cluttered parts, accessories and assorted tools, "Hello—I need you to help out for a minute. We need to get the Cadillac out and into the lot."

Rich had suddenly looked at me as a dark suspicion grew in his eyes. I had noticed the deep shadows to the back of the building and dreaded, no sensed that something might be lurking there.

"Clark—oh where is that man--," Al became visibly frustrated as he returned, and said, "He was here just a few moments ago. He must have gone off to the bathroom or out back for more parts?"

"Well, we really don't need him--," Rich had announced, "I can drive the car out of the garage."

"It's not that--," Al appeared embarrassed, as pointing back out and into the lot, he made us aware of a red 1959 Buick Electra that was blocking the driveway, "That car is moody, and doesn't seem to want to run."

"I'm mechanically inclined--," Jay offered, "Why don't you boys go and deal with the papers and insurance, and I'll see what I can do?"

"I would be truly grateful, sir--," Al fondled and fussed about Jay, "I'll even toss in a free car wash here in town, for your trouble."

"Sound's good to me—done deal." Jay motioned for Ole and the two of them hurried across the lot.

We had followed Al into his dirty little office, avoiding sitting upon the chairs. It looked more like a grease and oil smeared, dust covered booth in some old wrecking yard. While Rich finalized the papers and sorted out the insurance, I had gone over to the window to peer out. Jay fumbled from beneath the hood of the old Buick, and then waving, signaled to Ole who turned the key as it suddenly roared to life.

There was a huge sputter of blackened carbon and then a white cloud from both exhaust pipes. It rumbled like a Sherman tank as they warmed the engine for several minutes. Then, ever so carefully backing it out, they slipped in between a clutter of cars and disappeared from sight. A moment later and they both hurried past, as slipping and skidding across the ice, had gone back into the garage. Standing there and smiling foolishly, I admired the black convertible as they brought it out and parked before the office door. Cadillac and Duesenberg had always been my two favorite makers of luxury automobiles. There weren't simply designing cars for people, they were creating automotive art. Oddly, and as much as I appreciated the beautiful old classic, my attention kept returning to the darkness of the open garage door.

Allowing my thoughts to once more drift, I reached out with my mind and sensed something in the blackness of the shop. In the darkness between cluttered boxes and oil cans I had seen something lying from beneath the pile. At first it had appeared as nothing more than torn and fouled rags. But then, I had seen the slowly expanding crimson pool, and the bloodied hand that hung out from beneath... An accident with heavy machinery that had taken the life of the mechanic—or so it had been intended to appear... Furthermore, this was no vile act committed by our own evil, but rather a jealous employer having discovered the mechanic with his unfaithful wife. I now knew and sensed things even further, which I had chosen to disregard. These were the sins and evils that, constantly surrounding us, continued even as while we fought for our lives.

Peering to where Rich had anxiously fumbled through documents, I made eye contact with the manager. There was something cynical and even sinister in those shifty eyes. It was something that he'd been unable to disguise, even as while offering that false and toothy smile.

Caitlin had just looked over from where she stood beside me. It was apparent by her darkened expression that I had not been the only one aware of the mechanics brutal and mysterious death.

"Alright—we're done--," Rich beamed while victoriously waving the documents before him as he approached, "Let's get to a gas station and fill it up—and then hit that car wash!"

Al had followed him from close behind, and as I turned away from the desk, saw the sorrowful shadow of the mechanic standing there. In that moment I had sensed that his body was to be disposed of in an old wreck that was schedule to be crushed that afternoon. His corpse would forever vanish, his death would become a mystery and his murderer would be free to roam.

I'm not exactly certain of how it had occurred, but as I had made the decision to make an anonymous call, the shadow had looked up at me, and smiling, vanished into the wall...

"Rich—would you mind doing me a small favor?" I had asked while climbing into the passenger seat and closing the door, "I just need to stop over there--," I pointed to where my Eldorado was parked, and said, "I need to make a quick telephone call."

He had done so without even giving it much thought, and driving across the street, parked his new Cadillac beside the booth as I hurried out to the phone.

Dialing out the number for our connection at the Vancouver PD, I waited until Captain Markham had answered his private phone.

"Yes—it's Michael Schreiber--," I announced, "And there isn't much time. I want to report the murder of a mechanic at Al's used cars in Langley. The owner seems to have caught the man with his unfaithful wife, and killed him in the back of the garage in some hideous way. He plans to dispose of the body in a derelict car that's going to the wrecker this afternoon—please hurry."

Hanging up, I stood at the pay phone while looking over, and seeing Al watching from his office, as while waiting for us to leave.

"What's going on?" Rich climbed out of the car and hurried to where I stood, "Is there something going on here that I should know about?"

"You will shortly--," I promised him with a nod in the direction of the lot, "Just pay attention, you should have your answer in just a few moments."

It happened even faster than I had expected, as several police cars with lights and sirens came from several directions, and raced into the lot. Within moments they had Al in custody, and several officers ran from out of the garage shouting about having discovered something.

"What just happened...?" Rich stood and stared.

"Your friend has just turned in a murderer--," Caitlin called from the front seat of the car, "And released a lost soul in the process—which was very fortunate for you."

Turning to stare back at her in confusion, he asked, "But, why me?"

"Because the man responsible for killing him--," She raised an eyebrow, "Just sold you the victim's car..."

Shrugging as he had curiously turned toward me, I said, "It should be fine—his soul will pass on now that his murderer has been brought to justice..."

Looking back to where the police began searching the entire lot, he just shook his head and hurried back to the car.

Although it really wouldn't have mattered at this point, Rich had insisted upon taking it through the car wash. There had only been one place in town that had an indoor bay, and the job had only taken their team several minutes. I had not been expecting anything quite so extravagant from old Al, but was pleasantly surprised. When we pulled out of there it looked like a new car, and after what it had cost him, it certainly should have.

"Clark Edward Thomas--," Rich had spoken the name as though uttering some forbidden curse, "That was the name on the transfer papers--," He announced to everyone while appearing as though he had committed some vile crime, "I wouldn't have bought it, if I had known..."

"It needed a good home--," Caitlin reached over and across the seat from behind me, while gently patting him on the back, "I think that the old owner would have approved."

"You know something?" Ole leaned forward and looked between us from out of the back seat, "I don't think that I will ever be the same, if I survive this."

"At least you'll still be alive--," Tim sighed, "Which is a lot better than the alternative..."

"How did you know what was going on back there?" Jay was the first one to question the incident and my mysterious intuition.

"I'm not completely sure?" Answering quite honestly and glancing back at him, I said, "It was like an overwhelming suspicion that just stuck in my mind."

"I think that it's possibly far more than just that--," Biting down upon his lower lip, Tim spoke after a moment's thought, "Maybe after everything that's happened, you've developed some kind of a natural instinct for sensing and defining evil in all of its forms?"

"In which case it might be some type of psychical evolution--," Ole considered the concept, "They say that people suffering from traumatic events sometimes develop inexplicable abilities that science cannot explain."

"That might open up a whole new can of worms--," Jay warned, "Don't get him started, he's bad enough on his own, trust me..."

"This car sure is a beauty--," Choosing to ignore their comments, and admiring the black hood and sparkling ornament, I sighed, "It makes me miss Tim's '59 Eldorado convertible."

"So do I--," Tim frowned from where he sat in the back seat between Jay and Ole, "I was so depressed after everything that happened, that I let it go with the sale of the parlor..."

"Would you do something for me?" Rich had turned to look past me and at Caitlin.

"If I am able--," Raising an eyebrow in question, she asked, "What did you have in mind?"

"When we get back to the estate--," He adjusted the rearview mirror and then looking back at her, said, "Would you be kind enough take this car to the service station near our place, and leave the keys on top of the driver's side, rear tire?"

"Of course—," Agreeing she had looked back to him, and asked, "But what will you do without a car when it's time to leave?"

"If any of us are left and able to leave when its over--," Swallowing hard, he quietly said, "Maybe you could bring it back for those who need it."

"If I am able--," She gazed darkly back at him, "I will…"

Reaching for the chrome dial on the AM Wonder Bar radio, I switched it on and was amazed as the power antennae crept upward. It had only taken a moment, as through a field of fading static the music began.

"I know that tune--," Rich snapped his fingers with the recollection, "It's called 'The Mountains High' by Dick and Dee Dee."

It sent a shiver up my spine, as the haunting melody had reminded me of working night shift as a desk clerk at a hotel. It had been a wonderful time in my life with many magic moments that were spent with my dear Leigh. She had always loved that song, and sung along more times than I could have ever counted. The last time that I had heard it was on the night that she died…

CHAPTER TWENTY EIGHT

Suman Inn
2:15 p.m.
They had all gathered together to share a meal at the truck-stop diner, but this time few words had been shared. They simply ordered their food and drinks, and quietly watched as the sun struggled from behind the gathering clouds.

Looking up from his lunch, Scott had noticed a shadow lurking near their vehicles. Shielding his eyes with a hand, he squinted while attempting to define the culprit. Was it been a man, or just some shadow cast by a weather vane that he couldn't quite see from the window?

Noticing his odd behavior, Carrie had leaned closer, and peering out the window, curiously asked, "What's wrong—did you see something out there?"

"I don't know for sure?" Shaking his head, he scratched at his beard, and peering suspiciously between the vehicles, glanced back at her, "I thought that I saw something—but it's gone now."

"Could it be that creepy old guy sneaking around?" Having overheard them, Deb inquisitively looked to Scott, and asked, "Did you want me and Ray to run over there and grab the old fool?"

Carrie shook her head, "No, I think that it would be better if we all just stayed altogether. If we catch him poking around when we get back, I'll call the manager and we'll sort the old stinker out, once and for all..."

"Something really doesn't feel right." Maya looked between Scott and Carrie from where she sat across the table, and between Jen and Pam, "First that nasty old drunk goes after Danny—and then poor old Merlin, it just feels unnatural."

"We can't afford to blow our cool--," Deb warned Maya, sipping at a soda through a straw, and frowning as she said, "It'll only make things far worse for everyone involved."

"I agree with my wife--," Ray intervened, "But Maya does have a point, there are some very strange things going on around here."

"Let's get real here people. We don't have anywhere left to run or hide--," Putting down her cheeseburger, Jen looked over at Ray, "The only thing that we can do now is hope that the guys sort this thing out—and try to keep each other safe until that time comes."

"I know what kind of nightmares they're dealing with--," Sliding his coffee cup away, Scott frowned, "And there's no defense against those things that really works for long."

"So what would you suggest we do now?" Pam spoke quietly as the waitress hurried past to retrieve another carafe of coffee, and she asked, "Lock ourselves in our rooms?"

Scott had fallen into silent contemplation, clasping his hands together, as he solemnly gazed into the faces of his friends. He knew that no mere door or simple lock could hope to hinder the evil that pursued them all. As without a doubt, once darkness arrived, none of them would even stand a chance of surviving until the dawn...

"Dad--," Patrick looked to his father, "Is it coming after us now?"

"We don't know for sure--," Scott had refused to be dishonest with his son, but had no intention of starting a panic, as he said, "We're all a little edgy, and with good reason--," He looked among his friends, "But we're not sure of anything at the moment, so like Deb said, let's try to stay calm until we know more."

The waitress had startled Pam by accident as she approached from behind with more coffee. They had both gasped and then laughed, as Pam said, "I'm over-tired and jumping at my own shadow now—I didn't get much sleep last night."

"Oh—no worry there--," Amy had poured coffee for the others, and looking over at the hotel, said, "I'm surprised that anyone can even sleep in that place."

The comment having immediately caught Carrie's attention, she curiously asked, "Why would you say that?"

"Actually, I really shouldn't have said anything--," Amy leaned down to speak to Carrie more privately, and said, "But the original owner was a sick freak. He killed a bunch of young girls, and although they never found most of the bodies, he ended up dying in jail a few years back. His sister still owns and runs the place—and no one from around here would ever stay there, they say it's haunted..."

"Thank you--," Avoiding drawing any undesired attention, Carrie smiled as though nothing had even been said, and replied, "I'll certainly keep that in mind."

Scott had heard the entire thing and just gazed blankly at his wife. They had both sensed and suspected something terribly wrong about the place, but nothing like this.

Leaning close to Scott as though intending to kiss his cheek, she whispered, "I think that I'll have a chat with that old witch on the way back to our room."

"You and me both…" He agreed with a nod as she kissed his cheek.

"I hardly slept a wink--," Ray sighed while rubbing at his stomach, "That turkey dinner came back to haunt me."

"It haunted me too--," Deb glared at him, "You should've opened a window before you came back to bed."

"I slept—if you can call it that--," Jen nibbled at her French fries, "But geez—if they could turn my dreams into movies—no one would ever sleep again."

"I think that it might be a good idea if we make different sleeping arrangements--," Carrie stared over her coffee mug, "No one should be alone anymore—not even for a few minutes."

"That makes sense to me--," Deb turned to Ray, and said, "I'll miss you, but maybe you could stay with Danny?"

"Sure--," He agreed, as looking to the young man, he had said, "As long as you don't mind my snoring?"

"I'll survive--," Danny thanked him, saying, "But what about Deb?"

"I'll stay with her--," Anna volunteered, "Pam can stay with Maya and Jen, if that's okay."

"Of course—safety in numbers, I always say--," Pam agreed, "I grew up with two sisters, so it's nothing new."

"The pillow fights just won't be the same without you." Jen winked at Danny, as blushing, he grinned while shaking his head.

"I'm just curious--," Nervously tapping a finger at her soda glass, Deb peered over at Scott and Carrie, and asked, "If we needed to get out of here in a hurry—where would the safest place be?"

"Sanctified ground--," Carrie replied, "And anywhere that's been blessed."

"What—like a church or cemetery?" Jen sipped at her Vanilla shake.

"I guess that would work--," Pondering briefly, Scott said, "Michael said that thing can't cross onto hallowed ground in its energy form. So if we had to leave, we should be safe there."

"What about those dead things--," Carrie reminded him, "When it uses them it can go anywhere."

"But if it can't get into a cemetery in the first place--," Deb reasoned it out, "Then how can it possibly possess the dead?"

"Maybe it gets into someone first?" Jen finished her shake, and sliding the glass away and crossing her arms over her breast, said, "And then uses them to get into the place."

"Well it can't get into us as long as we wear these--," Carrie pulled the amulet from beneath her shirt, saying, "And if it's in physical form—it's not walking through any doors." Her recollection of the nightmare in Ireland made her shudder, but she felt confident, "It's just for a couple more days—and if we hold together, we can do this."

"We can do this--," Deb supported her while taking her husband's hand, and saying, "Michael and the others will make things right, and pretty soon this will all be over."

"I don't know if this is the same thing that we have all run from--," Anna had spoken rather reluctantly and surprised everyone, "Because, when I was in bed last night, I felt like someone was watching me from our window."

"It's just paranoia and completely understandable--," Carrie had attempted to soothe the younger woman's battered nerves, "I think that we all get that feeling now whenever it gets dark. I've been seeing things all over this place--," She admitted, "Even in broad daylight—believe it or not."

Danny had wanted to believe her, but when he looked up, his attention fell across the parking lot and to where the old man stared blankly back at him. But before he could utter a word to alert the others, the apparition had faded like a bad dream.

"Danny?" Pam had looked into his face, and then quickly to where he had been looking into the distance, and back toward their rooms. She hadn't seen an individual, but had noticed something moving in between their vehicles. They had glanced fearfully upon one another but neither had said a word. It had likely been nothing more than the workings of troubled and fatigued minds, and they hadn't wanted to make things any harder on the others.

When they returned to their rooms with the new sleeping arrangements, Danny still hadn't felt quite right. He didn't know whether it had been the absence of poor old Merlin, or simply sharing his room with a stranger. He could not have hoped for a better bunk-mate, because Ray was as pleasant and courteous as anyone could ever be. In the end, he realized to have just been homesick and that nothing else would ever feel right.

"Do you mind if I just slip over and say good night to my wife?"

"No, go right ahead."

Ray had quickly slid into slippers, and throwing a robe over his green flannel pajamas, waved as he hurriedly slipped out the door. For some reason, and although it was only nearing dusk, he now feared the thought of that unlocked door. Moving from the bed, he had walked across the room, but just stood there staring at the little, round brass handle.

"I can't lock it—how will Ray get back in?" Becoming anxious he looked between the parted curtains and then back at the door handle. The hair had stood upon the nape of his neck as a strange chill came in from under the door. Was there something out there? Slowly stepping away, he peered nervously all about the room. If anything should suddenly come through the door, he didn't even have anything to defend himself... So, creeping ever so slowly, he moved back to the door and cautiously reached out for the handle. With a gasp he had leapt back as the handle turned within his grasp, and a sudden force shoved it wide open before him!

"Sorry—did I frighten you?" Pam asked while stepping inside and noticing his terrified expression, "I just wanted to say good night—and make sure that everything was okay."

"Oh—no, I'm perfectly fine--," He shrugged, as a little embarrassed, sighed as he said, "I guess I'm just not feeling right after what happened with that old man—and after losing Merlin..."

Moving forward and gently hugging him, she patted him on the back while saying, "We've all been through so much—and lost so many over these past months. But it's going to be okay soon—just hang in there, buddy."

"I don't think that I'm ever going to be okay after everything that's happened--," He stepped back, and shaking his head, looked back at her, and said, "Especially after what happened to my mom and Dennis... I can't even sleep anymore—and when I do, it's all just nightmares ..."

She knew better than most, and after her experience with the bear, sleep came at a very high cost. There had been a movement behind her, and turning to look, she thought to have seen Merlin slinking beneath the bed.

"Merlin--," She put a hand to her mouth and looked to Danny in question, "But that's not possible—we buried him miles away from here..."

"It's just your imagination playing tricks on you--," Danny shrugged, and looking toward the bed shuddered with the thought, saying, "I thought that I saw him here earlier too—but it's just not possible." There had been a moment of doubt between them and it had been enough to arouse Danny's curiosity. Before Pam could even prevent him from doing it, he walked over and leaning down, lifted the covers and looked beneath the bed. Still blinded due to the daylight, it took several moments for his eyes to adjust as he stared into the deep shadows. It was just as he had suspected. There was nothing but darkness, and likely dust that had been left by a lazy cleaning lady.

"There's nothing under here--," He had turned his head to look back, and shrugging, said, "Like I said, we're all overtired and starting to see things."

"Maybe you're right?" She hadn't really agreed, but saw no sense in scaring him anymore than he already was, "We should get some rest."

"Thanks again--," He followed her to the door, and smiling, said, "For checking in on me...."

"You got it, sport--," She pinched his cheek, and pausing briefly to look back at him, said, "Sweet dreams."

"You too--,"Watching until she had gone back into her room and securely closed and locked the door, he quietly slipped inside. Shutting his own door, he had paused while he considered locking it, and then remembered Ray. Snapping his fingers, he sighed deeply, "Almost forgot about Ray, it wouldn't be nice to lock the poor guy out in his pajamas." He had giggled with the thought, and then stretching with a big yawn, wandered toward his bed and sat down.

The hot water, steam and soap suds had done Jen a world of good. It had soothed her aching muscles and relieved the tension that had almost become another nasty headache. She hummed one of her favorite 60's hits while rinsing her hair, and allowing the warm water to wash her worries away.

For just a moment, she had closed her eyes and just stood beneath the water in a final steamy rinse. Startled, a sudden draft from a slightly parted shower curtain had suddenly caused her to cringe, and turn to look down. At first it appeared to have been nothing more than the bathroom cabinet's shadow within close vicinity of the curtains edge. But then she saw it. It was a single, pale and bulging eye that horrendously stared up at her. It twitched with an excitement gathered from intrusive perversion and glistened while absorbing the sight of every inch of her naked body.

She attempted to scream, but not a single sound had come! Desperately grabbing at the shower curtain, she tore at it, as suddenly slipping, fell as it all came crashing down!

The bathroom door had been left slightly ajar at Carrie's previous request, and hearing the sudden commotion, both Maya and Anna leapt up and went running. Between the fallen curtain and flowing steam they saw Jen struggling, as gasping, she reached out to them in wide-eyed terror.

Maya had thrown a large towel about her fallen friend as they both helped her out of the tub. Supporting the terrified woman between them, they helped her across the room and to where they seated her upon the bed.

"What happened?" Maya knelt and looked up into her friend's staring and wild eyes.

"There was someone--," Jen stuttered as her jaw trembled while she attempted to speak, "There was someone—something—an eye looking at me!"

Anna had embraced her supportively, and looking to Maya, said, "Please have another look in there—maybe you will see something that might explain this?"

Without a word Maya had turned, and making her way back into the bathroom, began tidying up the fallen curtain and spilled shampoo bottles. As she hung the torn curtain as best she could, she took notice of a rounded bar of soap that rested upon the tub's edge, and within the cabinets shadow. Taking hold of this she had gone back out to where her friends still sat, "Is it possible that this might had started you?" She held it up before both women and Jen had just stared as she added in thought, "As exhausted as we all are, and in all that steam and in that dark corner, you might have just been confused?"

Shaking her head and looking up at Maya, Jen swallowed hard, "No—I know what I saw—and it sure as hell wasn't just some bar of soap."

"Should we get Carrie and Scott—and inform them of what's happened?" Deeply concerned, Maya nervously peered between her two friends.

"Not tonight--," Anna held Jen closer, and gently rocking her, said, "They asked that we stay in our rooms until daylight. We can tell them in the morning—and should be fine as long as we stay close together tonight."

"How do you feel about that, Jen?" Maya had offered her a bath robe, and draping it about her shoulders, said, "Will you be alright?"

"I'll be okay--," She whispered while looking fearfully between her friends, "But what if whatever that was goes after someone else?"

There had been a moment of hesitation as they all contemplated the thought, and then shrugging, Maya said, "Everyone has a roommate—they should be just fine."

Danny had quietly lain upon the bed while reading through some old horror comics that he had brought along. They were the boarded and plastic sleeved treasures that Michael had given him, and he was very careful in the way he handled them.

Ray had still not returned, but he understood how difficult it was for couples to be apart. He had seen his mother endure so many lonely years while pining for his father. Forcing the thoughts from out of his mind, he returned to the ghost story that he read in the comic. It concerned an evil old woman, a love triangle and family fortune.

There had been a sudden chill from under the bed that had caused his feet and toes to become bitterly numb. Drawing them upward, he rubbed at his cold flesh while suddenly unnerved by the long shadows in the room. The little lamp on the night table had offered a golden haze. It had been enough to read by, but was not nearly sufficient enough to brighten the entire room.

Intending to slip out from beneath the covers and quickly turn on the overhead light, he had halted while suddenly unsettled by the darkness beneath the bed.

"There's nothing under there--," He repeated it several times, "I'm just very tired—and nothing more… I'm acting like a scared little baby…" And he looked toward the door, muttering in thought, "Ray should be back here at any moment, anyway…"

Frustrated with his paranoia and exhausted, delusional state, he decided to put all his fears to rest, and dropped down again to look under the bed. Drawing the covers back, he peeked into the darkness beneath. The shadows ran deep and as his eyes adjusted, he could see the blackness at the very back of the bed.

"Nothing--," He whispered as he crouched down while still staring under the bed, "Nothing, it's just my own imagination and nerves from reading too many of those scary comics."

He had just been about to drop the covers and move, when a slight movement had caught his attention. As leaning down to closer examine it, a single and pale eye stared back from the darkness beneath the bed.

Leaping from off the floor and onto the bed, he pulled the covers close from all around him! His attention had gone immediately toward the window, as while contemplating a sudden burst of energy, and considered making a run for the door. With his heart pounding furiously, he was too terrified to even breathe for fear of making a sound.

The little lamp on the night table suddenly went out and he felt the room become deathly still. There was a bitter cold spreading outward from under the bed and it now slowly slipped beneath the covers as well. He shivered as, horrified, he attempted to cry out for help, but could make no sound. Trembling uncontrollably, he spun toward the door in the hope that Ray would return. But nothing greeted him there but the all-consuming darkness, as dusk faded from behind the closed curtains.

Terrified, he turned to look toward the lamp and the breath froze within his lungs. As standing directly before him and with pale and shining eyes, the thin and withered corpse of the old man stared ominously down!

Swiftly throwing the covers before his face and cringing as though he were still a child, he listened in the freezing stillness. The sound of his heart beating furiously caused the blood to thunder in his temples and he couldn't hear a single thing! Maybe it had just been a shadow and some odd reflection from a mirror from somewhere in the room? There was a moment of doubting, fearing and wondering as to whether it had all been some kind of horrible mistake. Shaking and terrified, he was just about to dismiss the whole hideous affair when he heard it... It came ever so faintly, but was the unmistakable sound of raspy and labored breathing coming from somewhere in the room. Still tightly gripping the covers close about his face, he wondered if it was possible that Raymond had returned. Maybe he had seen the light out and assuming that Danny slept beneath the blankets, had crept quietly back into the room?

The heavy breathing became louder, as wheezing from just beyond the covers, Danny's face and hands became bitterly cold. Unable to detain his terror any longer, he leapt up while tearing the covers away and stared blindly into the blackness of the room!

The pale moonlight cast a silvery veil through the parted curtains upon the floor and very edge of his bed. All about was in utter darkness, as from out of the very depths of the deepest shadows, something moved. Gasping for breath, Danny's heart pounded like a hammer and he feared that it might just explode. Shorter and shorter the breath came to him, as while the harder and louder his heart thundered! From out of the blackness he now heard the ghastly breathing again! It grew even louder than his own pounding heart, until he was deafened by the horrendous sound! He kicked off the blankets, and intending to leap from the bed, suddenly stopped exactly where he was... From just several feet away and at the foot of his bed, two pale and glassy eyes now stared back at him. Gasping and hysterical, he became paralyzed with fear! Desperately he tried to scream, but not a single breath escaped, nor would it return...

Ray had hurried back to their room while having lost track of the time... He had been a little startled to discover everything in complete darkness, and fumbled blindly for the switch. His fingers had crept along the side of the wall near the window, and locating the little button, promptly flicked it on.

Danny lay sprawled upon his bed with a gaping mouth, purple and hideously extended tongue, and wide, bulging eyes. His face was almost blue and his features and body still tensed within the throws of suffocation. As stiffened in the moment of death, his fingers still tightly clutched the covers that were still drawn closely about his face.

The sight had horrified Ray so much that he had attempted several times while trying to call out for help! When it had finally arrived it came as a long and wailing cry that shattered the stillness throughout the hotel and empty parking lot!

Pam and Jen had been the first to arrive and screamed at the horrendous sight. As suffering in absolute denial of the obvious, Pam rushed over and desperately attempted to revive the lad. "Danny—!" She shrieked while taking hold of his already stone cold hand, "Oh no, no no….. How is this possible? I just left him a few minutes ago—and he's already ice cold!"

"It's not!" Jen threw a hand before her mouth as she held back another terrified scream, gasping, "Oh my God, there's something else in this place with us—I knew it!"

Maya and Anna had appeared with Deb from behind the group and screamed when they saw the hideously splayed corpse.

"Oh my God--," Maya shrieked, as pulling the horrified Anna into a protective embrace, cried out, "Someone call an ambulance!"

"No—call the police--," Scott had appeared in the doorway behind them, and shouting, pointed to Ray, "Get on the telephone to emergency services right now!" Swiftly turning, Ray set off running as he had gone to make the call from Deb's hotel room.

"Oh no--," Throwing a hand before her mouth as she came in from behind Scott, Carrie shook her head in disbelief, "Not Danny—please God not him…"

"He's dead—he's somehow suffocated or choked on something--," Pam gasped in a state of utter shock, as gazing back with horror-stricken eyes, whispered, "How could this have happened—I was just here…"

Rushing to the bedside, Carrie gently took hold of Pam's wrist, and pleading, said, "Please, we need to go—there's nothing that we can do."

"But, we can't just leave him here--," Pam tearfully looked back at the dead youth, "Not alone—and not like this…"

Deb swiftly assisted Carrie, as taking hold of Pam's other hand, literally had to drag the hysterical woman from the room.

"Everyone out, please--," Scott forced them away from the door and promptly closing it, said, "I'm calling a meeting in our room, right now!"

"The police and ambulance are on the way." Ray returned from behind them, and staring aghast, said, "I was saying good night to my wife—and I wasn't gone that long."

Hugging her husband tightly, Deb sniffled as she led the distraught man away, "It wasn't your fault, sweetheart—I can't explain it, but there's just something terrible happening in this place…"

The fire department, police and ambulance had all attended the scene. The empty lot was flashing in red and blue lights, as the static sounds of emergency radios echoed throughout the place.

Reluctantly standing at the bottom of the steps in her pink bath robe, the manager had refused to come any nearer than that. Carrie had taken the opportunity in all of the confusion to catch the old woman by surprise. As taking her firmly by the wrist, forced her out of sight beneath the stars, and cursing, spat as she said, "You knew that there was something here and you didn't warn us!"

"I didn't want to give you the rooms--,"The old woman barked, "But you just had to have it your way—now didn't you? So if there's anyone to blame—you'd best take a long and hard look at yourself, sister!"

Pointing an accusing finger into the old woman's face, Carrie growled, "You're brother was a perfect and murderer of little girls—and he's still here—and we both know it…"

"He's dead--," The old woman's disposition softened as her black makeup now ran with the tears, "He died in jail two years—that sick and rotten, old son of a bitch…"

"You know something--," Carrie had sensed it from just being near the old woman, as squinting suspiciously, she asked, "What's keeping him here—what have you hidden…"

Horrified with the insinuation and shocked with Carrie's uncanny awareness of her crimes, the old woman pleaded, "He killed them—those three girls--," She stuttered, becoming hysterical, as she now begged, "I only hid the bodies, because I didn't want to get any further involved. I couldn't lose this place—it's all that I have left in this world."

"Where are they--," Carrie became more aggravated and furious by the moment, as tightening her grip upon the woman's wrist, she shouted, "Where have you hidden them!"

The rear lot behind the hotels was nothing but frozen and barren terrain, covered in tall grass and a few little trees. The entire area had been brightly illuminated by police flood-lamps as the coroners departed had excavated under the old woman's direction. Carrie and Scott had stood silently as while watching as authorities removed the remains of three bodies from the hardened clay.

"Ma'am--," An ambulance attendant had approached from behind with documents attached to a clip-board, "I'm sorry, but we can't locate the boy's mother and we'll need a signature before we can do anything with the remains."

"We'll take full responsibility for the boy--," Scott had turned, and accepting the clip-board, hurriedly signed the required documents.

"It's a real shame about the boy—I'm terribly sorry--," The older attendant had adjusted his glasses, and scratching at his mustache, thoughtfully said, "We don't often see cases of CCHS."

"What is that?" Shocked that there had been some feasible explanation to the event, Scott could only stare.

"It's called 'congenital central hypoventilation syndrome'--," The attendant had explained, "It's when a person starts taking shallow breaths, and there's a shortage of oxygen and build-up of carbon dioxide in the blood. It leads to suffocation—and from the looks of things, that's what we likely have here."

"You seem to be very sure about that--," Carrie sensed another reason for the man's suspicions, and said, "Don't they have to do an autopsy to substantiate cause of death?"

There was definite hesitation, but the attendant leaned closer and nervously said, "Well, off the record? This is the third case that we've attended at this location in the last two years, and the second in that room…"

Carrie's blood ran cold, as she turned to Scott and then gazed out and into the blinding lights of the excavation site…

There had been endless tears for the young man, as Ray kept blaming himself, and the women all wept. Patrick had sat silent upon a chair, as suffering from shock, stared as though having been mesmerized. Noticing this, Scott had immediately gone over and wrapping his arms protectively around his son, said, "Don't worry—I've got you, boy."

"Are you saying that we're dealing with some kind of haunting here?" Deb was astonished.

Sniffling, Jen wiped away the tears, muttering, "We ran right out of the fire and into the frying pan…"

"Please get all the furniture out onto the balcony--," Carrie directed Ray and Scott, "We don't need anything in here but the lamps and our own stuff."

"Take that bathroom door off its hinges and leave the light burning--," Pam pointed an accusing finger, and said, "We shouldn't take any chances…"

"What happened to that old lady that managed this place?" Hysterical with fear, Maya had gawked while turning to Carrie for an answer.

"I told the police that she'd confessed to me what her brother did--," Shivering uncontrollably, she slowly shook her head, "So, she won't be charged for obstructing the law in a criminal case, but they'll keep her for questioning tonight…"

"What are we going to do now?" Looking desperately between the others, Anna shuddered, "Are we going to still stay in this place, even after what has happened?"

"If we stay altogether, we'll be just fine--," Scott answered in a confident though compassionate tone, "Now that the remains of those poor kids have been removed, the old ghoul might stay clear of us…"

"It possessed that old man—the drunk outside Danny's door--," Jen contemplated the series of events, and then said, "It told him that ten came to this place and that only eight would leave. We've been involved in paranormal investigations like this for years—why weren't we watching him closer?"

"Because we were already out of our minds with fear over everything else--," Carrie looked among the group, as they sorted blankets and bedding upon the floor, "And even though we sensed things—we questioned ourselves instead of taking it seriously. There's no one to blame here—we're all only human."

"So where is this thing now—the one that killed Danny?" Wrapping herself into a blanket and resting her back against the wall, Maya looked up at her, "And how did the ambulance attendants explain what happened?"

"They have a medical term for what happened--," Scott grumbled while shaking his head and looking around at his friends, "It's called CCHS, and it's where people breathe in short gasps and their oxygen runs low, and carbon dioxide builds in the blood. The end result is suffocation…"

"So, no one is even taking this seriously?" Jen could only stare.

"The attendant that asked us to sign papers for Danny--,"Carrie stumbled over the words, "Told us that he was the third case of CCHS in this hotel over a two year period, and the second to die in that room."

"So, are we all going to suffocate in our sleep because of this thing?" Slipping deeper into the safety of her husband's embrace, Deb peered anxiously between Scott and Carrie.

"No—we'll be taking turns keeping watch through the night--," Carrie informed them quite confidently, and said, "At the slightest hint of trouble—or anyone's breathing not sounding quite right—I'll wake everyone up."

"How safe are we really?" Maya's eyes reflected darkly as they glimmered with tears.

"Michael always said that spirits can't properly manifest in bright light--," She nodded toward the lanterns, and said, "So, we'll be sleeping with the lights on—and keep the lanterns burning as well, just in case."

"And what if something should come in the night?" Anna trembled, as gazing back with wide and terrified eyes, muttered, "What if something tries to get to us..."

"Then we fight--," Carrie cursed under her breath, "And we keep fighting until we win—or every last one of us is gone..."

"This wasn't supposed to happen." Anna wept, "My husband said that we would be safe."

"And like so many others before him--," Carrie shrugged, "He was dead wrong..."

"We'll take the first shift--," Deb looked to her husband as she volunteered, "I've got enough coffee in my system to last a week."

"And I won't be sleeping anytime soon--," Ray agreed, "We'll wake you when we start feeling drowsy."

"Don't take any chances--," Walking over to where Scott still held their son, she turned to look back at Deb, "Keep in mind that if you drift off—it could cost us all our lives..."

The room had fallen into utter silence, as gathering extra lanterns and lighting them, Pam placed them in all corners of the room.

"If it's okay with everyone--," Pam peered into the faces of her terrified friends, "I would really like to say a prayer for Danny and for all of us in the days to come."

They had gathered without a word, and taking hold of each other's hands, bowed their heads as Pam recited the Lord's Prayer, and said, "God grant us the serenity and courage to continue—guard over our friends, and watch over the soul of our dear Danny, Amen..."

"Amen." Carrie felt her heart breaking but held back the emotions. It would be a very long and dark night and they would need strength, not tears...

Dublin Ireland
Christ Church Cathedral
8:00 p.m.
The story that old Lawrence had related to the clergy had brought about several instantaneous reactions. The first had been one of utter astonishment and horror, and the second being the question of several missing priests. In the third, there had been contacts made to secret organizations world-wide, and discrete, immediate intervention arranged.

"All that she gave me was this address--," Lawrence had offered them the page with Carrie's name, address, and the telephone number at Michaels home, "I wish that I could tell you more—but this is all that I know about them."

"The necessary correspondence has already been made --," Father Liam Grantham quietly explained, "And accordingly, members of our faction in that locale will be assisting in this matter in whatever degree possible."

"With all due respect, father--," Anxiously fidgeting with his cap between his hands, Lawrence swallowed hard, before saying. "But you should warn them, they have no idea of what they'll be up against..."

Clasping his hands together on the desk before him, Father Grantham spoke kindly, "My dear friend, the church has been aware of these 'unclean spirits' for centuries. Rest assured, they do not walk blindly or unarmed into peril."

"There are stories--," Lawrence became uncomfortable with the thought, and shrugging, peered nervously back at the priest, "That the clergy aren't what they used to be..."

The reaction had been one of extreme discomfort, as considering the statement and sadly looking back, he said, "Unfortunately, the road to sin is far simpler than those of morals and discipline. Even now, the tides turn against us as evil invades our sanctuary, defiling its followers and corrupting clergy, but there still remain a few of us who still fight in the name of that which is holy."

"Why is this only happening to us?"

"It isn't—but unlike the Buddhists who resist through positive thought, and the Muslims who fight through strict faith, I fear that we have faltered. There are many in our ministry whom know of this evil, and of which that very fear compels them to become desperate. As reaching out within warning, their sermons become intimidating and overwhelming, and even through their sincerest intention, they cause people to turn their backs upon the church. Even now we see a steady decline in attendance and a rise in the number of clergy committing vile acts against women, and even children..."

"So, this evil has gotten into everyone, everywhere?"

"It has always existed--," Father Grantham wearily rubbed at his eyes, "The bible is even filled with stories of vile things that exist in the darkness. So few people even question what occurs around them anymore. As blinded by the media, they simply follow like sheep to the slaughter. In the end, none dare question the source, but simply accept all as truth. And so, with the progress of ignorance comes the decline of faith in the world, and the end of mankind..."

"I'm ashamed to admit it—but this is the first time that I've set foot in a church since my wife passed away." Lawrence bowed his head, "Forgive me, father..."

Reaching across the desk and taking a gentle but firm hold upon the old man's hand, Father Grantham slowly nodded, "We often blame the world when we lose those we cherish most."

"I blamed the world--," Lawrence brushed away a tear within the memory of his beloved, admitting, "And I blamed God—for taking her away from me..."

"When the day comes—you will stand before the good Lord--," Father Grantham spoke kindly and with great confidence, "And be reunited with your loved ones. Until then—we must hold true to what we believe—and never relinquish hope or lose faith."

The tears ran freely as Lawrence had attempted to hide his face. Reaching over and gently drawing his hands away, Father Grantham quietly said, "We are all only human and there is no shame in tears. Have faith, dear friend—you are no longer alone..."

Looking to the priest, Lawrence had felt warmth and a strength that seemed to grow from deep within. There was a light of hope shining in the father's eyes. Illuminated by the sun's rays through the stained glass from behind, he shone like an angel in the golden light.

"God bless you--," Lawrence stuttered while wiping the tears from his eyes with a sleeve, "And thank you for being here for me and my friends..."

"That's my sole purpose in being here--," Father Grantham motioned for him to follow, as moving from the desk, he said, "Now let's get something to eat—and then I'll take you somewhere safe…"

"Is there really any safe place, anymore?"

"We have chambers where, created in mosaics, protective symbols and ornamentation guards us all against the evils of the night." Offering a reassuring hand which he placed upon the old man's shoulder, he said, "You are most welcome to remain here until this matter is properly dealt with. Father Mark Kokopelli Watkins is the senior advisor in Vancouver, and shall contact us with all news and any updates."

"Do you really believe that he can help them--," Lawrence's thoughts of Carrie and Scott ached deeply within his heart, "Before it's too late?"

"Father Watkins has considerable experience in these matters--," Father Grantham spoke with the utmost confidence, as looking down at Lawrence, he smiled kindly, "He is a man of great faith, resilience and dedication… And where this is faith, there is always hope…"

Walking together down the long corridor, Lawrence felt about in his vest for the little golden pocket watch. Then drawing it out and flipping open the casing, he lovingly admired the little picture within. It was as while passing beneath the illumination of the stained glass windows that he had suddenly looked up and into the light. As with the warmth of the sun gently caressing his face, he had suddenly felt his loving wife's presence again…

CHAPTER TWENTY NINE

Sanctum Arcanum
2:15 p.m.
We had driven home with the top down, as though still windy and cold, the sunshine had warmed our faces, hearts and souls. It had felt strange returning and pulling in through the tall and black iron gates. The estate had stood tall and dark as the sun drifted from behind it, and it suddenly appeared hauntingly sinister. In thought, I had remembered the first time that I had stood in the long shadows before the house of McCreary. As with its soaring towers, darkened windows and stone gargoyles, I suddenly realized to have returned… The thought sent icy shudders through my entire being as we had climbed out of the car and I stopped to look around.

"Please remain here until I have returned--," Caitlin called to me as, accepting the keys from Rich, and sensing my dismay, she had looked suspiciously at the house, "And though utterly consumed by fire—from its own ashes the dragon is reborn…"

She had swiftly pulled away, and speeding down the driveway and through the gates, soon vanished up the street. There was certain vulnerability within her absence, and it seemed apparent in the way that we had all gathered before the house that we must have all felt the same.

"I wish that I could have seen the McCreary estate just once--," Standing lethargically and pondering as he looked at my house, Ole sighed in certain disappointment, saying, "From your description it must have been an architectural masterpiece, even for all its dark nobility."

"It was the devil's playground--," Rich put an arm about Ole's shoulder, and thinking briefly, said, "A place of broken hearts, endless shadow and lost dreams…"

"I believe that was almost a direct quote--," Tim joined the conversation, and patting Ole on the back, said, "But don't feel as though you've completely lost out. Because as soon as it gets dark, everything that made the house of McCreary what it was—," He looked into the darkness of my house, "Will be reborn as Sanctum Arcanum…"

The ominous and romantic appeal had swiftly faded from Ole's eyes as, while realizing the horror of it all, he peered fearfully at the guest house.

"He's right, you know--," Jay gazed up and into the dark windows of the old manor, "In some ways, this place reminds me of the McCreary place— it's just not as big."

"This beautiful old house was left to me by the father of my first great love." I couldn't help but suffer with the emotions in reflection, as speaking quietly, I said to my friends, "Old Gordon financed my education and supported me after we lost her to a drunk driver, only months before we were to be married. He passed away several years later of pneumonia and left his house and property to me, along with a substantial amount of money."

"And you wrote short stories for that science fiction and horror magazine," Ole continued where I had left off, "Until your publisher convinced you to write your first masterpiece."

"It sounds like someone around here might be writing your autobiography?" Shooting me a skeptical glance, Rich thoughtfully put a finger to his lips, and said, "Or might possibly even take over from where you leave off?"

"I would hardly call it a masterpiece--," Politely bowing my head toward Ole for the compliment, I stared at the long shadows growing from all about us, and said, "But it was a beginning and we all have to start somewhere."

"Our dark angel returns--," Drawing our attention to the tall black iron gates, Rich appeared suddenly dismayed, "But not in the way that we are accustomed…"

With blackened wings folded and trailing behind her like a cloak, Caitlin had returned while hurriedly walking up the long drive. I had never seen her manifest the demon in this way before. As rather than becoming the beast entirely, she now controlled certain elements as required. The lean and reptilian legs carried her swiftly to where we stood, and the wings became a cloak while modestly concealing her vulnerability.

Moving close beside me, she had looked to Rich, saying, "The car is safely parked at the service station that you pointed out on the way back to the estate."

"Thank you, kindly--," Rich made a motion to remove his coat, but she had politely declined. As spreading her wings ever so slightly, revealed nothing but the demons muscular and lean form from beneath.

"That solves the modesty issue--," Ole had still politely looked away, "Although, I still find the demonic possession aspect of this quite terrifying…"

"It's necessary evil—and as disturbing as it may seem--," Tim looked between Caitlin and our shaken friend, saying, "Mark my words, before this is over, you'll be thanking God for the devil in her…"

"Someone is coming--," Caitlin spun, and looking back down the driveway, pointed a long and blackened claw, "Several men bearing weapons…"

We had just stood as the black 1975 Cadillac series 75 Limousine came up the driveway and then parked while blocking the gates. The doors had all opened and six men wearing black suits and overcoats slowly walked up the drive toward us.

Caitlin has seemingly vanished into thin air as they waved in greeting and the eldest and leader of the group called out, "Michael Schreiber, we are representatives of the Catholic Ministry and have been sanctioned by the archdiocese of Christ Church Cathedral in Dublin to assist you here."

"Members of the cathedral in Ireland where Carrie and the others stayed--," Rich reminded the group while quietly saying, "But how do we know they're really even human anymore?"

"Please stop!" Halting them with a raised hand, I politely asked, "How do we know that you have not been taken by the enemy, and have come to take us now?"

The elder had looked back to the others, and then accepting a long silver blade from one of his companions, walked toward us as his friends waited.

"This evil may take many forms--," He halted within several feet of us, and raising a palm into the air, crossed the knife across it, saying, "But it cannot disguise what it remains inside."

The blood ran from the sliced palm as he held it before us, and speaking in a loud and clear voice, said, "We have come in your time of need—and will sanctify these grounds and trap this evil here with us."

As we watched, each of the strangers had approached in turn, and using a long cotton cloth and bottle of isopropyl alcohol, purified the knife, and then sliced their palms in evidence before us. When the last had done so, the elder had held the knife and items before us, and said, "We ask only the same of you…"

"He wants us to cut our hands open?" Ole appeared suddenly pale.

"It's only fair—and makes perfect sense." Jay had moved forward, and accepting the blade, raised his hand while cutting it within evidence. The snow before us was red with blood as the knife was passed among us and each did the same.

"This mark--," The elder held his hand before him, while saying, "Shall distinguish us from those taken."

"Why didn't we think of that?" Rich appeared stunned.

"Because at the moment--," Tim whispered, "Most of us are so exhausted that we couldn't think our way out of a wet paper bag."

They had removed their coats, as wearing clothing of holy sacrament beneath, took out bibles and holy water as they began sanctifying the ground.

"I am Pastor, Mark Kokopelli Watkins--," The elder had approached me while extending his uncut hand, and smiling, said, "At your service, my dear friends."

He was an average build, balding and white haired, he sported a neatly trimmed beard and mustache. His eyes were the brightest of blue and sparkled with sincerity and faith, even within the face of almost certain disaster. I had liked him immediately, and his presence added an additional sense of confidence that had been previously and desperately needed.

"It's a pleasure to have you with us--," I had accepted his firm but gently shake, saying, "We don't have much time to explain, but there is a Beryllus which is a portal to another dimension in the vault of that building--," I had drawn his attention toward the guest house, and said, "And there is an evil that guards over it—as it's the only way that we have of sending it back into the void from where it came."

"And how do you intend to accomplish this?" He appeared confused but inquisitive.

"I have the Diabolus lapis--," His features had become drawn and pale as I explained, saying, "If I can get between the evil and that Beryllus—I know that I can draw and force it into another dimension through that mirror."

"Diabolus lapis--," The words were like a poison upon his lips, as staring, he pleaded, "You mustn't even attempt such a thing—the stone is infamous in mythology and always claims its bearer… Only rites of exorcism and prayer might hope to cast such a vile thing from out of our world."

"With all due respect, I realize that the ministry is aware of many things--," Pleading with his rational senses, I slowly shook my head, "But what we have here is well beyond mortal means to defeat…"

"If we told you that a demon has possessed one among us--," Speaking solemnly as the group gathered behind Father Watkins, Rich said, "And that it has been assisting us against this evil, would you believe us?"

They had exchanged glances that spoke of blasphemy and suspension of disbelief, but Father Watkins had just curiously looked back at him, and rather humbly, said, "And what evidence of this might you provide?"

Before anyone could utter a word, Caitlin, now having completely assumed the demons identity, slowly rose from behind them with burning eyes and outstretched wings. Her shadow had passed from over them, and blocking out the sun, caused them all too slowly turn and look behind them.

In that moment, weapons had been drawn and fired but she had vanished before them, unharmed and invisible again. They had fallen back, and staring aghast, Father Watkins had almost choked on the words, "How is this possible? Evil does not offer service until the greater good!"

"Not all that seems evil is our enemy--," Repeating Marlowe's gift of sublime wisdom, I pleaded that they understand, "And not all that are damned are beyond hope, or redemption."

Walking out from behind the trees, Caitlin had introduced herself to the unsuspecting Father, who had respectfully acknowledged her within greeting. She wore a green and hooded cloak that I had once seen in a dream, and her eyes flashed like emeralds in the sunlight.

"This is my wife, Caitlin—and the love of my life--," I had introduced them, and then slyly added, "And she is also the one that is possessed…"

Father Watkins had halted his men with a wave as they once more reached for weapons, and said, "Please, explain this so that I might properly understand."

"I wish that I could—but we're running out of time and daylight--," I had informed them all, and looking to the kindly older man, said, "All that I can promise you—is that she stands against the darkness beside us…"

There had been an obvious reluctance as the clergy found this unacceptable to say the very least. But after a moment's contemplation, Father Watkins had just nodded at me and turned to look back at his men.

"Gentlemen--," He had quietly requested, "Please collect your weapons— it is time…"

Without a word they had departed, and returning to the car, proceeded to unload gear and assorted weapons from the trunk. I had stood with Caitlin and Father Watkins as Jay and the others had gone to the house to collect the bows, lanterns, and other items that we might need. There was a strange and unsettling silence between us now. It wasn't so much the shock or even a sense of mistrust after what he had seen. It was only that it had gone against everything that he'd been taught or ever believed… I could relate to him in that moment in many ways.

"Father—I'm not certain of exactly how much you know?" Concerned, I felt it necessary to inform him of every possible detail, and said, "This thing that we're facing—it can assume shapes of any kind, and become any person. It can possess the living, animate dead flesh, and manipulate elements of decay."

"We have had the great misfortune of having encountered these terrors before--," Gently resting a reassuring hand upon my shoulder and shaking his head apologetically, he said, "But, as for the presence of a fallen angel in the service of God, this is very hard to accept... And it goes against all of our beliefs."

"None are beyond redemption--," Caitlin whispered from behind him and as though speaking to herself, "Father, would you deny absolution in the eyes of God?"

To this he could provide no answer, as silently looking down, he thought for several moments before looking back to her, and saying, "This is a matter for God him-self and not mortal men..."

Rich and the others had returned with weapons as Father Watkins team approached from behind. What had once appeared as a desperate gathering now looked more like a small army gathered before the gates of hell.

"The vault where the Beryllus is being guarded is in the sub-basement--," Rich spoke loud as he explained the details of the structure, "There are only two stairways from either side that we can use to get down there—and it's always dark. So, because of the reinforced foundations, there's little hope of blowing a hole through the walls to get any light in there. That being said, we're going to take out the entrance to the stairways on both sides--," He pointed to Caitlin and added, "That's where she comes in... Now, once she does that, we'll need to move really fast. We have no idea of what kind of horrors will be waiting for us in there..."

"I'll be going into the vault with Caitlin--," Removing the box from within my coat, I pulled out the stone and raised it for all to see, "The Diabolus Lapis—the summoning stone of all evil."

There had been silent awe among all who stood there, as with eyes fixed upon it, their mouths had dropped open.

"Caitlin is going to try to force the entity out of its physical form by destroying its body—and then I'll use the stone to draw it into the Beryllus. What I need from all of you—is to keep whatever nightmares it has protecting that vault away from us while we work."

"According to the illuminated manuscripts, the Diabolus Lapis will claim its holder--," Father Watkins appeared terrified, "Even if you can draw the entity into the Beryllus, you will also be taken and forever lost to oblivion..."

"We all have families and friends that are at risk if this thing escapes us here--," I had thought for a moment as the answer seemed clear, and said,

"If we don't stop it now—then it will hunt them down, and murder each and every last one of them. Now, I don't know about any of you? But if my giving my life in their defense is the cost here, then I'm willing to pay that price…"

"Your soul will be lost forever--." Father Watkins pleaded, "Surely, there must be some other way?"

"No--," Caitlin frowned, "It can never be destroyed. The only way is to force it out of its earth-bound shell—and cast it into another dimension…"

"Can I ask you all too please join us in a circle—and take one another's hands?" Father Watkins gathered us together, and bowing our heads, he recited the 23rd Psalm from memory. Caitlin had appeared somewhat uncomfortable for obvious reasons, but remained until he had completed the prayer. It had been something extraordinary to see a demon holding the hand of a priest…

"Gentlemen—and lady--," Looking among us all and bowing his head, he said, "God bless and keep all of you, Amen."

"Alright--," Looking to Caitlin, I directed her attention toward the guest house, and said, "Knock those walls out and light a way in for us…"

She had opened her arms, taking the form of the demon, and leapt into the air and soared upward with blinding speed. In that moment, we had all charged toward the building with weapons in arms, as she plummeted back downward, and curving suddenly, exploded through one wall of the building and erupted from our the other! Deafened by the sheer destructive force, we held lanterns high while rushing in through the shattered stone and billowing clouds of dust.

The sun had shone in from behind us. Leading the way, I was swiftly joined by Caitlin in demon form. She had peered over at me, and then racing ahead, confronted whatever awaited us at the bottom of the stairs.

The lights had suddenly flickered, flashed and then gone out. We had stumbled and were caught in utter blackness beyond the glow of the lanterns that we held.

There were sudden and blinding flashes as the priests cast down phosphor bombs and the light cast a brilliant glow through the corridor.

"Move—everyone follow me!" Rich had waved everyone onward as they continued to illuminate the passage as we went ever inward.

The attack had not been from the front as anticipated, but came from behind. The last man to have followed us screamed as he died being smothered in a blackened, acidic and pulsating filth! Terrified, we had fired into the hideous mass that now pursued us.

"Back off!" Rich had wailed, as drawing one of his home-made bombs from a belt beneath his coat, he shouted, "Everyone, stay down!" And with that he had tossed it outward and against the wall nearest the pursuing thing! The resulting explosions of the chemicals bursting into flames had created a wall of fire while blocking our escape!

"Keep going!" Rich had cried out, "We need to get ahead of the fire!"

"We're trapped and there's only one way out!" Jay choked on the billowing smoke, as partially blinded, desperately scrambled to the bottom of the stairs.

"Just keep moving!" Rich forced everyone onward and into the blackness, "We're almost there—it's just down this corridor and to the right!"

Unable to see Caitlin from before us and through the dense smoke, I blindly raced into the escalating madness. Rich and Jay charged valiantly down the dark hallway, and I could sense Tim and Ole coming up from directly behind. Father Watkins and what remained of his team were still firing into the blackness as while desperately attempting to guard the rear.

Once more we heard screams from behind, as shots were fired, and two more died horribly in the clutching tendrils of some unimaginable nightmare! With only Father Watkins and three remaining members of his team, we rushed into the corridor to our immediate right.

From out of the shadows they began to rise from all around us: Forms that had crawled from out of their worm-riddled coffins and now beckoned to their master's call. They were an ultimate blasphemy, and manifestations that mocked anything even slightly resembling humanity. Crawling and dragging bloated and rotting bodies, they twitched and flailed while turning upon us!

Dear God—the cane! I had forgotten it upon the mantel in the living room! We had no defense against these gruesome fiends!

"We can't fire on them!" Rich wailed, "The whole place will burn down around us!"

Gathering into a tight circle, we had faced them as they approached. The air was fouled by the sweetly sickening stench of decay, as they slithered and came at us from all sides!

The demon had appeared from out of the darkness, its eyes brightly ablaze as it waved its long and blackened claws. There was a flash of blue light that had appeared as lightning, and the corpses froze solid from all around!

"Run—run while you still can--," Rich once more led the group as we raced down the corridor and toward the vault door. An enormous shadow suddenly came down before us, as tentacles unrolled and seemingly sprouted from out of the ceiling! As halting suddenly, we collided and the impact sent us all crashing heavily to the floor!

Ole cried out as something swung down from the blackness, and dropping from the ceiling, leapt toward him! Moving swiftly, he fired an arrow that exploded against the horrendous thing. There was a brilliant shower of liquid flames, as rolling aside, he narrowly escaped!

Black and foul, it hung suspended from the ceiling, as blocking the vault entrance, swung a multitude of clawed and spiny tendrils from all about the room!

"We need to get into that vault!" I shouted as Caitlin fought desperately, but was unable to gain any ground.

Rich had halted both Ole and Jay as they had attempted to fire upon it, crying out, "Don't do it—or everything will burn, including the Beryllus!"

Father Watkins and his men began firing blindly into the immense and festering fiend, their sanctified bullets doing nothing but further enraging the beast. Lashing out, it sent tentacles in every direction, and ensnaring one of the unfortunate priests, tore the shrieking man limb from limb! There was an explosion of gore and steaming entrails, as dying, his life was ripped out!

The remains were sent crashing through a display case, as the shattered fragments exploded into the room.

Sliding through the gore imbued nightmare, Jay suddenly fell, as twisting and scrambling across the floor, he narrowly escaped the flailing tendrils. A priest caught him by the hand, and dragging him clear, threw themselves against the far wall.

"That's one I owe you father—," Jay gagged while wiping at the filth and gore that now soaked through his clothes, "I'm Jay Leonard."

"Father Jerry Langdon--," The young priest had said while brushing black filth from out of his short blonde hair, "God be with you, my son!"

"Father Whyte, answer me please—Jesse, are you still with us?" Father Watkins called into the blackness.

"I'm still alive, if that's what you mean, father--," The black priest had stumbled out from behind us while nursing an injured arm, "I think that my arm is broken—and I can't move my fingers."

"Father Whyte--," Father Langdon had hurried back toward his companion and immediately offered him assistance, "Are you okay to walk?"

"I'm not sure of how long I'll last?"

"Father Langdon--," Father Watkins called back to them, "Please get him out of here!"

"What about you, father?" Father Langdon was horrified and obviously unwilling to abandon the elder priest.

"Save yourselves--," He insisted as waving them out, shouted, "Now get going while you still can!" Then, dropping to his hands and knees in the putrid filth and blackness, he desperately crawled toward the blazing vault. His body ached, his lungs burned, and he was blinded between the smoke and flames.

"The vault--," He fought onward desperately, "Merciful God in heaven. Please grant me the strength to help these men. Be with us in our greatest time of need…"

Spreading her wings, Caitlin had leapt up and soared straight into the thing with such force that it had rocked the very foundations beneath us! The seething mass of tendrils and huge tentacles had only parted in the effort and then slammed down against her! Furious, the demon had fought back and torn great gashes into the hideous thing. As to our utter despair and total horror, the wounds filled with ghastly mucus and were whole once again!

"Shoot it—we have no choice!" Rich had wailed, "Just don't hit Caitlin!"

Jay and Tim hadn't required any further coaxing as the fiend now turned upon us. They aimed into the distance of the far wall and let their bolts fly.

With smoke billowing in from behind us, a brilliant white explosion rocketed against the far wall and ignited upon the monstrous thing! Although it felt no pain, it had struggled to escape the flames while obviously realizing that it might lose control. In those moments as its attention had fallen upon the inferno, we had rushed forward, and slipping between and among its tendrils, managed to gain entrance to the vault!

In the pale glow of the lantern's light we could see the Beryllus against the far wall. While hanging from all about it, the decayed limbs of horrendous things and claws that now flailed as we approached. The ceiling and walls glistened and moved as that festering fungus seethed while forming into figures from out of the floor. The smoke now worsened as the fire burned from behind us. Blindly we thrashed about while realizing that there was no escape from the old iron vault.

"Just burn it all and grab that damn mirror!" Horrified, Rich had finally given up all hope. It had only taken seconds and our companions had turned the whole room into a brilliant and blazing inferno. Through the utter madness and blinded and choking, we had fought toward the Beryllus, and miraculously taken hold of it.

"Let's get it out of here!" Pointing, Rich shouted, "We can take it back to the house!"

"No--," I held them back, and looking between them desperately, said, "I'm going to finish this here and now!"

Drawing the box from within my jacket, I pulled out the stone and held it up. Once more its light shone, even brighter than the surrounding fire, and a screeching could be heard from the darkness beyond!

"Get everyone out of here, hurry!" I shouted at Rich, "Once the portal opens, it'll be too late for everyone!"

"I'm not going anywhere!" Refusing to abandon me, he turned back toward the others and cried out, "Get out while you still can—I'll stay to make sure he gets back out!"

At first they had been reluctant to leave, but shouting at the top of my lungs, I said, "We'll be out just as soon as this thing goes into the portal— now go before it's too late!"

Reluctantly, they did as I had requested, as slipping from between the burning tendrils, escaped the fouled and burning room.

"You need to go, father--," I looked to the defiant elder priest, "When this portal opens—the vacuum will draw everything in!"

"I will not leave you—and if we must, then we go altogether and with God!" His expression was one of pure determination and absolute fear. He had wedged himself behind a large display unit within reach and clung for dear life, "We shall do this together, my friends!"

It was obvious that he was well beyond argument, and held fast to his faith and the old cabinet.

"Get out of here, Rich--," Fearing for my friend in those last moments, nothing else really mattered, "Go—Maya needs you! Don't throw your life away like this—not now!"

"I'm not leaving you here--," The tears ran as he realized that this might certainly be our ending, and he shouted, "We started this together—and we'll finish it!"

Caitlin had suddenly tumbled into the room, her wings aflame as she fought against the spiny tentacles of the enormous and horrendous beast. With a fury that I had never before witnessed, the demon ripped through the nightmare with such force that it fell in massive, charred and grisly clumps, twitching and crawling upon the floor!

Stepping before the Beryllus, I held the stone before me, and cried out to Caitlin, "Freeze it—force it out of its body—and into the mirror!"

Leaping back and from out if its grasp, the demon extended its claws, and extinguishing the flames in the room, began freezing the ghastly thing solid!

There was steam blowing from all about as the room suddenly became unbearably cold. The massive tentacles seizing, cracking and shattering, crumbling as the demon began smashing its way through the gruesome fiend.

"It's coming!" Rich gasped, dropping his glasses, as he clung to the Beryllus for dear life! The blackness had grown darker and deeper from all around us. I could still see the demon struggling to destroy the horror's body in the glow of the few lanterns that still lay scattered upon the floor.

Tim and Jay had rushed back into the room with Ole, bearing their bows, as they began smashing at the frozen mass. Having seen this, the demon fought ever harder, shattering the frozen body into shimmering fragments that littered and lay heaped upon the floor!

With its form utterly decimated and the stone drawing upon the entity, it suddenly could resist no longer. The foul form began vanishing, as absorbed into the surroundings, it returned to the ether. A sudden howling erupted from behind us and Rich leapt away as a vortex began forming! It was a circling form of shadows, which continually expanding, was emanating from an ethereal hurricane.

"Get out before it's too late!" Shouting above the raging storm which now grew from out of the Beryllus, I pleaded with Rich, "And take the others with you! Please—don't let everyone die after everything that we've been through!"

In that moment he had realized the inevitable and accepted that our time had finally come... With tears in his eyes he released his hold, and looking back at me one last time, fought his way toward the door!

Firmly pressing my back against the frame of the Beryllus, I struggled to keep the stone held out before me. It was finally happening... The darkness had become a shadow deeper than all others and was being drawn through the spirit hurricane and toward me... It would all soon be over. I just had to hold on a little longer!

Rich had narrowly escaped being drawn back, as gathered among the others, they desperately held onto one another! With an immense effort they had clung to the frame of the doorway and barely managed to pull each other from out of the room. Their faces were torn with emotion, as looking but one last time, I vanished from out of the doorway.

My entire body was thrust backward as I felt the power of the stone suddenly increase. The light shone ever brighter, becoming a blinding blue beacon as it had done before the mausoleums. It caused the storm to radiate with stellar lights that shone brighter and ever brighter! Father Watkins suddenly wailed, as reaching outward, caught my coat as I'd almost slipped and fallen into the Beryllus!

"Hold on—I will not let you go!" He fought with every ounce of strength that remained as we slid backward together and away from the brightly shining mirror.

Regaining my composure and place along the frames edge, I held the stone higher. The light exploded into the room and for a moment I was completely blinded!

Then it happened, the darkness slipped from out of shadow and erupted into a blinding, crimson flame! As darkly shining, it became an enormous head with white glowing eyes, fiery mouth, and blazing mane! From beneath crept every seething horror ever imagined, as gathered in the shadows between the flames, all manner of monster that we had ever encountered appeared.

"Do not gaze upon the beast!" Father Watkins cried out while desperately struggling to maintain his grip upon the cabinet and my coat, "For it only seeks to weaken you through fear. Stand firm—the time grows near—and the deed is almost done!"

Crashing heavily against the opposite side of the Beryllus, Caitlin spun toward me in sheer terror. She had returned to her human form, and appearing weakened, fought while barely able to resist the ethereal hurricane. Her eyes had fallen upon me in those last moments and shone with absolute terror. I could sense that it wasn't fear for herself at that point, but the horror of what would soon happen!

"Give me the stone!" Desperately reaching out, she grasped at my hands.

"No—I'm ending this here and now!"

"It will take you—and you shall both be forever lost into oblivion!" She shrieked while clawing at me, "Don't do this—don't do this to me!"

Her eyes were filled with tears as she fought to avoid being dragged into the Beryllus, but still struggled for the stone. The storm now flashed with lightning and ethereal sparks while raging from all around us. The darkness was drawing ever closer, as unable to resist the stone or storm any longer, was slowly being dragged into the Beryllus. It crawled in a blazing nightmare of every terror that was ever conceived, the snapping jaws and clawing limbs of a thousand horrors lashing out within mere feet of where we clung to the mirror!

The gravity of the vortex caught me in the process, as inch by painful inch, I could feel the world slowly letting go of me. It would just be moments now, as when the darkness was utterly consumed, until I would helplessly follow into oblivion...

"No—Michael--," Rich had wailed as he came rushing back into the room, and caught in the astral hurricane, was violently drawn into the storm! In the chaos of the moment, I had caught him just before he was dragged into the void. In a moment of absolute shock and dismay, I had fallen backward as the stone tumbled out of my hands!

A long and blackened claw had caught it before it hit the floor, and when I looked up, the demons fiery eyes stared back at me! Although having returned to its demonic form, from somewhere behind that burning gaze, I could still sense Caitlin.

"Don't do this!" Rich had pleaded while fighting to hold me down," Let it go!"

All of my efforts to escape his grasp had been futile, as fueled by fear-driven adrenaline, his desperation kept me pinned down to the floor.

The storm had reached its peak and as the darkness gathered mere inches from the Beryllus, Caitlin sorrowfully gazed back at me, "Forever shall I love you--," Her voice came as a whisper that echoed like a distant wind in my heart, "And through eternity—somewhere shall we meet again... Farewell..."

Wailing, I had reached out to her, as holding the stone upward, she touched the darkness and within a brilliant flash, they both vanished into the Beryllus!

"Caitlin!" The room flashed brilliantly with a boom of thunder, and then everything fell into utter and complete stillness.

The Diabolus Lapis rolled over and stopped mere inches from my face. It reflected coldly in the long shadows, and reaching out to take it, father Watkins had stopped my hand.

"No, my son—such things do not belong to this world. It must be returned to Clermont-Ferrand the black cathedral in France..." His bright blue eyes almost shone as he pleaded, "Only there can it be concealed within its obsidian tomb and guarded from those who might use it to cause harm."

Grabbing the stone and pulling it close, I slipped it back into its box, saying, "I swear on all that we hold sacred in this world--," Peering up at him, I spoke respectfully, saying, "That I will see to it that you get this back—just as soon as I am done with it. Please understand..."

There was a sublime compassion within his gentle gaze, as taking a firm hold of my hand and slowly nodding, he quietly said, "May God guide you in whatever path you now follow—I will be waiting, my friend..." Moving from where he had knelt beside me, he reached within his robes and offered me a card, "Please, feel free to call upon me, anytime."

"Thank you, father--," Bowing my head, I had looked up to him and said, "For everything."

Slipping the card into a shirt pocket, I turned to Rich, who still lay where he had fallen.

"I'm so sorry--," He wept within my loss and as while suffering within hers, "I just couldn't lose you, not like this and not here..."

"I know, my dear friend--," Hugging him tightly, I whispered, "I would have done the same for you..."

There was a movement in the shadows of the doorway and I gasped as a lantern now appeared.

"Michael—Rich, are you okay in there?" Tim had hurried inside with Jay and Ole following from close behind.

"Over here--," Father Watkins stepped back, and motioning to where we sat with our backs against the Beryllus, said, "They still live—though they have been through a living hell..."

"Are you okay, brother?" Placing down the lantern, Tim hugged me tightly, and whispering, said, "I wasn't sure of we'd ever see each other again."

"Where's Caitlin?" Jay curiously looked around.

Finally the strain of it all had been too much and Rich burst into tears, "She took the stone from Michael—and sacrificed herself in his place..."

"Oh dear God--," Ole looked back at the Beryllus, and noticing that the mirror had become utterly black, said, "It no longer casts any reflection..."

"The gateway is forever closed--," Slowly climbing to my feet and sorrowfully gazing upon the dark surface, I said, "Whatever power existed there has gone forever—and been lost with the darkness and Caitlin..."

"So it's all finally over?" Ole stared back in suspended disbelief.

Slowly nodding, I looked among the disheveled and distraught expressions of my friends, and quietly said, "It's over—and she's gone..." The shock finally began to sink in and I trembled with the realization, "She's gone..."

Blinded by the tears, Rich had looked up in complete horror, "Will you ever forgive me..."

"It's not you, my dear, dear friend--," I stared aghast, "But myself that I'll never forgive..."

CHAPTER THIRTY

Sumas Inn
Tuesday, February 11, 1975.
10:15 a.m.
Loading the last of the luggage into the vehicles, Scott had looked to Carrie as she wandered past with a hand full of keys, asking, "Did you want me to come with you?"

She thought for a moment, and then frowning, said, "No honey, I'll do this alone…"

All the others had already gathered into the vehicles, as sitting silently, they watched as she walked across the lot toward the little office.

Carrie knew that the police had released the old woman earlier that morning, and having filed no charges, she left the detachment a free woman. At the age of sixty eight and alone in this world, her cough would likely lead to a bad ending.

Walking in through the door, she heard the little bell ring, and approaching the counter, quietly waited. It only took a few moments for the old woman to appear, and she just looked at Carrie in utter confusion.

"You never told the police what I'd said to you--," She spoke in a quiet and polite tone, as closely examining Carrie, thought for a moment before saying, "If they'd known the truth—they would've sent me to jail…"

"I know--," Carrie dropped the keys onto the counter, and tilting her head, peered curiously at the old lady, "But the way that I see it—there's no prison on earth that could be worse for you than this place. Alone here at night for what's left of your life—and with that devil that you call your brother…"

Turning, Carrie had just walked away without saying another word as she heard the sudden sobbing from behind her…

Sanctum Arcanum
10:55 a.m.
There was a warm wind blowing the night we all stood and watched the guest house burn. Rich had gone over to the neighbors, and calling the police, notified the proper authorities to disregard the house-fire. In any

event, the vortex had drawn all the cursed and haunted artifacts from that vault into oblivion, and everything else now burned.

We spent the majority of the night out there, and with the morning we parted ways with dear father Watkins, Jerry Langdon and Jesse Whyte. As they pulled out of the driveway, Rich had turned, and pointing toward the house, asked, "When are we going to burn that?"

"We're not--," Looking to the others in a moment of thought, I politely asked, "Would you be kind enough to help me with putting the furniture back?"

"Michael--," Tim's eyes widened as he looked to the porch, and then asked, "You're not seriously considering staying here after all that's happened?"

"Why not--," Gazing back at the house and raising an eyebrow, I muttered, "It might still have one good story left in it..."

"We still have a day before the others return--," Ole shrugged, "So why not help him fix up the place? It's not like we don't have the time."

"Alright--," Jay offered Rich his crossbow back, and moving toward the furniture pile, said, "But let's do this quick, so that we have something to sleep on when we finally pass out."

"Wait--," Ole raised a finger in thought, "Shouldn't we remove the pails and mop up the mess that those horrid things have left first?"

"You won't find any evidence that they were ever here--," Rich quietly said, "And any that did exist--," He pointed toward the glowing embers of the guest house, "Was all destroyed in there..."

"I'll help with the buckets--," Tim walked toward the house, "I'm used to cleaning up the remains of the day..."

Exhausted, we worked like mindless machines, as removing the additional firewood and sweeping the floors, covered the pentagram with a Persian rug. We laid all the furniture back into its proper places, and no sooner had we achieved this, than were most fast asleep on the couches near the hearth.

"It's hard to believe that anything even happened here." Tim sat on the couch beside me while sipping brandy and watching our friends sleep, "So, what are your plans now?"

"I'm going to call a taxi--," I had quietly announced, "And go pick up my Eldorado."

"I'll call for you--," Suspicion had flashed in his dark eyes, and as he moved to make the call, he added in thought, "I'm too wound up to sleep anyway, so I might as well come along for the ride."

"What are you up to?" Awakened from a dead sleep and raising his head from the cushion, Rich looked up at me, "Where are you going?"

"I'm just going to get my car--," Glancing back at him, I spoke quietly so as not to bother the others, "Tim's coming with me—and we might stop for breakfast, so don't get worried."

"How come I still feel like this thing isn't quite over?" He squinted while trying to see without his lost glasses.

"You just get some rest--," Motioning for him to lay down, I said, "I need you to watch the telephone and house until we get back."

"Promise me something before you go?"

"Of course—name it."

"Promise me, that you're coming back—and that you're not going to chase down another portal to find Caitlin."

"Don't be ridiculous--;" Moving quietly from my seat, I had looked back at him, and said, "Of course I'm coming back..." Hurrying away before he could pursue the matter further, I made my way into the kitchen.

Tim had waved me over, as hanging up the telephone, he whispered, "They said that they'll be here in five minutes."

"Let's get going before we wake anyone." Hurriedly slipping into shoes, my black trench coat, and favorite grey scarf, I went for the front door, "Let's lock it—just to be safe."

The cab ride back to Langley, though lengthy and expensive, had passed quickly as we had both fallen asleep. As drifting in and out of consciousness, I caught brief glimpses of buildings and scenes, until finally gazing upon my black Eldorado.

The brief nap was sufficient enough to justify sharing breakfast at the hotel diner before leaving. We both ordered the vegetarian omelet and enjoyed several cups of very black tea.

"You know--," He grinned over his breakfast, and peering skeptically over at me, "I really wasn't expecting you to come back, if I'd allowed you to run off alone."

"And so you might have been right--," I quenched his curiosity and sadly said, "In all truth, I'm still having mixed emotions about the whole thing."

"Michael--," He took on the serious tone that he always adopted before some strict lecture, "I really don't feel that you should stay there—not after everything that's happened."

"Which brings us to my next question--," Evading his statement, I proceeded to share thoughts of my own, "Will you also be staying—or do you have something else in mind?"

"Well--," He chewed at his toast thoughtfully before saying, "I was thinking that I might get a little place of my own, and maybe settle down, now that things are okay."

"I'd be glad to help you get that new start--," Offering assistance, I smiled sadly, and said, "But it'll be a shame to see you go."

There were several moments of silence between us. Then, putting down his fork and clasping his hands before his face, he quietly said, "How have you been feeling? Well, what I mean to say—is how is your heart holding out after all of that excitement?"

"It seems fine at the moment."

"You've changed through this whole thing--," He looked between my hands and face, and squinting skeptically, said, "I'm going to be straight with you about this, but I'm very worried about you…"

"I'm as good as I ever was…" Breathing deeply I thought for a moment, and then said in reflection, "Maybe even better in some ways?"

"And what about Caitlin--," He watched me closely for any sign of betrayal, "And is there really no way of bringing her back from the abyss?"

"She surrendered her soul to the demon--," The words had hurt to even say, "I don't even know if she'd have wanted this any other way?"

"But, if she left this world--," He questioned the physics of the phenomena, "Then she also left her physical body and exists again in spirit. So, like before and like it was with Marlowe, would it not be possible to summon the demon and return them both here?"

"It's all over--," I looked to him, and sighing deeply, said, "And even if it might be possible, would it be worth the risk of possibly setting the darkness free in this dimension again?"

A shadow crossed before his face, as looking past him, I stared to where my Eldorado was now parked from just beyond the window. In memory I saw Caitlin loading the trunk, as she smiled at me before parting on that fateful day. In a wooden crate, and neatly packed among my most precious possessions, was a golden beryl that might hold the answers…

"So, you seriously don't have any plans to continue your previous research, or do investigations?"

Offering the most sincere gaze possible, I shrugged, and turning back to my breakfast, said, "I'm a fiction writer—and endlessly poking around for new ideas. That doesn't mean that it'll ever amount to anything…"

12:40 p.m.

It had taken three of us to lift the wooden crate from out of the trunk of the Eldorado, then four of us to take it safely up the stairs and then back into my office. There wasn't any need to ask for privacy within unpacking. They all simply promised to return for the crate when I was done, and closed the door in parting.

The effort had gone rather quickly, as it simply meant adding items back into their proper places. The last sorted were the crystals, the magnificent old student lamp, and the golden beryl. Dropping into the chair before the desk, I sat and pondered for several minutes. The ticking of the old iron clock beat to the tempo of my heart and my attention had drifted back to the empty chair where Caitlin had once sat. Closing my eyes tightly, I waited in darkness while vividly recalling her memory.

"After so much—how could I have lost you again—and this time forever..." The words had been spoken in thought, but also said in a whisper. My heart was utterly broken and my soul fell into the darkest of despair. There was no longer any Marlowe to offer guidance, or my dearest Caitlin's love to chase away the ghosts of bad memories.

Sliding a new page into the typewriter, I began documenting the course of events, cautious to change the names of the places and some of the people.

It all happened so quickly and without much effort, that within just a few hours the entire affair had been completed. The effort allowed me to relive the horror, heroic efforts of so many, and the final moments that now haunted my cold and empty heart. It also left me wondering, fearing the possible consequences of what any tampering into these events might cause? I thought to have sensed Merlin slipping beneath my desk, but realized that he was still with Danny.

The office felt so different now, so empty and utterly vacant of life. My senses had grown keener through those terrifying experiences, and something within me had changed forever.

It was apparent in several ways, as aside from the five senses, I was distinctly aware of a sixth. As closing my eyes and just allowing my thoughts to drift, I could sense and see my friends gathered about the hearth. In this same fashion, I was able to feel the grass beneath the fading snow, and the life being restored to the old Willow beyond my window.

And then, quite unexpectedly, Merlin appeared upon the chair beside me, and meowing as he always did, silently watched while waiting for me to take notice.

"Merlin—that can't really be you--," Opening my eyes, I was startled to see him still sitting there, and muttered, "You're off and away with Danny."

"No—he isn't..." The whisper came from out of nowhere, and startling me, caused me to look toward the draperies. Merlin suddenly scurried across the room toward a shadowy figure, and leapt into its open arms. Squinting in the dismal gloom of the early afternoon, I suddenly recognized the apparition, and gasped, whispering, "Danny?"

"We were taken--," He said sadly and in a barely audible tone, "By the shadow of the Sumas Inn..."

"No—this can't be—we've beaten the darkness, you should be safe and on your way home."

"There exist others in this realm--," He began fading, "Others that take the lives of the innocent and unwary in this world... farewell, friend Michael..."

"No!" Leaping from out of my chair, I ran to the window and stood staring, "This wasn't real—it couldn't have been? He's safe with the others—they both are."

There was a sudden knock upon my door, and answering, Rich had appeared in the open doorway.

"I just received a call from Carrie--," He informed me, "There's been trouble..."

"The Sumas Inn--," I had repeated the words of the apparition as Rich's face turned white.

Slowly nodding, he stuttered as while attempting to speak, "We've lost Danny—and Merlin's gone too..."

"Where are Carrie and the others right now?"

"They've loaded the vehicles and are on their way back here now."

"When they get back—please keep them here—there's something that I need to do..."

"Where are you going?" He had attempted to stop me, but frowning, I simply said, "I'll be back soon..."

Sumas Inn
9:35 p.m.
When I arrived at the old hotel and truck stop it was pitch-black and almost completely vacant. Parking the Eldorado before the doors of the main office, I slowly climbed out of the car and peered into the long

shadows that hung from all about. There was a sickly sour smell in the cool wind and I scowled while making my way into the office.

A little bell rang from above the door and I stood there for several minutes until an elderly woman answered. She was thin and dressed poorly, wore too much cheap makeup, and her white hair was tightly tied back. She croaked as she spoke, and coughing on cigarette smoke, said, "And what can I do for you?"

"I want to rent a room for the evening—and had one specifically in mind."

"Oh did you?" She took a long pull from her cigarette, and dropping it into an ashtray on the counter, curiously asked, "Which one and exactly why?"

"I want B9--," I spoke in an authoritative voice, as uninterested in her curiosity, said, "And I have my own reasons."

"I haven't had a chance to tidy up there yet--," She nervously looked around the office, "The last tenants just left today."

"That's just fine—I'm not concerned about that--," Staring intently upon the old woman, I insisted again, "I just want the room for tonight…"

There was an instant where I thought that she might refuse me, but then pulling out my wallet and producing the cash, she promptly turned and reached for the key.

"It's not the best room in the place--," Hesitating briefly, she held the key suspended above my open palm, and smirking, said, "And some might even tell you that it's haunted…"

"I don't believe in ghosts--," Grinning devilishly, I tilted my head, "The key please, Madame."

"Don't say that you weren't warned--," She dropped the key into my palm, "Check-out around here is at eleven…"

I stared down at the blue tag, and sensing Danny's presence there, shuddered while knowing that his soul was trapped due to his murder.

"A young man choked to death in there just the other night." She admitted while observing me toying nervously with the tag.

The comment caught my immediate attention, and I asked, "Oh, and exactly what happened?"

"No one knows for sure--," Shrugging, she butted her cigarette, and hacking, peered back at me, "A real shame though—for someone that young to pass away like that…"

"It really was…" Bowing my head for a moment, I waved good night and departed the office.

The walk to the B block section across the parking lot hadn't taken long. The night felt as though it was warming up, and a gentle breeze whistled among the empty stalls beneath the balconies. The snow that remained was mainly melting ice and reflected eerily in the dim glow of the pole lamps. I soon arrived at the building, and slowly climbing the stairs, paused while feeling a familiar presence. It was a distinct impression and I knew from the sensation that my friends had been there.

Walking slowly along the dimly lit balcony, I paused before B9 without even looking upon the number on the door. It was an impression that, growing stronger, caused an anger to swell within me, as turning and unlocking it, I swiftly opened the door.

"Danny--," The word was whispered as I felt his terror in that instant, and his soul was still lurking in the darkness of that room, "Danny—I'm here for you…"

The wind whistled in from behind me, as reaching within, I cautiously switched on the light. It was a pale glow which, emanating from an ancient overhead lamp, cast long shadows about the room.

Upon entering, I felt an immediate chill and stared without reason to the darkness beneath the bed. Blackness, as within that moment I decided to wander casually over and sit down while peering suspiciously out through the still open door.

Pulling the Eldorado keys from my coat pocket, I stared down at the little red rabbit's foot that Danny had given me, and Merlin's old collar.

"I know that you're both still here--," Whispering, I felt a familiar brushing against my lower leg and a shadow moved in the far corner of the room, "I'll set you free…"

The night was cool and the moon drifted ever so slowly from behind pale and luminous clouds. Utter stillness, as the shadows ran long from beneath the dim lights beyond the window. Drawing a small box from within my trench coat, I produced a pitch-black stone. This I held in my left hand while sitting silently and utterly alone.

It hadn't taken long before I heard the slight creaking of footsteps upon the stairway. They came very slowly, as ever so cautiously made their way in through the open door.

The figure had been lean and little more than a shadow as it paused in the stillness before the door. Gaunt and grim the deathly face now stared back through pale and shining eyes. The room flashed, as Merlin lay choking beside his dish and Danny died suffocating in the bed… I felt the horror of

Danny's death as the shadow of his soul now stood near the bed. A sorrow running deeper than all others now streamed like ice within my veins...

The thing in the doorway had crept inward and now silently glared back at me. It slunk cautiously forward, its bony fingers twitching, as preparing to pounce, it suddenly stopped. There was a moment of hesitation and then it looked down as I tapped my cane upon the floor, once, twice, and then three times...

Wednesday, February 12, 1975.

12:46 p.m.

It was a clear and fairly warm day as we all gathered in the driveway before my gates. Rich and Maya were reunited and he'd kept his promise to a dear friend. Jay was beaming like a kid while sitting in the front seat of his bright orange 1969 GTO Judge Convertible,

Anna held Ole as though they had been apart for many years. It appeared as though the horrific experience had brought them that much closer when realizing how easily life might slip away. They both stood proudly and smiled in the afternoon gloom, as resting against the black hood, admired their new Trans Am.

Carrie and Scott stood beside their Suburban, and Deb and Ray were with them. Pam and Jen had been silent, and seemed lost within bitter reflection. Standing quietly beside me, Tim could only shake his head as we all looked to one another within parting.

"I'll be closing the gates to this old place--," I had informed them all while shouting, "And be taking a vacation until I can figure out what to do with myself."

"Are you sure that you won't change your mind about coming away with us?" Rich appeared utterly disappointed, but I had just shrugged, and shaking my head, replied, "As much as I would love that, I think that this is something that I need to do alone..."

Carrie and Scott had walked over to where I stood, and hugging me tightly, sniffled while wiping away the tears.

"We'll be staying in Wisconsin with family for a little while--," She said with a sniffle as she looked up at me, "If you're ever in Eau Claire, be sure to look us up."

"I'll miss you both so very much--," The words had barely escaped my lips when I had to hide my eyes behind sunglasses to conceal the tears, saying, "But I understand that we all need an escape. It's so very hard to keep looking at the same old streets and places, they're a constant reminder of what's happened, and the friend's that we've lost here."

"And speaking of lost things--," Frowning, she had pointed to my breast, "I finally found out where that cross the first Caitlin gave you came from…"

Having entirely forgotten about the golden antique and removing it from around my neck, I held it before us while staring down upon its emerald jewel.

"Old Lawrence survived--," The words came like a miracle as she sniffled, and said, "He found us through the clergy of Christ Church Cathedral and called yesterday."

"So, something good came from all of this." The cross now shook within my trembling hands, "And what did you discover about this?"

Reaching out and gently touching the cross, she had gazed in utter awe, "I spoke with Father Liam Grantham at Christ Church--," She explained, "I told him that you'd been given this gift while at the house of McCreary." A strange light of fascination now flashed in her deep grey eyes, "When I described it to him—he'd known almost right away."

The suspense was almost unbearable…

"He told me that it had belonged to the clergy of St. Francis in Killkenny, and that it was lost when the last friar died in 1829." Her eyes seemed to shine as the sun peeked out from behind the drifting clouds, and she said, "He asked that I tell you to keep it safe—as it must have come to you by God's will, and he gave me his blessing."

"They're just some things that we'll never understand--," Scott looked down as the emerald glistened in the sunlight, "But not all of it was bad…"

Allowing the cross to gently fall back against my breast, I leaned forward and hugged Carrie.

"Thank you—I'd forgotten all about it and it would've haunted me forever, if you hadn't found its true origins."

"I know--," She stepped back and said through tears, "And I feel so horrible for just leaving you now—," Motioning back to the Suburban and where Patrick sat in the back with his face in his hands, she said, "He couldn't even come to say good-bye, because he didn't know how…"

"Never say good-bye--," Swallowing hard, I looked between Scott and Carrie, and whispered, "Only till then."

Scott fumbled for the words in parting, "You take good care of yourself, bro. And don't forget—pick up that phone once in a while, okay? Oh—hell," He grabbed me in an embrace that felt as though it might break us both, and said, "We'll come back to see you just as soon as we get things sorted out."

"My door is always open--," Wiping the tears away from where they had gathered at the bottom of the sunglasses, I said, "And I'm always around, somewhere…"

"We'll call you just as soon as we arrive in Wisconsin—," Carrie promised, and pointing a finger, sniffled and said, "You watch your diet and take care of that ticker—or I'll come back here and kick your butt."

"In that case, I'll have to toss out all my medication—and order pizza the moment you leave."

"I love you—you crazy bastard," She shook her head at me, and then turning, fell into her husband's arms. Looking back one last time, they had both waved as they made their way back to the Suburban.

"We'll be heading to Maine--," Deb and Ray slowly approached, and she suddenly hugged me, "You should come with us. It's a beautiful place and you could settle down in some new creepy old house and be a ghost writer."

"I'm not even sure if I'll be writing again after this last book--." Shaking hands with Ray, he had hugged me as well, as turning to look back at Deb, I quietly said, "But I'll make sure to try and stay in touch. Maybe we'll even see each again sooner than you think?"

"I sure hope so--," Ray pointed, and smiling somewhat sadly, said, "And you're always welcome in our home, if you change your mind about coming to live, or just want to get away."

"I've written down all the contact numbers--," Waving the little black notepad before them, I said, "And once things settle down for everyone, you can be expecting a call."

"God bless and keep you." Deb offered a final embrace, and then stepping back took hold of her husband's hand, saying, "I don't think I'll ever sleep right, ever again. But as long as I know that you're in the world somewhere, I know that we're all that much safer…"

"Evil exists from all around us and always will--," Looking upon them fondly, I sighed while saying, "But as long as you mind your own matters, and don't go poking around where you shouldn't, you should be perfectly safe."

"And are you going to go poking around again?" Peering at me suspiciously while extending a hand, Ray had gazed deeply into my eyes.

Accepting his firm but gentle grip, I had struggled for an answer, "Not in the way that you might be expecting--," I quietly replied, "Or anything dangerous—to anyone else…"

"Whatever you do—or wherever you might go--," Ray firmly shook my hand, "Always remember that you have family in Maine."

"God bless and keep you both--," Bowing my head and stepping away, I had watched, as slowly turning, they had embraced, and supporting one another, walked away. They joined Scott and his family in the Suburban, an adventure that they would share together, and a journey out of fear.

"If you're ever in Arizona—I'll be in Peoria with family," Pam wiped the tears from her bright blue eyes, "I'll always be kicking around somewhere—and always be happy to hear from you."

Gently embracing and and kissing her cheek, I looked deeply into her eyes, and said, "I hear that's its beautiful there, I have friends that retired in Scottsdale."

"It's hot and there are far too many spiders--," She cringed at the thought, "But it's bright and sunny, and I've had enough of the cold and dark for one life."

"And I've been a creature of the night for so long--," Gently taking her by the shoulders, I shook my head while saying, "That I'd likely melt into a puddle of me, in the hot sun…"

"In that case, I'd be glad to drag you around in a bucket--," She smiled while wiping at the tears, "If that's what it took just to have you around."

There had been an awkward moment of silence between us, and then embracing, she kissed my cheek before quietly stepping away.

"Well, I'm going back to Chicago--," Jen gazed up as tears filled her big and beautiful brown eyes, "But if you can guarantee no more boogeymen—I'll be happy to come back here to visit, anytime."

We hugged as she sniffled, and shaking her head, said in loving reflection, "You were all the greatest family that I ever had."

"And will always have—no matter what. Take care of yourselves--," Bowing my head again and waving, I watched as they sadly turned and went away. They both climbed into an Oldsmobile station wagon, a gift in a parting from our dear friend Jay.

"I'll still be staying here in town--," Jay walked over, and pausing to look at me, said, "So, if you're planning on getting into any more trouble, I'm only a phone-call away, brother." He slapped my shoulder, and hugging me tightly, winked as he went back to his car. The bright orange Pontiac stood out like an August sunset against the dismal grounds, and the pure joy that reflected in his eyes as he started the engine warmed my heart.

"I really have no idea of what to even say to you?" Ole stood next to his wife, and appearing utterly confused, looked back to me, "I suppose that I could be very angry about all of this--," He peered at his wife, and then sighing, said, "But I have to accept responsibility for sticking my nose where it didn't belong and almost losing it in the process… So, I will just thank you for saving both of our lives."

"I'm just glad that it's all over—and that most of us made it out." Firmly shaking his hand, I politely nodded as they slowly turned and began walking away. Pausing in thought, he reluctantly looked back and quite innocently asked, "Am I still going to be your editor, and how soon can I read what you wrote?"

"If you still want the position, I couldn't possibly think of anyone better." Looking to his wife and then back at him, I said, "And as far as the manuscript is concerned, you'll just have to wait until it's finished."

Smirking, he shrugged, and taking his wife's hand, slowly walked away

"Are you going to let me drive?" His wife offered an inquisitive, though obviously doubtful frown.

"We just got it my love—don't start with me already, please."

"I knew that you would get greedy about this--," She walked around to the passenger side, as stopping part way, Ole uttered an immense sigh. She had paused to glance back at him, as waving the keys and conceding, waved them at her, "Okay, you can drive, love of my life…."

Gleefully running over to the driver's side and snatching the keys from out of his hand, she hopped into the car while exclaiming, "I knew it—I always get my way!"

Hopelessly flinging his arms into the air, he grinned while peering back at me, "Women… I love her…"

Climbing into the car, I could hear him advising her to be careful, and her laughter resounded throughout the silent and empty grounds. For all of their little idiosyncrasies, it was plainly obvious that they had dearly loved one another.

"Do you have any idea of where you're going or when you plan to come back?" Tim casually sauntered over from the Cadillac and to where I stood. The black 1956 Cadillac series 62 Convertible had been a gift from Rich and was now loaded for a particularly long trip.

"At the moment, I couldn't really tell you--," I had looked to my dear friend with a shrug, and said, "Because I'm not really sure myself?"

"You know, you're really looking a lot younger these days." Suspicion had shone in his dark eyes, "Are you sure that being involved with all that ethereal energy hasn't affected you in some way?"

Patting at the sides of my face with both hands, I just smiled, "No, I just shaved off the sideburns—I thought that I'd try for a fresh look." It was a rather feeble attempt to disguise the obvious, as we had both known the truth. All the same, he didn't pursue the matter and had simply thrown his arms into the air.

"Of course—nothing strange or unnatural ever happens around you--," Frustrated with my eternal evasive tactics, he just smiled, "I'm going to miss you, brother."

We embraced and he'd slapped my back heartily, as a deep concern suddenly reflected in his dark eyes, "Are you sure that you're going to be okay alone in this place?" Inspecting the long shadows of the manor with fleeting glances, he swallowed hard as though still sensing some hidden threat.

"Oh, I'm never really alone--," I feigned a smile while saying, "I've got my ghosts, my books and a lifetime of memories."

There was a tear in his eye as he slowly nodded, and then looking back at me, said, "I'm going to follow the others across the border—and then maybe check out California and Mexico. Are you sure that you wouldn't rather just come with me?"

Glancing over my shoulder and back at the old house, I noticed a foreign shadow that now haunted one of the upper windows.

"I don't think that I'm quite ready for the real world—or might ever be again..." Shaking hands in parting, I said, "I'm sure that above all others, you understand that nothing really feels the same..."

Obviously concerned, he asked again, "Please consider moving away from this place—you really don't need to stay here anymore."

Looking back at the old manor, I had considered his words, and then quietly said, "I realize that it may be a symbol of fear and horror to everyone else. But to me, it's as beautiful and dark as it always was. It holds the best and the worst of everything and it's all that I really have left..."

"I'll be away for at least a month--," Sniffling and looking away, he cleared his throat, "Try to stay out of trouble—at least until I get back?"

"Trouble finds me and it always has--," Gently patting him shoulder, I paused thoughtfully, and looking back at him, said, "Take good care of yourself—and remember: Before turning down the lights, always be sure to look in the closet and beneath the beds..."

In that moment he had stared almost angrily, and then scoffing, said, "You know, as much as I love you, brother, sometimes you're a real son of a bitch."

Hoping to have avoided tears in parting, I sadly smiled, "Till then—my dear friend..."

"Till then—old friend..." Nodding in a knowing way, he slowly strolled back to his car. I watched, as climbing into the old Caddy, he started the engine and looked back at me. It was the same face that I had seen upon too many occasions and as while leaving Hedley. It was the parting glance of someone who now considered the possibility of never seeing one another again...

A chilling wind whistled among the pines and drifts as I slowly turned away. Then, reaching into my coat pocket, I pulled out the remote for the automatic gates. Swallowing hard, I pressed the button and watched as the tall and spiked iron gates began sliding open.

Then, stepping backward and onto the steps of the porch, I had silently watched from the front door. There was a moment while we had all looked at each other, time had suddenly stood still. In my heart, I had wondered if I might ever see any of them again in this life. Then, like a funerary parade, they all slowly pulled away, waving, as they drove up the street and out of my life. A cold wind whistled among the tall pines within that bitter-sweet parting and my heart ached to a raven's sorrowful call in the distance.

Friday, February 13, 1975.
12:20 a.m.
Sitting quietly before the typewriter, I sipped at a cup of tea while making additions and corrections to the manuscript. It was a particularly quiet night, and with a warm wind blowing from the east, I had opened the windows for a little fresh air.

I was feeling exceptionally worn out after spending the last few days attending to basic maintenance of the house. Aside from generalities, I had painstakingly removed all and anything that had been brought from the McCreary estate. This included the wonderful antique liquor cabinet and its entirely priceless collection of decanters and spirits. At one point, I had finally decided that it was all just too much for me and hired movers to clear everything out of the house! All that now remained were the contents of my office and an old kettle that sat upon the stove. It had once belonged to my uncle and now warmed the water for my tea.

The process of the entire cleaning had also been left to hired help. It wasn't that I had felt it was beyond me, but I just couldn't bear the responsibility of throwing away Raymond's things... To this were also added the trinkets and treasures of Gordon, Danny, Dennis and Tanya. In fact, I had been terribly shocked and broken while retrieving my comic collection from the book shop where Danny had carefully stored it. Pam had returned the few issues that he'd taken when they went away, but his memory and the comics now just left me in years. In the end, I had donated them all to a charity Christmas drive for the children's hospital...

After the house had been completely stripped and cleaned, I had purchased new wine-colored draperies for the entire place. These were also installed by hired help while I attended to other business. The bedroom that I had once shared had all been emptied, and I now slept in a new recliner that rested before the office window. I had no intention of ever filling the place again; it now existed as a barren reminder.

During this time there had also been a secret meeting arranged with authorities. Documents had been signed and files closed in matters concerning the events surrounding the deaths of the others. I had provided all the information in notarized form and the content had vanished along with the evidence and identities of those lost. In parting, the representative, who had refused to reveal his name, had assured me that no evidence or prior information of my involvement would remain anywhere in public records.

There had been some relief in discovering that accordingly, all evidence of previous offenses on my police record had also been erased. This meant that no one could ever trace my whereabouts in connection to previous investigations. It would all now appear as nothing more than a series of inexplicable accidents, unfortunate deaths, and that nothing else had ever happened...

A strange occurrence had been the ascending senses and awareness that still remained, even after Caitlin and the demon were gone. If I sat quietly and just focused, I could sense many things both here and in the hereafter. If an item or antique still had some connection to the dearly departed, I could sense it and became immediately aware. Most occurrences were harmless and simply a case of lost souls clinging to something familiar. In any event, I completely avoided such things and kept only what remained in my office.

In matters of my health, the doctor who had been assigned to me couldn't understand my miraculous recovery from a heart condition and ailment considered terminal. There had been some question as to misdiagnosis, and the medications were promptly cancelled. This of course had not caused me to change my diet. I felt more youthful, lighter, and sensed that I might require this body for a considerable time.

The gentle ticking of the old iron clock was my only companion through the seemingly endless nights. Utterly lost in most cases, the only thing that helped to maintain my sanity was the completion of the book. Dropping the last page of the completed manuscript into its basket, I looked over sadly into Caitlin's empty chair. It broke my heart, but I refused to dispose of it, sensing that some part of her still remained.

Placing a trembling hand upon the armrest, I whispered, "I love you more than life itself--," I remembered the promise, "And will never abandon you …"

It was a promise as empty and barren as the darkness that now filled my soul…

Moving to one side, I stared into the darkness at the far side of the room. The old mirror stood there staring back through a blackened face that no longer reflected. It was the only thing that I had secretly rescued from the guest house fire, that accursed Beryllus…

"Somewhere hidden behind your shadow lies a mystic doorway to my beloved… All that I need now is to solve the mystery of its key…"

Carefully bringing down the golden beryl, I placed it down upon the desk. It shimmered in the long shadows as though hearing the sorrow calling from within my heart, Caitlin... The diamonds danced within the shimmering heavens and its golden waves lapped at distant shores. Ever deeper I gazed, as flowing like a shining river from one dimension into another, it drifted into realms undreamed.

Extending my thoughts and allowing them to flow, I felt my entire being drawn into the shining stone. Then, traveling through a swiftly streaming multitude of galaxies at the speed of thought, everything suddenly became black. The sound of my own pounding heart now echoed, shining like a beacon through the cold darkness and unforgiving reaches of space.

Then, and in the utter blackness of where all light and hope failed, I saw an emerald glitter. Through the endless shadow of eternity she looked back at me, hope flashing in her brilliant, green eyes! My hands were upon the stone before I had even known what I had done! I was calling to her with all of my heart! I desired nothing more than to rescue or forever share the absence of eternity and oblivion with her!

A sudden flash and I awakened within my body and before the golden and shimmering stone. The tears flowed silently, bowing my head, as I realized she could never escape the void without unleashing the darkness…

Sensing a presence from out of the night, I suddenly turned to look about the room. Emptiness and utter silence… Only the draperies moved ever so slightly in a breeze that issued in through the open window.

A sudden movement from out of the shadows had been caught in the corner of my eye. It crept ever so slowly from out of the dark hallway and then made its way toward my desk. Looking down and into its big yellow eyes, I had leaned over while gently retrieving the little black kitten from the floor. It meowed affectionately and purred loudly, as holding it close to my heart, I had lovingly smiled, and said, "I was beginning to wonder if you would make it back up those stairs from your food dish? It's a long journey for such a little fellow. Welcome back, my dear little, Merlin."

Gently placing him down, he had stretched and yawned, and then waddled beneath the desk. In just a few moments he had found a warm and cozy place, and peacefully slept near the heating vent. I could hear the faint whistling of his sweet little snoring, as a short sigh had been caught in my heart. The recollection of our first meeting returning vividly, as swallowing hard, I thanked the fates for small mercies.

It happened the other morning and while backing the Eldorado from out from the alley behind the book store. Inexplicably, something had caught my eye in that moment. I had seen a black movement behind a dumpster from within the deep snow. Climbing from the car for no real reason, I had gone to investigate and been shocked as I looked down! For there, and caught in the ice and snow, I discovered the little kitten barely alive. It seems that the motion that I had seen was his last attempt while trying to escape a frozen grave…

Without a thought I had gently reached down, and plucking him from a frozen would-be grave, slipped him inside my coat. I had driven home like that, as while holding him close to my heart, attempted to keep him warm. It had been a long afternoon, as after feeding him what little that he would take, I watched over him through the night. In the morning I had been awakened, still holding him, as he meowed and his whiskers had tickled at my face.

For some reason and aside from all other things, I had never parted with Merlin's old dish or litterbox. These now became his after finding a home in my house and heart, we became fast friends…

Moving carefully so as not to disturb little Merlin, I turned down the light and went to the black leather recliner. I settled into the blankets before the parted curtains and silently gazed into the night.

The clouds drifted lazily across the blackened heavens as the stars glittered in hues of brilliant blues and white. Through the darkness, there had been just the faintest flash of emerald, and a familiar voice whispered, "Where there is love, there is always hope…"

"Marlowe…"

The adventure continues…

www.ingramcontent.com/pod-product-compliance
Lightning Source LLC
Chambersburg PA
CBHW021832010726
47493CB00005B/1359